THE BEATRICE STUBBS SERIES
BOXSET TWO

COLD PRESSED
HUMAN RITES
BAD APPLES

JJ MARSH

TRISKELE BOOKS

Cover design: JD Smith

Published by Prewett Bielmann Ltd.
All enquiries to admin@beatrice-stubbs.com

First printing, 2014

ISBN: 978-3-9524796-1-2 (MOBI)
978-3-9524796-2-9 (EPUB)
978-3-9524796-9-8 (Paperback)

Contents

Cold Pressed   1

Human Rites   217

Bad Apples   461

Dedications   699

A Message from JJ Marsh   700

Also by Triskele Books   701

COLD PRESSED

Chapter 1

That's funny.

Eva's guiding hand on the front door usually resulted in a gentle click, but tonight it slammed shut with far more force than she'd intended. A draught caught the back of her neck as she put down the carrier bag with a reassuring clink of bottles.

She locked the door behind her and stopped to listen. Rain beat on the roof, like fingers on drumskins, and a hollow dripping echoed from the guttering outside. The occasional hiss of wet tyres on tarmac. The hushed rush of the gas fire and the tink-tink of its ceramic surround from the living room. Her antique clock on the hall table echoing its woody tock with the regularity of a dripping tap. *Maybe I just don't know my own strength.*

Coat on the hook, boots off and slippers back on, she shuffled through to the kitchen, then remembered the carrier bag and shuffled back. The plastic was still wet. *I had an umbrella when I left, I know I did. Must have left it in the shop.* A foul night into which only a fool would venture. But when only a quarter of a bottle remains, it calls for desperate measures. She laughed out loud. *Desperate measures!*

Eva hummed to herself as she put two slices in the toaster and got the butter out to warm. A fresh highball from the cabinet, some ice cubes from the freezer compartment and a healthy slug, a good third of the glass, topped up with tonic. A slice of lemon would be nice, but she only had a couple of oranges and one of them had a covering of blue fur. A cold breeze brushed the back of her neck and she put down her glass with a slam. All the windows were closed. The draught came from the back door. Ajar by no more than an inch, with its peeling paint and rusted lock, the garden door allowed cool evening air and the smell of soggy grass to creep into her warm, cosy kitchen.

With a dismissive tut, she struggled with the ancient lock, but finally secured it. Very important, safety, for a woman living alone. She took a long sip of her drink, half-attempting to recall the last time she'd been out the garden door, but found she couldn't care less. Her memory wasn't the best, and anyway it was a peaceful neighbourhood.

Peaceful. Only the tiny chinking of ice cubes as she replaced her glass on the pine table disturbed the thick silence of the evening. Time to put the telly on; she was beginning to get the willies. The toaster ejected its contents with a jack-in-the-box metallic clatter, making Eva jump. She looked out at the darkness and made herself a promise, not for the first time, to get some curtains for the kitchen windows. The vodka was just beginning to work. Her cheeks warmed, her head lightened and a tune danced through her head.

She opened the fridge for the butter and remembered it was already on the table. The overhead fluorescent flattened everything but the light from the fridge door glinted on the lino. Water.

That's funny.

Two patches of water. No, four, five. Footprints. She stared at the pattern reaching from the back door to the hallway and laughed at herself. Spooked by her own wellies! She looked down at her feet, in dry sheepskin slippers. Her wellies were still in the hallway. She'd put them on to go up the shop and took them off when she came back. She hadn't made those prints.

Her head was muddled. That toast was going cold, so she closed the fridge and rubbed her arms against the chill. Time for a top up and her Saturday night entertainment. She scraped butter across the cooling toast and grabbed a quick slurp of Prussian magic. A slice of lemon would be nice.

A song. A singer. Tonight she'd try to vote, and fingers crossed she'd get through this time. She hummed to herself as she fetched a tray and ripped a piece of kitchen roll as a substitute for a doily. A movement in the hallway. She squinted into the dimness, wondering if she'd left the front door open as well. Darkness expanded and blocked out the hall light.

A man stepped into the kitchen doorway. Eva dropped her glass onto her toast and gasped so hard her bottom lip caught on her teeth. She tasted blood.

He entered the room, the light behind him, his face in shadow. Leather jacket, sunglasses, big chunky boots, black gloves and slick wet hair. He looked like the Terminator. She shrank backwards and his lips split into a grin, showing his teeth. Vodka and tonic trickled across the table and dripped onto the floor.

"Hello Eva," he said.

He didn't sound like Schwarzenegger. Strange accent. She swallowed some bitter saliva and tried to focus her thoughts.

"Who are you?" she asked, her voice trying for authoritative but missing it by a country mile.

He showed his teeth again. "That's what I've come to find out. I have a few questions for you."

She shook her head. "How did you get in here? I'm not answering questions from a total stranger. You come back tomorrow and we'll see."

"Sorry, Eva. Tomorrow's no good. You're not going to be here tomorrow." He took off his dark glasses. "So in the words of the King, it's now or never."

Eva's jaw slackened and her mouth gaped. She recognised those eyes.

Chapter 2

"I said to you, I distinctly remember, not to forget a screw of salt. I told you they wouldn't think of it."

"It's not the end of the world, Maggie. Eat your egg and stop fussing. Enjoy the view and the silence."

Maggie stared out at the Aegean Sea, an expanse of peacock shades, punctuated by white sails and wakes, the cliffs stretching away to their right and the harbour barely visible to their left. Distant misty calderas lay on the horizon like hump-backed whales. Sunlight sparkled from every angle, an omnipresent sprite banishing ill-will. Vast sky, endless sea and more shades of blue than she knew words for.

"It's a beautiful spot, I'll give you that. Just hidden away enough so we won't cross paths with any tourists. But I have never in my life eaten a hard-boiled egg without salt, Rose Mason, and have no plans to start now."

Rose selected a stick of celery and scooped up some hummus. "Just as I have always said, you're inflexible to the point of fossilisation. Have another look in the picnic basket. I'm sure I asked for salt."

Maggie adjusted her sunhat and returned to the hamper, placed in the shade of the chunky little moped. She pushed aside the empty wrappers and found something that looked like a pencil sharpener. In one end she could see ground black pepper, in the other...

"Salt!"

"What did I tell you? Now, is there anything else you want to grumble about, or can we enjoy our first civilised meal in a week?"

Clutching her condiments, Maggie arranged herself on the blanket and tucked her skirt under her knees. She inhaled and closed her eyes, savouring the warm citrus and herbal notes wafting from the hillside. A butterfly, freckled and rust-coloured, flitted from shrub to shrub on its own balletic mission. Rose poured two glasses of iced tea and handed one to Maggie.

"Thank you. I'll have my boiled egg now, if you'd be so kind. And to say this is the first civilised meal in a week is a wee bit harsh. I won't deny the conversation has bordered on the tedious at times, but I've no complaints about the food."

They gazed out at the beauty of the sea, its constantly shifting contours, accented by the graceful arcs of gulls.

"The food, I grant you, has been of superior quality." Rose sipped her tea and Maggie peeled her egg, bracing herself. She knew Rose was building up for an almighty moan. "But the deadly boring company gives me indigestion. I resent being told with whom and when I must eat. It feels like boarding school all over again. There is no reason on earth why we can't dine alone at a table for two and enjoy our meals rather than suffer more tales of unfortunate operations, dead or divorced husbands and overachieving offspring. Oh God, would you listen to me? We came up here to escape all that and what do I do? Bring it with us. Ignore me. Are you going to have some taramasalata?"

Maggie eyed the pinkish gloopy substance, the consistency of tapioca. "I might when I've finished my egg. Not all the other passengers are that bad. Mr and Mrs Emerson are pleasant enough. And that language fella, when he pokes his head out of his shell, can be entertaining on occasion."

She bit into her egg and absorbed the panorama, assessing photographic compositions with professional enthusiasm and an amateur eye. Rose's cornflower-print dress seemed to complement the colours, but looked incongruous amongst the scrubby flora of a Greek hillside. Her straw hat shaded her eyes and the 1950s sunglasses hid her expression. But Maggie could tell perfectly well Rose's eyes were smiling.

"Mrs Make-The-Best-Of-It is at it again." Despite her best efforts, Rose couldn't quite manage to make her voice sound stern. "You and I both know that a cruise is not our sort of holiday. We're trapped on a tub with people we'd actively avoid in everyday circumstances, fed at regular intervals and provided with something laughably called entertainment. On reaching dry land, we're dragged around a historic site in an air-conditioned coach, often sitting directly behind an incontinent nonagenarian and only let out for a three-minute photo opportunity. Maggie, I'm not being ungrateful and I'm happy to try anything once, but can we agree that despite our advancing years, we are still women of independent minds?"

Maggie wiped her fingers and picked up the camera as she considered her response. She caught several shots of the bay, zoomed in on a yacht then turned to her left to see what compositions the harbour might yield. Low white houses tumbled in Lego formation towards the sea, but the ridge hid all the port activity from view. In the distance, impossible to overlook, lay the *Empress Louise*, docked at the distant ferry port. She shook her head at the breathtaking scale of the thing. How something so vast could float around the world, operating with unfailing efficiency, still awed her.

She rounded on Rose with more theatre than passion. "How many years have we been holidaying together? Don't answer that, I can't remember either. How many of those holidays would have been anywhere but Brittany, Cornwall and Ireland, had it been left to you?"

Rose sniffed. "I have one word to say to you – Tenerife."

"Agreed." Maggie swallowed some iced tea. "A mistake you'll never let me forget. Neither will I let you forget the time we sailed along the Dalmatian Coast. Or the whales we saw in the Azores. Or that funny little place at the top of Capri."

"Yes, yes, I can see what you're doing. Sea, boats, adventures and some exceptional memories. This is not the same. In Croatia, we went off the beaten track. We made our own discoveries. Took our own stupid risks. A cruise ship offers no opportunity for... well, no opportunity for individuality. Yes, I admit I'm too old for camel-trekking, but holidays are supposed to make me feel younger than I am. This cruise makes me feel decrepit."

"You're being a snob, Rose. I'm sorry, but you are. As soon as I mentioned the C-word, you got all superior and made your mind up you would hate it. Well, I'm enjoying myself. I find the other passengers a curiosity and the only thing spoiling my fun is your moaning. So stick that in your pipe and smoke it."

Rose made a point of swivelling her entire torso towards Maggie. A hard stare, no doubt. Maggie kept her eye glued to the lens. She retracted the zoom from the ship to the sliver of bay visible below.

"And you're not being precisely the opposite? Dazzled by a 1920s mirage of charming bejewelled society folk doing the Charleston in the ballroom. Whereas the reality is bingo, aquarobics, whatever they are, dubious tribute bands and a desperate crowd of blue-rinsers colluding in the myth that... what are you looking at?"

Maggie didn't answer, twisting the magnification so she could pick out more detail in the middle distance. The vantage point, halfway up the cliff and beloved of coach parties, was empty. All the tourists had left, heading for the town's many restaurants for lunch. But one had come adrift.

An elderly lady wandered along the cliff path towards the car park. Her movements were irregular and she seemed disorientated or suffering from the heat. Maggie sat up straighter. They could scramble down there in minutes and help the poor old dear.

"Maggie? What is it? You look like a meerkat. Maggie Campbell, I'm talking to you!"

"There's someone down there. An old lady. I can't be sure at this distance, but it looks like one of the Hirondelles."

"I doubt it. Their coach passed us on our way up, so by now they've been herded into a local taverna to be force-fed moussaka. Why do you say it's one of them?"

"Same outfit. Blue blazer, white skirt, you know. Whoever it is, she looks distressed. We should help."

"Let me see. Where are the binoculars?"

Below, a second figure appeared and strode across the car park, heading towards the pensioner. He wore the classic white and blue-trimmed uniform of the ship's crew and reached out a hand to the woman.

"It's all right. One of the crew has found her. You'd think they'd do a head count before driving off. She shouldn't be wandering around alone at her age. He needs to get her out of the sun."

The pair were walking slowly back in the direction of the car park.

"Are you done, Maggie? Only I'll cover this lot up, I think."

Maggie took her attention from the camera to see Rose wave a hand at the abandoned tomato salad, shooing away flies which immediately resettled elsewhere on the picnic.

"Yes, best had." Maggie returned her attention to the couple in the distance, who had stopped to look out over the cliff.

The man was pointing along the coast, in the direction of the *Empress Louise*. While the little woman faced the ocean, he turned, apparently scanning the path in both directions.

"He should take her back and stop messing about; you can see she's had too much sun. Very irresponsible."

"Enough of your rubber-necking and help me put this lot away. Then I suggest a ten-minute snooze to aid the digestion." Plastic lids snapped and greaseproof paper rustled, but Maggie's gaze was fixed on the brilliantly white path and the mismatched pair facing the sea. As she watched, the man lifted the woman, scooping one arm under her knees and bringing the other up to catch her shoulders. A gesture almost playful in its gallantry. He stood that way for several seconds, holding her in his arms as he glanced behind him once again. Then he swung her backwards and with all his force forwards, releasing her frail form out over the cliff.

The woman fell in silence, with a few jerky movements like a puppet. The man remained at the cliff edge. Then, as if hearing some inaudible starter gun, he ran towards the car park and disappeared from sight.

Maggie sat frozen, her mind an uncomprehending loop. *I just saw... I couldn't have seen... he didn't... he did...* A sound like a chainsaw ripped through the silence and broke her petrifaction. Too late, she pressed the shutter and burst into tears.

Chapter 3

Nikos Stephanakis had wet trousers. The police speedboat had made a sharp turn as they approached the port of Athinos, hitting a wave broadside and spraying the solitary passenger down his left leg. Nikos gritted his teeth and pulled out his handkerchief. The irony was that if he'd still been in uniform, it wouldn't have shown. Wet black trousers look the same as dry black trousers. But his casual chinos were now beige on one leg and brown on the other. Could have been worse. At least it wasn't his crotch.

He got to his feet, hoping the sun and wind would hasten the drying process, but the boat had already begun to slow as they entered the harbour. And there, dwarfing every other vessel, loomed the *Empress Louise*. His eyes ranged across the expanse of white, drawn up and up towards the bridge. He squinted into the brightness, despite his police sunglasses. The speedboat drew closer and Nikos couldn't help but be impressed by the scale of the thing. A floating skyscraper. As the police boat nosed up to the quay, the liner's shadow fell over them. Nikos couldn't even see the top deck without craning his neck back as far as it would go.

In all the time he'd been with the Hellenic Police, he'd never actually set foot on one of these. He saw them every day, moored out in the bay, or like this one, a leviathan docked at the quayside. Like everyone else, he disguised his curiosity as contempt. Now, for his first assignment, he was entitled to board this sparkling, bustling world and ask all the questions he'd ever wanted.

A uniformed crew member checked his ID and motioned him up the gangway, with the assurance that someone would meet him at the top. A group of older women passed him on his way up. Some smiled, some greeted him with a quavering 'Good morning'. He responded in kind and for the first time, his enthusiasm for the case and his new role faltered. English. Ninety percent of the passengers were from the UK, and with an international crew the lingua franca could only be English. After two years living with a native speaker, his English was fluent and comfortable in the bar or when advising victims of petty crime. But at murder enquiry level? He sent a quick prayer to the Virgin – please let none of them be from Scotland.

When he and his guide arrived at the bridge after a long and confusing journey through the ship, the captain was on the phone. The huge room, which resembled an air traffic control centre, hummed with activity. Like a small boy, Nikos gazed around him, itching to ask questions about the consoles, screens and various items of equipment. The captain finished his phone call and swivelled his chair to face them.

"Captain Jensson, this is Inspector Stephanakis from the Hellenic Police, Cretan Region."

Nikos held out his hand to the huge Swede as he rose to his feet. The man was easily two metres tall, and to Nikos's surprise, wore no uniform cap or traditional captain's beard.

"Good morning, Inspector, and thank you for coming. I'm sorry to drag you all the way from Heraklion, but under the circumstances, I had no choice. Please, come through and I can bring you up to date."

Nikos smiled. So far, the captain's slow, clear English posed no problems. Maybe the language was nothing to worry about after all. He followed the man into an inner office with a desk, leather chairs and an old-fashioned globe. Sunken spotlights cast pools of warm light around the room and vast windows afforded a panoramic view out to sea. A delicate scent emanated from a vase of lilies standing on a column by the door.

"Rough trip?" asked the captain, with a glance at Nikos's trousers. "Would you like some tea?"

"Bad driver. Yes, please. No milk." The small talk came automatically, but details of sudden death were a different matter.

Nikos opened his briefcase and withdrew the file as Jensson

spoke into the intercom to order refreshments. Behind the captain's head hung a beautiful antique map, showing the two hemispheres surrounded by angels and exotic birds, with golden lettering in Latin. He soaked it all in, recalling his own grey office, with its strip lighting and plastic chairs, perfumed by coffee breath and sweaty shirts.

"So Inspector Stephanakis, how should we begin?"

"Can we start with the deceased? What can you tell me?"

"Esther Crawford, from Shaftesbury in Wiltshire, England. She was eighty years old. I don't know all our guests' ages with such precision, but she celebrated her birthday on our first day at sea. Part of a group called the Hirondelles, who apparently holiday together every year. She seemed very pleasant, and certainly active for her age."

"And the fall?"

"The ladies joined a tour of the island this morning. We offer a variety of excursions and they opted, as a group, for the pottery and sightseeing. It seems Ms Crawford became separated from the others and either fell, or according to one witness, was thrown from a cliff."

A knock at the door signalled a crisply dressed steward, who placed a tea tray on the desk, complete with an assortment of biscuits. Jensson waited until he had left before continuing.

"Your job will be to establish which of those it was." He rotated the teapot and poured the honey-coloured liquid into the first cup.

"Of course. Can I ask your opinion? Do you think it possible that someone threw her?"

Jensson stopped pouring and looked directly at Nikos. "No. I think it was a sad accident. The ladies who claim they saw a murder are a little over-imaginative. Not to influence your investigation at all, but I think it unlikely they can be sure of what happened. The distance, their age... to be honest, Inspector, I think we're wasting your time. But I am forced to take them seriously and report their statement. It's unfortunate, as I say. But having captained twelve of these cruises – this is my thirteenth – I notice old people have a tendency to die. Few as spectacularly as Mrs Crawford, thankfully."

Nikos took the tea from the captain. An unusual perfume wafted from the cup, but the taste was delicate. He took the opportunity of a pause to formulate his next question.

"Your thirteenth cruise? So you are not superstitious?"

Jensson shook his head. "Like most modern sailors, I believe there's no room for superstition at sea. Having said that, many of our passengers and certain elements of the crew feel differently. So it's a piece of information I have not made public. To all intents and purposes, this is my twelfth. For the second time."

"I understand. This morning's excursion – were there any men on the trip?"

"Yes. Several. Andros Metaxas, who was the tour guide, along with five male passengers, two off-duty staff members, but no crew. I have prepared a full list for you."

"There's a difference between staff and crew?"

"Most definitely. In the crudest possible terms, the staff interact with the passengers, front-of-house, as it were. The crew are operations. They run the ship."

"I see. Thank you for the list. I would like to talk to these people and the ladies who were travelling with the deceased. I also will need to visit the location. First priority is to meet the two ladies who think they saw a crime."

Jensson gave him a long look. His eyes, the pale green of shallow water, appeared to grow warmer. Nikos sensed his relief. Responsibility transferred, the death and allegation were someone else's problem now.

"All that can be arranged. I suggest you use the casino for your enquiries as it is closed during the day. One of the witnesses is still under sedation in the infirmary. When she's able to talk, you might want to interview them both together. The lady who says she saw something unusual is quite difficult to understand. She has a strong Scottish accent."

Nikos nodded. Of course she did.

"I appreciate your help, Captain. One more question, what was that tea?"

Jensson turned the label dangling out of the pot. "Earl Grey. Was it not to your taste?"

"It was delicious. I must remember the name."

Nikos took his mobile from his ear to look at the screen in exasperation. It didn't help. Chief Inspector Voulakis continued to talk, without pause for breath. Today he was in one of his moods. No matter what Nikos said, Voulakis would misunderstand. He placed the mobile back to his ear and looked around at the casino. Only the bar area was illuminated, low lights glinting off bottles and chrome. Thick carpet muffled all sound and the room smelt of furniture polish and air freshener. The voice in his ear was silent for a second, then repeated the question.

"No sir, that wasn't what I said. I can handle this case alone, I assure you. Another inspector is unnecessary. All I need is someone experienced with older British people. A native English speaker, ideally. I just need a bit of help with the language side of things."

He willed Voulakis to come to the obvious conclusion. If Nikos could get his girlfriend assigned as language support, life would be about as sweet as it could get. He closed his eyes as Voulakis embarked on another long recital of the burdens he bore and the impossible demands made of him. His eyes snapped open again as his senior officer swerved off on a different tangent.

"No, no sir. That wouldn't solve the problem at all. You don't need to bring someone from Britain. This can be managed locally. I was thinking more like a language consultant. In fact, I know at least one person..."

He may as well not have spoken. Voulakis rattled on with great enthusiasm while Nikos stared at the gleaming optics behind the bar.

"Sir, can I just..." but Voulakis had a call on the other line and promised to call back. Nikos hung up and swore. He didn't want a British detective treading on his toes and taking over. It was his case and he wanted to manage it alone. Maybe Voulakis would forget. Maybe the Brits wouldn't loan them anyone. Or maybe he should just achieve as much as he could in the next few hours and solve this problem on his own. He sat at a small table and picked up his briefcase. At least he'd remembered to download the dictionary app. He was looking up 'dementia' when there was a sharp rap at the door.

Before he could respond, the door opened and a tall man strode towards him with a scowl on his face.

"This is a waste of time. Yours and mine. I don't know what Jensson's playing at, calling in the police on the say-so of a pair of dotty old hens. I've already talked to the coroner and the local pathologist. It's clear that she fell. Sad, but nothing nefarious. My name's Fraser, by the way, Doctor Lucas Fraser."

Nikos shook the doctor's hand, trying to assemble some kind of meaning from the rapid-fire string of words. *Time, Jensson, police, sad...*

"Inspector Nikos Stephanakis. Pleased to meet you. Where are you from?"

"Fort William. Do you know Scotland at all?"

Nikos shook his head and wondered how soon Voulakis could arrange a British detective.

Chapter 4

The walk through the forest provoked a peculiar nostalgia in Beatrice as she kicked up piles of spice-coloured leaves. She stopped to admire sunlit dewdrops on a spider's web. Strands of mist still hung over the meadows and the low sun painted the landscape with an almost painful vivacity. A wood pigeon repeated its advice to sheep rustlers, *'Take TWO ewes, you fool,'* and a pair of magpies clattered off towards the village. Berries against the sky amid bare branches and a chilly breeze blowing parchment leaves across the path all combined to make her think of a phrase she'd not considered for decades. *Back to school.*

Matthew, his yellow woollen scarf wound twice around his neck, added to the dampness in the air by continuing to drone on about planning for the future. Beatrice changed the subject.

"Yes, well, as I've only just returned to work, retirement – early or otherwise – seems rather premature. What time did you book the table for tonight?"

"Eight o'clock. I know it seems premature now, but I'm talking longer term. One has to be prepared financially to give oneself the greatest range of opportunities."

"Eight? Isn't that a little late for Luke? I thought his bedtime was no later than seven."

An odd expression crossed Matthew's brow. "Luke won't be there. I told the girls that much as I adore them both, and of course, my grandson, I would prefer to spend the evening alone with you. Though I have invited them for Sunday lunch."

Beatrice stopped to look at him. His face was flushed with cold, and his hair blew around his head, giving him a boyish appearance, despite his insistence on talking about pensions.

"How very romantic of you! It's rather nice that after all these years we can still enjoy dinner à deux." She linked her arm in his and they trudged on. "I hope they've got that rabbit and prune pie on the menu tonight."

"They'll have some sort of game. Roger is a great believer in seasonal cooking. Isn't that your phone?"

Beatrice registered the sound and pulled off her gloves to reach into her pocket. Her heart sank as she saw her Chief Inspector's name on the screen.

"Oh God, it's Hamilton."

Matthew rolled his eyes and walked on. Beatrice answered the call.

"Good morning, sir. What can I do for you?"

"*Where are you, Stubbs?*"

"In Devon, sir. In a forest."

"*Damn and hell blast.*"

Beatrice followed in Matthew's wake, pressing the phone to her ear while she waited for Hamilton to continue. Distant muttering and computer noises were all she could make out. Hamilton's voice returned.

"*No, it's not going to work. Stubbs, you there?*"

"Yes sir?"

"*Listen here, apologies for the short notice etcetera, but how soon could you get on a plane to Greece?*"

Matthew held the gate open for her as they left the woodland for a sunny field. A few sheep glanced in their direction and went back to cropping grass.

"Greece? Monday, I suppose. I'm back in London Sunday night, so could be ready to travel first thing Monday morning."

"*Hmm. Bit more urgent than that. Suspicious demise of an octogenarian on a cruise ship. Any chance you could get back tonight? Fly tomorrow? I would consider this a personal favour.*"

Beatrice squeezed her eyelids together. "That's rather difficult, sir."

"*No doubt it is. But I need a trusted pair of hands. Nothing complex, only take you forty-eight hours or so. Should be able to compensate with time in lieu. And after all, two days on a Greek island in an advisory role is hardly six months in Siberia.*"

The cottage came into view as they descended the slope, smoke weaving from the chimney. She'd have to forego dinner tonight and Sunday lunch with Matthew's daughters and the always entertaining little Luke. But if she accepted the job, she could take three extra days next week to make up for it. What with next weekend, that made five full days of crosswords, forest walks, pub lunches and circular arguments about her future.

"Very well, sir. I'll catch a train back this afternoon. Could someone book me a flight for first thing tomorrow? And if you email the case details now, I'll study them on the journey back."

"*Tip top. Will do. All info to be sent soonest. Good show, Stubbs. Appreciate it.*" He rang off.

Matthew's head appeared to revolve as slowly as an owl's.

"You're going back to London." His intonation was as flat and hard as his eyes.

"I have no choice. Hamilton wants me to go to Greece for forty-eight hours. But I'll get time off in lieu, so I could be back by Wednesday. I'll cook dinners for us, we can spend time with the girls, teach Luke some new songs, visit the garden centre... oh Matthew, please don't be difficult. It's work, surely you can see that?"

He strode ahead, leaving Beatrice to hurry after him. She caught up as they reached the gate to the cottage and they trudged up the path in silence. Matthew unlocked the front door and sat on the bench to remove his boots. Beatrice stood in the doorway, determined to make him see the rationale behind her decision.

"Look, I know it's disappointing, but if I give a little now, I gain a lot more next week."

"Indeed. One must defer one's gratification. And it's not like I have any say in the matter, after all. Come on, pack your things and let's see if we can make the 12.23. What's happening in Greece?"

"No idea. Hamilton, cryptic as ever, said something about a suspicious death on a cruise ship."

"How awfully Agatha Christie!" Matthew's voice had a forced jollity, and as his head was bent to lace his shoes, she couldn't judge his expression. But she knew how precious their time together was to both of them.

"I am sorry, Matthew. I hate spoiling your weekend."

"It's not spoilt. I shall merely postpone my plans for a week. Now would you get your skates on? It'll take us a good half hour to get to the station."

She pecked him on the cheek and kicked off her wellingtons, her curiosity already piqued about exactly what her advisory role might be in Greece.

An extra five minutes spent looking for her hairbrush meant she missed the first train and had to wait half an hour till the next. Matthew bought her a baguette for the journey and stood at the ticket barrier to wave her off. She apologised once again for the interruption to their peaceful weekend routine.

"I'm used to it. Nothing involving you ever goes to plan," he said. "Now you'd better go. The quiet carriage is Coach C. And let me know when you're home."

She boarded the train, found a seat at an empty table in Coach C, unpacked her laptop and baguette and settled down to read Hamilton's email. He'd included flight details and information on her accommodation. She was flying to Heraklion, the capital of Crete, then travelling by boat to Santorini, where the liner was currently docked. An Inspector Stephanakis would meet her at the airport. It all sounded exotic and a world away from damp Devon mornings. She had no idea of distance or proximity of these places but their names alone set off all sorts of ideas. A quiver of anticipation ran through her as she imagined herself standing on a deck, watching the sunset, wearing a chiffon scarf and drinking a gin sling. She trained her attention on the case.

The situation at first glance appeared really rather simple. An old lady took an unfortunate tumble while on holiday with friends, and one of them seemed convinced it was no accident. Not the first time an excess of Sunday night television had affected perceptions in those with failing faculties. In the final year of her life, Beatrice's own mother had often ascribed incidents from *Downton Abbey* or *Coronation Street* to her neighbours, resulting in some awkward misunderstandings.

In such a non-starter of a case, Hamilton's request for her

assistance struck her as an over-reaction. Nevertheless, she would follow orders. If he considered it a personal favour, it probably meant politics were involved.

Her phone rang and she checked the screen. It was Marianne, Matthew's eldest daughter. Instantly, images of a white-faced Matthew in an ambulance flashed through her mind. Ridiculous, she'd only left him ten minutes ago.

"Marianne, hello. Is everything all right?"

Against a background of pop music, she heard Marianne's laugh.

"*I was calling to ask you the same question. Dad just phoned to ask if I'd like to join him at The Toad tonight because you had to go back to London. There's nothing wrong, is there?*"

"Not at all." She dropped her voice for fear of disturbing the other passengers. "My boss needs me to go to Greece to assist with an investigation, so I have to fly out tomorrow. Didn't your father tell you that?"

"*Yes, that's what he said. I just wanted to check he hadn't, you know, upset you or anything.*"

"Far from it. To be honest, I think it's the other way around. My dashing off has put his nose out of sorts. But he's being decent and has accepted it with typical grumpy grace."

"*He would. And there's always next weekend to put his plans into action. OK, so long as everything is fine between you two, I'll call Tanya to rearrange next Sunday. I'm so looking forward to this! Good luck in Greece and see you soon!*"

Beatrice ended the call and watched the fields flicker by, glowing as if irradiated in autumnal sunshine. Marianne's words suffused her with a sense of belonging, of acceptance and a depth of almost maternal affection she'd never expected to experience. Her phone beeped again. A text message.

Sorry to miss the big lunch! But can't wait for next weekend. Love, Tanya and Luke xoxo

So much spontaneous warmth made her smile and hug herself. That feeling took a long time to fade.

Until she started thinking.

A delay between Reading and Paddington meant she eventually got back to Boot Street at half past four. The City cast long shadows across the East End as shops and stalls began the process of giving way to the alternative landscape of the night. Impatient to discuss her theories, Beatrice was irritated to get no response from her neighbour's bell. On a Saturday afternoon, with a new boyfriend in tow, Adrian could be anywhere. Probably on the South Bank, dallying in a second-hand bookshop, pottering about in a craft market or enjoying good food by the river. The fact that she could have been doing the same things in a Devon village only made it worse. She stomped upstairs and started repacking her weekend bag. Greece, in November. What to wear? Which essential medicinal products to take?

She yanked out an article on wine she'd intended to share with Matthew and her conscience pricked. However, the conviction she'd arrived at on the train precluded a call. She sent a brief, upbeat text message assuring him of her safe arrival and opened the bathroom cabinet to find the Imodium.

Chapter 5

Unable to settle to television, book or case file, Beatrice opted for the Internet. Ostensibly research, but actually distraction. Images of Greek islands proved rather alluring. So much so that the doorbell gave her a real start. She picked up the intercom.

"Hello?"

"Oh, Beatrice, it is you. That's a relief. We saw the light and assumed the worst. Why are you back so soon?"

"Hello, Adrian. I have to work, unfortunately. What are you two up to tonight?"

"Clubbing, I think, but not till later. Now we're having cheese, crackers, a rich Bordeaux and *Strictly Come Dancing*. Want to join us?"

Beatrice weighed her loathing of reality TV against her urge to talk.

"I'll have a look in the cupboards to see what I can contribute. Then I'll be down in two shakes of a ham's tail. Are you sure I'm not intruding?"

"Don't be silly. Hurry up. I want to show you my new hair."

Holger opened the door and stooped to kiss Beatrice on both cheeks. He wore a tight lilac T-shirt with a tea-towel flopped over his shoulder and smelt of a crisp sea-breeze shower gel. He unbent to his full height and pointed with a frown at her carrier bag.

"You didn't need to bring anything. We have more than enough. Are you fine, Beatrice?"

She nodded. "Yes. I'm only back here because I have to fly to Greece in the morning. Did you have a lovely day exploring the capital?"

Holger gestured for her to follow him inside. "Perfect. The weather is good for photographs and I love to spend time in markets and art galleries."

"Me too. Did you go to Camden?"

"No, Adrian said it was too touristy. We went to Borough and Spitalfields."

His muscular bulk blocked out the light as they entered the living-room.

"Our guest is here!" called Holger, offering to take her bag.

"Hello, Beatrice! Come in and let me pour you a glass." Adrian, wearing a paisley-print shirt and jeans, stood at the kitchen island, uncorking a bottle of wine. His dark hair was spiked up into a mini-quiff reminding her of a young Tony Curtis.

"Hello you. Nice haircut. You look rather rockabilly."

"Do you like it? Couldn't do the whole James Dean thing but I fancied going a bit 'collar up' for a while. What's in the bag?"

"I brought oatcakes, Twiglets, some Godminster and one of Matthew's recommendations. It's a *Nuit Saint Georges*."

"You didn't need to bring anything, but seeing as you did, I'm glad it's something divine. Now sit down and tell me what happened. You haven't fallen out with Matthew, I hope?"

"No, no. Quite the opposite. Hamilton summoned me back so that I can be in Greece by tomorrow. A death on a cruise ship needs investigating. Looks straightforward enough so should only take a couple of days."

Adrian handed her a glass and pecked her on both cheeks. "Let's toast! To a glorious Sunday, whether in the East End, a Devon village or a Greek beach. Cheers!"

They repeated the toast, clinked glasses and drank. The wine was earthy and rich, and strangely soothing.

Holger gestured towards the living-room with his glass. "You two go and sit down. I'll add Beatrice's things and bring the tray in."

They did as they were told.

Adrian sat beside her on the sofa and dropped his voice. "I am utterly besotted. If I'd been given *carte blanche* to design my perfect man, I'd have never thought of some of those details. He's almost too good to be true."

"I must say, every time I see him, he gets better looking. When is he going back to Hamburg?"

"Monday. But two weeks later, he'll be back to stay for three months. He's got a job with an instrument-making shop in... where's that place again, Holger?"

Holger entered the room and placed a heavily laden tray on the coffee table in front of them. "South Thames College. I'm teaching advanced guitar-making. In Morden."

"Morden? Bit of a trek. Still, at least it's only one Tube line from here."

A look passed between the two men. "Um, Holger's not moving in, Beatrice. He has a place all lined up near Angel. But yes, it's still only one Tube line."

A blush crept up Beatrice's neck. "Sorry, I didn't mean to make assumptions. You're absolutely right to take things slowly. I mean, who knows what might happen in the next..."

Adrian laughed. "I think you'd better stop there before you dig yourself a deeper hole." He looked at Holger. "She means what she says about taking it slowly. How long have you and Matthew been together? Twenty years and they still haven't made the leap to cohabitation."

Beatrice forced a laugh to join in with Holger, despite a feeling of looming dread. Her observant neighbour picked up on her mood.

"Come on, let's eat. *Strictly*'s on in ten minutes. Beatrice, you said earlier, when I asked if you two had fallen out, you said it was quite the opposite. Are you going to elaborate? Has he popped the question?"

This time it was impossible to fake a laugh. It took a second for Adrian to notice her frozen posture and locked jaw, as he was helping himself to a slice of Godminster and an oatcake.

"Oh my God! Beatrice? He has!"

She shook her head. "No, he hasn't. Not yet. But he's going to, I know it. If I hadn't got the call from work, he'd be doing it now, across the table at The Toad. As it is, he'll find the right moment next weekend. What the hell am I going to do?"

Holger stared at her and Adrian put down his plate. "This is serious. Holger, top up the wine. I'll set the TV to record. Now, DI Stubbs, kindly start at the beginning."

It took some time to explain: Matthew's recent obsession with planning the future, the 'just the two of us' dinner plans, Marianne's call, Tanya's text message and the sudden realisation that every expectation was pinned on an imminent wedding. She finally stopped talking and Holger handed her a plate. Dear man, he'd already prepared a variety of cheeses, slices of fruit and selection of crackers. Sharing her concerns left her lighter, so she tucked into Brie on a water biscuit with a couple of grapes.

Adrian swirled the contents of his glass. He seemed lost in the deep colours. Beatrice and Holger both waited for him to speak. He looked up and nodded.

"I have to agree. It definitely sounds as if that is what he's planning. Your detective work is flawless, as always. The question now must be, what next? Holger, what do you say?"

Holger examined a Twiglet and replaced it on his plate. "For me, there is only one question. Beatrice, do you love Matthew?"

She nodded, her mouth full.

"So what is the difficulty here? Go to Greece, do what you need to do quickly and return to him. Wait for his question and answer from your heart. If you love him, if your relationship has already lasted twenty years, why not marry the man?"

Beatrice swallowed. That was the trouble with Germans. Always so logical. His argument made perfect sense and only someone wilfully perverse could disagree. She took a swig of wine and attempted to explain.

"You're absolutely right. The problem is that I can't help but see marriage as an end, rather than a beginning. I've spent over fifty years as an independent woman, and to give up now..." Her voice cracked and tears clouded her vision. Two bodies bundled close and draped arms around her back. She sniffed and yanked a tissue from her sleeve.

"Sorry, sorry. I know this is a problem of my own making. But I really don't know why things have to change. We've been happy like this for ages, so why rock the boat? I don't want to be a Devon housewife, tending courgettes and making jam and joining the Women's Institute. The very thought makes me hyperventilate. What the hell is the matter with the man? I don't know why he would propose now."

No one spoke for a few seconds. Beatrice thought back to one of her mother's favourite sayings, 'Old age don't come alone'.

Holger cleared his throat. "Are you sure you don't know why?"

She shook her head. "No, I do."

Adrian raised his eyebrows. "I think you'll find the generally accepted expression is just 'I do'. Might come in handy one of these days."

Beatrice gave a profound sigh. "Two little words that could change everything."

Adrian leaned forward to catch Holger's eye. "And you call me a drama queen?"

Taxi booked, online check-in complete, case packed and alarm set, Beatrice began preparing herself for bed. She was brushing her teeth when the phone rang.

"Hello?"

"*Stubbs, Hamilton here. All set for tomorrow?*"

"Yes sir. It doesn't seem especially complex. Is this more an exercise in cooperation?"

"*Yes and no. The fellow at the helm is new to the game and his grasp of the lingo is not the best. You're there as mentor. Play second fiddle, guide him in the right direction and only step in if he looks liable to bugger it up. And do it quickly, Stubbs. I need you back here.*"

"I'll do my best, sir. Is there another case on the agenda?"

"*Not exactly. Plan is, assign you to Operation Horseshoe, learn the ropes and take over from Rangarajan.*"

"Take over? But sir, Ranga's doing a great job! I don't understand why you would want to replace him now. Putting a white woman on the case instead of a senior Asian male seems counter-intuitive."

"*Of course you don't understand. Because as per bloody usual, Stubbs, you don't have the full picture. Rangarajan is taking early retirement at the end of this year. Horseshoe is an extraordinarily complicated operation, which requires a sensitive touch and a thorough understanding of cultural mores. When Ranga retires, I need a safe pair of hands on the tiller.*"

"Oh, I see. I had no idea he was thinking of early retirement as well."

There was an extended silence at the other end of the line. Beatrice winced. Another two little words.

"*I beg your pardon? Did you just say 'as well'?*"

"Sorry, sir. Nothing decided yet. Just an idea I've been considering."

"*Have you now? Well, you can damn well unconsider it. Do you have any idea whatsoever of the efforts I have made to keep you in your post? Of the political persuasion I've brought to bear in order to retain a person viewed by many as perilously close to being a loose bloody cannon? No, you don't. I refused to accept your resignation earlier this year because I believe in you. Sometimes, I wonder why. At your best, you are an asset to my team. At worst, you are a stubborn old coot who is a bigger pain than an infected wisdom tooth. On top of this, I am not prepared to lose two of my best senior detectives in one year. So please put all thoughts of premature retirement out of your mind and concentrate on the job in hand. Sort yourself out, Stubbs. Good night.*"

The disconnection tone beeped in her ear and she replaced the receiver. She sat in the window seat, looking out over Boot Street. Thirty years she'd lived in this flat. Twenty four years she'd been with Matthew. Coming up fifteen years she'd worked with Hamilton. In five years, she could officially retire. And then? Time trickled through her fingers and she could no more hold onto it than water.

With a shake, she pulled herself back from such unhealthy introspection. She checked her bags again, took her medication and she focused on what tomorrow held in store, while applying face cream. As she switched off the light, a thought occurred. Even if some of her colleagues did see her as a 'stubborn old coot', a cruise ship full of octogenarians would see her as a mere spring chicken.

Chapter 6

Her documents obviously marked her as an official to be respected, so her passage through Heraklion's airport was effortless. In the Arrivals area, she spotted a good-looking young man in shirtsleeves and chinos waiting beside a uniformed officer who held a sign saying STUBS. Beatrice raised a hand and offered a smile. The detective came towards her.

"Pleased to meet you, Detective Inspector Stubbs. How do you do?"

She shook his hand. "Very well, thank you. You must be Inspector Stephanakis."

"Correct. Welcome to Greece. How was your flight?" He relieved her of her bag, which he passed to the driver.

"Lovely. From London to Athens, I had the good fortune to sit next to the most fascinating lady. A sculptress who has lived there for over ten years. She gave me some very helpful cultural advice. For the first time I can recall, a flight went almost too quickly."

They followed the driver to the exit, where a police car was parked outside the door. The heat surprised her. London, when she left, had been a shivery five degrees.

Stephanakis opened the rear door. After checking she was comfortable, he went round the other side and joined her in the back. He shot some instructions at the driver in Greek and glanced at his phone. His chivalrous manner and clean-shaven face appealed to Beatrice. Very proper. He fixed his attention on her with a nervous smile.

"DI Stubbs, I am very pleased to meet you. I just got promoted to the role of inspector, and it is very exciting for me to work with someone with such a track record. But I must apologise in advance.

This is my first investigation and although it is not really complex, my boss thought my enquiries would benefit from an experienced officer, so..." He looked down at his phone once more.

Beatrice smiled, well used to preparing speeches before joining a new team.

"... I will need your patience. I know this area and police procedure very well and I hope I can contribute much."

"Don't worry, Inspector. I understand this is your first case. But they wouldn't have promoted you if you weren't competent. I trust you entirely to lead this case to its conclusion, and I want to stress, I'm assisting you. You're the boss."

He nodded, his uncertain smile and restless eyes expressing both gratitude and trepidation.

Beatrice smiled back and looked out of the window. This would be just the tonic she needed. A mini-break disguised as work, with sunshine, delightful scenery and an open-and-shut case. She'd think about Matthew when she got back.

The driver dropped her at the hotel to settle in and Stephanakis promised to return in time to take her to lunch. She dumped her bags and as always on arriving at a hotel room, checked the bathroom for cleanliness. Perfectly satisfactory. Even the end of the toilet paper had been folded into a neat triangle. She bounced on the bed, explored the mini-bar and took a bottle of water out onto the balcony. A sense of foreignness overcame her and gave her a sudden thrill of anticipation. The building opposite was cracked and crumbling, large chunks of plaster revealing the bricks beneath. Faded green shutters framed the windows and a cluster of mopeds were strewn rather than parked under the shade of a palm tree. Electric cables hung above the narrow street like necklaces in a costume jewellery store and a blue sign announced the name of the street in Greek. In a gap between dusty apartment blocks, beyond decorative balconies with plants in terracotta pots, past roof terraces with rattan furniture and pergolas, lay the sea.

Beatrice beamed and took a deep breath. Yes, in amongst the scent of petrol rising from the street and stale chemicals wafting from the air-conditioner unit, she could detect ozone. Closer to land the water was paler, the colour of cornflowers, deepening to an intense azure as it met the sky, which seemed bigger and bluer than it could ever be in London.

The telephone rang. Stephanakis was waiting to take her to lunch.

"It's nothing special, but a place I use a lot," he said, as he guided her along the pedestrianised street. "I thought you might be hungry."

Beatrice was admiring the sandy colours and the mosaic kaleidoscope created by the sea-blue shutters, white umbrellas, wrought-iron benches and lamps lining the avenue between the trees. Echoes of beach everywhere, as if it had crawled up the street and into the consciousness. She realised the young inspector was waiting for a reply.

"Hungry? I could eat a horse."

He gave her a look of mock alarm.

"Horse might be a problem, but I could arrange a goat."

"So long as it's dead and comes with chips, I'll eat anything. I am entirely in your hands."

Noisy and crowded, the taverna smelt delicious. Several people greeted Stephanakis and shot curious glances at her. Without warning, a cheery sort with a once-white apron shouted something incomprehensible at Stephanakis and grabbed Beatrice to kiss her on both cheeks. Stephanakis muttered a brief explanation and the man laughed from the belly.

"Detective Inspector Stubbs, this is Dinos. He owns this restaurant and cooks the food himself."

"God Save the Queen! *Kalimera!*"

"*Kalimera!*" she replied, grateful for the crash course from the sculptress on the plane.

Dinos found them a tiny table and Stephanakis checked the blackboard.

"Would you like me to translate the menu?"

"I eat everything and I am very hungry. So let's order the dish of the day, lots of bread, a jug of wine and get cracking."

Stephanakis stared at her for a second. Then he broke into a grin and relayed their order to Dinos, who evidently approved. He clapped his hands together, gripped her shoulder and said "Very good!" With a shake and a wink, he barrelled off towards the kitchen.

"Well, if the food is as hearty as the welcome, we're in for a treat. Good choice, Inspector."

"Dinos is a minor local celebrity and he's obsessed with your royal family. You should have seen how he decorated this place for that wedding. But he's mostly famous for his food. So don't worry, your meal will be delicious."

"I can't wait. And that is no idle platitude. Now, can we talk about the case? From what I've read, an elderly lady's tragic fall has been rather blown out of proportion by some of her companions. They suspect a deliberate attempt to harm her. Do you see any evidence of that?"

Stephanakis furrowed his brow. "That's not quite right. The ladies who saw the fall are not of the same party. We will interview the witnesses as soon as the doctor gives permission. But their story seems unlikely. The deceased was eighty years old; the witnesses are both retired and saw the incident through a camera. It's very hard to get a clear account of what happened. That's why I requested a specialist, someone accustomed to interviewing in English. So I'm happy you are here. My language skills aren't bad but I have real problems communicating with some of these older ladies or people with a strong accent. Your help is really appreciated."

As he spoke, Beatrice studied the young man. A smooth olive complexion, with cappuccino-coloured lips, shiny black hair and mahogany eyes added up to a very pleasing overall effect. Nascent wrinkles at the corners of his eyes added a feathery effect to his lashes. His polite manner and respectful attitude had already impressed her and now he had passed the first test. With careful diplomacy, he'd corrected her inaccurate assessment of the case, topping it off with a sprinkling of humility.

"I'm happy to be here," she said, and meant it. "Can you tell me anything else?"

"Esther Crawford was travelling with a group of friends from

England. Every year, they take a cruise together. Seven women, all in their seventies or eighties, who call themselves 'The Hirondelles'. The woman who claims she witnessed a murder is from Scotland and in her sixties. As far as I know, they had no contact with each other."

"Who else have you spoken to?"

"The captain, one of the ship's doctors, two of the deceased's companions and the Santorini police who recovered the body."

"So what is your plan?"

"Should we visit the site first?"

Beatrice cocked her head on one side.

He took the hint. "OK. First, we should visit the site and check the facts. Next, we interview the witnesses. If there is reasonable doubt, we conduct an investigation. I'm sure this can be resolved in a couple of days."

"Sounds like you have it all under control, Inspector. So should I act as interviewer while you take notes? Mind now, here's the food."

Dinos placed the plates on the table with a flourish. "*Stifado!*"

A rich-looking meat stew with jewels of oil floating on the surface, some roast potatoes decorated with cloves of garlic and sprigs of rosemary, a platter of bread and a generous terracotta jug of wine. The time to talk shop was over. She gave Dinos an approving smile and picked up her fork.

"How do you say *bon appétit* in Greek?"

"*Kali sas órexi.*"

"And the same to you."

The speedboat bounced over the waves and the island of Santorini grew larger on the horizon. Beatrice admitted relief. After the first half hour of sea spray, Mediterranean blue water, glittering sunshine and wind on her cheeks, exhilaration gave way to discomfort. Bless Adrian for insisting she tucked the Hermès headscarf he'd given her into her handbag. Without that, factor 50 sunscreen and her dark glasses, things could have been a lot worse. Stephanakis had stopped checking her every couple of minutes after it was clear she would not be regurgitating her lunch and now kept his eyes on the island ahead. She followed suit.

At first sight, the island did not live up to the pictures she had seen during her research. Stark, forbidding cliffs rose from the sea, while cruise vessels and ferries filled the busy harbour. A switch-back road scored a zigzag up the cliffs like a lightning strike. Not at all the kind of environment to host terraces of blue rooftops, pots of geraniums or ginger cats.

The police boat slowed and all the signs of a busy commercial port emerged. Filthy water, slicked with oil. Massive rusting chains upon which noisy seabirds perched, adding their own form of decoration. The fresh whiff of the sea was overpowered by diesel and exhaust fumes, and the sound of ferries, coaches, and larger boats drowned out the now-familiar buzz of their own engine.

Stephanakis left his post beside the driver and sat next to her. He raised his voice above the noise.

"This is Athinos, the ferry port. Most cruise ships use the Old Port, in Thira. But the only way up to the town of Thira is donkey or cable car. For the ladies of the *Empress Louise*, that was not an option. They travelled by coach to Fira, the main city, which is where everyone goes. The classic Santorini of the postcards. So we follow the same route. The pathologist will meet us at the dock."

"The island has its own pathologist?"

Stephanakis watched as the boat nosed a path towards a berth. "No, he is based in Heraklion, but he always takes the SeaCat. He has problems with small boats."

Not only small boats, it seemed. The hue and tone of Konstakis Apostolou's expression reminded Beatrice of a morgue wall. He exchanged pleasantries in English, a strong scent of peppermint on his breath, before climbing into the police car with less enthusiasm for life than of one of the local donkeys. Stephanakis, in the front, conversed with the local officer; Apostolou, beside Beatrice, rested his head against the window while she gazed out at the sea and the distant calderas. The switchback road provided a constantly shifting perspective, climbing higher and higher; each new turn giving more spectacular views. Something inside her seemed to lift; not her heart, and certainly not her stomach, but in her solar plexus; this place, this endless landscape, this miracle of geography filled her with a joy which threatened to boil up and explode.

The road levelled out and the driver trundled along the coast. Beatrice decided Apostolou needed a distraction. Normally, discussing a corpse with a queasy sort would be inappropriate, but in this instance, it was practically home from home.

"What a wonderful view, Mr Apostolou! But I'm sure you're used to it by now and bored by a tourist's chatter. Could we make the most of our time? Would you mind if I asked a few questions regarding your initial examination?"

His head swivelled in her direction. The cold black eyes and skin the colour of uncooked pastry made her think of a gecko.

"Yes. No. I don't mind."

"On initial examination and after the full autopsy, did you find any evidence to make you suspect anything other than accidental death?"

He wound down the window a few centimetres and breathed. His goatee beard was a masterpiece of precision.

"No, nothing at all. She obviously overbalanced, lost her footing and fell over the edge. No one could survive such a fall. At eighty years old, she probably had a heart attack before hitting the ground."

Beatrice gazed out at the bay, maintaining her smile.

"You say 'probably'. In all my experience of pathology, that's a word rarely used in physiological terms. When hazarding a guess as to circumstances or perpetrators, perhaps. But as to the definitive state of a corpse? Do you believe Esther Crawford had a heart attack? Before or after she fell?"

He tilted his head to the incoming breeze. Colour, if only a faint peach, returned to his cheeks.

"My investigation is not complete. I can tell you only that an elderly woman fell to her death from a cliff. A post-mortem on such a body will take time, especially with the complications of her being a tourist. And a two-hundred-metre drop makes any examination problematic. Regardless of what we find, one old woman's delusions will not reanimate the deceased."

Stephanakis leaned around to face them. "We stop at the site of the incident now, and then proceed to Fira, which is where the coach party stopped for lunch. We follow their route. But this is the place where Mrs Esther Crawford died."

The driver pulled into a parking area, an ideal spot for tourists to take photographs.

"You said Fira is the main tourist town?" Beatrice asked.

Apostolou answered. "The main tourist town is Oia."

"Here? But this is a car park."

"No," Stephanakis smiled. "He's talking about the town of Oia. It's pronounced 'ee-ya'. Famous for the sunset views and very popular with tourists, especially honeymooners. Many people come to Santorini to get married. It is a perfect location for a wedding."

Wedding locations were not a subject that interested Beatrice in the slightest. Several large coaches were lined up against the cliffs; huge protruding wing mirrors gave them the appearance of enormous soldier ants. Their passengers spread along the viewpoint, posing, snapping and pointing while their drivers smoked in the shade of the vehicles. Apostolou got out of the car and rested against the bonnet for several seconds while Stephanakis and Beatrice made for the edge.

"I'm puzzled, Inspector. There's a safety barrier all along the front. So how on earth did she manage to fall? And if she was pushed, how would you get an eighty-year-old over that without being seen?"

"It wasn't here. The incident happened further along the path. The barrier is only at the beginning. Mrs Crawford fell from the unprotected section."

"I see. Still, there are so many people hanging about, surely such an incident could never go unnoticed. I imagine this place has a constant stream of visitors throughout the day."

"Yes, it does, but between twelve and two is always a quiet time. It's the same with most scenic sites. The islands operate on a tourist timetable. Coach companies work with the restaurants to deliver all their passengers in shifts. So places like this are usually empty over lunch. Mrs Crawford died at quarter past midday."

"So what was she doing here? Why was she up here alone?"

Apostolou joined them. "Her party failed to realise she had been left behind. No one noticed until a head count was taken at the restaurant. She probably got lost and missed the departure time. I presume I'm using the word 'probably' in an acceptable way this time?"

Beatrice shot him a look, but his eyes crinkled as he smiled. Apparently recovered, he had a dapper, genial air with an observant expression.

"Yes, that is acceptable," she replied. "Time of death is 12.15? That's awfully precise considering your post-mortem is unfinished."

"Inspector Stephanakis can be more precise than I. There were witnesses."

Stephanakis nodded slowly. "Not the ladies up on the ridge, who claim she was thrown." He pointed above the coaches. "Although one of them took a photograph just after the incident. Nothing to see, of course, but the time was 12.16. But down in the bay, a couple of... what is the name for diving without the oxygen tank? Just with breath?"

"Free diving. There were free divers at the bottom of the cliff?" Beatrice asked.

"On a boat. These cliffs are the walls of a volcano. They go down a further 400 metres. The free divers were preparing to jump when they saw, and heard, someone hit the ground. They raised the alarm."

"That was at 12.20," added Apostolou. "The local police retrieved the body an hour or so later and I attended the mortuary at 17.00. Mrs Crawford had all the injuries consistent with a long fall. Broken neck, severe abrasions, various fractures and almost complete destruction of her internal organs. It's not the first time I've seen this sort of thing."

The party walked single file down the path until Stephanakis indicated they had arrived at the spot. The two men flanked Beatrice as they gazed down at the sheer volcanic rock, waves crashing spume into the base. Out of the corner of her eye, she saw Stephanakis cross himself, with a quick and practised gesture.

"Now," she said, "let's have a look at the witnesses' picnic spot and see what kind of a view they had."

Stephanakis looked at her feet.

"What?" she demanded.

"Nothing. It's very good. You are a detective. Of course you wear the right kind of shoes."

They clambered up the cliff path, Beatrice wondering why such a description of her footwear made her nose throb.

Chapter 7

It was hard to comprehend the proportions of the *Empress Louise*. Standing on the quayside, eleven floors were visible and there must have been more below the waterline. It was as tall as a cathedral and ten blocks long – a skyscraper on its side. The pristine whiteness and uniform patterns suggested a vast hotel complex, which was probably close to reality.

Beatrice looked at Stephanakis. "Big, isn't it?" she said.

"Big is one word for her. She carries just over two thousand passengers and another thousand people in terms of crew and staff. Fifteen decks, eighty metres high and two hundred and eighty metres long. She has eleven restaurants, four pools, three theatres, four bars, a nightclub, two cinemas, a casino, a place of worship and a shopping mall. The *Empress Louise* specialises in 'seniors', so she has a substantial medical centre, plenty of wheelchair accessible cabins and a morgue."

"Been doing your research, Inspector?"

"I'm fascinated by the scale of the thing. You know, this ship is bigger than the village where I grew up."

"Same here. Let's hope we don't get lost. Shall we make a start on these interviews?"

Greek speakers to Stephanakis and English speakers divided between them. The casino was easily large enough to accommodate two interview areas. Stephanakis occupied a table near the bar, close to the door. Beatrice walked further back, past the serried lines of slot machines, the roulette wheel and the various card tables before she found what she was looking for. An elevated relaxation platform with comfortable banquettes and two highly polished tables that would serve as both work station and rather sophisticated interview room. The distance and the amount of wood and carpet between her and Stephanakis would ensure no conversations could be overheard. She unpacked her briefcase and gazed around the darkened space, curious as to how different it would seem with all the flashing lights, glamorous people, champagne, laughter, cheers and noise. She decided she could probably live without the experience.

Her first interviewee was Captain Jensson. Tall and blond in his impressive uniform, with Nordic blue eyes, yet disappointingly without a proper captain's beard. Nevertheless, he was clearly a professional. He had come prepared. Printouts of the itinerary, the passenger list from the excursion highlighted by gender, a file on the deceased including medical records and a photograph of the dead woman. He'd thought of everything.

Next up, Dr Fraser. Belligerent, impatient and judging by the difficulty of their exchange, possibly hard of hearing. He brought nothing but attitude, adding very little to what she already knew of Esther Crawford. His one revealing remark was his dismissal of the witness as senile. Beatrice pressed him as to the medical accuracy of such a statement, which he brushed off as a joke.

The Hirondelles followed, Esther Crawford's travelling companions. In their late seventies to mid-eighties, they were all visibly distressed by the death of their friend. Talking to a police officer alarmed them still further. Beatrice tried interviewing them in pairs, hoping they might feel less intimidated, but the effect was an echo chamber of cliché and emotion. After talking to four out of the six, the only useful piece of information they'd given was that Esther Crawford had been a bird-watcher and often wandered off during excursions.

Once they'd left, she wrote up her notes, the beginnings of a headache thumping behind her eyes. The darkness, at first so calming and discreet, now felt oppressive and cloistered. Beatrice needed some air. She waited till her colleague's interviewee had departed, then suggested a break and comparison of notes so far. A bright young man, he welcomed the idea immediately. It served her less selfish agenda as well. She could ensure Stephanakis needed no additional support while getting an essential boost of sugar and caffeine. Her role as mentor was to lead by example, after all.

It was a strange experience to emerge from the ship's casino into brilliant sunshine. They chose to sit outside at The Boardwalk, one of the smaller restaurant-cafés on an upper deck, and share their findings. The sea breeze eased her headache before she'd even ordered coffee, plus something honey-soaked to boost her sugar levels. She dug out her sunglasses, settled opposite Stephanakis and absorbed the view, allowing herself to relax.

"What an afternoon! I feel like I've had the same conversation with four different people. I'm not sure I learnt anything more than what a sweet person Esther Crawford was. What about you? How were your interviews with the crew?"

"I didn't learn much either. Some of the staff and crew had gone ashore, but not to the tourist areas. No one saw anything and none of them seemed very interested. I have the feeling all the passengers are just one big faceless group to them."

"Not surprising, I suppose." The waiter brought their order: *baklava* and cappuccino for her, an Earl Grey tea for him.

Beatrice lifted her face to the sun while Stephanakis flicked through his notebook. Back home, she'd be donning her wellies to walk through the rain with Matthew. She changed thought tracks and focused her mind on the present.

"That doctor I spoke to. I don't think much of his bedside manner, do you?"

Stephanakis smiled. "Dr Fraser? He seems in a bad temper all of the time, if that's what you mean. But I can't be sure because I only understand about one word in ten."

"Yes, he has an accent all right. And a tendency to shout. Perhaps that's from talking to so many people with hearing problems. I believe he might have one himself. I'm sure a constant stream of old folks' ailments can be tedious, but if you work on a ship like this, what can you expect?"

"Did he tell you he never actually treated Mrs Crawford? She saw

Dr Weinberg once about her low blood pressure, who prescribed iron tablets. But the nurse..." he opened his notepad and checked. "Sister Bannerjee said that she came back two days later because the tablets made her sick."

"Low blood pressure can cause fainting. I must ask her colleagues if she suffered from dizziness at all. Although even if she did, I can't see why she was wandering about alone or how she could fall over the edge of the cliff." She picked up her fork and tucked into her sticky-looking dessert.

A shadow fell over their table. "Sorry to interrupt."

Beatrice looked up with a start. "Dr Fraser, hello again."

"Just to let you know, I've given the all-clear for you to speak to the ladies who think they saw the bogeyman. Mrs Campbell is still very shaken, so don't expect too much. You may get more sense out of her companion, Rose Mason. She seems to have her head screwed on. Of course, she didn't actually see anything. Probably because there was nothing to see."

"Thanks for your permission, doctor. We'll visit them as soon as we're done here."

"Very good. Go to the infirmary reception. They're expecting you." He strode away.

Stephanakis watched him go. "What is a bogeyman?"

Beatrice stirred her coffee in irritation.

"A non-existent scary creature designed to frighten children. Dr Fraser is being very patronising. His perspective is relevant, of course, but if he discredits witnesses before we interview them, that is prejudicial. If he continues like this, we'll have to ask him to keep his opinions to himself."

After their coffee break, Beatrice and Stephanakis went in search of the infirmary, following the map they had been given. It was the first time they'd moved around the ship without a guide and soon found themselves completely lost. Stephanakis looked from the map to the signage in increasing frustration. Beatrice, as she always did on such occasions, asked a passer-by. A well-dressed man approached, wearing a navy houndstooth-checked blazer, pale trousers and open-necked shirt. He was carrying a book. Always a good sign In Beatrice's estimation.

"Excuse me. Do you speak English?"

He stopped and looked down at her with warm, light-brown eyes. "I do. Can I be of assistance?"

"We're looking for the infirmary, but seem to have taken a wrong turn. Would you happen to know where it is?"

His forehead creased and unfolded. "As a matter of fact, I know exactly where it is. You're almost in the correct place, just one deck too high. If you go down to the end of this corridor, you'll find stairs down to the next level. Double back on yourselves and you'll see the door on your left." He smiled, his tanned skin wrinkling into well-worn grooves. Beatrice smiled back. He reminded her of someone. She couldn't recall who, but it was definitely someone she liked.

"You're very kind. Thank you."

He wished them both a pleasant afternoon and continued up the corridor, stooping to duck under the doorway.

Maggie Campbell finished her story and took a moment to compose herself. Her companion, Rose Mason, reached for her hand. Marguerite and Rose. Beatrice briefly wished she'd been born in an era when it was fashionable to name one's children after flowers or precious stones. The two women could have been sisters. Both wore hyacinth shades of blue, had soft grey hair, pale powdery skin and bright eyes. Mauve shadows swelled under Maggie's eyes as she battled tears. She won. After several swallows, she was ready to speak again.

"Detective Inspector Stubbs, I'm not at all surprised people don't believe me. I still find it hard to credit myself. But I swear on all I hold dear, I saw a man throw that lady off the cliff, so help me God. I couldn't identify either of them, but she was wearing the Hirondelle uniform and she recognised him. He was tall. When he met her, she seemed relieved to see him. She wasn't surprised, though. The sort of reaction you'd have if you'd lost someone and then found them again." She scrunched up her eyes and clenched her fists. "That poor, poor woman. Dr Fraser told me she'd celebrated her eightieth birthday on board. Why would anyone do that to a harmless pensioner?"

Stephanakis met Beatrice's eyes. The four of them sat around a small table in the infirmary lounge; Stephanakis taking notes, Maggie giving her statement, Beatrice asking the questions and Rose Mason supporting her friend and gently prodding her to remember the details.

Rose spoke. "That's what the police want to find out, Maggie. So you have to help them as much as possible. Do you remember you told me one of the crew had found her? You seemed very sure the man was from the *Empress Louise*. Can you remember why you said that?"

"It was only an assumption. All I can remember is that he was a lot taller than her and wore white. Or it could have been cream, I suppose. The midday sun tends to bleach everything. I couldn't tell you his hair colour as he was wearing that hat they all wear. It looked like the white uniform and because she seemed to know him, I thought he had to be a crew member. But I definitely have no evidence for that and would want to make no accusations."

Beatrice glanced at Stephanakis, with a slight twitch of her eyebrow. He got the message and cleared his throat. "Thank you, Mrs Campbell. Can you think of anything else about the man which might help us? Did you see where he came from?"

"From below where we were sitting. But that's where all the coaches park, so it doesn't really help, does it?"

Beatrice nodded her reassurance. "Do you mind if I ask why you were up there? Why you chose to take a picnic off on your own?"

Maggie sniffed and jerked her head in the direction of Rose. "Ask her."

Rose gave an embarrassed smile. "Cruises aren't really my thing. I agreed to try it, as Maggie was so keen, but I am not enjoying the experience, to be truthful. The whole thing feels a bit stage-managed. We snatch every opportunity to go ashore and do our own thing. We try to escape the coach tours, go in the opposite direction to the herd and avoid anything that looks like a tourist spot. When we docked at Santorini, we hired a moped and took a picnic up to the cliffs, deliberately choosing a spot where we could appreciate the view, but no one else could see us. It sort of backfired this time."

"You hired a moped?" Stephanakis asked, a note of disbelief in his voice.

"Yes, I like scooters." Rose's face cleared. "They remind me of the good old times on the south coast. I used to be a mod, back in the day."

"Me too. Or at least I wanted to be. Never really had the looks." Beatrice shared a complicit smile with Rose, aware she was excluding Stephanakis. The bond and trust with the witness came first. She could explain to him later.

"Where did you get the picnic?" asked Stephanakis.

Maggie answered. "You can order them aboard and they have it ready for just after the ship docks. All beautifully presented in a wee hamper. They even remember the salt."

"And while you watched the man throw the woman through your camera, Mrs Campbell, you didn't take a photograph?"

"No. I wasn't ready... I just watched." Maggie pinched her lips together.

"And you saw nothing at all, Mrs Mason?"

Rose shook her head. "No. I'm not sure if I should be glad or sorry about that. Seeing how much it has traumatised Maggie, part of me is relieved. But I also wish I could back her up with something more concrete when people like that bully of a doctor make it clear they think she's doolally. To answer your question, Inspector, no. I was packing away the picnic and listening to her commentary. But I have no doubt whatsoever that Maggie saw what she says she saw. She was not suffering from heatstroke, she wasn't tipsy and she is in full possession of all her marbles."

The two women exchanged a look which made Beatrice soften. But she had to state facts.

"Thanks for your testimony. I have to be honest and say you are our only witnesses. Inspector Stephanakis has to find proof of what you saw or the case will be deemed accidental death. The pathologist can find no evidence of anything other than a fall. Circumstances suggest she wandered off looking for birdlife and became disorientated and she suffered from a medical condition which may have caused dizziness. Do you see why we have to explore every last detail?"

They both nodded and reached for each other's hands.

"I know reliving the incident is painful, but please, think very hard once again and if you recall anything, give one of us a call. I will be here tomorrow morning, but unless something turns up, I will have to return to London. The Hellenic Police and I really would like to help you, but we have less than twenty-four hours before this will be filed as an accident. Inspector Stephanakis and I will give you our cards."

Back in the casino, her early start, the weight of that cake, the quiet darkness of the casino and the futility of this case threw a torpor over Beatrice. Maggie Campbell's story was wholly convincing, but without proof it was a non-starter as a case.

In several of the late-afternoon interviews, Beatrice struggled to keep her eyes open. More of the coach trip passengers expressed the same platitudes – couldn't believe it... lovely woman... eightieth birthday... only spoken to her half an hour earlier. Why did that make a difference? Why did people always express astonishment at how recently they had communicated with the deceased? As if that phone call, chat in the supermarket, hug before parting conveyed special protection for at least a fortnight.

These were strangers, wedging themselves into the centre of events by dint of being a bystander. Or bysitter, as they had all been on the same coach. They added nothing to the case but much to Beatrice's misanthropy.

Last on the list were the final two Hirondelles. Miss Joyce Milligan, the trip organiser, was the first in the chair. For eighty-one, the woman was remarkable. Quick on her feet, if a little stooped, beady-eyed and with a firm handshake. They progressed through the necessaries. Couldn't believe it ... lovely woman... known her for over fifty years... eightieth birthday... only spoken to her at breakfast... family informed. Saddest Hirondelle cruise they'd ever had.

"Indeed, very sad. Especially, as you say, just after celebrating eighty years of life. Do you know if Mrs Crawford's low blood pressure ever caused dizziness?"

"Not that I know of. She never mentioned anything like that. I know she had poor circulation. Ten minutes in the pool and Esther used to go blue. Esther Williams she was not. She had tablets from the ship's doctor but didn't get on with them."

"Can you tell me a little more about the Hirondelles? How did you all meet and where does the name come from?"

Joyce looked confused for a second. "Oh, has no one explained yet? Well, I have to confess the name was my idea. Most of us, not all, were teachers at the Swallows Hall Academy in Wiltshire. Private girls' school, long since turned into a conference centre. Headmistress for twenty-two years, you know! Before I got the top job, I was originally the French mistress. Doesn't take a detective to work out what 'swallows' is in French." She gave a wheezy laugh. "A gaggle of us became good friends whilst chaperoning the girls on school trips. We had quite some adventures in those days. I could tell you stories that would make your hair curl!"

"I can imagine." Beatrice warmed to the infectious laugh. "So you've been holidaying together for a long time then?"

"We have. Many of us never married, you see. And even those who did rejoined the fold after their chaps died. It's a very special kind of club. We take good care of each other. For many of us, we're all we've got."

The piercing truth of that shook Beatrice fully awake. "I understand. And Esther..."

"Founding member. One of the original Swallows. Of all of us, she was perhaps the healthiest and most full of life. This is why it's so hard to believe. And coming so soon after Beryl, the whole group is grief-stricken and shocked. I'm organising a memorial service for them both because we have to celebrate our happy memories and all the good times we had together. It will help us overcome our sadness now and find a way of coping with future losses. I doubt I'm the only one who's aware that at our age this sort of situation will become more the norm. Every one we lose moves the rest of us further up the queue."

Beatrice looked up from her notebook. "Beryl? Are you saying another of your group died recently?"

"No one told you that either? Beryl Hodges passed away not twenty-four hours after leaving port. Just after Esther's eightieth birthday party. I really don't know if poor Esther fell or was pushed but it's not the way I'd want to go. At least Beryl went peacefully in her sleep. I'll tell you one thing, Detective Inspector, this has been the unluckiest Hirondelle holiday we've ever had."

Chapter 8

Andros Metaxas couldn't speak Greek. The few phrases he did know were delivered with no real attempt at an accent and he made mistakes most school kids would ridicule. Nikos switched to English. It was less painful.

"You're not actually Greek, are you?"

Andros held up his hands in mock surrender. "It's a fair cop, guv."

Nikos frowned. The expression made no sense.

"Oh, come on. Don't look like that! The Brits and the Yanks want the genuine article, your average Spiros from a village with olive groves, a donkey and a couple of legends. They also want someone who speaks English and understands their sense of humour. Ta-da! Andy Redmond becomes Andros Metaxas and everyone's a winner."

The guy reminded Nikos of a TV presenter. Everything he said was designed to raise a laugh or a round of applause. His long legs stretched out in front of him, he leant back in his chair, projecting the image of someone completely at ease.

Nikos kept his head down, writing nonsense notes in Greek, and allowed his other senses to take over. Andy was a smoker. The scent of tobacco mixed with something sweeter emanated from his leather jacket. His ankles twitching against one another could indicate something as innocent as nervous energy. Or not. Nikos looked at him, directly in the eyes. Bloodshot, red-rimmed and constantly shifting. All useful information to be filed.

"Your nationality is not important in itself. Your decision to create a false identity is significant, however. Is your boss aware of this deception?"

Andy pulled an exaggerated expression of stupidity. "Umm, duh, let's see. He has my passport so I guess he does. Listen, it's part of the deal. The excursion staff, the waiters, the sports coaches, the entertainers, we're all playing a role here. This is a pantomime. Glossy front, cardboard back. Give the punters what they want and everyone goes home happy."

"Not Esther Crawford. She goes home in a box."

Andy sat up in his chair. "The worst you can pin on me regarding the old girl's fall is forgetting to do the head count when they got back on the coach. When she took her tumble, I was trying to seat forty-six grandmas in a Fira taverna. I have loads of witnesses."

Nikos's attention was distracted. At the other end of the casino, Detective Stubbs gathered her things and escorted her most recent interviewee to the door.

She came back to his table with a polite nod towards Andy.

"I have to go up to the bridge. I wonder if you could take my last Hirondelle interviewee? Doreen Cashmore." She placed a manila folder on his table. "You'd better read that first."

"Of course."

She walked towards the door, then looked back and gave a reassuring wave in his direction, although her expression was grim.

He turned back to the dopehead in front on him.

"Yes. The worst we can pin on you is causing the premature death of an elderly woman by neglect. That roll call would have saved her life. Whether your omission was due to laziness, incompetence or to mental impairment as a result of consistent drug use is not for me to say."

Andy's eyes looked everywhere but at him. "Yeah right. Classic police tactics. Try to stitch me up for drugs and make me the fall guy..."

"Shut up, Andy." Nikos lowered his tone, but maintained his emotionless expression. "I can ask a staff member to search your cabin right now, and in less than five minutes, no 'stitch-up' would be required. Please understand, that is not my objective. I am here to find out what happened to Esther Crawford while she was under your supervision. Any information you can provide will be useful."

Andy's TV persona slipped away and he hunched forward. "Can I have a glass of water?"

According to the file Beatrice had given him, not seven but eight Hirondelles had boarded the *Empress Louise* just over ten days ago. Nikos wondered why no one had mentioned the name Beryl Hodges up to now. The ladies ranged in age from seventy-seven to eighty-one, all active and lively despite various infirmities. The unexpected departure of Mrs Hodges made it seven and now there were six. As if the shock of losing two of their companions wasn't enough, one death was being investigated as murder.

Fear hung on Doreen Cashmore like a damp coat. One of the youngest at seventy-seven, she told Nikos they had discussed abandoning the cruise and flying home to England.

"My son says not to be so daft and enjoy my holiday, but how can we enjoy ourselves when they're not even cold? We'll miss their funerals and we've always been there for each other. A memorial service is a nice idea, but it's not the same. Any road, no one can relax without knowing what really happened to poor Esther. Why would anyone want to harm her? She wouldn't hurt a fly."

"That's what we want to find out. It seems a silly question, but can you think of any reason why someone might benefit from your friend's death? Would there be anything in her..." Nikos stalled, searching for the word to describe the document. It wasn't testament, not bequest, it was...

"Past?" Doreen's face changed. Her eyes dropped to her hands, where she fiddled with her antique rings. Then she shook her head repeatedly, a gesture designed to be emphatically believable, which had the opposite effect.

"No. Esther and Beryl were both good-hearted, decent women and everything they did was for the best."

Confused, Nikos said nothing, processing her reaction. Doreen rushed to fill the silence.

"Not that Beryl's passing has anything to do with it. It's just bad luck and very sad to lose them both so suddenly, that's all."

The word came back to him. "Do you know if Mrs Crawford and Mrs Hodges had made a will?"

Doreen blinked. "Yes, I think we all have. We often discuss the best way of leaving our affairs in order for when the time comes."

Nikos touched her arm. "Mrs Cashmore, are you sure there's nothing else I should know? Anything from the past that might be relevant?"

She shook her head quickly and withdrew her arm. "I'm sorry. I really can't help you." She placed her hand over her eyes, pulled a tissue from her sleeve and dabbed at her nose.

Nikos recognised ham acting when he saw it. "Thank you, Mrs Cashmore. I think that's all for now. Do you want me to get someone for you?"

"No, no. The others are waiting outside. We'll be fine." She got to her feet and snatched up her handbag, eager to get away.

Nikos watched her leave, his mind replaying her words and in particular, the use of the first person plural.

Chapter 9

Captain Jensson's private rooms were situated right behind the bridge, to Beatrice's surprise. He stood in the doorway, waiting to meet her.

"Great minds think alike. I intended to send someone to find you and invite you to dine with me at the Captain's table this evening. And I would also like to discuss the issue of accommodation and movement. Please come in. Shall I arrange tea?"

"Thank you. No, I'm not thirsty just now. But I do have an urgent question. I've just discovered that Esther Crawford was not the first woman to die on this cruise."

Jensson motioned her inside, pointed to the L-shaped sofa past the desk and closed the door. Beatrice, sufficiently intimidated by the grand surroundings, sat. He pressed a few buttons on the desk phone and came to sit opposite.

"Have you ever enjoyed a cruise, Detective Stubbs? Probably not. I expect a detective is always too busy for real escape. And now, your first encounter with the concept of luxury sailing is to investigate an accidental death. That is really a misfortune."

"Captain Jensson, my question was..."

"Yes, I understand. The reason I ask is not irrelevant. Once you have experienced a cruise, you learn something about crowds. About crowd behaviour. This ship has the size and personality of a small town. I am not exaggerating. We have the same population as many small towns in Western Europe. And all that goes with that. Gossip, sickness, rumour and moods sweep through such a community with astounding speed. There is something physical at the root of this, of course. So many people in an enclosed space. But far more powerful is the psychological reason for sudden paranoia."

Beatrice's irritation grew to bursting point. "If you intend to give me a lecture on discretion, Captain, I will apologise now so we can get to the point."

He shook his head, his serene features not in the least ruffled. "No, that was not my objective. The truth of the matter is I find this collective mentality quite fascinating and hoped to share my enthusiasm. But I see now is not the time. Your question was about the earlier death. What do you want to know?"

His affable manner infuriated Beatrice. "For a start, why were we not informed? A member of the Hirondelle party dies mere hours out of port and no one mentions it when another one falls off a cliff? Surely you can see how it might have been helpful to bring this up earlier."

He got up to reach a leather-bound journal from his desk drawer. After flipping through several pages, he brought it to her. She scanned the list of names, dates, vessels and causes of death.

"Are these...?"

"The people who died under my captaincy. Although I am not directly responsible, I still feel a superstitious obligation to remember these souls. And as I captain ships specialising in pleasure cruises for the elderly, my book rarely reaches our final destination without another new addition."

Beatrice fixed her gaze on him. He gazed steadily back. In the lamplight of the casino, she had assumed his eyes were blue. Now, in the brightness of the sunlit bridge, she could see they were more of a faded green, like a dollar bill.

"What has that got to do with crowd mentality?"

"I am very pleased you asked. This is my point. Cruise ships are an exercise in collective belief. An illusion maintained by mutual will. We promise the 'ultimate luxury experience' and every effort is made to deliver precisely that. The crew are trained to anticipate your every need, catering staff spend months planning menus to suit all palates, entertainers rehearse intensively to ensure a smooth performance, the procurement department ensures a steady supply of far too much food and we all uphold the fallacy that this is the holiday of a lifetime.

"The truth is resolutely ignored and if anyone attempts to face facts, he or she is simply smiled into submission. Because the truth is, this is a sparkling, shiny, hugely expensive, floating rat run. You are given the impression of free will and endless choices, but in reality, you are shuffled from one activity to the next and gently parted from your cash at every opportunity while the message is continually reinforced: you are having such a marvellous time! In exchange for your spending money, you bank images and anecdotes as currency to distribute on your return home as hard proof that it was indeed the holiday of a lifetime."

Beatrice stared at him, speechless.

He smiled. "And you know the saddest thing of all? Many people come back. They like the fact that it's a glorified old people's home with guaranteed good weather. They are completely content with having no real decisions to make. They actually believe the hype and fork out another chunk of their savings to collect another set of photographs, dine with another group of strangers and buy another load of overpriced junk to foist on friends and family.

"Now, you asked about crowd mentality. I've just explained how it usually works. A group delusion keeps us all happy, within our closed community. As long as we all play the game. But closed communities share the same flaw. Just like sickness spreads through the ship faster than gossip, so does discontent. People do not want to be reminded of reality while they're living the dream. And there is no starker reminder of the fragile and temporal nature of our dream than dying. When the average passenger age is over sixty, the spectre of mortality casts a still-longer shadow."

Reflections of sun on water played a blithe denial of Jensson's words across the ceiling. The whiteness, the golden light, the sanitised perfection of their environment... Beatrice could understand the importance of upholding that mythology of the moment.

"So when a person dies, you try to keep it quiet rather than upset the apple tart?"

"We try to minimise disruption for everyone on board. For friends and family, we offer free transfers home and assist with transportation of the deceased. Dr Fraser is a registered coroner and we have a ship's morgue, so if an incident should happen at sea, we can begin the process of formalising the death certificate.

It is in everyone's interests to try to isolate the distress and grief of those affected. With heart attacks, strokes or simply passing away in their sleep, that's relatively uncomplicated. Beryl Hodges was one of the latter. Not only that, but it was early into our voyage, and one of the easier ones to manage. However, Esther Crawford's fall set the passengers on edge, even more so when the rumours of homicide came to light. This is why I'm so keen for you to close the case quickly. This kind of atmosphere can poison an entire cruise."

"I appreciate that, Captain, but I am extremely surprised you didn't mention the previous lady's demise to me or Inspector Stephanakis. You say she died in her sleep?"

"Yes. Fraser may have a complicated name for it, but as far as I know, she just stopped breathing. I know nothing of her medical history, but I recorded her death as 'natural causes'. I myself hope for such a calm departure from this life. People fear change. And there is no change greater than death."

Jensson's melancholic world-view began to drag on Beatrice's mood. "I'll look for Dr Fraser now and get the facts. You mentioned accommodation, Captain. There's no need, as I have a hotel in Heraklion."

"Yes, that will be convenient as the *Empress Louise* is sailing to Crete tonight. Generally, we only stay one or two nights in each port, and our delay in Santorini has forced a schedule rearrangement. My question was whether you would like to dine aboard as my guest and sail with us this evening. We have fully equipped guest rooms."

It was tempting. She'd never spent a night on a ship, not even a ferry.

"May I consult with Inspector Stephanakis? I am assisting him in this investigation, so he might have other plans for me."

"Of course. And the offer also extends to him. I would very much enjoy your company. You can send a message via any member of the crew. I believe tonight's menu is shellfish, if that helps persuade you."

On the way back to the casino, Beatrice tried observing the ship through Jensson's jaded eyes. An older couple dozed on sun loungers in the shade; a group of ladies played backgammon under an umbrella and a foursome laughed helplessly as one of their party missed a shot on the crazy golf course. She looked down at the deckchairs and met the eyes of a woman around her own age, who was holding a hefty paperback and reaching out for her cocktail.

She smiled and the woman smiled back, raising her glass. As shiny rat runs go, it could be worse. She decided to stay for dinner. She was partial to a bit of seafood.

Chapter 10

Maureen, my girl, this is the last time. Never again. She even said it aloud.

"Never again, I swear."

No one could say she hadn't tried. She gave it a go but it wasn't for her. If she had her 'druthers, she'd be on a plane home already. It wasn't just the seasickness that ruined the trip. Even when she'd recovered enough to face the others in the dining-room, something she ate upset her stomach all over again. And then that nurse asking what she'd had for lunch. She'd held her tongue and just said she didn't actually know what it was, when what she really wanted to say was 'some foreign muck and rice'. So after a full ten days, she'd barely left the cabin. Holiday to remember indeed.

After all that, today had just about put the tin hat on it. Weak as a kitten, she was, and they'd had her traipsing round old ruins in the midday sun. All she'd said was a cold drink in the shade would be nice and Audrey bit her head off. Called her a Moaning Minnie. It was all very well for her; she and Pat were having a marvellous time, gallivanting around with those jolly-hockey-sticks women, while Muggins was laid up in bed.

Her mouth was dry and her nose half blocked. She sat up and reached for her glasses so she could see what time it was. Quarter to nine. She'd missed dinner. Her own fault for having a nap as soon as she got back. She hadn't really intended to sleep, it was more about making a sulky exit, but a short lie down these days could last for hours. And now she wouldn't be able to sleep tonight. It would be an idea to eat something, just to keep her strength up, but it was very complicated calling cabin service and she had no idea where her hearing aid might be. Maybe she should just take a sleeping tablet and get up early for breakfast.

In the tiny bathroom, she had a cat's lick of a wash, put her teeth in to soak and blew her nose. She took a Benadryl for her congestion, a Restoril to help her sleep, a vitamin C pill and her blood pressure tablet. *Shake me and I'd rattle*, she thought. A good night's sleep and in the morning, she'd apologise to Pat and Audrey for being such a wet blanket. That should make them both feel guilty. She filled a glass with mineral water from the mini-bar because tap water was bound to give her the trots.

Back under the duvet, she set her glass of water on the nightstand, said her prayers and switched off the light. Only another week to go and she'd be home in her own bed, with Herbie curled up on her feet. She missed him, funnily enough. But he wouldn't be missing her. Whenever she left him with Juliet, he came back fatter than ever. She spoilt him rotten. 'I can't resist, Mum. It's that pitiful miaow he makes.' Yes, he had her wrapped around his paw, all right.

A light crossed her eyelids. It took a second to register and she opened her eyes. All in darkness. The ship was lit up like a Christmas tree all night long, so she always closed the curtains. The room was never completely dark, the way she liked it at home, because those wretched floodlights were so bright. She preferred the curtains shut during the day, as the view of sea, sea and more sea got a bit dull after a while, and the glare made it harder to see the telly...

Her eyes flew open. She could smell aftershave. She stiffened and held her breath. Someone was in her cabin. The room seemed full of shapes that could be human; her jacket on the door, the shadow cast by the desk chair, that lump at the end of the bed. Then the lump moved.

She sat up with an intake of breath, her head muddled and dizzy. A man was standing at the foot of her bed. He said something she didn't catch. She reached for her spectacles but couldn't locate them. Instead, she knocked over her glass of water. He came closer.

"Don't touch me! Stay away!" Her voice sounded muffled and querulous. "Who are you?"

Her words came out indistinctly. What with no teeth and her sleeping tablet, even to her own ears she sounded drunk.

He spoke again. Although his voice was low, he sounded polite and unthreatening. She made out the words 'Waitrose' and 'best regards'. A crew member, perhaps, with some sort of delivery?

"Go away now. It's not convenient." Her neck was too weak to support her head. She rubbed at her eyes and forced herself to focus. "Do you hear? You have to go. Goodnight."

Instead of retreating, he came closer. The light spilling through the window illuminated his face. His smile seemed vaguely familiar. He sat on the bed and she noticed his hands. He wore white medical gloves. An orderly from the infirmary come to check on her progress? His smile faded as he looked into her eyes. This time she heard him quite clearly, repeating her words. "No. It's you that has to go. Goodnight."

In one swift move, he shoved her roughly back down on the bed, while clasping his right hand over her nose and mouth. Her arm flew out and hit the nightstand. Purely out of instinct, she grasped the cord of the telephone. He loomed over her and pressed his knee onto her chest. Her lungs convulsed, the impulse for air desperate. She writhed and kicked and twisted, yanking the telephone to the floor. The crushing pressure on her chest increased as she rained feeble blows on her attacker. White spots appeared in her vision and she seemed to be falling, through the mattress, through the floor, through the bowels of the ship, through the deep blackness of the sea, down and down and down to where it was finally, truly dark.

Chapter 11

Chief Inspector Voulakis sounded pleased.

"*So tomorrow you can file the report? Accidental death, unreliable witnesses, positive outcome of collaboration with London. That is music to my ears!*"

Nikos shifted the phone to his other ear as ran up two steps at a time and unlocked his front door. Karen's singing reached him from the kitchen, along with a delicious smell of roasting meat and rosemary.

"No promises, sir. But we've made a thorough investigation. Doctors, witnesses, travelling companions, crew. Apart from one lady's account, there's no evidence of foul play. Detective Stubbs is staying on board tonight, but unless something turns up tomorrow morning, we'll have no choice but to close the case."

"*Excellent! Good work, Stephanakis. By the way, the Scotland Yard detective. Stubbs. What's she like?*"

"Smart. She's really easy to work with. It's actually been a pleasure."

"*Enjoy it while you can. The next case is bound to be a bastard. Come into the station tomorrow evening and we'll have a beer to celebrate your first successful result! Have a good evening.*"

Karen watched him from the kitchen doorway, her eyes curious and a smile hovering in the wings. He replaced his phone in his jacket and put his briefcase on the chair.

"So Inspector, how was your day?" Her voice was husky. "Have you solved The Murder on the *Empress Louise* yet?" She slipped her arms around his back and pulled him to her, tilting her face for a kiss.

He obliged.

"This time tomorrow, my love, it will all be over. Voulakis will be buying me beer and I'll be celebrating my first case not only filed in Greek but also in English."

She hunched her shoulders with excitement and kissed him again. "How's it going? Is the Scotland Yard woman being kind to you? She's not sexy, is she?" Her eyes narrowed in faux jealousy.

"She's nice. She keeps reminding me that I'm in charge and doesn't play power games like most of the men I've worked with. She doesn't even correct my English when I know I'm making mistakes."

"Nice deflection. I asked you if she's sexy. How old? What does she look like?"

"No, I wouldn't describe her as sexy. But I do like her as a person. I'm not good at guessing ages. Mid fifties? She's short, but very upright and always alert, like a squirrel. Bright eyes and funny hair."

"Oooh-kaaay. So now I'm picturing a rodent in a clown wig." Her arms circled his waist.

"Not exactly. I'll find a photo on the Internet. It's a pity this case will be over so soon. I'm learning a lot from working with her. A few more days would be perfect. Why is it British women always teach me so much? Talking of which, how was your day?"

"Boring. The Director of Studies has increased class sizes, my Proficiency group wants individual feedback and the receptionist has got nits. Who cares?" She looked at him under her lashes. "My man is home. I've put lamb and potatoes in the oven, but that will take another twenty minutes. So why don't we go upstairs and I can continue your education?"

She led him by the hand up the narrow staircase. On the landing, he caught sight of himself and his gleeful expression in the mirror. It made him laugh.

Beatrice too was grinning into the mirror. Who'd have thought the frumpy detective would scrub up so well? Despite having left all her clothes, jewellery and most of her make-up at the hotel, the ship's housekeeping staff had come to the rescue. They proved priceless.

A charming lady checked her sizes and hurried off to the formal hire facility. Jensson was not exaggerating – this really was a small, perfectly equipped town. From the selection she delivered, Beatrice opted for a long black dress with a short spangled jacket. Her assistant assessed the outfit, and went off to seek jewels, shoes and a handbag. Meanwhile, the original lady made her an appointment at one of the various hair salons for a blow-dry and make-up session. In less than an hour, Beatrice was transformed into someone worthy of the Captain's table.

She tore her eyes from the glittering stranger in the mirror and looked around her cabin with some regret. It would be so indulgent to stay here, order room service and lounge around on this wonderful bed, admiring herself in the full-length mirror. But this five-star guest suite was thus named because its occupants had guestly duties. And her host awaited. She gave her reflection one last arch look, practised a gracious smile, picked up her key card and ventured onto the deck.

Halfway down the staircase leading to the Grand Dining Room, she hesitated. One could not fail to be impressed by the opulence. Chandeliers, starched napkins, gilt pillars, flower arrangements, two tiers of balconies as if it were a theatre, polished wood and the sparkle of crystal glassware managed to be simultaneously enticing and forbidding. She wanted a second to squeeze her eyes shut so she might imagine herself in the past, and also to stifle a giggle.

"Good evening. I presume this is your first visit to the Grand Dining Room? Most new arrivals need to stop at this point, if only to decide on their own responses to such flamboyance. Some say awesome, others say awful. Have you made up your mind?"

Beatrice recognised the man as the one who had given her directions to the infirmary earlier that day, although he was now dressed in black tie. It suited him. "Good evening. I'm not sure I have. I suppose the one thing one cannot accuse them of is false advertising."

"Very true. I believe we're dining at the same table tonight, unless my guess is wrong and you are not the police detective from Scotland Yard."

"Yes, that's right. Beatrice Stubbs. Pleased to meet you."

"Oscar Martins. Likewise. Did you find the infirmary in the end?"

They shook hands and then he offered his arm in a curiously old-fashioned gesture. Amused, Beatrice placed her hand on his forearm and they proceeded down the steps.

"We did, thank you. Your directions were spot on. Lord knows how long we would have been wandering about otherwise. This ship must be full of lost souls trying to find their way home."

"A description uncomfortably close to the truth, I'd say. Here we are. Good evening, Captain Jensson. By happenstance I met Detective Stubbs on the staircase and took the liberty of escorting her."

At the circular table sat a middle-aged couple, a scowling elderly lady, and between the captain and Dr Fraser, a pretty Japanese woman.

Captain Jensson stood to make the introductions. "Mr and Mrs Simmonds from High Wycombe, Ms Ishii from Kyoto, Dr Fraser is our senior medical practitioner and this is Mrs Bartholomew who lives in Boston. Ladies and gentlemen, I'd like you to meet Mr Martins from Cambridge and Detective Inspector Stubbs, who's just joined us from London."

Beatrice followed Oscar's example, nodding and smiling around the table, with a general, 'Nice to meet you' before taking her seat. Mr Simmonds, a bland-looking individual with wholly forgettable features, rubbed his hands together.

"Lucky me. I get to sit next to Miss Marple. I've always wanted to pick the brains of a lady detective."

Mrs Simmonds giggled. "Don't be naughty, Don."

Beatrice smiled. "And I'll be happy to share whatever you'd like to know. With the obvious exception of the case I'm here to investigate, of course."

A beat of silence, then the frowning lady spoke. "We were all looking forward to hearing about your progress. It's the only topic of conversation aboard. Surely you can share a few little tidbits amongst friends?"

"It would be extremely unprofessional for a detective, lady or otherwise, to discuss ongoing enquiries. So I'm afraid 'tidbits' are off the menu tonight. But I understand we'll be dining on shellfish, Captain, is that correct?"

Jensson picked up his cue and the conversation moved onto the quality of Greek crustaceans. Ignoring the stony glares from at least three of the party, Beatrice attempted to involve the Japanese woman in conversation, but after extracting the information that Ms Ishii was a classical pianist, Mrs Bartholomew interrupted.

"Detective Stubbs, why are you here?"

Before Beatrice could gather her thoughts, Dr Fraser jumped in. "Good question. I think Captain Jensson over-reacted a wee bit. Even if you do need to take an old lady's imagination seriously, I can't for the life of me understand why you'd involve Scotland Yard. The local boys are perfectly capable of digging about, finding nothing and recording a verdict of accidental death. Waste of time and resources."

The first course arrived, an oval dish with tiny dabs of baba ghanouj and hummus, punctuated by mini falafel and dolmas, decorated with olives and a salad garnish. A waiter placed a basket of warm pitta bread between each pair and began pouring the wine.

Jensson seemed at a loss as to whether to ignore or respond to the physician's comment and the party watched the waiter's progress in silence. Finally, as the captain's glass was filled, Oscar raised his.

"Regardless of why we're here, let's enjoy fine food and good company. Cheers everyone!"

Beatrice, relieved at Oscar's gracious behaviour, lifted her glass to join the others. The lines on Jensson's forehead smoothed. The Bartholomew trout's did not but she toasted anyway. Timing was of the essence. As soon as glasses were replaced on the table, like a crack team trained in the art of diplomatic small talk, Oscar enquired as to the weather in Boston, Jensson asked Ms Ishii's opinion of the string quartet and Beatrice turned to her neighbour.

"So tell me, Mr Simmonds, what are house prices like in High Wycombe?"

The seafood platter surpassed all expectations. Shells, claws, the remnants of lemon wedges and well-used finger bowls littered the table, while compliments poured forth in abundance. Their party began to break up almost immediately. Dr Fraser was called to an emergency, Mrs Simmonds wanted to get a good seat in the auditorium for the evening's Rat Pack Repertoire and Ms Ishii excused herself, claiming further practice was required for tomorrow's recital. Beatrice felt increasingly relaxed by each departure. Oscar sat back to allow the waiting staff to clear his plate.

"My favourite kind of meal: varied, perfectly cooked, reasonably healthy and incredibly messy. Tell me, do I have any scales stuck to my face?"

Beatrice laughed. "Not that I can see, but the lighting is subdued. It really was a feast, I agree. I'm very glad I stayed for dinner. And I must remember to make a note of that wine."

"Indeed. Deceptively light, but it works its magic." He glanced in the direction of Mrs Bartholomew, whose face was flushed, but not softened as she bent the captain's ear.

Beatrice dropped her voice. "And I thought avoiding icebergs would be the worst part of the poor man's job."

"Icebergs can take many forms. Now I'm going to respect my waistline and decline dessert. However, an espresso and a digestif might round off the evening rather well. I plan to head for the Club Room. No entertainment other than some muffled Mahler, but they do decent coffee and their collection of single malts could bring tears to your eyes. Would you like to join me?"

"I would, but is that not terribly rude?" She flicked her eyes towards the beleaguered captain.

"Captain Jensson? Detective Stubbs and I have enjoyed ourselves enormously. Thank you for a truly memorable meal. We would like to round the evening off with a little dancing. Could we tempt you and Mrs Bartholomew to join us? The Kit Kat Club has an excellent jazz band."

"Thank you, Mr Martins, but I'm afraid my evening is dedicated to the usual routine checks. But I hope you enjoy the music. I am a big fan of jazz." Jensson looked genuinely regretful.

"Oh, of course. But how about you, Mrs Bartholomew?"

"Dancing? In the middle of a meal? My doctor advises nothing more strenuous after dinner than retiring to the couch since my operation. I wonder if it's conducive to digestion at any age, to be honest. No, I intend to withdraw to my cabin, order room service and enjoy my dessert in peace. I bid you all a pleasant evening."

They all stood to say goodbye. Jensson's relief at Mrs Bartholomew's departure was almost visible. Almost. He shook their hands, offered them a hint of a wry grin and hurried off in the opposite direction.

Beatrice faced Oscar. "And what if they'd said yes?"

He shrugged. "We'd have been forced to go dancing. A risk I was willing to take. It's been a while but I can still remember how to lindy-hop. Come on now, you've been rescued. Let's make the most of it."

The Club Room, as promised, was a real haven from the sensory assault of the Grand Dining-Room. Leather wingback chairs, wood panelled walls, thick carpet, green velvet curtains, hidden spotlights and a gleaming oak bar all combined to create the illusion of a traditional London gentleman's club. Beatrice even fancied she could smell cigar smoke. A few other people populated the place, the majority male and sitting alone with a newspaper or mobile phone, with the occasional couple tucked away in one of the booths. Oscar indicated a small table to their left.

"Ideally situated. Clear view of the bar, well positioned to observe newcomers and high-backed chairs to protect us against draughts."

A waiter, perfectly turned out in waistcoat and tie, appeared at their side with a drinks menu as they seated themselves. Beatrice opted for a decaffeinated coffee and chose a port wine from the extensive list. Oscar didn't need the menu, but ordered a Macallan to go with his espresso. He was evidently a familiar face, addressing the waiter by name, and nodding to a pair of bespectacled gents as they'd entered. He settled back with a contented smile and rested his gaze on her.

"So, let's hear a bit about Beatrice Stubbs. How long have you been a 'Lady Detective'?"

She chuckled. "I shouldn't get so frosty about it, really. Being called a lady detective is better than how my superior officer usually refers to me, which is either a 'bloody woman' or a 'stubborn old coot'. Let's see, I've been a detective inspector for almost fifteen years now."

"Oh, an inspector? Excuse me, I was unaware of your full title. A detective inspector from Scotland Yard. Here, on a cruise ship, in the Club Room. It's all a bit Cluedo, don't you think?"

"Coupled with the suspicious death, I suppose it is. I've never been on one of these ships before, so I'm finding it all rather an adventure. But I get the impression you are quite the seasoned cruise traveller."

"Your impression is correct, Detective Inspector. I am a veteran of these trips and have been ever since I lost my wife seven years ago. Ah, and here are the drinks. Thank you, Alex. While she was alive, we were adventurers, exploring less-travelled paths and making discoveries. After she died, adventuring seemed too much like hard work. I booked my first cruise with the aim of having everything done for me. And although I found giving up all freedom of choice too much to bear, I grew to like the itinerary being taken out of my hands. So when we dock, I hire a car and go off and do my own thing. But come back to join everyone again in the evening and sail onto the next port. And I have met some fascinating people on board. Someone like yourself would fall into that category."

Beatrice stirred a brown sugar lump into her coffee. "Nice of you to say so. Tell me, what do you do when you're not sailing the Mediterranean?"

"I'm a language historian, or a historical linguist, I'm never quite sure which. Semi-retired, in that I do very little teaching these days. But I publish in various journals and occasionally write articles for magazines, while continuing the Sisyphean task of completing my book."

"Ooh, a writer! What's the book about?"

"You'll be surprised to know it's about the history of language. Or to be precise, the death of it. I have previously completed two modest volumes, one called *Stories of the Atlantic Arc*, all about the linguistic connections between the Celts. The second was called *Mother Tongue: The Word of God*, which explores the relationship between language and religion. Hugely popular with insomniacs, apparently. Shall we toast? To inspiration and resolution!"

"I'll drink to that," said Beatrice, and lifted her tawny port towards the chandelier. The light in Oscar's laughing eyes matched the colour perfectly. They chinked glasses and held each other's gaze as they drank. *Nothing more than good manners*, she thought.

Velvety tones of sweet fat grapes danced on her tongue, a hint of sherry wood teased her nose and a gentle warmth spread down her throat and across her chest.

"Now that is an absolute jewel of a digestif. I only chose it because I liked the name, but it's delicious. What was it called again?"

Oscar checked the drinks menu. "Offley. Sounds more Irish than Portuguese. Not a name you'd forget, in any case."

"Nor a taste. Somehow robust and delicate at the same time."

A smile elevated Oscar's cheeks. "A charming description!"

The young waiter hovered at the table, his demeanour anxious. "So sorry to interrupt. Captain Jensson needs Detective Inspector Stubbs urgently. He asked if you could meet him at Cabin C343. It's on level C3. Would you like someone to show you the way?"

Oscar stood and reached into his pocket. "No need, Alex. I know C3 very well. I can escort the detective. Thank you and have a good evening." He pressed a note into the young man's hand, drained his whisky and gestured in the direction of the door. "After you, Detective Inspector. The devil waits for no man. Or lady."

Chapter 12

Typical of his luck. Instead of a successful conclusion and celebratory beers with the boss, Nikos was woken the wrong side of midnight and instructed to get to the port, ready to meet the *Empress Louise*. A second fatality had occurred during the sailing from Santorini.

This time there was no doubt. Maureen Hall had died a violent death. The telephone had been yanked from the wall, a water glass shattered on the floor and – a detail which emphasised the victim's frailty – a pair of senior citizen spectacles had been crushed underfoot. On first inspection, the doctor confirmed the body showed all the signs of having been smothered.

Nikos withdrew from the sad scene in the little cabin, leaving the forensics team to find what they could. At least Captain Jensson had been smart enough to prevent anyone other than DI Stubbs from entering after the initial discovery. She knew better than he did how to manage a crime scene. Now that the body had been removed, the little room was filled with people and light. He yawned as he turned the corner of the corridor, feeling guilty as he did so, and found himself face to face with the two ladies who had 'witnessed' the death of Esther Crawford.

"Inspector...?"

"Ladies, you should be in bed. I can tell you nothing at this stage."

The taller one interrupted. "You don't need to. Why else would this corridor be filled with police and people so early in the morning? We know someone is dead. Sheer common sense will tell you all this fuss means it's unlikely to be due to natural causes."

"I must ask you to vacate the corridor now. I am sorry and I understand your concern, but until we find out what happened, it makes no sense to talk about it. Do you understand why I must ask you to leave?"

The little lady from Scotland shook her head in regret. "We'll let you do your job, Inspector. But please get to the bottom of this. Something is very wrong here."

He bowed his head. "I am going to do my best."

Her friend looked at him intently. "Are you on your own now? Did Detective Stubbs go back to Britain?"

"No, she's still here. It seems she will stay on a few days if she can get permission. Please can I ask you now to return to your cabins...?"

"... and lock the doors? Oh yes, we most certainly will. Goodnight, officer, and good luck."

Nikos watched them walk away down the corridor, heads bent in conversation.

They were right. Something was indeed very wrong here.

Maureen Hall. Seventy-four years old, a widow with one daughter, born in Yorkshire and lived there all her life. Confined to her cabin for the majority of the voyage due to illness. Travelling with two friends, first cruise experience. No apparent connection to Esther Crawford or the Hirondelles or anyone else aboard. Retired to her cabin after returning from an excursion at 17.50, according to the key card records. No further activity until another entry at 22.08. The telephone system indicated an attempted call at 22.14, but no number was dialled. The ship's switchboard staff, geared to anticipate the needs of its population, relayed the aborted call to the cabin attendant service, who sent a member of housekeeping to check all was well. Nina Sousa attended at 22.21. On receiving no reply, she returned to the staff room to collect her access card and notify her line manager of her intention. At 22.24, Maureen Hall's key card was replaced in the main socket which controlled the cabin's electricity. When Ms Sousa returned and entered the cabin at 22.31, she found the inhabitant deceased and evident signs of a struggle.

Nikos sat on the bridge, watching the dawn break over Heraklion, his home and a place he'd never seen before from this angle.

The liner had arrived three hours ago, after sending news of the sudden death of Maureen Hall, to interrupt another night's sleep. He hoped DI Stubbs would achieve her aim in insisting the *Empress Louise* remain at anchor for another twenty-four hours. She faced a formidable opponent in Jensson. A company man, his concern was for the shareholders and stakeholders, should their schedule be disrupted. The paying customers seemed of lesser importance.

Dr Weinberg delivered the ship's medical records for Maureen Hall with a sombre greeting. Nikos appreciated it, not being one for small talk at eight in the morning either. After the quiet Austrian had departed with an equally curt farewell, he trawled through the details. Only two things the dead women had in common: blood pressure problems – but in opposite directions; one low, one high – and the fact they had both attended the ship's infirmary.

He bought a coffee from the buffet counter and took it out onto the deck. He needed some space to think. Wiltshire and Yorkshire. He pulled up a map of Britain on his phone, but saw the two counties were sufficiently far apart to make the geographical connection unlikely. He checked records of elderly deaths in each, which was when he encountered the name of Dr Harold Shipman.

The case rang a distant bell. The doctor who administered fatal doses of painkilling drugs to elderly female patients. A serial killer of 250 people, infamous in Britain, well known around the world. Nikos looked at the image and tried to imagine the motivation. None of the articles he skimmed indicated the doctor had given any kind of explanation for his actions. A twisted version of mercy killing, despite the fact so many of his patient-victims were healthy and happy? The jewellery, the savings... was his motive mercenary? Or born of altruism, a desire to save people from pain?

And here, on this peaceful, harmless cruise, why would someone wish to end the lives of these particular women? Esther Crawford and Maureen Hall led quiet lives, enjoying their retirement, until someone decided their time was up. He made a note to check the beneficiaries of their wills and ask the doctor a lot more questions about the death of Beryl Hodges.

Nikos sat back and watched early rays of sun cast long shadows across the harbour. He slugged the remaining coffee from his cup and thought back over the past two days.

Dr Fraser and his anger at everyone, including the police. The coroner, Apostolou and his quick decision regarding the fall. The clear resentment towards him and DI Stubbs from many of the staff on board. Jensson's assertion that old people tend to die. Conspiracy theories were part of a police inspector's job, but he still couldn't find the motive for any of these men to commit murder. Older people, ladies in particular, were the life blood of the cruise ship system, so killing them off would be senseless. Apostolou took care of his elderly mother himself, so he would sympathise with the hazards of old age.

He looked back at the expressionless face of Harold Shipman. No, neither the doctor nor the captain could possibly be in the frame. Even as he thought it, Nikos planned the investigation of both.

Beatrice Stubbs, despite her dramatically different appearance, looked tired and irritable as she returned from the bridge. Nikos was waiting for her outside her guest cabin, at her suggestion. The casino was not an option and both were reluctant to use the captain's office.

She gave him a humourless jerk of the head in greeting as she unlocked the door.

"What a bloody awful situation!" she said, flinging her handbag onto the table. "Please make yourself at home, Inspector, I'll just be a moment." She closed the door to the bedroom section and Nikos stood at the floor-to-ceiling windows, watching as the coastline came to life and signs of activity began in the morning light. Somewhere over there his beautiful girlfriend lay under a blue cotton sheet, her hair spread over the pillow, soon to wake up alone.

A knock brought him back to the here and now. He opened the door to a cabin attendant, who carried a tray of coffee and pastries. He thanked the man and took it with a smile. Detective Stubbs might have spent a sleepless, stressful night, but she was in no danger of losing her appetite.

She emerged from the sleeping quarters dressed in shirt and trousers with a towel around her head.

"Oh good, the coffee's here. Right, I'm ready to begin. Where shall we start?"

Nikos hesitated, but only for a second. "I'd like to hear what the immediate plans are. Did Jensson confirm the sailing time?"

"He did. The ship has to depart this evening. Their schedule is extremely tight since the hold-up in Santorini. They must set sail for Rhodes at midnight. Help yourself to milk and sugar. What about the body?"

"Taken to the city morgue for a complete post-mortem. We should have the results sometime later today. Then arrangements can be made to fly her home. I agree with your initial assessment of the scene. It looks as if the perpetrator was disturbed. On top of that, I think he was still in the cabin when the maid knocked. In the time it took her to fetch an access card, he managed to get out and disappear."

"What makes you say that?"

"I got the printout of the cabin's card activity. Inside the room there's a socket, just like this one in yours. After you open the door, you slot the key card into that socket and all the electricity works. If the card is removed, the lights don't work. It was removed at 22.08, and replaced at 22.24." He stirred his coffee. "That's not long to kill someone."

Beatrice looked up from her croissant. "Long enough. What about how the intruder got in? Any records on that?"

"A staff access card was used at 22.06. One of many used by housekeeping. They are not assigned to individuals and if you are a staff member, they're easy to find."

They both remained silent for several seconds. Nikos searched for a way of broaching his thoughts on potential suspects, but first he needed to know how much longer he would have his British back-up.

"I suppose it was too early for you to contact Scotland Yard?" he asked.

She chewed and swallowed. "No. I managed to get hold of Chief Inspector Hamilton, and I'm afraid there's good news and bad news. I am permitted to stay and work on this case, but the powers-that-be would like me to take a more active role. What happened tonight has raised the goalposts. We're talking about a potential serial killer of British citizens, albeit on Greek territory. My boss would like me to lead the investigation and unfortunately, he intends to contact your superior officer today."

Nikos tensed his jaw. He should have expected this. Voulakis would agree, of course he would. In fact, he would be stupid to argue.

"I understand, Detective Inspector Stubbs. But I hope I can continue to work with you. I'm learning a lot."

"Listen." She dusted flakes of pastry from her hands. "Depending on what your superior says, this is what I propose. A collaborative investigation, jointly led by British and Greek agents. Partners, if you like. I will need your local expertise, but I believe I can bring a certain amount of experience to bear. What do you say?"

Nerves made Nikos clumsy and he clattered his cup back onto the saucer. "I say that is a very generous proposal. I would like that very much."

"But I do have one thing I need to get off my chest. On my return from the bridge, I met our two witnesses, Mrs Campbell and Mrs Mason. They were on their way back to their quarters in some state of alarm. Apparently, you had advised them to stay in their cabins and lock the doors. I appreciate the good intention behind your advice, but in an environment such as this, it might be better to avoid generating panic."

Nikos deliberated over what to say, aware of the heat creeping up his neck.

"DI Stubbs, I asked them to leave the corridor where we are investigating. I suggested they go back to their cabins, mainly because it was so early. They were the ones who mentioned locking doors. I can assure you I was not trying to alarm anyone."

"I see. Captain Jensson has a point. It is terribly easy to spook a flock like this, especially when they're looking for a reason to get hysterical. I'm sorry. I had my doubts but thought it best to check. And one other thing, if we're going to be partners, can we drop the formalities? My name is Beatrice."

"No problem. Call Nikos."

"Nice working with you, Nikos." She offered her hand and they shook.

"You too, Beatrice."

"Now, tell me your thoughts on how we proceed."

He was ready for this and had thought of nothing else since he'd received the call. "While we wait for the crime scene results, we research the three deaths on this cruise. We need to find out more about Beryl Hodges and make one hundred percent certain her death was natural."

"My thoughts exactly. I will call London and get them to organise a PM. I hope to God they've not buried her yet. Or worse still, she might have been cremated."

"If so, we'll have to look for the information elsewhere. Next, we seek connections between Esther Crawford and Maureen Hall. I think we should interview the doctors again, Fraser in particular. I also want to talk to the captain. Something about that book you mentioned, his deaths record, makes me uncomfortable. And the ship's security team must have information about who we can eliminate from the crew by providing alibis. The only thing..." He tailed off, not wishing to admit it.

"Motive?"

Nikos nodded. "Exactly. I can't understand who would benefit from killing two elderly women."

"So that's what we need to work out. When we know why, we will find who."

Chapter 13

None of the infirmary's medical staff had enjoyed an uninterrupted eight hours sleep, and a large percentage of the passengers found themselves afflicted that morning by a variety of nervous disorders, requiring a visit to the morning surgery. Short fuses were to be expected. Dr Fraser's air of barely contained rage had an oddly soothing effect on Beatrice. The more he spluttered and swore, the calmer she became. Nikos impressed her by not rising to the doctor's aggression, and simply restating their requests for information.

"Just to be clear, the death certificate for Beryl Hodges was signed by you and Dr Weinberg? Did the other doctor actually examine her or did you alone determine she died of natural causes?" asked Nikos.

"You have the certificate in front of you! It's there in black and white! As senior physician and official coroner on board, I have every right to make a professional assessment without wasting my colleague's time. She died peacefully in her sleep. The woman suffered from obstructive sleep apnoea. She used a CPAP machine at home but didn't bring it with her. The condition means you stop breathing for a few seconds during the night, but then your system, or machine, kicks in and you clear the blockage. If you don't, for whatever reason, it causes oxygen deprivation, and eventually leads to asphyxia. When someone dies of asphyxia aboard, there is always a concern about insufficient ventilation, or exposure to noxious gases. So I check thoroughly. Yes, obviously for insurance, but also because I'm a professional physician and my own reputation is at stake. The truth is the woman was old, she had asthma and her lungs couldn't cope. Congestion added to the frequent blockage to her breathing and her system shut down due to a lack of oxygen."

His strident voice and expansive gestures echoed around his compact consulting room. Nikos wrote detailed comments in his notebook, but Beatrice kept her eyes on the doctor. His hostility, his easy explanation, his curious refusal to see a connection made her wary. She studied his manner. His eyes, with all the warmth of pack ice, shifted constantly between her and Nikos. He often ran his bony hands through his thick hair, dislodging flakes of dandruff onto his shoulders. While she and Nikos sat still and calm opposite him, he shifted and twitched with extraordinary impatience.

Beatrice waited till he'd finished speaking. "We believe Maureen Hall was smothered. Correct me if I'm wrong, but wouldn't an obstruction over the face asphyxiate a person in much the same way as sleep apnoea? Were there any other marks on Beryl Hodges that could support that theory?"

Fraser rolled his eyes. "How many times must I tell you people...?"

"Dr Fraser. Sorry to interrupt." Nikos sat forward, his palms open in appeal. "We are not trying to cause problems for you. Two ladies died in a similar way, one of whom was murdered. Police procedure is to seek any connection which leads us closer to finding who killed Maureen Hall. As we have another suspicious death to add to this case, the job of the police is complicated and difficult. We want to work with other professionals as a team, not make enemies."

Fraser considered, his physical fidgeting in abeyance. "Fair point. It's just this calling of my professional competence into question... Look, there was no need for a detailed post-mortem on Beryl Hodges. As I explained, her sleep disorder coupled with asthma explained why she stopped breathing and I had no reason to look any further."

Beatrice gave a sympathetic smile. "Understood. And as it was over ten days ago, I doubt you'd remember any unusual injuries."

Nikos shot a sly glance sideways at Beatrice and bent his head over his notebook.

"The problem with women of that age is their susceptibility. Their bones are fragile, their balance is unreliable, their digestive system is inevitably problematic and their skin... their skin can tell many stories, but we don't know which is which. By that I mean injuries heal far more slowly than they do in the young, they bruise easily, and often tend to cause themselves more damage than others."

"By which I gather Beryl Hodges bore some marks you could not explain?" asked Beatrice.

Fraser ran his hands through his hair once more. "There was a certain amount of bruising to her face, especially the left side of her jaw. Any number of explanations for that, so it wasn't worth including in my report. Cause of death was clear."

"I see." Beatrice closed her files. "Doctor, can I ask you, when you have a minute, to think about that incident once again? In the light of what has just happened, and the pathology report on Maureen Hall, I think it might be worth turning every stone. Even those already turned."

"Yes, I'll think about it in the unlikely event I get a minute. Now I really need to start on the backlog of paperwork." Fraser picked up a pen and Beatrice noticed his hands were unsteady.

"Just for the record, doctor. You left the captain's table at around quarter to ten. I believe you were called to an emergency?"

"Are you telling me I need to provide an alibi?" His grey-blue eyes were incredulous.

"Only so we can eliminate you. Or we wouldn't be doing our job," said Nikos.

"There was no emergency. I just had to get away from that Bartholomew woman. Her accent drove me up the pole."

Beatrice could understand that. "So where did you go, if you don't mind my asking?"

"Back to my cabin. Stayed there the rest of the night." The man spoke through clenched teeth.

"Thank you. We'll let you get on."

"About bloody time."

Exhaustion aside, Beatrice's respect for the young Greek inspector kept growing. He showed great timing and excellent instinct, even though he'd been dragged out of bed in the small hours. Nikos Stephanakis, she decided, was destined for great things.

Beatrice and Nikos split up to interview the nurse, Sister Bannerjee, and Assistant Physician Dr Weinberg. She sat opposite the weary little nurse who was so washed out even her bindi looked faded. Beatrice began her introductory speech.

"Sister Bannerjee, the only reason I am here is to clarify..."

"Detective Inspector, I am very sorry for my rudeness and for my disloyalty but I have to tell the truth to a police officer. Dr Fraser is not a good doctor and makes many short cuts. The routine here is 'P and PO'. Excuse my language, but this means 'Prescribe and Piss Off'. We have to push the medicines of our sponsors, encouraging injections and vitamin supplements and we send our patients away with a packet of pills and no idea of the root cause of their problems. I have spoken to the captain about this issue on several occasions, but this whole enterprise is only about making money from the weak and vulnerable. DI Stubbs, on this ship, something is rotting. Now at last, it eventually floats to the surface."

The sincere face opposite astonished Beatrice. Beneath the mask of friendly efficiency lay an anger and passion which had found its voice.

"I see there is a great deal to discuss. But first, Sister, I have a question regarding Beryl Hodges. Did you happen to see her body? Dr Fraser tells me there was some bruising to her face."

The horizontal frown lines on the nurse's forehead contracted into sympathetic verticals. "I assisted at the medical examination and yes, I saw the bruising. Chiefly on the left side, on her cheek and jaw. Older people bruise easily."

"So you didn't think there was anything suspicious about her death?"

The woman's eyes widened and Beatrice detected a flash of anger. "Let me guess. He told you about the bruising and the fact she was asthmatic. Did he say anything else?"

"Anything else regarding the body? No, I don't think so."

"Perhaps he forgot to mention the Emerade."

Beatrice stopped writing and lifted her head very slowly to meet the nurse's eyes.

"I beg your pardon?"

"Mrs Hodges had several doses of Emerade in her cabin's fridge.

It's an adrenalin auto-injector. People who are at risk of anaphylactic shock, those with allergies to insect stings or certain foods, need to be prepared to inject epinephrine or adrenalin directly into their systems to counter the effects of anaphylaxis."

"The sort of swelling-up and can't-breathe effects?"

"That's part of it, yes. Asthmatics are a particularly high-risk group. Dr Fraser performed tests on her lungs to ensure there was no inhalation of toxic fumes but did not test for symptoms of anaphylactic shock. To be fair to him, it would have required laboratory conditions and a full post-mortem. He said it was unnecessary and saw no need to add it to the report."

Beatrice put down her pad and thought. Then she walked over to the examination table in the spotless nurse's station.

"Sister, I am going to lie down here and I want you to attempt to force something into my mouth. Let's do this in slow motion. Remember, I am old and feeble and probably asleep. How would you do it?"

Sister Bannerjee stood, blinking for a moment. Then she exhaled sharply with a nod.

"OK. First thing, Mrs Hodges had an interior cabin on B1. That means her bed was against the cabin wall. You need to turn the other way. If I was going to attack her, I would have no choice but to come at her from the right." She placed herself at the foot of the examination table. "One minute please, I need to lower it. This table is much higher than the beds on board."

Adjustments made, she gestured for Beatrice to get into position.

"She would have been sleeping on her side. I think. On the back is the worst way for someone with her condition to sleep. Now, I come into the cabin and..."

She pulled Beatrice's shoulder gently, rolling her onto her back. Beatrice opened her eyes. The nurse pressed her left arm against Beatrice's windpipe and used her right hand to steady Beatrice's jaw. She lifted her left hand and prised Beatrice's teeth apart, picked up an imaginary object and poked it into her mouth. Beatrice, in character, bulged her eyes, struggled weakly and began to choke. Sister Bannerjee used her body weight to hold Beatrice down and brought her right knee up to press on her victim's chest. They made eye contact and the nurse's fierce expression of concentration dissipated. She released Beatrice and stepped back, straightening her uniform.

"Perhaps I should have locked the door before attempting to kill a police detective," she said, an awkward smile surfacing.

Beatrice swung her legs off the table and sat up. "You're right-handed. Any marks made by your fingers would be on the left-hand side of my face."

"Yes, but anaphylaxis rarely works that quickly. It depends what allergies Mrs Hodges had, but if that is what killed her, it is far more likely she was stung by something or ingested a trigger at least an hour earlier. Leaving her time to get up, inject herself and call for help."

"So why would someone need to hold her face?"

The nurse opened her palms. "I just don't know. She might have even made the marks herself. Who knows? Now it's too late to do a complete post-mortem examination."

"Perhaps. Thanks for your assistance, Sister. I think I should talk to the senior physician again. One last thing..."

She shook her head. "No. Dr Fraser is left-handed."

Captain Jensson did his best to persuade Beatrice to stay another night on board, dangling the offer of a place at his table, but she remained steadfast in her determination to return to her hotel. Even lamb kebabs could not sway her. There was the meeting with Nikos's superior to be navigated, she had several phone calls to make and if the truth were told, the atmosphere on board was stifling. As she followed Nikos down the endlessly looping gangway, she reflected on the ridiculousness of such a feeling. On a ship where she'd got lost twice, she felt boxed in. It was purely psychological, she knew, but the sense of lightness as she stepped onto the dock and into the police car was absolutely real. The *Empress Louise* would sail at midnight, destination Rhodes. Beatrice and Nikos would join them tomorrow, hopefully finding the same number of passengers as when they'd left.

The journey though Heraklion – the frenzied traffic, errant mopeds, graffiti on corrugated tin, blasts of music from passing cars, the scent of a fish stall, a jumble of vegetables outside a shop, children chasing each other round a fountain, an unruly cypress tree reaching out from a park – all grounded Beatrice with a re-assuring sense of real life unpredictability. Here, anything could happen and she felt all the safer for it. When a rain shower spattered the windscreen, she rolled down the window to inhale the smell.

Meanwhile Nikos relayed the limited results of his interviews with the housekeeping crew, outlined Dr Weinberg's opinions and shared his own reaction to the showdown with Fraser.

"Anyone who works on the ship can access those cards. The only record they keep is who signed for which card for security purposes. If there are any accusations of stealing, for example. The card used to open Maureen Hall's room had not been signed for and it hasn't been returned. No surprise. Weinberg has very little respect for Fraser, although he was complimentary about the nurse. As for Fraser's behaviour, I'm not sure if it's his professional reputation he's trying to protect or if he's hiding something, but he behaves like a guilty man. Did he apologise for being so rude to you?"

"Eventually, and with bad grace. Yes, you're right to say he has something to hide, but as to whether it's connected to criminal activity or just incompetence, I'm not sure."

Nikos flipped open his notebook again. "Something else that doesn't add up. He said he went back to his cabin. I checked. His access card was used to enter the infirmary at 21.53. He didn't return to his own cabin until 22.37."

"Good thinking," Beatrice said, in with genuine admiration. She hadn't thought to check the doctor's alibi. "Right, I want to talk to Fraser again tomorrow and I'll also ask Jensson about him. There's something unhealthy about the captain's unquestioning acceptance of everything Fraser does. If both Weinberg and Bannerjee doubt the doctor's methods, Jensson really has a responsibility to take it seriously. But he allows himself to be bossed and bullied by the man."

"Yes, he does. But you don't," said Nikos, with an amused respect in his tone. "I think you made both of them very nervous by saying they were still under suspicion."

"So they should be. Heads in the sand, hoping the problem will go away. Unless they wake up to what is happening and start to cooperate with us, both their careers are likely to end in under a week. They're typical of people who've been in a job too long. Bored and resentful, going through the motions, wishing they were somewhere else..."

She stopped, aware how cynical she sounded. "Now, tell me about Inspector Voulakis. What kind of man is he?"

Nikos looked out at the activity on the street for a few seconds.

"He's been in the job too long. He's bored and resentful and going through the motions, wishing he was somewhere else." Nikos echoed Beatrice's words with a rueful smile. "He's deadened by administration – always hoping for a bit of action, as long as it doesn't involve hard work. He sometimes likes to divide people or encourage tension between his officers. I don't know how he will react to you, Beatrice. He's a real Anglophile but..."

"But what? How do you advise me to play this?" Another battle with someone else's baggage was the last thing she needed.

He shrugged, with an apologetic grin. "One one hand, you are exactly the kind of exciting challenge he loves. On the other, you represent a whole pile of problems."

She grinned back. "Story of my life, Nikos."

Chapter 14

Rose was right, it was time to get out. Maggie knew her reluctance to leave the cabin was becoming unhealthy. After two days of sympathy and room service, she'd sensed Rose's patience beginning to fray. Even Joyce Milligan's kindness in visiting twice, as a representative of the Hirondelles, only made it plainer that life went on. Rose was bored, and if Maggie were honest, so was she. There was only so much entertainment to be gained from people-watching, and as their inner balcony overlooked the pool the scenes below had grown repetitive and dull. Rose told her they were turning into curtain-twitchers. Time to get out and do their duty, she said. Detective Inspector Stubbs needed their help, she said. Rose could be very persuasive.

"Between five and seven is the best time to venture out. The excursions have returned and will be either resting or refreshing in their cabins." Rose made it sound like an adventure. "Fewer folk on deck. The crew tend to use the facilities more at that time, so we can keep our eyes peeled for someone of the right height and build. The man we're looking for is tall..."

"Yes," Maggie agreed. "A good six-footer. Although Esther was a tiny woman. He may have looked bigger beside such a wee thing. But tall and strong, of that I have no doubt." She suppressed the image of the jerky body in freefall.

"So we go for a walk, greet anyone we meet, keep our opinions to ourselves and watch. Avoid the Hirondelles if at all possible, and dine at The Sizzling Grill. We'll find none of those biddies in there."

"Don't be rude, Rose. I hope I have as much energy as Joyce Milligan when I'm her age. And we're not far off biddies ourselves.

I'll just say again, if it feels too much, if I start to feel panicky, I'm coming back here. No arguments."

Rose sat in front of the dressing table, dabbing lipstick onto her bottom lip. "Yes, of course, but that's not going to be necessary. You're the observer, collecting information on all the male crew members on this ship. You're the only one who's seen this man. You have to give DI Stubbs something to go on. Especially after Maureen Hall."

Maggie, standing by the door, gathering all her courage, stepped back into the room and sat down on the ottoman with a thump. Maureen Hall. That poor elderly, infirm and ailing woman, smothered in her sleep. *How could anyone, why would anyone...?* her thoughts began the same futile circuits as before, so she called a halt. Rose was right. Time to get out.

The heat came as a surprise as did the brightness and the noise. Squeals and shrieks of laughter from a group of youngsters in the pool competed with a group singing *Happy Birthday* from the deck above. Maggie recoiled, only to meet the resistance of Rose's guiding arm and positive voice.

"Fresh air! I feel better already. So, let's start with a walk around the deck – right or left?"

Maggie pointed away from the pool and Rose led the way. A few people dozed on the loungers and chairs, paperbacks or magazines propped on their chests. Maggie's paranoia subsided as she saw that no rubber-necking mob of ghouls was camped outside her cabin. In the first few minutes, no one took any notice of her at all. Maggie relaxed her shoulders, raised her head and gazed out to sea. The sun sank, filling the sky with ripples of colour; tangerine, violet, blush and scarlet reflected in a mercury sea. An outrageous display enjoyed by covetous eyes for the briefest of moments, but never captured. Like the flash of a Moulin Rouge underskirt.

She looked at Rose. "The world doesn't care, does it?"

Rose's optimistic expression faded.

"No, no, I mean that in a good way. Whatever tragedies and dramas we endure down here, the world turns, the sun sets and life goes on, relentless and oblivious. As it should be." Maggie reached out to squeeze Rose's hand briefly. "I know I've not been much fun these past few days. So I'm giving myself a good shake. Look."

She shook herself from head to toe, wobbling her cheeks for comic effect. "From this moment on, I stop feeling sorry for myself and do everything in my power to identify the man I saw. It's the least I can do for Esther, for DI Stubbs and for you. Shall we start by the staff pool?"

Many staff and crew members used the quiet period between passengers' daytime activities and evening entertainments to swim, sunbathe or use the gym in their own private, less well-equipped section of D deck. Rose and Maggie positioned themselves in the shade and watched the high jinks as waiters, maids, chefs, entertainers and sailors let off steam in the water. The age-old signs of flirtation had not changed, Maggie observed, as she watched the interaction among the young. A bunch of men organised an impromptu water volleyball match, hastily unrolling a net across the pool and yelling instructions at each other.

A great hairy individual Maggie didn't recognise clambered out of the water and fetched a ball. She assessed his build and height, and nudged Rose. "That's about the size of him."

"That one? But he has a beard. You'd have spotted that, wouldn't you?"

"I'm not saying it is him. But he was about that size. And at that distance, I couldn't see his face at all clearly, although I can't picture a beard."

Rose pulled her sunglasses down her nose to observe the big man leaping into the pool after the ball. "Some people have more than their fair share of hair."

Maggie looked over her shoulder and recognised a passer-by. "And others were at the back of the queue. That language fella should either wear a hat or put some sunscreen on his bald patch. I'll mention it at dinner."

They both watched Mr Martins walk along the deck, jacket over his arm, purposefully making for the Reception Area.

Rose spoke. "Make that breakfast. By the look of him, he's off out for the night. Plus you and I agreed on The Sizzling Grill for dinner, to avoid any nosey parkers and... Oh hello, Captain Jensson!"

Maggie jumped at the unexpected presence of the captain.

"Good afternoon, ladies. I'm very happy to see you out and about. How are you both?" The captain's smile was as glittery as the pool.

Maggie assumed a smile. "Better every day. Just trying to get back into the swing of things."

"I'm very happy to hear that. And your timing is perfect, because tomorrow we arrive in Rhodes. So much unforgettable history to experience, you really shouldn't miss it. Could I invite you to the Captain's Table tomorrow evening?"

Rose stepped in. "We're not yet up to braving the dining-room, but thank you for the invitation. This evening, we're going to the grill. Small steps, you see."

"I quite understand. The food at The Sizzling Grill is delicious, incidentally. Kostas takes extraordinary pride in the freshness of his selection. An asset to our team, who works hard and as you can see, plays hard."

He gestured to the pool.

"That hairy one is a chef?" asked Maggie.

"Most certainly. But I can assure you he wears clothes in the kitchen." The captain winked and departed.

Maggie watched him move along the deck, stopping to greet the occasional passenger with a friendly observation. She could spot a poor actor a mile off and his false bonhomie galled her. She turned to Rose.

"Similar heights, the captain and that chef. And I feel sure as eggs is eggs, the man who threw Esther Crawford off the cliff had no beard."

"The captain? Now, don't get paranoid. He has to be above suspicion. He spends all day and every day on board. Still, we can keep our eyes peeled for lookalikes."

"Hmmm. I'm fed up with watching this lot and their tomfoolery. Let's go up onto the observatory deck."

The way the world had tilted on its axis reminded Maggie of September the eleventh, 2001. The shock of those attacks in America changed how she looked at the world, and not for the better. Aircraft, usually nothing more to her than noise or vapour trails, had taken on the form of instruments of death. The rhetoric of 'terrorism' and 'war' left a manipulative taste of political engineering in her mouth, but the images had made their mark. September 11th changed the way she saw the world. The way she saw the sky.

Two days ago, what she'd witnessed changed the way she saw people. Now every smile hid a hint of ill intent and everyone wore a shadow. Words like 'evil' floated like storm clouds through her mind. A crew member's good manners in allowing them right of way on the steps appeared predatory; a fellow passenger's comment on the weather rang an ominous note. Her nervous system was yet to disable the alarms.

She and Rose leaned on the railing and gazed out at Crete. As the evening darkened, lights sparked into life across the port of Heraklion. Restaurateurs would be readying tables, bands tuning up, taxi drivers preparing for a busy night. A peculiar sadness stole over Maggie. She wanted to rush down the gangway and fling herself into the midst of it all, but at the same time she was happy to hide, appreciating the ship's protection, the distance from real life. She sniffed, mostly in disgust at herself.

Rose inclined her head. "Funny how a view changes as you get older. Here's you and me, standing here looking at a beautiful Greek island. Look at all the others here, all gazing out at exactly the same place, at exactly the same time. But I'll bet not one of us is seeing the same scene. What are you seeing?"

"Life," said Maggie, without hesitation. "Or rather other people's lives. I'm standing here, imagining how much fun they're all having. I'm envious and a bit of me wants to hurry down there and join them. And another part of me is saying 'Go home, old lady. Jigsaws and knitting is all you're good for.' That's what I see. How about yourself?"

Rose's brow twitched, somewhere between concern and annoyance but before she could speak, another voice interrupted.

"In which case, you should run down there this minute and

throw yourselves into the middle of the action. Which would be just the thing to fill you with lust and life and mischief. For one thing, it would kick all that 'too old' business into a cocked hat. The downside? You'd miss my show. Which is something else to fill you with lust and life and mischief. Especially lust."

The man was tanned, smiley and had eyes worthy of Frank Sinatra. Maggie found herself smiling back.

"I recognise you. You're Toni Dean. 'The Man with the Golden Voice'. I've seen your picture on those posters."

"Hush now. We don't talk about *those* posters." He darted a glance behind him. "Oh you mean the ones for the show? Fair dos." His eyes danced with teasing fun. "As for the Golden Voice, that wasn't my choice of marketing line. I wanted 'The Voice of an Era'. See, I don't sing any of the modern stuff. All classics - Tony Bennett, Dean Martin, Tom Jones, Howard Keel, Paul Anka, Bing Crosby... they don't make 'em like that any more. Have you two charming ladies seen my show?"

Rose's expression brightened along with each name the man quoted. "No, not yet. We've spent a lot of time ashore and haven't had a look at the entertainment. But we're just beginning to take advantage. Did you say you'll be singing tonight?"

"Nine o'clock, The Empress Grand Ballroom. Consider it a first step. Tonight, music and laughter. Tomorrow, another island and another day. And Rhodes might be an inspiration. You'll feel brave enough to go exploring and find an adventure!"

Maggie's smile was a weak effort, she knew, but she'd had her fill of adventures. Rose's response held far more enthusiasm.

"Nine o'clock, then. If we're still full of beans after our dinner, we'll come and hear you sing."

"If you're full of beans, don't you come anywhere near me!"

Rose laughed, almost a giggle. "You know what I mean. See you at the ballroom."

He bowed like a typical showman. "Look forward to seeing you there. And even if you don't make it, promise me you'll remember this: You are never too old. If you feel like it, do it. That goes for jigsaws or gigolos!" With a mock-shocked face, he waved and backed off towards the steps.

After he'd descended from sight, Rose gave Maggie a nudge.

"What do you think? He's just like an old-fashioned Redcoat, or one of those Saturday Night at the Palladium entertainers. Old-school with the personal touch. It might be good fun."

"Yes. Exactly what I feel like tonight. Something familiar and unthreatening. Not to mention an hour or so in the dark. I'm game."

"Me too. Adventures can wait till tomorrow."

They linked arms and headed downstairs to The Sizzling Grill.

Chapter 15

Chief Inspector Voulakis and Detective Chief Inspector Hamilton. Her stiff, unsmiling, immaculate boss seemed worlds apart from this amiable chap with his large belly, loosened tie and five o'clock shadow. He carried a peculiar but not unpleasant scent about him, which Beatrice could only associate with roast potatoes. Where Hamilton projected a judgemental chill, this man radiated warmth and bonhomie. Hard to imagine as it was, the two had been great pals for sixteen years, according to Nikos's voluble superior.

He greeted Beatrice with a huge smile and shook her hand in both of his. He showed surprisingly little interest in the details of the case and accepted Beatrice's suggestion that she and Nikos Stephanakis should work as a team without demur.

"Why not? If you are happy to share the role, who am I to argue? I know this will be a great learning experience for Inspector Stephanakis. I myself learned so much from working with Hamilton in that one year alone. I will never forget how much I improved as a detective. You know, we were two of the first officers to award an ASBO. They'd only just been introduced and we used them to break up two hooligan firms associated with Millwall FC. Groundbreaking work."

"I didn't know that, sir. Congratulations. Although I'd say we no longer think of ASBOs as 'awards' these days."

The man's grin just grew wider. He sat back with his arms behind his head. Beatrice looked away from the sweat patches and spotted a leather cord around his wrist, threaded through a single blue bead.

"Ha! My English police vocabulary was never the best. Yes, I am sure you will teach Stephanakis much. I wanted to send him to

London, you see, but secondments like mine are much harder to finance these days. This will be the next best thing. I owe Hamilton yet another debt of gratitude for sending you. How is he, by the way?"

"Very well, if a little bad-tempered. He expected me back in London this week, but that is unlikely to happen now."

Voulakis burst into laughter, smacking his hand on the desk. "His loss, my gain. He will never do me a favour again in his life. Tell me, is he still a confirmed bachelor or has he found a lady friend yet?"

Beatrice hesitated. She abhorred rumours and speculation about her colleagues' private lives, having seen first-hand how damaging it could be. But as the two men had a personal connection, it might appear rude not to pass an innocent comment.

"As far as I know, sir, DCI Hamilton prefers to remain independent. But I am not the best informed on office gossip."

He sighed, shaking his head and gazing into the middle distance. "Such a shame. You know, he is the reason I married my wife. That's where I met her, in London! She was a second-generation Greek immigrant and a neighbour of Hamilton's. He introduced us, thinking it would cheer me up if I could speak Greek with someone. Cheer me up? I fell in love! Every time he comes to visit, I try to find a nice woman for him, but it never works. You know the expression, 'he bats for the other side'? Well, that's what my wife thinks. But that is not the truth."

Despite herself, Beatrice's curiosity took the bait. "Really, sir? Several of my colleagues would agree with your wife."

Voulakis folded his hands over his substantial stomach and shook his head. "No. It's a sad story. He doesn't often talk about his private life, but one night we drank a bottle of brandy, and he told me he'd fallen in love. The lady was unavailable, unfortunately, but his feelings never changed. Every time I ask him if he's met someone else, he says no one ever comes close. Perhaps one day he will forget her and move on. It's never too late."

The temptation to snort arose, but Voulakis wore an expression of such heartfelt sincerity, that Beatrice opted to change the subject instead. How people love to extrapolate, turning a probable brush-off into an operatic tragedy.

"Captain Jensson has offered both Inspector Stephanakis and myself accommodation aboard for the rest of the investigation, as the ship needs to proceed with its itinerary. Is that acceptable to you?"

Voulakis widened his eyes. "To me, yes, but Stephanakis! What about your girlfriend?" He winked at Beatrice. "She's British as well, you know. Very romantic. She was his English teacher and she fell madly in love with him."

Nikos rolled his eyes, but softened the gesture with a smile. "Karen will understand the practical reasons for staying aboard. And it's only for a few days."

"Perhaps not even that long," Beatrice said. "I want to wrap this up quickly and return to Scotland Yard. But looking at it realistically, we think we have a serial killer on our hands, so we'll need to keep a close ear and an eye to the ground. So aboard the *Empress Louise* is where we should be."

"Are you going back tonight?" asked Voulakis, his question apparently born of enthusiasm rather than supervisory rigour.

Nikos replied first. "No sir. We'll join the cruise tomorrow. Tonight, I would like to prepare for a few days away and tomorrow DI Stubbs will check out of her hotel. We both need some rest after last night and I think a few hours away from the ship will do us good."

Tired, tetchy and a little claustrophobic, Beatrice looked over at Nikos and mentally transmitted her gratitude.

It was quarter to five. The sun filled her hotel room with butterscotch light and threw intersecting triangles across the tiled floor. With every intention of explaining the reasons for her extended stay to Matthew over the phone later that evening, Beatrice took a shower, drew the curtains and lay on the sheets to get an hour's rest. She checked her phone and picked up a voicemail.

"*Message for DI Stubbs. Dr Bruce of Beech Avenue Surgery, Salisbury here. Bad news, I'm afraid. Beryl Hodges was buried on Friday. No post-mortem carried out, but I did examine the body, at the family's request. Cause of death determined as asphyxia brought on by anaphylactic shock exacerbated by asthma. The lady had suffered previous violent reactions to shellfish, so in my estimation, that was what provoked the allergic response. Hope this information is useful, call if any questions."*

Which brought her no closer to deciding if Hodges had been killed deliberately or had made a mistake with her choice of starter. If the woman had medication in her fridge to counter such a reaction, surely she'd be extremely careful? In which case, how would someone make her eat the very thing that might kill her? She imagined trying to poison someone with prawns, recalled an episode of *Masterchef* involving fishcakes and her eyes closed.

When she awoke, the clock said half past eight and her stomach said dinner-time. She decided to go out for some food and call Matthew on her return. Due to the time difference, he'd barely be home from work yet and she needed a bit more practice on her breezy update.

The lobby, which had been awkwardly full of guests checking in earlier, was now peaceful and almost empty as she made for the exit. She handed her key to the receptionist, clearing her throat to disguise her growling stomach.

"Good evening, Mrs Stubbs. Your visitor is waiting in the bar."

Beatrice raised her eyebrows. "Sorry?"

"He said not to disturb you and he would wait until you are ready. Through there."

She followed the pointing finger and entered a small room, dimly lit and sparsely populated. At the bar, a familiar figure sat reading a paperback, an almost-empty glass of red wine at his elbow. She approached, feigning a frown.

"And what do you think you're doing here?"

Oscar Martins's face passed from surprise to puzzlement to pleasure as he brought himself back to reality. She could identify with that feeling, so lost in a book that reality comes as an intrusion.

"What do you think I'm doing here? Stalking you, of course. I ruthlessly pumped Inspector Stephanakis for the name of your hotel. But I'm on a break right now, so the time seemed right to enjoy a glass of the local grape. Can I tempt you?"

"Certainly not. On an empty stomach and three hours' sleep, I would be swinging from the chandeliers. I was on my way out to find something tasty and substantial. With chips. Have you eaten?"

"No. I saved myself in case I happened to bump into you. My Machiavellian plan was to track you down and invite you to dinner." He slipped his book into the right inside pocket of his jacket and Beatrice recognised the cover. *An Empty Vessel*, by Vaughan Mason. One of Matthew's favourites. She made up her mind. She'd refuse to be drawn on any aspect of the case, but some company and discussion on literature wouldn't hurt.

"Come on then, let's waste no more time. You're due back on board at eleven. I'll ask the concierge for a local recommendation."

"No need. I found the perfect place, just around the corner. A good stalker should do his homework. I do have one request, if you don't mind?"

Beatrice tilted her head to indicate she was listening.

Oscar clasped his hands under his chin and lowered his brow. "I must ask you not to talk about or allude to your investigation in any way. I warn you now that if you should attempt to share sensitive details about this case, I shall stick my fingers in my ears and sing Demis Roussos until you stop."

"I rather like Demis Roussos. But thank you, I accept your terms. Can we go now? I'm absolutely starving."

"This way."

Oscar's evident pride in having found a charming little local taverna was somewhat punctured on their arrival. Dinos spotted her instantly and rushed to kiss her on both cheeks.

"Again! You come back! You love my food! Welcome, Police Lady! Welcome, mister. Sit, sit!"

A flush of happy anticipation suffused Beatrice as they sat at a battered table, but she sensed Oscar's confidence had lost some of its ease.

"Inspector Stephanakis brought me here for lunch when I arrived. You obviously have an eye for the right kind of eatery. If the *stifado* is on the menu, I'd strongly recommend you try it."

His face creased into a knowing smile. "And you have a knack for tact. Not to mention notoriety. It seems you're not easily forgotten."

Beatrice glanced across at Dinos behind the bar, who was roaring with laughter at one of his own jokes. The whole room turned to watch, his laugh an entertainment in itself.

"I believe Dinos is what we'd call a local 'character' and one of his quirks is a peculiar fascination with the British Royal Family. That's why a London detective is likely to stick in his mind. Now, why are you lurking about hotel bars when you could be attending the 'Introduction to Rhodes' lecture on the *Empress Louise*?"

Oscar stroked an imaginary beard. "I was paralysed by choice. What should I do? The lecture on a place I have visited three times before, aqua-aerobics in the main pool, a retro sing-a-long in the piano bar or fifty percent off having my legs waxed? When you have so many opportunities, sometimes it's easier not to decide. Plus, our conversation from last night remains unfinished. You were..."

"Meatballs!" boomed Dinos. "Special today, very good. Yes?" He plonked a basket of bread and carafe of red on the table and rubbed his hands together. "Yes?"

Oscar shrugged helplessly while Beatrice laughed.

"Meatballs. Yes." She waved a finger between herself and Oscar to indicate they would both succumb to the house special. She had every reason to trust their host.

"Very good!" he bowed and gave the thumbs-up.

Beatrice watched him roll back to the kitchen, the loose sole flapping from his trainer. A man in his element, at home in his world. Not rich in the conventional sense, but respected for himself, and apparently happy with his lot. She compared him with Jensson, whose job ascribed greater status and certainly accrued greater wealth. And yet the outlook of the two appeared diametrically opposite. She checked herself. Making assumptions about two men she'd met a couple of times. The worst kind of mindset for a detective.

She focused on her dining companion. "I hope you didn't mind my ordering for you. Well, acquiescing for you. Dinos seems to be rather a steamroller, so I just gave in. I also tend to trust the dish of the day when all the locals are tucking in."

Oscar poured wine into two beakers. "Me too. And I'd never have been brave enough to argue even if I had wanted *stifado*. So let's toast going local. Cheers!"

"Cheers!" The wine, like Dinos himself, was rough, unpolished, full bodied and warming.

Oscar took a sip and his eyes widened. Instantly his tanned cheeks began to glow.

"Oh dear," said Beatrice. "Do you hate it? We can order something else."

Oscar shook his head and drank again. "No, not at all, I like a wine that gives you a bear hug. I feel more manly with every drop. And what better partner for homemade meatballs? As I was saying, our conversation was interrupted by last night's incident. And, if I may make so bold, rather unfair. I told you about my profession, my marital status, my cruise habits and my shameful habit of writing books. You, with classic professional cunning, revealed nothing more than your full title. Well, I'm not a man to give up easily. Tonight, DI Stubbs, I'm asking the questions."

The meatballs, as predicted, were a triumph. The second carafe slipped down smoothly as more and more people packed the taverna. Departing diners struggled and wrestled their way to the door. Heat and condensation increased, yet tempers remained friendly and cheerful, while the noise level made any conversation less than shouting impossible.

Oscar paid the bill, claiming it as his treat. Dinos insisted on taking a group selfie and bestowing more kisses in their effusive goodbyes. Beatrice didn't argue with either of them, but expressed her thanks with absolute sincerity for an excellent evening. Once on the street, the night air cooled her cheeks and she slipped into her jacket. Traffic, people, lights and music seemed to spill across their path, flowing, bouncing, bumping and perpetually moving. Oscar shielded her from a group of shrieking girls tumbling from a bar, but Beatrice's sense of goodwill remained unshaken. She smiled at the girls, at Oscar, at the world. Dinos's house wine should be available on prescription.

"Your hotel, madam. Thank you for your company and I will see you tomorrow, I'm sure. Good luck with the investigation, not that you'll need it. I should hurry and get a cab. Look, here's my card. Give me a call. Sleep well."

He took her hand, drew her to him and kissed her lightly on both cheeks.

"Goodnight, Oscar, and thank you. Yes, it's getting late. Don't miss the boat!"

He gave a surprised laugh. "My sentiments exactly."

He stepped into the street and hailed a taxi immediately, causing a cacophony of horns behind the cab. He turned for a last wave and ducked inside. Beatrice waved back and watched the vehicle careen off into the direction of the dock.

She released a happy sigh and looked at her watch. Half past eleven. In Devon, it was half past nine, a perfectly reasonable time to call someone. Then she should pack, perform ablutions and bed. The flight to Rhodes was due to depart shortly after seven. She tucked Oscar's card into her pocket and picked up her key from reception. As she made for the stairs, she congratulated herself. Not only had she relaxed and stopped thinking about the case, but she'd made a new friend. For someone who'd spent the whole previous night awake investigating a murder, it was a respectable night's work.

"Good evening, Professor Bailey speaking."

"Matthew, it's me. Sorry to call so late."

"Hello, Old Thing. Didn't recognise the number. How's Greece?"

"The place itself is very pleasant. However, the case itself has taken a turn for the worse. There's been another fatality and this time, I'm afraid there is no doubt."

"Oh dear, that's most unfortunate. I understand you can give no details, but from a purely selfish perspective, I presume it means you won't be back on Wednesday."

"Highly unlikely. The aim is to clear this up in the next couple of days, but you know how unpredictable such a situation can be."

Matthew's voice, when it came, was profoundly weary. *"So long as you hold Hamilton to his word and insist on days off in lieu. We need some uninterrupted time together."*

"I will try. The only thing is, he wants me to take over another operation, so I'm not sure how flexible he'll be."

She stood at the French windows, watching the patterns of lunar light on the ocean. A moon bridge, from this world to another. Seconds passed as she waited for his response.

"Matthew?"

"What takes priority, Beatrice? Really, it's a genuine question. Are Hamilton's needs more important than yours? Than ours?"

She pressed a hand over her eyes and grimaced. "No." Her buoyant mood leaked away, leaving an uncertain void. "As a matter of fact, I broached the subject of early retirement. He wasn't happy and told me to forget the idea for next year. But the year after, I'm sure he'll be fine, because he'll have two detective sergeants in..."

"To be completely frank, I could not care less about Hamilton's problems. I'm more concerned with ours. I begin to feel you actually prefer our being apart and have no inclination to change that. My attempts to discuss our future are met with evasion or absence. For my part, let me be clear. I would very much like to spend my dotage with you. Ideally in the same house, but I'd settle for the same county."

"Matthew..."

"What do you want, Beatrice? That is not a rhetorical question. Think about it and give me your answer on your return. Whenever that may be. I wish you a goodnight and a swift resolution to your case. Take care, Old Thing."

Beatrice returned his wishes, put the phone down and leant her forehead against the window. Her relaxed and positive frame of mind had been ousted by a malign and familiar unease. She was being irresponsible, hiding her head and hoping the problem would stop knocking. She winced at the idea of identifying Matthew as a problem. The one person who had loved her, supported her through the worst of times, made so many sacrifices and only wanted a future together. What was wrong with her?

She thought about his question. What did she want? The best of both worlds. Matthew's love and companionship, Hamilton's respect, her own peace of mind and equilibrium. Even if it came in the form of medication. There had to be a compromise. All she had to do was find it. But before that, she had to call James. Her counsellor of two years was unfailing in his patience yet unforgiving in his persistence, never letting her twist off the hook.

Yes, she would call James. It was not quite a decision, but a decision to decide, which would have to suffice.

Chapter 16

Winds buffeted the city of Rhodes, shaking trees and whipping tourists' hair into their faces. As they drove along Papagou, Nikos pointed out the Palace of the Grand Master of the Knights of Rhodes, just visible through the trees of Platia Rimini. Beatrice seemed impressed, exclaiming her admiration of the ancient edifice. They drove under an arch in the city walls and alongside the harbour, where the wind flailed masts and whipped flags. He kept up his tourist guide commentary, but his mind was elsewhere. He had mixed feelings about this place.

On the island of Rhodes, Karen had changed from being his teacher to his lover over one highly charged weekend. Incredible memories he hid away so as not to wear them out. Yet Rhodes was home to a piece of shit he'd rather forget. There were several people on this planet Nikos never wanted to see again, but only one he actively wished dead. Demetrius Xanthou, schoolmate, colleague, rival and now an inspector for the South Aegean Region of the Hellenic Police. Acid roiled in Nikos's gut.

The awe-inspiring architecture changed in stature as the police vehicle turned away from the beach and rolled down Akti Sachtouri into the commercial port. Three vast cruise ships dominated the skyline, anachronistic and intrusive, like contemporary hotels in mediaeval towns.

By the time they arrived at the *Empress Louise*, breakfast had finished and many of the cruise passengers were descending the gangway, keen to begin their exploration of the island. Nikos took a deep breath and with a nod to Beatrice, led the way onto the boat in the opposite direction to the silver-haired tide.

Captain Jensson looked less than rested. When he greeted them at the bridge, he reported no disturbances other than a great deal of seasickness amongst the passengers. High winds had made the sailing the most turbulent so far.

"We weren't even sure if we'd be able to dock. So the medical team have their hands full. I don't think Dr Fraser will be able to spare you much time today, if any. How do you want to proceed, detectives?"

Nikos looked at Beatrice, but she gave a minuscule nod for him to take the lead. So he did.

"DI Stubbs received news last night that Beryl Hodges died from anaphylactic shock, very likely a reaction to seafood complicated by her asthma. This may be coincidence, but we have to keep in mind the possibility someone knew of her allergies. Our plan is to search for links between the dead women and identify potential suspects. We'd like to interview their companions, talk to you and your team once again, and we will need to speak to Dr Fraser at some stage. Do you mind if we use the casino again?"

"The casino is available for today, but then we will need to make other arrangements. As for another interview, I'm not sure what more I can add. I rarely do more than pass the time of day with most passengers. And the Hirondelles, travelling as a group, would not be invited to dine at my table. Not out of any kind of prejudice, but we don't like to split up a party."

"Did you meet Beryl Hodges?" asked Nikos.

"No. The Hirondelles arrived in the afternoon, held a birthday party in one of the restaurants for Mrs Crawford that evening, and unfortunately, the Hodges woman died during the night. I never even saw her."

Beatrice jumped in. "Do you know which restaurant they chose for their party? It could be relevant, given cause of death."

"If I remember correctly, that would have been The Sizzling Grill. Esther Crawford told me she had a particular fondness for the Sticky Chicken Wings."

Nikos wrote 'grill' and 'chicken wings' in his notebook and would find out how to spell the other words later. "Did you have any contact with Maureen Hall?"

"Mrs Hall was sick for most of the voyage. I'm afraid I hadn't even spoken to her."

"But presumably Dr Fraser had seen her, as she would have been a patient?" asked Beatrice.

Jensson frowned. "Usually the nurse sees to everyday problems such as nausea and blood pressure issues, so I doubt it."

"Well, that's something we can check with him personally. We'll let you get on, but perhaps you might find time for us later this afternoon?" Beatrice's voice, while polite and friendly, contained an underlying firmness Nikos admired. A fleeting frown crossed Jensson's face.

"Detective Inspectors, I don't mean to be difficult and obviously I want this situation resolved. But I have received a succession of visits since you left us in Crete. Firstly our Human Resources manager, delivering a series of complaints from staff about police intrusion. Then Nurse Bannerjee, representing herself and Dr Weinberg, whose workloads have increased substantially. Apparently, many passengers no longer wish to be treated by Dr Fraser as he seems to be the focus of the enquiry. Finally, the head of entertainment would like to have the casino back. He has not been able to keep up his regular maintenance and cleaning since you've been here. Morale amongst the staff is visibly low, everyone has their suspicions and the atmosphere is becoming sour. I urgently need to demonstrate some progress before this gets out of hand."

Nikos resisted the urge to look at Beatrice. "Believe me, Captain, our aim is to solve this as fast as we can. But we cannot demonstrate progress if we don't make any. We can give you an update later today if you like."

A uniformed crew member hovered behind Beatrice, trying to catch Jensson's eye. When he succeeded, he pointed to his watch.

Jensson raised a finger in acknowledgement. "I have to go. My afternoon break is at 15.30. I can see you then."

Nikos watched him walk away and return the sailor's salute, back straight and head high. One of those men who had an innate authority and commanded respect without even trying. Nikos wondered if he would ever get to that stage.

One of the worst things about interviewing friends and relatives of the recently and suddenly deceased is ascertaining the root cause of their guilt. Because they are all guilty. In Beatrice's experience, that guilt could be as pertinent as having wielded the murder weapon or as irrelevant as being less than complimentary about that morning's pancakes.

Audrey Kean and Pat George, the travelling companions accompanying Maureen Hall, were most definitely guilty. They outdid each other in self-recrimination, seeking and finding more reasons to feel terrible about their friend's unfortunate end. But they didn't kill her. Beatrice knew that from the outset. What she had to do was assume the role of grief counsellor while plucking the occasional useful nugget from the cascade of self-flagellating misery.

Maureen, a widow, had lived her entire life in Yorkshire. She had no connection with Esther Crawford or Beryl Hodges and had met none of the Hirondelles. Seasick, and probably homesick, for the majority of her first cruise, she'd been cabin-bound for almost a fortnight. Her only trip ashore was on Monday. The heat and exercise were too much for her and she'd complained. Which, according to Audrey, led to 'words'. The threesome had parted ways on their return to the ship. That was the last time they saw her.

After the women left, tearful and wretched, Beatrice took a few minutes to order her impressions and knowledge of the facts. Cabins of the deceased in completely different areas. Two women belonging to the same party, the third with no connection. Two very different methods of killing, one very narrow age range. But was this really a serial killer? Or simply a series of coincidences which made two deaths and one murder appear connected? Beatrice lay back on the banquette, covered her eyes with her hands and started all over again.

The ship's records on who was aboard and who disembarked at each port had been rigorously maintained. Nikos ran several reports on the data and noted the vast majority of passengers who left the ship at every port joined official excursions. A tiny percentage chose to make their own way, including Rose Mason and Maggie Campbell, a small group of architects and a few individuals, such as Oscar Martins. For each possible murder, Nikos cross-checked the locations of the individuals concerned. Everyone was aboard when Beryl Hodges expired. When Esther Crawford plummeted into the sea, the tourist buses were parked outside the tavernas, the architects were attending a lecture on archaeological reconstruction, Rose and Maggie were picnicking, and only Oscar Martins was somewhere on the island alone. No one else remained unaccounted for. When someone smothered Maureen Hall, most people were dining in the ship's restaurants, including the architects. Oscar Martins was in the Club Room with Beatrice, and Rose and Maggie had ordered room service in their cabin.

But that only narrowed down passenger movement. The person who took the housekeeping key card to Maureen Hall's room knew where to go and what to get, indicating a level of inside knowledge. And as for who was where and when in terms of staff and crew, Nikos needed help. He stood up and looked across the silent expanse of casino to Beatrice. No one there. She hadn't passed him so she must have gone to the bathroom. He folded up his laptop, tucked it under his arm and set off for the bridge.

A deadly combination.

Lying down in a darkened room, with a firm cushion beneath her after nights of insufficient sleep, it was no wonder she'd dozed off. Beatrice blinked up at the ceiling, massaged her face and checked her watch. 11.40. She'd only been asleep for around twenty minutes and just hoped her catnap had not involved snoring. Still, Nikos was far enough away not to have heard. She held her breath and listened. Not a sound. She lifted herself onto her elbows and peered across the room. No sign of him. He'd obviously taken a break.

She flopped down onto her back and tried to relocate her thought-process regarding connections between the killings. But her stomach released a creaking, snapping groan, as if an alligator had opened its jaws. A scanty breakfast of yoghurt and fruit at six in the morning was barely enough to keep body and soul together. She was starving. Another creak, this time from the end of the room. Good. Nikos was back. She'd propose an early lunch over which they could share notes. She shoved herself upwards again, her eyes at table level and blinked into the darkness of the casino.

A man, much taller than Nikos, was pacing silently along the bar. He scanned the room and bent over Nikos's table, turning some papers to face him. With a brief check back at the door, he then withdrew a phone from his inside pocket. Beatrice squinted but the light from the bar rendered the individual nothing more than a large silhouette. He tilted the phone over the table and Beatrice understood.

"Can I help you?" she yelled, the volume of her voice even scaring herself. The man shot backwards and was out the door before she'd even got her feet on the ground.

She hurried after him and burst out into the corridor, startling an elderly couple walking past.

"Sorry, didn't mean to alarm you. A man just came out of here, did you see him?"

They looked at each other, back to her and shook their heads, like nodding dogs in the negative.

"Did someone pass you? In a hurry? Someone tall?"

They shook their heads once again. Then the woman spoke. "We didn't see anything. All we heard was a lot of noise. Just now, down there." She pointed at the opposite end of the featureless corridor.

Beatrice ran, assessing the risk of leaving the casino, her laptop and notes, against getting a description of whoever wanted to photograph police evidence. She turned the corner to see a maid collecting the contents of a cleaning trolley from the floor and muttering in some Eastern European tongue.

"What happened?"

The maid's irritation segued into apology. "Sorry, madam. I leave my trolley here and someone comes round this corner too fast. Knocks everything all over the floor. I am in the cabin, changing the towels and I hear a big crash. So I come out here and look at this mess! Nothing wrong with my trolley. This is correct parking according to housekeeping rules."

"Did you see who it was? Can you describe the person?"

"No. He is gone when I come out. Hear feet running. Big man, for sure, and he says a lot of bad words. Some passengers don't know nothing about good manners."

She picked up her feather duster and mini-shampoos, shaking her head in disbelief or disgust or possibly both.

Beatrice thanked her and returned to the casino.

Coincidence could now be ruled out. Whoever had targeted these three women was on the ship and not only aware of the investigation, but watching them. How else did he know Nikos had left the casino?

On her return, the cavernous, shadowy room was quiet and suddenly sinister. The shadows and recesses now made her skin prickle and she wished for Nikos's reassuring presence. His table was empty, but all his papers were still there. She didn't touch anything, aware of the possibility of fingerprints, but bent to see what had interested their visitor so. The uppermost page listed the Hirondelles: name, age, home address and cabin number.

Chapter 17

Rose had been waiting forty minutes by the time Nurse Bannerjee called her name. In that time she'd grown increasingly uncomfortable among so many sickly faces, most with a greyish pallor.

An elderly man with a dressing over one eye released regular sighs, the hairy chef held a bandaged left hand against his chest while using his right to press buttons on his phone, two middle-aged women with dyed blonde hair held a whispered conversation, interrupted frequently by the smaller of the two's frame-shaking cough. All eyes assessed Rose with curiosity, as she appeared perfectly healthy. She jumped to her feet on hearing her name and left the waiting room in relief.

"Come in, Mrs Mason. Close the door. How is Mrs Campbell today?"

Rose folded her hands in her lap. "Much better. I feel bad for taking up your time when I can see you're rushed off your feet, but Maggie needs some more sleeping tablets. She's doing fairly well during the daytime, but still having restless nights. It's only a repeat prescription I'm after."

The nurse made a note on the pad in front of her. "She couldn't come herself?"

"She slept badly, partly to do with the rough crossing. She's getting some rest, so I said I'd come on her behalf."

"I see. Mrs Campbell is Dr Fraser's patient. Shouldn't you see him?"

Warmth crept up Rose's throat. It would be tactless to say she didn't want to bother him, but she could hardly tell the nurse the truth – that Dr Fraser was rude and aggressive and she hated dealing with him.

She cast around for a suitable reply, but Nurse Bannerjee didn't seem to expect one.

"I'll get her files from his office," she said.

"There's no need, I know the sort she takes. I brought the packet with me."

"I'll need to record it, Mrs Mason. Wait there."

Rose did as she was told, feeling more uncomfortable than ever. She hated to be a nuisance. The nurse was usually cheerful and pleasant, but today she seemed uncharacteristically short-tempered. After last night's crossing and the stream of patients, that was to be expected. *It's not all about you, Rose*, she told herself. *You're just the latest in a long line of irritants.*

Sister Bannerjee took a long time and Rose found her thoughts wandering, so that when the door swung open, she actually jumped.

"Sorry for the delay, I couldn't find the file. But Dr Fraser has signed a prescription for your friend's medication and agreed to release it to you. Here you are."

The scrawled handwriting was difficult to decipher, but Rose could read it well enough to see the name was different to the packet she had in her hand.

"Oh, this is not the same. Is this a weaker dosage, do you know?"

The sister took the piece of paper and the empty carton and compared. "No, it's a bit stronger if anything. I'm not sure why he'd do that. Well, today is extremely busy, so I'm going to write Mrs Campbell a repeat for the time being. I'll keep this and talk to Dr Fraser later, when we've located these missing files. If we need to change anything, I'll let you know."

Rose waited while the sister wrote the prescription, thinking over what she had said. "Is there more than one file missing?"

"Not really missing. Just been put in the wrong place, I expect. It happens when we're very busy. Don't worry, everything's on database, so we can always make a copy. Here you are."

She held out the chit.

"Thank you. On Maggie's behalf as well as mine. I'm sorry to be a nuisance, but the missing files don't include the ladies who recently passed on, do they?"

The nurse shook her head. "No, no. It seems we've misfiled a few under the letter C. Mrs Campbell, Mrs Cashmore and Mr Chester have all gone walkabout. They'll turn up, don't you worry. Give my best to Mrs Campbell."

Rather than returning to their suite, Rose went in search of the casino. She argued with herself all the way, but the voice of reason drowned out the whispers of self-doubt. And even if they did see her as a flapping, paranoid old woman, it would be better than not saying anything. She knocked lightly on the door and waited until the young Greek inspector opened the door. Although he was very nice and friendly, she persisted in her request to speak to Detective Inspector Stubbs. He advised her to wait on deck, as his colleague was conducting an interview. Rose did as she was told and had just sat down on a deckchair when DI Stubbs arrived. She greeted Rose warmly, despite looking worn and harassed.

"Thanks for coming, Detective Inspector. I really am sorry to drag you out of an interview."

"No problem at all. I needed a break. Inspector Stephanakis says you might have some information."

"It's probably nothing. But it struck me as odd and I thought you should know. I picked up a prescription for Maggie at the medical centre this morning. Her file has gone missing, along with a Mrs Cashmore and a Mr Chester. The nurse thinks they've been mislaid."

The detective nodded and waited for her to continue. Rose swallowed. "Now normally I wouldn't think twice about something like that. But the name Cashmore rang a bell. I had a quick look at the passenger list again and realised who she is. Doreen Cashmore is a member of the Hirondelle party."

The detective didn't clap her hand to her mouth or go goggle-eyed. Instead she lifted her face to the sunshine and closed her eyes. "This weather is sublime. Such a change to rush hour in wintry London."

"I'll bet it is. Shame you're here for so brief a stay."

"I have a feeling it will be just about right for me. Thanks for letting me know about the ship's medical files. I will check them myself. No detail is insignificant, and I'm glad you spotted that. How's Maggie?"

"Better every day. Now it's just the nightmares. She had a bad night so she's napping as we speak. Most of the ship was up last night, though. Dreadful crossing. I'm glad we have two days on Rhodes to recover. We're planning to go ashore tomorrow. It looks like a lovely city."

"Good idea. Can't miss an opportunity like this and they say the architecture is worth the trip in itself. Thanks for the tip-off, Rose. I'll keep you posted."

Rose lay back in her chair as the detective's heavy shoes clumped along the deck. She'd done her duty. There was nothing in it, she was sure, but her whole body felt lighter for having relayed her concerns. Now, time to get back to Maggie.

After the initial explosion, Dr Fraser's bluster and outrage had blown itself out. The computer records held by the receptionist indicated that of the 243 registered visitors to the medical centre, only 232 physical files could be located. Those missing included one member of the staff, German swimming instructor Hans-Rudi Burkhard; retired couple Ken and Pam Miller, on their second honeymoon; Jonathan Chester, an IT engineer suffering from burnout; and Maggie Campbell, witness to the death of Esther Crawford. The others belonged to the six remaining Hirondelles.

Nikos and Beatrice faced each other over the printed spreadsheet. Her frown carved two deep vertical grooves in her forehead as she used a highlighter to mark the absent folders. Nikos watched the pattern emerge.

Beatrice looked up. "I think you're right. Whoever took the files was in a hurry and grabbed those he wanted, accidentally picking up a few extras in the process. Look. Deirdre Bowen and Doreen Cashmore, both Hirondelles, were alphabetically separated from one another by Burkhard and Campbell. Chester was next to them. And Mr and Mrs Miller happen to be the only names between Vera Melville and Joyce Milligan. The other two gaps are Nancy Palliser and Emily de Vallon, the remaining Hirondelles. The person who took these has no interest in the swimming instructor or the honeymooners or the IT chap. But I do wonder if Maggie Campbell was entirely accidental."

Nikos lifted his head to look over Beatrice's shoulder. "As the one person who actually saw our suspect, probably not. She needs protection and under the circumstances, I'm not comfortable with using any of Jensson's crew. I want to ask Voulakis for some support. For her and the Hirondelles. I think we now have evidence someone is targeting that group."

She frowned again. "If it is a single individual, and I'm not sure it is, then Maggie's not the only person to have seen him. The man in the casino? I could only see his silhouette, but I was a lot closer than Maggie."

"True. So we need to be very careful. I will act as protector for you, but we can't ensure the safety of these women without more officers."

"Would it not make sense to use some of the local force?"

Nikos wrestled with himself. Personal loathing should not get in the way of an efficient investigation.

"Yes, possibly. I'll make some calls and see if we can have at least two uniforms."

"Jensson won't like that."

Nikos shrugged. "No, but any more deaths and he'd have to cancel the cruise. His choice."

"He might have to anyway." Beatrice folded up the spreadsheet. "There are no secrets on this vessel. The news about the medical centre is all over the ship already, and it's likely to fuel suspicion and hostility towards Fraser. Nikos, I suggest we take him ashore to 'help with enquiries'. For his own benefit, and because I strongly suspect more than one person is involved in these deaths."

"Good idea. Maybe we should offer the same opportunity to Maggie Campbell? She'd be easier to keep safe on the island."

Beatrice revolved the highlighter pen in her hands, her gaze distant.

"Beatrice? You don't agree?"

"What? Oh yes, absolutely." She placed the pen on the table and stretched as if she'd just woken up.

"Let's get Maggie and Rose off the boat and under protection. It's better to divide our chickens. I just can't understand where Maureen Hall fits in. I have to talk to the Hirondelles again. Firstly, to warn them of the seriousness of this. And to find the connection. There has to be one. Have we talked to all of them?"

Nikos consulted his notes. "Between us, yes. One woman I interviewed didn't actually say anything but I got the feeling she wanted to."

"Doreen Cashmore."

Surprise at Beatrice's astute guess made him sit up straighter in his chair. He tipped an imaginary hat in her direction. She smiled and inclined her head in acceptance.

"Yes. Doreen Cashmore. It's only an instinct, but I know she was lying." He replayed their conversation in his mind. "I wanted to ask her about Mrs Crawford's will, but couldn't recall the word. I asked if there was anything in her... and she finished my sentence with the word 'past'. Why say something like that? She's another one hiding something, but I don't think she'll tell me. You might have more luck."

"I can but try. Perhaps if I talk to her unofficially?"

It amazed him how Beatrice seemed not only on his wavelength but one step ahead. In a feeble attempt to keep up, he shared his latest discovery.

"There's one other thing. Beryl Hodges didn't get to use cabin service much in her first few hours aboard, but after she left the birthday party, she ordered a drink. I checked the records. A glass of warm milk with a sachet of Ovomalt was delivered to her cabin at 21.49. The cabin attendant's name was Vicky Morton. Nothing special about her, apart from the fact she is the current girlfriend of Andros Metaxas."

"The tour guide who forgot Esther?"

"Yes. His real name is Andy Redmond. I need to ask some more questions."

"We both do." Beatrice tapped the pen against the back of her hand. "Where do we go from here?"

"How about this for a plan? I'll call Voulakis and the South Aegean Force, while you tell Fraser we're getting him off the boat.

You find Maggie Campbell and persuade her and Rose to leave. I'll talk to Andy and his girlfriend separately. I want to get a feeling for how much loyalty there is. Talk to the Hirondelles together and ask if they too would like to leave in the circumstances. Then get Doreen Cashmore alone, while she's feeling scared and vulnerable. Offer support, a safe place to hide and all the help she needs if she can just give us some idea of why they are under threat."

Beatrice's smile stretched across her face as she nodded her approval. "You, Nikos Stephanakis, have all the makings of an excellent inspector. And a devious human being. Let's go."

Chapter 18

Beatrice and Jensson compromised. He gave permission for two South Aegean sergeants to come aboard only after Beatrice had agreed they should operate in plain clothes. The two officers worked with the *Empress Louise*'s own security staff to identify any crew members without an alibi for one of the three deaths. It was not a substantial list. Nikos made a rota of interviews for the sergeants while he escorted a subdued Dr Fraser ashore, along with Maggie and Rose. The two women had jumped at the chance to leave the ship and Beatrice detected as much enthusiasm from Rose as from Maggie.

She spent forty minutes trying to persuade Joyce Milligan to take her Hirondelle party ashore, but they seemed determined to stick it out. Not only that, but a memorial service was imminent so there was no question of leaving. The Hirondelles extended a most cordial invitation for Beatrice to join them.

Under a cloud of reluctance and defeat, Beatrice returned to her cabin to change into her grey suit. A little on the warm side for this weather, but suitably sober for the Hirondelles' memorial service. The *Empress Louise* had a multi-faith place of worship. No full-time chaplain or priest was attached, so it operated on an ad hoc basis. Occasional ordained passengers consented to hold services such as Mass or Shabbos, if sufficient interest existed.

Joyce Milligan, with indefatigable determination, had rooted out a Church of England priest willing to say a few words and persuaded a couple of the entertainment staff to sing some carefully chosen songs for the two departed Hirondelles.

The ladies were already seated when Beatrice arrived at the small room on E deck. She made a rough calculation and determined the room would hold no more than forty people. Currently, it hosted half that number. Four rows of pine benches took the place of pews and a neutral altar provided a point of focus. Someone waved. Maggie and Rose were sitting behind the main party along with half a dozen individuals Beatrice didn't recognise. She waved back and parked herself on the end of the last bench so as to observe proceedings. No sign of Captain Jensson, which she found disappointing. The priest, Reverend Melvyn Price, had just begun to welcome the congregation when the door eased open and a man sneaked in and stood by the gauze curtains flanking the doorway. Toni Dean, the crooner from the Rat Pack Revue. Oh dear, thought Beatrice, a Sinatra impersonator at a funeral can only mean one thing.

In front of the altar, another low table bore three photographs, propped up against white wooden cubes. The central picture was a group photograph of the Hirondelles, in a formal pose, all wearing their bowls-club style uniform of A-line skirt and peony-blue blazer, with a stylised swallow on the pocket. To the left, a less than distinct image of Esther Crawford laughing at the camera. Her short, neat haircut gave her the appearance of an ancient elf. The picture of Beryl Hodges, on the opposite side, was better technical quality but lacked atmosphere. Owlish glasses, a worried expression and standard issue set-and-blow-dry. She looked like half the occupants of the ship.

The priest, who'd caught a bit too much sun in the past week, read some endearing memories about each lady and invited mourners to pray with him. One of the young entertainers sang *Amazing Grace* in a pure, uplifting soprano. Several of the ladies reached for tissues. None of this breached Beatrice's defences. Then Joyce Milligan gave a short reading.

"Not, how did she die, but how did she live?
Not, what did she gain, but what did she give?
These are the units to measure the worth
Of woman as woman, regardless of birth.
Nor what was her church, nor what was her creed?

But had she befriended those really in need?
Was she ever ready, with words of good cheer,
To bring back a smile, to banish a tear?
Not what did the sketch in the newspaper say,
But how many were sorry when she passed away?"

The words, the rhythm and the sentiment might all have left the casual observer unmoved. Yet Joyce Milligan's voice, fighting emotion to deliver a powerful, heartfelt eulogy to her friends, had goose bumps creeping over Beatrice's skin by the second line.

The priest thanked her and introduced the last element of the service. 'One of Esther and Beryl's favourites'. He signalled to the back of the hall. The latecomer made his way down the aisle, bent to shake hands with all six of the Hirondelles and expressed his condolences with sincerity. Beatrice watched him operate. Blond hair, a deep tan, a charming if somewhat feigned manner. He took his position behind the photographs and nodded at the priest, who pressed a button on the CD player. The intro to *My Way* burst thinly into the space and Beatrice's toes curled. Then Toni Dean began to sing and her cynicism melted into chocolate marshmallow with caramel on top.

"Beautiful service. Lovely idea. Such a touching way to say goodbye. Thank you for inviting me. So sorry for your loss. Beautiful service. Very moving. Not at all, happy to be of help..."

The litany continued as the party milled about before the dead women's photographs. She praised the young soprano and admired Joyce Milligan's reading. She was working her way towards Doreen Cashmore when Toni Dean stepped into her path.

"Detective Inspector Stubbs. Just wanted to say hello. Toni Dean, entertainer. Very pleased to have you with us even on such a sad occasion. If today tells us anything, it's how much these dear ladies touched lives. I wish you great success with your investigation."

"That's very kind. I enjoyed your song very much. You do have an extraordinary voice."

"Thank you. When Miss Milligan asked me to sing this song for this occasion, I bit her hand off. It's a lovely way to say goodbye to someone you..."

Over Dean's shoulder, Beatrice saw Joyce Milligan and Doreen Cashmore leading the way to the exit.

"Indeed. Nice to meet you. Thanks again," she said and hurried off in their wake.

Doreen Cashmore was happy to join in the general approval of the service, compare the detail with other funerals she'd attended and reminisce about Beryl and Esther, but separating her from the rest of the Hirondelles proved a challenge. Ostensibly as a supportive gesture, the women had made a vow – that none would be left alone – not even with an officer of the law. Gentle persuasion and an emphasis on Beatrice's own role as protector met with polite resistance from the surviving ladies. She chose not to insist, although she had every right in her investigative role, as she wanted to elicit the information without recourse to pressure. Despite all the friendliness and encouragement to attend the service, Beatrice registered the atmosphere of closed ranks. Less vulnerability, certainly, and less chance of anyone veering from the party line. An opportunity would arise, eventually. All Beatrice needed to do was keep her eyes and ears open.

By teatime, Nikos had still not returned to the boat, but the South Aegean sergeants were ready to report the results of their interviews, such as they were. Of the fourteen individuals who had left the ship in Santorini, only five could not prove their movements; two women, three men. Yet when Beryl Hodges and Maureen Hall died, Efthakia Dellas was at her post in the communications room, Toni Dean was running through his Rat Pack repertoire onstage in the ballroom, Kostas the chef was in the kitchen, and senior stewards Lukas Karagounis and Susana Iliou were supervising evening service in the Grand Dining Room. No single staff or crew member remained without an alibi for at least one of the deaths.

Beatrice sat alone in her guest cabin, her focus switching fruitlessly between the various PDF versions of the ladies' wills, the spreadsheet of suspects on her computer and the view of the

Aegean. No surprises in the list of beneficiaries. Children, grand-children, a cancer charity, a sister. She had put in a request to the Wiltshire police to see if they could establish any connections but held out little hope.

Two methods of murder. Two people? One favours smothering and chest compression. You don't have to be especially strong to suffocate an octogenarian, so this person might have quite a dif-ferent build to the man seen on the cliff. It could also be a woman. Experience had taught Beatrice the danger of gender assumptions. The cliff man had greater brute strength and a sense of opportun-ism. One ensures the alibi whilst the other performs the act. At least one might be staff or crew, explaining access to key cards. She made a note to cross check the alibis and anything linking all five staff visitors to Santorini.

If a passenger were an accomplice, it would make sense to ob-serve the police investigation. The Hirondelles had not sought her out, but accepted her presence with a similar skittishness as a flock of sheep might show towards a collie. Apart from Maggie and Rose, only Oscar had made any friendly overtures. Yet he had actively prevented her from discussing the case and asked no searching questions.

Whether the killer was a passenger or ship employee, whether he worked alone or with a partner, the fundamental question re-mained. Why? Precedents existed, such as the Californian woman who killed and buried her tenants then claimed their benefits. The Tunisian who murdered more than fifteen elderly women in Southern Italy eventually confessed to sexual gratification as his driving force. As for The Stockwell Strangler, whose oldest victim was ninety-four, his motivations were both financial and sexual. None of the women on the *Empress Louise* had been molested, and if there were no monetary advantage, what would make someone go to such lengths to end the lives of ladies enjoying the third age?

The telephone in the cabin lit up and emitted a purr.

"Hello, this is DI Stubbs."

"*Hello Beatrice, Oscar here. Congratulations! We thought we'd given you the slip in Crete, but you tracked us down.*"

Beatrice smiled. "Elementary, my dear Oscar. Equipped with a detailed itinerary and scheduled arrival times, tracking this great white vessel was a doddle. How are you?"

"*Frazzled. Been out exploring and actually feeling my age. I'm planning a nap, can you believe? But before I surrender to The Sandman, I wanted to enquire as to your plans for dinner. Last night's conversation, scintillating as it was, seems unfinished. Especially as bellowing over the background row of the average taverna tends to obscure the nuances. Could I lure you ashore, or failing that, into one of the less pretentious eateries aboard?*"

Beatrice considered. He really was good company and helped her forget the case. Which was currently the last thing she needed.

"I'd love to. I really would, but tonight I plan to treat my partner to dinner in return for picking his brains. Perhaps another evening?"

"*Ah, the handsome Inspector Stephanakis. I stand down. I could never compete with such rugged good looks. I wish you an educational evening. And should our paths cross tomorrow, I would consider myself blessed.*"

Beatrice's laughter was genuine. "Talk to you tomorrow, Oscar. Bye for now."

She focused once again on her spreadsheet, only to be interrupted by a knock at the door. She opened it to see a pretty blonde girl in a cabin attendant's uniform.

"Hello?"

"Detective Stubbs, my name is Vicky Morton, Cabin Attendant Service Personnel. I spoke to Inspector Stephanakis earlier today about the death of Beryl Hodges."

Beatrice remembered. The tour guide's girlfriend. "Oh yes, I know. You delivered her drink."

"That's right. I did. I wasn't much help, I'm afraid. Anyway, Inspector Stephanakis said if I thought of anything, any detail I could remember, I should let him know. But I can't find him."

"He's gone ashore. If you have something to say, you can talk to me. Come inside. Does this mean you've remembered something?"

Vicky followed her into the room and closed the door. "Sort of. When Mrs Hodges let me into the cabin, she was in her nightgown and she'd already taken her teeth out. Ready for bed, I thought. So I put the milk on the table and I saw a slice of birthday cake."

"Yes, she'd been to Esther Crawford's eightieth birthday party."

"Right. But she wasn't going to eat cake without her teeth. She told me to put the milk on the bedside table and draw the curtains for her. I asked if I should put the cake in the fridge and she waved her hand, you know, like the Queen."

Beatrice said nothing. The girl had thirty seconds to get to the point or would be noted as a timewaster.

"I wrapped it in a plastic bag and popped it in the fridge. It was the only thing in there."

"And? Why do you think this is relevant?"

"Inspector Stephanakis mentioned that Mrs Hodges was allergic to seafood and kept an EpiPen in her fridge in case of a reaction. Thing is, when I put that cake inside, the fridge was empty. I mean empty, like it had never been used."

"There could be several reasons for that. She had only just arrived, so she might not have unpacked it yet. Or if the injection device needed to be chilled, perhaps it was in the mini-bar instead."

"That's what I thought, but Inspector Stephanakis definitely said the fridge. Anyway, I just went down to G Deck and asked the cleaning crew. They were the ones who cleared the room after the body was removed. They told me they found four of those EpiPens on the top shelf of the fridge next to a slice of cake. What I'm saying is they weren't there at half past nine the night before. If she had a reaction in the night and went looking for her medicine in the fridge, it wouldn't have been there."

Chapter 19

Of all the crappy luck. Two years after he thought his nemesis had gone for good, his very first case as inspector had to involve Rhodes, the South Aegean Region and Demetrius Xanthou. It was as if Fate was laughing at him.

Once Mrs Campbell and Mrs Mason were settled in their hotel, he drove Dr Fraser to the police station with dread in his stomach. However, an interview room was prepared, the desk clerk expected him, an English-speaking sergeant was waiting to assist and Xanthou made no appearance. Nikos began to hope they might actually avoid each other. The second surprise was Fraser's willingness to talk. He hadn't expected much more than a repeat performance from the defensive Scot, so his humility came as a shock.

"Inspector, you should know that my career as a physician is now over."

"If that is the case, I'm sorry. I'm afraid we had no choice but to remove you from the ship. It was a decision made jointly with the cruise line management."

"I know. Jensson told me. You were right to do it; I'm not stupid enough to deny that. To be honest, I'm relieved. This situation has gone on too long and is not sustainable. When it begins to harm others, it's time to face the problem." He fiddled with his coffee cup but did not drink. "I have an addiction, Inspector. OxyContin, an opoid-based painkiller. It's the only thing that gets me through the day."

Nikos took a second to process that information. "How long have you been dependent?"

"Since a back injury in 2009. It happens a lot. I'm not the only one. Doctors are trained to look out for the repeat prescription seekers. Whereas doctors themselves don't need a prescription and we hold the keys to the medicine chest, so there's nothing stopping us."

Nikos tore off a sheet of paper from his notepad. "Please could you write down the name of the drug for me?"

Fraser scribbled something and then wrote several more words in block capitals beneath. "Medical name and brands. Over five years, I've not paid for one pill but this has cost me everything. My marriage fell apart, my career atrophied, I lost several jobs, the offers dried up, my colleagues in the medical profession avoid me and I know I've been guilty of negligence."

Nikos, scrambling to comprehend, tried to formulate a question but the doctor hadn't finished.

"My kids would rather I didn't visit and most of my friends have drifted away. Not Jensson, though. We met years ago, doing the Norwegian routes. Great man, full of ideas and intelligence. We played chess when we could and enjoyed the occasional debate. Our paths only crossed once in a blue moon, but we kept in touch. He's a pal, the kind of friend you call when you're up Shit Creek. He put his own neck on the line to offer me the Senior Physician post on this cruise. He trusted me."

A strange chill blew across Nikos's neck and he knew without doubt Xanthou must have entered the observation room behind the mirrored glass. He tried to push those judgemental eyes from his mind and focus on the man opposite.

"Do you feel you deserved his trust?" Nikos asked, wishing the other person in the room was Beatrice, not a blank junior officer, and that his interviewee would speak simple English.

Fraser clenched his hands together as if in ferocious prayer. "From the minute I wake to the minute I lose consciousness, one single thought process dominates my brain. How to get it, when to take it and how to hide it. No, I didn't deserve this post; I'm barely competent and better practitioners than me are still in medical school. As for the deaths of these ladies, I take full responsibility for a less than thorough post mortem on the Hodges woman. That's all. I didn't kill her. I can hardly focus on the conveyor belt of habitual daily complaints, let alone plan a succession of murders."

"Do you think you misdiagnosed the death of Beryl Hodges?"

"Very likely. And in doing so I lost any chance of redemption. Worst of all, I've probably lost the only friend I had left." His head dropped onto his knuckles and Nikos gave him a moment.

"Dr Fraser, you're free to go now. I'd like you to stay in Rhodes for the time being while I corroborate your story with Captain Jensson. Please leave contact details and the name of your hotel with the desk clerk. Thank you for your time. And good luck."

Fraser stood up and held out his hand. "Thanks to you too. I'll be in touch. All the best."

The sergeant escorted him out and Nikos collected his notes, waiting for Xanthou's big entrance and the dick-waving showdown, which could only be seconds away. The door opened.

"Nikos Stephanakis! Good to see you again! How long has it been, three years?"

Someone once told Xanthou he looked like John Travolta. Nikos often wondered who it was, as he would like to hunt that person down and punch them in the face. The most misguided statement ever, not least because it was absurdly far from the truth. In full ignorance of the fact that Travolta was at least half a metre taller, Xanthou had taken it to heart, growing sideburns, combing back his hair and dyeing his eyebrows. Now, in jeans, black shirt and denim jacket with the collar turned up, he looked like a low-rent Elvis impersonator.

Nikos mentally rolled up his sleeves and donned his superhero mask.

"Demetrius Xanthou. Two years, I think." Neither man offered his hand.

"Really? Feels longer. Congratulations, by the way. I hear you finally made inspector." (*ZAP!*)

"Thanks. Yes, really pleased with my first case. Teamed with a senior inspector from Scotland Yard." (*ZIP!*)

"So I hear. Having a woman as your boss? Very modern. How's Karen?" (*POW!*)

"Great. Karen and I are a team, equal partners, in the same way I'm working with DI Stubbs. Pretty effective together." (*WHACK!*)

"Yeah. Which is why you need the help of the South Aegean

force. I have to get on, but if you can't cope, you have my number. Give my love to Karen. Wait, I have her email, I can do it myself! Those days, huh? Happy memories." (*KAPOW!*)

Xanthou was out the door before Nikos noticed his interview notes were crumpled in his clenched fist.

He found an empty office, forced himself to relax and called Beatrice. She answered on the first ring.

"*Nikos. Where are you?*"

"Still at the station. I made sure Rose Mason and Maggie Campbell checked in OK, and then interviewed Dr Fraser at the station. Interesting outcome. He's addicted to prescription drugs. A painkiller called OxyContin."

"*I know it. Same sort as Vicodin and that has plenty of fans. Yes, that explains some of his behaviour.*"

"He functions, at a basic level, but got sacked from several previous posts and it's damaged his personal life. Jensson is an old friend, so this position was a kindness and a last chance for Fraser."

"*Wouldn't painkiller addiction make him less mentally adept?*" Beatrice asked.

"That's what he said. When he's had his fix, yes. When he needs more, it makes him agitated and aggressive. Neither situation fits the profile of the calm, well-planned serial killer we're looking for. I'll check out his story, just in case."

"*Yes, better had. Addicts can be very cunning. Still, his planning and methods will have an entirely different target.*"

"Exactly. I can't see a motive either. I really don't believe Fraser's connected. Did you talk to Doreen Cashmore?"

"*I've not been able to get her alone. The Hirondelles are joined at the hip. But I got the results from your South Aegean colleagues.*" She conveyed the unexciting outcome of the crew interviews. Nikos listened intently, occasionally asking for clarification and making notes.

"OK, thanks. I agree with checking for connections and testing those stories. I'm just going to Pathology for the forensic results on Maureen Hall's cabin and the papers he touched in the casino. Then I'll be back."

"*Let me know as soon as you get anything. Do you have plans for dinner tonight? I thought we could chew over theories and a steak at The Sizzling Grill.*"

"Good idea. Let's talk to the stewards and the communications officer before dinner, say hello to Kostas the chef, and then attend the Rat Pack Revue. That way, we can cover all those alibis."

"*Sounds like quite a plan,*" said Beatrice. "*But I've had my fill of crooners today, so might seek out Mrs Cashmore and leave you to enjoy Ol' Blue Contact Lenses.*"

"He certainly looks the part. So I'm interested to hear if he can actually sing."

"*He can sing, I'll vouch for that. He did his bit at the memorial service. Apart from his voice though, everything about the man is fake, from tan to accent.*"

Nikos looked up at the police personnel board. Xanthou's face smirked back at him. "I know exactly what you mean."

As he left the station, he got a text message alert. Karen.

Missing you. Any news? How's Xanthou? Kxxx

He stopped on a street corner to write back.

Miss you too. Some progress. Still an arsehole. Nxxx

Chapter 20

The only hole in any of the alibis, at least so far, seemed to be Kostas's assertion he had been in the kitchen all evening when Beryl Hodges and Maureen Hall were killed. As *chef de cuisine*, he was responsible for all dishes leaving the kitchen, and personally approved each plate before it went through the swing doors. Yet service ended at 10pm, leaving only desserts, supervised by the Pastry Chef. Kitchen staff turned their attention to cleaning surfaces and storing unused food, while Kostas took a break. According to the *commis chef*, he usually disappeared for half an hour to forty minutes, returning to approve the standards of cleanliness. Plenty of time for a cigarette, a drink or even a visit to an old lady's cabin.

Beatrice dawdled over her chocolate mousse and coffee, chatting to her waiter and digesting her conversation with Nikos. His assessment of motive was rather astute. Elderly women and sudden death usually suggested money. Or less commonly, revenge. The absolute lack of forensic evidence in Hall's room and on the documentation in the casino had bothered Beatrice more than she liked to let on. He'd worn gloves. There was nothing haphazard about the way this man operated.

Nikos had left just before nine in order to catch the opening number of the Rat Pack Revue. A wave of diners had departed around the same time. A new batch descended shortly afterwards and Beatrice was reminded of Jensson's words.

You are given the impression of free will and endless choices, but in reality, you are shuffled from one activity to the next and gently parted from your cash at every opportunity while the message is continually reinforced: you are having such a marvellous time!

The thought depressed her and she made Rorschach patterns

on her napkin with spilt coffee. A vampire bat, a cross of thorns, a broken heart... my, she was morbid tonight. She paid the bill, left a generous tip and went in search of Doreen Cashmore.

To her surprise, the cabin door was opened by Joyce Milligan, who wore a lilac leisure suit and a hairnet.

"Detective Inspector Stubbs? You're either here because you've heard the rumours about my cocoa or you have arrested a suspect. Have you got someone?"

"I'm afraid not. I'm sorry to disturb you so late, but wanted to check all was well and have a quick word with Mrs Cashmore."

Joyce shook her head, like a horse refusing a jump. "Not right now, Detective Inspector. She's had the most dreadful day. Poor Doreen suffers with her nerves, you know. Under the circumstances, we thought a milky drink and an early night best. I'll stay with her. We look out for each other, you know."

Her huge hand, with bony, veined knuckles, rested on the cabin wall. A relaxed posture, but one which also barred entry. Strangler's hands, thought Beatrice.

"Of course. You're very lucky to have each other."

"And lucky to have you looking out for us. It was jolly decent of you to come to the service today. We all feel better for having said our goodbyes."

"It was extremely touching. Your reading and Mr Dean's Sinatra both had me welling up."

"He's got a fine pair of tonsils, hasn't he? I was quite overcome by his generosity when he approached me and offered to sing. I'd never have dared ask."

"Ah, I thought it was all down to your powers of persuasion. Give Mrs Cashmore my very best and I hope you both sleep well. Goodnight."

"Same to you, hope the bed bugs don't bite."

Beatrice returned to deck and stood watching the shore as she considered the possibility the Hirondelle Hunter could be one of their own. The idea was totally ridiculous. Joyce Milligan was eighty-one years old. The sort who may well have wrestled bullocks in her youth, but nowadays, she was nothing more than a protective mother hen.

Laughter rang out from a table at one of the bars on the entertainment deck, generating a spike of envy in Beatrice. In one of her rare sociable moods, she had no one to talk to. Nikos would not leave the show till ten and then he would tail Kostas, so they'd agreed to debrief in the morning. She could return to the cabin and call Matthew. Except she really didn't feel like any more intensity. Her mind was all over the place and she had the urge to do something. Her mother's voice whispered on the Mediterranean wind, 'The Devil makes work for idle hands'. Beatrice hunched her shoulders against the breeze and turned in the direction of her cabin. She'd watch some television, empty her mind and take one of her pills, as several signs of rapid mood cycling were in evidence.

Pills. The news of Dr Fraser's addiction had sparked a nagging concern, once again. James had assured her more times than she could count that her mood stabilisers were not an addiction but a necessity. The alternative, allowing her condition to dictate her life, was much more alarming than taking one tablet a day. This she knew. This she understood. She fought a daily battle with her thought processes and with the recurrent urge to miss a day. Just to prove she could do without. It inevitably backfired and she'd regret it, but the temptation to rebel, to revolt against what was best for her returned again and again. Grow up, woman, she told herself. Get back to your cabin, take your tablet and reattach your stabilisers.

As she ascended the stairs, she heard rapid footsteps from the deck above and when she arrived at the top, she saw Oscar hurrying in her direction.

"Quick! This way!" he hissed with some urgency. He turned her around, guiding her by the elbow, and they trotted back down together. At the bottom, he took another sharp angle, drawing her with him until they were tucked side-by-side under the steps in a dark alcove. He pressed himself back into the shadows and listened.

Deck lights between the rungs threw horizontal stripes across his face, making her think of film noir and Humphrey Bogart. Beatrice looked at him for an explanation and was just about to open her mouth when Oscar boggled his eyes and pressed a finger to his lips.

An American woman's voice carried on the night air. "... usually found in the Club Room after dinner. Well, if Mohammed won't come to the mountain..."

"The Club Room? Wouldn't you need to be a member?"

"Perhaps. If so, we'll join. It's only a question of greasing palms. Do you know, I found a concierge service in Boston..."

Two pairs of feet clanged down the metal steps and a rustle of evening gowns brushed past their faces. The ladies proceeded, still talking, across the deck below. Beatrice left Oscar in the shadows and tiptoed across to the railings. Mrs Bartholomew and another woman marched towards double doors diagonally opposite without a glance behind.

Beatrice looked over her shoulder and laughed to see Oscar flattened against the wall. "What does she want with you?"

Oscar closed his eyes with a mock shudder. "She has some 'totally awesome' family stories which really should be in my book. Or maybe this material might merit a book all its own. I'd have to sign a confidentiality agreement, blah, blah ... oh spare me, please. And now my sacred retreat, The Club Room, is off limits. I always said there should be a door policy. I am cut adrift."

"Don't be so dramatic. There are plenty of other cafés and bars to hide in. You're spoilt for choice."

"I beg to differ. For an old codger who desires good conversation in a peaceful setting with a quiet glass of something elegant, there are precious few."

Beatrice spoke without thinking. "The ship's guest cabins each boast a substantial mini-bar, muted yet tasteful music and I was quite fancying a nightcap. Or would our reputations be forever tarnished if we were to withdraw unchaperoned?"

"My good lady! Let us make haste and to hell with the rumours. Which way?"

Lamps lit, a bottle of red opened, a concerto wafting from the speakers and Oscar relaxing in the armchair; the scene soothed

Beatrice. She kicked off her shoes and sat on the armchair diagonally opposite him, so they both faced the panoramic window and the city, which from this distance looked strung with fairy lights.

"Does that happen a lot?" she asked.

"Being pursued by women? All the time," he said, with a regretful shake of his head.

She raised her glass. "Cheers. I meant the offer of material for a book."

"Cheers. Oh, I say. That's fruity. Yes, sadly, all too often people believe an apocryphal anecdote about their granny's comical expressions is worthy of inclusion in a serious academic study on language. I've fallen victim to this phenomenon so many times, I now flee at the first warning signs. Mrs Bartholomew sent a summons for me to join her after dinner, including the details I mentioned earlier. I politely declined, claiming a prior engagement. But the woman is indefatigable. She made a bee line as soon as she saw me down cutlery, and I had to quit the dining-room with unseemly haste. I knew I should have gone ashore. It's always on the last leg of the journey when one's fellow passengers become insufferable."

"Oh dear. What will you say when she finally catches up with you? She will, you can guarantee it."

"I'll deny all knowledge of running away, or claim forgetfulness. I cultivate that air from first impressions. Sitting at the wrong table, unable to recall people's names, searching for my glasses when they're on my head. The dotty professor act."

"You didn't fool me."

"I didn't try to. What is this wine, please? It's quite lovely."

Beatrice fetched the bottle and handed it to him. He removed his glasses to read the label.

"Ah, a Portuguese Dão. I went on a tasting tour up the Douro valley two years ago. Loved every drop. Have you been?" He looked up at her. Lamplights reflected in his hazel irises and dark lashes framed his eyes, surprisingly naked without his glasses. She returned to her seat, leaving him with the bottle.

"No, but it's on the list. Last time we went wine-tasting was to Hungary. That was a revelation."

"I'm sure it was. I've heard great things." He sprang out of the chair in a supple movement and placed the bottle back on the table. Whilst on his feet, he approached a print depicting a Greek fishing village. He stood in front of it with his hands folded behind his back, in the style of Prince Phillip.

"I must say guest suites certainly have the edge. Wine, space, artwork and soft furnishings are all quite superior. But I suppose the view is the same for us all. And what a view it is." He replaced his glasses and walked to the window. Beatrice felt a peculiar sense of relief at having a barrier between her and Oscar's eyes.

She joined him to gaze at the Palace of the Grand Master of the Knights of Rhodes, as imposing a sight over the city as Castle Rock over Edinburgh. They sipped their wine in appreciative silence.

"You said '*we* went wine tasting'. I presume you're referring to Mr Stubbs?"

She shook her head and returned to her spot, tucking one leg under herself, wishing the conversation would take another turn. "There is no Mr Stubbs."

"I'm so sorry."

He sat in the armchair once more, waiting for her to continue, his brogues keeping time with the Brahms.

"No, no. I meant we're not married. Matthew and I have been together over twenty years but never..."

"Got around to it?" offered Oscar.

"No, no. Made it official, I was going to say. I'm sure marriage is a wonderful thing for some people. It just never appealed to me."

The piano and cello reached a crescendo, as if attempting to score the conversation. Oscar rested his chin on his hand and studied her. She scratched her temple, swilled her wine around the glass and willed him to look away.

He smiled, as if sensing her discomfort. "So that poor man, besotted by this elusive and brilliant butterfly, proposes every year on Christmas Eve, hoping in vain to capture the object of his desire. But no. She flutters into his garden, accompanied by sunshine and rainbows, stays awhile, but refuses to be netted."

The wine had gone to her head and she flushed. "I'll tell him about that image. He'll find it hilarious. Especially the butterfly bit. One of his daughters refers to me as Beatrice the Bull Elephant ever since an awkward incident in a Totnes delicatessen. We were admiring a display of exotic spices in a glass case. Unfortunately, a rather forceful sneeze took me by surprise. My forehead hit the glass and it shattered, exploding colourful spices everywhere. That was seven years ago and I still occasionally find grains of turmeric in my ear."

Oscar threw back his head and laughed, a warm, deep sound. His shoulders shook and his stomach bounced.

"If I could exchange all the money I paid for this cruise just to have been present at that moment, I would do so twice. Those shopkeepers are probably still telling that story."

"I wouldn't know. Unsurprisingly, we've never been back."

Oscar got to his feet. "I feel duty-bound to have one last glass of the Dão before leaving you to your rest. You will join me, DI Stubbs?"

"I should coco. A wine like that cannot be ignored. Are you peckish? There's nuts and whatnot in the cupboard."

He offered the wine and she held out her glass. He kept his eyes on the carmine stream, only glancing at her as he finished. Again, she felt the jolt of adrenalin. Danger, yes. But what kind? He settled back in his place and refilled his own glass, still with a slight smile.

"Thank you, but after bolting three courses to escape The Boston Badger, not even nuts and whatnot could tempt me. How about you? Did Inspector Stephanakis enjoy dinner with the boss? Where did you eat?"

"I'm not his boss. We're equals on this one. We went to The Sizzling Grill. We both had the ribs but with different sauces. I never want to eat anything else. Ever."

Oscar's face creased into another laugh. "My wife used to say the same thing. After every holiday, every memorable meal, every concert she'd enjoyed. Always vowed to move there, or eat, drink and listen to nothing else." He gazed into his wine, his face soft in recollection.

"If you don't mind my asking, how did you meet her?"

Oscar looked up in surprise. "Many people start a question the same way, but they want to know about the end, not the beginning. As always, Beatrice Stubbs is different." He raised his glass in an ironic toast, then sipped.

"She was a mature student. Not one of mine, I stress. I had rules about that sort of thing. But she assisted me at a couple of conferences. One evening, I wanted to return to my hotel room to prepare some slides. She challenged me. Language, she said, is a living thing. You cannot study it from behind a microscope. Come out in the city with me, let's listen and talk and get Jane Goodall with the natives. She bullied me out of the library and into an all-night cafe in Copenhagen. We continued adventuring for sixteen years until bowel cancer took her in 2007. Without her, I have regressed to my natural state. Playing it safe."

The CD came to an end and silence swelled to fill the space. Beatrice realised she had deflated the mood.

"I'm sorry you lost her so early. I'm also glad you found someone so remarkable and enjoyed her company for many years."

His smile was that of a weary child. "Yes, I know how lucky I've been. The problem is that she showed me the joy of life. Now I'm back behind the microscope, observing but not getting involved. My daughter despairs of me and still holds out hope that someday I'll meet someone to break through the glass. Good Lord, we've turned maudlin. I'd best cede the floor to you as your spice cabinet mishaps are far more entertaining."

"Mishap. It was only the once. Thank you for being so honest and I'm sorry if I dragged up old wounds. Shall I tell you the story of the time a bee flew up my trouser leg?"

He smiled but shook his head. "Fair's fair. I told you mine. Now I want to hear about Not-Mr-Stubbs. How did you meet?"

The words were out of her mouth before she'd decided to speak.

"I stole him."

Chapter 21

Beatrice looked at her wine glass as if it had betrayed her. Several well-rehearsed fabrications lay at her disposal, and other than those directly involved, few people knew the reality. She'd not even told Adrian. So why this sudden impulse to share the less palatable elements of her past with a near stranger? After twenty-four years, the burden of truth didn't get any heavier. If James were here, he would ask her to examine her motives before saying any more. But he wasn't here. It was just her and Oscar.

He set down his glass, crossed his legs and folded his hands around his knee. A patient listener. She took a large swig of wine and began.

"I grew up in the Gloucestershire countryside. Stone walls, quaint towns and charming hedgerows. Quiet, just the way my parents liked it. They had accepted their childlessness and I believe they had begun to enjoy it when I came along. I was a solitary child; content to read, listen to adult conversation or play with an elderly Labrador called Horace. On my first day at school, I sat next to a pretty blonde girl called Pamela Pearce. Without even asking my name, she informed me she was an only child and her two favourite things were steamed pudding and picking scabs. With so much in common, we naturally became immediate friends. Ersatz sisters, I suppose, throughout our school days.

"When we got older, she attended my graduation ceremony and I was her bridesmaid. She was the first person I called when I was accepted into the CID. She made me godmother to her eldest. While I thrived on the daily battle that is life in London, she was content to be a housewife and mother in the country, joining the school committee and all that. Her husband was a university don and a lot older than us, but he seemed pleasant enough. Pleasant, if rather dull. I liked visiting for the occasional weekend, seeing the girls, enjoying Pam's company, although I was always relieved to get back to my little flat in the East End. Pam travelled up to see me once and was terribly anxious the whole time. What's the phobia where you are afraid of crowds?"

"Agoraphobia."

"Is it? I thought that was open spaces. Well, she had the most awful time and we both agreed it was better if I did the visiting."

Oscar listened with complete attention, not even touching his wine. Beatrice took another swig and pressed on. The story seemed desperate to be told.

"In 1988, Professor Matthew Bailey gave a series of weekly lectures at The British Museum. Pam pleaded with me to look after him. I think she was projecting her own experience, because he was perfectly at ease alone in the city. He actually preferred his own company. I made excuses the first couple of times, but then caved and took him to the Docklands. A bunch of art students had put on an exhibition in the Port Authority Building. I thought he'd hate it. He didn't."

"You mean...?"

Beatrice brought herself back over the decades and focused on her companion.

"Yes. No one had any idea how significant it would turn out to be, least of all me. Anyway, I bought him fish and chips and felt I'd done my duty. Of course, his typical old school manners meant he had to return the favour, and pretty soon it became a weekly event. He'd come up on the train, give his lecture and then we'd do something cultural and argue about it. It's hard to explain. He was so different. You see, my life was made up of answers. Matthew was all about questions."

She fell silent, recalling how reluctance, by imperceptible degrees, shifted to anticipation and eagerness.

Oscar's voice almost startled her. "You fell in love." His tone was comprehending and sympathetic, with no hint of judgement.

"Yes. It sort of crept up on me. One evening, as we said our polite goodbyes at Green Park, I saw the same thing in his eyes.

Nothing happened. No passionate kisses in the rain or a tearful flight across a photogenic bridge; it wasn't a bloody Richard Curtis film. I just looked at him and knew this was it. The best and worst thing in my life. I'd fallen in love with my best friend's husband, so my choices were destruction or destruction."

Oscar stood and poured a little more Dão into her glass. "An impossible position. What did you do?"

Beatrice realised she was scratching at the scar on her wrist. She laced her hands in her lap. She had to finish the story and get Oscar to leave. Her desire for solitude whined like the spin cycle of a washing-machine.

"I stopped seeing him. I told him I was too busy, volunteered for overtime, spent every waking hour at work, refused his calls, the whole five yards. It was agony. His lecture series finished and I thought I was in the clear. Then Pam invited me to Marianne's first communion."

"Your god-daughter?"

"Yes. I couldn't refuse. I spent weeks counselling myself and practising detachment. The second I saw him, everything fell apart. I was so jumpy Pam even asked if I was taking anything. Can't recall anything of the communion, just a blur of white dresses, singing, fizzy wine, ribbons and this pulsing presence I had to ignore. Matthew was supposed to take me to the station. He said nothing but drove us instead to a beauty spot by the river. We sat on a bench and talked. He loved me, I loved him and neither of us had done it on purpose, but there it was. A few days later, he told Pam, and then the girls. He moved out to a cottage nearby. I stayed in London and we gave the relationship a trial period, just seeing each other at weekends. That trial period has lasted twenty-four years."

"And Pam?"

An ancient pain, like a once-sprained muscle, flared into life.

"She never spoke to me again. After a period of ugliness and spite, things settled down. Now we take turns at family events. The girls ensure our paths never cross. I always intended to build a bridge once the dust had settled. But what words do you use to say 'I'm sorry I had to ruin your life to find mine'? I'm still searching."

Oscar rubbed his forehead, pushed himself out of his chair

and stood at the window, facing the view. Beatrice joined him, her stomach inexplicably fluttery.

"Look, I'm sorry about all that. I normally lie when people ask me that question. Other than those involved, you're only the third person I've ever told all the details. And one of those was paid to listen. Tonight, it just all whooshed out, for some reason. I have no idea why."

Oscar kept his eyes on the lights of Rhodes but a faint smile smoothed his face. "I think I can hazard a guess. This is a genteel form of sabre-rattling. You are fluffing your feathers, shaking your quills or baring your teeth. The entire display, possibly not even on a conscious level, is designed to make me retreat. The message here is two-fold. Firstly, you belong to another. And secondly, you want me to think badly of you, as The Other Woman. Either way, your unusual candour is a warning. I understand. And I'll back off."

A rush of anger erupted in Beatrice. She stalked to the table and refilled her glass, counting to ten in her head. Rather than having the intended calming effect, the numbers fuelled her temper.

"In point of fact, I pay a professional counsellor to help me analyse my behavioural patterns. He's very good at guiding me towards an understanding of my own motivations. The one thing he never does is tell me why I act a certain way or attribute a gesture to his own deeper comprehension of my psyche than I have myself. So when I share a secret with someone who then imposes some cod psychology on my words, intimating my embarrassing truth is nothing more than some primitive fan dance, I find it infuriating to say the least. If I wanted you to piss off, Oscar, believe me, I would have no hesitation in saying so!"

His expression, backlit by the lamp, was unreadable. Another surge of emotion swelled as she debated asking him to leave. The problem was, now she didn't want him to go. He came towards her and placed his hands on her shoulders.

"Beatrice, I'm sorry. That was incredibly arrogant of me. For you to share what you describe as 'the embarrassing truth' must have been painful and I should have been more sensitive to the compliment. But with classic egotism, I interpreted your honesty only in relation to myself."

His eyes searched her face. She replayed his words and understood what he was saying. Her anger collapsed. Her voice, in complete contrast to her most recent outburst, was hushed.

"I wasn't telling you to back off because I didn't realise you were..." she discarded several alternatives and still the right expression eluded her.

Oscar's lips twitched. "Coming on?"

She couldn't reply, her senses muddled by the heat of his hands, the scent of his cedar wood cologne and the expression on his face.

He shook his head, his gaze never leaving hers. "In that case, I'm seriously concerned about your skills of observation." His pupils expanded, a few fireflies of colour floating on the edges.

A pulse beat at her throat as his thumb brushed her collarbone, sending whispers across her skin.

"Can I just clarify one thing, Detective Inspector? Do you, or do you not, want me to piss off?"

A voice in her head began making a series of statements.

This is the perfect time to laugh, apologise for shouting and tell him not exactly to piss off but that it is getting late. Your moods have been erratic all day and you have not yet taken your stabiliser. Sudden flares of lust and lack of good judgement are, as you well know, sure signs of your condition. Break his gaze and speak, woman.

The roaring in her ears drowned it out. When Oscar bent to kiss her, her body moved to meet his, as if she had no say in the matter. The touch of his lips triggered a simultaneous liquefying sensation and intoxicating euphoria so that his steadying hands on her shoulders seemed the only things keeping her upright. She released a huge, shivery breath as his mouth moved to press butterfly kisses on her neck and the diminished voice in her head floated clean away.

Then he stopped. He lifted his head, looking over her shoulder. "There's someone outside the door," he whispered.

An envelope lay on the mat. Oscar broke the clinch, wrenched open the door and looked both ways up the corridor. Beatrice, light-headed and dizzy, picked up the white *Empress Louise* stationery.

"No one there," he said.

"They can't have got far. You go left, I'll go right. Quick!"

She rushed barefoot along the corridor, shaking with a maelstrom of emotions. As she turned the corner, the envelope clutched in her hand, she collided heavily with someone coming the other way. Doreen Cashmore had the air of a wild animal exhausted by the hunt.

"Mrs Cashmore, are you all right?"

"I changed my mind. I was coming back to get the letter. I shouldn't have written it. It's not my place but it's been on my conscience, you see. That poor woman had nothing at all to do with it. I can't, I just can't..." Her face screwed into a wretched grimace and she began to weep dry hitching sobs that sounded like a gate blowing in the wind.

"Come. Let's sit down and sort this out. You really shouldn't be wandering about alone, especially not at this hour. This way."

Doreen allowed Beatrice to manoeuvre her back along the corridor and pulled a tissue from her sleeve to blow her nose.

"I couldn't get out before. I had to wait till Joyce went to bed. But she was playing cards on the computer till late and... oh!"

As they approached the guest cabin, Oscar stepped out of the door, glancing quickly at the elderly lady and back to Beatrice.

"Ah. I was just coming to find you." His eyes locked onto hers.

Beatrice's stomach effervesced and she forced herself to look away. "Mrs Cashmore, this is a friend of mine, Oscar Martins. Oscar, Mrs Cashmore is a bit upset, so we're going to have a chat in my cabin, if you don't mind."

"Of course not. I'll leave you in peace. I hope you feel better soon, Mrs Cashmore. And perhaps we can continue our discussion tomorrow, Detective Inspector?"

Mrs Cashmore was still blinking at Oscar so didn't spot the transformation of professional police officer into fourteen-year-old girl.

"I... umm... well... yes, that's a distinct possibility. See you tomorrow then."

"See you tomorrow. Sweet dreams. Goodnight, ladies."

They watched him walk down the corridor until Beatrice came to her senses and ushered Mrs Cashmore inside. While making her guest some tea, she splashed cold water on her face, took her stabiliser and prepared to concentrate on the job. She'd save thoughts of Oscar till later.

Chapter 22

Finding a place to make a private call with no danger of being overheard by the police patrol or anyone else was impossible. In the end, Nikos walked all the way back to his cabin to call Karen.

It might make him late for the cabaret, but it was worth it. Of all people, Karen would understand why today's encounter with Xanthou had got under his skin. With her usual perceptive analysis, she said Xanthou's behaviour showed him to be insecure and threatened. His problem, and no one else's. No, she'd received no emails from the cocky little git, but if she did, she'd delete them. She wanted Nikos to come home. She missed him and when he got back, she would chain him to the bed to stop him leaving again. By the end of the call, he felt warm, righteous and a little bit horny.

He checked his watch. The show had already started. He hurried back to the entertainment decks and The Man with the Golden Voice. Fortunately, the ballroom was laid out in cabaret, rather than theatre style, so Nikos's late arrival caused the minimum of disturbance. A waiter showed him to his seat and took his order for still water. Toni Dean was coming to the final chorus of *King of the Road*. Behind him, spotlights picked out the backing vocalists, two tuxedo-clad men and a woman in a black sheath dress singing into a single microphone, while two showgirls in sparkling swimsuits and an abundance of feathers struck poses every few bars. The band, at the back of the stage, consisted of a piano, drums, a trumpet and a saxophone, along with a double bass and a synthesiser. Dean swayed from foot to foot, convincingly Sinatra-sounding, flashing his teeth at every opportunity.

Nikos settled back and wondered what wicked observations Karen would make if she were here. She could always puncture the artificial and pretentious with a well-chosen barb. She'd have something to say about the showgirls' eyelashes and fixed grins, for sure, not to mention Toni's perma-tan. She insisted on watching the Eurovision Song Contest every year, 'for comedy value'. If only she was here. He loved the way she reduced Xanthou so effectively to a 'cocky little git'. Voulakis, when he'd been their senior officer, could see there was a problem, but laughed it off as professional jealousy. In fact, he used to fan the flames, in the misguided belief that competitiveness would make them both work harder. He had no idea how personal and destructive Xanthou could be.

Toni (Frank) was introducing the cast with a showman's patter. The crowd applauded and whistled as 'Sammy Davis Junior' and 'Dean Martin' strolled onto the stage to join in with a rendition of *A Lovely Way to Spend an Evening*. Nikos, already bored, browsed the glossy programme and realised that each entertainer would have a section of the show to himself, beginning with Frank and ending with a finale involving all three. So what did Toni Dean do while his colleagues took the stage?

Nikos made some rough calculations and decided to leave at the interval and miss the start of the second half. He'd just have time to find out what Kostas got up to after ten o'clock before returning to watch the offstage movements of Toni Dean. He sat back to listen to *My Kind of Town* and found himself humming along.

Kostas, clearly in a hurry, left the kitchen with a bag. Nikos almost lost him a couple of times as he slipped around corners and through doorways. Tailing an experienced staff member round a cruise ship without alerting said individual to his presence – Nikos could remember easier gigs. The chef, whose familiarity with layout far exceeded his own, ducked into a crew elevator and the doors closed. Nikos waited several seconds before approaching to watch the numbers descend. G Deck. Below sea level and where crew quarters were housed. Kostas was staff, so certainly had a cabin on A Deck or above. All staff and crew facilities, including mess, buffet and recreation facilities were in A Deck. The only things on G Deck were laundry, refuse, engines and the lowliest quarters. What would he need down there?

As a senior member of staff, Kostas had access to all areas. Crew, staff and passenger facilities were at his disposal. So what would draw him to visit the most basic, below-sea section, where engineers slept on bunks and shared a toilet? In the same crew lift he'd seen Kostas take, Nikos pressed the button for G Deck, wondering if he'd emerge into a full-fledged ceilidh with Kate Winslet dancing the polka.

He didn't. The gangways stood silent, every door closed and apart from the far louder sounds of the engines and the smell of cooking fish, no different to six levels above. He turned left, for no other reason than he sensed that was where the smell came from.

The first open door led to an empty cabin, with two unmade beds and laundry hanging from a makeshift line across the sink. The second opened into a communal area, where a few men played cards and others argued or laughed in small groups. They turned to stare as he crossed the threshold. One man shook his head and pointed towards the ceiling.

"No place for you. Go back upstairs." Nikos withdrew, opting not to use his police badge. Kostas was nowhere to be seen. He retraced his steps to the lift and decided to turn one last corner in the other direction, before abandoning hope of finding the vanished chef.

Storerooms and offices. Each bearing an abbreviation: HT/HR Office, LC/LS Store G2, IT/ITS, PLCPO, C/S/C Storage. Nikos tried every door. No indication as to meaning or usefulness and each one locked. A fruitless exercise and now he'd have to hurry not to miss the Rat Pack changeover. Back to the elevator. As he watched the numbers descend, he heard a door open, a soft goodbye in Greek and footsteps coming his way. Kostas started at the sight of the inspector. Nikos noticed the chef's jaw harden and saw the bandage on his hand. He assumed a relaxed pose to counteract the chef's folded arms and greeted him in Greek.

"Yeah, I followed you. It's my job. I have to check each staff and crew member's alibi. Yours, in the kitchen from six till eleven, didn't stand up. I know you leave during dessert and only come back to check the cleaning. I can't remove you from suspicion until your alibi is proven. You're not being persecuted. You're not the only one."

Kostas cursed under his breath. "No such thing as privacy. Just like a TV show. Performing, all the time."

"I don't know. Not my area of expertise. What did you do to your hand?"

"Cut it. Meat cleaver slipped. Do you want to see?"

"No. All I have to do is make one hundred percent sure that you were somewhere else when three elderly ladies died. You told the Rhodes sergeant you work in the kitchen till eleven pm. You don't. See my point, Kostas? I need to know what you do between ten and half past."

"Come." Kostas jerked his head back up the corridor. Nikos checked his watch. 'Frank' would be handing over to 'Sammy' about now, and heading off to do what exactly? He shrugged and followed the chef.

Kostas rounded the corner and knocked on a cabin door and called out. "Tsampika? It's me again."

The door opened and a tall, gaunt woman peered out. Her expression darkened when she saw Stephanakis and looked to the chef for reassurance.

"This is Inspector Stephanakis. He's not interested in you, he's checking my alibi. He wants to know what I do in the break. Will you tell him?"

She addressed Nikos with a resentful glare. "He visits me. Every night."

Stephanakis could guess the reason but had to get confirmation. He winced at the indelicacy of the question.

"Can I ask why?"

Kostas answered. "It's the only chance I get to see my sister."

"Your sister?"

"Yes. Tsampika is crew, on the laundry team. Since her husband lost his job and their savings got swallowed by rent increases, she has to work. On the ships, she earns enough to keep her family by leaving them for two weeks every month. It's not the worst job in the world. I gave her a reference, but not as her brother. Some people down here know we're related but the powers-that-be don't know anything. Crew are not allowed on passenger decks, so if we spent time together on A Deck, it would raise eyebrows. That's why

I visit her in her cabin and bring her some decent food when we both have free time. She doesn't have much."

"Food or free time?"

"Both."

"I'll need your full name, Tsampika. I won't cause you any problems, I'll just check this out quietly."

She chewed her thumbnail and looked up at her brother.

Kostas lowered his brow. "I'll give you her name, but know this. If you tell any senior management or anyone at all in HR, she'll lose her job. Mine could be in danger, too."

"I will make sure your sister is not implicated in any way and will keep my investigations general. I don't want to cause harm here. I just want to stop someone killing the passengers."

He thanked Tsampika and wished the siblings goodnight. While he waited for the elevator, Kostas caught him up. They rode in silence to the entertainment deck.

Nikos spoke. "Kostas, you're an experienced cruise veteran. In your view, is the person who's targeting these women a passenger, a member of staff or crew?"

Several seconds passed and the lift doors opened. They stepped out onto the deck and Kostas paused.

"It's not anyone on the crew. They all know these people are our livelihood. Staff? Many of us could happily kill the occasional passenger, of course, but how stupid would we be to bite the hand that feeds? Passengers, I couldn't say. In my experience of eighteen cruises, at least fifty percent are borderline crazy."

"Thank you. I'll leave you now and I promise to be discreet."

"That would be most welcome. Goodnight, Inspector."

Nikos held out his right hand.

The chef shook it.

Backstage at the Ballroom was surprisingly shabby. Worn carpets, peeling photographs of earlier performances, empty coffee cups and labelled rails of costumes. Nikos knocked twice on Toni Dean's door but no one answered. He tried the door, which was locked. The Stage Manager was unconcerned.

"Gargling in the bathroom? Gone out for fresh air? He's a wanderer, that one. The entertainers spend so much time indoors in the dark, soon as they get more than five minutes break, you'll usually find them on deck. With Toni, he's a free spirit. He's a biker, you know. When we're docked, every chance he gets, he's off out on his Harley. Couple of times he's only just made it back in time for the show. Gives me grey hairs, that one."

A pressure lifted. Subject to checks, the chef was simply a loyal brother and the crooner relished a bit of freedom from routine. Not only that, but Nikos was growing increasingly convinced the predator was a passenger. He made a note on his phone: Oscar Martins – any history?

He ascended the stairs to the observation deck, scanning the strolling passers-by for a man with a tan and extraordinarily white teeth. The evening air, cool and fresh, energised him. Somehow, he felt secure. It had taken a while, but he was now an inspector. He'd encountered Xanthou and risen above any attempt at patronisation. Despite being promoted two years later than his rival, he was working his first case with an experienced detective from Scotland Yard, who treated him as an equal. Best of all, he'd got the girl. Karen, his fantasy woman, had chosen him. Perhaps it was premature but the world looked pretty good to Nikos Stephanakis.

A man was smoking at the end of the deck, looking out at the island. Nikos approached, gauging the man a little short to be his target, although the tuxedo looked familiar. As he approached, he spotted the goatee beard, the paunch and the round glasses. Not Toni Dean, but Dr Weinberg. No wonder he was hidden from sight. A doctor with a cigar?

"Good evening, Doctor."

Weinberg acknowledged him with a half nod and continued his contemplation of the city of Rhodes. "A man could never get tired of Greece, I'm sure."

Nikos leant his arms on the rail beside him and tried to see the view through foreign eyes. "Not sure. Give me another thirty years."

Weinberg laughed, a gentle, restrained sound from one side of his mouth, blowing smoke away in a considerate gesture. "To live here, in the lap of the Gods, with history and beauty and knowledge surrounding you. You are fortunate to be born Greek, Inspector."

"Thank you. I think so. Though the general atmosphere, at the moment, is not one of feeling lucky."

"Are you referring to the situation on board or the morale of Greece as a whole?"

"I was thinking about my country," Nikos replied, preparing his defences.

Weinberg exhaled downwind and fanned the smoke away with his hand. "With good reason. The current climate is to be expected when austerity measures weaken the vulnerable still further."

Surprised, Nikos checked the doctor's face for sarcasm.

The ship's floodlights reflected in Weinberg's glasses as he turned to meet Nikos's stare. "Oh yes, Inspector, I'm serious. I cannot claim comprehensive knowledge, as my interest is medicine. But I follow the news in my field. I know about the increase in HIV infections, the malaria outbreak, the infant mortality rates and number of male suicides. What has happened to Greek healthcare in the past five years is a retrograde step. This makes me sad. Sad and very angry. You see, when I'm not working, I volunteer with *Médecins Sans Frontières*, or used to."

"Why did you stop?"

"I didn't stop. But I had to stop working in Greece. My last tour of duty was in Mozambique. Very different, but another beautiful country."

"I don't know it. Why can't you work in Greece?"

The doctor extinguished his cigar. He used a small tin cup complete with lid to dispose of all traces of his habit. "Some people, including many members of the crew, blame Germany for the EU bailout conditions. As an Austrian, I'm regarded as more or less German as well. The accent, you see. So I am the enemy. Today, they had no choice. But I think both the engineer and the chef would have preferred Nurse Bannerjee to me."

"A chef? Was that Kostas, from The Sizzling Grill?"

"Correct. Broken finger. Easily set with a splint."

Nikos's phone, switched to silent since entering the ballroom, vibrated. He checked the screen. Number unknown.

"Excuse me, Doctor. I have to take this call. It was good talking to you and I wish you a nice evening."

He walked across the deck and answered professionally. "Stephanakis?"

"Inspector Stephanakis, I'm sorry to disturb you. This is Captain Jensson. Could you please join the emergency team in Deluxe Cabin 254 on the Aegean Deck? It seems there has been another attack."

Nikos began running and talking at the same time.

"On my way. Another of the Hirondelles?"

"The lady in question is a member of the Hirondelle party, but fortunately the attack was incomplete. An alarm alerted neighbouring cabins and the man escaped before help arrived."

"Where's DI Stubbs?"

"Here. One moment. I will pass her the telephone," Jensson said.

"Nikos? Where are you?"

"On my way. Who did he attack? Doreen Cashmore?" He rushed up the stairs to the next level.

"No, because Doreen was in my room. He assaulted Joyce Milligan. But she fought back. Her injuries look pretty nasty, but she'll survive. By God, I hope so. Nikos, listen. Doreen's spilled the beans and now I know why. The only thing we don't know is who."

Chapter 23

Dear Detective Inspector Stubbs

I am writing to you because I feel there is something important you should be aware of regarding the Hirondelles and Swallows Hall. I apologise for not talking to you earlier, but we thought it best not to speak of the matter as it seemed irrelevant. However, recent circumstances have convinced me that it is most definitely something the police need to know. Not all my companions agree, which is why I am writing this letter rather than coming to you in person.

When I secured a position as house mistress at Swallows Hall in the winter of 1961, Joyce Milligan was Head. It was a prestigious school and we were all proud of our reputation for academic standards and propriety. It was the place for nice girls. Several of our pupils came from important families and two of the girls' fathers were MPs. In the spring of 1965, Eva Webber, a fifteen-year-old whose family were well-respected landowners in Surrey, came to me with a problem. She was pregnant.

I consulted with Joyce immediately and we held a teachers' meeting to decide the best course of action. If the news became public, it would be a disaster for all concerned. The girl would lose her good name and stain that of her family. Parents the length and breadth of the country would doubt Swallows Hall as an appropriate moral institution for their daughters. The child was too young to marry and in any case refused to reveal the identity of the father, who could and should have been prosecuted. As a Church of England school, we could not consider terminating the pregnancy. Even if we had, she was too far along.

We were lucky in one respect. The school hosted day girls and boarders. Eva was one of the latter, which made it easier for us to keep her condition quiet. We told her to write to her parents asking permission to join summer school and stay over the holidays. I had the task of accompanying the girl to the French Alps, to a sympathetic convent school where we used to take our winter sports holidays. She spent the rest of her confinement there, and as far as I could ascertain, maintained her education. In the meanwhile, Joyce and Esther located a private adoption agency to find a family for the baby.

Eva gave birth on the first day of July. Thankfully, without complication. Although the nuns had experience in midwifery, several other teachers and I travelled to Isère just in case. Joyce and Beryl took the child back to England as quickly as possible to minimise upset for Eva. Unfortunately, she had already formed a bond with her child. Removing the little boy was a deeply upsetting experience all round. I remained with Eva until she had recovered in both body and mind, then we returned to school and tried to put the episode behind us.

It is my belief our actions brought a curse upon us and we are being punished for what happened in 1965. Moreover, I believe that the killing of Maureen Hall was a terrible error and it should have been me. I became Mrs Cashmore in 1972. Before that, my name was Miss Doreen Hall.

Yours sincerely
Doreen Cashmore

Dr Weinberg would not be drawn on a prognosis until he had seen the X-rays. Joyce had a suspected broken collarbone, and possibly a broken rib, plus extensive bruising to her face as a result of her defensive injuries. After consultation with the staff at Andreas Papandreou Hospital, it was decided she would be better served by a smaller private clinic in Sgourou, where security would be easier to arrange. Exhausted, frustrated and shaken, Beatrice watched the ambulance leave and returned to the bridge.

At first glance, she assumed the man in conversation with Nikos was one of the entertainers. Leather jacket, quiff and old-fashioned sideburns. She picked up the tension as soon as she saw Nikos's face.

"DI Stubbs, this is Inspector Xanthou from the South Aegean

Region of the Hellenic Police. Xanthou, this is Detective Inspector Stubbs of Scotland Yard."

The man's eyebrows arched and despite being the same height as her, he managed to look down his nose.

"Right." He shook her hand with minimum effort and turned away to continue speaking Greek.

Nikos interrupted. "Xanthou, this investigation is a cooperative effort between the UK and Greek forces. So that everyone can understand, we speak English."

"Fine. I'll repeat myself in English. I find it amazing that two senior officers, supported by two of my own men, cannot protect five old ladies. My resources are stretched to the limit, so I can't offer you any more assistance. This is a farce."

Beatrice had an urge to giggle. A farce indeed. This ridiculous bantam cock of a man, attempting pomposity while dressed as if he were busking in a skiffle band.

"Pleased to meet you, Inspector Xanthou. I fear 'five old ladies' is a serious underestimation of the task. This ship carries two thousand passengers, all of whom deserve our protection. Your sergeants understand that much and have patrolled the entire vessel. My suggestion, if you're in agreement, Inspector Stephanakis, is to entrust the protection of Joyce Milligan to Inspector Xanthou, whilst we proceed with our investigation. Let's hope the South Aegean force can protect one old lady." She faked a laugh and prodded Xanthou's shoulder, for no other reason than she knew he'd hate it. "Excuse me gentlemen, I need to talk to Captain Jensson."

By the time she'd finished discussing the logistics of removing the Hirondelles with Jensson, Xanthou had left. Nikos stood outside, talking on his mobile. When he saw her, he signalled for her to follow. He led the way to the empty cafeteria and bought two coffees from the vending machine, still conversing in Greek. They sat at a window table and he ended the call.

"Well?" he asked.

Beatrice cradled her coffee. "Jensson's staff will book six seats on a charter flight to London Gatwick for lunchtime today. Five

Hirondelles and myself. We'll need an escort to the airport and specialised transport for the ladies. From there, I'll hand over to the Wiltshire police. Can you arrange for a briefing room at Gatwick where I can talk to those officers and any relatives we can get hold of?"

"You're leaving?"

"No. Just ensuring the ladies get home safely, then I'll be back. Someone on this ship is our man and we are this close to finding him." She held up finger and thumb in a narrow pinch.

"You said Doreen Cashmore told you what all this is about. You went to her cabin?"

"She came to mine. She delivered a letter around the same time Joyce was attacked in Doreen's room. The first thing you should know is Doreen's maiden name was Hall. She is firmly convinced that Maureen Hall's death was a case of mistaken identity and that she was the intended victim. She thinks the Hirondelles are cursed because of something which happened almost fifty years ago."

"Cursed? Come on."

Beatrice took a sip of coffee. "It might not be as far-fetched as it sounds. They're called the Hirondelles..."

"Because of the school. I know. Swallows Hall."

"Yes, a girls' boarding school. An underage pupil fell pregnant in 1965. Obviously a scandal in those days. Not just for her but also for the school. The teachers, under the direction of Headmistress Joyce Milligan, hushed it up. They hid the girl away until she reached full term and gave the child away for adoption. Doreen believes they're now being punished."

Nikos snorted, blowing foam off his cappuccino. "By whom? The mother would be in her sixties now."

"Yes, and unlikely to be a serial killer. Doreen's conscience led her to keep an eye on the girl after she left school, but she hasn't seen her for several years. It seems the woman suffered from depression and became an alcoholic. I have the last known address, which I intend to check while I'm in London. I'll also visit the adoption agency which took the baby."

"What about the father?"

"They don't know who the father was. The girl wouldn't say. The only men the girls had contact with worked at the school. All the teachers were female, so that left only a caretaker, a priest and two gardeners. Doreen thinks it could have been a local boy she met while in town. Why would he suddenly pop up after fifty years?"

"Hmm. How about the child they gave away? Who would be forty-eight, forty-nine? The HR department must be able to give me a list of employees of that age."

"Definitely worth checking, because we have a birth date. 1st July 1965. You'll also need to check where our suspects were at the time of the attack."

Nikos made a note on his phone. "I will. I made progress with Kostas, but still need more information on Toni Dean and Oscar Martins."

"I can help you with the latter. Oscar was having a drink with me last night."

Nikos's head snapped up. "Where?"

"In my cabin." She tried not to sound defensive.

"You had Oscar Martins *and* Doreen Cashmore in your cabin?"

"Oscar first, who left when Doreen arrived." She picked up her coffee cup to hide her discomfort.

Nikos tapped his phone against his chin. "So he knew Doreen was with you and Joyce was alone. He could easily have gone to their cabin and attacked Joyce Milligan."

"It's not their cabin, only Doreen's. He didn't know Joyce was there. I only knew because I went to talk to her after dinner and Joyce opened the door. So the person who attacked Joyce was looking for Doreen."

"You sound very convinced," Nikos frowned. "I don't understand why you would invite a murder suspect to your room."

Beatrice finished her coffee. "I wanted to find out a little more about the man, that's all. Anyway, he's ten years too old to be that adopted child."

"You didn't know about that then."

"No, I didn't. Fair enough. Go ahead and interview him again. Should we get back to the bridge? I have a batch of calls to make then I'd like to grab forty wings before we leave for the airport."

"You're hungry?"

"What? No, I just need a short nap, you know, rest my eyes."

Nikos sat back and appraised her. "If there's anything going on, it might be better to tell me now, for the sake of this case."

"There's nothing going on. Yet I get the feeling that is not true of you and Inspector Xanthou of the South Aegean Force. Is this something more than local rivalry?"

"Nice deflection. Yes, there's history, but it has no bearing on this case. If it did, I'd tell you."

His chin lifted, dark with stubble. Beatrice held his eyes and heard a faint echo of James's voice. 'So would you say that when you are emotionally pressured, you tend to look for a scapegoat?' A pang as familiar as thirst plucked at her and she had a thought.

"Nikos, I apologise. It's none of my business and you're right. Only when the personal affects the professional is it worth discussing. We have a job to do, so let's get on with it. I plan to spend about twenty-four hours in Britain, so with a following wind, I'll be back tomorrow afternoon. Meanwhile, this end of the investigation is in your hands."

He rested his cheek on his fist, all the defiance gone out of him.

"Yes, of course. I'm sorry for being suspicious. I guess we both need some sleep. Why can't serial killers keep to civilised hours like the rest of us?"

"Civilised hours?" She thought about it. "Yes. He works late and sleeps late. Bear that in mind when you're checking alibis. You know what, that bastard is probably tucked up in bed right now."

"Wish I was."

"Me too. But first I need to make sure Joyce is all right. Can we trust him to look after her, do you think?"

"Who?"

"Danny Zuko. Sorry, I meant Xanthou. He seems to be pursuing another agenda."

"He's got ego issues. But I think he'll make a point of protecting Joyce Milligan. Who's Danny Zuko?"

Rarely had Beatrice been so relieved to hit the tarmac. Fretful and querulous without the steadying presence of Joyce Milligan, the five Hirondelles in her charge behaved like a flock of giddy geese, vacillating between alarm and absent-mindedness, with Beatrice as the hapless gooseherd trying to guide them safely home. Even the stewardesses' patience had frayed.

By the time the little beeping airport trucks deposited them at the conference centre after a protracted toilet break, Beatrice was ready to snap. However, seeing the emotional reactions of the families and the efficient organisation of the briefing, she managed to remain professional and helpful throughout. She kept to the vaguest of terms regarding the investigation. The Wiltshire detective, on the other hand, went into fine detail of how the relatives and carers should keep their charges safe. At first, his pedantry irritated Beatrice, but the effect on the families was a panacea. She answered several questions, ranging from naive to aggressive, then at a signal from the detective, called a halt. She made a hurried general farewell, thanked the representatives of the Wiltshire force and rushed out across the terminal to the taxi rank.

"Can you take me to Islington? I have an appointment in Upper Street. Just across from the Hope and Anchor."

The driver folded his paper. "Course I can, darling. What time's your appointment?"

Beatrice clambered through the rear door, amused and reassured by the casual endearment. "Four o'clock."

"Plenty of time! Sit back and relax."

She did as she was told. Her head fell back against the seat and she took three deep breaths, intending to open her worry box in a moment. Within minutes, she was fast asleep.

When she awoke, it took her a few moments to orient herself. The taxi was parked but the driver was absent. Islington flowed past the window and James's practice was across the street. She checked her watch. 15.43. Despite a stiff neck and dry mouth, she actually felt better. She sat up straight, checked her purse and mobile - both present - and found a packet of wet wipes to refresh her face. She was smoothing her hair in the wing mirror when a mechanical click announced the unlocking of the doors.

"She's awake! All right, sweetheart? Didn't mean to scare you, just thought I'd let you sleep for a bit. Your appointment's in a quarter of an hour, so I fetched us both a coffee." He handed her a cardboard cup and placed his own on the roof.

Beatrice blinked in disbelief. "That's very kind of you. How long have I..."

"We got here about half an hour ago. I'm not in a hurry so I thought I'd have a break and let you get some kip. You'd only been asleep an hour, see. Bad time to wake someone. My daughter, she's cabin crew with BA, told me how it works on long-haul trips. Forty-five minute cycles, innit? Have a nap for minimum three-quarters of an hour. Or if you got time, an hour and a half. The old 'grab an hour's shut-eye' is the worst. You wake up even tireder, see? How you feeling?"

The milky coffee, cheerful chatter and kindness from a stranger comforted Beatrice so easily, she wondered if her appointment with James was as urgent as it had felt several hours and another country ago.

"I feel vastly restored. It really is very decent of you to let me rest, not to mention bringing me a coffee."

He grinned. "As my missus always says, do as you would done by or dooby-dooby something or other." He raised a hand as another cabbie tooted.

"Well, I'd like to pay you for your time." She glanced at the meter, which was switched off.

"Let's call it forty quid. Cheers my darling. You have a good afternoon, now, all right?"

Chapter 24

James had changed receptionists. Another good sign. No matter how sanguine these discreet, polite people were, Beatrice always managed to rub them up the wrong way. She knew the endless reorganisation of appointments and short-notice cancellations was a nuisance, but on top of that the urgent requests for a last-minute slot meant she invariably became one of their least favourite patients. This one, a young man with Joe 90 glasses and too new to be jaded, gave her a pleasant smile and told her to go on in.

Not for the first time did Beatrice feel a surge of relief and affection on seeing her counsellor. She quelled the urge to rush over and give him a hug.

"Beatrice. Right on time. Did David offer you coffee?" His gentle smile and cool blue eyes acted like a cold flannel on her forehead. She couldn't wait to begin.

"I just had one, thank you." She settled into the chair. "And I appreciate your making time for me, despite the fact it's unscheduled."

"Yes, we do have our regular slot next Wednesday, but I assumed you had something pressing you'd like to discuss."

In an instant, the weight of all the time she'd known James seemed oppressive and suffocating. He knew everything about her relationship with Matthew, always advised truth in emotion and set great value in trust. How could he do anything but judge her? After all, she'd even judged herself. Once again, she wondered if she should change counsellors. Maybe someone closer to her own age. Silence dragged on and although there was no clock in the room, Beatrice heard ticking.

James spoke. "If you don't feel ready to discuss what brought you here, could we begin by dispensing with the formalities? How is the medication working for you?"

"James, I am a horrible person. Selfish, immature, greedy, unbalanced and just plain horrible. I can no longer bear to be in my own skin. If only I were religious."

He watched her, attentive and concerned. "How would religion help, do you think?"

"Because it's always so black and white. This is right, that is wrong. Punishment on earth, rewards in heaven. Actions count, not feelings. But if you have no system telling you how to behave, if you're carving out your own code of conduct, you only have yourself to blame."

"Hmmm. That's an interesting choice of word. 'Blame'. Something I tend to associate with judgement."

Beatrice studied him for a second. She really did wonder if he could read her thoughts.

"Or responsibility. You do something wrong. You accept the consequences. You take the blame."

"OK. Can we return to that in a moment? I ask because I feel I've missed a stage in your reasoning. You said 'do something wrong'. If we're not applying the rules of religion or law, who makes that call?"

"I do. According to my own principles, which happen to tally with those of most civilised people, I have done something wrong. Therefore I am culpable."

James tugged at his earlobe, a deceptive gesture Beatrice knew well as signifying serious thought.

"I'm wondering where I fit in, Beatrice. As both defendant and jury in the High Court of Stubbs, you have reached a decision and accepted your own verdict. Would you like me to pass sentence? I'm happy to do so, but feel the penance must fit the crime. As yet, I'm unaware of the deed, the motivation behind it, any extenuating circumstances or other offences to be taken into consideration."

It took her almost half an hour to tell him. Not least because he constantly interrupted her statement of facts to enquire as to her feelings. Unusually for one of James's sessions, she didn't cry. She squirmed and winced and fidgeted, but would not allow herself the indulgence of tears. She didn't deserve them.

Finally she stopped and James left a pause before speaking again.

"Can you see any correlation between recent events in Greece and what you think Matthew is planning?"

Beatrice stared out at the traffic on Upper Street. "God, I am so tediously predictable. Kicking against the traces at my age. It's pathetic."

"Pathetic, predictable, horrible, selfish. I think it's time the tenor of the language changed. You may feel angry about your behaviour, but I cannot allow you to be abusive to one of my clients. Even if it is yourself."

"Don't you ever get bored, James? Is it not bone-wearyingly dull listening to all these people, each of whom thinks they're special, who make the same set of clichéd mistakes as everyone else?"

"That's almost the exact opposite of how I see my profession. I also recognise your question for what it is – a classic Beatrice wriggle of evasion to avoid taking the last step. You've told me what happened and how you feel about it. You've acknowledged the thought processes which led you to behave in a way you deem reprehensible. The unaddressed issue is how you plan to deal with it."

A sigh so deep it was practically a groan escaped her. With the inevitability of the phases of the moon, here was the last part of the pattern. She wanted James to tell her what to do. He wouldn't. She'd sulk and then finally, if there was any time left in their hour, she'd face the fact she had to clean up her own mess. This time, she'd just skip to the end.

"I will separate my ego from my emotions. I will tell Oscar I made an error of judgement and keep my distance. I'll say nothing to Matthew and instead engage in a serious conversation about our future. And I'll stop trying to hide."

James nodded as the speakers emitted a soft sound, waves or rain or somesuch, but it was the indication that their session was drawing to a close. "Definite progress, Beatrice. I will ask two more questions, if I may? The medication?"

"No side effects and so long as I take it at the same time, the swoops are softer. Still there, but softer."

"Good. Let's keep the dosage the same and talk next week. You still want to honour next week's appointment?"

Beatrice stood up. "Definitely. I have to go back to Greece tomorrow but I expect everything to be done and dusted by Sunday. Monday latest. See you next week and thank you so much."

"You're welcome. You did all the work. One last thing I'd like you to think about between now and Wednesday. To what extent are your fears about marrying Matthew related to your fear of becoming Pam? One to chew over. See you next week and good luck in Greece."

Rush hour had begun and Beatrice battled through the crowds towards the Tube. Dusk was falling and the gloomy onset of evening mirrored her mood. Becoming Pam? Where the hell had he got that from?

Chapter 25

DEATH STALKS THE AEGEAN!

Three women dead, one hospitalised at the hands of the Cruise Killer!

One of the most reassuring sights is a Chevalier Cruise Liner sailing majestically along our coastline. These leviathans of the Mediterranean represent luxury, comfort, five-star service and the best way to experience the joys of the Greek islands for visitors – and let's not forget, a steady source of tourist income for residents.

Strangled in their beds! Thrown from a cliff!

Since the *Empress Louise* sailed from Athens two weeks ago, three elderly ladies have been brutally murdered in shocking circumstances. Two smothered in their beds, another thrown from a cliff top in Santorini. And last night, the killer tried to strike again. Joyce Milligan, 81, fought off her attacker and rang the alarm, alerting the ship's crew. Doctors at Sgourou's Kalithea Clinic say her injuries are serious but she is comfortable. A source close to the case said the cruise has been abandoned, with the ship detained indefinitely at the commercial port in Rhodes harbour. The Cretan Regional Police, who have made little progress with their investigations despite the support of a British detective from Scotland Yard, have asked the South Aegean Region for assistance.

Read related stories here...

Nikos dropped his head into his hands and let out a string of the worst curses he knew. He'd never have checked the *Dimokratiki* news site if the cabin steward hadn't mentioned the story when delivering lunch. He shoved the paperwork to one side and picked up his phone. Who to call first? Beatrice couldn't read Greek and anyway she wouldn't touch down in London for another hour. Voulakis? He should know there was a press leak. No, the first person he would seek out and speak to would be Xanthou, because everything about this stank of his involvement. Before he could dial, the phone rang.

"Stephanakis."

"Inspector, this is Captain Jensson. Could I ask you to join me on the bridge at your earliest convenience?"

Jensson's uniform was neatly pressed and his face clean-shaven, but his eyes showed his exhaustion. He did not look pleased to see Nikos.

"Inspector, I would have preferred it if the police had consulted me or the cruise line before going to the press. As it is, my team must field questions from journalists and families with little information and no preparation, and the PR damage to Chevalier Cruises cannot be underestimated. Plus, the information printed is incorrect. The cruise has indeed been cancelled, but I have orders to sail to Athens this evening so that passengers can be flown home."

"I had nothing to do with this, I assure you. It must have come from the South Aegean Region police press department. I apologise on behalf of my colleagues, because you certainly should have been consulted."

With a flick of the wrist, Jensson waved aside the apology. "So the right hand has no idea what the left is doing. Aren't you a force that's supposed to work together? It doesn't fill me with confidence that you will be making an arrest any time soon."

Underneath his tiredness and embarrassment, a boiling rage seethed in Nikos. Xanthou. This had gone on long enough. Only someone as petty and self-serving would undermine Nikos and the entire investigation just to score points.

"Inspector, can I ask what do you intend to do now?"

"I will speak to the South Aegean Regional force and ensure all communications are approved by a Chevalier Cruises spokesperson from now on. I'll continue my research on the HR documents and security records, and by the time DI Stubbs returns tomorrow morning, I hope to have a suspect in custody."

Jensson's face was blank. "The ship sails at twenty-two hundred hours. Please do what you have to do before then." The captain turned to the instrument panel and addressed the officer operating the map screen. Nikos had been dismissed.

He walked in without knocking. Xanthou was on the phone. He gave Nikos the once-over with an expression so supercilious it could have been pantomime and pointed to the chair with his pen. In no hurry to end his call, he doodled on his notepad, swivelled his chair to look out of the window, made weak jokes and laughed at every one.

Nikos folded his arms and waited, running over his speech, stoking his ire. The conversation, full of affected machismo, finally drew to a close. Xanthou hung up and focused on his computer screen.

"So, Nikos. Didn't have time to shave this morning?"

"Shut the fuck up."

Now he had his attention.

"What did you say?"

Nikos laughed. "Oh, stop it. I don't find you intimidating so drop the menacing looks. Act like an adult for just a few minutes. Look, I can tolerate all the digs and snide remarks, even if I think there's something quite sad about you still crowing two years later. Yes, you're younger than me. Yes, you got promoted before me. Yes, you're Karen's ex-boyfriend. Get over it. I have. This is not about some puerile jostling for position any longer. We have to work together to catch a serial killer who is still at large. And thanks to you, now has the name of the hospital in which his latest potential victim is still recovering. Going to the press to criticise the Cretan

Regional Force is sabotage. Is your ego that desperately fragile that you'd rather make me look bad than prevent any further deaths?"

Xanthou tilted his head to one side in a gesture of sympathy. "It really is eating you up, isn't it? Jealousy becomes paranoia."

"Don't patronise me. Who else knows as much about the case and stands to benefit from bad-mouthing the Cretan police?"

"Well, let's see. The failure of an expensive collaboration with Scotland Yard has upset a lot of people. Could be the press, the ship's crew, the cruise line management..."

"The collaboration is not a failure and I know damn well this leak has your fingerprints all over it!" Nikos stopped, aware he was shouting.

"If you can't control your temper, I'll have to ask you to leave my office. The journalist could have got that information from a number of sources. For the love of God, you only have to hang around the bar of Hotel Kyrios and buy that drunken doctor a whisky. He tells anyone who'll listen how he was wrongly accused."

Nikos hesitated. Dr Fraser had not even crossed his mind.

Xanthou pressed home his advantage. "So, better get back to that extensive list of suspects, bring them in here and let's start interrogating. Because to be honest, Nikos, you're wasting my time."

"There are only three suspects, but I'll interview them on board. The ship sails to Athens tonight, and I'll be on it."

"No. The ship is impounded and will stay in Rhodes until we make an arrest."

Nikos rolled his shoulders to release the tension. "This is not your case. You are assisting. DI Stubbs and I make the decisions. I'm going back to the ship and if I make an arrest, I'll bust my balls to make sure the suspect is taken to Athens. Or Crete, or even London. Anything to avoid being hamstrung by you and your ego."

"This may be a bad time to mention it, but I've filed a report on your mishandling of this case and registered a vote of no confidence in you and DI Stubbs. Thankfully, your behaviour today confirms my judgement as correct. Sorry, Nikos, but you just aren't inspector material. I need to make some calls so I'd like you to leave now."

Nikos sat back, his arms behind his head. "Maybe you're right. If all I had in my life was my job, I really would consider myself a failure. Have a good day, Xanthou."

His smile lasted until he'd closed Xanthou's door.

Hotel Kyria had seen better days. The bellboy, smoking in the shade of the awning, did not lift his eyes from his mobile as Nikos passed. Inside, the interior decor was what Karen would call 'Louis d'Hotel', faux grand, ornate, gilt but most of all, dusty. A sign indicated the way to the bar, which was empty but for a solitary figure with a newspaper and a glass of orange juice. He spotted Nikos and straightened in anticipation.

"Good afternoon, Dr Fraser. No news yet I'm afraid. Hopefully we'll make an announcement later today."

The light in the doctor's eyes dimmed and his face sagged. He suited the shabby atmosphere perfectly, as did the newspaper, a two-day old copy of *The Daily Telegraph*.

"If there's no news, this must be a social call." He caught the barman's eye. "Anything for you, Inspector? Spiros squeezes a mean orange."

"Not for me, thanks. The reason I'm here is to find out how the press got hold of the *Empress Louise* story."

"The press?"

"It's the lead story on the main Rhodes newspaper site, *Dimokratiki*."

The barman placed a fresh drink on Fraser's coaster.

"*Efharisto*, Spiros."

Nikos waited for him to drink and continue.

"Yes, I can say 'thank you' in Greek, but that is the extent of my knowledge. I've not read the paper or its website, but I heard the story's out. So you put two and two together and decided the Scottish addict must have been rambling to some hack."

"On the contrary. In fact I'm sure the information came from another source. I just need to be able to prove that."

Two young men entered and sat at the bar, each performing an elaborate handshake with Spiros.

Fraser took a long draught of his juice and licked his lips. "Chevalier Cruises cancelling this particular trip is a shame for the grannies. Bit of a bugger for staff and crew, too. Still, the worst they'll suffer is a couple of weeks unexpected holiday before the next batch of pensioners arrives and it all starts over – hopefully with fewer deaths, mind. The one person who'll struggle to recover from this is Jensson. His captaincy is tainted and his career is just about over. That man has been a solid friend to me. Why would I shoot the poor bastard in the foot?"

Nikos inclined his head. "You knew the cruise had been cancelled?"

"Jensson called earlier today to ask if I wanted to sail with them to Athens at ten this evening. I refused. I have a flight home on Sunday and I'm checking into a clinic. I can't help you, Inspector. Yes, I had the opportunity. Journalists drink here regularly and I drink with them. You could even say I had a motive. Bitter that my career is over, I wanted to destroy my friend's. The fact is that I didn't and I wouldn't. But how can I prove that?"

"I think you just have. You know the ship is sailing tonight. The person who leaked the information didn't." Nikos rose from his seat and held out his hand. "Doctor, I wish you all the best."

Fraser heaved himself up and returned the handshake. "Same to you, Inspector. Listen, I wrecked my own career. Jensson doesn't deserve to crash and burn because of some sick bastards who are out to get old ladies."

"Bastards? You think there's more than one?"

"I don't know. But if it is just one man, I hope to God I never meet him."

Chapter 26

The 18.39 from Waterloo disgorged its passengers at Bookham Station just before seven. By the time it had pulled away, the platform was empty. Commuters hopped into waiting cars or unlocked their bikes or trotted off up the lane. Everyone had a purpose and knew where they were going. Beatrice checked the map on her phone and set off through the cool, damp evening air towards Church Street. Well-lit pavements, people walking dogs, a hairdresser's, an art gallery and neat front lawns; here was suburbia at its finest. Fife Way lay to her left and the house was easy to find in the quiet cul-de-sac. To Beatrice's relief, the lights were on. Repeated calls had received no response.

She withdrew her badge and knocked on the door. Seconds passed with no sign of movement within. She knocked again and listened. After today's discovery that the adoption agency no longer existed, this was her last hope. She was bending down to look through the letterbox when a voice behind her made her jump.

"Can I help you?"

A woman in her late thirties wore a padded jacket over a Co-op supermarket uniform and held a heavily loaded carrier bag.

"I'm looking for Eva Webber. I understand she lives here."

"What do you want with her?"

Beatrice held up her badge. "DI Stubbs, CID. I'd like to ask her a few questions in relation to an investigation I'm conducting. I believe she might be able to help."

The woman tilted her watch to the street light. "Should've come earlier. You won't get much sense out of her now. She just called up for more supplies." She raised the carrier bag. "Smirnoff, tonic, fags and a sliced white. Come on; let's see what we can do."

She moved a miniature watering-can from the windowsill and picked up a key. The *Eastenders* theme came from the living-room as forcefully as the stench of cigarette smoke and stale air. Eva Webber lay on the sofa, a knitted patchwork quilt over her legs. Beside her stood an occasional table, almost entirely hidden under an empty plate, two remote controls, a mobile phone, a bottle of vodka with a third remaining, two empty tonic bottles, a packet of Marlboro Lights, a lighter, an ashtray, a dirty glass and a pile of magazines. Her slow gaze flickered over Beatrice and came to rest on the Co-op carrier bag. The room was uncomfortably warm.

"You are good to me, Jen. How much do I owe you?" Her voice, hoarse and low, had an indistinct looseness, as if she'd just woken up.

"Receipt's in the bag. We'll sort it out tomorrow. Eva, this lady is a detective from the police. She wants a word."

Eva blinked slowly. "About what?"

Jen shot a sympathetic look at Beatrice. "Nothing to worry about, I'm sure. I'll be off now and pop round in the morning. Good night, DI Stubbs, and best of luck."

As the door clicked shut, Eva began pouring herself another drink.

"Please sit down, officer. How can I help?"

The affected sobriety struck Beatrice as the most illogical be-haviour when all evidence pointed to the contrary. She sat, taking in the room. The dust, the stains on the carpet, the gas fire and old-fashioned cushions piled on every chair.

"I'm sorry to call so late, Mrs Webber."

"Miss." She pulled the kind of haughty look only a drunk can manage.

Beatrice made a rapid decision. "I'd like to talk to you about what happened at Swallows Hall."

The trajectory of glass to mouth did not falter. She sipped twice and cradled the glass to her chest as if afraid Beatrice might steal it.

"Swallows Hall? Haven't thought about that place in years. What do you want to know?" Her gaze rested on the flames of the gas fire.

"I want to know about your baby, the one they made you give away."

Eva's expression did not change. "Jen's very good, but she never thinks to get the tonic from the cold cabinet. There should be some ice in the freezer compartment."

The kitchen was messy, but not actually dirty. Beatrice found a clean teacup, popped out the last three ice cubes and opened the back door for some fresh air. When she returned, Eva was lighting a cigarette. She tipped the ice into her glass and swirled the contents with such little coordination that some spilt onto her lap.

"Thank you. You'd better tell me why you want to know."

A blanket of tiredness overcame Beatrice, exacerbated by the warm room, fug of smoke and lack of sleep. She wanted to walk out the door and leave this wretched woman to drink herself into oblivion. Instead, she turned off the television.

"That's not how it works. I ask the questions, you give me answers. If you don't want to talk, we'll go down to the police station. Of course, you'll have to leave the bottle behind. I know about your pregnancy, what the teachers decided, who was involved and how your baby was given up for adoption. What I don't know is anything about the child. I want you to tell me if it was..."

"He. Not it. I had a baby boy." She stirred the ice cubes with her middle finger, a tinkling sound providing a counterpoint to the pings of the gas filaments. "I never even held him."

Something in her tone checked Beatrice's exasperation. The woman wasn't talking to a police detective, she was talking to herself. Beatrice would need to sympathise, tease out, engage and encourage – but never demand.

"It must have been very hard for you. You were so young."

"I was fifteen." Her face collapsed into a grimace and Beatrice scrabbled in her bag to find tissues. By the time she'd found them, Eva was blowing her nose on an ancient handkerchief.

"I understand it's painful to bring all this up again. I wouldn't ask if it weren't important."

"They ruined my life. And his. I'll never stop wondering what might have been."

A thin line lay between emotional truth and maudlin sentimentality. Beatrice had to keep the woman focused or all she'd get would be a series of country and western clichés.

"I suppose you still think about him, wondering where he is now."

"I know where he is." For the first time, Eva looked directly at Beatrice. The rain cloud of grief left her face, leaving an expression of beatific joy in its stead. "He found me."

Her words pulsed through Beatrice like a shot of caffeine. The chill breeze from the kitchen pierced the stale air. Still in uncertain territory, Beatrice knew she was very near to getting the information she needed.

"How extraordinary! It's much harder to do that via private adoption agencies. He must have been very determined."

"He was. He said he'd never tried before, but he'll be fifty soon, so he decided to find me before it was too late. Fifty years." Eva was shaking her head as she reached for the Smirnoff.

Beatrice seized her opportunity. "How did he contact you?"

Her eyes were unfocused as she looked past Beatrice with a soft smile of reminiscence. "He came here. He sat right where you are sitting now."

"I cannot imagine how it must have felt to meet your son after all these years."

Tears spilt from Eva's glassy eyes as she laughed. "Nor can I. Not really. He turned up late and I'd had a few. When I found out who he was, I had a few more. I must have fallen asleep, because when I woke up, he'd put a cushion under my head and a blanket over me. He'd gone. I didn't get to say goodbye."

Beatrice tried to halt the slide into self-pity. "What can you remember, Eva?"

She sniffed. "He asked a lot of questions. He wanted to know why I gave him away. I didn't! Not willingly, I never had any choice! I told him that. I told him the truth about what they did."

"Did you tell him who was involved?"

Eva broke eye contact and shifted her focus back to the fire. "I don't remember. I said a couple of things, but..." The downward pull of her mouth reversed suddenly. "I tell you what, though. He's a looker. A real heartbreaker. Tall, handsome and he looks just like him."

"Like who? His father?"

Eva scowled and narrowed her eyes. "You're all the same, aren't you? They tried that. They tried every trick in the book. Threats and bribes and trying to catch me out, just like you. Didn't work. I didn't tell them who his father was. Never have and never will."

"Actually, I'm not really interested in his father. What I do want to know is who your son is and where he is now."

Eva hummed a few notes, a tune Beatrice couldn't make out. "I named him, my baby boy. I knew he was a boy and I knew I'd have to give him up and they'd most likely call him something else, but before he was born, I used to talk to him, sing to him and tell him stories. I called him Frankie. They all thought I was daft at school, you know. Me and my LPs. The other girls were crying and screaming over 45s of The Beatles and The Hollies and The Stones, but not me. I was an old-fashioned girl in many ways."

"Eva, your son? What name does he use now?"

She burst into loud cackles, pushing Beatrice's annoyance to the limit. She wanted to slap the silly old lush, who was rocking back and forth in amusement.

"You'll never guess what he does for a living! At a caravan park, in Dorset somewhere. When I told him why I'd named him Frank, his face was a picture."

Beatrice was already on her feet. "You called him Frank, after..."

"Ol' Blue Eyes. And now my little Frankie is..."

"A Sinatra impersonator." She walked into the hall and dragged out her mobile, leaving Eva mumbling the words to *New York, New York*.

The church bells struck the hour at exactly the same time as Beatrice's phone vibrated in her hand.

"Nikos! I was just about to call you. I need you to make an arrest. Take Toni Dean in for questioning and I'll gather all the evidence we need to charge him. Nikos? Are you there?"

"*Yes, I'm here. Beatrice, we have a problem.*"

"What is it?"

"*The ship is due to sail, but two people are missing. One is Toni Dean. The other is Oscar Martins.*"

Chapter 27

He smelt him before he saw him. Voulakis, as ever preceded by the smell of onions, entered the bridge, shadowed by Xanthou. Nikos acknowledged neither, concentrating on making notes and listening to Beatrice's voice at the other end of the line. Their third call in the space of an hour.

"*... two key aspects of concern. If they're working together, are they planning a second attempt on the life of Joyce Milligan, or returning to the UK to pursue the surviving Hirondelles? Or have they split to do both? What extra measures have you taken?*"

"Alerted all border controls, doubled hospital security and Forensics are in the process of analysing both their rooms, as you advised."

"*Good. Keep me informed of every development. I'll get a flight back as soon as I can, hopefully tonight. The taxi is approaching the airport now.*"

Nikos revolved his chair to face his colleagues. "Beatrice, one other thing. Chief Inspector Voulakis has taken over as senior investigating officer, so he'll be your key contact. I am currently in an assistant role. He's just arrived, in fact, so perhaps you should speak to him."

He heard her swear with surprising force. "*Why the hell has he stepped in?*"

Nikos summoned all his resources of diplomacy and hoped Beatrice would pick up the subtext. "After a complaint from Inspector Xanthou of the South Aegean Region, the Police Supervisory Board asked Chief Inspector Voulakis to take charge. The case is still a collaboration between the Cretan Regional Force and Scotland Yard.

The Chief Inspector has chosen to retain both myself and Xanthou as assistants. Would you like to talk to him?"

"*What I'd like to do is to kick Xanthou's arse. Bloody weasel. Still, at least they didn't give the case to him. Yes, put Voulakis on.*"

Trust her to get it first time. Nikos grinned, with no attempt to hide it, and handed the phone to Voulakis. He circled the name Toni Dean on the pad in front of him and vacated the seat to put some space between them.

"DI Stubbs, hello." Voulakis settled into the chair and looked at the paper. He beckoned Nikos. "Yes, a few changes in recent hours. And just ten minutes ago, I received a call from the airport police in Athens. They have detained Mr Oscar Martins, attempting to board a flight to London. I'm sending Inspector Stephanakis to interview him now."

Xanthou exhaled a sound of disgust and folded his arms. Neither Nikos nor Voulakis paid any attention.

"Yes, of course you can, if you can get a flight this evening or early tomorrow. I'll inform Stephanakis you'll join him in Athens. Here in Rhodes, Inspector Xanthou will take charge of hospital security and protecting the injured lady..."

Nikos scribbled her name on the pad.

"... Joyce Milligan. The *Empress Louise* must sail in approximately twenty minutes, but forensics teams are searching the cabins. I understand you have information about Toni Dean?"

As demotions go, it could have been worse. You could say a lot about Voulakis, but his management of the situation was both professional and partisan. Nikos was in position to make an arrest, while Xanthou was babysitting an old lady. Which must have been almost as infuriating as sharing his office with a senior Cretan officer with a passion for garlic, onions and olives. Each time fatigue hit Nikos while he waited in Athens Police HQ for Beatrice, he pictured that supercilious face wrinkling in disgust. It boosted his spirits without fail.

For the third time, he tried to focus on the Wikipedia biography of Oscar Martins. A respected professor with several publications to his name, a widow and father, nothing to link him to Dean or to Swallows Hall, and no police record. He tried the opposite route. Toni Dean's website ¬– *The Voice of an Era* – contained photographs, videos, testimonials and reviews but gave no personal information apart from contact details via Sunnyside Caravan Park in Weymouth. The ship's HR records were more useful, confirming Beatrice's findings, and showing Dean's age as fitting the profile of the Swallows Hall child. Yet none of his previous cruise ship contracts had coincided with voyages taken by Martins, so where did they meet? What would make two such men work together, if indeed they had?

A door opened. A uniformed officer, talking to someone out of sight, gestured towards Nikos. Beatrice. Her hair was wilder than usual as she marched across the deserted room, but her ready smile and bright eyes reassured him.

"Have you had any sleep since I last saw you?" he asked, holding out his hand.

She shook it and sat on the edge of the desk. "Enough. You?"

"No, but I can catch up. Depends on how long this takes."

"It won't take long. I'm quite sure Martins is unconnected to this case. We must make certain, of course, and exhaust every avenue of enquiry. Is there any news of Dean?"

"Nothing concrete, but the Wiltshire force sent an email this evening. Doreen Cashmore has received two anonymous phone calls. She found the first message on her answer phone. A male voice saying 'Welcome home'. The second call was more threatening. When she picked up, a man said 'Hello Doreen. You can run but you can't hide'. She's gone to stay with her family for a few days."

"Could they tell where the calls originated? This might be a smokescreen."

"They're working on it. All they know is the caller did not dial an international prefix. Whoever called her is in the UK."

"Hmm. Until we have proof he's followed them, let's work on the assumption he's still here. Now we really should get this interview over with. I'd prefer to observe, if you don't mind. I think it might complicate things if I were in the room."

She stood up but he remained seated and looked up at her. "Have you told me everything I need to know, Beatrice?"

Her eyes flicked downwards and she exhaled.

Tiredness made Nikos take a risk. "Voulakis said I would like working with you. He was right. Not what I expected but definitely an education. I respect your judgement. What I don't understand is why you'd risk being alone with a potential killer. Everyone on board knew who you were and why you were there. Martins engineered situations just to get close to you. Taking him to your room was..."

"Stupid. I agree. I feel more foolish than you know. Perhaps there is one thing I should say. Oscar Martins expressed an interest in me."

"I know. That's what I said."

"No, I meant a different kind of interest. Of the... er... romantic nature."

Nikos kept his expression blank. "He made a pass at you?"

"I suppose you could call it that. He kissed me."

"And what did you do?"

She dragged her gaze to meet his. "I kissed him back."

For the want of any better ideas, Nikos wrote that down. "Right. I see. In that case..."

"Yes. It's better if he doesn't know I'm here. You conduct the interview, I'll observe from behind the glass."

Either Oscar Martins was telling the truth or he maintained one of the best poker faces Nikos had ever encountered. No, he'd never met Toni Dean nor seen his act. No, he had no connections with the Hirondelles and had not dined with them once. Swallows Hall was not a name he was familiar with. He could offer little evidence of his activities ashore, as he explored the islands alone. Yes, he had left Detective Inspector Stubbs immediately prior to the attack on Joyce Milligan. Surely the *Empress Louise* had CCTV cameras which would prove his assertion that he had returned directly to his own cabin?

The *Empress Louise* had no CCTV, but Nikos knew key card

records would confirm if anyone had entered Martins' cabin at that time. Whose hand used the card was another question. Was he playing dumb? The man appeared eager to help and perfectly calm, so perhaps it was time to push him.

"We'll check. My problem is this. I have a list, not a long one, of people I wanted to question further. In one day, two people on that list disappear. No official check out, no request for a refund, nothing. When someone does that in the middle of a murder investigation, it makes me suspicious. So to eliminate you from my list, I need an explanation, Mr Martins."

"Of course. I apologise." He studied his hands for a moment. "Here you are, interviewing me, when far more pressing problems demand your attention. Particularly as I presume your colleague is still in the UK, handling that end of the investigation?"

Nikos said nothing.

"So then, let us be brief and you can get on with your job. I chose to leave the cruise for wholly selfish reasons. Since losing my wife, I tend to steer clear of personal relationships. Cruise ships such as the *Empress Louise* are stuffed to the gills with lonely folk on the prowl. As far as I'm concerned, they're welcome to each other. All I want is some occasional conversation, a change of scenery and plenty of peace and quiet.

"On this occasion, I encountered someone unexpected, in pursuit of something far more intriguing than a replacement spouse. I found myself drawn to her. She wasn't the slightest bit impressed with me or my books, which made me like her all the more. The same evening the unfortunate Milligan lady was assaulted, I made two startling discoveries. Firstly, the object of my affection was in a long-term relationship. Secondly, I'd fallen in love with her. What a silly old fool.

"In the cold light of day, I saw the situation as hopeless. Staying on the ship would only make things difficult for her and painful for me. I took the easy way out, Inspector. Better to leave immediately and do my best to forget her."

Nikos scratched his stubble, wishing there was a way round the unavoidably embarrassing question. "For the record, Mr Martins..."

Martins looked up and past him at the mirrored window. "I

think we all know I'm talking about Detective Inspector Beatrice Stubbs."

04.02. Beatrice was awake in her hotel room, staring through the darkness at the ceiling. Once again, Oscar's face flashed into her mind, looking directly at her as if the mirrored glass did not exist. Once again, she felt her colour rise, even as she lay alone in the dark.

Nikos had joined her in the observation room immediately after Oscar's confession and she'd been grateful for the lack of light. They agreed to release him without charge and Beatrice, the unforgivable coward, stayed where she was until a car had taken Oscar to an airport hotel. Hiding was gutless, certainly, but the alternative was too awful to contemplate. The pain in his eyes had been almost unbearable when she was in the next room. If they'd come face to face...

She turned over, towards the column of blue light from the hotel's neon sign seeping through the curtains. The feeling was unbearable precisely because she knew it only too well. She'd made her decision to cut off all contact with Matthew almost a quarter of a century ago but the agony of emptiness that followed was as raw in recollection as it had ever been. The hollow sense of nothing to look forward to, the conviction she could never be happy again, the constant ache of missing him and knowing he was going through the same. No matter how much she told herself she'd done the right thing, it made no difference and she banished all thoughts of alternatives.

And now Oscar was in another hotel room across the island in the same misery, wishing he'd never boarded the *Empress Louise*. She squeezed her eyes shut and forced herself to address the question of her own feelings. The discomfort and embarrassment, the fillip to the ego, the guilt and sadness all mingled together to echo what she'd said to James. *I can no longer bear to be in my own skin.*

Her attraction to Oscar was undeniable and she'd sensed the danger from the start. Yet she spent time with him, enjoyed the attention and even, if she was brutally honest, took some gratification from his attempts to charm her – all the while ignoring her partner of twenty-four years and his plans for their future together. The pattern of behaviour was not new. Immature, evasive and rebelling against... what? She scrunched up her eyes and tried to block out the question James had put. His voice and image took shape in her mind like a hologram.

To what extent are your fears about marrying Matthew related to your fear of becoming Pam?

The problem with truths is once they're inside your head, you cannot block them out. The time she spent with Matthew was perfect. Growing runner beans. Village life and knowing everyone's business. Bickering over breakfast. Cooking together and entertaining the girls. Mushroom-picking and walks in the forest. Sunday afternoons doing the crossword in the conservatory. She relished it all, at weekends. Much more so because she could still be the outsider with the exciting busy job in the city. She could escape.

To what extent are your fears about marrying Matthew related to your fear of becoming Pam?

In a whisper, she answered Hologram James as truthfully as she could.

"Because if that part of me is gone, there's nothing left to chase. All the time he can't have me, he'll keep trying. Once I give in, I've played the final card and I've been netted. Then all I can look forward to is a slow withering of interest until someone more exciting and lively catches his eye.

"My God. I'm actually afraid of myself."

She turned over again and tried to empty her mind by doing a few half-hearted yoga breaths. She had to be up in three hours. Her internal cinema screen replaced James with a close-up of Oscar's eyes. The colour of real ale in the firelight, crinkled up with laughter. Hypnotically intense and magnetic. Flat and deadened behind the glass.

Her mind flitted back to the taxi driver, and his 'Do as you would be done by.' When faced with personal gratification or the honourable thing to do, Oscar had chosen the latter.

Which made him a better person than her.

Chapter 28

The taxi hurtled along route 95 to Sgourou. Maggie nudged Rose and smiled. She was relieved to get a reassuring nod back. Rose had not been keen to spend their last day in Greece on a hospital visit. It had taken all Maggie's persuasive powers to drag her along, citing her own experience in a foreign hospital, thousands of miles from home, frightened and weak and very alone.

Maggie could not explain the sense of responsibility she bore to the Hirondelles, but she had to do something. A kind of atonement. After breakfast, they sought police permission to visit Joyce Milligan. The inspector, dressed more like a Brighton rocker than a detective, granted it easily.

The hospital had the air of a private nursing home and the approach bore out what the officer had said. This little clinic was much easier to keep secure than that sprawling great place in the centre of Rhodes. It had its own driveway, a small car park and none of the attendant chaos that comes with A&E facilities. The security checks at reception were rigorous and Maggie appreciated the inconvenience for Joyce's sake. An orderly escorted them to a private room, which had an officer outside and nurse within.

Perhaps because the safety arrangements had absorbed her attention, Maggie was unprepared for the emotional impact of seeing Joyce. Her face was a nightmarish patchwork of grey-blue bruises and raw pink abrasions, stitched together with ugly black thread. Although she was sitting up in bed, a tube ran into her nostril and a neck brace supported her head. Her wintry blue eyes looked pitifully vulnerable without her glasses. Maggie's throat swelled, preventing speech.

Rose never had that problem. "Joyce, we're so happy to see

you!" She stood at the foot of the bed, her tone cheerful. "Looks like you've been in the wars."

A familiar light danced in Joyce's eyes and her voice surprised Maggie with its strength.

"You should see the other fella."

The nurse smiled at their laughter and stood up to leave. Maggie was glad, as her presence and that of the orderly made her self-conscious.

"Not lost your sense of humour, then?" she asked.

"No, just my teeth."

Maggie couldn't swallow her gasp. "He knocked your teeth out?"

"Knocked them over, strictly speaking. They were in a glass by the bed. Fortunately, I always carry my old ones as spares ever since my sister's bulldog tried them on for size."

She flashed them a cheesy grin, provoking more laughter.

Rose parked herself at the end of the bed. "We thought a visit from us might cheer you up. How come it's the other way round?"

"You're very considerate and I'm grateful. Seeing two friendly faces is an absolute tonic. Now, where's the gin?"

Maggie glanced at the door and dropped her voice. "Even if you were allowed, which I doubt, we'd never have smuggled it past security. They're ferocious."

Joyce followed Maggie's sightline. "Spoilsports. No, I can't complain, they are taking very good care of me. I reckon they'll be glad to see me go, though, I must be a terrible nuisance. If the old bellows hold up after today's tests, I get a police escort to the airport and a first class flight home, courtesy of the cruise line. Speaking of which, shouldn't you be en route to Patmos by now?"

Rose explained the most recent developments, remaining factual and neutral about their departure and the cancellation of the cruise. Maggie leant against the windowsill to admire the grounds. It was nice to see a bit of greenery after all the sea and sunshine. Flowers and shrubs alongside brightly coloured benches surrounded a cluster of sun umbrellas over a patio. Maggie could think of worse places to convalesce. Several people in dressing gowns or uniforms strolled the path, a motorcycle courier walked back up the drive and an ancient Volkswagen took three tries to fit into a parking space. The driver finally emerged, a bent old man carrying a string bag of oranges who didn't bother locking the car.

That was when she heard it. The chainsaw rattle of a big bike, tearing through the silent afternoon. The sound distressed her for some reason. She had a feeling she'd heard it before.

After a late lunch back at the hotel, during which Rose chattered on enough for both of them, they retired to their room. Since beginning the cruise, they'd fallen into the habit of having an afternoon nap. In Greece, it seemed rather continental and modern, as opposed to sad and wasteful at home in Edinburgh. But today, Maggie had too much on her mind to sleep. She lay in silence for a few minutes then sat up and looked over at her friend's bed.

"I want to go back, Rose."

Rose, on top of her duvet, her hands folded across her stomach, didn't open her eyes. "Me too. I'm about ready for home. If we'd known Joyce was going back today, we could have booked the same flight. Never mind. We'll be on our way tomorrow."

"That's not what I mean. I want to go back to that day on Santorini. I want to remember everything that happened."

Rose opened her eyes and frowned. "And the point of that would be...?"

"I have a feeling I forgot something. Today, a wee memory popped up and I want to go over it again. Just to be sure."

With a deep sigh, Rose rolled to face Maggie. "Marguerite Campbell, it'll guarantee more nightmares, I warn you."

"Humour me. We wanted to explore Santorini on our own and we ordered a picnic."

"Very well. Yes, the picnic. We rented that moped and went looking for a spot where no one else could find us."

"Those narrow roads and all the tourist coaches made me nervous."

"Then we found that little lane up the cliff."

"You had your cornflower dress on."

"And you had a sun hat. There was a smell of rosemary."

"I saw a butterfly. I couldn't find the salt."

"We thought we were so clever, avoiding the crowds."

"We argued about the cruise. It was so quiet."

"Yes, the silence. The peace." Rose closed her eyes.

"Then I picked up the camera and saw those two people in an empty car park. I recognised the Hirondelle uniform. The man was a member of staff, I thought. You said I was rubber-necking. He picked her up and threw her and I couldn't understand what I was watching and I pressed the shutter just after he'd gone and I cried and you asked me what's wrong and it wasn't quiet any more because..."

"The motorbike."

"Yes, a big snarly noise..."

"... like a chainsaw."

"You remember!"

"Yes, I do. Because you could hardly speak and I couldn't even hear you when you did."

"The thing is, Rose, it's a special kind of motorcycle. I can almost see it. Handlebars high up, long sort of body and the people who ride them always have beards and sunglasses."

"Choppers. Like in *Easy Rider*. You're spot on. How peculiar we should think of that now. When we gave our statements, I was so busy talking about what we'd seen, I never thought about what we heard. I'm not sure it's important, but we should inform the police anyway. How about we go to the station after our nap?"

"I think we should go now."

Chapter 29

Nikos owed Beatrice a break. She put up a bit of a fight, but the combination of exhaustion and the awkwardness of last night soon prevailed. He insisted she get some rest. He'd slept better than she had, that much was obvious. Her face was shadowed and worn, like an ancient gravestone. He offered the use of his hotel room, which she eventually accepted. It would be another long day and she needed to get some sleep before escorting Joyce Milligan home that evening. Nikos took the Martins report and the details she'd found in Britain into the station.

In his pre-caffeinated state, he opted to avoid Xanthou and instead, in a corner of the police cafeteria, he reported directly to Voulakis. The reaction was not what he expected. Voulakis, jubilant, assured him they would both be home in Heraklion tomorrow. The suspect had been identified and traced to Britain; the Martins lead proved a dead-end and he could not wait to tell Hamilton that Beatrice Stubbs was breaking old romantics' hearts. As soon as Joyce Milligan was off Greek soil, they were home and dry. It was over to the Brits. They should both expect some high-level recognition for a job well done. He hurried off to call a photographer.

Nikos, unconvinced, got another coffee and found an empty space in the open plan office where he could use his laptop. Before recording the events of yesterday, he read the case notes, updated this morning by Xanthou. Something was wrong. Doreen Cashmore's answering machine had recorded another threatening phone call, this time traced to a payphone in a Dorset shopping centre. Three calls. No action. On the ship, three murders and one attempted with no hint of warning. This man used surprise to his advantage, so why advertise his intentions now? The result would be a terrified target, increased security and fewer opportunities for him to strike. It had to be a distraction. Attention on the Cashmore woman left him free to attack any other of the Hirondelles.

He had no choice but to call Xanthou. The response was typically unhelpful. No, he had not requested CCTV footage from the shopping centre in the UK. That would be a job for the British police. For the Hellenic Force, and the Rhodes Region in particular, this case was over. And he had a lunch appointment with his new girlfriend, so if Nikos didn't mind...

What a *malaka*. Nikos ignored the attitude and sent a rapid email to his contact in Wiltshire, asking for advice on getting images of the payphone or caller from the shopping centre security team. He called the hospital and checked Joyce Milligan was fit for travel. He bribed a sergeant into bringing him a falafel salad from the canteen and reread all his notes on Toni Dean. His eyelids were beginning to get heavy when his email pinged. Wiltshire's DS Helyar confirmed that Dorset Police had requested the footage from Brewers' Quay Shopping Centre. Security officers at the centre partially identified the caller at the precise time Doreen Cashmore received her third threat. The individual in question was known to security officers as an occasional nuisance, harassing schoolgirls, smoking joints and drinking alcohol on the premises. His name was Jez Callaghan, he was approximately twenty-five years old and his place of employment was Sunnyside Caravan Park, Weymouth.

Nikos checked Dean's website. The same caravan park. An indistinct image was attached. Baseball cap, angular bones, baggy jeans. Difficult to get too much of an impression of his face, but it was obviously a young man who looked nothing like Frank Sinatra. He emailed back, with a polite request that Jez Callaghan be brought in for questioning.

When Voulakis and Xanthou returned from their respective lunch meetings, Nikos was on the phone to Beatrice, who was impatient to be involved. He waved his notepad with some urgency and caught the cynicism in Xanthou's sly look. On the other end of the line, Beatrice announced she would come into the station to discuss procedure and hung up. The phone rang again immediately. It was the front desk.

Nikos got to his feet and addressed Voulakis. "There are two witnesses at reception who say they have some information about this case. I'll go. Just need to update you quickly first."

"No, no, you sit down. Xanthou can handle the witnesses. His English is fluent. But of course, he had an excellent teacher!"

He laughed at his own joke, eliciting the first unified response from his inspectors since the case began. Voulakis didn't seem to notice their cold lack of amusement and continued grinning at them both. Xanthou shook his head in disgust and left the room.

Voulakis heaved himself into the chair opposite Nikos, exuding goodwill and the unmistakeable scent of coffee and ouzo. That explained it. His boss's humour, crude at the best of times, reverted to schoolboy when he'd had a drink. He nodded and scratched his belly while listening to Nikos explain his discovery.

"Excellent! You are an exemplar to us all. The fact is, we can now hand this case over. We write up all our findings and hand it over. Successful conclusion for us! We should celebrate!"

"If Toni Dean is not in the UK, there is nothing to celebrate. He could still be here. When Xanthou returns, we need a briefing before the police escort departs for the airport. Everyone must be aware of this threat."

"Nikos, relax. You never stop! It's over and you did a great job. I'm giving you a glowing report. Let the Brits take it from here and we can get back to Crete. I don't know about you, but I find the food here very bland. We leave at four, pick the old woman up, take some pictures and send her off to the airport. Tomorrow's front page will be all about the heroic joint efforts by the Hellenic Police to keep the dear old thing safe from a nasty lady-killer. Let's just finish the paperwork and we can get a flight home tonight."

Although far from fresh when she arrived at the station, Beatrice looked better than she had that morning. When Nikos returned with a coffee for her, she was sitting bolt upright opposite Voulakis. A worried frown pinched her brows as she listened to the arrangements.

"A single outrider doesn't exactly qualify as a police escort, Inspector."

Xanthou entered the room and spoke before Voulakis could reply. "It's all we can spare. There's a summit at the Palace this week, involving several VIPs. It requires a lot of extra security."

"And don't forget you have Inspector Xanthou himself, who is trained in personal protection. It's not a long journey and we really have no reason to expect any problems," said Voulakis, with a reassuring if slightly patronising smile.

"As you say, it is not a long journey, and if you and Inspector Stephanakis are coming as far as the hospital, could you not come to the airport with us?"

Voulakis raised his shoulders to his ears and shook his head with exaggerated regret.

"Sadly not. We too have a flight to catch this evening, so must return to file our reports and close the case from the Greek side. I'm sure you understand how important the paperwork is." He wandered away in the direction of the coffee machine.

Beatrice followed him and continued talking. Nikos wished her luck, but held out little hope. If his boss could take the lazy route, he would.

Nikos looked at Xanthou. "And the witnesses?"

Xanthou ignored him, checking his emails.

Nikos cleared his throat and spoke louder. "Inspector Xanthou, what did the witnesses want?"

"Nothing. A waste of time. God, I am so looking forward to seeing the back of all you old women."

The one positive thing about the journey to Sgourou was having Beatrice as his sole passenger. Voulakis wanted to ride in the Jeep with Xanthou and examine the security features himself. An arrangement that pleased everyone.

She was quiet at first, looking out of the window. After about ten minutes, she spoke. "I wish it were you taking us to the airport."

"So do I. But so long as Xanthou and the other officer stay with you until you're in the Departure Lounge, I don't foresee any problems."

"No. Although I'd be a lot more relaxed if we knew Dean was definitely in the UK. Yes, you're right, the man would be insane to try anything here. You know, I am heartily sick of flying. When I get back, I am point blank refusing to travel anywhere which involves airports for at least a year. By which time, I hope to be retired."

"Retired? Already?"

"It's early retirement, if I can take it. I've had enough, Nikos. Time to leave it to hungry young talents like yourself. And I wanted to say, I really do think you are a talent. Working with you was a pleasure."

Nikos kept his eyes on the road but couldn't hold back the grin. "Coming from you that means a great deal. For me, it's been a real learning experience."

"Mostly on how to be unprofessional when it comes to suspects, I imagine." She returned her attention to the passing scenery of garages, ceramic factories and furniture stores.

"Shit happens, Beatrice."

She didn't respond, her forehead leaning against the window. The light industrial units petered out, leaving trees and shrubs.

"Listen, I'm not going to judge you. I wouldn't be with my girl-friend if we hadn't bent the rules a little. Do you ever think you'll come back to Greece? I'd like to introduce you to Karen. I think you two would get along." He indicated and pulled into the hospital driveway.

"Thank you. Yes, I think I probably will, one day. But it won't be on a bloody cruise liner. And I would be delighted to meet Karen. If you two ever happen to be in London, give me a call. I'll show you some of the city's best-kept secrets."

"I'll take you up on that. Oh shit, look at this. God help us."

Voulakis, Xanthou, a motorcycle outrider, two doctors and a nurse stood around a seated Joyce Milligan in front of the hospital door, while a photographer rearranged the tableau.

It took half an hour to get a sufficient variety of poses to satisfy Voulakis and do a formal round of thanks and farewells. Nikos ground his teeth. They could have dispensed with this whole PR job, escorted their guests to the airport and been on their way back by now. It was strangely sad to say goodbye to Beatrice, especially with an audience. Thankfully, Joyce complained that she'd received no cheek kisses and raised a laugh to break the moment.

The cases were stowed in the Jeep, Joyce Milligan was stretched out in the back seat, the staff waved on the steps, the motorcycle outrider was in position and the party was finally ready to depart. Voulakis belted himself into the passenger seat and sighed with satisfaction. The Jeep pulled away, the bike behind it, and with one last wave at the medics, Nikos followed them down the drive. An impulse tugged at him to turn left instead of right, but he gave a quick toot of the horn and turned back towards the city, watching them recede in his rear-view mirror.

"Relax, Nikos. They're in radio contact and we can keep up with them every step of the way."

"We could have been with them every step of the way if we'd skipped the photographs."

"Getting good PR for both regional forces and Scotland Yard cannot be underestimated. Yes, I was on the fussy side with the photographer, but it's important to project the best image of all of us. I wasn't going to let Xanthou, and therefore the South Aegean Region, grab all the limelight."

Nikos knew this was an appeal to unite against a common enemy and wished he had the maturity to resist. He was thinking about how to frame a response when Voulakis started laughing.

"What?"

"You know what he did? This morning, when I said we'd take pictures for the press, Xanthou went out at lunchtime to get his hair cut. The vanity of the man! I was coming back after lunch and saw him come out of Antonis the barber's."

Nikos joined in the laughter. "He told me he was lunching with his new girlfriend."

"Some girlfriend! Antonis is fifty-seven and has a moustache!"

"He's so false. Smiles and charm with Joyce Milligan for the pictures, but did you see the way he shoved her into the Jeep? At least Beatrice is with them. She'll look after her."

"I think he's had enough of old women today. Well, he can go back to preening himself in front of tourists from tomorrow."

"Yes, best place for him. Why has he had enough of old women? This case?"

Voulakis yawned. "I suppose. Not glamorous enough for him. Plus those two ladies came in this afternoon, the original witnesses, and he had to listen to their chatter for over an hour."

"Over an hour? Why?"

"Nothing important. They'd remembered something from the Santorini incident."

"Did he tell you what it was they remembered?"

"A noise, apparently. After seeing that man throw the old lady off a cliff, they heard a motorbike start. They heard it again this morning and recalled the sound. As Xanthou said, it's probably the closest thing to excitement in their lives, so they have to wring out every last drop."

Nikos snapped his head to look at Voulakis.

"A motorbike?"

"So they said. It's just a way of getting involved. That's why they went to visit the Milligan woman. Desperate to be part of the action."

Nikos indicated and pulled over into a concrete merchant's yard. "Wait. They visited Joyce Milligan?"

"Why are we stopping?"

"They heard the same sound of a motorbike? When? Where?"

"Today. At the hospital."

Nikos reversed into a three-point turn and started the siren.

Chapter 30

Joyce sighed as the car turned the bend and they lost sight of the hospital staff.

"Such lovely people. I wonder if I can come back next year, perhaps with fewer injuries."

Beatrice swivelled in her seat. "Even if you turned up bouncing with health, I'm sure they'd be delighted to see you. Are you comfortable?"

"Well, I'd rather be back there, riding pillion with him." She jerked her head at their escort. "I asked him if he was married, but he went all coy."

Xanthou, unsmiling, said, "He doesn't speak English."

Joyce pushed herself round to look out the back and gave the outrider a girlish wave, a ripple of gnarled knuckles. Beatrice chuckled to see him lift a gloved hand in response.

"You see, the language of love is universal." Joyce winced as she returned to her original position.

Beatrice frowned. "Joyce, are you..."

"I'm right as rain, my dear. Don't worry. Might just give the surfing a miss next weekend."

Xanthou indicated and took a quieter road uphill towards the centre of the island. The Jeep climbed to greener areas and Beatrice regretted the onset of dusk. Peaceful roads, forests and views of which they would see very little as the light faded.

"This is a quicker route than going back through the city, I assume?"

Xanthou nodded once, like an extra not paid enough for dialogue.

Beatrice tried again. "The journey takes around twenty minutes, I believe?"

"Depends on traffic."

So that would suffice for small talk. They rode in silence for several minutes, Beatrice inhaling the scent of evening foliage. She looked back at Joyce.

"Warm enough?"

"Snug as a bug in…" The remainder of the rhyme was drowned out by the roar of an overtaking motorcycle, startling Beatrice and causing Xanthou to touch the brakes.

"Idiot!" Xanthou spat.

He was right. Even on such quiet roads, overtaking on a bend was a stupid and unnecessary risk.

"Definitely," Beatrice agreed. The sound of the bike's engine faded into the distance.

"Drivers like that will be dead soon," said Xanthou.

"But sadly they take others with them." She flipped down the sun visor to look in the vanity mirror. "You all right in the back there?"

"Fine, Beatrice. A bit peckish is all."

"We'll have time for a snack at the airport. Our last chance to sample…"

Three things happened at once. Beatrice realised the road behind them was empty, with no sign of their escort. The police radio burst into life, urgent voices speaking Greek, and her mobile rang. Caller display showed Nikos Stephanakis. She hooked a finger in one ear to block out the background noise and answered.

"*Beatrice! Stop immediately. Dean may be lying in wait or following. I believe he's still in the area. We're about five minutes away, so stop now and turn around. We'll meet you. Tell the outrider to keep his position at the rear.*"

Beatrice looked behind them. "OK, we'll stop right away. But our outrider has disappeared."

Nikos swore. She ended the call and tried to attract Xanthou's attention. He was yelling into the police radio and driving faster than was safe.

"Stop the car, Inspector! We have to turn around!"

"Don't be stupid. This is a few old ladies creating a fuss over nothing. And Stephanakis is one of them. We're going to the airport as planned. And if Dean is following us, turning round delivers the chicken straight into the fox's jaws." He turned the radio volume to a background buzz and drove still faster.

"Inspector, I am senior officer here. You obey my orders. Stop the..."

Xanthou braked sharply, causing Beatrice to drop her mobile. On the road ahead, stark in the glare of the headlights, lay a motorcycle and its rider. The torso was clearly visible while the lower body seemed trapped beneath the chassis. There was no sign of movement. Xanthou switched off the engine, unclipped his seatbelt and withdrew his gun.

"No!" Beatrice caught hold of his jacket. "If this is an ambush..."

Xanthou shook her off. "... then I am armed. If not, I can help. Call an ambulance." He got out of the car, his gun trained on the stricken biker, and approached.

Beatrice scrabbled for her phone and scanned the surrounding woodland. The silence, the forest, the cool evening air stretched her senses to screaming point. Once she'd located her mobile, she twisted to reassure Joyce, who was staring past her at the road ahead.

"Beatrice...?"

"Don't worry, he'll be fine. He's..."

A shot blasted out, ringing round the trees and shocking both women into silence.

Xanthou crumpled and hit the ground.

The body under the bike remained inert, but out of the trees, a figure emerged. Dressed in a black ski mask and a leather jacket unremarkable in its lack of identifying features, the man trained his gun on the Jeep.

"Joyce, get down. As low as you can." Beatrice opened the glove compartment, but found no gun. She dialled Nikos on her mobile with shaking fingers.

"Officer down," she whispered. "Passenger safe. Armed man approaching."

The figure moved towards Xanthou, his focus still on the Jeep. Beatrice glanced to her left and checked the ignition. Xanthou had left the keys there. Faintly she could hear Nikos's voice from the mobile and Joyce's uneven breathing. A brace of sitting ducks. She released her seatbelt. His gun still trained on the car, the man kicked Xanthou's prone body and looked down. There was no response. He snatched up Xanthou's gun, straightened and began to approach the Jeep. His mask hid his features but she caught a flash of white teeth in the headlights as he yelled in her direction, his gun aimed at Beatrice's face.

"Stubbs! Put your hands where I can see them!"

Beatrice dropped the phone into her lap and raised her palms to the level of her head.

Joyce's shaking voice came from the back seat. "Go, Beatrice. Get out now and God bless you."

Beatrice did not move. "I'm not leaving you."

The man paced towards them.

"Go on. He's not interested in you. Get out and go. Please don't ask me to meet my Maker with you on my conscience." Her voice broke.

Beatrice's whole body shook, but she remained where she was. "No. I have a duty of care."

"So did I." She was crying, her words hard to make out. "We thought we were doing the right thing. Please, Beatrice..."

The gunman opened Beatrice's door.

Chapter 31

As the car rounded the corner, Nikos took in the situation in a millisecond. In the headlights, a bike and a body. The outrider. The temptation to ride on past and find Dean arose but Nikos slammed on the brakes, hit the hazard flashers and drew his weapon.

The motionless uniform lay at the edge of the road, his bike on its side about twenty metres farther ahead. Nikos handed his mobile to Voulakis, instructed him keep listening to Beatrice and to call an ambulance. He got out of the car and approached the uniformed man. The headlights illuminating his movements made him a perfect target if anyone was lying in wait. He crouched beside the motorcycle officer, whose name he couldn't recall and holstered his weapon. The helmet was scratched and scuffed. He lifted the visor, holding his breath. No blood, eyes closed, breathing regular, strong pulse.

"Can you hear me? Are you hurt?"

No response.

He squinted at the car and saw Voulakis setting up a POLICE warning sign on the bend. When he looked back down, the motorcyclist's eyes were open.

"Hi, hello? Can you hear me?"

"Where's my bike?"

"Here. It's fine. Do you know what happened?"

He tried to sit up. Nikos put a hand on his shoulder. "Stay still. Wait for the ambulance crew."

The rider relaxed onto the ground.

"Someone hit me. A biker. He tried to overtake and I signalled to stand back but he did it anyway and hit me with I-don't-know-what. I came off the bike and..."

"What's your name?"

"Tsipras."

"What day is it?"

"Thursday."

"What kind of bike do you ride?"

"Honda Transalp, XL700V."

"You'll be fine, Tspiras."

"Is he hurt?" Voulakis had joined them.

"I can't tell. He needs to be checked by an expert. Let's leave the helmet in place." Nikos rested his hand on the rider's arm. "How are you feeling?"

"Weird. Dizzy. Shit! What happened to the ladies?"

The very question tearing at Nikos. He stood up and faced Voulakis.

"Sir, I'm going after the Jeep. Dean is on two wheels and while I'm in pursuit, I want the same advantages. I'll take Tspiras's bike; you stay with him and keep trying DI Stubbs. Radio and mobile. I'm going to need back-up so move the police vehicle to one side."

He grabbed his mobile and ran for the Honda. It had been a while since his motorcycle cop days, but this kind of bike and Nikos were made for each other. He heaved it upright and swung into the saddle. Seven words pulsed through his mind as he gunned the ignition. Beatrice's voice, professional and calm. "*Officer down. Passenger safe. Armed man approaching*".

Beatrice heard Joyce flinch as the gunman wrenched open the door.

"Get over and drive. Do it quickly and don't make me hurt you."

He shoved her shoulder with his left hand, while the right continued to aim his gun at her. She clambered over the gearstick and lifted her legs after her.

"Mr Dean, my driving skills..."

"My name is not Mr Dean. Now fucking move!" He turned the police radio off.

She started the car, put it into first and moved forward, easing around the fallen bike, its dummy rider and the immobile shape that was Inspector Xanthou.

A strong smell of ammonia hit her nostrils. Joyce Milligan's fear had manifested itself. The man swore and opened his window. In the mirror, Beatrice couldn't see Joyce at all and assumed she was still in the foot well.

"Come on, speed it up." A bass, rough, West Country accent through gritted teeth. In only five words, this voice revealed itself as far from the transatlantic syrupy timbre of Toni Dean. If not Dean, who the hell was under the mask?

She accelerated and changed gear. He slid down in his seat and reached for something on the floor. Beatrice's mobile. He tossed it out of the window without taking his eyes from her.

Dusk had departed and night crept over the landscape. The scene was monochrome and sinister in the headlights, trees casting long-fingered threats across the grey tarmac.

"Slow down. Now turn right. Don't indicate! Yes, that track there. Go on."

Sandy and overgrown as it was, the track was no match for a police Jeep. They bounced and lurched away from the main road, branches and brambles scratching at the windows, causing Beatrice to duck more than once. Moonlight made visibility surprisingly clear. Nevertheless, Beatrice switched to full beam, mainly to advertise their own visibility. Her concentration on the terrain concealed frantic activity in her head.

How to get him off guard, how to alert the rest of the force to their location, how to protect Joyce without getting herself hurt in the process, how to convince the gunman she was no threat.

After a few minutes, in which Beatrice grew increasingly concerned by the total absence of sound or movement from the back seat, the track descended steeply into a small clearing with a stone-built herder's cottage in the centre. It seemed long abandoned, although there were signs of recent activity judging by the amount of tyre tracks in the dust.

She brought the Jeep to a bumpy halt, but didn't switch off the engine.

"Don't stop here. Pull up to the hut."

A memory, or rather the resentment of one, surfaced in Beatrice's half-consciousness. A police driving instructor, who thought he was a Marine drill sergeant, teaching her to drive. *What are you doing?! Put it in first! No, don't accelerate yet, you moron! Hear that? That's the gearbox screaming! What is wrong with you!?* He'd tried to humiliate her into tears. He failed, she passed. Most importantly, she learned more about power games than driving.

She pressed down on the accelerator and clutch simultaneously, then tried shoving the gearstick into first. The graunching clash of metal made her wince.

"For fuck's sake!"

"I'm sorry," she sniffed, breaking her own breaths to sound nervous and emotional. "Driving isn't really..."

"Right. Stop the car here and get her out."

"Mr Dean, can I say something?"

"MY NAME IS NOT FUCKING TONI DEAN! Just shut your mouth. If you keep quiet and do as you're told, I'll leave you out of it. Just get her out of the car. Do not talk to me and DO NOT get in my way!"

Spittle flew from the gap in the ski mask. Beatrice could not see his eyes, which under the circumstances, was a good thing. She opened her door.

Contrary to expectations, Joyce was conscious. She said nothing and her eyes were unreadable in the dark. Her skin was both moist and cool, a smell of urine emanated from her clothes and she doubled over in pain as Beatrice helped her from the car. Yet her grip on Beatrice's hand was as strong as ever. The man watched them from a short distance, his gun as still as a signpost and his Maglite pointed to the entrance. He gestured with his head for them to go inside.

The building resembled a bunker. Squat, square with a flat roof and thick walls, a rough wooden door and deep-set windows without shutters. Outside, a few large rocks circled the remains of a bonfire.

Beatrice shoved open the door into blackness and immediately thought of spiders. She supported Joyce as they stood just inside the doorway. With an impatient exhalation, the man pushed past and lit an old-fashioned kerosene lamp. A weak yellow glow reflected off the whitewashed walls. No spiders, breadcrumbs on the table and the scent of a recent fire. So this was where he'd been hiding. The barrel of the gun directed them to the single bed against the wall. Beatrice and Joyce sat, clutching each other's hands. The man paced to each window, listening and checking, his gun cocked. Finally he turned to look at them. He let the gun fall to his side and seemed to be waiting for them to speak.

The mask induced a disproportionate amount of fear. Beatrice tried to convince herself it was only a stage crooner under there, a man who dyed his hair and bleached his teeth and should have been in Butlins. It didn't work. They waited for him to say whatever it was he needed to say. Whatever it was that had made him kill three elderly women and attempt to murder a fourth. What drove him to shoot one police officer and abduct another. He would need his moment. They always did. Whether to camera, to victims, to YouTube, they needed their fifteen minutes.

Right on cue, he slipped his hand under the neck of the ski mask and eased it off his head. A feeling of vindication and sickness swept over Beatrice.

Nikos was right. Toni Dean. The tan, the teeth, the bleached hair. She clenched Joyce's hand so hard she heard the poor woman whimper. He'd just shown his face to two witnesses. Which implied that after tonight, no one would be left to identify him.

Chapter 32

Each time Nikos took his hand from the throttle, he could hear distant sirens behind him, growing louder. Ambulance? Back-up? He hoped it was both. The road wound upward, the temperature dropped and moonlight through the trees created a cinematic effect. He needed another pair of hands. Not just an officer in support but two more limbs with opposable thumbs to hold his gun while he steered.

On the straight, he drove as fast as he dared. At every corner, he slowed, not only for safety but to avoid announcing his arrival. On an awkward bend, he thought he saw a light flash through the forest but when he looked again, it had disappeared. His inattention to the road, even for a second, was a bad idea. Ahead, stark in the single beam of the headlight, lay two bodies, one under a Harley Davidson Chopper. Nikos braked, dismounted the Honda and readied his gun.

The decoy under the Harley did not concern him. Xanthou, on the other hand, lay on his back with his hands pressed to his chest. His eyes were closed and his lower jaw spasmed, chattering his teeth together.

"Xanthou!"

No response.

Nikos checked his pulse and noted the blood seeping through the clothes beneath his clenched hands. He ran back to the bike to radio Voulakis.

"At the scene. Xanthou has a serious gunshot wound to the chest. This injury is life-threatening so make this the ambulance's priority. The police Jeep is missing, as are its passengers and there

201

is no sign of Toni Dean. They can't have gained too much distance, so I am going in pursuit."

He tore the Mylar blanket from the first-aid kit and rushed back to the shivering detective. The reflective material would keep him both warm and visible.

"Xanthou, listen to me! Medical help is coming." He tucked the blanket around his body and patted his face. "I have to leave now. Dean has taken Joyce Milligan and DI Stubbs. You'll be fine and the ambulance is only a few minutes away. I have to go. Sorry. Just... hang on."

He kicked the Honda into life and drove away, clenching his teeth and wishing his medical training would stop the cold hard facts pounding through his brain: chest-wound, internal blood loss, patient into shock, lungs fill. Cause of death – drowning in own blood.

Nothing you can do but get him to hospital. If you stay and hold his hand, you'll only be there to watch him die. Find Beatrice. Find Joyce. Find Dean.

They must have taken the Jeep but how the hell was he supposed to know where? The Filerimos forest boasted many tracks up and around the monastery.

A small blue glow, like a pilot light, shone from the verge. Nikos drew alongside, donned gloves and picked up the phone. Missed calls: Voulakis, Voulakis, Stephanakis, Stephanakis, Stephanakis. All callers trying to contact Beatrice Stubbs.

Astride the bike, Nikos closed his eyes and concentrated with an intensity he'd never used before. Why hadn't Dean shot them there and then and left them to bleed to death like he had Xanthou? He intended to kill Milligan, Nikos had no doubt. Why the hiatus? Dean had taken them somewhere else for a reason. Torture? Interrogation? Whichever, it couldn't be public and it couldn't be far.

Nikos bagged the phone and stuffed it in his jacket. He was just reaching for the radio when he heard a sound. An ugly crunching of gears, the sort of noise you'd make when driving a strange vehicle. It came from the forest.

The police Honda purred cautiously along the road, Nikos watching for any kind of right turn into the woods big enough to accommodate a Jeep. A siren further down the route grew closer. An ambulance, please God. He crossed himself and offered a prayer for Xanthou's health. Then a break in the trees, tyre tracks and a right turn. Nikos crossed himself again.

Uneven terrain and an uncertain reception made him cautious, clashing with the imperative to roar ahead and prevent whatever Toni Dean had planned. The dusty, stony track ascended to a peak and Nikos knew his headlamp would shine over the ridge like a searchlight. He killed the lights and edged up to the ridge as quietly as the bike would allow. Below, a squat stone cottage sat in a clearing. The Jeep, parked in the shadows, appeared empty. Nikos scanned the area but the only sign of life was the dim glow coming from the cottage. He switched off the police radio and called Voulakis on his mobile. He kept his voice low. Voulakis promised caution and assured him that back-up, mere moments away, would approach with stealth. Nikos pulsed the throttle once and allowed the impetus and gravity to propel him towards the stone building.

Close enough. He left the bike behind the Jeep; accessible for a rapid escape, but sufficiently hidden from the windows. There was no glass in any of them and sounds up here would carry like goat bells. Communications devices on silent, Nikos withdrew his weapon and emerged from the cover of the Jeep.

Inside the cottage, a shadow crossed the window. A weak solitary light barely cast enough illumination to create a reflective square on the ground, yet Nikos focused his whole attention on the dim ochre gap as he crept forward.

"Stubbs, stand up and turn around." Dean stood in front of her, a roll of masking tape in one hand, and his gun in the other. With one last squeeze of Joyce's hand, Beatrice did as she was told. He wrapped the tape around her wrists, yanking painfully on her shoulders to test it was secure. She made no attempt to pull her wrists apart once he'd finished, knowing it would induce panicky feelings of impotence. Instead, she sat beside Joyce and took calm breaths.

"Right. Better safe than sorry. You are a copper, after all. See, you shouldn't even be here. I've got no beef with you. But you can't stop interfering, can you? That's what you're all about. Interfering in other people's lives."

He walked away, facing the window. Joyce laid her hand on Beatrice's arm. A gesture of reassurance, but her trembling set Beatrice off like a mimosa tree. He cleared his throat as if to prepare himself and dragged a chair from the small table. He sat opposite, resting his right hand – the one with the gun in it – on his left. Close up, the Dean sheen was less polished than usual. The contact lenses were missing. His trademark baby blues were a pale grey, reddened and bloodshot as if he'd not slept. His dyed hair lacked its flyaway, freshly shampooed bounce and hung limp across his right ear. The only sign of the showman was a smudge of mascara beneath his eye. So whether on stage or planning an ambush, the man still enhanced his eyelashes. Beatrice began to see how little she understood this person and his motives.

"And you, Joyce Milligan, you'd know all about interfering, wouldn't you? Playing God and ruining lives. Do you know how long I've spent wondering why? Give or take a few months, thirty-eight years. They told me the summer before I started secondary school. 'In case I found out from someone else.' Thirty-eight years wondering why my parents didn't want me. What a waste. I went through every scenario. I'd been kidnapped and sold. They'd been killed in a car accident and I somehow survived. He was famous and handsome and secretly watched me grow up from afar. She died in childbirth and he couldn't cope alone. He'd left her and she'd turned to prostitution. They were desperately poor and wanted the chance of a better life for me, but giving me away broke their hearts and they died of consumption. Yeah, right."

He beat the gun against his palm. Beatrice searched for something to say. Dialogue would buy time.

"Many adopted children..."

"SHUT UP! Shut your trap right now or I'll shut it for you. In fact, fuck it. This is not about many adopted children, it's about me. And it's none of your fucking business."

He jumped to his feet and grabbed the tape, tore a stretch off with his teeth and slapped it violently across Beatrice's mouth, knocking her backwards. The smack reverberated through her head, inducing tears of pain and the taste of blood where she'd bitten her tongue. He pulled her upright by her hair and pressed his face close to hers.

"You never listen. None of you. Can't tell them, 'cos they think they know best. If you can't tell them, you got to show them. One more time, Stubbs, and I will teach you the lesson you fucking well deserve." He brought his tensed fist to her cheek and snarled into her face.

Beatrice tried to stem the panic, breathing through her nostrils, inhaling Dean's sour breath. Beside her, Joyce whimpered, distracting his attention.

"Shut up, Milligan! Or you get the same. Listen, I could have killed you in the car. The only reason you aren't dead yet is because you have to understand what you did. You wrecked my life, and hers. Have you seen her lately? She's a fucking mess. Your fault! Everything I've ever done has turned to shit because I spent my life wondering why I wasn't good enough. It was your fault! Now I'm pushing fifty and I'm still doing the rounds on floating retirement homes. Your fault!"

He walked away, shaking his head. Beatrice watched his heaving back as he tried to get his emotions under control. He spoke, his voice calmer.

"I stopped wondering and decided to find out for myself. A private detective got the info in about ten days. My father wasn't a movie star. My mother wasn't dead. He was 'Unknown' and she was a fifteen-year-old schoolgirl. That was all there was to it. Some silly little slut got up the duff, gave the baby away and forgot all about it."

He turned back to face them, his eyes wide and an unsettling smile on his face. His gun rested in his hand, pointing away from them for now.

"The detective was worth the expense. Her home address was in his report. So I went there, with one thing on my mind. I wanted to wreck her life like she'd wrecked mine. To make her take responsibility. But she wasn't responsible, was she, Joyce?"

Hyperventilating through her nostrils was making Beatrice

light-headed. She willed herself to slow her breathing down, inhaling deeply and relaxing into the release. She had to stay conscious. Beside her, Joyce seemed catatonic, hypnotised by Dean. Her body, pressed against Beatrice, no longer shook with fright and she shed no more tears. She seemed patient and resigned to her fate.

"No. Responsibility belongs to The Hirondelles. A fucking bunch of dried-up spinsters took her choices away. And mine too. You conniving hags, with no life of your own, you destroyed us. You might as well have drowned me at birth. But you didn't and I found you and made each of you pay."

He cocked his weapon, aiming at Joyce's forehead. "It's finished now. You are the last."

"I'm not the last."

"You are. The Hall woman is going to live the rest of her life terrified of her own shadow, which is exactly what she deserves. Couple more calls should bring on a heart attack, I reckon. So yes, you are the last."

Joyce spoke, her voice weakened but steady. "You killed two of my friends and then you sang at their memorial service."

A flash of those teeth again. "Yes, I enjoyed that. Nice touch, wasn't it?" He opened his mouth and sang the first line of *My Way*, not taking his eyes off her.

Joyce stared right back.

"Me too. Few regrets. Just the one. I really wish I had."

Dean's expression did not change. "What? Wish you had what?"

"Drowned you at birth."

Waiting for the right moment was a matter of assessment, opportunism, snap judgement and a cool head. The lighting was poor and Nikos found it impossible to judge the layout at such a distance. At one point, Dean came to the window and stared out into the darkness. Nikos could not see the man's gun and without any knowledge of the scene inside, dared not pull his own trigger. Nor did he dare move in case he gave his position away.

Dean retreated and Nikos heard shouting. This was the right moment. In a low ducking run, he reached the window and flattened himself against the wall.

Dean kept up a monologue, of which Nikos heard snatches. 'My father wasn't a movie star,' 'Responsibility belongs to The Hirondelles,' but the content was of less importance than the sound. Each time his voice became less distinct, Nikos knew he'd turned away from the window. He edged closer and moving his torso like an Egyptian dancer, managed to get his eye and gun around the window frame.

Dean had his back to Nikos, whereas Beatrice and Joyce faced in his direction. His blood raced as he saw the tape across Beatrice's face and her hands behind her. Neither woman could see him, their attention held by the man towering over them with a gun dangling from his hand.

Joyce Milligan said something and Nikos detected a change in atmosphere. Dean's voice rang out in song, an eerie sound in the moonlit forest. Nikos watched him step back and aim his gun at Joyce Milligan. He had to take the chance. He aimed for the right shoulder, an attempt to disable rather than kill, and upwards in case the bullet continued its trajectory. He pulled the trigger and for the first time in his life, shot a man in the back.

Dean jerked forwards, the gun slipped out of his grasp and clattered onto the flagstones, and he went down, first onto his knees then onto his left side, and collapsed.

Nikos pressed his hands onto the windowsill and heaved himself up. He climbed over the sill and landed softly on the ground beside Dean. He picked up the handgun and clicked on the safety catch, stuffing it in his belt.

Beatrice's breathing was shallow and her eyes bulged. He holstered his own weapon and went to release her. She shook her head and used her eyes to indicate Dean. He looked over his shoulder. The man was inert and posed no threat. He tore the tape from Beatrice's mouth.

"He's got Xanthou's gun!"

A rush of movement behind Nikos set off an automatic reflex. In one fluid movement, he withdrew his weapon, twisted over his shoulder and without a second's hesitation, pulled the trigger. Dean jolted and slumped back.

Above his own ragged breathing in the shocking aftermath of the gunshot, he heard Joyce Milligan reciting the Lord's Prayer.

Blood trickled like a meandering stream from a bullet hole on the right shoulder of the leather jacket. But the fatal shot was to the neck, an ugly wound now pulsing blood in gouts. In Dean's left hand, a police issue Heckler and Koch. Due to the nature of the injury, Nikos did not attempt to check the carotid pulse, instead taking Dean's gloveless right hand to confirm what he already knew.

Nikos Stephanakis had just killed a man.

Chapter 33

Joyce Milligan's wish to return to the Kalithera Clinic in Sgourou was granted far sooner than she could have imagined. Beatrice doubted the staff had sufficient time to change the sheets. Distressed and emotional, the octogenarian was cleaned up, given a sedative and as much reassurance as possible. Reduced yet visible security remained in place. While Toni Dean would be committing no further acts of revenge, the question of an accomplice had not been resolved.

Beatrice wanted to go to the Andreas Papandreou Hospital to see Xanthou. His condition was critical and her collegiate loyalty compelled her to his side. But she also wanted to remain at the scene to gather evidence with Nikos and the crime scene crew. After all, she had been the only person to witness who, what, when and how. Plus she knew why.

In the end she did neither. Voulakis insisted she go to the clinic with Joyce and get checked by a doctor. He escorted Xanthou to hospital, and Nikos took charge at the scene. The Hirondelles had been informed so as not to prolong the agonies. For the moment, Beatrice was redundant.

After Joyce had finally let go of Beatrice's hand and submitted to sleep with a grudging resentment, Beatrice bit her tongue and underwent a full examination. Her mind was full of Xanthou's waxy pallor, the terror of facing a masked gunman, the shock of watching a person killed in front of her and the constant voice reminding her of all her mistakes. She needed to be with Nikos. Her white angel repeated *Dean's dead. It's over. He can't hurt anyone else.* Her black demon said nothing. He simply shook his head.

At eight o'clock she arrived at the police station to find Nikos alone in the canteen, bent over his laptop. He saw her and stood up to pull out a chair.

"Are you OK? Shouldn't you be at the clinic?" he asked.

"I'm fine. The doctor said so. A bit shaken, obviously, but I had to come here. Any news?"

His shoulders sagged. "No. Critical is the last I heard."

"Why are you in the canteen? I went looking for you in the office."

"Guess how popular I am with the Rhodes officers? While one of their inspectors is fighting for his life, I have to report him for misconduct. He dismissed two important witnesses and ignored key evidence which could have averted the situation. Not only that but disobeyed an order to turn around. The South Aegean Division of the Hellenic Police is going to hold an inquiry. Here, in Rhodes. Voulakis and I will have to testify."

"What happened to the outrider?"

"Dean broadsided him and he crashed into the forest. Concussion and some stitches is all. He'll have to take the stand as well."

Beatrice waited for his eyes to stop roaming. "Regardless of Xanthou's injuries, you wouldn't be doing your job if you didn't accurately report what happened."

"If that stupid bastard dies, he'll be a hero and we'll look like cheap rivals trying to score a point."

"You couldn't have done otherwise. The truth has to come out."

"I know." He formed a visor with his hands and looked down at his keyboard. Beatrice waited. That was one of the main reasons she was here. Sharing their joint experiences and the emotional impact was an essential part of the debrief. It should never be rushed.

He looked at her sideways, his deep brown eyes clouded. "I'm the one who should really be under investigation. I shot a man."

"Was that the first time you've had to kill someone in the line of duty?"

His jaw clenched and he nodded once.

"Don't worry. I'm not going to say anything as trite as 'It gets easier'. It doesn't, at least not for me. I've been put in that situation twice, where you're forced to choose your own life over someone else's. I chose mine and those two people's deaths, or rather lives-that-might-have-been, still haunt me. The fact is, you shot someone who would have shot you, or me, or Joyce instead."

"I didn't know that at the time."

"You did. I told you he was armed."

"I didn't see the gun. I couldn't see his left hand. The light was bad, he wore a black glove and I just reacted to the movement. He could have been unarmed and asking for help."

Beatrice observed the muscles work in Nikos's jaw. "In an extremely pressured situation, you made a judgement call. It was the right one. Beating yourself up over whether it might have been wrong is pointless and a waste of energy. So stop it."

The silent, empty, darkened canteen seemed to echo her words. The laptop screen illuminated Nikos's eyes.

"Is it that easy?"

"No. I told you. It doesn't get easier. You have to fight it every day. Ask yourself what would have happened if you hadn't shot Dean when you did. Right now, I'd be on the phone to Karen, breaking the news of how a second's indecision led to the premature end of your career. Of your life."

He said nothing and Beatrice let the image play out in his mind. Eventually he looked at her again, resignation ageing his smooth features.

"You're right. Thank you. As first cases go, I could have had an easier one."

"But would you have learned as much? About yourself, I mean."

"Maybe not but at least I'd be able to get some sleep. This week..."

The display lit up on his phone. He answered and Beatrice watched his face for clues as the conversation, monosyllabic and in Greek, told her nothing. He didn't talk for long and placed the phone back on the table. His jaw muscles began pulsing again.

"That was Voulakis, at the hospital. Xanthou died twenty minutes ago."

Chapter 34

Admin Assistant Melanie squealed when Beatrice walked into the office at New Scotland Yard on Friday afternoon.

"You been in Greece!" she said, in the same tone one would use when congratulating a person on a promotion or pregnancy.

"Yes, I have. Why..."

"It's on my shortlist!"

Beatrice took a second to re-enter the alternative world of Melanie. "Ah, the honeymoon destination shortlist."

"No, Beatrice! You're getting scatty, you are. This is for the Hen Weekend. Honeymoon's been sorted for ages. Luxury Caribbean cruise for three weeks."

"Oh yes, cruise ships. I've heard they're lovely."

"Holiday of a lifetime. So, dish the dirt on Greece, then. Food, people, toilets, air-conditioning, door handles, quality of entertainment and safety levels for single women?"

"Melanie, let's have a coffee one of these days and I'll fill you in on... did you just say door handles?"

"Too right. Couldn't get on with them in Milan. Me and my sister got stuck in the restaurant bathroom for half an hour 'cos we couldn't figure out how the door handle worked."

"I see. The thing is, I need to talk to Hamilton. Is he in his office?"

"Yeah. In a right antsy mood an' all. Best of luck."

For the first time, Hamilton's scowl actually lifted when she entered the room. Rather than their usual arrangement – she opposite as if in the headmaster's office – he stood up and gestured to the visitor corner. With a certain discomfort, she sat in the leather armchair while he opened a cabinet.

"You're not driving, are you, Stubbs?" he asked.

Door handles, driving... she was beginning to feel as if someone had changed the code and forgotten to tell her.

"No sir. I don't, if I can help it."

"Good. It's Friday evening, almost, so I think a small toast to your achievement might be in order. I presume you drink whisky?"

"Yes, sir." Her unease grew. Hamilton in 'a right antsy mood' was offering her a drink and using expansive terms such as 'achievement'? Something was wrong.

He handed her a crystal glass and raised his own. "A job well done. Serial killer apprehended, case closed and satisfied collaborators. Your good health!"

"Good health," she replied and took a sip. The taste was strong, peaty, smoky and warm. It made her think of wild coasts and heretics.

Hamilton eased himself into the chair opposite and crossed his legs. "Chief Inspector Voulakis is very pleased. The loss of the South Aegean Inspector was a damn shame, but as far as I understand, that was largely his own fault. Operation closed and most satisfactory. Apparently you and the Stephanakis chap made a jolly good team. Might be able to offer him something here at a later stage."

Beatrice tried a quick smile. Hamilton's brow creased.

"What is it, Stubbs? Come on, spit it out."

"I agree, sir, the case was brought to a conclusion of sorts and I'm pleased the remaining ladies are safe. Inspector Stephanakis made a superlative colleague. I'd very much like to work with him again. It's just that witnessing two fatal shootings tends to spoil the mood for celebration somewhat."

"Hmm. Full picture, Stubbs. On the instructions of Inspector Nikos Stephanakis, Wiltshire police arrested one Jeremy Callaghan, identified as the anonymous caller. Also known as Jez. Didn't take much for him to buckle. Seems he and Dean, real name Keith Avis, have worked at the same caravan park for the past five years. This Callaghan character gave DS Helyar some illuminating information."

"How do you mean, sir?"

"Avis was a dangerous mixture. Towering ego. Possibly a case of over-identification with his act. Believed he should be pulling crowds in Vegas. Not only that, but a bully, a blackmailer and an extreme right winger. Member of more than one questionable organisation. Usual paranoia about immigrants and homosexuals bringing the country to its knees, and strong views on the role of women."

Beatrice thought about that. "Who was he blackmailing?"

"Several entertainers at the caravan park and Callaghan himself. Provided them all with recreational drugs then threatened to expose them. Gained confidences only to use the information."

"Nice man."

Hamilton flicked his finger against his glass, creating a dull echo. "According to Callaghan, he'd given up on Britain and planned to emigrate to America. He was refused a visa, which he blamed on an incomplete birth certificate."

"Was that the real reason he was refused?"

"Hardly likely. His affiliations already marked him out as undesirable. Fuelled some sort of fire, nevertheless. Very angry man looking for someone to blame."

"His birth parents."

"His birth mother. In his mind, it was all her fault. As I said, odd ideas about women. So he sought her out, with every intention of 'ruining her life'. Callaghan said he was no more specific than that. Whatever happened when Keith Avis aka Toni Dean met Eva Webber we'll never know, but we can safely assume she told him about Swallows Hall, the names of the teachers and the summer of 1965. All he told Callaghan afterwards was that he'd changed his plans."

Beatrice pondered the golden liquid in her glass. "Thank you for the bigger picture, sir. It helps, a bit. Would you share that information with the Hellenic Police? I'd like Inspector Stephanakis to know we appreciate his investigative rigour."

"Fair enough. Tell me, what did you think of Voulakis?"

She chose her words carefully. "He seems a little less precise than I'm used to, but he made me most welcome. I liked him. I had no idea you had been friends so long."

"Indeed. We go back a long way. I introduced him to the woman who is now his wife."

"So he said."

Hamilton inhaled the aroma of his Scotch. "What else did he tell you?"

"That you and he 'awarded' the first ASBOs ever issued."

He gave a short snort of laughter. "True. We did. Probably even used the word 'award' in those days. Now, look here, Stubbs. You and I need to have a chat about your future. I'm chairing a meeting with you, Rangarajan and his DS for this coming Monday to discuss the logistics of handing over Operation Horseshoe."

"No, sir." She placed her drink on the low table, making sure to use a coaster. "Firstly, I won't be here on Monday. I am taking a week off in lieu and will return the following Monday after I have discussed and decided my future plans with my partner. Secondly, if the result of those conversations means early retirement, I am absolutely within my rights to be taken seriously by my senior officer. Loose cannon or not. Until I know what I want for my own future, I will make no plans or commitments to any projects I may not be able to fulfil."

She lifted her chin to Hamilton, daring him to argue. He sat back and swirled his drink around his glass, studying her.

"Don't waste it, Stubbs. That's a sixteen-year-old Lagavulin. A week in lieu is acceptable. We'll schedule a bilateral meeting for the following Monday and take it from there. On a personal note, I hope you'll postpone retirement. You are an extraordinary detective inspector and an asset to my team. A loose cannon and a bloody nuisance without a doubt, but someone I would prefer to keep."

She sipped at her whisky to hide her smile. "Thank you, sir."

Back home in Boot Street, she paused outside Adrian's flat. Sounds of *La Cage aux Folles* drifted into the hall, so she decided against disturbing him and stuffed a note under his door. Upstairs in her own place, she threw a laundry load into the machine, repacked her case for a week in Devon and checked her messages. A voicemail from Rose Mason, announcing their safe return to Edinburgh and inviting Beatrice to join them on a weekend jaunt to Wiltshire for a 'survivors' reunion'. Beatrice smiled at the sardonic inverted commas. She was copied in, along with Chief Inspector Voulakis on an email from Hamilton. The main recipient was Nikos Stephanakis and the content conveyed warm gratitude how influential his work had been.

Satisfied, Beatrice had a shower, brushed her teeth and although it was only ten past nine, crawled into bed. She set the alarm on her phone and finally made the call she'd been planning all day.

"*Beatrice?*"

"Hello, Matthew. I'm back."

"*Hurrah! And the case?*"

"The case is closed. Semi-satisfactorily. I'll tell you the sordid details when I see you. Listen, I've told Hamilton I'm taking a week off to think about my future. May I come to Devon? I thought we might talk this over together."

"*Of course. Nothing would make me happier. You sound very... chipper.*"

"I am. You asked me to think about what I want. And I did."

"*Ah. Good. So do you know what you want, do you think?*"

"I do."

Human Rites

Chapter 1

A controversial decision, placing a forty-five quid bottle of German Syrah at the top of the tree, but in Adrian's opinion it was justified. He tied a glass golden star to the neck with red ribbon and angled the spotlight to hit it directly in the middle. Warm and luxurious was what he was aiming for, to create desire in passers-by. He clambered out of the window display with great care, put the spare decorations on the counter and went outside to assess his handiwork.

"Oh yes," he murmured. Tapering tiers of wine bottles sparkled dark green under the lights, the claret and emerald baubles spoke of sophistication and the gold star caught the eye as if to say *here's what you've been looking for*. He waited till a black cab had rattled past and crossed the street to get another perspective. The bottle tree looked beautiful and enticing and seasonal without being tacky. Not an easy feat. Thankfully the garish street lights depicting cartoon reindeer were limited to Shoreditch High Street so nothing detracted from his display.

He folded his arms against the chill and pretended he was a weary office worker, trudging home in the dark. It was ten to four but dusk had already fallen, and Harvey's Wine Emporium stood out in the gloomy grey of Bethnal Green Road, a glittering temptation. Shivering but satisfied, Adrian crossed over and checked the alignment of the labels. One pinot noir could be shifted a millimetre to the left, but other than that, it was precision stacking.

As he came through the door, Judy Garland's voice warbled from the speakers. One of the many things Adrian detested about the festive season was the bombardment of truly dreadful Christmas songs from every outlet, but on this occasion, Judy wishing him a merry little one seemed entirely appropriate. He sang along as he adjusted the pinot noir then nipped back outside to be certain of absolute perfection.

Damp air penetrated his sweater, but the window looked exactly as he'd pictured it. He rubbed his upper arms as he smiled at the rows of hand-picked reds and congratulated himself. That was when he sensed he was being watched. He adjusted his focus. Reflected in the glass was a nun, standing on the opposite pavement, gazing at his shop window. Adrian turned to face her with every intention of fishing for compliments but she'd already begun walking away, her face averted. Embarrassed to be coveting forbidden fruit, no doubt. He returned to Judy, delighted his seasonal arrangement was already having an effect.

At five o'clock, Catinca arrived for her shift and they worked together for an hour to cover the evening rush. Adrian advised an older couple on dessert wines and directed a stressed suit towards the Date Night selection, while Catinca chirped and cackled at the till. No matter what age or gender, she got a smile or a laugh from every single customer. Adrian suspected some regulars delayed their purchases until after five, so they could enjoy the added bonus of her irrepressible good humour and personal transformations. This evening, the electric blue hair and indigo jumpsuit were no more than a memory. Now she resembled Marlene Dietrich with her dinner jacket, white shirt and a blue-black Mary Quant bob. The only constants were her Converse trainers and Bow Bells-meets-Bucharest accent.

"Get out of it! You worry about calories? Rubbish! Look at you. And wine is grapes so part of five a day. Cheers mate, here is change."

"You like it? Ta very much. No more purple. Is colour of bishops and suicide. Kettle chips go well with cava, want to try new flavour?"

"Adrian! This lady wants port wine. Tony, not Ruby. Go over and see him, darling, one in stripey jumper."

When the activity died down, Adrian fetched his coat from the office and prepared to leave.

"Catinca, I'm off. Any problems, give me a call. I'm at home tonight. And book a cab to take you home, OK? Just remember to get a receipt."

"Yeah, yeah. I never forget. Your window looks cool."

"Do you think so? It took me most of the afternoon but it's certainly turning heads. Hey, do you know whether nuns are allowed to drink?"

Catinca thought about it. "Yeah, must be. Is a wine called Blue Nun, innit?"

"True. Right, have a good evening and I'll see you tomorrow."

"Cheers, mate. Laters. Don't forget Christmas card."

"Thanks. First one I've had this year."

The Christmas card situation occupied his thoughts on the bus journey home. It wasn't the first one he'd had, but most of the cards on his mantelpiece were from suppliers, colleagues and the occasional client of the Wine Emporium, all delivered to the shop. In previous years he'd had to clear the windowsills and use the top of the TV to house his collection of robins, snowmen and glittery greetings. But it was mid-December and he'd not even received one from his mum. In fact, he wasn't sure when he'd last had any post at all.

When he got home to Boot Street, he immediately checked his mailbox in the communal hall. Empty. Not even any junk. He pushed open the slot bearing the name B. Stubbs. Stuffed to overflowing. He tried S. Fasman. Empty. What was it with the ground floor? He rang Saul's bell.

The door opened to a smell of frying onions and Saul wiping his hands on his customary grey jogging suit. Adrian reflected for a second on the irony of the name. Saul was no more likely to jog than Adrian was to take up cage-fighting.

"Hello Adrian. All right?"

"Hi Saul. Sorry to disturb you. Just wondered if you've had any problems with the post? Has your mail been getting through?"

"Yeah. I've had all the usual crap, mostly bills and pizza flyers. You waiting for something important?"

"Not really, it's just weird there's been nothing at all for days."

"Days? Nah, you had a delivery yesterday. Or was it this morning? I had to buzz the postie in. Package for you. I knew you weren't home so I said to leave it in the hallway."

"When was this?"

Saul lifted his chin and scratched his rust-coloured beard. "Must have been today, 'cos I was busting a gut to meet my Friday lunchtime deadline. Someone buzzing at the door was the last thing I needed."

"But there's no package out here. No post for me at all. I've just checked."

"That is weird. Maybe Beatrice picked it up for you?"

Adrian shook his head. "She's not home yet. She hasn't picked up her own mail. He didn't ask you to sign for it, did he?"

"Who?"

"The postie."

"No, no, I just pressed the buzzer and let her in."

Adrian thanked him and went back to his own flat, planning to call his mother to ask if she'd already sent her cards. He switched on the light and as he closed the door, he noticed a piece of paper on the mat.

At first he thought it was blank, but when he flipped it over, there was something typed in the middle of the page.

Romans 6:23

He frowned. Was that a TV schedule, a football score or a bible reference? None would make any sense to him. Without even taking off his coat, he took the paper into his study, opened his laptop and typed the word and numbers into a search engine.

He clicked on the first search result for The King James Bible and there in big red letters was the verse.

For the wages of sin is death
but the gift of God is eternal life
through Jesus Christ our Lord.

Chapter 2

Beatrice buried her nose deeper into her scarf as she trudged down Dacre Street, needle-sharp raindrops assailing her forehead. The Cayman Islands would be nice. Some gentle little money-laundering scam to investigate, then fly home once the crocuses come out. Perhaps she should ask Hamilton for a transfer.

"Sir, since we've agreed I can take early retirement by the end of next year, could you assign me to something relaxing in the Caribbean for a few months?"

Even in the dreary gloom of her Monday morning commute, the thought of provoking Hamilton's apoplexy raised a smile. Until she remembered the meeting. Operation Horseshoe and zero hopes of escaping a London winter. She stopped off for a bucket of caffeinated milk and entered the office with a nutty croissant and a scowl.

"Morning, Beatrice! Don't forget it's Secret Santa today! You got your pressie all wrapped?" Melanie sat behind the reception desk, an elf hat perched on top of her headset, waggling long false nails encrusted with crystals.

"Morning, Melanie. Yes, it's in my bag. When are we doing this?"

Melanie let out a bubble of laughter. "When do you think!? Christmas lunch, just before the pudding. You'll never guess what..."

"No, I won't because I cannot be arsed. It's Monday bloody morning, I'm wet and cold and I have a meeting with Hamilton in ten minutes. What?"

Melanie's face drooped into a sympathetic pout as she tilted her head to one side. "Awww. Bless. You do look a bit parky. Anyway, Hamilton's in hospital, so that's one thing off your plate. The meeting's still on for nine though, with Ranga as Acting Superintendent."

"Hospital? What's the matter?"

"Dunno. Got a message this morning." She clicked the mouse and read from her screen. *"Unexpected hospital attendance required. Updates as and when. DCI Jalan please take helm."* She looked at Beatrice, her artfully painted eyes huge. "You reckon it's his teeth again?"

Ranga spent several minutes of the team meeting on small talk, asking Dawn Whittaker about her house move, joking with Russell Cooper about his latest rugby injury, soliciting Beatrice's opinion on cheeseboards and enquiring after Joe Bryant's new puppy. The atmosphere grew warmer, softer, and every face around the table relaxed. Beatrice knew he would be such a perfect boss and wondered if there was a way to persuade him not to retire. If so, maybe she'd follow suit.

"Now then, down to business. I am not exactly sure what is wrong with Superintendent Hamilton or when he is likely to return to work. I have asked Melanie to send flowers and I will call the hospital later to find out more. Nevertheless, we have to move on in his absence. We need to make staffing decisions regarding Operation Horseshoe. Next Monday, I have a meeting with three out of four of the religious leaders involved. I would like to introduce them to whoever will eventually take over.

"Relationships with the community are the cornerstone of this op. This team is especially trained to be culturally sensitive in order to communicate with a broad range of ages and backgrounds. Given the long-term nature of public liaison, we're looking for a capable manager to develop this unit in the future. Beatrice, I know Hamilton wanted you for this one, but given your own plans to retire next year, my view is that it could be counter-productive to switch the senior detective in twelve months' time."

Beatrice nodded. "That's exactly what I said. To me, it makes far more sense for Dawn to head this op. She's got a great track record of forming alliances and proved her mettle in the knife crime operation. Plus, unlike me, Dawn's just reaching her prime."

Dawn laughed and a faint blush tinted her cheeks. But rather than speak, she opened her palms to her colleagues to offer their opinions. An offer Russell Cooper could not refuse.

"No-brainer as far as I'm concerned. Dawn's perfect for it. She was solid gold on knife crime and can talk to anyone, young or old, black or white, vic or perp and even if she does lack management experience, six months working alongside you will sort that out. What do you reckon, Joe?"

In contrast to Russell's trombone tones, Joe Bryant's softly accented Cornish speech was a tin whistle.

"Yeah, if Beatrice really is going to retire..."

"I am."

"Damn shame, but we've had that discussion. It's logical to assign someone who'll take it on for longer. I'll stick my hand up and vote for Dawn. Does that mean we can have Beatrice for the trafficking enquiry?"

Ranga smiled. "One second, Joe. We've heard from everyone but Dawn herself. How do you feel, DI Whittaker?"

Beatrice watched her friend's face. She was glowing like a child presented with a birthday cake. "On condition my apprenticeship satisfies Ranga and the other community leaders, if I achieve all the targets set during the training period, as long as my colleagues and the Super approve and Beatrice doesn't see me as a cuckoo then yes, I'd love to join Operation Horseshoe."

Beatrice could tell from Ranga's beam that her decision was what he wanted. She watched Dawn laugh and enjoyed a huge swell of vicarious joy. After years of unhappiness following public betrayal, humiliation, loneliness, grief, and bitter resentment, Dawn was rebuilding her private life. Plus her dogged hard work was proving a success at the Met. Not that she or any of her colleagues would comment publicly, but this year had been a turning point.

"I guess we have to wait for Hamilton's green light first?" Dawn asked.

Ranga shook his head. "I'm DCI and currently Acting Superintendent, so the decision is mine. Plus we have no idea when he will be back. DI Whittaker is assigned to Operation Horseshoe. As of now."

The team burst into a brief round of applause before Russell Cooper's voice drowned it out.

"Good on you, Dawnie! You've had a shitty few years with the divorce and kids and everything. But look at you now! New bloke, new flat and taking over a major op!" He stuck his hand across the table. "And I tell you what, that haircut takes years off you. Put it there, mate!"

Ranga, Beatrice and Joe stared at Russell in disbelief. But Dawn crumpled into laughter and took Russell's hand.

"Good luck in the Diplomatic Corps, Cooper. Thanks everyone. I really appreciate the vote of confidence."

Ranga gave a satisfied sigh and turned to Beatrice. "How do you fancy something relaxing with a bit of travel, DI Stubbs?"

Beatrice stared at him. "Acting Superintendent Rangarajan Jalan, you couldn't have made me happier unless you included a slice of Christmas cake."

"Would *Stollen* suffice?"

"Ah. When you said a bit of travel, I pictured the Caribbean. But as it happens, I'm extremely partial to *Stollen* and Germany's lovely at this time of year. What's going on?"

"Art theft. An incident in Richmond last week may have a connection to two similar robberies. One in Hamburg, another in Amsterdam. I'd like you to follow up and report your findings to the Interpol Cultural Protection Task Force. I have a file prepared for you and meetings already lined up. Interview the victim, take detailed notes on the circumstances, hop over to Germany, compare notes and spend the weekend visiting Christmas markets. We get Brownie points for cross-border collaboration and the insurance company here will be satisfied. How does that sound?"

"Like a piece of cake."

Chapter 3

Monday was Adrian's day off. When he started his business, he'd worked twelve hour shifts, six days a week. Now he could afford to employ Catinca for the evenings and they both worked Saturdays. In order to give himself a proper break he closed the shop on Mondays. He loved the freedom of having half his weekend while everyone else was at work. It was also an opportunity to indulge his latest hobby: gourmet cooking.

His upstairs neighbour's loathing of Mondays was well-known, so he'd fallen into the habit of creating something extravagant or adventurous for Monday evening and inviting Beatrice to pass judgement. She said it made starting the week bearable. Today's menu was Salmon Wellington with asparagus and Swiss chard. In the oven, his concoction changed colours. The sliver of fish visible between the pastry edges turned from raw and grey to golden pink, matching the evening sky. A South African Chenin Blanc chilled in the fridge and the table bore a Nordic theme, as close to festive as he could bear.

He'd just begun preparing the vegetables when he heard the external door slam shut. All his calm and positive thinking dissolved in a second. He dropped the knife, rinsed his hands and hurried to the hallway, drying his hands on his apron. On tiptoes, he crept up to his apartment door and looked through the peephole but the vestibule was pitch dark; whoever was out there hadn't switched on the hall light. Adrian waited, straining to hear over his own pulsing heartbeat. Silence. It occurred to him that the door may have indicated an exit rather than an entrance. He switched off the living-room lamp and rushed to the window. Purposeful figures strode along the pavements, wrapped up against the weather, intent on getting out of the cold.

He began to relax. People were allowed to enter and leave the building. One disturbing note should not make him this jittery. His post had arrived as normal over the weekend and his mantelpiece was now crowded with cards. A Royal Mail hiccup and someone's idea of a joke would not affect his equilibrium. And he had asparagus to blanch. He turned back towards the kitchen, inhaling the scent of fish, pastry and dill. He was just reaching for the lamp when he glanced out of the side window and froze.

Under the street light on Coronet Street stood a nun, looking straight at his window. Totally still, hands clasped to her chest, her eyes were fixed on his apartment. Adrian stepped closer to the glass and saw she was not completely immobile. Her lips moved rapidly as if she were reciting a litany. He leaned forwards once again and the orange sodium glow hit his face. She registered the movement and ducked away behind next door's wheelie bins and into the shadows. At that precise moment, the doorbell rang and Adrian jumped like a hare.

He checked the peephole and opened the door. "Beatrice!"

"Yes. The person you invited for dinner."

"Of course, I'm just... you're early."

Beatrice checked her watch. "Ten minutes late, actually. But even if I were, you look like you've just seen Lord Lucan wheeled in by Elvis. Whatever's wrong?"

"Nothing! Nothing at all. Just a little bit behind with my preparations. Come in, sit down and tell me about your day."

Beatrice perched on a breakfast stool, opened the wine and chattered about the big religious unity police thing while Adrian boiled the water and chopped the chard, all the while acting attentive. Every time he passed the window, he checked. The nun had gone.

"Ooh, the smell! I'm positively drooling. Thank you for cooking for me."

"You're most welcome. Tuck in. Why are you in such a good mood on a Monday?"

"I've just been telling you. The outcome of today is that everyone's a winner. Ranga's got his replacement, it's a feather in Dawn's hat and I'm assigned to something cushy involving European art galleries. Berlin on Wednesday, then Amsterdam and on to Hamburg. After that I'm going to stay for the weekend."

An unexpected surge of disappointment mixed with envy rose in Adrian's chest. They'd planned a Tate Night on Friday and he didn't want to go alone.

"Lucky you! Can I come?" he asked, not entirely joking.

"This is absolutely delicious! The pastry is superb. Is this spinach?"

"Swiss chard. Thank you. There's hollandaise to go with the asparagus in the gravy boat."

"Such extravagance for a school night. I wish you could come with me, actually. You'd be the ideal companion for poking around galleries and markets. Pity you have to work on Saturday."

As Beatrice poured the custard-coloured sauce in a zigzag over her spears, Adrian had an idea.

"Will Matthew be joining you over the weekend?"

Beatrice, mouth full, shook her head.

"Tell me if this is a stupid idea, but what if I left Catinca to mind the shop on Saturday and flew over to join you? That's exactly why I hired her, to give myself more freedom. I fancy a mini-break somewhere different. We could visit galleries, pick up some unusual gifts in the markets, drink mulled wine and if we're in Hamburg, we could say hello to Holger."

Beatrice swallowed, her eyes bright. "Quite the opposite of a stupid idea. That would be the cherry on the cake! Matthew can't come as he's got two university Christmas soirées to attend, so your company would be most welcome. Shall I check which hotel they've booked me into and we can stay in the same place?"

Adrian's first bubbles of excitement surfaced at the thought of a spontaneous getaway and a change of scene. "Yes, do. And I'll call Catinca and Holger to make arrangements tomorrow. This could be fun!"

"You should ask Holger for some restaurant tips. How is he? Have you two been in touch?"

"We chat every once in a while, send each other silly postcards, that sort of thing. Just because the relationship didn't work out, it doesn't change the fact he's a really nice guy."

"He is. It would be lovely to see..."

Adrian straightened at the sound of the building's door buzzer, raised a finger to hush Beatrice and went to the peephole. A pizza delivery driver entered the hallway with a cardboard box. Adrian watched until Saul had opened his apartment door and only then returned to his seat.

"Sorry, just wanted to check who was coming in. Saul's having a takeaway. Not quite to the standard of our meal, I'm afraid." He refilled their glasses, aware of Beatrice's gaze.

"I can't imagine many takeaways reaching these heights. It's beautifully cooked and the vegetables go with it so well. I'm going to treat you to a couple of indulgent meals while we're in Germany to say thanks for these Monday marvels."

"There's no need. I told you I like having someone to enjoy it with. Then again, I never say no to an indulgent eating experience."

They ate in near silence for a few minutes; the only sounds the odd murmur of appreciation.

"By the way, did you hear anything else about the disappearing post?" asked Beatrice, adding another blob of hollandaise.

"No, nothing. Deliveries have been completely normal since Friday. The mystery package hasn't turned up yet and no one in the building knows anything about it. So it seems your theory was correct."

"Perhaps, perhaps not. Though I will say it tends to happen a lot in the run up to Christmas. Someone rings a random bell and claims they've got a connection with another person in the building. Other occupants will often press the buzzer out of trust, laziness or lack of thought. The stranger then scopes the place and checks for opportunities such as keys under doormats."

"Or packages sitting in the hallway."

"Or packages sitting in the hallway. But I didn't mean to un-nerve you. If you like, I can get some police-approved wording for a security leaflet. We could stick one in everyone's letterbox."

"Might be an idea. We could all do with being a bit more careful."

Beatrice scooped up the last of the pastry and placed her knife and fork together. "That meal, in my opinion, trumps the savoury choux puffs. Exactly what a body needs on a December night, but not too heavy. A triumph!"

"Thank you. It was certainly tasty and pretty to look at." He prodded the remains of his food and decided to finish it later.

"Adrian, is everything all right? You seem awfully on edge. I've bent your ear often enough with my problems, so if something's bothering you...? Tell me to mind my own business if you like."

Adrian smiled. Beatrice was a great listener and had always taken him seriously. The trouble was, he didn't even take himself seriously. His imagination was sometimes his worst enemy.

"The only thing bothering me is how to plan for a German mini-break in only four days. I'll need to check the weather and plan my wardrobe. I'm thinking wool and tailoring. And as I intend to bring back presents, should I put the expandable suitcase in the hold, or limit myself to hand luggage only and use my travel-sized toiletries? There's so much to consider. Not least what to eat. Is there a Hamburg speciality, apart from the obvious?"

"Fish, I expect. It's a port, so we'll have seafood coming out of our ears."

"Wonderful. Fish, art, markets and a good companion. I am so looking forward to this!"

Chapter 4

Richmond's Roedean Crescent was a far cry from Boot Street. This was where money lived. The police Vauxhall Insignia eased along the road, offering Beatrice glimpses of gated detached properties shielded by neat hedges or strategically planted trees. Most driveways were empty, but occasionally she spotted a Mercedes, a Range Rover or a Jaguar.

DS Pearce continued his briefing without taking his eyes off the road. It was unnecessary, because Beatrice had familiarised herself with the file, but she chose to listen to Pearce's version. He might have picked up something she'd overlooked, and anyway it was better than making laboured small talk. Pearce was not known for his sense of humour.

"You can see for yourself, plenty of space in the driveways and lots of cars on the street. Easy enough to park up and watch the household's routine. It's pretty regular. A driver arrives to take him into the City at seven every morning. He's a senior asset manager with an investment bank. She takes the kid to school in the Volvo just after half past eight. She's home by nine, and two days a week she lets the cleaning company in. Then she hits the gym, goes shopping and has lunch with a friend. Always back here before the cleaners leave at half-one."

"Is it always the same people from the cleaning company?"

Pearce indicated right and reversed into a space in front of some impressive white gates. "No. Depends on the rota. The two Filipinas are the most regular, but they're not always available." He turned off the engine. "Ma'am, I'm expecting a hostile reception. This bloke's already given a statement twice and he's got a serious attitude problem. If he starts getting arsey, I'll do the same. Leave you to do the charm stuff."

Beatrice raised her eyebrows. "Thanks, Pearce. I'll do my best."

The door was open by the time they'd crunched across the gravel. No butler, no underling, just the master of the house. Chet Waring stood in the portico, wearing a navy suit and a smile fit for Santa Claus. Against his tanned face, his teeth were startlingly white. Beatrice marched up the steps, ID in her left hand with her right outstretched.

"Mr Waring, my name is DI Stubbs. Thank you for making the time to see us. My colleague DS Pearce I believe you already know."

"It's my pleasure. Really. Knowing you guys are taking this seriously is such a relief for me. Yes indeed, DS Pearce has been a rock during this investigation and I couldn't be more appreciative of his thorough approach."

A cool, firm handshake and a warm smile of welcome. Pearce gave no reaction. After many years of practice, he had perfected the neutral mask. But Beatrice was curious. What attitude problem? They followed him into a magnificent hallway, half filled by a gargantuan Nordic pine that almost obscured the grand piano nestling under the stairs. Waring took their coats and ushered them into a large living space full of expensive paintings, arty knick-knacks and a choice of sofas. Knitted socks hung from the mantelpiece, each with a nametag, while Bing Crosby crooned from hidden speakers.

As soon as they were seated, a young man entered with a tray bearing a coffee pot, jug of milk and a selection of pastries. Waring took it and placed it on the table in front of them. A whiff of nutmeg wafted past Beatrice's nose. Spices, carols, stockings, a pine tree... A Child's Christmas of Clichés.

"Thanks Simon, that's all for now. Coffee, DI Stubbs, DS Pearce? Please help yourself to muffins or whatever. Don't know about you guys but I can't work until I've had my morning sugar fix. The amount I've contributed to Caffè Nero's profits this year? I shoulda bought shares."

"Thank you. I'll have mine with milk, no sugar and perhaps one of those mini Danish affairs. As for business, Mr Waring, we're not here to go over old ground. I'd just like a few more details about the painting itself so we can make comparisons to other art thefts around the world. I must stress this is part of a larger operation and may not be of material use in your particular case. However, all reports of art theft have a wider benefit when reported accurately."

Waring poured coffee for Beatrice and Pearce, listening and nodding with such intensity that Beatrice was tempted to laugh. Instead she bit into her sugar-glazed cake.

"Too right. Cultural artefact databases are the collector's best friends. I already reported this to the Art Loss Register. How can I help?"

"Tell us how you acquired the piece. And why."

"Sure. The painting was in my possession for just over three years. I bought it at auction in New York and paid one million, one hundred fifty thousand dollars for it. Today, that's around three-quarters of a million in sterling. I bought it as an investment, obviously, but also because it's an amazing piece. It packs a real punch. Not everyone likes it as much as I do, of course, but they all notice it. That's why I'm so desperate to get it back. It's the centrepiece of my collection."

"Has anyone else ever offered to purchase it from you?"

"Not that I can recall," Waring replied. "Anyhow, I'd never sell."

"You're insured for the full amount, I assume?"

"Yep. Every artwork I own is covered at the professionally assessed value. I'm pretty risk-averse. I guess that's the norm with people in my line of work."

Pearce spoke. "Why do you think the thieves only took this one painting? As you say, you've got plenty to choose from." He looked around the room, his eyes narrowing. "I'd say those horse figurines on the mantelpiece are Lalique. Not only worth a fair bit but easy to carry. Or these little snuffboxes. Russian, aren't they? Major market for these and not as hard to shift as an original Otto Dix."

Waring's grey eyes widened and his face expanded into a broad smile. "You know your stuff, Detective Pearce! The horses are Lalique. And the snuffboxes, mostly Russian, are worth between three hundred and eight thousand dollars each. But let me assure you, I did a careful inventory, as did my wife, and nothing else is missing. My theory is the thieves were stealing to order. Some wealthy oligarch is amassing German Expressionist art from the 1920s and needed a Dix for his collection. The depressing fact is that if I'm right, I'll never see the painting again."

The smallest twinge of sympathy touched Beatrice at the pain in his voice. Rarely had she grown so attached to an inanimate object that its loss would have caused her grief. Yet she recalled the silver bracelet Matthew had given her on her promotion to Detective Inspector. It was an antique, with tiny golden ivy leaves embossed on the surface. During some rather enthusiastic participation in a New Year's Eve ceilidh, it had come adrift, never to be seen again. It wasn't the bracelet so much as its talismanic significance imbued by emotion.

"Do you have a photograph of the painting, Mr Waring?"

He seemed to bring himself back from an unfocused emptiness and reignited his smile.

"I have a file with all the documentation regarding provenance and the original catalogue, plus various images of the whole picture, detail and frame. Help yourself to more coffee. I'll just be a moment."

The door closed behind him and Pearce got up to examine one of the other large canvases on the wall between the windows. Beatrice leaned back to see what had attracted his attention. Roseate flesh and entwined limbs writhing on a chequerboard floor. Exaggerated features and a lack of restraint spilling out across the rigid geometry. It somehow made her think of Liza Minnelli. Pearce wrote something in his notebook as Waring returned.

"What do you think, Detective Pearce? Quite a talent, wouldn't you say?"

"I take it you're a fan of the Expressionist school?"

"Darn right. Are you?"

Pearce sat beside Beatrice and nodded once. "I find certain aspects of the movement have a powerful impact. The social commentary after World War One in German art and British poetry is excoriating."

Beatrice tried not to stare. She knew Pearce specialised in

culturally-related crimes, but had never spoken to him on the subject.

Waring's eyes lit up. "My thoughts exactly! You know what, you'll totally get why I miss this painting. Someone with such an appreciation of art is going to understand. This is *The Salon II.*"

He opened a glossy catalogue and indicated an A4 print of the original on the right hand page. Beatrice took the brochure and shared it with Pearce. The painting depicted a room, shell pink, with ruby velvet curtains parted to allow the viewer access. Six prostitutes in various states of undress sat around a table. Breasts spilled, stockings slipped, curls escaped pins, lipstick smudged, cigarettes drooped and stains marked the cloth. At the head of the table, a sun blasted out black, grey, puce and golden rays, the light reflecting off each weary woman's face.

The most shocking thing about the piece was the women's eyes. Each face was turned to the viewer, as if they had been surprised. Some eyes were fearful, some glittering, some suspicious, some hopeful, some vacant and resigned. The image made the viewer the object of attention and asked a simple question. *What do you want?* The more you stared, the more complicit you became.

Beatrice pushed the catalogue back to Pearce and stood up. "I see what you mean about it packing a punch. May we keep this file?"

"Sure."

"DS Pearce will continue to handle the robbery line of enquiry, whereas I will pursue the art theft connection. Thank you for your time, Mr Waring. One more thing. Your cleaners – I understand one was hurt. How is she?"

"She's recovering. A bunch of stitches but no permanent damage, thank God. I paid to have her treated privately. Here's my personal card, DI Stubbs. Please feel free to call me whenever you need. Thanks so much for your help."

Back at Scotland Yard, an odd electricity charged the air. Melanie was on the phone and merely pushed a plastic folder towards Beatrice. It contained the details of her flights and accommodation in Germany. Pearce trudged off into the main office to photocopy Waring's documents. Beatrice was hanging up her coat when behind her someone wrenched open a door.

"Stubbs! In here, now."

Hamilton's face, pale and lined, was tight with tension.

"Hello sir. I didn't realise you were back. How are you?"

His only reply was to walk back into his office. Beatrice followed. He winced as he lowered himself into his chair and gestured for her to close the door.

"Bloody furious is how I am. Sit down. You knew perfectly well I wanted you on Operation Horseshoe. I fully expect my team to follow orders whether I'm here or not. Then I find that after being out of action for twenty-four hours, I've been undermined by you, Whittaker and Jalan. What the hell were you thinking? I said, sit down!"

Given the intensity of his anger, Beatrice sat. "Sir, there was no intention to undermine you or anyone else. We simply discussed what was best for the operation itself. Ranga said he wanted someone on board for the longer term and seeing as I will be leaving..."

"You seem very sure of that. I do not recall agreeing to your proposal, Stubbs. I said I would think about it, so please do not make assumptions."

The injustice of his remark stung. "Sir, I had your assurance..."

"And I had yours that you would step up to support Jalan in Operation Horseshoe. Now I find you've forgotten that obligation entirely to flit off on another European investigation."

The heat suffusing her face could have been just the effects of coming in from the cold and nothing at all to do with her rising temper.

She took a deep breath and exhaled with some force. "Your detective inspectors collectively agreed that the best allocation of resources would be for DI Whittaker to assist DCI Jalan. She's looking for a longer career with the Met and taking her experience into account, she is the perfect fit. This art theft collaboration with Interpol can be wound up within a week. But if you'd prefer to reassign me to something else, sir, that is your prerogative."

"You were supposed to be assigned to Horseshoe! I believe I

made that clear. Why do you always want the jobs that'll get you out of the country, Stubbs?"

"Out of the country? I accept whatever cases I am given, sir. But in light of my intention to retire..."

"In light of your intention to retire, yes indeed. What are you going to do then? Without the job to provide you with opportunities to escape, how long will it take before domestic bliss loses its allure?"

Beatrice took two deep breaths and stood up. Hamilton's grey features seemed twisted and ugly, like those of a gargoyle.

"Thank you for your concern, sir, but I don't believe my private life is any of your business. For the record, whether or not you agree to my departure is immaterial. If you don't grant me early retirement, I will resign. One way or another, I will be leaving at the end of next year. As for allocation of duties, Melanie has booked me a flight to Berlin for tomorrow. Should I tell her to cancel it?"

Hamilton looked down at his desk. Beatrice clenched her fists. He shook his head. "No. Go to bloody Germany and get out of my sight."

She stalked out of the room and made straight for the ladies' toilet.

Five minutes later, Dawn Whittaker poked her head with exaggerated timidity round the bathroom door. Beatrice leant against the wall, her arms folded. She met Dawn's eyes in the mirror. She didn't smile.

"Can I come in?" Dawn asked.

Beatrice nodded.

Dawn closed the door behind her and hoisted herself up to sit between the sinks. "Two hours ago, I was doing exactly that, in exactly the same spot."

"The miserable old bastard had a go at you as well?"

"Ranga got the worst of it. But yes, he had a go at me too. He questioned my competence, accused me of elbowing you out of the way to further my career and stated I was the last person he would have selected for this op. That said, he's decided not to change anything. I think he's just reminding us he's still in charge."

Beatrice shook her head. "I can understand him having the hump because we didn't do things his way. It's just the personal nastiness I find so offensive. What the hell has got into him?"

"The question on everyone's mind. Ranga called the hospital this morning to check on his progress only to find he'd discharged himself last night. The doctors were very concerned and want him readmitted as soon as possible. Obviously they're not giving out any medical details, but they said if he came to work, we were to ask him to return to hospital."

"I pity the poor sod who delivered that message," Beatrice said and ran the taps to wash her face.

"Ranga. Who else but the reigning monarch of diplomacy? I don't know what was said but Ranga came out of there looking more shaken than the time we raided that basement flat in Bermondsey."

"Poor Ranga." Beatrice patted her face dry with paper towels, her outrage deflating as she began to realise Hamilton's anger wasn't just directed at her. "So we still don't know what's wrong with him, apart from being a vicious old git?"

Dawn shrugged. "One thing I know. He's in pain. He's hunched over and tense and he's having problems walking. He really should be in hospital."

"Definitely. At least he couldn't take out his foul temper on us from there. But if he won't listen to Ranga, neither of us has a rat's chance in hell of persuading him."

"No. Let's just get on with the job." Dawn jumped down and checked her hair in the mirror. "Did your art theft victim give you much?"

"Not really. Although I think his stolen painting will give me nightmares. Listen, I'm off to Berlin in the morning. Fancy a drink tonight?"

"On a Tuesday? Too right I do."

When Dawn suggested La Cave at London Bridge, Beatrice knew there must be gossip. One of the pubs local to the office would have been their usual haunt. Dawn's casual rationale for her choice was that the Northern Line was handy for both of them. Beatrice north to Old Street, Dawn south to Clapham.

Beatrice wasn't fooled but the choice of venue made no difference to her. The place served wine and that was all that mattered. Comfortably settled at a window table with two glasses of Rose de Syrah and view of the river, they toasted Dawn's new role.

"So when's the flat-warming?" Beatrice asked.

"After Christmas. But I want you to come round for lunch one weekend. So I can show off the flat and introduce you to Derek."

"Ooh, yes please. I'm dying to meet him. Is he still fabulous?"

Dawn put a hand to her heart in a mock-swoon. "He just gets better. You know what? He actually offered to drive all the way down to Southampton to collect Finley for Christmas. Not that the ungrateful little shit will appreciate it."

"I was just going to ask about the kids. Any improvements?"

"Don't let's spoil a nice after-work drink." Dawn surveyed the Thames, rather festive with its reflections of Christmas lights glinting off choppy waters. "Better views than The Speaker or the Blue Boar, don't you think?"

"Not to mention more private. Come on, whatever it is, cough it up. I know we're not here to discuss the view."

"You're like a truffle pig, you are. If it's there, you'll root it out." She sipped at her wine, drawing out the moment. "I had lunch with Ian today."

"Ex-husband Ian?"

"The same. We meet up about once a month, talk about our horrible children, coordinate strategy and all that. And share any office gossip. The thing is, he knows a lot more about the Met's internal politics than me. Apparently," she glanced around for eavesdroppers, "the board are seeking a replacement for Hamilton."

Beatrice put down her glass. "No! Why? He's always been the golden boy. Half the board are alumni of his old school. Or university."

"I don't know why, but it goes some way to explaining this morning's shit-storm."

"It certainly does. If they want him out and he doesn't want to go, he'll be like a boar with a sore head. What else did Ian tell you?"

Dawn's expression was that of a poker player revealing a royal flush. "He told me that both you and Ranga are slated for the post."

Beatrice burst out laughing. "Perhaps the board should do a bit more research. I'm only a DI and Ranga wants to take early retirement. Pity. I was only thinking today he would have made a great Superintendent."

"Their thinking is that if either of you were offered the role of Super, you'd change your minds. Less field work, more management, comfy chair..."

Beatrice swallowed a large glug of wine. "Ranga might."

"Operation Horseshoe is not quite what we thought it was." Dawn leaned in, holding Beatrice's eyes. "It's a testing ground for a trainee Superintendent because it's all about management skills. No wonder Hamilton was so keen for you to take over from Ranga. He must have blown a gasket when he heard it was me."

"Don't be ridiculous. Hamilton would rather gouge out his own eyes than see me as Superintendent! Or even DCI. He thinks I'm a loose cannon."

"Not according to Ian. Hamilton was the one who put your name forward."

"He must be mistaken. No, Ranga is the obvious choice and to be honest he's the only one I'd vote for. The board should approach him now, and when he hands over Horseshoe to you, he can get the comfy chair. He'd be brilliant. I might even..."

Dawn pounced. "You'd stay if Ranga was Super? Are you serious?"

"I didn't say that."

Like synchronised swimmers, they both reached for their glasses and drank, gazing out at the rolling river and the glitter of new London's money lights twinkling from its surface like a shower of silver coins. Finally Dawn tilted her head, her expression inquisitive.

"Whatever Hamilton's opinion on the matter, the decision is up to the board. If they promoted you to DCI and offered you Super in a year's time, would you stay?"

The greedy hog of Beatrice's ego immediately played a slide show of her as DCI, firm yet kind and as well-loved as Ranga. She saw herself making a speech on Ranga's retirement and making a joke about filling his shoes as Superintendent. Office hours and no personal risk, meetings with the suits upstairs, press interviews, a talented, well-managed group of detectives. Awards, accolades, an increase in salary and status.

She would hate it.

And what of Matthew? What of their plans to cease battling the daily grind; hers the criminal world, his the semi-literate levels of bottom-rung academia. Their dreams of peace, pottering and enjoying the fruits of their labours. Together.

Beatrice watched a Christmas party pleasure cruiser sail past. Enticing warm fairy lights, laughter, music and dancing. The reality, she knew, would horrify her if she were actually aboard. The music at a volume threshold of pain levels that hurt her ears, the flimsy clothing, risky and risqué behaviour of the celebrants, the face-ache of forced jollity. She was too old for all that. Too old for everything.

"No, I wouldn't. If the board selected me as Superintendent, I'd have serious doubts about their judgement. I've scraped by so far and all I want now is a quiet life. I've had enough, Dawn. And if that information finds its way back to the board, I shouldn't mind at all."

Chapter 5

Spheniscophobia: the fear of nuns or penguins. Adrian didn't believe it for a second. Who on earth could be afraid of penguins? It would be like having a fear of teddy bears. No way. It had to be a made-up word.

He'd been having nightmares again. Last night's involved the pursuit of a monochrome woman through the rain-blurred colours of Soho. She kept disappearing and reappearing in impossible places until he caught her by the neck and beat her head against a parking meter. Violence. Blood. Neon. Hitchcock meets Polanski. Perhaps he should pitch the idea to a film studio. The thought cheered him and he drained his tea, closed the browsing window listing phobias and went back to researching the top ten attractions of Hamburg.

The sleigh bells Catinca had insisted on attaching to the door tinkled as a customer entered. Adrian looked up with a welcoming smile. The shop had been especially slow, even for a wintry afternoon. Every week, The Square and Compass pub next door had a beer delivery around two o'clock on a Wednesday, requiring a huge dray to be parked on the pavement for at least an hour, hazard lights flashing while barrels and crates were unloaded. Adrian's shop was hidden from the casual passer-by, and in the unlikely event that customers made the trip especially, they would have to dodge the delivery men, ramps and open trapdoor leading to the pub's pungent cellar. Few were up to the obstacle course and those who chanced it didn't linger.

The lorry had blocked out daylight till three pm, when ominous clouds took over, filling the narrow strip of sky visible above the street. So this customer was a pleasant distraction. On second glance, more than pleasant. Tall, balding, neat facial hair, tight jeans, a suggestion of musculature around the upper body and a knowing smile.

"Can I help you or would you prefer to browse in peace?" asked Adrian.

The smile grew broader. "Both. I also want to buy some wine."

Adrian blinked, a sense of unease flickering. "In which case, you're in luck. I'm sure we have the odd bottle knocking about somewhere. What sort of wine are you looking for?"

"Red. Full bodied. Maybe South American." His unsubtle tone tipped from flirtatious into leering.

"You'll find some robust Chilean reds over there or I can recommend the Argentinean Shiraz you see on special offer by the door. Check them out." He gave a brittle smile and returned to the screen, aware of the man's movements in his peripheral vision. Clearly not a serious customer, he sloped around the displays with an absence of focus, casting meaningful looks in Adrian's direction before grabbing a bottle at random and approaching the counter.

"Would you recommend this one?" He thrust it by the neck, like a piece of game he'd just shot.

Adrian placed one hand under the bottle's base and cradled the back, with as much tenderness as if regarding a newborn. "There's not a wine in this room I would not recommend. This is a very drinkable Chilean Pinot Noir. Plenty of depth, competitively priced and it goes with everything. Not to mention a stunning label. Is it for a special occasion?"

"Nope. Unless you're free tonight?" The man rested a hand on the counter and loomed over Adrian.

"I'm afraid not. I have to prepare for a weekend away with my partner." He began wrapping the bottle in tissue paper. "That'll be eight pounds ninety-nine. Thank you. I hope you enjoy the wine."

The transaction was completed with no further eye contact. Without saying thanks, goodbye or even 'Have a nice day', the man took his bottle and left. He stopped just outside for a moment and Adrian thought he might come back in. But after a second staring at the window display, the man shook his head and walked away. Harvey's Wine Emporium's only customer in two hours hadn't got what he wanted. Outside it was almost dark and rain began to spatter the window. Adrian switched on the outside lights. Raindrops could be miserable drizzles of water or excellent reflectors of rainbows. It was all a state of mind.

He was in the middle of preparing a Christmas selection hamper when the door opened with such force the sleigh bells hit the floor. Catinca, dressed as a Tartar princess in a soggy faux fur parka and ornamented boots, opened her palms and lifted her shoulders so high she appeared to have no neck.

"What the hell! This shit? Wrong on every level. You crazy? Where this leave me? What you thinking, mate?"

She'd left the door wide open. A wintry draught circled the shop and street noise overpowered the subtle sounds of Chet Baker. She pointed a gloved finger at the window in an accusatory gesture. With an uncomfortable sense of dread, Adrian walked past his irate employee to look at the shop from the street.

On the bottom third of the window, illuminated by internal and external lights, ugly red graffiti drew attention from his bottle tree. The scrawled message read:

HERE SODOMY

He stared in confusion and disbelief, clapped one hand to his mouth and shook his head. Catinca yanked him back into the shop.

"First time you seen it?" She held him by the shoulders.

Adrian nodded, unable to speak.

"You here all day?"

He nodded again.

"Arseholes!" she yelled and slammed out the door. The connection between her curse and the graffiti burst a bubble and a snort of high-pitched laughter escaped him. The confusion drained from his mind and he assessed the day in a selection of stills.

Arriving in the morning and taking a moment to admire the pristine façade. Locking up for twenty minutes while he went to Pret-a-Manger for a soup and a sandwich. Sitting in the gloomy shadow of the brewery dray looking up the word for a fear of nuns. The interminable afternoon. The unsubtle customer.

He picked up the sleigh bells and reattached them to the door. Then he went back to sit behind the counter, unable to act, his thoughts as slow as treacle. It was impossible. No one could have sprayed the shop without him noticing. Although when he was sitting at the counter, the wooden dresser in the centre of the room obscured most of the window. Surely someone must have seen who did it? And what was HERE SODOMY supposed to mean? He'd had homophobic reactions more times than he cared to count when he was younger, but never via the shop. Where had Catinca gone? He stood up, wondering what on earth to do.

Two older women came in, looking for something Italian to go with their book club choice. Adrian recommended a Pinot Grigio. He had just finished advising an endearing young couple on vinho verde when Catinca burst back in, breathing heavily and carrying a clear plastic bottle. The couple departed with their purchases, regarding Catinca with some apprehension. Once the door had tinkled shut behind them, she began.

"No one seen nothing! You call police and get CCTV. John over the road gave me this for to clean. White spirit. I'm gonna start. Call police."

Adrian did as he was told and was passed to a Community Support Officer who asked a series of questions to ascertain if it was a one-off or regular occurrence. He sounded as puzzled as Adrian by the message itself. Since the cleaning had already begun, he told Adrian to photograph the damage and report to him if there were any future incidents.

He put on his jacket to take over from Catinca. She shouldn't have to kneel on a wet pavement scrubbing at red spray paint. But when he got outside, she was pacing around, talking to someone on her mobile, her cloth and bottle of white spirit abandoned. The paint seemed untouched. He took several photographs, his mind muddled.

"OK. See you then, mate." She ended her call and pointed at the bottle. "That shit don't work. Can't get it off, so we gonna hide it, right?"

"Hide it? I suppose we could tape some cardboard to the outside until I can get a professional cleaner here tomorrow. Downstairs I've got boxes for recycling..."

"No. Not cardboard. Not cool. It's organised already. Mates coming. Artists. We gonna graffiti over it, innit?"

Rain dripped down Adrian's neck. His elegant, subtle display with its hints of taste and expense was to be covered in graffiti. Maybe he should just shut the shop, pull down the metal grille and get a glazier in on Monday.

"Catinca, I'm not sure..."

"Adrian?" Across the street, John from the art café called out from his doorway. "Can I do anything?"

Before Adrian could open his mouth, Catinca replied. "We got it sorted, mate. Gonna cover it up. But you know what?"

The phone inside the shop was ringing. Adrian went inside to answer and give this week's order to the wholesaler. By the time he'd finished and served two more customers, he could see considerable activity outside. He followed the last customer into the street.

Catinca was giving orders to three young men with identical haircuts. A variant on the short back and sides, this was more no back nor sides, leaving just a thick black thatch on the top. John was setting up three of his café umbrellas to protect the foursome from the rain. Catinca jerked a thumb at Adrian and said something to her three friends. They nodded at him and one gave the thumbs-up. Adrian responded in kind, a deep weariness overcoming him.

"John, thanks for the loan of these. Catinca, exactly what are you going to do to the window?"

"Me? Nothin'. The crew gonna fix it up. Don't worry. It'll be tasty."

"Tasty?"

"Posh, innit? I know what you like. Don't worry, chief, we gonna do it right for the shop. I reckon you wanna keep it after you see. Go inside. Customers."

He shrugged his shoulders, feeling helpless, and went to attend the evening rush. John came over with coffees for the 'crew' and a cinnamon latte for Adrian. The steady clientele kept Adrian occupied but their curiosity about all the activity under the umbrellas drew his attention time and again to the door. At least he could answer honestly each time someone asked him what was going on.

"I have no idea. Catinca has a plan."

The many exaggerated expressions of concern did nothing to reassure him. He chose to keep his head down and manage the ebb and flow of customers as he tried not to think about it. Around half past eight, things quietened down and the temptation to look around the dresser increased like an itch. Instead, Adrian selected a bottle of wine for each of Catinca's helpers. He wrapped them in tissue paper and added ribbons, feeling a little lost. What did young graffiti artists drink these days?

With a tinkle of sleigh bells, the door opened and Catinca came in, her nose red and her cheeks shining. She took off her gloves, stood behind Adrian and put her cold hands over his eyes. He didn't resist. She guided him out of the door, across the street and turned him to face the shop.

"Ta-da!" she said and took her hands away. Adrian's mouth opened. Forming a festive circle to frame his bottle tree was a graffiti wreath of holly leaves, berries, mistletoe and glinting lights. The original message had been completely obliterated, replaced by an urban ring of red, green, gold, silver and white. The corners of the window were untouched, allowing the warm glow from the interior to spill out while the spotlights on the bottle tree drew the eye to the centrepiece of the display. The effect was magical. He clasped his hands in front of him, mesmerised.

"It's beautiful," he said, and meant it.

Catinca pulled down her fist in a gesture of triumph while the graffitists exchanged some sort of complex handshake. John shook his head, grinned and nodded, in a mixture of disbelief and awe. Adrian thanked everyone at least three times before returning to the shop to fetch their gifts. Catinca followed.

"Mate, you gonna give them twenty quid bottles of wine? You know what, just twenty quid will do."

Adrian took her advice and pulled sixty pounds from the till. It seemed to please them and they left after taking several shots of their handiwork on their phones. Catinca took over the shop while Adrian helped return John's umbrellas and handed him a sublime Moscato grappa. John tried to refuse, emphasising the neighbourly support philosophy but when Adrian mentioned how well it accompanied quality coffee, he accepted with good grace.

Catinca's face was flushed. Whether through achievement or warmth, Adrian couldn't tell. He waited till she'd finished serving a chatty regular and leaned on the counter with a smile.

"You are amazing. That was one hell of a save. I'm not going to insult you with twenty quid or a digestif. But I have to do something to thank you. What would you like? Be honest."

She beamed back at him, her rain-smudged eyeliner softening her feline features. "Make me part of team. Design side. I gotta good eye. You know you can trust me, right? Gimme more responsibility. I could open shop on Mondays for you. Day off for you, more money for me, good for shop. Make me proper assistant, innit?"

He didn't even need to think about it and held out his hand. "Deal. Shall we start after Christmas?"

She shook his hand with a delighted grin. "Why not now? Trade is busy before Christmas, not after. And when is quiet, I can do displays. Next Monday?"

"Why not indeed? Sure, start on Monday. Don't forget I'm away this weekend, so it's good practice for you to handle the shop alone on Saturday."

"I can handle it, mate. Don't worry. Now, you go home. Yeah, yeah, I'll get a cab and keep the receipt. One more look while it's quiet?"

They stood on the pavement, leaning against one another, gazing at the window and grinning like loons.

"You get the CCTV?" she asked.

"No point. The pub had a delivery lorry parked in front this afternoon. Whoever did this had a good hour to act unseen."

"Arseholes."

As he walked down Boot Street, he saw Beatrice's lights were off. Eager to tell her of the evening's triumph, his stomach dipped with frustration until he recalled she was already in Germany. Still, he would be there in two days, eating cake and drinking mulled wine and regaling her with his story. He fumbled in his pocket for his keys and opened the gate, only to see a knot of people in the hallway. Saul looked round as he approached.

"Here he is!" Saul's voice betrayed relief.

The instant the two men in overcoats turned towards him, Adrian knew they were police. His first thought was Beatrice. Plane crash? Kidnapped by German art robbers? High-speed motorway accident on an autobahn?

"Good evening, Mr Harvey, my name is DI Quinn and this is my colleague, DS Marques. Could we have a word?"

A series of images flashed across his mind, both real and imaginary but all equally potent. Two plain-clothes police officers, his post box stuffed with mail, Saul's concern and curiosity, tonight's choir with an empty space in the tenor section, the sheet covering Beatrice's body in a German morgue, a Christmas wreath on a window, the thin wall between him and his own chaise longue.

"Is something wrong?" he asked.

"No, no, we'd just appreciate your assistance with an enquiry. Could we go inside? Thank you for your help, Mr Fasman."

Saul gave Adrian a worried look and retreated inside. Adrian opened his own flat door and led the police in, aware of the smell of last night's garlic. They wouldn't sit.

"Thanks Mr Harvey, but we'd better get on. Would you mind bringing your computer and mobile phone down to the station and answering a few questions? It's nothing more than eliminating people at this stage."

"Eliminating people from what?"

DI Quinn's eyes held his, steady and reassuring. "I'm afraid we have received an anonymous accusation. We're pursuing anyone in possession of images of child pornography in connection with a wider operation. I'm sorry to say your name has come up on two separate occasions and we need to eliminate you from suspicion. It won't take long, sir, and best get it out of the way."

Speechless, Adrian fetched his laptop, put his coat back on and followed the detectives out to their car, conscious of Saul peering out of his front window.

He was released without charges at quarter past twelve. They kept his laptop and smartphone overnight to be subjected to further checks in the morning. He sleepwalked along the street, unaware of the direction he was heading, inhaling the petrichor smell of rain on pigeon shit. Up ahead, a black cab came out of a T junction, its yellow sign glowing. Adrian yelled 'Taxi!' at the top of his voice. The driver's head snapped around and the right indicator blinked.

He bent to the window. "Boot Street, please."

The driver unlocked the doors. Adrian sank into the leather back seat and stared out at the shadowy, rain-lashed streets.

"Horrible night," the taxi driver observed.

Adrian met his eyes in the mirror. "You got that right."

Chapter 6

Frau Professor Doktor Edeltraud Eichhorn. Beatrice tried to envisage the bearer of such a moniker, but failed. The Frau part of the title was useful, as the name Edeltraud gave Beatrice no clue as to gender. The theme from *The Magic Roundabout* danced through her head as she walked along Hardenbergstrasse in the sunshine. The Universität der Künste Berlin stretched along one side of the dual carriageway, a mixture of imposing old architecture and low modern buildings, flanked by trees and flags. Very impressive.

Beatrice checked her watch. Twenty past eleven. Professor Eichhorn's email specified the appointment as eleven-thirty and emphasised the importance of punctuality. She passed a row of bikes and entered the main portal. Calling it a door would have been a disservice to the twin columns either side of an ornate sculptured motto held aloft by stone eagles. Inside, the reception looked like any other university hallway. Notice boards, groups of young people chatting, scuffed floors, a reception desk with a glass window and a waiting area whose only occupant was a little old lady. Beatrice approached the receptionist but before she could announce herself, the old lady appeared at her side.

"Detective Inspector Stubbs?"

"Yes."

"You are ten minutes early. However, that is better than being late. My name is Frau Professor Doktor Eichhorn." She held out a hand. Dressed entirely in black, she only came up to Beatrice's shoulder. Her pewter-coloured hair was cut in a sharp geometric style reminiscent of the 1980s, and her features were highlighted dramatically. She wore deep red lipstick and her peony blue eyes were framed by eyeliner and mascara. For a seventy-five year old, she looked cooler and more stylish than Beatrice had ever been in her life.

Beatrice shook her hand with a smile. "I'm very pleased to meet you. Yes, I wanted to arrive a little early in order to find your office. I didn't expect to find you waiting for me."

"We are not going to my office because I don't have one. I retired completely last year and continue my research at home. The reason I asked you to meet me here is that it is a public place and I have to be sure you are who you say you are. You could be dangerous. Can I please see some kind of official identity?"

"Of course." Beatrice reached into her jacket for her badge, rather taken aback. "Have you had much experience with dangerous detective inspectors?"

The woman scrutinised the badge and handed it back. "Sometimes those who profess to protect us can be the most lethal. Since we have established your identity, I suggest we retire to the office where you can ask your questions in privacy. I dislike the main cafeteria here as it is unpleasantly loud."

"I thought you didn't have an office."

"I borrow one when it is necessary. Wait quickly." She spoke in German to the receptionist, who handed over a key.

"This way." Beatrice followed her along the corridor and into a lift. She cursed her very British trait of being uncomfortable with silence.

"This is a lovely building," she said.

"I suppose it is."

"How long have you been a professor here?"

"I'm not a professor. I already told you I retired. I studied with UDK and after a few years' travelling, I came back to lecture here for forty-three years."

"Forty-three? You must miss it."

"Yes, I suppose I must. Not in a good way. This is our floor."

The image of a university office as cluttered, chaotic and romantic was instantly dispelled as Professor Eichhorn opened the door. The room looked more like a surgery than a seat of learning. Books were filed neatly on shelves, the desk was clean and uncluttered, four discreet paintings hung from the pure white walls.

"Sit, please."

Curious as Beatrice was to take a closer look at the chosen artwork, she obeyed her host, sat on the sofa and took out her notebook. The diminutive ex-professor opened a cupboard and clattered about with something mechanical. An optimist would have guessed it was an espresso machine.

On the coffee table in front of her lay a stack of beautiful Taschen art books. She scanned the titles: Kokoscha, Grosz, Beckmann, Schmidt-Rotluff and most importantly, Dix. Instinct advised her not to touch and she waited until Eichhorn returned with a teapot and two cups. She sat beside Beatrice, folded her hands and looked straight ahead.

"So, Detective Inspector Stubbs, your questions."

"Sorry, but what should I call you? If you're no longer a professor, is it simply Frau Doktor Eichhorn?"

"Frau Eichhorn is sufficient."

"Right. I hoped you could help me formulate my questions. As I said in my email, I have a series of aggravated burglaries to investigate. In every case the target was an example of fine art. The details of all the thefts were in the attachment. My intention is to talk to security experts, victims, insurance companies and art experts such as yourself. I'm a detective so I'm looking for a pattern, for connections. The thefts we associate with violent housebreaking are not limited to a single country, although all of the stolen art originates from Germany."

"That is not strictly true. Tea?"

"Yes please. Milk, no sugar."

"It's peppermint. Milk would be disgusting. The artworks in your file originate from a movement, not a country. Largely a German movement, that much is correct but it encompassed artists across many countries, with western Europe as the locus. All the stolen pieces were created by Expressionist artists. Do I need to start from the beginning or are you aware of the Expressionists?"

She poured the tea and waited for Beatrice to respond.

"I know a little. Artists who worked between the wars and

expressed their feelings about their subjects via distorted depiction. I admit I'm more familiar with Expressionist film than fine art, Frau Eichhorn. So maybe you should start at the beginning."

Eichhorn placed the cup on a coaster and looked directly at Beatrice. "Good. To admit ignorance opens the door to intelligence. Can I commence with a question? What do you understand by expressionism?"

The sensation of being back at school, put on the spot with the holes in her knowledge exposed, left Beatrice speechless, her brain scrambling for any kind of association.

"Crudely, I understand the term as meaning a reflection of an individual's subjective experience as opposed to trying to create an objective impression for the viewer."

Eichhorn inclined her head a few millimetres, her eyelids reducing the blue to a mere slit.

"Umm... the artist attempts to convey his own sentiments," Beatrice blustered. "In the most basic terms, it's a question of perspective. If the painter feels oppressed and intimidated by a person, building or even a feeling, he depicts that figure as huge, throwing a shadow across the image. It's an expression of inner thought. And influential across all kinds of media."

"Yes, that is very basic, but we have to start somewhere. Drink your tea and I will show you."

A faint smile softened her face and gave the distinct impression she was looking forward to delivering her first lecture of the year. Beatrice settled back and sipped her milkless, minty tea.

An hour and a half later, she had filled twelve pages of notes. Her mind was full of the stark, exaggerated images of George Grosz's lurid streetscapes, Oskar Kokoschka's troubled eyes, the harsh sketches of Otto Dix, James Ensor's masks, the haunting depravity of Max Beckmann. So many evocative names such as *Die Brücke* and *Der Blaue Reiter* echoed in her ears. Several paintings were familiar but took a new sense of the political with Eichhorn's passionate contextualising. She needed some time to process all this information.

A vague sense of distress tensed her brow and she recognised the signs of over-empathising. Sensitive, intelligent men sent to fight, who experienced extreme brutality and horrors, returned home broken, damaged and ignored. And when they depicted such cruelty with visceral brushstrokes or woodcuts, they met with outrage and disgust. Less than a generation later their artworks, and in some cases livelihoods, were removed by the Nazi regime, labelled subversive.

Beatrice closed her notebook, unable to absorb any more. "Frau Eichhorn..."

"Yes, yes. You must be hungry. I understand. Go and find some food. I also need a rest. We can continue after a break."

"No, that's not what I was going to say. This is all incredibly helpful. I'd like some time to think about it and read some of the material you have given me. Right now, I feel saturated. Would you mind if we stopped here and continued our conversation at a later stage?"

"It depends when. I am free this afternoon but tomorrow and Friday I will be researching. I could meet you on Saturday for a short time. How long do you stay in Berlin?"

Beatrice shook her head. "I have to leave for Hamburg in three hours. Could I call you on Saturday with more specific queries?"

Frau Eichhorn pushed back her metallic grey fringe. "A question for you, first. Do you like these?" She flourished a hand across the open books with all the élan of an Italian traffic cop.

Beatrice looked at the pictures, trying to assemble some kind of cohesive response. Her feelings would not fit into words, so she answered with the clumsy truth.

"I couldn't say I liked them. They are powerful and affecting, certainly. In a strange way, they make me feel a little ashamed or even shocked. It's as if these artists lifted up the rug and showed all the dirt underneath."

"I think they would be pleased to hear such a response. For a police officer, you show some comprehension of what art can do. Yes, you can telephone me on Saturday. Not before, please. Can you find your way out by yourself?"

Beatrice assured Frau Eichhorn she could, expressed her thanks and they shook hands once again. As she turned to wave goodbye at the door, the small figure remained bent over the woodcut prints of EL Kirchner with the intensity of someone reading a love letter.

When she stepped out of the plane in Hamburg, snowflakes tumbled out of the darkness onto her hair, shoulders and face. No one else seemed at all enamoured of this Christmassy spectacle, so Beatrice kept her enthusiasm to herself. She hoped the snow would continue till the weekend. Adrian would love it. The other passengers hurried across the tarmac to the waiting bus, but a man intercepted Beatrice at the bottom of the steps.

"Detective Inspector Stubbs, my name is Herr Jan Stein, detective with the Hamburg police force. We spoke on the telephone."

Beatrice stared at the impossibly handsome man in front of her. Surely jaws as square as his only existed in comic books? She shook his hand.

"Hello Herr Stein. Good to meet you."

"Likewise. You can clear immigration this way. You have hand luggage only?"

"Yes. Just this." She lifted the handle of her wheelie case.

"I take it. Come. It is snowing." He picked up her case and gestured for her to accompany him. Not exactly a smiler. More of the tall, dark and brooding type. His physique made Beatrice think of a word she would normally ridicule. Hunk.

She followed him through the terminal building, showed her passport and police badge to an official and emerged out of a side door once again into a snowy courtyard. An unmarked Mercedes was parked against the wall. Stein unlocked it and indicated she should get in while he stowed her case. He hadn't said a word since they left the aircraft.

She opened the passenger door only to find a steering wheel in the way.

"You want to drive, Detective Inspector?"

"Oh, of course. So sorry." She gave him a look of contrition and was surprised to see him smile.

In the correct seat, she fastened her seatbelt. He started the car and circled away from the terminal building towards the barrier.

"Did you have a pleasant flight?" he asked.

"Yes, thank you. Very short."

"Good. And your meeting in Berlin was successful?"

"Hard to say. I hope it will prove to be. Perhaps when I meet the cultural crime unit, I'll have more of an idea."

"Ah yes. Unfortunately I have bad news. Herr Meyer had to postpone tomorrow's meeting until Friday. I apologise for the short notice."

"Oh. That's disappointing. I'd hoped to meet him before I go to Amsterdam."

Stein glanced at her. "I suggest changing your schedule. We can organise a flight to Amsterdam in the morning so you can complete that part of your investigation. When you come back tomorrow afternoon, you can use a room at the police department here. On Friday, a meeting is scheduled for two-thirty with the BKA."

"Baker-what?"

"Sorry. That was German. Bravo-Kilo-Alpha. *Bundeskriminalamt* or Federal Criminal Investigations in Wiesbaden. DI Stubbs, it's getting late so I can take you directly to your hotel if you wish. Alternatively, I can take you to meet Herr and Frau Köbel. They were the victims of the first theft. It might help provide some context."

Beatrice thought about it. "Not exactly tired, detective, but the professor gave me a crash course in the Expressionist art movement and I'll need a bit of time to get all that straight in my own head. I'm not sure how much more context I can absorb today."

He didn't take his eyes from the road as he indicated left. "This is a different kind of context."

They only stayed for twenty minutes, during which Stein acted as interpreter for Herr Köbel. Stein's translation of his words lent Köbel's story a haunting sense of helpless melancholy, reflecting Beatrice's impressions of the paintings Frau Eichhorn had shown her earlier. Stein's rendition of the old man's story echoed in her ears.

"He met her at school, fifty-two years ago. Both were good

students. They fought and argued and competed with each other to get the best grades. He was in love with her, but was too timid to speak. When he returned from military service, she took control. She asked him to marry her. He says he nearly ruined everything by bursting into tears. In his whole life, he was never happier than on their wedding day. She had her own medical practice, he worked for Deutsche Bank. They had three children, a beautiful home and a passion for collecting art. She had exceptional taste and when her father left her fifty thousand Deutschmarks in his will, she bought the Schlichter. It was her most precious possession. They were planning a trip around the top European art galleries for their fortieth wedding anniversary.

"The night of the robbery, he was attending a business awards ceremony. His driver brought him home late. He found her in the hallway."

Köbel clasped his hands together and closed his eyes. Stein filled in the details in English while the elderly man composed himself.

"Forensics established the basic outline of events. The thieves rang the doorbell. When she answered, they attacked her with a blunt object. She suffered severe head trauma, broken ribs and internal bleeding, indicating she had been repeatedly kicked. From the hallway, they went to the painting in the dining room, removed it and left the way they came. No other rooms disturbed, no searching for anything to loot and none of the neighbours saw anything. The house has a security system with alarms and security cameras. Only active while the owners are absent."

Herr Köbel was listening. He gave Stein a nod of gratitude and continued in German. Stein relayed the content to Beatrice.

"He says she spent half a year in hospital. Physically, she made a full recovery. According to the doctors, there's nothing wrong with her brain. He says he is not a doctor but he is an expert on his wife. She is not there. Her personality, her opinions, her spirit are all gone. She eats, sleeps and likes everything. This is a woman who used to throw shoes at politicians on the television and swam naked in the lake. She shouted at him for buying *foie gras*, smoked marijuana in the garden and cried so hard at a sculpture in the Prado that he had to take her outside. He asks me to tell you this: she loved that painting. Whoever took it also took his wife. He knows he'll never get either of them back."

Beatrice swallowed. "Please tell him we'll do everything in our power to bring these people to justice and restore the artworks to their owners."

Before Stein opened his mouth, the old man spoke in English. "I understand. Thank you. But the owner of that painting is gone."

He reached for the hand of the woman next to him on the sofa. Her eyes left the muted television and she tilted her face to him with a warm smile. She squeezed his hand, nodded at their guests, patted the cat and returned to a quiz show she couldn't hear.

Herr Köbel walked them to the door and stood, frail yet upright, in the cold evening air to wave them off. Beatrice got into the Mercedes, now covered in a gauzy layer of snow, and waved back. Stein drove away in silence, possibly glad of a rest after twenty minutes acting as interpreter. The snowy streets, the streams of brake lights, the festive decorations, traffic signals and shop windows drifted past, making no impression on Beatrice. Her mind was still in that warm little room listening to Herr Köbel's polite, patient repetition of a story he had told countless times while his gentle wife with the sweetest smile watched a silent TV and stroked a tortoiseshell cat. Detective Stein steered the Mercedes into a parking space and turned off the engine. Beatrice brought herself back to the moment.

"Is this the hotel?"

"Yes. It has a very good seafood restaurant I can recommend. I hope you sleep well and a car will collect you at eight in the morning. Do you need anything else?"

"Just my bag."

They exited the car into wet slush. Beatrice buttoned up her coat while Stein fetched her suitcase.

"Thank you. I really appreciate your showing me the context of the robbery."

"It's not easy, I know. But if we don't see the detail, we don't see the big picture. Have a nice evening, DI Stubbs."

She watched him drive away and dragged her case up the hotel steps. An empathetic, good-looking, intelligent detective? He wouldn't last long.

Chapter 7

He dreamt about his hair falling out. Clumps of it on his pillow, bald patches on his scalp. That was a new one. Usually when he was having a nervous or insecure phase, Adrian dreamt he'd lost his teeth. On the plus side, if he was having bad dreams, at least it meant he was getting some sleep.

He woke at six, packed and prepared for the 'ifs'. If the police gave him back his laptop, if Catinca could cover Friday, if he was permitted to leave the country, if he could get a flight to Hamburg tonight... He occupied himself with the practicalities of if to drown out the whine of the who and the why.

There was little he could do without his computer or phone, so when the eight o'clock pips came on the radio, it was time to leave for the shop. Adrian checked all the windows were secure, watered all the plants, turned off the heating, picked up his expandable suitcase and locked the flat. He had written a note for Saul, but as he could hear the sound of breakfast television from inside, he rapped three times on the door.

Saul was in his dressing gown and Tigger slippers, a circle of ginger hair sticking up around his bald patch. His head looked like a gas ring.

"Adrian! Didn't hear you come in last night. Everything all right?"

"Not really. Someone made unfounded allegations. The police won't say who or what exactly. Anyway, as soon as they've finished checking my computer, I'm in the clear. Look, Saul, I hope you know..."

"Hey, I told them you're a decent geezer who wouldn't harm a fly. Don't worry about it. Anything I can do?"

"Yes, if you don't mind. I hope to get away for the weekend, just for a mini-break. Could you keep an eye on my flat? Don't buzz anyone in on my behalf and let me know if you see any..."

He couldn't bring himself to say the word. Nuns. Even to himself he sounded paranoid.

Saul finished his sentence. "Anything out of the ordinary?"

"Exactly. Thanks Saul, you're very kind."

Adrian spent the morning making arrangements with Catinca, Lufthansa and the Hotel Europaeischer, with irritating interruptions from customers. Just before lunch he tried to get hold of Holger, one of the few people on earth without a mobile phone. He called his home and workplace and left messages. He emailed Beatrice to let her know of his potential early arrival and intended to spend his lunch break retrieving his computer from the police station. But just before midday, the police detective from the previous night, DI Quinn, entered the shop carrying a laptop case.

"Morning, Mr Harvey. Brought this back for you. Your mobile's in the front pocket. Apologies for the inconvenience. Do you have a minute?"

"Yes. One sec." Adrian locked the door and turned the wooden sign to 'Closed for lunch'. He faced the detective, his arms folded.

DI Quinn placed the case on the counter with a reassuring smile. "We're not taking this any further. There's no evidence of your involvement in anything to do with illegal images of children."

"Of course there isn't!" Adrian's relief made his voice sound harsh and raw.

The officer's relaxed manner remained unchanged. "Mr Harvey, we believe you were the target of a classic misassociation and, more than likely, the subject of a random prejudicial attack. We see this more often than we'd like. There's nothing in either accusation to suggest this is personal. Unless you can think of anyone who might want to cause you problems?"

Adrian shook his head.

"No other incidents you think could be connected?"

"Connected to child porn? I get the odd homophobic comment

now and then, or aggressive attitudes in the street. We even had graffiti on the shop yesterday. But associating me with paedophilia because I'm gay? That's sick."

"But not unusual. You'd be surprised at the people who know nothing of statistics but are expert at making assumptions. If any other events come to mind, let me know."

Adrian flicked his eyes to the window and the busy street devoid of nuns.

"Mr Harvey? Is there something else you want to say?"

"Yes. Am I allowed to leave the country?"

"Bit extreme, but of course you can. No charges, no criminal record, you're free to go where you want. Lanzarote's not bad at this time of year."

The last if.

Adrian stood and shook the sergeant's hand. "Thanks for returning my laptop. If I think of anything else, I'll let you know."

"Yeah, you do that. Here's my card. While I'm here, I'd better take a decent bottle of red for dinner. That Argentinean Shiraz looks like a bargain."

The police sergeant hadn't even closed the door with his bargain before Adrian was on the phone.

"Beatrice? I'll be there tonight!"

Whether it was the journey, the stress of the previous twenty-four hours or the two gin and tonics he and Beatrice had consumed in the hotel bar last night, Adrian slept better than he had in weeks. His dreams, if he'd had any, did not involve the loss of any body parts or uncharacteristic violence. The Hotel Europaeischer was quiet and restful, despite its position opposite the main train station. He rolled over to check the time. His watch showed twenty to nine, but that was still GMT. Here it was twenty to ten and Holger would be arriving at eleven to take him on a tour of the city. Adrian sprang out of bed, switched on the mini coffee machine and jumped into the shower, where he launched into a lusty version of *Do You Hear The People Sing?* from Les Mis.

True to form, Holger was punctual. Adrian was waiting in the foyer and had just sent Beatrice a *Bon Voyage* text for her trip to Amsterdam when a tall figure approached.

"Holger!" Adrian bounced out of the leather sofa and opened his arms for a hug. With a moment's hesitation, Holger embraced him with slap on the back then stepped away.

"Adrian, it's good to see you. Are you well?"

"I feel better than I have in a long time. Must be the Hamburg air. How are you? How's the instrument-making business?"

Holger put his hands in the pockets and shrugged. The padded jacket made him look even bulkier than he was and a beanie hid his blond hair, but his eyes, the colour of oxidised copper, were warm and familiar.

"For a change, very good. I'm repairing as well as building and working six days a week. I actually have an urgent job to finish today. Is it OK if we have lunch and I leave you to explore? At the weekend, I'm free, but I wasn't expecting you so early."

Adrian smiled. "I know and I'm sorry. Just fancied getting away as soon as I could. Yes, I had no breakfast so I'm starving. Let's have something to eat then just point me in the direction of the cool places. I'll be quite content to amuse myself before Beatrice gets back this evening."

They took the U-Bahn a couple of stops, a short trip during which Holger used Adrian's map to point out where to go and how to get there. When they emerged at Stadthausbrücke, Holger led the way to a bright bar with hefty wooden tables like a school refectory. It was a bit early for the lunchtime rush, but a few customers were perched on stools looking out the window, drinking coffee and working on their laptops. The bar smelled of herbs and coffee beans, making Adrian feel right at home.

Holger spoke in German to the barman who made a friendly 'help yourself' gesture towards the tables. They took off their coats, settled on a spot in the middle and sat down to pick up the menu. Adrian put it down again, unable to understand a word.

"OK, the lunch deal here is two kinds of pasta, one meat, one veggie, or the house salad. The pasta is homemade, the sauce is freshly cooked and the salad comes with goat's cheese and fig mustard. What I usually do is half and half. Half salad, half pasta.

The sauces on offer today are tomato and basil, or lemon chicken."

Adrian, for once, opted to be guided. "Perfect. I'll have half and half too, with the veggie sauce."

While Holger spoke to the waiter, Adrian looked around at the art on the walls, the cool concrete bar and the orange lettering on the window.

"I ordered you a glass of house red. I take water, because I must work this afternoon."

"The perfect accompaniment. Thank you. What does that say?" Adrian pointed to the words on the window, giving up on trying to read an unfamiliar language back-to-front from the inside of the bar.

"*Erste Liebe* is the name of the bar. It means First Love. That sign says *Die Erste Liebe vergisst man nie*, which means..."

"You never forget your first love."

Holger gave a bashful smile. "Yes. I thought it was appropriate."

Adrian reached across and squeezed Holger's arm. "I'm touched. Although it's probably more accurate to say your first experience."

"No. You weren't my first gay experience. I've been in love before and had sex with both genders, but I'd never fallen in love with a man until I met you."

The waiter brought the drinks, giving Adrian a moment to catch up with the sudden intensity of the conversation. He replayed their entire relationship in the time it took for the waiter to pour their drinks. The initial attraction, the sexual compatibility, the sad and relentless chafing of personalities and the bitter taste of defeat. He looked into the pale turquoise eyes of his ex.

"Well, thank you. I feel privileged. And even more so that we managed to stay friends after we split up. I really am very pleased to see you again."

"Likewise. I have a lot to thank you for."

"You can redress the balance this weekend. I shared all my best London tips and hard-won secrets with you and expect a local's guide to Hamburg in return. Beatrice and I are both keen on fish, so where would you recommend?"

"I made a list of places for you. Here. And I invite you both for lunch on Sunday. I'm babysitting my god-daughter, who you must meet. My plan is to cook lunch for us all, then go to the animal park."

"Lovely idea! How old is she?"

"Nearly seven and she speaks English. As well as German and Danish."

"Oh God. Linguistically shamed by a child. Here's the food."

The waiter wished them *Guten Appetit* as he placed the plates before them.

"*Danke.*" Holger ground some pepper onto his pasta. "Yes, but it wasn't tourist tips I wanted to thank you for. It was for letting me be myself."

"Mmm, fresh basil." Adrian's inhalation masked a sigh. He recognised all the signals. Holger had Something To Say. "What do you mean, be yourself?"

Holger's fork hovered over the plate. "Allowing myself to be gay. Before I met you, I believed I was straight and just occasionally experimented with men. Two conversations with you made me realise I wasn't."

"Really? I love these kind of revelations! Come on then, what did I say? Maybe I should start some kind of blog. The Gay Guru." Adrian speared a cherry tomato and popped it into his mouth.

"It wasn't what you said, it was your attitude. You have a sense of... entitlement. You believe that you can have everything you want in life. That being a homosexual is not a minus."

Adrian frowned, the evening spent answering questions at the police station shadowing his thoughts. "Of *course* it's not. In fact, it's completely the opposite. I couldn't have everything I want in life if I wasn't gay." His reply sounded rather sharper than he intended. He softened his tone. "Although I suppose if I wasn't, I wouldn't want that in the first place. But you know what I mean."

"Yes, now I do. It's hard to explain to someone like you."

"Someone like me?" Adrian wished they could just eat their lunch and talk about the weather.

"Someone whose background was very different. My family were not exactly homophobic, mostly left-leaning and liberal, at least for Bavaria. Although they didn't condemn gay people, they taught me a strong sense of pity. They never said it in so many words but their attitude was that homosexuals can't help themselves. We should be kind to them, compassionate and never persecute a person for what he is, but they can never have the social advantages straight people have. It was as if being gay was a kind of disability."

The pasta was going cold. Adrian had stopped eating and Holger hadn't started.

"What on earth do you mean by social advantages?"

"Love, marriage and children. Social acceptability. Equality. All the kinds of things a bourgeois son of a councillor believes are the key to satisfaction. If I am completely truthful, I thought if I ever came out, I'd be throwing myself into a ghetto. You showed me another side to the story. You and Beatrice."

"Beatrice isn't gay. A total commitment-phobe, perhaps, but definitely straight." He scooped up some goat's cheese with a piece of bread. "Will you eat? I can see you've got something to get off your chest, but that can be done without wasting a lovely meal."

With a half-smile, Holger cut up a chunk of chicken. "You're right."

They ate, appreciating the food.

Adrian took a sip of wine and said it for him. "You want kids."

Holger nodded and shook his head simultaneously, an evasive gesture.

"Don't avoid the question. I know you do. And why not? You live in Germany, in a progressive city where I bet you can marry and adopt and bring up a child in a happy community with bike lanes and crèches and gay parenting support groups."

"In Hamburg, yes that's true. The laws here are progressive and the people have an open mind."

"So your biggest worry is what the parents will say? Holger, you cannot let your upbringing dictate your life. Your family taught you a lot of good things, such as respect and manners and responsibility, but there comes a time when you can teach them something about how the world has changed. One of the worst things you can do is to live the life your parents wished for you, because it will never be your own. Seriously, I know what I'm talking about."

Holger shook his head, this time a definite no. "That is not my biggest worry. My family will accept it or they will not. I will be sad if they don't, but it's up to them. My biggest worry is that I'm thirty-five, I just realised who I am, and I only ever met one man I loved. I want children, yes, desperately. But as myself, in a loving relationship with someone who wants that as much as I do."

Adrian put down his cutlery and dabbed his mouth with a napkin. "I don't suppose we could compromise on a Schnauzer?"

Holger smiled but didn't laugh. "I wasn't suggesting you. We're not right for each other, I know that. I'm just afraid I'll never meet someone who works with his hands, who has a feeling for nature, who takes care of those he loves, who wants to raise a child and is someone I can respect."

"You will. You are a lovely person, not to mention hot as hell. There is someone out there fantasising about their dream man this minute and you tick all the boxes. I promise you'll find him. Believe it and it will happen."

"Thank you. Can you give me some idea of when?"

Adrian closed his eyes and pressed his fingers to his temples. "February the second. That gives you just enough time to join the German equivalent of Grindr, ditch the timewasters and start meeting a whole new bunch of friends. I'll compose a profile for you this afternoon because trying to express one's own fabulousness is impossible. I know because I've tried."

Chapter 8

Geert de Vries was not happy to see Beatrice. He opened the door to his beautiful red-brick home on Apollolaan in Amsterdam's Oud-Zuid district with all the enthusiasm of a dead fish. A small man with a thick steel-grey hair, he asked for ID, examined it and only then shook her hand, a cold, limp gesture. He led her to a morning room at the back of the house overlooking a wide canal.

All the relevant documentation was spread on the table and he pulled out a chair for her to sit down. He offered no refreshments.

"I am afraid your visit here is wasted. I can add nothing to previous statements, which were exhaustive." His voice was tight, rehearsed and passive-aggressive.

"Thank you for making the time to see me. I apologise for the change in schedule."

"I should be at a business meeting in St Petersburg right now. Instead I had to cancel my plans to repeat myself to the police. I have nothing more to say about the loss of that piece."

Beatrice gave him a patient smile. "I'm less interested in the practical elements of the theft, Mr de Vries. I'm working with the BKA to establish any links between a series of art robberies. Could you tell me a little about the painting?"

His eel-like eyes flickered over her. "It was one of my most expensive acquisitions. One point four million Euros. An original Max Beckmann can go for much more. One sold for twenty million dollars at action in New York. The self-portraits of his exile here in the 1930s are in demand. Those and his nudes."

"What attracted you to the piece?"

"I'm a professional collector. I buy and sell with a view to appreciation in value. Beckmann is one of the most highly prized artists in certain circles. I had intended to sell *Portrait of an Exile* in the next two years."

"I assume you liked it? As it was a picture of Amsterdam as well."

His lip pulled up into a sneer. "I deal in art. I handle many pieces I do not personally like. Collecting artworks because they depict your home town or favourite animal is for old ladies. I am a professional. That said, this piece was a favourite and I hung it in this room. The thieves got in through that window and escaped via the canal. It seems either the intruders disabled the alarm system or the security firm were negligent. However, I was fully insured so I have been financially compensated."

"If the piece surfaced again, would you buy it back?"

De Vries narrowed his eyes. "Why would I do that?"

"You said it was a favourite."

He gave a dismissive shake of his head. "Tastes change. I am now focusing on more contemporary European artists."

Beatrice changed tack. "I notice from your statements you have been burgled before."

"Unfortunately, yes."

"It is odd that on both occasions only one piece was taken, don't you think? I understand you lost a Paula Rego in 2010."

"Which was underinsured. I made a loss and learned my lesson. Do you have many more questions? I have a lunch appointment."

"Just a few, I won't keep you long. That Rego painting, *The Schoolgirl*. Was it stolen from this room too?"

His cool grey gaze didn't waver. "No. That picture hung in my bedroom."

"I see. So the casual visitor would have been unlikely to know it was there."

"The criminal element knows I have an expensive hobby."

"Mmm. Let's just hope the criminal element doesn't do it again, shall we? Otherwise it might look rather like a pattern. Now, can I ask about the provenance of the piece?"

Her hint found its mark and two smudges of colour bloomed on his cheeks. He held out a folder. "It's all here. What more do you need to know?"

Beatrice made a pretence at reading the document for appearances' sake. She already had what she needed to know.

After she left the unpleasant little man, she had a couple of hours to potter around Amsterdam before catching her flight back to Hamburg. She wandered along the canals until she saw a cafe with green-clothed tables and chairs in the sunshine. She stopped for coffee and a waffle, entranced by the spectacle of a young couple taking a small black piglet for a walk. On her way back to the station, she found a patisserie selling alphabet letters made of chocolate. She bought an M for Matthew, though the chances of it surviving the weekend intact were slim.

A melancholy settled on her as she looked into windows of homes decorated for Christmas, gazed at gabled roofs reflected in canals and stepped out of the way of bicycles. When she was younger, everywhere had the potential to be a place she might live one day. Not any longer. Her future was mapped – retirement to the English countryside. It was exactly what she wanted. Yet however well-travelled she might be, she'd never experienced the adventure of becoming a local in another country.

She sighed and stopped on the apex of a bridge. A glass-roofed boat passed beneath and tourists waved up at her. She waved back, wondering if they thought her Dutch. Somehow making a choice was cause for regret in itself. It was the same sensation she often encountered when handing back a menu. Those other dishes, tastes and sensory experiences were no longer an option. All the things she could have tried, all the places she could have known, all the lives she could have lived. You open one door and a hundred others slam shut behind you.

She dallied at the skating rink behind the Rijksmuseum, where her attention was caught by a Chinese couple. Hopeless skaters, giggling and clutching each other, they spent more time horizontal than vertical. In the couple of minutes she watched them, he fell over four times and took her down with him. Her thin legs skittered about like those of a newborn foal, shooting off in all directions. The man clambered to his feet and held her, standing still as the swirl of skaters passed by and in their own little eye of the storm, they kissed.

A wave of loss hit Beatrice, as forceful a sensation as when one's stomach gets left behind in a dropping lift. She wanted Matthew, here, this minute. Exploring a foreign city was no fun without someone to exclaim and point and take pictures with. This time next year she would be in Devon, adding brandy to her cake mixture, mooching about in markets, hiding presents from him and preparing their very first Christmas as cohabitees. Twelve more months and she would be handing back the menu and enjoying the dish of her choice. She should be happy. So why could she hear the echo of slamming doors?

Her job was done, if not to her satisfaction. By Friday morning she had completed her task in Hamburg's police department and was fully prepared for that afternoon's meeting. She'd checked connections, interviewed victims, sifted evidence and collaborated with local officers, but nothing stood out. That lack of substance niggled at her all morning. She finished typing and sat back to stare at three walls of her borrowed room covered in art prints, documents, photographs and a blown-up map. Where was the connection? She went over it all one last time.

The paintings. Apart from belonging to the same art movement, they were all quite different.

Hamburg. Rudolf Schlichter. *Frau mit Zigarette und Katze*. 1932. White background, smoking woman in green dress, black cat, both gazing at the viewer with absinthe green eyes.

Amsterdam. Max Beckmann. *Portrait of an Exile*. 1939. Man on bridge. A canal in the background, signs of wear and tear on face and clothes. Eyes cast left in fear as locals look on.

London. Otto Dix. *The Salon II*. 1921. The prostitutes at rest, staring at the intruder, breath held, waiting to see which way their fate would go.

The paintings had as little in common as the robberies. Brutal attack leaving woman permanently damaged early evening. Break-in while family on holiday. Mid-morning assault on cleaner. The thieves had done thorough research on the occupants' routine as well as the precise location of the paintings. In each case, nothing else was taken. Not even in the Oud-Zuid incident in the Netherlands, where the security system was disabled and the burglars had all the time in the world.

The owners were all wealthy, but seemed to have varying levels of passion for their acquisitions. Yesterday in Amsterdam, the haddock-faced art dealer saw dollar signs instead of brushstrokes, where Frau Köbel, according to her husband, had loved the painting with the same passion she used to have for many things in life. The American in London, Chet Waring, had given the impression of enjoying the controversial content while fully cognisant of the piece's value.

Beatrice stretched and stood up. Perhaps there were no connections and she should stop trying to invent them. She looked out through the glass wall at the activity in Hamburg's open plan police department office and wondered what to do about lunch. Her mobile buzzed. An incoming message from Adrian with no text but a photograph. A selfie, wide-eyed, jaw dropped and one hand clasped to his cheek, standing underneath a street sign: Reeperbahn. She smiled. So he'd found 'The Sinful Mile'. His mock shock reminded her of Edvard Munch's most famous work. Another Expressionist.

Someone rapped a knuckle on the glass door. Mr Mills and Boon stood outside waiting for her to beckon him in. In a crew-necked jumper and jeans, Stein looked twice as handsome as when she'd first seen him. She motioned for him to enter with her right hand, smoothing her hair with her left.

"Hello Detective Stein. How are you?"

"Thank you, fine. Is everything in order? Do you have all you need?"

"Absolutely. Just making the final preparations for our meeting, then I'll remove everything from the walls and tidy up before I leave."

"You leave us today?" His jaw, shaded by planes of stubble, jutted forward, making her think of a snowplough.

"I should say so. I've discovered nothing new, so once I've reported back to Herr Meyer, I'll get out of your way."

"You are not in anyone's way. Do you have plans for lunch or would you like to come with me to the police canteen? My team are keen to meet you. The menu on Friday is usually fish."

"Yes please. I'd be delighted to meet your colleagues. As a matter of fact, I love fish and I've eaten it at every meal since I arrived – including breakfast."

She packed up her laptop and cleared away her notes, looking forward not only to some food, but also to sitting opposite Detective Stein. Pleasant scenery guaranteed.

Stein's team were a friendly bunch, if a little reticent to begin with, who soon began asking general questions about Scotland Yard, London and Interpol, gradually getting more specific and related to her current case. She tucked into a fish pie and answered as best she could. Two of the sergeants, Rudi and Kurt, could have been catalogue models, both blond and bland. The youngest of the group was Margrit, a tomboyish young woman with a ready smile and an expression full of curiosity. The remaining members of the team were Berndt, a retired detective, acting as a consultant and Tomas, the IT specialist. Neither of the latter two said much and Beatrice suspected they were uncomfortable speaking English.

Stein worked the table like a professional cocktail party host. DI Stubbs might be interested to know that Rudi (Blond No. 1) had studied in London. Cue conversation on locations and impressions. When it came to languages, Margrit was their star. How many was it, he asked her.

"Five. This is mostly luck of birth, DI Stubbs. My mother is Danish, my father is a Finn and I grew up in Germany. I learned English in school and spent summer camp in Spain. If you have two languages, it just gets easier."

"I'm sure you're right. I do admire people who speak more than one language. I can barely say good morning in any other tongue but English."

The IT expert, Tomas, lifted his head from his plate. "You don't need to. English is the world's second language."

"Yes, that is true. But I imagine Spanish or Chinese would also be useful. Are you multilingual too, Tomas?"

Margrit laughed. "Yes! He speaks German, English and HTML!"

Everyone joined in her laughter although Tomas contributed nothing more than a close-mouthed smile. Beatrice observed him in her peripheral vision while responding to a question about her opinion of Hamburg. He bent his head over his food, clearly listening but reluctant to participate. She watched as he cut off a portion of fish, added a potato cube and a dab of spinach and forked the arrangement into his mouth. His skin had a wan, unhealthy pallor, not helped by the grey jumper and stone-washed jeans.

Beatrice added a comment designed to include everyone. "And I'd appreciate some advice from you locals. One thing I plan to do before I leave the city is visit a Christmas market. I hear you have several."

Margrit, Rudi and Kurt shouted over each other to tell her which was the best, and even Berndt proffered an opinion by nodding his head. Tomas reached into his back pocket for a fold-out map, which he handed to Beatrice. She opened it.

Stein stood up. "Plenty of advice there, DI Stubbs. I need more water. Can I get anything for anyone else?"

They all shook their heads and he glided off across the room with all the grace and strength of a ballet dancer. Beatrice admired his impressive physique over the top of Tomas's map.

"Have a look at the backside."

Beatrice snapped around, mortified, aware of her colour rising. Tomas reached across and turned the map over.

Margrit shrieked with laughter and broke into German. "*Dass war toll! Tomas hat eben gesagt 'Schauen Sie mal am Arsch'!*"

The blonds and Margrit slapped the table in amusement, Berndt chuckled but Tomas had blushed a livid red. Beatrice, excluded from the joke, did not smile.

"Sorry, DI Stubbs," Margrit wiped her eyes. "I was explaining Tomas's mistake. He didn't know that 'backside' has a different meaning in English. He was trying to tell you to look at the back of the map, but you understood 'Look at the arse'! Your face was so funny. I wish I had my Handy."

The honking of the blonds and Margrit began to grate on Beatrice's nerves.

"The mistake was mine. I should have realised. Sorry Tomas."

Stein returned with his water bottle. "What's the joke?"

Tomas pushed his plate away and wiped his hands, preparing to leave.

Beatrice placed her knife and fork together. "Another example of my linguistic incompetence, I'm afraid. But while we're on the subject, Margrit, the correct word for your communications device would be mobile phone. Cell phone in the US. Handy has quite a different meaning in English. Well, that meal was quite delicious. I must say you are lucky to have such an excellent canteen. I can't remember the last time I ate at Scotland Yard. It always smells of frying."

Margrit's grin had disappeared, Tomas's blush returned, the blonds and Berndt looked to each other for some indication of how to react, and Stein picked up his cue with effortless style.

"Good to know, thank you. Our canteen also has a reputation for delicious desserts. Would you like to select one? Then you and I can take a coffee and discuss how we approach this meeting."

"Yes, please. Nice meeting you all and thank you for your hospitality. Have a pleasant afternoon." She bestowed a general smile as they wished her the same and followed the broad shoulders of Detective Stein in the direction of the dessert counter.

Herr Meyer represented the central Federal Criminal Investigations Office, but was also a member of Interpol's Expert Group on Stolen Cultural Property. He listened with silent attention as Beatrice reported her lack of findings. He asked several questions of her and of Stein, courteously using English so everyone could follow. His line of questioning focused on the insurance cover for each painting and he showed scant interest in the background of the artists. He took Beatrice's report and placed it straight into his briefcase.

She reined in her irritation. He had not apologised for postponing their meeting, nor had he attempted to provide her with any guidance. Thus she had been left alone to work her own line of enquiry. Now it seemed she had wasted her time. She aimed for a polite, conciliatory tone.

"I'm far from an expert," she said, "but the only visible element connecting these three thefts is an art movement. My task here is complete, but if I had the chance to continue, I'd want to pursue those links. Or perhaps I'm being naïve? Do you believe this is nothing more than an insurance scam?"

Meyer checked his watch and addressed Stein. "Will you arrange a car for me? My flight is in ninety minutes. Thank you."

Once Stein had left the room, Meyer faced Beatrice with a smile. The same sort of smile a dentist or clinician might wear while delivering a diagnosis.

"I wish you could continue, DI Stubbs. If I had the budget to pay an art expert or committed detective inspector to 'pursue these links', I would. Our problem is that there are two main reasons for art theft. The myth of the ruthless collector is the most glamorous and the least plausible. I'm not saying that discerning, wealthy and amoral collectors do not exist. They do. Unfortunately, so do organised gangs of thieves, fences, lawyers and corrupt white-collar individuals.

"Our experience is that most thefts are in fact 'art-napping'. Thieves steal to order, keep the piece in a safe place for up to three years, then via a third party, offer a ransom to the owner or the insurance company. No insurers admit to paying ransoms, of course. But artworks are frequently returned, their condition generally worse."

Beatrice frowned. "But that makes no sense. Why would an insurance company pay out twice? Surely the owner has already been compensated?"

"Yes, but rarely for the full amount the piece is worth. Few museums and only the richest collectors can afford to insure all their works for their market value. So it's in the interests of the collector or insurer to pay whatever the art-nappers demand, usually ten to fifteen percent of the true value. The owner regains an invaluable artwork, the insurance company writes off the loss, and meanwhile the notoriety of the theft increases the value of the painting substantially, increasing the insurance premium." Meyer smiled again. "A scam with no losers."

Stein returned, spoke in German to Meyer and lifted an eyebrow to Beatrice. She gave him a tiny nod of reassurance.

"That is fascinating, Herr Meyer. I had no idea it was so organised."

"Most lucrative crime is. My investigation so far has been into the insurance companies and the art-nappers. But the increasingly violent nature of these robberies adds considerable pressure. I am very grateful for your input and will study your report with great care. Thank you for your time, DI Stubbs. Herr Stein, *Ihnen auch*."

He shook her hand and Stein escorted him out. Beatrice watched them cross the office towards the lift, a dull grey official beside a comic book hero. She turned back to her temporary quarters and set about removing all items she had stuck on the walls. First, the reprints of the stolen artworks. She laid the three images side by side on the table and studied the harshly rendered features, the fleshy colours, the eyes.

The eyes.

The prostitutes, staring at the viewer with optimism, lust or fear.

The woman and the cat, green-marble orbs with black slits for pupils, their unblinking focus on the observer.

The self-portrait, the man's eyes cast left, looking over his shoulder at the row of Dutch houses, the canal and the open-mouthed gawpers.

Eyes. Was that it?

A rap once again on the glass door. Stein really did take formality to the max.

"Come in. No need to knock," she called, squinting at each painting in turn.

A cough.

Beatrice turned to see the young IT expert standing with his laptop clasped to his chest.

"Hello Tomas. I thought you were Detective Stein."

"Is he gone?"

"Stein? I think he's just escorted Herr Meyer to his car. He'll be back in a minute if you want to wait."

"No. I want to show you something. Can you, before you leave, come to me?"

His intense, hooded stare bothered Beatrice. Under the circumstances, she erred on the side of caution.

"Once I've finished with Detective Stein, perhaps you'd like to come back? I need to clear this room this afternoon. Is that OK with you?"

He glanced over his shoulder at the rows of desks and blue-lit faces. "Maybe. My number is in the directory. Tomas Schäffer. Till later."

Stein helped her detach her material from the walls, making a neat pile beside her briefcase.

"Are you disappointed with Meyer?" he asked, as he unpinned the map.

Beatrice looked up in surprise. "Not at all. He's got the experience and I know when to shut up and listen. I'm just disappointed I can't take this further, as it was about to get interesting, but I know what it's like where funding is concerned."

"So do I. A shame, as you say. It would have been good to keep you for a few more days."

Beatrice turned to the wall to hide her smile. "Thank you."

The clear-up was completed without further conversation and once the room had been restored, Stein held out his hand.

"It was a pleasure working with you, DI Stubbs."

They shook hands and Beatrice experienced a fleeting wish that Germany was one of those countries where people kissed each other all the time, like Spain or France.

"Same to you. Thank you so much for all your help. I wasn't very useful, I'm afraid, but I genuinely enjoyed my experience of Hamburg."

"You were useful. I found your handling of my team over lunch impressive, by the way. Berndt explained to me what happened and how you managed Tomas and Margrit."

"Talking of whom, Tomas came in a few minutes ago. He said he wanted to show me something. He's not the most socially skilled man, so I asked him to come here, mainly because this room has a glass wall."

Stein's eyebrows rose. "You are honoured. Tomas rarely shares his findings. He once asked me to pass them onto Herr Meyer, who I'm sorry to say was dismissive and patronising. Since then, Tomas has not spoken of it to anyone, as far as I know. It's the bigger picture, so to speak. You might find it informative. A word of warning – Tomas lacks social skills but he's certainly no threat. He tends to get very absorbed in his work. He'll talk for hours unless you stop him. Don't let him make you miss your flight."

"Thanks for the tip. I'm not flying till Sunday, so I should be safe enough. Have a good weekend, Herr Stein and I am most grateful for your help."

"Likewise. Goodbye."

She watched him leave and sighed. Never mind Bette Davis eyes, he had Cary Grant eyelashes. She opened the translation app on her phone. *Stein*, she had a feeling, was German for star. Which could not be more appropriate for a man with matinee idol looks. She tapped in the letters and bit her lip as she saw the results. Not star, but stone. Detective Rock. That would do.

When Tomas Schäffer arrived, he set up his laptop without looking at Beatrice or addressing her in any way. Her instincts told her not to attempt chit-chat, so she waited until he was ready.

He sat in front of the machine tapping in commands, and eventually looked up. He tilted the computer slightly to his left and looked at the chair next to him. Beatrice sat down, her attention on the screen.

"This is not a police project. This is something I do in my spare time. Herr Stein found it interesting. Herr Meyer did not. I don't care if you think it is useful or not but it is my duty to share this information."

"Thank you. I appreciate your trust."

His glance darted sideways, as if he suspected sarcasm. "This is a database containing all the information on art thefts in Europe during this year. I have another for the previous year. The data is available in police records but what is different about this is the way I broke it down. Every element of each theft is entered separately. This means the search functionality can find data patterns we might not see. You can search using any combination of criteria. For example, paintings stolen from museums, artworks from 1921, by a particular artist, in the city of Hamburg, worth between one and two million Euros, whatever you want."

His fingers fluttered across the keys and new screens appeared, each with a list of search results.

"That's extremely impressive. Does it work the other way? Could it find any connections between the three thefts I'm investigating?"

"I already ran reports and printed them for you. I don't see anything obvious, but perhaps with your knowledge...?" He handed over a plastic folder. Beatrice took it and studied the papers while he pattered away at the keyboard.

"At first glance, my knowledge seems less than adequate. Can I keep these? There's someone I'd like to talk to whose knowledge is far superior."

"Of course. In respect of this database, all the information is here. It is only a matter of asking the right questions."

Beatrice stared at the mass of data on the screen.

"Tomas, do you think you could spare me an hour tomorrow? I know it's a Saturday, but with your skills and my contact's expertise, we might find a way to exploit this superb resource between us. I just have the feeling something is staring me in the face and I just can't see it."

"Yes. That is exactly how I'm feeling also. I am free tomorrow. When you know what time, call me and we can meet here. I will give you the number of my..." He coughed. "... mobile phone."

His eyes flickered to hers and his lips twitched into the merest hint of a smile before he looked back to the screen.

Chapter 9

Yesterday, a mile of sin. Today, a mile of art. Adrian strolled along the lakeside promenade, hands tucked into coat pockets. The wind whipped across the Binnenalster, shattering the reflections, stinging his cheeks and making his eyes water as he lifted his face to a hazy sun. Maybe Holger was right and all five museums in one day would be too much to take in. Beatrice's attention span hadn't held out for two. But to be fair, her mind was still on her work. For someone normally held rapt by Monet and Cezanne, she'd got all excited about some Expressionist painters at the Hamburger Kunsthalle and scuttled off to the office.

Adrian set off down the lakeside with a heady enthusiasm, intent on seeing the Bucerius Kunst Forum. The combination of good company, art, food and a new city to explore had filled him with energy. He stopped and gazed across the water. Pleasure boats, grand architecture with uniform rows of windows, archways, floating bars, bridges, wide pavements along wider streets, ornate spires and so many expanses of water! Hamburg had a lot of space. Unlike the cramped, narrow backstreets of London, everything was broad and open to the sky. He could breathe here. He could live somewhere like this. Maybe he and Holger should talk about their differences and try again. Weekend markets, art galleries, the sea, all in the company of a beautiful, sensitive man... Adrian could do all that. There was only one thing he couldn't do. Kids.

Daydreaming. He shook his head and retrieved his mobile from inside his coat. The navigator app said the museum was just past the next bridge. Snowflakes began falling, fat and wet, melting on impact with the ground. He held out his gloved hand to catch one and raised his face to the sky, sticking out his tongue. A silent white barrage pelted onto his face, hair, shoulders and shoes, and finally into his mouth. He took a selfie with the lake as a backdrop, pulling a pantomime expression of wonder. He wasn't sure who for. The wind and cold started to seep through his clothes. He shook himself, patting his coat to dislodge the settling flakes and looked behind him to see if anyone had noticed his childish behaviour.

Less than a hundred yards away, on the other side of the street, stood a nun. She was staring directly at him, her arms folded over a black coat, an expression of disgust on her face. Through the snowflakes, like some slow-motion automated mannequin, she shook her head three times. Adrian's breath caught in his throat, the cold going far deeper than his clothes. A huge tourist bus rumbled past, blocking his view and he looked up to see faces pressed against the coach windows, peering down at him as if he were part of the tour. He made a decision. He would not be hounded by some judgemental stalker, whatever her motive. She was the one who should be afraid.

Once the coach had passed, he dodged through the traffic and vaulted over the central reservation. His coat flapping, he splashed through a puddle and tore across two more lanes to confront her. A sudden gust of wind forced snow into his face, making it hard for him to see. He reached the point where she'd been standing. No one, nothing. Not even footprints as the snow was too wet to stick. He ran as far as the corner but there was no sign of her.

In the middle of the tree-lined avenue, snowflakes spinning around his head, he couldn't be sure she'd even been there at all.

His feet were wet and his trousers spattered with mud. He decided to forget the museum for now and get back to the hotel to change. Cold and unsettled, he made his way to the U-Bahn, seeking the comfort of ordinary people.

To Beatrice's relief, Frau Eichhorn had accepted the invitation without hesitation, despite the explicit instructions not to disturb her before Saturday. Yes, she could come to Hamburg. Yes, she'd be glad to help the police explore their data. Yes, she could fly the following morning. Twinges of guilt pierced Beatrice as she left

Adrian to his own devices, but her attention would not be drawn from the case. The potential alchemy of mixing these two specialists had such exciting potential that Beatrice had been awake since four in the morning.

She met Tomas at the police station and although a Saturday afternoon was a lot quieter than the previous day, several people were working in the open plan detectives' office. Officially, she did not have permission to enter the building, so she marched through the place with a purposeful air, reoccupied her borrowed room and helped Tomas set up the computer so the results would be visible on the wide screen. A nagging concern bothered her. Before flying an expert witness in to assist, Beatrice should have cleared the expense with Hamilton, or Ranga at least. She hadn't. It would cause ructions on her return, but worse, wilfully going against protocol was often a sign that she was entering one of her mood cycles. The last thing she needed. She added a reminder in her notebook. Mood stabiliser – 11pm.

When Frau Eichhorn's taxi arrived, Beatrice was waiting in the foyer with a visitor's pass. She watched the small woman exit the cab and survey the police station. Today, the ex-professor wore a poppy-red riding coat and black leather boots with flat heels. She looked like something from an up-market perfume advertisement.

Howard Jones. Out of nowhere, the name Beatrice had been trying to remember came to her. Frau Eichhorn's haircut reminded her of Eighties' pop star Howard Jones. She went to greet her with genuine enthusiasm.

"Frau Eichhorn, so nice to see you again. Thank you for coming."

"Detective Inspector Stubbs. You're welcome. It's been many years since I came to this city. I could never live anywhere else than Berlin, but occasionally I like to visit the sea. I brought you a present. My own book on the Expressionist movement and its contemporary ramifications. Even if I say so myself, this is the definitive work on the subject."

Beatrice took the weighty book. "That's an extremely generous thought, thank you. Come this way. I'm very keen for you to meet my colleague and hear about his work."

The first thing Beatrice noticed when they entered the

glass-walled room was the smell of coffee. Tomas stood awkwardly to attention and Beatrice made the introductions. She watched them appraise each other as they shook hands.

"I was just going to ask where we could get coffee on a Saturday, but I see you're ahead of me. Thanks Tomas, that's very thoughtful. While I pour, perhaps you could explain the database to Frau Eichhorn?"

He drew out a chair for the professor and seated himself at the computer. Beatrice listened to the German explanation, understanding very little apart from the occasional word such as '*hier*' and '*so*'. The screen filled with various search results and Frau Eichhorn started asking questions. Beatrice placed the coffees on the table and waited as Tomas appeared to try out various combinations at Eichhorn's request.

By the time they concluded their experiments and remembered Beatrice was in the room, she'd finished her coffee and Eichhorn's had gone cold.

Tomas switched to English but didn't look up from the laptop. "Frau Eichhorn suggests adding several new fields to the artwork labelling. This way we can drill down further into the art movement sub-sections. It could take a little time."

The professor nodded her approval. "It's a useful resource and intelligently assembled. But any program can only be as good as the quality of its data. Herr Schäffer's police information, I assume, is perfect. The definitions of stolen artworks need some refinement. I suggest you give us an hour at least, DI Stubbs. Why not go for a walk? But before you do, can I have some more coffee?"

Beatrice had been dismissed.

The U-Bahn 3 went via Mönckebergstrasse, Hamburg's main shopping street. Rather than head straight back to the hotel, Adrian chose to alight there. He was glad he did. A mellow sense of seasonal spirit crept up on him as he emerged from the underground station. Hamburg's Christmas lights were white, delicate and a far cry from England's cartoon reindeers. The still-falling snowflakes, the warmly wrapped shoppers, the festive windows and the smell of roasting chestnuts chased away his jitters and replaced them with a mixture of embarrassment and optimism. So what if a sour old God-botherer had caught him fooling about in the snow and shook her miserable head. It was just one of those things. Nothing to do with the events in London, which were probably unconnected anyway. He really had to get a grip. Germany had nuns too. Look at *The Sound of Music*. Or was that Austria? Whatever. Regardless of what some joyless crone thought, he was on holiday and intended to enjoy himself. He'd been working too hard, and he was feeling a bit run-down and paranoid. Forget it and move on. He had another two hours before meeting Holger, which left him just enough time to see what Hamburg offered in the way of retail therapy.

He dallied in department stores, browsed a few designer outlets, bought a beautiful scarf depicting an old map of the Hanseatic League for Beatrice and a pair of stylish yet tough walking boots for himself. In a café bathroom, he changed into the boots, as his leather loafers were not built for this weather. Dry of foot and internally warmed by caffeine and Kirsch, he stood in shop doorways to take pictures: a spectacular glittering Christmas tree, candlelit street stalls selling Glühwein and fairy-lighted trees with a dusting of snow. At twenty to three, happy and restored, he bought a cornet of roasted chestnuts and set off to meet Holger. He was turning over the problem of a suitable gift for his ex-boyfriend when he heard something which made him stand still in the street.

Voices. Uplifting, beautiful and harmonious male voices. In a pedestrianised street to his left, against a backdrop of a bus stop and a bike rack, stood around twenty men, all wearing dark coats and red scarves, singing 'Hey, Big Spender'. A crowd had gathered to watch in admiration and amusement as the choir entertained them with their comic choreography routine. A tall man with a beard conducted the group whilst another passed out flyers to the watching shoppers. Adrian accepted one of the leaflets with a smile and folded it into his back pocket. He applauded along with the rest of the crowd as they ended the song with a flourish. He stayed where he was and listened with a critical ear. Their star tenor was not up to his own performance standards, although he did have a greater range. By the time the choir had sung and danced their way through 'Super Trouper', he'd finished his chestnuts. His nose, cheeks and knees were frozen. But inside he was warm and fizzing. He'd found the perfect place to start seeking a husband for Holger.

"Entartete Kunst. Degenerate art," said Frau Eichhorn, pacing the room as if it were a lecture hall. "From what we have learned from Herr Schäffer's data, I have come to the conclusion that someone is collecting a particular kind of artwork. The police information shows us that a portrait by Kokoschka was stolen earlier this year from a private gallery in Munich. Oskar Kokoschka, like the other artists involved, was labelled a degenerate by the National Socialist regime. The term degenerate was not just an insulting word. Artworks were seized, artists forbidden to paint or even purchase painting materials, and museum directors sacked for exhibiting anything which promoted 'cosmopolitan or Bolshevik' attributes. Many artists escaped to live in exile; Beckmann to the Netherlands and Kokoschka to your own country. Under Culture Minister Frick, art's sole function was to illustrate Nazi ideals and glorify the state. Can you imagine?"

Beatrice couldn't but had no time to reply.

"Goebbels had the idea for the infamous *Entartete Kunst* exhibition in 1937. A kind of public disgracing of such artworks and a hugely successful propaganda exercise. It is worth remembering that many of these pieces, confiscated by the state, were still acknowledged as valuable and later sold abroad or kept by senior officials in their personal collections. It is my view that someone is ordering the theft of such pieces to amass a collection of degenerate art. The fact that it was banned by the Nazi regime has a strange attraction for some people."

Beatrice absorbed the information and Frau Eichhorn's conclusions, a frisson of excitement bubbling in her stomach. "I see. From the criminal perspective, how far does this Munich theft fit our limited pattern?"

Tomas glanced at Beatrice, shrugged and shook his head. "From the criminal perspective, not really. No violence. The painting was stolen at night along with several other items. And because there were no signs of forced entry, suspicions revolved around the security team. The other difference is that the painting was recovered. It was under-insured and the gallery owner paid an undisclosed amount to get it back."

Beatrice watched his expression. He was stating facts, not opinions.

"And what do you think, Tomas? A wealthy collector with a fascination for the forbidden who decided that Kokoschka was not to his taste?"

He didn't look up from his screen. "Herr Meyer said the idea of the wealthy collector is a glamorous fantasy."

"Yes, he said the same to me. As he's a cultural crimes expert I took his opinion on board. I'd like to do the same with yours."

He shrugged again. Beatrice waited. She suspected avoidance rather than evasion, as well as a fear of certain ridicule.

Tomas finally spoke. "My theory is different. I think Frau Doktor Eichhorn is correct. Someone with money and influence is looking for specific pieces to complete a collection. The Kokoschka is not part of it. From the angle of an art movement, it makes sense. From the police records on comparable criminality, not."

A loud buzzing noise startled Beatrice.

Frau Eichhorn took out her telephone. "My alarm. I must leave for the airport. Will you please arrange a taxi? Herr Schäffer, why not run two types of analysis? If the Kokoschka is not part of this, your job becomes easier. Add two other artists to your list – George Grosz and Christian Schad. These were the left-wing 'verists' of the *Neue Sachlichkeit*." She turned to Beatrice. "New Objectivity in English. Check the art registry for where works by these artists are held and who owns them. I'm sure you can operate a kind of protection for potential targets.

"If the collector is picking and choosing from pieces which fell under the umbrella of *Entartete Kunst*, you have a far larger problem. No definitive catalogue exists, the artists come from all over Europe and their works are similarly dispersed. I can give you the name of a curator in Berlin who has written a book on the subject. Thank you for inviting me, it was nice to meet you and now I must leave."

She shook Tomas's hand and said something in German which made him blush. Beatrice escorted Eichhorn downstairs and saw her safely into a cab before hurrying back to the office to call London. She needed more time.

Outside the restaurant, Holger bid Adrian and Beatrice goodnight with kisses on both cheeks and a reminder of his address for tomorrow's lunch. They watched him cross the street and returned his wave before he descended into the U-Bahn. Adrian shoved his hands in his pockets and Beatrice linked her hand through his arm as they trudged back to the hotel. It was snowing again, this time tiny little balls that settled on his coat like polystyrene pellets.

"I have decided," Beatrice announced. "I like Hamburg. I'm quite partial to ports in general, but this city has something rather special about it. More waterworks than Venice, apparently."

Adrian corrected her with a wry smile. "Waterways."

"That's what I meant."

She'd been in an excellent mood all evening, discussing German artists with Holger, praising the rich food, teasing Adrian about his squeamishness regarding sausages and exulting in the fact she had permission to stay another week.

"Me too. I've had such a lovely day. Art, cakes and the market Holger showed me were so magical it was practically a Christmas fairytale. We must have a look at that tomorrow morning."

"After your description, I wouldn't miss it for all the Wursts in Hamburg."

Adrian laughed at her high spirits. "Is that really the plural of *Wurst*?"

"No idea. But I will always remember how to say *Blut-und-Leberwurst*, just in case I ever get the opportunity to eat it again."

"Oh stop. The name was enough to put me off. Isn't that typically German? Call it what it is in graphic terms, no matter how hideous it sounds. Blood and liver sausage. I don't know how you and Holger could face it."

"One could equally well say how typically British that we use a euphemism like black pudding instead."

"I wouldn't eat black pudding either. The pork chops were delicious and they looked far nicer than that monstrosity you ate. Funnily enough, I was just about ready for some meat. I'm glad Holger persuaded us. He is the perfect host."

"Lovely man. I have to say, I think he's definitely my favourite of your exes. Certainly one of the best looking. Those eyes!"

"True." He hadn't missed all those admiring glances from both genders in their direction in the markets, on the street, at the restaurant. "I do wonder occasionally if perhaps we gave up on the relationship too easily. Mind out, it's icy just here."

They picked their way over a patch of frozen overflow on the pavement and turned into Kirchenallee.

Beatrice looked up at him. "Not tempted to try again? He told me while you were in the loo that he's still single. I wasn't prying; it just came up in conversation."

Adrian gave her an arch look. "The day Beatrice Stubbs isn't prying will be the day hell freezes over. No, I think Holger and I make better friends than we do lovers. And anyway, he wants to be a father."

They walked in silence till they saw the lights of the hotel. Adrian was relieved. It had been a fabulous day, but after all those hours walking, shopping and standing around in galleries his feet were killing him, his face was smarting from the cold and that heavy meal of meat and potato made him yearn for his bed.

At the entrance, Beatrice stamped her feet to dislodge the snow. "If it's all right with you, I'll skip the nightcap and try to catch Matthew before he turns in. I feel I ought to explain personally why I need to stay a few more days."

"You read my mind. I'm going to turn in too. Being a tourist is exhausting."

Choral renditions of German carols were playing in the lobby as they entered. Beatrice said her goodnight with a light buss of his cheeks and trotted off down the corridor. Adrian took the lazy option of the lift. His bed had been made up, fresh fruit delivered and the mini-bar replenished. Best of all, it was warm. He hung up his damp coat and took off his boots. He was just undressing to get under a hot shower when he spotted a white envelope inscribed with his name lying on a silver tray. He slipped his finger under the flap and withdrew the typewritten message.

Go home.
You are not welcome here.
Go home.
Repent and ask forgiveness.
Go home.

All feelings of safety and comfort evaporated as the cold reclaimed him from the inside. He dialled Beatrice's room, but she was engaged. He threw the card on the table and called reception. After an interminable wait while they located the clerk on duty, he learned that the envelope had been delivered by bicycle courier.

Enough. This was tangible evidence. Someone was trying to frighten him and mess up his life. He replaced the card in the envelope and sat on the bed, staring at the silver salver.

He called Beatrice again. This time she answered.

"Yes?" Her voice was sharp.

"It's me, sorry. Were you asleep?"

"No, just about to call Matthew. I've not had chance yet. My bloody boss was on the phone and is insisting on coming here in person to ensure I'm not having a jolly at the Met's expense. The man is quite unbelievable."

"Oh no. When's he coming?"

"Wednesday or Thursday. I have to get this case either resolved or handed back before then. I will not have him breathing down my bloody neck. Anyway, I need to talk to Matthew now. What was it you wanted?"

Adrian hesitated. "Oh, nothing. I just realised I forgot to thank you for dinner."

"Don't mention it. See you at breakfast. Sleep tight."

The line went dead. Adrian replaced the handset, checked the door was locked, windows were secure and the wardrobe contained nothing more than his clothes. He took a scalding shower and wrapped himself in a bathrobe, then poured himself a gin and tonic while flicking through the channels to find some music, colour and comfort.

He got under the duvet with an extra blanket over his legs. The gin spread flames across his thorax and he clutched the glass in both hands. He didn't scare easily, but whoever sent that note had followed him from London. And that thought chilled him to the core.

Chapter 10

For a six-year-old, Asta had strong views on domestic creatures. She approved of the fact Beatrice owned no pets because she worked long hours and lived in a flat. It wouldn't be fair to the animal. A hamster might work, she suggested. Beatrice promised to take the matter under consideration.

Asta chewed on some coleslaw and regarded Adrian. He smiled with some awkwardness and shook his head.

"No pets either. I live in the flat under Beatrice's. But I have always wanted a Schnauzer. Maybe one day, if I move to Wales."

Holger addressed his goddaughter in English. "Bread, Asta?"

She shook her head without taking her gaze off Adrian, her Jean Harlow hair catching the light. "Thank you, no. Why do you want a Schnauzer?"

"I don't know. They have a lot of character. If I was a dog, I'd be a Schnauzer."

She placed her fork on the table, her left hand on her hip and her right under her chin as she studied Adrian. "No, you're not a Schnauzer. You're a Weimaraner. And Holger is a Labrador. He hates it when I say that, but it is true. Beautiful dogs, both of them, but a Labrador is more useful."

Beatrice and Holger burst into laughter, Adrian's eyes widened and Asta resumed her lunch.

"What kind of dog would you be, Asta?" asked Beatrice, helping herself to another slice of ham.

"I don't think I can answer that question. I can't see me from the outside. Even if I could, I'm only seven years old next birthday and not any kind of dog at all yet. In dog terms, I'm still a puppy."

Beatrice nodded, trying to maintain a serious expression. "Yes, you are very similar to a puppy. Bright, cute and with surprisingly sharp teeth. Ham?"

Asta turned to Holger. "*Was heisst* 'cute' *auf Deutsch*?"

"*Herzig.*"

She looked back at Beatrice and gave her a gracious nod. "Thank you. Yes please. One piece is enough. I always eat too much when I'm with Holger. He makes very good food and never tries to give me 'children's meals'. He knows I hate fries."

She grinned at her godfather with endearing warmth. He smiled back and Beatrice could almost see a cord sidewinding across the table, joining the two with a tangible commitment. Adrian shoved back his chair.

"Sorry, can I use your toilet?"

"Of course. First door on the left."

Adrian left the table and Beatrice turned to Asta.

"Holger tells me you speak Danish as well as English and German."

"Yes. My father is Danish and my mother is German. We spend our holidays in Denmark, so I can practise. When I am adult, I will live there all the time and have a farm with horses."

"And dogs?"

"Yes. Many dogs."

Holger stood up to clear the table. "Who would like some *Rote Grütze* for dessert? Beatrice, it's a kind of red fruit salad, served with cream. Quite light and sweet."

"Yes please."

"Asta?"

"Yes please. It's my favourite!"

"I know." He looked up as Adrian came back. "Adrian, dessert?"

"No thanks. But I wouldn't mind a coffee."

Beatrice studied her neighbour across the table. His eyes seemed bloodshot and his skin was the colour of dirty snow.

"Are you feeling OK?" she asked. "You look a bit peaky."

Adrian attempted a smile. "Tired, that's all. Couldn't get to sleep for ages and when I did, I had a succession of nightmares."

"You should have said. We could have skipped the market this morning and had a lie-in."

"We could, but I'm glad we didn't. I'm completely sorted for Christmas now."

Asta was listening and when Holger placed a bowl of berries in front of her, she tilted her face up to him.

"*Was heisst* 'nightmare'?"

"*Ein Albtraum.*"

Asta giggled, showing tiny white teeth. "Nightmare. *Ein lustiges Wort.*"

Holger raised his eyebrows. "Yes, I suppose it is a funny word. I never thought about it. Cream or vanilla sauce?"

"Vanilla sauce, please. When I have my farm, I will have a black horse and I will call him Nightmare." She giggled again and all three of them joined in. Beatrice gazed at her. She was the dearest little thing, a heart-shaped face framed by a dead-straight, silky platinum bob. Her eyebrows, mere hints of golden hair, danced above her crystal blue eyes as she looked from one to the other.

Holger offered Beatrice a jug of custard and spoke to Asta. "But what if he understands English? He might behave like a nightmare. You might be better to buy a white horse and call her Daydream."

Asta burst into peals of laughter and showed berry-stained teeth. "Horses can't speak English! I think I will have both. Nightmare and Daydream!"

"Your parents will think I've given you ideas. Come on now, eat your dessert. I'll make the coffee then we're off to Hagenbeck!"

Asta took a big spoonful of fruit and custard, her cheek apples shining as she gave Holger the thumbs-up. Beatrice turned to share a smile with Adrian, but he was checking his phone.

The Tiergarten Hagenbeck had an unusual system. The animals were separated from visitors and each other not by cages, but by wide moats, so one could see creatures moving in layers, part of a three-dimensional landscape. Asta, a regular visitor, knew exactly how to show guests the full experience. She took hold of Beatrice's hand, talking non-stop.

"Today is cold, so maybe we will not see everything. The animals sometimes stay at home. We start with the elephants. Then we go to the Africa panorama through the old door. Zebra, lions, monkeys, I like Africa. After that is the Ice Sea, with animals from Antarctica. Do you like penguins?"

"Very much."

"Me too. And then we go to my favourite place, the children's zoo. You can feed the animals and touch them and ride the ponies. But maybe not today. The snow, you know..."

"Probably a good thing. It's a long time since I went pony-riding."

Asta laughed, a clear bright sound like winter birdsong. "Me, not you! You're not a children. I must practise for my farm. Holger!" She looked back towards the entrance, where Adrian and Holger were strolling slowly behind, and indicated her intended route. Holger raised a hand in acknowledgement and inclined his head back to Adrian.

Beatrice watched them, deep in conversation, the Weimaraner and the Labrador, before Asta dragged her onwards. Adrian was not on his best form. Perhaps he really was lovesick. Since Holger, there had been very few boyfriends and none had lasted more than a month. A light inside him seemed to have dimmed and his innate joy in every pleasure life offered was lacking. She made up her mind to draw him out over dinner tonight. A small voice broke her concentration.

"Look, Beatrice! The elephants!"

Beatrice looked, astounded to see so many vast pachyderms within touching distance. Grey, leathery skin, long eyelashes, prehensile trunks and such expressive faces, the herd shoved and rubbed against each other, scooping up hay and tucking it into their mouths. A simply jaw-dropping sight in the middle of a North German city in the middle of winter. She widened her eyes, looked down at Asta and neither of them could stop laughing.

The zoo was larger than she expected and the wintry chill was so piercing that Beatrice wasn't surprised when after an hour Adrian suggested a break for coffee. Several refreshments areas were closed, due to the season. So they made their way back to the main restaurant at the entrance via the Himalayas and Australia, where

Beatrice stopped to take a photograph of a kangaroo. She'd never seen a real one before. Holger engaged Asta in conversation while Adrian and Beatrice went to the counter to get drinks. The heat of the café warmed her cheeks and she decided on the ideal beverage to complete her restoration.

"Hot chocolate with cream. And you?"

"Triple espresso and a hot water bottle for my bum. I've never been so cold in my life."

"I'll get some cakes for us all too. If you're in Germany at Christmas, it would be a sin not to have *Stollen*, don't you think?"

"What?"

"*Stollen*. German Christmas cake. Adrian, what on earth is wrong? You look like death warmed up."

"Nothing. Sorry, just really tired and cold and in need of a sugar rush. Yes, let's get cake. Then can we go back to the hotel? I'll be useless company this evening if I don't have a nap."

"Of course we can. Holger needs to get Asta back to her folks by five, anyway. She's an adorable child, isn't she?"

"Yes, very sweet, if a bit precocious. I can see why Holger got broody."

Beatrice gave their order in halting German, but the cashier appeared to understand and rang it into the till.

Adrian nudged Beatrice out of the way. "My turn. And I'm taking you out to dinner tonight. Seeing as I can't cook for you on Monday."

"You'll be far too busy to cook, checking up on Catinca, the shop, the stock and comments on the website. Anyway, I'll be back Thursday or Friday. If you miss me that much, I wouldn't say no to a hot dinner when I get in."

He didn't respond. Beatrice looked up to see him staring at the doorway, a twenty-Euro note in his hand. She followed his sightline. Just a bunch of people coming in from the cold. A Sunday family, two nuns and one of the animal park staff wearing a fluorescent tabard.

"Adrian?"

"Yes? Oh, sorry, here." He thrust the note at her and Beatrice paid. She handed him the change, picked up the tray of drinks and jerked her head at the second tray with plates and cake.

"Are you sure you're all right?"

Adrian shook his head, his jaw tight. "Not here. Let's talk about this over dinner. I'm beginning to think I'm going a bit mad."

He led the way back to their table, past a young woman who was eating a doughnut with one hand and rocking a pushchair with the other. The rocking was doing nothing to soothe the infant. His face was screwed up and his lips were almost violet as he screamed with a shrill fury. Beatrice gave the woman a sympathetic smile. The gesture seemed to wake her from her glazed and vacant state. She looked down at the child, tore off a piece of doughnut and popped it into his mouth. The screaming stopped instantly.

"Asta has done a drawing for you, Beatrice." Holger held out a paper napkin on which was drawn a strange hunched animal with large ears, some sort of dorsal fin and foreshortened front legs.

"How lovely! Is it a platypus?"

Asta's laughter gurgled as she shook her head. "It's a kangaroo! There's its pouch and that's its tail."

"Of course. It's lovely. Look, Adrian."

His attention was distracted, so Beatrice touched his arm. He looked at the picture and smiled at Asta. "A kangaroo. You're very good at drawing animals."

"I'll do one for you too. How about a penguin?"

Adrian opened his mouth to reply but the screeching infant on the next table started up again. The bench began to vibrate, caused by Adrian's leg bouncing under the table.

"No, not a penguin. How about a tiger?" He raised his voice and his smile was forced. Beatrice caught Holger's eye and exchanged a look of concern.

"Coffee and cake, that's what we need," she said, distributing the drinks. She bit into her slice of *Stollen* and watched Asta concentrate on colouring in stripes on a big cat. Adrian wasn't eating, but had twisted around to look behind him. Beatrice assumed he was frowning at the heedless mother until he leapt up and jolted the table. Hot drinks spilt everywhere, scalding Beatrice's hand and soaking Asta's napkin. Holger's glass of green tea smashed to the floor.

Adrian whirled around to face two approaching nuns carrying trays.

"Leave me alone! Just leave me alone! What is your problem? Stop stalking me! This is harassment and I've had enough. I swear on everything I call holy – and I'll tell you now, it isn't the Bible – if I ever see you again, I'll report you to the police! Now FUCK OFF!"

Everyone else in the café fell completely silent, even the screaming child. Then Asta began to cry. The nuns' shocked faces showed a mixture of incomprehension and fear. Beatrice, clutching her throbbing hand, elbowed herself to a standing position.

"Adrian..."

His head snapped towards her, his eyes both haunted and enraged. He looked at Asta, cringing beside Holger, as if seeing her for the first time. Then he picked up his jacket and stalked to the exit, ignoring the stares.

Chapter 11

The cafeteria staff applied a cooling spray and cling film to Beatrice's hand and covered it with a light bandage. The procedure absorbed so much of Asta's attention that her tears dried up. Holger apologised to the nuns, although Beatrice couldn't imagine what he could say to excuse such behaviour. People threw them curious looks as they left, but Asta recovered her chirpy humour and took Beatrice's undamaged hand to lead her out into the sunshine. There was no sign of Adrian.

"Does it hurt very badly, Beatrice?" Asta asked again.

"Not since they put the spray on. It feels sort of numb."

"Do you want to see the rest of the Tierpark?"

"I do, but not today. I should get back to the hotel."

Holger zipped up his coat. "Yes, good idea. And I'll take my favourite god-daughter back to her parents."

"I'm your *only* god-daughter!" Asta laughed.

"And my favourite," he teased. "Beatrice, I'll meet you at the hotel later. Can you find your way?"

"Oh yes, easily." She held out her bandaged hand to Asta. "It was lovely to meet you and thank you for showing me the park. I won't shake your hand but perhaps you could shake my finger as a substitute."

Asta grinned and with great care, moved Beatrice's index finger up and down. "Lovely to meet you too, Beatrice. Have a good time!"

No one mentioned Adrian.

By the time Beatrice exited the U-Bahn, the sun had sunk, leaving the streets colder and greyer. It matched her mood. The welcoming lights of the hotel offered a sense of relief and trepidation, but mostly warmth. She made straight for her own room, kicked off her shoes and dialled Adrian. After six purrs, he answered, his voice sleepy.

"Hello?"

Beatrice closed her eyes and exhaled. "You're there. Thank heavens for that. How are you feeling?"

He took a long time to answer.

"Not great. I took a zed."

"A what?"

"Sleeping tablet. I need to get some rest."

"OK, you do that. Just so long as I know you're here and you're safe. It's ten past four now, so shall I come round at seven?"

"Yeah, seven is good. Bye." The phone went dead.

Beatrice replaced the receiver and stared out of the window, replaying the afternoon's events until her stomach reminded her of the missed hot chocolate and *Stollen*. She picked up the phone and called Room Service.

At ten to seven, someone knocked at her door. She switched off the TV and hurried to unlock it, expecting Holger. It was Adrian, freshly shaved and dressed in a white shirt with an aubergine jumper. He held out a small box, marked with the hotel livery.

"Chocolates. As an apology for making you miss your cake."

Beatrice searched his face. Not the nervous wreck he'd been earlier, but his brightness rang hollow. "Thank you. I ended up having some back here, actually, but chocolate never goes to waste." She reached out for the box.

He saw the bandage. "What have you done to your hand?"

"You spilt coffee on it. A minor scald, that's all. Come in, we need to have a chat."

His brittle demeanour cracked. "Oh shit, I am so sorry. I hurt you, made Asta cry, pissed Holger off and terrified two people who couldn't even understand what I was saying. I feel so stupid and ashamed of myself."

On impulse, Beatrice stepped forward and pulled him into a

hug. He clutched her to him, like a child with a teddy bear. They stood for several seconds, drawing comfort from the contact. He wore a spicy scent, like freshly plucked rosemary. She released him and looked into his face.

"Thank you for the apology. But I'd prefer an explanation."

He rubbed a hand over his face and sat on the sofa. "I owe you that. Can we have a glass of wine?"

She grabbed two little bottles from the mini-bar, poured them into glasses and handed one to her guest.

"Cheers." They raised their glasses and took a sip. For the first time in Beatrice's memory, Adrian did not comment on the wine. Instead, he released a huge sigh and began to talk.

Beatrice concentrated on his voice, reminding herself this was her friend, not a witness, not a complainant or a victim. But her police training could not be silenced for long.

"What did you do with the note?" she interrupted.

"Which one?"

"I meant the one delivered here, but both."

"Binned. I didn't occur to me to keep them."

"Can you remember if they were in the same kind of font, similar paper, anything to indicate they came from the same source?"

He shook his head. "They were typed, that's all I can say for sure."

"And when you were taken in for questioning about those accusations, you didn't tell the police about the Bible verse or the nuns?"

He rotated the stem of his wine glass. "No. I thought it would sound like paranoia, plus I wasn't even sure there was a connection. I just wanted to get out of there as soon as I could. I've got the sergeant's card though." He pulled his wallet out of his back pocket and flicked through the cards. "Do you think I should call him and report all this?"

Beatrice hesitated, weighing up the situation through the eyes of a detective inspector. It didn't look good. If a man made a complaint about being stalked by a nun with almost no evidence, Beatrice would have asked a lot of questions to ascertain his plausibility. Catinca could confirm the graffiti but no one else had seen the notes and as for the nun sightings, it could be coincidence. Before she could formulate a reply, there was a knock at the door. Adrian's demeanour changed from nervous to downright fearful.

Beatrice opened the door. "Hello Holger."

"Hi Beatrice. I just came from Adrian's room. There was no reply."

"He's here. Come on in."

Beatrice only half listened to Adrian's apology and summary of the situation for Holger while she looked up Detective Sergeant Quinn on the police database.

She tuned back in to the conversation and the contrition in Adrian's voice. "So when I saw two of them today, I lost it. I'm really sorry for making such a scene, especially in front of Asta."

Holger shook his head. "Asta's fine. It's you I'm worried about. This doesn't make any sense. You think a nun put graffiti on your shop?"

"I know. It sounds insane. But I promise I'm telling the truth. Someone is trying to scare me and has travelled from London to follow me here. Don't you find that weird?"

"The nuns at the zoo. Did you recognise either of them?"

"I've never got a good look at the one who's been following me, so I couldn't be sure. Although they did seem a bit older."

Holger shook his head, frowning. "It just sounds so..."

"Unbelievable? This is exactly why I didn't say anything to the police. I'm having trouble believing it myself. It's a horrible feeling when you don't trust your own mind. And now the two people I thought I could trust suspect me of delusions."

Holger, sitting on the bed, looked across at Beatrice. "I don't suspect you of anything. Beatrice?"

Beatrice closed the laptop and came to sit on the arm of Adrian's chair. She'd have been more comfortable next to Holger, but with what she had to say, it might look like they were ganging up.

"I think we should look at this in two ways. Firstly, we take the idea of a stalker seriously and keep any evidence that someone is following Adrian. If we're going to report this, we'll need something more concrete than what we've got. Secondly, when is the last time you had a holiday? You've spent so long building up the shop and working late and worrying, I wouldn't be surprised if you were feeling a bit burnt out. Why don't you go somewhere lovely, get some sunshine and take a week off? Now you've promoted Catinca to assistant manager, there's nothing stopping you."

Adrian stopped fiddling with his glass. "So you think I'm imagining things and it's nothing a week in Tunisia won't cure."

"No. I believe you're unsettled by what's happened and could do with a break. Not least because if someone is behind this, they're unlikely to follow you to a holiday destination. Anyway, some distance from your routine might add some perspective."

He didn't reply, still staring into his wine. Holger caught Beatrice's eye while they waited for a response.

Adrian finally answered. "I can't take a holiday now. Christmas is around the corner, Catinca's only just started in the assistant role and I'll never be able to book anything at this short notice."

Beatrice hid her satisfaction. If his objections were only practical, the thought had already taken root. Holger clicked his fingers and pointed at Adrian.

"I have an idea. It's not Tunisia and the weather is even worse than here, but my grandparents have a holiday house on the island of Sylt. They usually spend the summer there. It's right on the beach and a beautiful, wild, peaceful place. Anyone in my family can use it whenever they want, but my brother and I are the only ones who do. I can call my grandmother now to see if it's free. Trains go every hour so I could take you there tomorrow. No traffic, no Christmas songs, just waves and seagulls. The perfect escape."

The faint sound of the train station tannoy and occasional honk of a horn could be heard outside the silence of the room. While they waited for Adrian to respond, Beatrice's stomach growled. She shot a glance at the chocolates. Now was not the time.

A smile crept across Adrian's face and he looked up at Beatrice. "Funnily enough, I just bought some hiking boots yesterday. Looks like it was meant to be."

"Fantastic! Holger, call your relations. Adrian, get onto Catinca. Let's get this organised and then can we go out to eat? I'm absolutely starving."

Chapter 12

Tomas Schäffer had clearly worked all over the weekend. His results were broken down across several spreadsheets and in two languages. It took over an hour to explain his analyses. As he could not stop talking, Beatrice finally asked for some time to let the information sink in, ideally with the aid of some coffee. He conceded and left for the canteen.

The amount of data was intimidating. She started with the smallest set, planning to work her way up to the rest. *Neue Sachlichkeit*. New Objectivity. Five artists, the locations of most of their works, insurance cover, security measures and likelihood of theft. She focused on individual collections first, since they weren't sure if the museum robbery had skewed the inquiry.

The names Frau Eichhorn had suggested featured prominently. Schad and Grosz, alongside Dix, Schlichter and Beckmann, were available to view at various galleries around Northern Europe. Only two known examples of Grosz were in private collections, one in Bremen, another in Geneva. Several homes boasted a Schad, at least two in Berlin, one in Munich and another in Salzburg.

She called Ranga's mobile, specifically to avoid Hamilton, and got permission to approach Interpol. Then she spent twenty minutes talking to Herr Meyer. He said surveillance at six properties was impossible but if intelligence provided sufficient reason, he would fund one. Finally, she sent a message summoning Schäffer back. She wanted him in the room before calling Frau Eichhorn.

He arrived so quickly she suspected he'd been hovering outside the door. She called the ex-professor, whose voice rang out from the speakerphone.

"*Detective Inspector Stubbs. I was expecting your call. Herr Schäffer's material is very interesting.*"

Beatrice shot a look at Tomas and muted the microphone. "You already shared this with her?"

His expression was defensive. "It's mine. I didn't include any police information, only the art-related elements. Sharing my own research is legitimate."

Eichhorn continued, oblivious. "*All these works are potential targets so I suggest adding extra security to each home. If it was up to me, I'd ask each owner to put a fake in its place, but I understand time and effort may not allow for that.*"

"Which ones do you think might be the most likely targets? I doubt I'll get funding to supervise all these places, so if I have to choose, I'd like to make an informed decision."

Tomas's eyes flickered over hers as they waited.

"*Schad. If they go for a Grosz, others might make the connection to the verists and increase security levels. In my opinion, the thieves will take a Schad next and wait for calm. That could take years. Then they'll steal a Grosz and the set will be complete.*"

"Thank you, Frau Eichhorn. I appreciate your help and I'll be in touch."

Beatrice hung up and turned to Tomas whose fingers were already flying across his keyboard.

"What are you doing?"

"Searching for images of the Schad paintings."

"Good idea. Pay special attention to those with eyes. I'm going to find Detective Stein and ask if I can officially borrow you for the week. If that's OK with you?"

His focus didn't shift from the screen. "Of course it's OK with me. What do you mean about those with eyes?"

"Check out the other thefts. I have a feeling there's something to do with gaze, eye contact, windows to the soul and all that."

"You have a hunch?" he asked, his lips twitching.

"I don't believe in hunches. What I have is an instinctive feeling with no supporting data."

His eyes met hers for a full two seconds before he returned to his computer with a poorly-concealed smile.

Stein's agreement was easily obtained and Beatrice sensed an enthusiasm in his voice. Whilst grateful for his acquiescence, she declined his invitation to lunch and waited till Tomas left for the canteen before settling down to read Frau Eichhorn's book in peace. She needed time to immerse herself in this world, to let her subconscious loose.

Each page drew her in. Unable to read the German commentary, Beatrice absorbed the artworks for what they were. In the quiet of her glass-walled room, the pictures became both familiar and more strange. Many of these pieces she'd seen before, in galleries and as reproductions, yet now she looked at them through a different filter. The sensation reminded her of an occurrence on her daily commute. A young man who had shared the same route for years suddenly broke their unspoken etiquette – a brief nod of acknowledgement and return to their respective newspapers – and struck up a conversation. She recalled the feeling of breaking glass, a simultaneous sense of possibility and dismay for something that could never be the same again.

Tomas returned and stood in the doorway, his expression unusually bright. For the first time, he made direct eye contact and did not look away.

"Good news."

Beatrice put down her book. "Just what I need. Come in and tell me."

"BKA intel just in. WBC with two owners of Schads at fifteen hundred. Can you be there?"

"I think I'm suffering from some kind of sugar withdrawal. My brain processed almost nothing in that sentence. Something is happening at three o'clock? In which case, I will rush out for a sandwich and come back so you can explain slowly in small words."

"I brought you a brown bag lunch package from the canteen. Sandwich, fruit, dessert and juice. I know you have had no time to eat. And I can bring an espresso from the machine when you finish."

Beatrice held out her hand for the bag. "That is most considerate and welcome. Now start at the beginning. We have some new intelligence?"

The six-person web conference ended at twenty minutes to four. Tomas and Beatrice were joined by Stein in person, Meyer from Wiesbaden and the two art collectors on video link. The threat to their artworks was made clear by Meyer, the danger to their loved ones clearer still by Stein. Both German speakers, the two collectors had myriad questions, which Stein and Meyer handled, while Tomas muttered translations for Beatrice's benefit.

The team identified Frau Kruger as the most vulnerable. Her property had easy access from a prestigious Berlin street and her painting, *Die Wolken*, had recently featured in a high-profile Schad retrospective. She eventually agreed to an extra security patrol and the installation of an alarm system.

Regardless of the practical considerations, however, Beatrice knew that Frau Kruger's painting was not the target. The minute Tomas indicated the next picture – *Nina in Camera* – a jolt of recognition shot through her. The eyes. Huge, liquid, limpid and exaggerated, the girl's gaze induced a feeling of vertigo. They were eyes you could fall into. Viewing the painting under glass, you would see the reflection of yourself in the velvet depths of her irises. A powerful conviction took hold that this painting was linked to the others by more than just the art movement.

So she paid particular attention to Tomas's translation when the painting's owner was speaking. Herr Walter would put his own security team on high alert, since he was currently skiing in Davos. Beatrice twitched and whispered a question to Tomas.

"When did he leave Munich?"

"*Entschuldigung, Herr Walter, wann sind Sie nach Davos gefahren?*"

"*Freitag abend. In privatjet. Wir kommen am Mittwoch morgen züruck.*"

Tomas whispered to Beatrice. "They flew Friday evening and will come back on Wednesday morning."

Stein met Beatrice's eyes with a certain curiosity. He waited till Meyer thanked the participants for their time and the guests had disconnected before speaking.

"According to Herr Meyer, we can afford to carry out surveillance on only one of these paintings. Which would be your choice, DI Stubbs?"

She didn't hesitate. "Munich. The owner is absent, it's a Schad and it's got the eyes connection. I am quite convinced this is the next target. If he's away for a couple of days, now is the perfect opportunity for the thieves to act. On top of all of that, it's just two days of watching the property."

Meyer, on screen, nodded. "That's all in order. I will talk to the Munich force and ensure they are fully briefed. I will also follow up with the other potential burglaries. Congratulations everyone, this is good work. Have a nice afternoon."

The screen went dark, Tomas's attention reverted to his computer but Stein was still watching Beatrice.

"Coffee, DI Stubbs?"

"What an excellent idea."

She reached both arms behind her head to massage her neck. It was like kneading stale bread.

Stein asked Tomas a question in German, picked up the phone and as far as Beatrice could understand, ordered coffee. Then he stood behind her.

"That won't work. If you have tension, you need another pair of hands."

He brushed her hands away and applied his own to the solid knotted mass of muscle between her shoulders. Soothing palms, hard thumbs, pressure and warmth unlocked all kinds of physical reactions. Thankfully, he continued talking, so that Beatrice's little moans could be disguised as grunts of agreement.

"Herr Meyer will organise extra patrols in the area of the Munich house. We can implement a similar intelligence search for all the other pieces by Schad and Grosz, adding addresses, owners and other terms in our database. Isn't that right, Herr Schäffer?"

"Exactly what I'm working on right now," Tomas replied, hunched over his screen.

"So what we need to do is mine the data. Find the cross references... oh sorry, did I hurt you?"

"No, just found a hot spot. Carry on."

His hands spread across her back again, manipulating the musculature. Heat moved across her skin. He continued talking but her concentration was divided between her neck, where his thumbs applied pressure to either side of her atlas vertebra and his voice, saying something important about mapping.

Her phone rang, seconds before she dissolved entirely, so she was actually grateful to see Hamilton on caller display.

"Thank you, Herr Stein. You're rather good at that. I must take this call. It's Detective Superintendent Hamilton. Excuse me."

She took the phone outside, hoping the wintry air might cool her cheeks.

"Good afternoon, sir. How are you?"

"Stubbs. Any progress?"

"Some. Just finished a phone conference with the Cultural Crimes unit and two potential targets. We'll be collaborating with forces in Berlin and Munich to add extra levels of protection. Everything is under control and even if I've made no progress by Friday, I'll hand over to Herr Schäffer to pursue the investigation. Whatever happens, I'll fly back to London on Friday evening and be back at work on Monday."

"That would be appreciated. Going to need all hands on deck next week. But I will be in Hamburg on Thursday and thought you and I could have dinner."

"Dinner, sir?"

"Yes, Stubbs. A meal one traditionally has in the evening. See if you can't find a decent restaurant and book a table for two. There's something I need to discuss with you."

Beatrice's heart sank. Not only an evening spent making small talk with Mr Irascible, but he'd probably insist on talking shop, putting out feelers on the whole replacement Superintendent issue. A horrible thought struck her. Would he expect to accompany her back to London?

"Certainly, sir. Have you already booked your return flight?"

"Onward flight, in point of fact. Flying out again on Friday morning."

"Oh, I see. Is that for business or pleasure?"

He took a moment to respond. "This is not work-related."

In other words, mind your own business. Beatrice changed the subject. "Are you feeling any better now, sir?"

"A little. Thank you for your concern. Now when you book a

restaurant, make sure it serves something other than fish. Steak, ideally. See you Thursday, Stubbs."

"I'll look forward to it," she lied.

Chapter 13

Tell the truth and shame the devil, his granddad used to say. Get the weight off your conscience and rest easy. So after sharing all his fears with Beatrice and Holger, arranging business as usual at Harvey's Wine Emporium and anticipating an impromptu holiday while escaping the excesses of Christmas preparations, Adrian thought a good night's sleep should be his by default.

It didn't work like that.

Once under the duvet, he turned out the light with a sigh, only to switch it back on within seconds. He made a note on the hotel notepad: *security system – remind Catinca to change password.* He spent the next ninety minutes envisaging every possible disaster which could befall his business and finally, at ten past two, decided to cancel his trip. He would call Holger at seven and say he'd changed his mind. Go to the airport, get a flight to London City and be back behind the counter of Harvey's Wine Emporium by lunchtime. Decision made, he set the alarm, switched off the light and willed the onset of sleep.

Two hours later, sweaty, clammy and with a sore throat, he woke from a nightmare. The dream had taken place in his hotel room, with shadowy figures around his bed, pressing down on his limbs. He'd tried to scream, but it felt as if his mouth had been glued shut. He put the light back on, checked the door was locked and searched the room thoroughly. Prickles and itches all over his skin made him scratch, so he took a shower and decided he may as well pack.

By the time he'd shaved and was completely ready for his return home, it was four-thirty in the morning. He turned off his alarm as he had no hope of sleeping anyway. Finally, fully clothed on top of the duvet, he drank a camomile tea and watched music videos with the sound down.

Traffic. Car horns. A siren. The dawn chorus. Adrian opened his eyes and realised the hotel room phone was ringing. His watch said twenty to nine.

"Hello?"

"Adrian, it's Holger. I'm downstairs in the lobby. Sorry I got here a little late. I stopped off at the main station to get our tickets. I thought we could have breakfast on the train. Are you ready?"

Adrian blinked at his suitcase and dismissed his night frights in an instant.

"I'll be down in two minutes."

The journey lasted almost four hours and Adrian loved every second of it. The crisp blue light of winter, the landscape growing wilder by the mile, the rail causeway to the island, sweet houses that reminded him of Amsterdam and ever-changing but always thrilling views of the sea.

They arrived at the island's main town, Westerland, and switched to a bus to take them north along a coast road. Adrian was in awe. He'd never seen a winter beach before. The composition of dune grass against blue ocean trimmed with pristine white snow seemed like a fairytale setting. He could imagine a unicorn galloping through the surf or out towards the horizon, a dolphin leaping out of the water in a slow-motion arc.

He constantly exhorted Holger to look, which he duly did. Holger seemed to enjoy Adrian's excitement and offered insider tips on the *Strandkörbe* or beach basket-seats, the expensive celebrity holiday homes in Kampen and the marine life so treasured by the islanders.

Just after one o'clock, the local bus service deposited them at the end of a sandy track. Adrian felt as if he'd arrived at the end of the world. Once the bus had gone, he stopped to breathe the clear cold air and to listen. Other than seagulls, the wind through the dune grass and the distant sound of the rolling sea, the peace was complete.

Holger inhaled and stretched. "I miss this place. This is my first time back since the summer. Come on. Let's get to the house and light a fire. The wind is sharp."

They set off in the direction of the sea.

"Just remember, this is a holiday house. Don't expect too much. There are all the basic conveniences and unbeatable views, but it is pretty simple. List, that town we just went through, has shops and restaurants and everything you need, only a twenty-minute bike ride away. You know, I never spent time here in winter. It feels very different. I hope you will be OK. This is not London."

Adrian took a huge breath of sea air. "Thank God for that. Stop worrying. All I want is nature and solitude and this looks like the place to find plenty of both. Oh! Is that it? No way!"

The house at the end of the lane had a peaked roof, descending from a top point to flick out over the eaves like a schoolgirl's hair. The red brick seemed warm and inviting against the backdrop of windswept dunes and the bleached horizon. Shuttered windows gave it a sleepy look, as if it was dozing until their return.

"Yes, that's it. When we were kids, we lived every summer at this house. This place is my childhood."

Gulls screeched as the wind buffeted them towards the building, encouraging them onward. Beyond the rectangle of garden lay the empty beach and constant tumbling waves, rushing up the sand and receding in a soothing rhythm.

Adrian inhaled and closed his eyes. "I'm going to like it here. I already know."

"I hope so. Strangers sometimes suffer from *Inselkoller* – island rage. Just remember you can leave at any time. Buses to Westerland are regular and then you can catch a train back to Hamburg. Don't stay if you feel uncomfortable."

"You should have been a travel agent. 'How to Sell a Place', by Holger Waldmann. Let's get inside, my face is freezing. I need some tea."

Holger unlocked the door, switched on the lights and deactivated the alarm. Adrian heaved his case over the threshold. It was almost as cold inside as it was out until the door slammed, shutting out the wind. A vague aroma of vanilla drifted through the air.

White walls, a driftwood sculpture, an open-plan living-room with a corner sofa, a beech wood kitchen with an island hob, parquet flooring with pastel rugs and sunken spotlights illuminating the cleanest, most Adrian-friendly environment he'd ever encountered outside his own flat.

"I don't believe it. This is the original IKEA house!"

Holger looked around as if seeing it from Adrian's perspective. "It is pretty Scandi, I guess. My grandparents bought this place way back in the 60s. They lived in it for twenty-seven years. If they sold it now, it would be worth millions. The decor is their taste. Light, clean and functional, but my grandmother has a homely eye. Come upstairs. I will switch on the heating and show you the bedrooms."

Patchwork quilts on ironwork beds and a pine grandfather clock. The final detail to convince Adrian he should live here and never move for the rest of his life. Holger went around the building, opening all the shutters, and lit a fire. Adrian hummed Doris Day's *Just Blew In From the Windy City* as he unpacked the food and assembled a picnic lunch on the dining-table. The sun shone directly into the living room, turning the wooden floor the colour of honey.

As they ate the cold meats and cheeses with a white loaf and gherkins, Adrian encouraged Holger to reminisce about his childhood summers on the island.

"What did you do here as a kid? I want to hear stories. Tell me!"

Holger gave a dismissive laugh. "Nothing to tell. Same as every kid, I was an explorer. My brother and I were mad about making things. When we were very small, it was a den or a wigwam or a tree house, where we'd occasionally be allowed to sleep. Whenever we did, my sister wanted to come with us but she never lasted the night. She always got scared and had to be taken back to the house. Then we discovered the sea. Growing up in Bavaria, we had forests and castles and mountains, but the sea was something almost foreign. We built kayaks and learned how to sail. One year my grandfather bought an old wooden sailboat which we fixed up. I got so sunburnt while we painted it I had to stay indoors for two days. At that age, it felt like forever."

"Are you the oldest?"

"No, I'm the one in the middle. My sister's the oldest by five years. Joachim and I were born within a year of each other and we're extremely similar in looks and temperament. People often thought we were twins. He's the one member of my family who still treats me exactly the same way since I came out. It honestly doesn't matter to him."

"What about the rest of your family?" Adrian asked.

"My grandparents, the ones who own this place, are cool with it but sort of too much, if you know what I mean. Always asking if I've met a nice man. Very interested in you and excited that I'm bringing you here. They just want me to be happy. My sister, Patricia..."

Adrian cut another slice of bread and when Holger didn't continue, offered a prompt. "Your sister doesn't want you to be happy?"

"She is a person of extremes. She made a lot of effort to make me change my mind. I refused and now she will not speak to me. My parents are accepting but worried."

"Why are they worried?"

"They fear I'll be beaten up, they think it's a phase, They wonder what they did wrong, and they believe I'll suffer from prejudice or AIDS. The usual."

Adrian shook his head in exasperation and poured more tea. "They expect the worst. You have a duty to show them the best. Make them happy for you."

Holger tore a chunk from Adrian's bread and bit into it. "I want to make me happy first. The family comes later. Finished? Are you ready to look around?"

"Have we got time for a walk on the beach?"

With a glance at his watch, Holger stood up. "Maybe later. Now I want to show you how everything works. We can walk back to the bus stop in an hour. Come. You're going to love the sauna."

They strolled up the lane as the sun sank into the sea, the sky all the shades of a volcanic eruption. Adrian was speechless. Almost.

"It beggars belief. I've never seen such an outrageous sunset in my life and I've been to Bali twice. I really can't thank you enough for introducing me to this place, loaning me the house and not giving up on me. You're so patient. I know I've not been the best company these past few days. When you talk to your grandparents, please tell..."

A car horn beeped as they reached the main road. A Jeep pulled to a halt and the window rolled down to reveal a bearded face with a big smile.

"Daan!" Holger dropped his rucksack, the driver jumped out and the two men embraced. Despite not understanding a word either said, Adrian deduced from the smiles and easy affection that this was a long acquaintance. The big hairy man looked at him with curiosity. He had deep-set green eyes and a monobrow.

"Daan, this is Adrian, a friend of mine from London. Adrian, meet Daniel Knutsen. We met when we were eight years old. Daan lives on the west coast and repairs boats for a living."

Adrian took Daan's outstretched hand and returned the strong shake.

"Pleased to meet you."

"Hello Adrian, you too." He had a wide, generous smile with teeth like tombstones. He reminded Adrian of Captain Haddock crossed with Bluto.

Daan pointed an accusing finger at Holger and spoke in English. "Why didn't you let me know you were coming?"

"Because we only decided last night. I'm not staying, I have to work. But Adrian will be here for the week to get away from it all. Maybe you could come over once or twice? Just to make sure he is OK?"

"Sure. I'd be happy to do that. If you feel like some sightseeing, Adrian, I can give you the guided tour."

"Thank you. I definitely feel like some sightseeing." Adrian hoped it wasn't just a friendly platitude.

"Holger, when are you leaving?"

"As soon as the bus gets here."

"Get in the truck. I'll take you to Westerland and we can have at least half an hour to talk. It's been too long."

Before Holger could reply, the bus came down the road. Daan rushed back to his Jeep, which was blocking the way. Holger hugged Adrian, picked up his bag and jumped into the passenger seat. Within twenty seconds, the two men drove off, waving and miming phone calls. Adrian watched the truck turn the corner, followed by the bus, and he was left alone.

He gazed behind him at the sunset for a moment and strolled back along the track to his holiday home. The sun had dropped below the horizon and the sharp twilight air brushed his neck. He was glad they'd left the lights on. The glow reassured him, as did the motion sensor triggering the outside floodlight. *I feel safe and comfortable. I will not get spooked by any strange noises. I have an alarm and a security system. I am perfectly safe.* He closed the door, checked all the windows and doors, put on the Scissor Sisters to drown out the sounds of the North Sea wind and started unpacking his case. He was going to be absolutely fine.

Beatrice left the office early, in a hurry to get back to the hotel in time for her scheduled telephone chat. This was one conversation she wanted to have in private.

"Hello James."

"*Beatrice, good to hear from you. I was surprised to receive a phone call request so soon after our last session. How are you?*"

"Fine, completely fine. Mindful, self-aware and taking the tablets. Thanks for making the time for me. The thing is, I need some advice, in a sort of 'off the record' kind of way. This isn't about me, you see. But don't worry, I'll pay for this as if it were an official session."

"*I see. Before we go any further, I can't offer any professional insight on a police investigation. It would...*"

She interrupted, well prepared for his objections. "... be completely unfair to even ask. This isn't about my investigation, I assure you. But a friend of mine is displaying peculiar behaviour and I wondered if you could offer some guidance as to where I could seek help."

There was a pause. "*What precisely does 'peculiar behaviour' mean?*"

Beatrice smiled. She'd expected more resistance. Her counsellor was punctilious in his professionalism so she'd thought long and creatively about the exact phrasing to excite his curiosity. Her deviousness had paid off.

She outlined the episode at the zoo and tried to deliver Adrian's later explanation without leaving out any crucial details. James, as always, began with questions.

"*Has your friend had any previous experiences like this?*"

"Not that I know of."

"*As he's joined you and his ex-boyfriend for the weekend, I assume he's not displaying antisocial tendencies.*"

"No. Quite the opposite. He was outgoing and lively until Sunday."

"*I don't suppose you know if he's having trouble sleeping?*"

"He did mention he'd had a bad night, yes. He was very tired and irritable and sort of disengaged. And I found out yesterday he's taking sleeping tablets."

"*Any other recent behavioural changes?*"

A familiar instinct to hide, dissemble and protect surfaced. Beatrice fought it, knowing that without honesty there could be no help. That applied to Adrian just as much as it did to her.

"He's been jumpy. He thinks his post went missing, he worries about who's coming into the building, he seems much more nervous than usual and contacts me on a daily basis. Just cheerful little check-ins, but that's not normal."

"*Hmm.*" Rustling scratchy noises indicated James was writing. Beatrice visualised the white-blond head bent over his paperwork in his light, white room and longed for her next appointment. Once a month seemed far too infrequent.

"*I'm going to send you a list of people he could see when he gets back to London. Many are experts in the field of paranoia but some simply use CBT to realign thinking patterns. I suggest you present the idea to him as physiotherapy for the mind. Interesting as this case is, I can't take him on, as there's an obvious conflict of interest. I hope he finds the right person, but if not, come back to me.*"

"Thank you, James. He won't be back for another week, as he's spending some time in his ex-boyfriend's holiday home. I wish I could go too. A remote island in the North Sea where people speak Danish and wear patterned jumpers."

"*He'll be with his ex-boyfriend?*"

"No, Holger has to work. And Adrian could do with a bit of time out. He hates the whole Christmas excess, crowds, pressure, food, so a week alone on an island is just what the doctor ordered."

"*As I said, I can offer no diagnosis on your friend. But with my background and understanding of mental health I feel that if someone is suffering a depressive episode and potentially experiencing anomalous incidents, the last thing he needs is a week alone on a remote island where he can't even speak the language. My advice would be to get him back to London and into a specialist's surgery. I'll send an email with contact details immediately. I'll leave it up to you how to deal with that.*"

Abashed, Beatrice said nothing.

James picked up on her silence. "*I don't mean to be alarmist. However, the fact you had enough concern to call me indicates this man is important to you.*"

"He is," she agreed, only then realising how true that was.

"*Beatrice?*" His voice changed register, a more urgent tone than his usual practised distance.

"What?"

"*Remember how important your friends have been during your low points. At the time you found them bullying and controlling, but now you appreciate their loyalty. They stuck around. They held on no matter how much easier it might have been to let go. If this person is important and he needs your help, be a bully if you have to, but don't let go.*"

His words hit home. "I won't. Thank you, James."

After fifteen minutes repeatedly trying Adrian's mobile and receiving the unobtainable message, she tried Holger. The only number she had was for his work, a studio in a shared building. A brusque, male voice answered and she left a semi-comprehensible message in jumbled German. She faced facts. She'd left it too late. Adrian had already gone.

Chapter 14

On Tuesday morning, Beatrice awoke in a terrible mood. A wretched night of fidgeting till four in the morning led her to oversleep and miss breakfast. She was worried about Adrian, regardless of his cheerful assurances. The investigation was too big, too complex and as concrete as a spider's web. It was all bloody pointless. She considered handing over everything to Tomas and just going home. Better her tail between her legs than her head against a brick wall.

She'd no sooner opened her office door than Stein followed her in, carrying two cups of coffee.

"Good morning, DI Stubbs. It seems you were right."

Beatrice unbuttoned her coat. "Good morning, Herr Stein. Is one of those for me?"

"Yes." He helped her out of her coat and hung it on the chrome stand. "Latte macchiato. I know you can't think before your first coffee."

"You have no idea how grateful I am." She took the cup and inhaled. "Right about what?"

"The painting in Munich. The owner left a message for me this morning. He instructed his security team to be extra vigilant and in response they mentioned some unusual activity. The normal routine is that one officer patrols the grounds, while the other sits in the security lodge, watching the camera footage. One of these cameras is trained on the road outside the house. It seems a black van with Dutch plates parked outside on three consecutive nights around four in the morning. No one got in or out, and the van drove away just before six."

Beatrice wiped some foam from her lip. "That's very interesting. I wonder…"

"You wonder what?"

"We now have extra reason to believe this piece is an imminent target. Therefore it might be worth investing in more than surveillance. The thieves are looking for the easiest time to pull a heist. That's likely to be overnight. Basic security cover, fewer potential witnesses, cover of darkness for vehicles. We even have a probable timescale. Could we stage an operation with a secondary undercover cordon to ensure we trap this gang in the act?"

He sat down and rotated his coffee cup, thinking for a moment or two.

"We can present Meyer with a suggested plan and then approach the Munich force. We'll need BKA support or they'll never agree."

There was a knock on the glass and Tomas entered with his laptop bag slung across his shoulder and two cups of coffee in his hands. He glanced at Stein and nodded to Beatrice.

"Morning, Tomas. What's the news?"

He held out a cup. "I got you a coffee. Herr Stein told you there's an update on security of the Munich painting?"

"Thank you." She took the cup and placed it placed it next to the one Stein had given her. She smiled inwardly at the courtesy of her foreign counterparts, remembering the kettles and the jars of pound-shop instant in her own office, the open milk cartons she'd have to sniff before risking. "Yes. We were just discussing if it is feasible to set a trap."

Tomas set up his computer while talking. "All the signs point to this theft happening over the next two days. Setting up a trap is a lot of expense and effort but on this occasion, it might be worth it."

Beatrice picked up her first coffee and drank from it. "Herr Stein, what do you think? Increased surveillance and a team on standby?"

"That sounds practical but expensive. Let's work out what to say to Meyer and if he agrees, I'll need to talk to Munich as soon as possible. This means a lot of work for them. If we go ahead, I'd like to be there in person. I want to be present when we catch this group. Would you like to come with me?"

"Yes, please. Catching these violent thugs in the act would make me very happy. Not to mention convincing Scotland Yard I'm not a timewaster." Beatrice sampled the other coffee, in the interests of fairness. "Tomas, anything else we need to know?"

"The Swiss and Austrian police have warned the owners their paintings are at risk. They gave no more detail apart from telling them to take 'extra precautions'. Frau Doktor Eichhorn sent me a message last night with factors regarding composition. She confirms your feeling, DI Stubbs. Of the six items we have identified as being on a possible hit list, only two Schads and one Grosz have subjects looking directly at the observer. One of those is *Nina in Camera*."

"The one in Munich. What about the other two?" asked Stein.

Tomas typed some commands on his keyboard. "There's a Grosz we already know about in Bremen. It's called Äusserer Schweinehund. But one other Schad we hadn't considered. This one is in Lübeck. Not in a private home but in a small gallery shared by a group of collectors. Less expensive than the others, although it's insured for a million Euros. It's called *Jäger,* which means hunter. You can see it here."

Beatrice and Stein moved closer to look at the screen. Once more, eyes dominated the picture even though this was a full-length portrait. Hard and somehow malign of feature, the man wore a felt coat and a green hat, peaked at the front and uptilted at the back. His britches were tied at his knee and the nuanced nature of the paint gave a vivid reality to both colour and texture. His right foot rested on a dead boar, gutted and muddy. His grey eyes challenged the viewer to congratulate him as he cradled his shotgun over his knee. The sensory power was such that Beatrice could not only feel the fabric of his coat, but smell the ripe gamey odour of the wild pig. She hated it.

"Not what I'd want in my living room, but each to his own." She took the other coffee once again and swigged. "Do you have an image of the Grosz?"

Tomas reached for the mouse and stopped.

"What is it?"

He spoke without turning from the screen. "This is not nice. Sometimes, you wish you hadn't seen something. Are you sure you want me to show you?"

Beatrice swallowed more coffee, managing nerves, curiosity, irritation and a refusal to be patronised. "Thanks for your concern, Tomas. A detective's job is to turn stones. We may not like what we find underneath them but it's our duty to look."

Tomas gave a sharp nod. He clicked a few times and a garish image filled the screen. A caricature of a fat man, dressed in a three-piece suit, with porcine eyes and florid cheeks, a cigar protruding from lips pulled back in a grin, showing his stained teeth to the viewer. His right fist held a rope, the end of which was tied around a woman's neck. She was on her knees, her arms hanging limply by her sides. She wore a gauzy top, torn so her left nipple was visible, and no underwear apart from stockings, revealing a dark triangle of pubic hair. Her face was covered by a white bag. The fat man's left thumb jerked behind him, at two figures in uniform bending over a bloodied body on the ground. One muscled arm was bringing down a club, the other's foot was drawn back for a kick.

Beatrice found it repulsive, but she refused to react. She focused on the fat man's eyes. Once again, they had a message for the viewer. *Look at this. Feel shock. Feel injustice. And there's nothing you can do.* It was a direct challenge.

Stein took a deep breath. "As a social commentator, Grosz didn't hold back. DI Stubbs, does this fit the pattern you and Frau Eichhorn identified?"

"I think it does. I'd like to discuss it with her again because I see a transactional factor in these works. A gauntlet laid down by artist to viewer, communicated by the eyes. Thanks, Tomas, I've seen enough. You're right, though. Some things you wish you could unsee. What does the name Äusserer Schweinehund mean?"

Stein frowned. "It's hard to translate. *Innerer Schweinehund* is a common expression, meaning 'inner pigdog'. The lazy demon inside you that makes you stay in bed rather than go jogging, who offers excuses rather than encouragement. It tells us not to try anything because we will fail. We all have to overcome our pigdog if we want to achieve anything. Naturally it's 'inner' because it's a part of us we keep hidden. Äusserer Schweinehund is a twist on that expression which would mean 'outer pigdog'. My interpretation is

Grosz is making a statement – here is the worst part of humanity openly exposed."

"Sounds like a rational analysis to me. Right, gentlemen, let's get to work. I need to call Berlin."

After calling Frau Eichhorn, Beatrice made some notes for Tomas, who was still on the phone to Herr Meyer. She signalled ten minutes and made a little walking gesture with her fingers. Tomas nodded and she went out into the street. She didn't go far as the cold made being outside more of a struggle than a pleasure, but she needed time to think. The concepts she'd discussed with the art professor batted around her mind and her solar plexus glowed with the conviction she was right. With Eichhorn's help, the police were now able to think like the art aficionado who employed such vicious means to assemble his collection. And therefore stay one step ahead. They were going to catch this gang and find where the trail led.

Yet not all the optimism and excitement she experienced was related to the case. She had just discovered a powerful weapon to wield in her own fight and wanted a few moments to process the idea. Stein's description of the *Innere Schweinehund* – the personal demon – thrilled her to the centre of her being.

Beatrice had always prided herself on clear-eyed self-assessment – she knew she was nothing special. Hard work and application had enabled her to rise through the ranks of the Met, because her intelligence was no more than the upper end of average. Talent, kindness and wit, albeit mediocre, were in evidence, as were selfishness and greed. Her looks would never turn heads, apart from her hair, and that caused more alarm than admiration. She lacked vanity despite possessing a sizeable ego, but on the whole she'd always quite liked herself.

Since her diagnosis with bipolar disorder, that had changed. In the same way she might regard an old friend in a new light after a betrayal, she realised she could no longer trust herself. She had become her own enemy; one who would never give up trying to destroy her. One who had almost succeeded by convincing her the only thing to live for was endless misery and offering an escape route via a bottle of pills. Those black dogs who padded around the peripheries of her subconscious, waiting for their moment to attack her soft, white underbelly were her own monstrous creations. She had long since lost her grip on the leash.

Now this exhausting battle had taken on a new dimension. The unpredictable mood swings, the energy-sapping inertia, the conviction of life's futility against an incessant tide of cruelty and injustice, the hyper-cycling euphoria which would drop her at any second into a void of numbness, the smothering duvet of absence – none of these was Beatrice Stubbs. Her enemy now had a name and an otherness. An *Innere Schweinehund* she could visualise, personalise, separate and therefore defeat.

She had a Pigdog.

Chapter 15

In the upmarket area of Gruenwald in Munich, the streetlights remained on all night. Not that it was necessary. High walls and electric fences bristled with security cameras and movement-triggered floodlights. These luxurious villas and their occupants and contents could not have been better protected. Especially this evening, as a dozen plain-clothes police officers were stationed around the vast corner property on Waldstrasse. Most officers carried the badge of the Munich City Police, apart from two, who were sitting in the back of a surveillance van, drinking coffee. The time was 04.41.

Stein checked in with all units, and although Beatrice didn't understand the German, she picked up the bored intonation over the airwaves. Nothing happening. The operation was due to run till eight am but everyone knew the optimum hours would be between four and six. Tension built and the clock seemed to slow. *Do it. Do it now!* Beatrice closed her eyes and willed their targets to act.

"DI Stubbs, if you need a rest, you could lie down on the bench for half an hour. I'll wake you if anything happens."

Her eyes flew open to see Stein's brown eyes and shadowed jawline angled towards her with a kind expression of concern.

"Thank you. I'm fine. How about yourself? More coffee?"

"No more coffee. I need to freshen my mouth. Perhaps there's water or juice in that fridge behind you. Only another three hours to go. We will survive."

Beatrice gave a tired laugh and opened the mini-fridge to find cold water, all kinds of energy drinks, a variety of juices and assorted chocolate. She selected two bottles of juice and a bar of Lindt to share between them. They sat side by side, watching the screens, listening for input and snacking on their impromptu picnic. Waiting, watching.

Stein spoke, his focus on the monochrome images of gates, doors, gardens and streets on screens.

"It's like looking at an empty stage. This is the place where anything could happen."

Beatrice swallowed some chocolate. "I know what you mean. The stage is set and we're all in anticipation. But when nothing happens for hours on end, it's no more exciting than watching pants dry."

Headlights swept across the screen and they both sat up, stowing their drinks. The car drew closer and Beatrice spotted the unlit taxi sign on the roof. She got a clear view of the driver and passengers while remaining invisible, thanks to the police vehicle's tinted windows. A couple kissing in the back seat, an uninterested driver and nothing to draw their attention. Nevertheless, Beatrice followed its trajectory. At the junction, the cab turned right, not left and removed itself from suspicion. The clock read 04.53.

"Coming home at this time of night? Munich is obviously a party city." Beatrice rustled open the rest of the chocolate.

"Less so than Berlin or Hamburg, unless it's Oktoberfest. Isn't London even more of a twenty-four hour party zone?"

"Probably. I wouldn't know. My clubbing days never really began. Even in my twenties, I was usually in bed by eleven."

Stein raised his eyebrows with a smile.

"To clarify, in bed with a good book. Are you a party animal, Herr Stein?"

"Sometimes. I play guitar in a band at weekends, so late nights and socialising are part of the package."

"Really? What kind of music do you play?"

"Jazz, funk, some of our songs are more pop, but it's all easy listening. The important thing is that when I'm playing, I'm completely absorbed, concentrating on what I'm doing at that moment. I can forget whatever happened during the day and focus on the music. It always makes me feel better. In a job like ours, I find that's vital."

"I agree. One can get very weary when dealing with the less attractive side of human nature on a daily basis."

"And you? What do you do to relax after..."

The floodlights around the house burst into life, throwing a harsh brightness across the grounds. Stein picked up the radio and checked in with each patrol. After a few moments, a security guard exited the gatehouse and made a circuit of the garden, checking the gates, shining a torch into corners and generally putting on a display of 'doing my job'.

A realisation dawned, draining all the tension from Beatrice and leaving in its stead a sense of being played for a fool. "We're onto a loser here. The security team know we're watching and this is all part of the show. Nothing's going to happen."

"But it was the security team who alerted us," said Stein. "That doesn't make any sense."

Beatrice sighed with frustration and tiredness. "No, it was *one* of the security guards who reported the activity. Probably a senior member of the team. Then we told the owner we'd be here tonight, watching. Despite our warning him not to do so, he's obviously told the security firm. Look at that bloke. He's acting the part! If the thieves have one of the guards on their payroll, which is highly likely, they know they're under surveillance and they're miles away, laughing at us or stealing someone else's painting."

Stein watched the poor performance and nodded slowly. "I think you might be right. *Scheisse!*"

Five hours sleep and one flight later, Beatrice was fractious and upset. During the telephone conference, Herr Meyer did not mince his words and called the Munich operation 'poorly planned' and 'rushed without sufficient thought'. He asked for a full report and analysis before committing to further surveillance. It was a rap across the knuckles and Beatrice could only hope Hamilton would not get to hear of it before he arrived on Thursday. Fat chance.

She spent the rest of the afternoon incorporating Eichhorn's expert opinion, Tomas's data analyses and her own unsubstantiated views into a report and delivered it to Stein. His face seemed shadowed and fatigued, but the warmth in his eyes was genuine as he thanked her.

She left the office at five and walked to the hotel, wishing Adrian was still in residence. She needed to offload. On a whim, she took a detour and jumped on a U-Bahn to Holger's studio. It would have been polite to call first, but he had no mobile. If he wasn't there, she'd go to his flat. Further than that, she hadn't planned.

The studio complex, *Made im Speck*, was an old brick building which showed signs of a previous life as an industrial plant. She looked for a bell or door knocker, then pushed open the door and called a hello. No reply. The place seemed empty, although all the lights were on. It didn't surprise her. These collective art/work spaces seemed to operate on a very relaxed system of trust. Beatrice wandered from studio to workshop, encountering all kinds of eye-popping creations, but not a single artist. No caretakers, no security guards, no Holger.

Finally a bearded male in overalls emerged from a doorway, smelling so strongly of dope that she reeled.

"*Guten Abend. Ich bin... um... Holger Waldmann?*"

He spoke in English with a Mancunian accent. "Holger? I don't think he's here today. You can check his studio. Up the stairs, second door on the left."

"Thanks."

She found Holger's workspace more by luck than the hipster's directions. The second door on the left was a photographer's studio, containing some rather disturbing nude close-ups. She closed the door in a hurry and checked the other side of the corridor. The second door on the right opened into a viaduct arch with a carpet of wood shavings and sawdust. This was the right place. The body of a violin lay on the workbench, oddly vulnerable without its neck. Unvarnished, limbless, bare of strings: an instrument embryo.

Beatrice stroked its curves with one tentative finger, before drawing back out of respect. The room gave little away. Tools hung from the walls in neat racks and a wooden chest of drawers, each compartment neatly labelled, reminded her of a spice cabinet. She smiled. A scent of pine, nutmeg and tar ebbed and flowed as she wandered the room, a fine dust disturbed by her footsteps. A workshop, a place to use one's hands, with few indications as to the craftsman himself.

On a small table in the corner, there were books and papers and several box files in no discernible order, and a selection of photographs pinned above the desk. Photographs of guitars, violins, a double bass. A smiling Holger with two men in overalls holding a certificate of some kind. Another one showed Adrian and Holger on a London bridge. She pulled out the pin and picked it up, looking past their beaming faces to ascertain which bridge, but the background was out of focus and indistinct. As she went to stick it back in place, she spotted a postcard which had been obscured by the one in her hand.

The image looked like a monastery, austere and withdrawn from the world. Old-fashioned script under the picture read *Kloster St Ursula, Rosenheim, Mai 2009.*

On the back were hand-written words.

Open your heart and return to the path of righteousness. Forgiveness is yours for the asking.

Voices could be heard echoing in the yard below, so she reached for her phone, took a photograph of the back and the front of the postcard, then replaced both images as she had found them. Time to go. Her urge to seek a friendly face had melted away in this peculiar building. Now she had an insistent need for some uninterrupted thinking space. In any case, Matthew would be home from university in an hour and she could bend his ear instead.

Outside in the frosty air, she hailed a taxi and gave the driver the address of the hotel. First priority, order room service. Then Matthew. After that, a little bit of research on Kloster St Ursula in Rosenheim.

Chapter 16

In forty-eight hours, Adrian had not spoken to a single person – apart from the checkout staff at the supermarket in List, a couple of texts exchanged with Catinca, a call to Holger, two to Beatrice and a bit of banter with friends from the Gay Men's Choir on Twitter. He was practically a hermit.

Being alone was such a grounding experience. He walked on the beach, paying attention to detail by collecting beautiful shells and jewel-like pebbles. He paid homage to the immense and ever-changing canvas of sky with photographs which caught a mere sliver of the colours and expanse. He cooked meals for one with local ingredients, some more successful than others. Herrings, he decided, would never be a cupboard staple. He read his book, cycled along the coast road and adjusted to enjoying experiences for their own sake, rather than capturing them to post on Facebook. He had changed gear, put himself in a different kind of Cruise Mode.

In the evenings he lit a fire, poured a glass of red wine and caught up with some European films on his must-get-round-to-watching list. He slept deeply and could remember none of his dreams. His island escape was working wonders and he made up his mind to escape the commercial horrors of Christmas every year.

A storm hit the coast on Wednesday, which put paid to any cycling as the rain lashed the house and a gale shook the building with the force of a meteorological tantrum. When a Jeep bounced down the track late Wednesday afternoon, he was surprisingly relieved to see another human being. He opened the door to greet his visitor and recoiled at the strength of the wind.

"Hello Adrian!" Daan yelled as he slammed the driver's door shut. His shaggy hair whipped across his face, obscuring his smile.

He swept it away in practised gesture of exasperation and crammed on a trapper hat, then advanced with his hand outstretched.

"Remember me? Holger's friend? I'm on my way home after buying some food. So I thought I'd ask if you want to join me. Let's go indoors. Shouting over this wind is a waste of time. What kind of crazy person comes to Sylt in December? Have you got any beer?" He grabbed Adrian's hand and shook it with an alarmingly powerful grip.

"Hello! Nice to see you again. Come in, come in, you're getting soaked!" He closed out the screeching gusts and punishing rain. "My God, Sylt really knows how to put on a show."

Inside the house, Daan seemed even larger. His black beard, waterproof jacket and ear-flap hat seemed to fill the small hallway, carrying a smell of the sea. Although he had brought the outdoors in, his smile radiated good humour and warmth.

"It's going to be like this for a couple of days. That's why I stocked up at the supermarket today. If I have to stay indoors, I want to enjoy myself. Good food, plenty of drink and entertainment. So, where's that beer?"

"Oh, yes, sorry. I don't think I have any beer, but I have got a smooth red wine which is very warming. Shall I get you a glass?"

Daan narrowed his eyes. "No beer? OK, good job I went shopping first. You don't mind dogs?" He didn't wait for an answer, but opened the door and battled his way back to the truck, using his shoulders against the wind like an American footballer. Adrian watched from the threshold as he hefted a case of cans in a fireman's lift and threw some items into a carrier bag. He jerked his head and a husky leapt from the back seat, ran straight past Adrian's legs and shook itself in the hall.

The door banged wide open and Daan blocked out the light. He held out the case of beers with another huge grin. "If I'm cooking for us both, here is as good as anywhere." Adrian lugged the cans into the kitchen while Daan took off his outdoor gear.

"The dog is called Mink, but just ignore her. Don't try to make friends. She doesn't have a lot of time for humans. If she likes you, it's her decision. Just put down a bowl of water where she can see it and let her make up her mind. Are you Jewish?"

Adrian filled a ceramic bowl with water and solemnly placed it in the hallway, observed by a pair of ice-blue eyes. He considered the relevance of the question and tried to answer honestly.

"Um, no, not committed to any religion to be honest, but..."

Daan, now in thick socks and a fisherman's sweater, gave him a powerful pat on the back. "Nothing to do with religion. But on the menu tonight is my speciality. Pork, parsley and potatoes. How does that sound?"

"Lovely! I eat everything. It's very kind of you..."

"I like to cook for people. And I should have called you before. Holger said you were alone. How about we have dinner this evening and if the storm is over, I'll take you on a tour of the island on Friday? Mink and I will sleep in the spare room tonight if that's OK. I never drive drunk but never eat pork without beer and akvavit. Shit! The pork! We need to switch on the gas. The meat takes at least two hours and it's getting dark already."

He barrelled into the kitchen, leaving Adrian and the dog in the hallway, both avoiding eye contact.

Daan moved around the kitchen with an easy familiarity, talking and drinking beer as he prepared the joint of meat. Mink watched from the doorway, her glacial gaze fixed on Daan's hands as he massaged spices into the scored pigskin. In an attempt to be useful, Adrian sat at the table, peeled the potatoes and listened.

"Yes, I've known Holger for years. We met when I was around eight years old. His family and mine spent summers here, which I hated at first because I had to leave my friends at home. In fact, it was because I wanted to play with him and his brother that I learned German."

"How come you didn't speak German?"

"I'm Danish. Daan the Dane from Odense. Do you know Odense? It's a port. I grew up with boats and the sea and never wanted to do anything else. I did my apprenticeship in maritime technology in Britain, you know. A boatyard in Plymouth."

"Plymouth? How funny. I thought you had a touch of a West Country accent."

"I loved Devon! And Cornwall. Cornish pasties are the best invention in the world. But I always planned to live on Sylt. As soon as I got my diploma, I moved here to start my own business. The island changed a lot, but no matter how many rich idiots in SUVs swarm here in summer, it's still wild and natural."

As if to prove the point, a machine-gun volley of raindrops hit the window with impressive force. Had Adrian been alone, the ferocious weather would have unsettled him. Daan's company was most welcome.

"Holger mentioned you repair boats. So your work is also your passion. Same with me. I sell wine. It's never going to make me rich, but I love what I do."

"Exactly!" Daan heaved the meat into the oven and clanged the door shut. He set the timer, stamped on his empty beer can and flung it into the recycling bin before opening another. "Beer for you or are you staying with the wine?"

"I'm fine with this, thanks. How many more potatoes do you need?"

"Do the whole bag. Even if we don't eat them tonight, they are delicious cold. Yes, I love what I do and I'm good at it. On Sylt, I can make good money. All these wealthy fools who think this is their playground are very careless with their toys. In the summer months, I often have too much work, fixing their stupid mistakes. So I earn as much as I can in the summer which takes me through the winter, when there's not much demand. Why did you choose wine?"

He sat at the table and picked up a paring knife to help Adrian.

"To show off, at first. But then I found myself reading more and more on the subject and accidentally became the go-to guy for wine recommendations. I got a job in an upmarket hotel and learned from a master sommelier."

"Sommelier? What's that? A wine waiter?"

"Well, a bit more than that, but yes, an expert on wines. Then I became a buyer for a chain of off-licences and the manager of one of their stores. Eventually, I took the risk of starting my own business and this is the first real holiday I've had since then."

"Why did you and Holger split up? You two seemed perfect for each other."

Adrian stopped, surprised at the sudden lurch towards the personal. Daan continued peeling, an open expression of enquiry on his face.

"We have... differing hopes for the future. Basically, he wants kids. I don't."

"Shame. You make a lovely couple and I know he was mad about you. But I'm with you on the kids thing. Didn't even want a dog, but she was abandoned by some selfish moron and left to starve. Typical of these people. They dabble. Buy a boat and all the gear, sail a couple of times, damage it through incompetence and move on. Get a dog, expensive pedigree, don't train it or give it enough exercise, so it gets bored and starts causing damage. Then they chuck it out. Bastards."

They both turned to look at the wolf-like shape in the doorway. Since the meat had disappeared, Mink lay with her nose on her paws, watching the two men.

"She is a beautiful animal. I've always wanted a dog, but living in London..."

Mink got up, stretched her front paws out with her bottom in the air and walked over to Adrian. She sniffed at his foot and up his calf, rested her chin on his knee and looked up into his eyes.

Daan grinned. "That means you're allowed to touch. Offer her the back of your hand and give her a stroke. Under, not over. Don't go for the top of her head. It still scares her."

Adrian nervously obeyed the instructions and caressed the soft fur under her jaw. He did feel a bit stupid speaking to her in English, but hoped she understood the tone.

"You're a gorgeous girl, aren't you? Look at those ears. What a fabulous coat. Like a Siberian landscape in the shape of a canine. Oh my God, her tail is wagging."

"And if you give her a piece of your pork crackling later, she'll love you forever. Right, that's the potatoes done, now we can have a break before I start the sauce. Why don't you prepare a fire and I'll make up my bed in the guest room. I know where everything is, don't worry. And I might just break with tradition tonight, seeing as I'm dining with an expert and drink wine with the pork. Choose something for us. Mink! *Fuss!* Come on, we need to sort out our bed."

The dog loped after him, wolf following bear, and Adrian found himself smiling.

The meal was an unqualified success. Moist, succulent pork, perfect roast potatoes and a piquant parsley sauce accompanied by a chilled dry Riesling all worked in harmony to deliver comfort, taste and balance. Mink lay in front of the fire, sated by her plate of leftovers and crackling. Adrian's usual urge to clear the table and tidy up immediately had deserted him, and the two men sat amongst the remains of the roast, savouring the satisfaction of a great meal and pleasant company.

The weather continued to batter the house, but inside the atmosphere glowed. Daan had a disarming technique of engaging in small talk one moment and segueing into politics or personal details the next.

"What did you see of Sylt so far?"

"Why do the British always put fruit with meat? It's weird."

"When did you realise you were gay?"

"What was your impression of Hamburg? Full of dickheads?"

"Why are the British so hung up about class?"

"Have you ever been sailing?"

Adrian thought about that one. "I've been on a boat but I wouldn't call it sailing. To be honest, it wasn't an experience I'd want to repeat."

"Let's see how the weather behaves. I'd like to show you a different side to the island, if it calms down. Mink won't even get on the boat when the sea is choppy. That dog has good sense. We can tour the whole of Sylt in the Jeep whether this storm continues or not, but the boat is best. I want to show you my place. It's nothing sophisticated, apart from being the most beautiful location in the whole Northern hemisphere, I guarantee."

"And you live alone? Apart from Mink?"

"Yes. I have relationships now and then, but my last girlfriend told me there is no room in my life for a partner. I can't argue with her. Company is great, but on my terms. I need time alone to feel rooted. Not many people understand that and end up getting frustrated or angry with me. Best to keep it casual. With plenty of variety." He laughed loudly and clapped his hands together, waking the dog. "Now! Time for the akvavit!"

Adrian stacked the plates and took them into the kitchen, while Daan uncorked the hooch. When he came back, his guest was standing at the fire, peering at pictures on the mantelpiece. He thrust a glass at Adrian.

"Here! Cheers! I hope Sylt brings you everything you want."

Adrian threw back the firewater and coughed.

"Sip it. There's a taste as well as an explosion. Here, look at this. Do you recognise me?"

The mantel was covered with framed photographs of children, dogs, boats, happy family units and picnics. Adrian scanned the various assemblies and spotted a dark-haired child on top of an upturned canoe. Every other head was blond.

He pointed. "You're not the average Dane."

"Marauding Celts along the coast. Powerful genes. How many generations does it take to fade black hair and green eyes? Not to mention charm. You ready for another?"

"Go on then. Is that Holger?" He indicated a white-blond kid holding a paddle.

"No, that's Joachim, his brother. That one's Holger." Another white blond, cross-legged in the sand, squinted at the camera. "We spent that whole summer on the beach, rebuilding a boat."

Other pictures showed freshly-caught fish, seventies fashions and family meals. There was another blond, a girl with plaits who stared out of the pictures with a resentful glare.

"Is this Holger's sister?"

Daan's smile shrank to nothing. "Yeah. Patricia. Horrible sow."

His terminology made Adrian laugh, attracting Mink's attention as she raised her head from her fireside spot. Daan poured two more glasses of akvavit.

"She was! She ruined everything. Always hiding and listening to us so she could run to Mummy and tell tales. Whenever we had an adventure planned, she'd want to be part of it, but as the dictator, not part of the team. She spoiled everything. Bossy, sneaky, poisonous. We used to lay Patti-traps, early warning signs that she was near. That was my first close-up experience with women. It's a surprise I didn't turn gay."

Adrian laughed harder. He suspected he might be borderline drunk.

"What?" Daan demanded.

Adrian attempted to focus his thoughts. "I don't think it's a negative experience with a particular gender that flips a switch. I see it as more of a positive thing, like good taste. I know the kind of wines I prefer which suit a particular dish. I know the kind of people I prefer who suit a particular experience."

"Good point. Cheers!" They toasted again. This time Adrian repressed his cough because Daan had already launched into a story about the time the three boys tried making their own alcohol.

"So sick, all of us. My stomach wasn't just upset, it was outraged!" He thumped his thigh and laughed, a huge infectious booming sound which made even Mink's tail thump.

The evening passed so pleasantly in terms of conversation, food and ambience, Adrian was amazed to see it was after one in the morning. He was warm, happy, expansive and pissed.

"Daan, I need to go to bed. I'm drunk as a skunk. God knows what's in that akvavit but I'm not surprised it gets you through a Scandi winter. Are you and Mink OK to put yourselves to bed? I need to douse the fire, locks the checks and make sure we're safe."

Daan bellowed with laughter and clapped his hands. "How about I lock the checks? Yes, you're obviously new to akvavit. Go to bed, we'll make sure the house is safe. See you in the morning for the full Danish. I hope you have some decent coffee. Sleep well, Mink and I will be fine. Drink some water before you go to bed or your head will hurt tomorrow."

Adrian did as he was told, dimly conscious of Daan chuckling and talking to the dog as he secured the doors. He filled a beer mug with water and ricocheted up the stairs to his room. After taking off his clothes, he did a lazy mouthwash, drank some more water and hit the pillow like a manatee.

Adrian opened his eyes and ran an inventory. Head throbbing, stomach queasy, mouth dry and a pressing need to urinate. He sat up and drank several gulps of water, registering the LED digits. Just before six in the morning. The storm had either taken a break or blown itself out.

He got up and fumbled his way to the toilet in darkness. He emptied his bladder and washed his hands with his eyes barely open. On the way back to his bedroom, he stopped, listening to an unfamiliar sound. Snoring. He walked on the balls of his feet to the door of the guest room, which was wide open. Inside, lit by strips of moonlight lay the wolf and the bear, back to back, one on top of the duvet, one underneath, both snoring. He tiptoed away to his own room and as he turned the door handle, he heard a more familiar sound. The creak of the front door.

The sound took a second to register, by which time his eyes were wide open. He stood still and listened in the gaps between snores, feeling the cold wood of the landing beneath his bare feet. He switched on the hall light and padded down to the living room. Nothing. In the fireplace was a mound of ash, the front door was locked and empty glasses littered the table. Down here it was warmer and Adrian's heart rate returned to normal. He checked the kitchen, just to be sure, and stood in the hallway wondering what else could have made the sound he'd mistaken for the door.

That was when he saw the mantelpiece. All the photographs he'd looked at a few hours earlier had gone. Instead, right in the middle, was a large wooden crucifix.

Chapter 17

"It was an inside job."

Judging by the number of empty cups, Tomas had been in the office for some time. Cables snaked across the desk to two laptops and a third device which looked like something from a Bond movie. He didn't even look up when she entered the room but delivered his evaluation directly at his screen.

A thought crossed Beatrice's mind. If she had set Tomas onto the connections between Holger Waldmann and a nunnery in Rosenheim, she need not have wasted last night chasing one dead-end after another in front of her screen. But she shook off her personal preoccupations and focused on work.

"Good morning to you too. There was no 'job', inside or out. What do you mean?"

"The security guards tipped off the thieves minutes after the conversation with Herr Walter. Look at the timeline. Incoming call from the boss advising extra security at sixteen ten. Outgoing call from same mobile at sixteen twenty-three. The number dialled is located in The Hague. Three more text messages from that number that afternoon and evening. The metadata shows us this Dutch number is the kingpin."

"*Was soll denn das werden? Was fällt dir ein?*"

Beatrice and Tomas both jumped as Stein's voice whipcracked around the room.

A rapid-fire exchange in German ensued with Stein repeatedly indicating the Bond box. Tomas's body language gave the impression of defensiveness but without apology. Stein repeated the word 'knee' three times with all the conviction of the final word. She watched the exchange like a tennis match, mildly entertained and admiring the sparks off Stein.

Tomas jerked his head towards Beatrice. "*Was meint die Chefin?*"

Stein's expression turned volcanic. "DI Stubbs, I'm sorry about this. I needed to say something to Tomas regarding his unauthorised use of police equipment."

Tomas protested. "It is authorised. The Munich force has clearance to use the FlyTrap for specific purposes. And I am permitted to use the data. This meets all the official..."

"*Halt die Klappe!* This surveillance equipment is still restricted under European law. Our policy is to use this only in cases of terrorist activity, human trafficking and drug smuggling. Art theft does not qualify."

"That's not for you to say! DI Stubbs is in charge of this investigation."

Beatrice held up her hands in surrender. "I have no jurisdiction here and in any case, I feel under-informed. Can one of you tell me what the problem is? Tomas, explain this box of tricks."

"The FlyTrap. You don't know it? This is an IMSI device which captures data from mobile phones. It intercepts mobile traffic by imitating a base station. You can listen in to conversations and read all SMS data, in fact anything going out of or coming into a mobile. This technology is controversial, especially since Snowden, because you don't need a warrant. This is why Herr Stein is uncomfortable."

Beatrice exhaled, relieved she was not as far out of the techno-loop as she imagined. "Yes, I'm familiar with the technology. We just call it by a different name."

"So you know that it is legal and one of the best techniques we have to track the electronic communications of organised gangs."

"Which is exactly what we're dealing with. So your issue is the legality of data-gathering, Herr Stein?"

"No. I know it's legal. I'm far more concerned about civil liberties and privacy issues. Just because we believe a painting to be under threat, the police have no right to listen into conversations coming from that house."

Tomas shook his head. "Herr Meyer disagrees."

Stein's head snapped round with a furious glare and Tomas looked away.

Beatrice cleared her throat. "I'm confused. If this imitates a mobile phone base station, how can it possibly work from here?"

Tomas was eager to explain. "The data didn't come from this machine. I asked Herr Meyer if we could use this technology as a back-up to the physical surveillance. He gave the instruction to the Munich team, not me. All I have is the data they gathered. It takes a long time to find the relevant information and I had to ask a communications analyst, but I found it and we are in a far better position than before. The only problem is here in Hamburg. We have the technology." He indicated the box. "But Herr Stein refuses to let me use it."

"If Meyer and the BKA approved its usage, I don't see the problem. Herr Stein?"

"Munich can make decisions regarding data-gathering according to their own policy. Ours is only to use communications interception in clearly defined circumstances. This is not one of them."

Beatrice sat down, partly to defuse the tension but mostly because she had not yet recovered from a night drinking coffee and watching an empty house. She yawned.

"If I understand you correctly, this FlyTrap shows a certain amount of telephone activity from a mobile phone belonging to one of the security officers at the Munich house. We assume it was a warning to potential thieves not to attempt the heist that night. If that's the case, and as yet we have no other evidence, surely we'd want to use this machine to eavesdrop on the Netherlands operation. So I don't see why you need it here in Hamburg."

Tomas, eyes glittering, tapped a couple of commands into his screen. "Listen to this. It's in German, but I will translate."

A voice recording came from the computer's speakers. Beatrice made out a few words but kept her attention on Stein's face. His frown eased as he listened and as the speakers ended their conversation, he nodded.

"That's clear. The caller doesn't identify himself but says their 'appointment' for the evening must be postponed because his boss asked him to do overtime. The person at the other end, who speaks German with a strong Dutch accent, asks if the caller is being watched. The caller says that eyes are everywhere. He then suggests an opportunity over Christmas, when the place is empty. The Dutchman says he'll talk to his people but confirms our suspicions by saying 'Tonight, Nina stays home'. Tomas, you said there was an SMS?"

Tomas tapped at the keyboard, his complexion pink with excitement. This man evidently loved his job. "The first one is from the same mobile and more or less the same location, on the outskirts of The Hague. It says 'Due to increased levels of interest, his client prefers to withdraw his offer. Thanks for your help and I will be in touch.' The security guy replies 'A temporary withdrawal, I hope? As mentioned, access over the Christmas holiday will be no problem.' There's a two-hour gap in communications before the Dutchman sends a final text. 'Other options I need to investigate. Thanks for the information and I will contact you if we decide to proceed'. So, they're looking at other paintings. This means we have to get as close as we can to the other pictures on the list."

Stein sat opposite Beatrice, his expression thoughtful. "DI Stubbs, how do you see it?"

"I assume we know who owns the Munich mobile, Tomas?"

"Yes. The other calls and texts show it is the younger security guard, Udo Katzmann."

"So in theory, we could bring him in and lean on him a little. He's obviously an amateur or he'd have used a separate mobile for communication with this gang."

Stein shook his head. "That risks alerting the nucleus we're onto them. Tomas has a point about using the FlyTrap, but I cannot authorise this. Nor can you, DI Stubbs. I will ask Herr Meyer for his decision and we can proceed in conjunction with the Netherlands police."

"That's fine with me. On the same issue, Tomas, employing a secondary tactic was an interesting idea. However, it is totally unacceptable to do so without asking permission from Herr Stein or myself. Going over our heads to Meyer was a poor decision and I'm surprised Meyer allowed it. It will not happen again. This unit functions as a team, and as such it offers its members the courtesy of full disclosure."

She resisted the urge to ask for agreement and opened her laptop. She could feel Stein's eyes on her, but kept hers down.

The morning passed quietly with the three officers absorbed in their own tasks. Apart from the occasional request for confirmation, they worked in silence. Stein's phone rang just before eleven. He picked it up, glanced at the display and left the room. Beatrice decided it was coffee time.

"Tomas, I'm going to the canteen for my caffeine fix. Can I bring you anything?"

He looked up. "Thank you. I'd like an espresso. And..." He hesitated.

"Yes? I'm having a pastry so I'm happy to get one for you too."

"No, not a pastry. I want to apologise. Meyer told me to inform you and Herr Stein about using the FlyTrap. It was my choice not to do that because I know how much Stein hates the idea of covert interception. He would have stopped it and we'd have zero results after last night."

"That doesn't sound much like an apology. More of an excuse."

"It's both. I am sorry I didn't inform you." His eyes met hers, slid away and looked back from under his brow.

"Accepted. I hope you'll do the same to Herr Stein. It might be a good opportunity to talk about your different approaches to the FlyTrap. As I understand it, he's only following the official policy for the region."

Tomas waved his head from side to side, in an 'I'm not so sure' gesture.

"Well, I'll leave it up to you. But we're working as a team, so no secrets. Now do you want a pastry or not?"

Tomas caved in and requested a Berliner.

On the way to the canteen, Beatrice stopped at Margrit's desk. The girl looked up from her screen with a bright smile.

"Hello DI Stubbs. How's it going?"

"Very well, thank you. I wondered if I could ask you a favour."

"Of course. I'm on Herr Stein's team so it's not a favour, it's my job."

"It's not actually work-related. You see, I've been looking into retreats for my holiday next year. I want somewhere peaceful, where I can meditate and contemplate but nothing overly religious. Someone recommended this one in Rosenheim, but the website's all in German. Would you mind having a look and tell me what you think?"

Margrit took the piece of paper with the URL written on it.

"Sure. Do you want me to do it now?"

"No, there's no hurry. Just when you have a spare five minutes. Thanks Margrit, I appreciate it."

By the time Beatrice got back with the cakes and coffee, Stein had returned. She approached the room with caution, trying to read the body language between the two men. Tomas's humble posture and Stein's relaxed attentiveness suggested an apology was in progress, so she went back to the canteen and added a latte and a croissant for Stein. On her return, both men were working on their computers so she decided it was safe enough to enter.

"Elevenses time!"

Stein smiled, his face unlined and open. "A good time for a break and a discussion of procedure. Thank you, DI Stubbs. That was Herr Meyer on the phone. He's spoken to detectives in The Hague and the decision has been taken at the European level to commit to telecom interception in three locations: the house in Bremen which houses the Grosz, the gallery in Lübeck with that Schad painting of a hunter, and at the location in The Hague. It's been identified as a light industrial unit which imports and exports fruit. We're responsible for Lübeck and Bremen. As Tomas knows the FlyTrap pretty well, I suggest he oversees both operations, keeping us informed at all times, naturally."

A look passed between the two men.

"Good. Glad to see you two have buried the ratchet. I agree, I think Tomas deserves a role of responsibility after all the effort he's put in."

A look of confusion passed across Stein's face but cleared as

Beatrice passed him his coffee. Tomas bit into his doughnut, careful not to sprinkle sugar on his keyboard.

"I have one area of concern," said Stein. "Do we warn the owners of the house and the gallery? They are potential victims, not suspected criminals, so perhaps they should be aware that every personal call or SMS might be scrutinised."

Beatrice thought about it as she tucked into her apple strudel. "Did Herr Meyer have an opinion?"

"He said that after the Munich non-event, he would advise not informing them. We might be sabotaging our own operation by doing so."

Tomas nodded vigorously. "Exactly. We don't know if the security teams and owners are involved in some way. This is our chance to find out. I say no. We listen, assess any relevant data and pinpoint the next target. From there, we can use traditional methods of surveillance."

"I tend to agree," said Beatrice. "We delete any information which is not pertinent to this case, but we listen to all of it." She rammed home her point. "We are very close to identifying a gang who don't simply steal works of art but use violent means to do so, ruining lives in some cases. As far as I'm concerned, we put every possible means we have into catching these people so we can find who pulls the strings. I believe we owe that to the victims."

She was pushing Stein's buttons, she knew. Evidently, so did he.

"Thank you, DI Stubbs. I had not forgotten the victims. It seems I'm in the minority, so I'll accept that. For this operation, we do not warn innocent people their personal conversations are being monitored. Tomas, can I leave you to arrange the two local units and report back to DI Stubbs and myself on how you plan to analyse the volume of data?"

Shoving the rest of the Berliner in his mouth, Tomas nodded, still chewing, and started work immediately.

Stein's gaze rested on Beatrice's face. "I'd like to discuss a few points with you in more detail. Do you have plans for this evening? I think it might be a good idea to get out of the office and share our thoughts on the management angle of our collaboration."

Beatrice flushed. There was something extremely intimate

about the way he used the word 'you' instead of her name. This was practically asking her on a date. Then she remembered her commitment and grimaced.

"Oh hell. I'd really love to, but my boss is arriving tonight. He wants to have dinner and I'm not in a position to refuse. Could we do lunch instead?"

"Your boss is coming from London? Must be important. Of course we can have lunch instead. But we get out of the building, OK? I know a nice place a short walk away. Can we say twelve-thirty?"

"Yes, I'll look forward to it. I had planned to speak to Frau Eichhorn about the paintings in question, but under the circumstances, perhaps I shouldn't mention them. What do you think?"

Stein gazed at her until she began to feel awkward. "Shuffle the cards. Ask her about a lot of paintings and slip those into the middle somewhere so as not to attract attention. Oh." He leaned forward and picked a piece of apple strudel off her jacket.

"I was saving that for later," she said.

"Too late!" he replied and slipped it into his mouth. "See you at lunch."

She watched him walk away with a heartfelt sigh, the scent of his aftershave lingering in her nostrils. It was probably for the best they couldn't have dinner together. Her imagination was likely to run away with her. Instead, she had to spend several hours with Hamilton. Her smile faded.

Chapter 18

Daan wrapped his hands around the coffee mug, took a sip and swallowed, his gaze resting on the mantelpiece. He shook his head again. A scratch at the door indicated Mink was ready to come in. Adrian opened the door and she bounded back across the threshold, leaving wet pawprints in her wake. Outside the light was weak and yellowy, but the storm had gone, at least temporarily, leaving a trail of broken branches and drifts of tobacco-coloured leaves in its wake.

Back inside, Daan was still shaking his head. "This makes no sense. We both stood here last night, looking at those photographs. We identified me and Holger. I even remember noticing the dust when I picked one up. Last night, those pictures hadn't been touched for months and there was no crucifix anywhere in this room. This morning, the pictures are gone, the surface has been cleaned and there's a huge cross in the middle."

"And the door was locked. When I thought I heard it close, I came down and checked. It was locked. I'm one hundred percent certain."

"Two people in this house with the door locked. So it must have been you or me. I don't think I've ever sleepwalked. Even if I did, I wouldn't know where to find a cross in this house. Holger's grandparents don't have such a thing, as far as I know. They're Calvinists and reject all kinds of iconography."

Adrian rubbed his face. "It wasn't you and it wasn't me and it certainly wasn't Mink. I wonder why she didn't bark?" The dog's tail whisked back and forth across the floor as she faced the two men.

"Because she sleeps like the dead. Useless guard dog."

"That's true. When I heard the door close, it was impossible to hear much at all over you two snoring. You were both out cold, like I'd been. Where did the pictures go? Where did that cross come from? Who the hell has access to this house and why would they come in during a massive storm to replace family photos with a crucifix? And what's up with Mink?"

The husky's eyes were fixed on Daan and her tongue lolled as her tail made rhythmic sweeps of the rug. Daan broke his focus on the cross and shifted his attention to the dog.

"She's hungry. Me too. We should have some breakfast and then I need to... shit, look at the time! I've got to go! No time for the full Danish. I'll shower, you fry an egg and put it in a pork sandwich to take with me. Give Mink some leftovers. No bones! I don't want her farting in the Jeep all day. We have a long drive."

He thundered up the stairs, cursing the time. Mink followed Adrian into the kitchen and watched as he prepared her breakfast.

"Here you are, girl. Eat up. I'll wrap some bones for later. Now, he wants a fried egg and what?"

The mechanics of making the sandwich only occupied half of Adrian's attention. His gaze was drawn to the window and the patterns in the swirling leaves conjured by the wind. Someone was trying to scare him and doing a pretty good job of it. Staying on a stormy island in winter was perhaps not the smartest move. He should be at home, with friends, with crowds, London Transport, Catinca, the shop. He shouldn't be alone.

Daan barged into the kitchen, poured himself another half cup of coffee and drank it in one. "Sandwich ready? You fed the dog? OK, listen. I don't know how that happened." He jerked his head in the direction of the living-room. "But it is a bit freaky. At this time of year, Sylt can be a bleak place. I have a job today, otherwise I'd stay. Still, there are two things we can do. One, I've just set the CCTV cameras to record. They don't usually run during the winter, but this counts as special circumstances. If anyone is creeping about the place, we can see them. Two, how about I leave Mink with you? At least you'll have some company."

Mink's head angled at the mention of her name. Daan dropped to his haunches and spoke soft words, unintelligible to Adrian, as he scratched her neck. Her tail drooped and her ears folded back. She didn't want to stay.

"Are you sure? She doesn't look happy."

"She'll sulk for half an hour. Then take her for a walk on the beach. Give her a bone when she gets back if you can cope with the farts. Take her out again this afternoon and feed her when you eat. She'll be fine. Make sure she has water and I'll come by on Friday morning to pick you up for the tour. OK? I have to go. Thanks for dinner!"

He grabbed his bags, scratched Mink's chin, hugged Adrian and ran out the door. They watched as he executed a three-point turn and drove off with a toot. Adrian looked down at Mink.

"Do you want to go for a walk? Walkies?"

Her head dropped, she turned tail and curled up in the corner of the hall, refusing to look at him. Adrian locked the front door and before he could dither, removed the cross from the mantel and put it in the cleaning cupboard. His stomach rumbled and he decided Daan's breakfast recipe sounded intriguing. He set some butter to melt in the pan and started shredding some pork. He'd got halfway through a rendition of *To Know Him Is To Love Him* when he sensed a presence at his side. A pair of serious blue eyes studied him as Mink's nostrils flared in the direction of the counter. Adrian unwrapped a bone and placed it in her gentle jaws. She took it into the hallway and started gnawing.

"Eat that now and then we can both fart outside."

The wind was still powerful as Adrian and Mink crested the dunes and he had to lean into it to make any headway. Mink ran ahead, chasing sea birds with a gleeful bark. The cold air blew away the last traces of his hangover and he ran down the other side of the dune to join the dog. The vast arc of beach stretched away towards the distant town of List to his right, with a spit of sand curving out into the sea. The voices of two horse riders reached him, as they conducted a shouted conversation as their mounts kicked through the surf. Further along, a man threw sticks for a small scruffy terrier. To his left rose a headland topped with dune grass, deserted but for gulls.

He whistled to Mink but his breath was whipped away. He trusted her to follow and picked his way across the beach, his boots sinking into the soft white sand, to the edge of the sea where the footing was firmer. Clouds tumbled across the sky set to fast-forward, creating constant patterns of light and shadow on the ground below. Adrian shielded his eyes from the sun and gazed out at the waves.

The colours of the sea changed constantly, from a brushed steel grey to the dark blue of a naval uniform, only to break into bubbles of white as the water crashed on top of itself and rolled up the sand. He took a step to avoid getting his feet wet and Mink charged past him, straight into the water. She pranced, bouncing off her front paws, and landing with a splash, again and again. Adrian laughed aloud at her playfulness. After a few minutes she trotted out of the water and shook herself so hard her face seemed to rearrange itself. Then she pushed her shoulder to the ground and fell into a roll, wriggling and kicking her legs in the air.

"You're going to get filthy!" Adrian yelled against the wind, but she was on her feet and rushing into the sea once more. They proceeded along the beach like this until she found a piece of wood in the shallows. She picked it up, threw it with a sideways jerk of her head, grabbed it and shook it before bringing it to Adrian and dropping it at his feet. She didn't look at him but stared intently at the wood, nosing it towards him. He picked it up and flung it along the sand, watching her rush after it. When she was almost upon it her forepaws lifted and she leapt into the air to dive on it in an almost catlike pounce.

Adrian wiped away tears of laughter. For such a serious animal, she certainly knew how to have fun. Man and dog kept each other mutually entertained all the way to the set of rotting posts stretching into the sea, presumably the skeleton of a long-destroyed pier. Even in their ruin there was something beautiful about them, like standing stones.

The cold air, so bracing and clean at first, now began to infiltrate his jeans, so he turned back to the house, wondering if there was an old towel he could use to dry a large, wet, sandy dog. He planned to make a hot chocolate, read his book and maybe have a nap on the sofa. Being awake since six after a drunken sleep was not sufficient rest. But his fear and paranoia in the small hours was under control. Tonight, he would have the dog and security cameras, and Daan would be back in the morning. He might even take a sleeping tablet to catch up on his rest.

A bit of digging about in the laundry cupboard unearthed an old blanket and a towelling sheet with holes in it. Adrian used the latter to dry Mink, amazed at how much water a dog's fur could hold, and made a blanket bed for her in the middle of the rug. She circled it several times, dug it into an acceptable shape and curled into a ball, her nose on her tail. Adrian's mobile beeped. A text from Beatrice, asking him how his holiday was so far. He sent a rapid reply.

Weather dramatic, scenery divine, food and company excellent. Ax PS: I want a husky!

He checked the doors were locked and made a hot chocolate, then settled down on the sofa under a fleecy blanket to read. Within five minutes, his eyelids started to droop.

When he awoke he was sweating and couldn't move, and a damp and putrid stench filled his nostrils. He turned his head to see a mound of grey fur, each hair tipped with black, beside his head.

"Mink!"

A furry tail bounced off the cushions, followed by more of the revolting smell. Adrian struggled upright and shoved her onto the floor.

"Oh my God, Daan was right about the farts. Why did you have to point the business end in my direction?"

She scratched behind one ear then shook herself again, the cloud of fine hairs she released visible in a shaft of sunlight.

"Right. Time for lunch, another walk and then I'd better clean up after you. I had no idea you'd be such a full-time job. Come on."

Omelette for him, a tin of meatballs for her and *OK Go* playing on his iPad, with sunshine streaming onto the pale wood of the kitchen. All these elements combined to put Adrian in the best mood he'd enjoyed for weeks. Then he bundled himself up in his warm jacket and took Mink out to explore the other end of the beach. They walked over the headland and looked out at the tip of the island with its lighthouse. Adrian threw sticks, watched a distant ferry heading for Denmark and gawped at what he first assumed was someone swimming in the bay, until he realised it was a seal. He'd never seen one in the wild before. The seal was joined by several more and they bobbed and dived in the waves before heaving themselves onto the sandbank to enjoy some rays of afternoon sun. He wished he had binoculars.

A cloudbank swelled from the east and the sky on the horizon seemed to join the sea in a wall of smoky grey. Mink was digging in the dunes but lifted her sandy snout out when Adrian clapped his hands. She dashed to join him as the first fat raindrops pockmarked the beach and they broke into a run through the dune grass and back to the house. They weren't fast enough. All his efforts at keeping her out of the sea were wasted. She was now as rain-soaked as he was. Puffing and dripping, he dried them both in the hallway and went upstairs to change his clothes. From his bedroom window, he saw the cloudbank chase the last tiny sliver of sunshine until it was swallowed by the sea. Raindrops pelted the roof above him and he hoped there were enough logs downstairs that he wouldn't have to go back out to the wood stack.

Once he was dry, he checked all the windows and made Daan's bed. It occurred to him he had no idea where the Dane was or how to make contact. He'd just have to wait till he reappeared tomorrow.

It was already darkening when he got downstairs so he switched on the lights and dragged the vacuum from the cleaning cupboard. Mink disapproved of the sound, slinking out of the room with her ears flat. The wooden floors were easy to clean and the whole floor took only twenty minutes to restore to photo-shoot charm, with a quick spray of Febreze to counter the whiff of wet dog. He put the vacuum back and froze. That morning, he'd taken the wooden crucifix from the mantelpiece and put it in that very cupboard. Now it had gone. He rushed back to the living-room. The mantel remained empty.

He searched every room in the house, in wardrobes, under beds, behind doors, but found no trace of the cross. Mink found the whole exercise a game, trotting after him, nosing under beds and snuffling behind furniture, occasionally glancing at him as if to say, 'What are we looking for?' A vein in his neck pulsed and his breathing became laboured.

He returned to the lounge and lit a fire, less than reassured by the pile of logs that remained. He'd have to go outside again later. Mink curled up on her blanket and Adrian took a moment to breathe deeply and think. This tornado of thoughts was blinding any attempt at logic. He imagined explaining the situation to Beatrice, which calmed him. He sat at the table and wrote down the facts.

Pictures removed, crucifix substituted. Daan could bear witness to that. Crucifix relegated to cleaning cupboard, now disappeared completely. No witnesses, apart from a very clear memory of shoving the vacuum to one side so he could fit it in. That's how he'd known where to find the cleaning materials this afternoon. Doors locked on both occasions. It was pointless to wonder why, he just had to focus on how.

Perhaps someone had been hiding in the house last night? But how did they lock the door after leaving? There was no one here now; Adrian had just spent the last half hour searching the entire building. The only occupants were himself and a large snoring husky.

So whoever it was had a key. He checked the doors again and noticed the front door had a chain. So even if someone did have access, he could stop them getting in. The back door didn't, but it was opened by an old fashioned key, so all Adrian had to do was leave his key in, tilted so it couldn't be pushed out, and no one could insert one from the other side. No one was in the house. No one could get into the house. Bingo.

Now the question remained, who had a key to the property? Holger said his grandparents lived here in the summer and loaned it as a holiday home the rest of the year. The logical thing would be to leave a key with a local. Adrian checked the time and called Holger at home. No reply. He left a message on his answerphone.

Hi Holger, just checking in from Sylt. Everything's lovely and the place is a delight. Daan and his dog came round for dinner and we're off on an island tour tomorrow. One odd thing, a crucifix appeared on the mantelpiece overnight. Bit weird but generally I'm fine and feel safe. Can you give me a call when you get this? Bye bye.

How can anyone on the planet survive without a mobile? No wonder they were incompatible, the man was a troglodyte. He pondered calling Holger's studio, but you never knew who would answer the phone. Instead, he uncorked one of his favourites, a Châteauneuf-du-Pape, and took some photos of the label, the ruby glass aglow with firelight and the sleeping dog in the background in a set of still life images guaranteed to inspire envy. At least he could make his life *look* perfect.

Chapter 19

From the sublime to the ridiculous. Lunch with Herr Stein had been everything she needed. Their surroundings were not exactly five star – an upstairs room in an Imbiss – but the fact they were alone, dropping bits of kebab and lettuce on the paper plates and eating with their fingers seemed to fit the occasion. Gloves off.

Stein appeared relaxed and willing to share his thoughts, with the proviso that she did the same. Their conversation was a delicate two-step, each exchange a quid pro quo. He acknowledged her detective work and hoped she understood his adherence to policy. She complimented him on his ethical standpoint and emphasised the importance of compromise and mutual respect in multi-national collaborations. He praised her instincts regarding his team and suggested unified thinking on their plan. Then she got a chilli caught in her throat. He leapt to his feet and patted her back till she stopped coughing, then poured her a glass of water.

"Thank you. You obviously have healing hands. Sorry, I was attempting to agree with you. We have no choice but to join up our thinking. We need the Dutch police, the BKA, two teams on the ground here in Germany, ourselves and Tomas overseeing the data. Do we..."

"Trust him?"

Beatrice shrugged in apology.

Stein shrugged back. "In the interests of mutual respect, I don't honestly know. Tomas is untried in the field. My hope is he will rise to the challenge, but I've never seen him under pressure, making decisions with human beings rather than data. Having said that, I noticed he brought you coffee and a lunch bag this week, and volunteered an apology. Not a big deal for most officers, but in Tomas it shows an unusual sensitivity and awareness of other people's feelings."

Beatrice chewed the last of her kebab and ruminated. "If you want my nine eggs, everyone needs the chance to prove themselves. Tomas's data is the cornerstone of this investigation, so he should be central to the investigative team. He'd benefit from guidance when it comes to fieldwork, but you can watch over him."

Stein opened his book and made a note. "I'll make arrangements. Would you like anything else?"

"No thanks. Apart from that awkward chilli, I enjoyed that. How was yours?"

"Dirty but satisfying. I'd planned to take you to a sophisticated Asian restaurant tonight. Instead, we're in an Imbiss, eating a kebab which nearly killed you."

Beatrice sighed. "I have nothing against dirty and satisfying. Nor sophisticated Asian either. If I had a choice, I'd much rather have dinner with you than get the third degree from my boss. But when it comes to Hamilton, no is not an option."

"Why is he coming here?" Stein asked, gnawing on a toothpick.

"To check up on me. He thinks I keep taking foreign assignments to run away."

"Run away from what?"

"Reality, I suppose." Beatrice rubbed her eye and immediately wished she hadn't. The remnants of chilli irritated her cornea and made her eyes water. "Sorry, I need to wash my face."

"Let me see."

Stein in close proximity to her garlic breath was a horrifying thought. "No, no, all I need is a rinse. Shall we get the bill?"

"You're invited. I'll pay while you use the bathroom. That chilli's determined to get you one way or another."

Beatrice thought back over their conversation as she stared at her reflection in the mirror over her hotel room desk. Tomas did have many of the identifying features of a geeky misfit with antisocial tendencies. But as Stein said, he was also showing behaviour which counteracted that. Apologising. Engaging. Bringing her coffee.

She agreed with herself. He was certainly worth trying out on an operation. Apart from anything else, it would broaden his horizon from theory on a screen to action in the field.

Her hair was disobedient and the dour black dress made her look like a Portuguese fishwife. Good job she'd be sitting opposite her own crotchety boss, rather than Germany's equivalent to George Clooney. Hamilton would only take exception if her outfit contained any colour.

She applied lip salve but not gloss, put in her black pearl earrings and gave herself a final check in the floor-length mirror by the bathroom. Sober, boring, steady and anything but a loose cannon. She would do. In her handbag, she slipped an executive summary of the case to save her a lengthy explanation and give her a few minutes off the hook. With a deep sigh, she left her room and went to find a taxi.

When she arrived at Estancia, Hamilton was already sitting at the bar. She was five minutes early and only a third remained of his water, so he'd been waiting a while. His expression was neutral as he watched her approach. His greeting took the form of an inclination of the head.

"Stubbs." He pulled out a bar stool.

"Good evening, sir. Sorry I'm late."

"Five minutes early, for a change. Drink? G&T if memory serves?"

Hamilton proposing alcohol? She kept her eyebrows under control and gave a gracious nod. "Thank you, sir, that would be just the thing. Are you joining me or sticking with water?"

"Don't mind a drink when not on duty. This is my second." He drained his glass and a whole new level of concern opened up. She'd never seen Hamilton drink and had no idea what might happen if he did. These uptight sorts were often the worst when they let their hair down. He gave some kind of hand signal to the barman as if he were at home in his club, while Beatrice hauled herself onto a bar stool.

"Did you have a good flight, sir?"

Hamilton ignored her in favour of watching the ceremony of drink preparation.

The barman presented two tall glasses: ice and lemon and an innocent looking fizz. "Two gin tonic, sir. On the tab?"

"Yes, thank you. Here you are, Stubbs. Cheers!"

"Cheers to you too." She took a small sip and studied Hamilton's posture, colour and general demeanour. "You look better, sir. How are you feeling?"

A silence ensued and Beatrice's stomach sank in dread. A whole evening of these social power games. Her trying to make small talk, him refusing to engage. To think she could be chatting to Herr Stein over spicy noodles.

"How am I feeling? Surprisingly good. Yourself?" He didn't look at her, but studied the array of optics behind the bar.

"Optimistic. I believe this case could be solved within days. We have a great deal more information and a cross-border collaboration agreed. I wrote a summary for you, if you'd like to read it?"

"Not now, Stubbs. In fact, hang onto that and give it to Jalan. I'm taking some time off."

Irritated, she shoved the folder back into her bag. "So I understand. Is this a holiday, sir? I imagine you could do with one."

"Not exactly. Planning to catch up with some old friends."

He beckoned the maître d' to enquire about their reservation, forestalling any further questions. Beatrice bit her lip, sipped her drink and watched the beautiful people enjoying themselves.

A waiter escorted them to their table, insisting on carrying their drinks, and parked them in an alcove, next to an impressive pillar. Hamilton sat with his back against the wall, forcing Beatrice to sit opposite, with little to absorb her gaze other than her boss and some decorative cow horns attached to the wall. She snapped open the menu and looked for the most expensive dish.

"Stubbs, I've already decided on the food. We'll have the best quality steak and chips. Medium rare for me. You tell the chappie how you'd like yours. Might want to decide on an appropriate wine while you're at it. That's one area where your expertise outstrips mine."

Her molars pressed together, tensing her jaw, as she scanned the wine list. In point of fact, she did want steak and chips, but loathed it when others decided for her. She took her revenge via the wine.

When the waiter arrived, he gave their order. She added a Malbec with a hefty price tag and instructed the chef to cook hers medium to well done with a pepper sauce. In the last year, she had gone off bloodied meat. The napkins, the tasting of the wine, the addition of cutlery and the enormous effort it took to find a suitable subject for small talk wearied her and she decided she'd had quite enough of eating in restaurants for a while. Tomorrow, she would go to a supermarket and picnic in her room.

"Did you get the chance to have a look around Hamburg, sir?"

Hamilton tasted his wine. "That's jolly pleasant. Good choice. No, all I've seen is the interior of a taxi and my hotel room. Too damned cold to go exploring."

"It's certainly chilly. Perhaps you'll have a bit of time tomorrow. There are some lovely spots along the..."

"Doubt it. Flight at midday. I'm not here as a tourist, you know."

Not as a tourist, not as her boss, so the question was unavoidable. Why was the crabby old bastard here?

He narrowed his eyes. "Something wrong?"

"Not at all, sir. Trying to store the name of this wine, that's all. It's very good."

"So it should be, for the amount it costs."

She did not retort, but sat back and surveyed their surroundings. Let him come up with some chit-chat if he could be bothered.

"If you could choose anyone across the team, including yourself, who do you feel would make the best Superintendent?" he asked, his focus on his glass.

Hardly chit-chat, but better than sitting there in silence. She'd been expecting this and needed to tread a careful course between pretending she had no idea what he was talking about and pushing the idea of Rangarajan Jalan as the ideal.

"I thought you were planning a break, sir, not leaving us altogether."

"Playing for time, Stubbs? Answer the question."

"Not playing for time, sir. I've no reason to do so. Personally, I believe Rangarajan Jalan has all the management experience, diplomacy, decisiveness and interpersonal skills to be an outstanding Superintendent. If all you wanted was my opinion on a successor, sir, you could have asked me over the phone and saved yourself a trip."

Hamilton smiled, with all the warmth of a shark. "How odd. When I asked Jalan, he recommended you. Some sort of pact, I ask myself?"

Beatrice's temper changed colour. Up till now, she'd been in zone amber with the occasional flare of red. Now she shifted into magnesium white-hot. This arrogant, upper-class arse chose to make assumptions and patronise her as if she were a sixth-former. He'd already spoilt her evening and would continue to do so unless she showed her teeth.

"Sir, can I just say something?"

"No. Just for once, Stubbs, shut up and listen. I asked you to take over Operation Horseshoe for more than one reason. One, I thought you were perfect for the position and could learn a great deal about diplomacy from DCI Jalan. Two, I hoped the engagement would reignite your enthusiasm for policing in London and quash your desire to leave the force. Three, the role would be closely observed by the Chief Super and the board with a view to a promotion. Can you not see that I was trying to do you a favour by manoeuvring you into the job? But with your usual short-sighted urge for immediate gratification, you wriggled out of it to come here. I care very much about who will take over as Superintendent and the only possible candidates thus far are both determined to retire. Frankly, I find it very disappointing when an officer hasn't got the mettle to finish the job."

The man had offended Beatrice on every possible level and she considered simply getting up and walking out. Perhaps throwing her wine in his face to boot.

"Ah ha! Finally, the food. Move your elbows, Stubbs. Medium to rare? That's for me. The overcooked one with sauce is for her. Can you wait while I try this? Then I can send it back if not to my taste."

He sliced into the middle of his steak, parted the meat to check the colour and cut off a small section and chewed it with care. He looked up at the waiter.

"Cooked to perfection. The chef should be commended. Top up, Stubbs?"

Beatrice said nothing but watched as the waiter poured.

"Thank you." She spoke only to the waiter.

Hamilton lifted his glass. "Bon appétit. Cheers!"

She reciprocated, unsmiling, took a sip and returned her attention to the food. The sauce came in a mini jug beside a huge lump of meat and the chips looked crisp and chunky. At least she could enjoy the food, if not the company. She attacked her plate with vigour. He nodded his approval, apparently at ease, and they ate in silence. The sound of conversations, laughter, crockery and high heels on tiles eddied around them, filling the gaps.

After a while, Beatrice noticed how little Hamilton had eaten. She was a good two-thirds through this beautiful piece of meat, but he'd barely had more than a few mouthfuls.

She looked into his face. "Not to your taste, sir?"

"The food is delicious. As is yours, evidently." Hamilton leaned back, rotated the stem of his wine glass and fixed his stare on hers. "You want to know why I'm here."

"I did wonder. It seems a long way to come for a chat about human resources." She carried on with her chips.

"What did you expect?"

In her head she said *power games and politics.* Aloud she said, "I expected you to grill me and demand proof I'm not wasting police time."

"Are you wasting police time?"

"No, sir."

"Good. Consider yourself grilled."

He picked up a fat chip, reached over and dipped it in her sauce. He bit it in half, chewed and swallowed. Beatrice began to wonder if he was drunk.

"Not bad, if a little heavy on the cream. Fact is, Stubbs, I'm sorting out my affairs."

Beatrice refused to react. Hamilton always had loved his melodramatic language and half-statements, with the express intention of eliciting a question.

"Really? I found it rather well balanced with the Marsala to add that touch of punch and sweetness."

He topped up her glass, without asking her. "Not to my taste. As I say, I'm ticking boxes and dealing with unfinished business."

She put down her knife and fork and stared him in the eye.

"Sir, if you have something to say, please say it. All this 'sorting out affairs', 'unfinished business' sounds very dramatic."

Hamilton looked directly at her, all geniality gone. "It does rather, doesn't it? Truth of the matter is, I'm dying."

Chapter 20

It was always bittersweet to reach the end. Adrian closed his book and lay back on the sofa to consider the sense of loss. Reading is a strange experience, he thought. You dive into the world of another, adjust to their terms, begin to feel at home and then it's over. You're alone with a bundle of emotions and no means of return. Rather like a failed relationship. Or being kidnapped by aliens.

The fire's earlier blaze had dwindled to a glow, so he got up and checked the weather. Darkness limited his view but it didn't seem to be raining. He seized the moment to go wood-gathering. He borrowed a waxed jacket and an Aussie-style hat then grabbed the hatchet from the tool cupboard. Cold wind hit his face as he opened the back door and he was glad of the porch, keeping the rain off and providing enough illumination for him to work. He loaded the log basket then set about chopping some kindling on a wooden block. The effort warmed him and he found himself relishing the swing of the blade and the split of the wood as he indulged his inner lumberjack. After one last look at the starless sky, he lugged the loaded baskets back inside, locked the door and attached the chain. Mink was sitting in the hall, her tail thumping as she awaited his return.

He looked at the clock. Five past seven. "I've been out for less than fifteen minutes, you soppy creature!"

She ran to him and bunted her head against his legs.

"Yeah, OK, I missed you too. Come on, let's build the fire. Then I need a shower before we think about dinner."

He knelt by the fireplace and built a tepee of kindling around some scrunched-up copies of the *Sylter Rundschau*. While he selected some dry logs, an odd sensation crept up the nape of his neck. He was being watched. He snapped around to the window facing the sea. Nothing but navy darkness. He looked behind him into Mink's blue eyes and caught the smallest movement at the kitchen window. Without switching on the light, he walked silently across the hallway and up to the glass. Balletic grasses swayed in the wind and trees waved their branches as if in some sort of interpretive dance. The floodlights hadn't been activated so it was probably something light blowing past, like a plastic bag.

He returned to his task and finished his preparations. Then he ran up the stairs, peeled off his layers and jumped into the shower. He rejected the creeping fear of a stalker, determined to conquer his own paranoia. Focus was essential. He mentally began preparing two quite different meals for himself and his guest.

Daan worked late to get the job done. It hadn't been a good day. The first attempt at repairing the damaged section of the gunwale had resulted in bloodied knuckles and a good deal of swearing. All because the imbecile had given him the wrong dimensions. He drove to a nearby metalwork shop to get a replacement panel cut to fit, then started again. Finally, he tightened the last of the screws and looked at it from all angles. A professional job. He was hungry as hell and just as soon as he'd done clearing up, he was heading for his favourite restaurant in Rømø. Tonight, he planned to enjoy live music and a large burger. He'd missed the last ferry, so he'd have to sleep in the Jeep and get the first one in the morning. Without Mink, it was going to be a cold night.

He was sweeping up the last pieces of detritus when his mobile rang.

"Daan Knutsen."

"Daan, it's Holger."

"Hey! How are you?"

"Good, thanks. Just calling to ask if you've seen Adrian at all."

"Yeah, we had dinner last night. Nice guy, although for a wine merchant, he can't really hold his liquor."

"How did he seem to you?"

"Nice, like I said. We had a fun evening. I can see why you liked him. If I was gay, he'd be just the sort I'd go for."

Holger paused. "I can't imagine you as gay. No, what I meant was his behaviour. When he was in Hamburg, he seemed a bit para- noid and nervous. He sometimes imagines things. Today he left a message and said something which worried me. I hoped the rest would do him good, but I think he's still having these delusions."

"I didn't notice anything strange, but I've nothing to compare it to. He was good company. I cooked my pork speciality, we got drunk and I stayed over. He was a bit freaked this morning but he wasn't the only one. All the pictures on the mantelpiece had been moved and there was a wooden cross there instead. Weird."

"You saw that?"

"Yeah. He must have done it himself, sleep-walking or some- thing, The brain can do some weird shit."

"Daan, will you keep an eye on him for me? I'm really concerned he's having some sort of breakdown and all this... stuff... is a cry for help."

"Of course. I'm taking him on a tour of the island tomorrow, in fact. And I left Mink with him."

"What do you mean?"

"He's got the dog. She's not a Rottweiler or Doberman, but she'll help him feel more secure tonight."

"Why, where are you?"

"Rømø. Doing a shitty job in some crappy village but at least there's a good restaurant. I wanted to get back this evening, but the last ferry's already gone."

"..."

"Holger? You still there?"

"Yes, just thinking. I called Adrian a few minutes ago, but there's no answer. That's not normal. He's always got his mobile nearby. I'm wondering if I should get up there."

Daan looked at his watch. "I don't think you'd make it. What time is the last train? Anyway, Mink is there to keep him company. If he is ill, being responsible for an animal is a good thing. It switches his focus away from himself."

"Maybe. Listen, I'm going to call him again. If there's still no answer, I'll check the trains and see if there's any way of getting there tonight. I can't help feeling I've made a mistake. I thought calm and isolation would be the best for him. Now I'm not sure he should be alone."

"I'll be there first thing tomorrow, so don't worry too much. Let me know if I can do anything."

"If neither of us can get to Sylt tonight, we'll just have to put our trust in Mink."

Two days' growth had given him more than stubble. Adrian spent ten minutes checking the advance of grey, trimming the edges of his not-quite beard and cleaning his fingernails. In the last two days, his attention to personal grooming had seriously slipped. Fortunately, like a well-kept lawn, the damage was easy to repair. He hummed along to the sound of Lady Gaga coming from the living room as he clipped his toenails. Mink barked. And again.

At first his body tensed before he understood this was a request for attention, not a warning.

"Demanding dog," he muttered. He wrapped a towel around his waist and came out onto the landing. "What?"

There was no reply. He pattered halfway down the stairs to see her sitting at the bottom, her tail wagging.

"Nearly done. Then we'll have dinner."

Toilette complete, he dressed in jeans and a long-sleeved T-shirt, and descended the stairs with enthusiasm. Mink was waiting, tail sweeping the parquet floor like a windscreen wiper.

"I know, I'm hungry too. Where are you going?"

The husky trotted into the living-room and sat in front of the unlit fire, an expectant look on her face.

"Yes, yes, when we've eaten. Come on, it's dinner time!"

She bounded ahead of him into the kitchen, her collar tinkling. He put enough rice on for both of them and prepared a chicken piri-piri à la whatever was in the cupboard for his dinner. She would have chicken scraps and rice with a handful of peas. He was opening a bottle of Chilean Sauvignon Gris when he happened to look into the reflective surface of the oven and saw a white face at the window. He whirled round, pinching his skin in the corkscrew.

The window was completely dark; there was nothing more than raindrops on the other side.

Pain drew his attention. His right index finger was already sprouting a blood blister and he realised he was clutching the bottle so tightly his nails had imprinted livid grooves in his thumb. The house was silent, apart from rice bubbling in the pan.

This had to stop. He turned the gas down and walked all around the house closing the blinds. He lit the fire and switched on some random news channel, just to feel a connection to the rest of the world. Then he unplugged his phone from the charger. The screen blinked on and announced two missed calls from Holger in the last half hour. He hit redial as he went back to the kitchen and ignited the heat under his chicken. The phone rang for a full minute. Holger was not at home.

The DVD selection was surprisingly eclectic. Presumably each family member had contributed some of their favourites. Adrian discarded anything at all scary, opting for the familiar and well loved. He was debating over *The Grand Budapest Hotel* versus *Brokeback Mountain* when Mink started growling. Her hackles stood up in a ridge along her back and her attention was fixed on the front door. Adrian's hairs rose too.

"What is it, girl? Did you hear something? The wind, I expect. It's still pretty lively out there. Nothing to worry about." He was reassuring himself, he knew, but the dog's ears twitched towards him and she laid her muzzle back on her front paws, still watching the door. He set up the film and picked up another log to throw on the fire. That was when the doorbell rang. Mink burst into an alarming volley of barks and Adrian dropped the log on his foot.

"Ow! Shit! Mink, shush now. MINK! It's probably Daan. Sssh. Come here."

He caught hold of her collar with one hand and opened the door, chain on, with the other. The porch light was still on from his wood collecting foray but there was no one at the door. He craned his head to see alongside the house, but all was in darkness. Mink thrust her nose through the gap and sniffed.

"Hello? Hello?" he called, his voice sounding feeble against the wind.

He pulled the dog back, closed the door and switched off the porch light. She was still growling. He checked the back door. Locked, with his key inside. He tried Holger again. No reply. He went into the unlit kitchen and looked out at the blackness. It was a long way to come to play knock-down ginger.

The blackness. If someone had rung the doorbell, why hadn't the floodlights come on? Thinking about it, he realised they hadn't come on while he was chopping wood, either. At the time, he'd been absorbed in his task with the porch spilling enough light on the log pile. He had no idea where the electrics were or how to operate them. He picked up the phone to dial Beatrice and dropped it in fright when a hammering came at the side window. Mink went berserk, barking and scratching and digging at the front doormat.

Adrian chickened out of approaching the window. If someone was there, a face at the glass, his heart would probably give out. Instead he crept into the kitchen and looked out. Light from the living-room lamps glowed through the windows onto the wooden walkway. No one in either direction, as far as he could see. Mink's barks grew angrier. He snatched the hatchet from the tool cupboard once more.

"No, I'm not opening it. No. You can't go out there. Somebody is playing silly buggers and trying to scare us. No, no, come and sit down now. I need to find a number for Daan."

He sat on the sofa and tried to think above the thumps of his heartbeat and Mink's incessant growling. There must be a phone book. He dug through the magazine rack with shaking hands and found a local directory. But Daan the Dane was unlikely to be listed. Had he ever heard Daan's surname? He must have, when Holger introduced them. What the hell was it? Mink padded out into the hallway and gave the front door a thorough sniffing, then commenced another marathon growlfest.

Perhaps under boat repairs? What was the German for boat? Or repairs? The only person he knew on the island who had even entrusted him with his dog and he didn't even know the man's name or number.

But the dog did.

"Mink, come here. Come, there's a good girl. Now sit." He reached around her neck, trying not to tremble, feeling for the small silver disc he had seen on her collar. He found it and tilted her to the firelight to read. One side was engraved with a single word: MINK. On the other, another word and some digits. He couldn't read at this distance and Mink had begun to growl once again. He knew it was directed at the disturber of their peace but wasn't comfortable with his face so close to hers.

"Can I take this off? Good girl. I only want it for a minute. There's a good dog."

He unbuckled the leather and drew it slowly through her fur. She seemed unconcerned and returned to her lookout post while he read the disc. Knutsen! That was it. Adrian reached for his phone when Mink released a volley of enraged barks. A jolt of fear rushed through him as he heard the unmistakeable sound of running footsteps on the wooden porch, which sent Mink into a frenzy.

He pocketed his phone and stood behind the door, trying to listen over his ragged breathing and Mink's noisy outrage. With a double check the chain was still on, he opened the door and something thudded at his feet. The crucifix was back. It must have been propped against the door and now it slid sideways into the gap, preventing him from closing the door. He tried shoving it away with his foot, impeded by Mink shoulder-charging him out of the way.

He reached for her collar to hold her back, rolling his eyes at himself when he realised it wasn't there. Instead he pushed her backwards and told her to sit. He squeezed the door as near to closed as it would go and released the chain. Then he opened it enough for him to crouch down, pick up the crucifix and fling it off the porch. The next second a massive blow to the back of his knees shoved him onto all fours. Twenty-two kilos of furious Siberian Husky shot past him and away round the back of the house.

"Mink! MINK! MINK!!!"

He went back inside, pulled on his boots and a coat, checked the back door was locked, then picked up a torch and went out through the front in search of the dog.

He could hear no barking and she was nowhere near the house. He did three circuits, cupping his hands round his mouth to call her name. He struck out towards the beach, his increasingly desperate calls snatched away by the wind.

Chapter 21

Beatrice set down her knife and fork, searching for the right words.

"Sir, I'm so sorry. I don't know..."

"... what to say? Not many do. Generally speaking, 'That's a shame' is preferable to 'Thank God for that'. More wine?"

"I had no idea things were so serious. I mean, I know you've been ill, but none of us was sure what the problem was."

"Not really a topic for the water-cooler. Cancer of the prostate. Unpleasant but rarely a killer when diagnosed in the early stages. When it isn't, one is subject to many more complications, especially when it spreads. I'm part of the latter unhappy band of souls."

Beatrice took a sip from her freshened glass. She tasted nothing. Hamilton's restless eyes moved from her plate to the window, to his plate, to the bar but rarely made it to her face.

"Eat up, Stubbs. Just because I've put a dampener on the evening, no need to let good food go to waste. In fact, I'll give that sauce another go. May I?"

She nodded and instead of using one of his own untouched pile, he purloined one of her chips with an uncharacteristic smile.

"You could hardly say no. Denying a condemned man his last wish."

Beatrice faked a laugh. But the shock of Hamilton's news had not sufficiently sunk in for her to appreciate his gallows humour.

"What about treatment, sir? I understand the complications, but surely there are things they can do?"

"Hmm. Still say that's overly rich for such a beautiful piece of meat. Less is more, Stubbs. Unless it comes to the wine." He studied the label and emptied the bottle into their glasses. "Yes, there are things 'they' can do. Alleviate my symptoms, prolong my time, ease the pain, providing I'm happy to spend my remaining days in an oncology unit."

"You said 'remaining time', sir. Would it be incredibly crass of me to enquire as to what that means?"

Hamilton smiled for the second time in two minutes, a warmth suffusing his face as he looked at her, his eyes softened by the candlelight glinting off his red wine.

"Crass, no. Blunt, impetuous, direct and classically Stubbs, but not crass. That, never. As for how long this thing will take to kill me? The consultant says I should celebrate this Christmas to the hilt. That, combined with words such as 'palliative care', 'will and testament', and 'keep me comfortable', indicate this is likely to be a matter of months. Like that Pratchett fellow said about his own illness, it's an embuggerance."

Tears flooded Beatrice's eyes and she reached into her bag for a tissue. Her phone screen indicated a missed call but now was not the time to check. She dabbed her eyes as discreetly as she could while the waiter cleared their plates.

"Sir, I can't tell you how sorry I am. I just want you to know that if there's anything I can do to help, although I have no idea what that might be, I would be honoured to do so. You only have to ask. I'm sure the rest of your team would say the same."

Hamilton stared into his glass. "I should like a coffee and a dessert. But first I must find the bathroom. Order whatever you want and something with chocolate and cream for me. Obviously accompanied by an espresso and a quality port wine. Then we do have something to discuss."

He levered himself to his feet with an almost imperceptible wince and gave her a polite nod. Beatrice sat back, staring at the ceiling, her thoughts and emotions a mess. Twenty minutes ago, she'd have cheerfully killed him with her bare hands. Now his vulnerability and attempts to promote her after he'd gone brought a painful lump to her throat and she scrabbled for another tissue. The vibration and glow of her phone caught her attention. Adrian. She picked up the dessert menu and her handset at the same time.

"Adrian? Are you all right?"

For several seconds she could hear nothing but breathless sobs and incoherent babbling, occasionally punctuated by recognisable words.

She sat bolt upright. "Adrian! I can't understand what you're saying! Are you all right? Has something happened?"

He was silent for a second and Beatrice thought she'd lost him. Then he repeated his story, still panicky and breathless, but with more attempt at being understood.

"Slow down, I can only catch about half of this. What dog? When? Where are you now?"

The waiter approached the table and Beatrice held up a hand to indicate she needed more time.

"Adrian, listen. "Go back indoors immediately. I'll call Holger and I'll call the local police. Get in and stay there. Don't move till I call you. Adrian… Adrian!" but the line had gone dead.

Beatrice was still shouting into the phone when Hamilton came back. Other diners' heads began turning towards their table. She looked up at Hamilton, saw his eyebrows arch in an unspoken question as he registered the concern on her face. She slammed her mobile down onto the table with too much force, then picked it up again and called Holger's home number.

"Something the matter, Stubbs?" Hamilton asked.

"A friend's having a crisis. He came with me to Germany… oh, shit!" she said as Holger's answering machine cut in. "Sorry, sir. I was trying to get help from a mutual acquaintance but he's not home."

"By friend, you mean your partner, I assume?"

"What? No, not Matthew. This is my neighbour. I think he's having some kind of breakdown. He's on his own and he needs my help."

"Then you must go to him, DI Stubbs."

"But sir, your news…" Beatrice was torn, uncertain of how to react to such an unprecedented situation.

"Go," Hamilton ordered. "There's nothing I have to say that won't wait. Might just pop some thoughts on paper, in fact. Probably best, can't stand a fuss. Go to your friend, Stubbs, that's an order."

Beatrice made up her mind. She shouldered her handbag and picked up her phone. "I am so sorry."

She looked up at her boss and saw his face had lost all the warmth of earlier. She wondered if she'd imagined the light in his eyes.

"Sir, this is terrible timing and I wouldn't dash off if it weren't an emergency. I really am sorry. Thank you for such a lovely meal. I just want to say again I'm shocked and saddened by your news but you can count on my full support. Have a lovely break and I look forward to seeing you on Monday." She held out her hand.

Hamilton shook it and held on for a moment. "My flight leaves at lunchtime. Perhaps we might have breakfast, presuming all is well with your friend?"

"I don't think I'll make that, sir. I need to travel north tonight, towards the Danish border. See you bright and early Monday morning."

A waitress arrived with a large chocolate cake. Beatrice gave it a lustful once-over then allowed the waiter to help her into her coat.

"Thanks again for dinner. Your pudding looks delicious."

"Thank you for being with me. Goodbye, Stubbs."

"Goodbye, sir." She hurried to the door, pressing the waiter for advice on the nearest taxi rank while tapping her phone for directions as to the best way to get to the island of Sylt.

Stein entered the station bar, peeled off his thick navy coat, hat and gloves and strode towards Beatrice. She put down her phone and pulled out her earpiece, so relieved she could have hugged him.

"Thank you so much for coming! I'm sorry to disturb you so late, but this is uncharted territory for me."

"Any news since we spoke?" he asked.

"Yes, I managed to get hold of Adrian a few minutes ago. He's in a terrible state. He thinks someone got into the house while he was looking for the dog. I told him to get a taxi into the town but he won't leave while the dog is missing. And I can't see a way of getting there tonight. Is it possible the island is actually cut off overnight?"

"Train and ferry access stops overnight. But it's not exactly cut off."

"But if the causeway is railway only, it's not possible to drive onto the island. So I have no chance of getting there before morning? What about a helicopter?"

"DI Stubbs, would you authorise use of a Metropolitan Police helicopter for a nervous man and a runaway dog? Out of the question. We cannot get to List tonight. But he is not cut off. I called the Sylt police force and asked officers from Westerland to attend the scene. They will ensure he is safe and assist in looking for his dog. I suggest we have a coffee and wait for their report."

"How close can I get? To List, I mean. If I can get nearly there, I could get the first train in the morning. Herr Stein, this is important to me. I need to get moving. Is there a train that will take me most of the way?"

Stein rubbed his eyes. "I'll drive you. Come on, let's get a coffee to go."

"Are you sure? That's so kind of you. I'd feel much better with you beside me. Right, you order the coffees but I insist on paying. A small sort of thank you."

She picked up her phone to tell Adrian the good news.

Chapter 22

Daan wasn't answering. Twice his calls went to voicemail, but Adrian couldn't find the right words to leave a message. He paced from front door to back once again, peering into the darkness, willing a lupine shape to appear.

Since Mink had disappeared, the disturbances had stopped completely. He'd wandered up and down the beach, combed the length of the lane and called the dog non-stop. Without gloves, his hand soon became too cold to hold the torch, so he alternated. One in his pocket, one shining a light across the darkened dunes. He returned to the house every ten minutes to check if she was there, afraid she would miss him and run off again. The fourth time he came back, he saw a rectangle of light spilling over the wooden steps leading to the kitchen. The front door was wide open. As he approached, the floodlights came on. That was when he called Beatrice.

The relief of hearing her voice burst his bubble and his voice cracked as he tried to explain. Practical as ever, she told him to go indoors and call Holger. He did as he was told, reluctant to disconnect and lose the human connection, especially as he dreaded what might be inside. He locked the back door, went straight into the kitchen and grabbed a jointing knife, feeling foolish and prepared in equal measure. Apart from the open door, nothing seemed altered. No crucifixes, front door locked and embers glowing in the hearth. No Mink.

He phoned Holger, expecting the answer machine, which was exactly what he got. Then he searched the house, knife in hand, working himself into a state of terror every time he opened a wardrobe door. The house was empty. No one, nothing under the beds, behind the shower curtain, in the utility room or standing between the rack of winter coats. He steeled himself to open the back and front doors and found no huskies, religious icons or murderous psychopaths lying in wait. He stood on the front porch and stared out into the night.

Icy crystals hit his face as he watched snowflakes swirl in changing patterns at the whim of the wind. Where the hell was Mink? She'd freeze to death out there. Siberian Husky she may be, but this was a domesticated dog who loved the fireside. A bitter blast of Nordic wind made him recoil and he retreated inside. No Daan, no Holger, Beatrice hours away and that beautiful dog out there in the dark and cold at the mercy of whatever kind of freak was tormenting him. A bone-chilling shiver ran through his whole body and he wondered if he'd ever feel warm again. If he could transport himself to a Moroccan hammam... He stiffened as he recalled a snatch of conversation.

"You're going to love the sauna."

Adrian stopped his pacing between the two doors to the house. What sauna? By the time Holger had shown him the heating system, the bathrooms, the spare blankets, the oven and how to use the entertainment console, it had been time to catch the bus. He'd never seen a sauna in the house and had no idea where it was.

He took one more look outside and walked back along the hallway. There was no room unaccounted for, so unless the sauna was in some kind of outbuilding he'd yet to see, there was only one place it could be. Underground. He'd seen no unusual doors, no indication of a cellar or access to a basement. He stopped to think. If you have a sauna, you will get hot and sweaty and need a shower. He made for the downstairs bathroom.

Whiteness, pine furniture, stone tiles, a toilet, bidet, dual sinks and a shower big enough for two. It was large, as bathrooms go. But no evidence of another door. He ran his hands along the walls, a cursory examination, his ears attentive to any sounds anywhere in or outside the house. Two wall panels had a circular disk at handle height. Adrian bent to study them more closely. Silver recesses with a semi-circular pendant. He hooked his finger into the loop, pulled it out and twisted it. The door opened smoothly, revealing shelves of towels, toilet paper and disposable guest slippers. There was also a pine bucket with a wooden ladle. Exactly the sort you'd use to pour water on the coals of a sauna.

He tried the second door. A silent black space which made him clutch his knife tighter until he saw the rattan flooring and a dangling pull switch to his right. He pulled and saw a spiral staircase leading down to a bright, whitewashed room, two pine recliners and several artificial plants. The atmosphere was so wholesome and enticing he'd got halfway down before he realised he was enacting exactly the kind of horror movie cliché he despised. He scuttled back up the stairs, switched off the light and jumped as his phone rang. He closed the door and answered the call.

"Beatrice?"

"Yes. Just to let you know we're on our way. The local police should be paying you a visit shortly to check out the premises and help you find the dog. Are you all right?"

"Umm. Yes and no. I just discovered a sauna in the basement. A whole room I didn't know existed."

"Is there anything down there?"

"Not sure. I was just checking it out when you called."

"Don't! Can you secure the door or block it in some way till the police arrive? And did you get hold of Holger or the owner of that dog?"

"Holger and Daan aren't answering. The sauna room is inside a bathroom so I'll lock the door from the outside. How long will it take you to get here?"

There was no answer.

"Beatrice?"

"We're not going to get there till early tomorrow morning. I'm estimating six o'clock. But local police will be with you as soon as they can. Adrian, listen to me. Stay safe. Don't open the doors to anyone unless you see police ID. Not even the dog. It could be a trap. The dog will find a place to shelter and we'll find it tomorrow. Do not open the door unless it is to a police officer. Is that clear? Secure that basement now and I'm going to call you every half an hour to make sure you're fine. I'll be there in the morning, I promise."

Adrian looked at his watch. Eleven pm. Seven hours to go. He locked the bathroom door and went back to his vigil, peering out of the kitchen window, back to the living-room, checking his phone, waiting for something to happen. Every gust of wind rattling the door, each creak of the roof or pockets of wet wood popping in the fireplace set his nerves jangling. Pacing between one side of the house and the other, he had to pass the locked bathroom door, which wound him up to snapping point. He wanted to listen to music, drown out the silence and distract himself, but needed to be alert. He had to be ready. His promise to Beatrice was hollow. If Mink returned, he would let her in and deal with the consequences.

Twenty minutes later, he was straining to see out of the front window when a flash of headlights lit the dunes. A car bumped down the track, frequent red glows from the brake lights indicating the driver's caution. Adrian's tension became a trembling anticipation of relief. The police patrol car pulled up and two officers got out. The driver stayed in the car. Adrian watched from the window as they approached the house and he rushed to open the door, forgetting everything Beatrice had said.

Both officers were tall but there was no mistaking who was in charge.

"Mr Harvey? My name is Herr Rieder and this is my colleague, Frau Jenssen. We understand you had some problems this evening. Can we come in?"

Adrian opened the door wide, relief at human contact and the presence of authority rendering him unable to speak.

It took over an hour to give a full statement of recent events, during which time he and Herr Rieder drank two pots of mint tea and Beatrice called twice. The policewoman and driver went out looking for Mink while Adrian sat on the sofa and tried to be as chronologically clear as he could. That meant he'd already been talking for fifty minutes before mentioning the locked bathroom and sauna.

Herr Rieder's disbelief was evident. "If I understand you correctly, there is a locked room in this house which may contain the dog?"

"No, I told you. Mink went outside. She couldn't possibly have got back in the house on her own, let alone open the sauna door. I doubt there's anything at all down there now, but it is somewhere a person could have hidden. I didn't dare open it alone, I just locked it and waited for the professionals."

"Show me, please."

Adrian led the way to the bathroom, wishing he had some kind of excuse not to accompany the man. He unlocked the door and jolted as he saw Herr Rieder remove a gun from his holster. His nerves approached hysteria and he began to sweat. Rieder motioned him away, shoved open the door and switched on the light. The bathroom and its mirror reflected innocence and emptiness. The reflection of his washed-out self and an armed cop seemed ridiculous in the spa-like sanctity of the space.

Rieder found the door to the sauna without instruction. Perhaps most houses had a similar arrangement, Adrian thought. He watched the officer open the door, call an order in German and wait. No response from the darkness.

Rieder entered and switched on the light. The wooden staircase creaked with each step as he descended into bright cleanliness. Adrian followed on tiptoe. The room was empty, peaceful even, with the one area of uncertainty. The sauna itself. The small wooden block, like a sinister Wendy House, sat in the corner with its one window in darkness. Adrian's hair stood on end and every sense screamed at him to retreat. Rieder did a 360° check and moved towards the sauna. Adrian held his breath. The officer threw back the door with his left hand, keeping his gun cocked in his right.

Silence. The door swung back and forth from the momentum but afforded enough visibility to see the space was empty. The only thing apart from pine slats, a heating unit with artificial coals and a laminated instruction sheet was a pile of picture frames. Rieder took out gloves to examine them and the photographs they contained. He showed them to Adrian.

"Those were the ones on the mantelpiece. My guest will tell you. We stood there and talked about them."

"The guest who stayed the night?"

"Yes, I told you, the owner of the dog. Daan Knutsen."

"Who gave you so much strong alcohol you had to go to bed, leaving him downstairs. A man very familiar with this house, who would know about the sauna."

"Daan didn't do this. He was as freaked as I was. And he left me his dog!" Desperation roughened his voice and he bit his lip, determined not to cry.

A loud knock sounded from upstairs, making them both start. Rieder indicated Adrian should take second place as he climbed up the staircase.

"My colleagues. I hope they have your dog."

The door opened to three people. Two cold, tired, snow-dusted police officers and in the middle, Holger. An optimistic shot of adrenalin pumped though him at the sight of his friend but he could not help but scan the background for Mink.

Frau Jenssen shook her head to dash any hopes. "We looked everywhere, including the owner's house in case he made his way home, and sent out an appeal to officers nearby. Don't worry, he'll be fine. In this weather, he will find somewhere to hide."

"It's a *she*," said Adrian and fell into Holger's arms.

The officers sat by the fire and took a statement from Holger while Adrian made more tea. Beatrice called again to announce her arrival in Knee-Boo or something, which was where the car shuttle would begin at five am. She and her colleague had checked into a motel to catch a few hours' sleep. The news of Holger's arrival seemed to ease her mind and she advised him to get some rest.

When he got back to the living room, the police had gone and Holger was poking at the embers in the grate.

Holger looked up, his face full of concern. "Are you OK?"

"I feel a whole lot better since you arrived. Where'd the police go?"

"They answered another call. We can go into the station tomorrow to add to our statements. Anytime, doesn't have to be early."

"I have to be up before first light. Beatrice will be here at six." Adrian placed the tray on the table and sagged onto the sofa.

"Beatrice? I didn't know she was coming to Sylt."

"I called her when I couldn't get hold of you." Adrian had barely enough energy to lift the teapot.

"I couldn't get hold of *you*! After I got your message, I phoned you twice. When I got no answer, I decided to come here. You always answer your phone. When you didn't, I assumed there was a problem. Then I phoned Daan but he's on a job in Denmark. So I ran for the train. And if you use this as another opportunity to persuade me to get a mobile..."

"You spoke to Daan?" Adrian rubbed his itchy eyes. "Did he tell you about the crucifix?"

"Yes, he mentioned it."

"See, it's not just me! Daan saw it this morning and didn't understand it either. He thought it was creepy. That's why he put on the CCTV cameras and left me Mink. And what did I do? I went and lost her."

Holger stared at him. "Daan activated the cameras? And you didn't tell the police?"

A huge sense of embarrassment followed by relief washed over Adrian. How could he have forgotten the CCTV? Finally proof that he was not imagining things.

"I forgot. I was worried about Mink."

"Stay here and listen for the dog. I'll check last night's recording and find out what the hell is going on." Holger stomped up the stairs.

Adrian poured more tea but didn't drink it. Instead, he checked the thermometer on the kitchen window. Minus 7°. He paced round all the windows, imagining Mink outside, shivering in the snow and freezing rain, the light in her blue eyes growing duller.

A warm hand on his shoulder woke him.

"Adrian?" Holger crouched by the sofa. "Do you want to get ready for Beatrice? It's nearly seven in the morning."

He blinked several times and took in his surroundings. He was lying on the sofa, covered by a fleecy throw. The fire had gone out. His brain circuits crackled into life. "Mink?"

Holger stood up and shook his head. "She's still not back. No point in going out yet, it's still as dark as the inside of a cow's arse."

"What did you see from the cameras?"

Holger shrugged and looked away.

Adrian sat up. "What? What is it?"

"The camera footage shows nothing. No one going in or out of the house. No one outside the building. No dog. Nothing registered between 18.00 and 21.00. The first images show up at 21.39 when you arrive at the kitchen door."

Adrian rubbed his eyes with his palms. "Wait, what? No footage at all? None of me collecting and chopping the logs? None of the crucifix? You're not telling me it didn't pick up Mink knocking me flat. I ran round the house three times, it can't have missed that!"

Holger knelt beside him. "We'll work this out later. I'm as confused as you are. Something's wrong, I just don't know what."

A light flashed outside the window and by the time Adrian had risen to his feet, he could hear the sound of an approaching engine.

"That must be Beatrice. Listen, Holger. I agree that something's wrong. But it isn't me. This is not my imagination."

Chapter 23

On the journey across the sea and up the island, Beatrice bounced between various emotions. Concern for Adrian, for his well-being and mental health. Residual guilt at abandoning Hamilton after he'd taken the time to deliver his news in person. Professional embarrassment at dashing off across the country with a senior detective just as her case was coming to a head. Irritation at how Stein appeared lean, rested and fresh while she had all the appearance of an uncooked doughball. And an undertow of worry about her medication, left behind in her Hamburg hotel bathroom. A day or two will make no difference, she told herself, trying to block out an image of James shaking his head.

Stein spoke little, which suited her. For all she could see in the inky pre-dawn, Germany's picturesque playground for the rich and famous could have been a back road in Norfolk. Blackness, a bit of sea, a glimpse of village and more blackness. A flash of irrational anger blazed at Holger for suggesting somewhere so remote and impractical for Adrian's rest cure. Occasional sleet showers spattered the windscreen as she checked her phone again. Nothing new from Adrian. She gnawed at her thumbnail and leant over to see the SatNav.

Stein spoke. "Three kilometres, DI Stubbs. We're there, almost. Are you OK?"

"Yes, thank you… No, not really. Four hours sleep and no idea of what's really going on is making me extremely nervous. You shouldn't be here, for a start. I've already broken an entire file of protocols by asking my colleague to drive through the night to help a possibly delusional friend of mine. In the cold light of, well, not-yet-day, I think my judgement was off. I should not have…"

"You asked me for advice and I gave it, as your colleague. I offered to drive you here as your friend. I'm very happy you accepted. Attention! Here's the turning. Look out for the dog."

The car bumped down the track to the isolated house at the end. Silver streaks of dawn were just beginning to pierce the night sky as they parked. The door burst open and Adrian rushed out to meet them. He hugged Beatrice.

"I am so glad you're here."

"Are you all right?" she asked.

"Yes, since Holger turned up I feel much safer. Still no sign of Mink though. The police searched but found no trace of her."

"We'll look again when it's light. This is Herr Stein of the Hamburg police. He very kindly drove me all the way here. Herr Stein, Adrian Harvey."

The two men shook hands. "Pleased to meet you, Mr Harvey. Let's go inside, you must be cold."

Holger, standing in the doorway, raised a hand in greeting. Beatrice made the introductions and Holger closed the door, shutting out the wind.

Stein glanced around the interior and said something in German. Beatrice couldn't pick up any of the words but recognised the appreciative tone. Holger nodded and replied, then said a word Beatrice certainly did know.

"*Kaffee?*"

"Ooh yes please," she said.

"I'll make coffee for us all and let Adrian tell you... his story."

Adrian shot him a look Beatrice couldn't read.

Ever the professional, Stein took notes while Beatrice pressed Adrian for precision. "How long did it take you to get dressed to go after the dog?"

"Only a couple of minutes. I put on my boots, grabbed a coat and found a torch, locked the door and left."

"Was the crucifix still there?"

"I don't know. I didn't see it, but it must have been. I only just chucked it off the porch. But it was dark and..."

"No outside lights?" asked Stein.

"They weren't working. The first time they came on was when I got back and I found the kitchen door open."

Stein made a note. "And that was at what time?"

"I can check," said Beatrice, scrolling through her phone. "Here it is. 21.41."

Holger entered with a tray. "Yes, that matches what's on the CCTV footage. I can clearly see him pacing and talking on his phone at that time."

Stein looked up. "There's CCTV?"

"Yes. But the problem is that it shows nothing. I checked everything it recorded from six o'clock last night. The first activity it picked up was Adrian leaving by the back door." He looked at Adrian. "I'm sorry."

Beatrice frowned. "How is that possible? Are some of the cameras faulty?"

Holger shrugged and shook his head. "They recorded the police arriving, me turning up and everything. Just no dog, no activity outside apart from Adrian."

The room fell silent and Beatrice sensed Stein's surreptitious assessment of Adrian. She tried not to do the same, despite her urge to study his face and gestures for clues. To give herself time to think, she poured coffee for everyone. Sunlight crept across the room and the only sounds were the stirring of spoons and ticking of the clock for several minutes. Then a creaking, bouncing and honking of a horn announced the arrival of a vehicle.

"It's Daan," said Holger. He stood up. "I'll go and tell him what's happened."

"No. I'll do it. I lost his dog, so I should be the one to tell him." Adrian pushed himself to his feet and went to open the door. He looked utterly wretched.

The big Dane took the news in his stride. He greeted everyone with a general wave and listened to Adrian's explanation with every appearance of calm.

"Probably chased off after something and got lost. Maybe she tried to make her way to my place. I'll go home and check. It's a shame she's not wearing her collar, but many people would recognise her anyway. You go out, look around and call me if you find her. If she's not at home, I'll be back to help in around forty minutes."

He jumped straight back into his Jeep and rattled off up the lane. Then his brake lights came on and he began reversing. He rolled down the window.

"Take her collar with you!" he bellowed.

Holger gave him the thumbs up and he rumbled away.

Adrian, Holger and Beatrice prepared to search, while Stein left to talk to the local police. Since the sun had come up, Beatrice could appreciate the beauty of the place. Last night, it had seemed bleak, miserable and almost deliberately inaccessible. This morning, the expanse of golden pink sunrise reflected on a snowy beach would have taken her breath away if the cold hadn't got there first.

She took the stretch of beach to the left, reaching towards the headland, leaving Adrian to cover the middle and Holger to take the right. As she crested the dunes, she could see the rough outline of a coast in the distance and she wondered whether it was still part of Germany or if she was actually looking at Scandinavia. Birds screeched and swirled, and the early sun highlighted the drifts of snow on the leeward side of the dunes. The wind whipped her hair across her face, but her eyes scanned the landscape and she let out her infamous whistle. Two fingers in her mouth, a lungful of air and she could make an impressive noise.

But no dog or anything else came running. She'd covered the headland and was making her way back towards the house when she saw the Danish man's Jeep pull up outside. She squinted and watched him jump from the cab with some kind of box in his hand. He strode off down the beach. So the dog hadn't made it home yet. Chilled by the wind and pained by her impractical footwear for beachcombing, Beatrice decided to explore further inland. She kept up her whistling while turning over the nagging worry that Adrian's story was only partially true. There had been a dog; the collar was evidence. But if it hadn't gone missing when he said it had, what had really happened? Why would he go to such lengths as to bring Holger all the way here from Hamburg, to worry Beatrice herself enough so that she would travel half the night?

Half an hour later, her eyebrows frosted and thighs like slabs of ice, she returned to the house. As she opened the front door, she heard Holger's voice, speaking German. His head whipped round when he heard Beatrice come in, so she shook her head regretfully, so as not to raise his hopes. She removed her outerwear while he finished the call. He lifted the coffee pot in enquiry.

Beatrice was just about to answer with enthusiasm and politely suggest some toast when her phone rang.

"Adrian?"

"We found her! She was shut in a shed. She's OK but she seems a bit woozy. Daan's carrying her back. Where are you?"

"Oh that's wonderful news!" She took the handset from her mouth. "They've got the dog!" Holger closed his eyes and sagged with relief.

"I just got back to the house. Holger's here too."

"Good. Can you find some blankets and stuff so we can keep her warm? What? Oh, Daan says to heat some milk too. We're about ten minutes away."

"I'll do it now. See you in a bit."

By the time the odd procession reached the porch, Beatrice had assembled a bundle of blankets, put some milk in a pan over a low flame, instructed Holger to light a fire and was waiting at the door to welcome them.

The dog, a great furry thing like the ones that pull sleds, bobbed along in its owner's arms, wrapped in his puffa jacket. Adrian's lips were blue with cold, but his recent worried frown was only a trace of itself and in his hand was a box of dog biscuits.

Daan laid the dog on the blankets and removed the coat. Beatrice fetched the milk and gave it to Adrian, who crouched beside the two big hairy heads.

"Mink? Here you go, girl. I expect you're thirsty. Nice warm milk for you."

The dog's sleepy blue eyes watched him set the bowl down and she got unsteadily to her feet. Her back legs remained in a crouch but she sniffed the milk and began lapping. Four humans watched, each wearing an indulgent smile.

Holger spoke first. "Where did you find her?"

Adrian looked up from his kneeling position. "In one of the out-buildings on the next farm. Daan was calling and whistling and we heard her bark. Just once. So we searched all the barns and found her in what looked like an old chicken coop."

Daan nodded. "You know it, Holger. That shed on the Lemper farm. We all used to play in there as kids. Though I can't remember the Lempers ever having chickens."

"How did she get in there?" asked Beatrice.

Daan's voice deepened, although his focus remained on the dog. "She didn't. The door was bolted from the outside. Someone shut Mink in there deliberately. My guess is she went after some meat. She'll do anything for food."

Beatrice was beginning to feel the same way.

"It looks like she was drugged or sedated somehow," added Adrian. "See, it's just like she's come round after an anaesthetic."

The dog had finished her milk and seemed to have dozed off, still standing up.

"Perhaps she should have a check-up," said Beatrice, partly out of concern and also to disguise her rumbling stomach.

Daan guided the dog back down onto the blankets, mumbling gentle words in a foreign language. Then he got to his feet and smiled.

"Let's see if food, time and a warm fire make her feel better. If there's no change in two hours, I'll take her to the vet. First, I need coffee and breakfast. Dog-carrying on an empty stomach is never a good idea. I'm hungry and I don't think I'm the only one." He grinned at Beatrice. "Adrian, will you stay with Mink? Beatrice and I have work to do in the kitchen."

He rubbed his hands and led the way. Beatrice followed without hesitation. She had already decided she was going to like Daan.

After a substantial plate of smoked salmon and scrambled eggs with toast and a large milky coffee, Beatrice felt fully restored. So, apparently, did Mink. She appeared in the kitchen doorway, nose twitching, followed by Adrian with an empty plate.

"She's already had half of mine but I think she fancies seconds."

Daan studied the dog with a smile. He opened the fridge and tore off a few strips of chicken, under a pair of blue watchful eyes. Her tail wagged and she sat obediently as he fed her one slice after another.

"Let's see if she keeps that down. I have a feeling she will be fine." He looked at Adrian. "Can we postpone our island tour till tomorrow? I should stay home and watch her for the next twelve hours or so."

"Of course. She needs to be supervised after such a horrible night. I'm happy to wait till tomorrow."

Beatrice stared at him. "Adrian, you can't possibly be thinking of staying."

"Why not? If you and Holger are here..."

Holger shook his head. "I have to get back to Hamburg today. I have a meeting this afternoon and a lot of work to catch up with. You should come back with me. You can always visit Sylt again in the summer."

"He's right," Beatrice agreed. "I can't stay either, because I'm in the middle of a major investigation. I could get myself and Herr Stein in trouble for being here now. Why don't we all go back to Hamburg together?"

Adrian's face fell and Holger reached over the table to put a hand on his arm and give it a squeeze. "It wasn't my best idea, leaving you up here alone. Especially when you're unsettled. Better to come back to the city."

"What do you mean by 'unsettled'? There's nothing wrong with me."

Beatrice could sense trouble brewing. "Adrian...". Her appeal to common sense was curtailed before it could begin, interrupted by the ring of her mobile. "It's Herr Stein. Excuse me."

She stepped over the supine dog and went into the living-room to take the call. "Hello, Herr Stein?"

"DI Stubbs, we need to get back to Hamburg. Our sources indicate that this evening will be of vital importance. I'm coming to pick you up now. Can you be ready?"

From the kitchen she heard voices rising and tried to eavesdrop and converse with her colleague simultaneously.

"Yes, of course. How long have I got?"

"Thirty minutes. Maybe a little more, I need to stop for fuel. Is your friend fine? Did he find his dog?"

She dropped her voice. "The dog's here, but I'm not sure whether he's fine or not. If I can persuade him to come, do you think we can take him and Holger back to Hamburg with us?"

"That's probably the best thing for him. Sylt is not an easy place in the winter. See you in half an hour."

"See you then."

She rang off just in time to hear the words 'pig-headed and stupid!' and the front door slammed. As she hurried to the kitchen, Adrian stormed past her and took the pine stairs two at a time.

In the kitchen, only one man and his dog remained. Beatrice boggled her eyes at Daan. He rolled his head in a loose, evasive gesture.

"They had an argument. Adrian wants to stay, Holger wants him to go. Adrian asked if he was throwing him out and then I messed up."

"What did you do?"

"I said he could stay at my place."

"But Holger wants Adrian to go for his own good."

Daan slumped against the sink. "I'm better with dogs than people." He looked down at Mink, who thumped her tail once. "Shitty shit, this is the Friday from hell. I'll find Holger, you talk to Adrian. If you think it's best for him to go, I will support you. I trust what you decide. You remind me of my mother."

With that non-sequitur, he went into the hall to don his outdoor things.

"Mink! *Fuss!*" he commanded. The dog padded to his side.

Beatrice checked her watch and trudged up the stairs. She stood in the doorway of a bedroom, watching Adrian pack in an obvious rage. He must have been furious or he'd never have treated cashmere that roughly. She waited a few seconds to allow him to ignore her or shout, but he whirled around and glared.

"You've come to tell me I'm not right in the head as well?"

"You think I'd ever say something like that? To anyone?"

He faltered for a second. "I had a row with Holger. He's playing the 'I know best' role, which I hate."

"Yes, well, that's between the two of you. On a practical note, there's space in the car if you want to join us on the journey back to Hamburg. I won't push you, but I will say this. I'm short-tempered and fractious because I had very little sleep last night. Didn't we all, you might say. Yes, but I left my boss in the middle of dinner, possibly exposed a colleague to criticism, drove through the night and spent several freezing hours wandering a North Sea island looking for a dog. Why? Because I was worried about you. Tonight, I may well be involved in a complex operation which I will be unable to leave at the drop of a cat. So I'd feel vastly more relaxed if I knew you were safely across the city in a cosy hotel room, rather than on an inaccessible island five hours away, in an empty house which scared you half to death last night."

Adrian had the good grace to look ashamed. He continued packing and spoke through a clenched jaw. "You're right. I am scared of being alone. But I won't be chased away."

"Well, what are you going to do?" she asked.

"Daan says I can stay with him."

"Why is it so important to..."

"Because I will not be fucking bullied! And..."

"And what?"

"And... no more running and hiding. I've reached the end of the line. I'm going to stay and face this. It's not just the fact that someone's stalking me, I need to get my own head together. This is the right place, I can feel it."

They stared at each other for a second until the sound of Daan's mighty lungs reached up to the first floor.

"Beatrice!"

She gave Adrian a reproachful look and trotted down the stairs.

Daan stood in the hall with Holger's bag. "I'm taking him to the train station. He wants to get back. What's Adrian going to do?"

A voice came from above her. "Adrian is going to stay, if you don't mind."

Daan looked up the stairs at Adrian, back at Beatrice and

shrugged his enormous shoulders. "Right, fine. I'll be back in an hour or so. Beatrice, do you need a lift?"

"My colleague is due in about twenty minutes, so I'll travel with him. Nice to meet you and Mink. Look after him." She jerked her head up the stairs.

Daan embraced her in a smothering hug. "Short but sweet. *Tschüss!*"

As he yanked the door closed, Beatrice wondered exactly what his words were referring to.

"Beatrice!" Adrian hissed.

"What? I feel like I'm in some horrible nightmare where voices keep calling my name and I have no idea what they want."

"You understand security. Come up here, quick!"

She ascended the stairs again. "Stein will be here soon."

Adrian's voice came from a different room. "I know. Get a shift on!"

The room was an office and Adrian sat in front of a computer with various icons on the left hand side. "CCTV. How do I check the footage from last night?"

"Holger already did."

"So he says. I want to be sure."

Beatrice didn't like the tone of paranoia in his voice. "All these systems are different, I'm not sure I can..."

"Just try." He vacated the seat and batted a hand at her.

It took her a good five minutes to familiarise herself with the recording system, and only then because she recalled a case in Finsbury Park where cameras had proved crucial. Last night's footage was broken into three-hour chunks. She started at 18.00 and watched a minute in real time before fast-forwarding. The system had 'markers', indicating when some kind of motion had occurred. The two cameras were fixed, showing one view of the front and one of the back porch. The light changed as the night grew darker and once an owl or piece of paper flapped past the front camera. Other than that, nothing.

She sped the tapes back and forth, finding no activity on either. She opened the next batch – 21.00 till midnight. The first thirty minutes showed nothing until Adrian arrived at the back door at

21.39. They watched him, a strange sensation. She on the other end of that line, trying to calm him. He, obviously frantic, desperate for help. Where had he been? The tape sped on to the police arrival and Beatrice hit pause.

"He's right. There's nothing on here."

"That's just not possible." Adrian rotated the chair so that Beatrice was facing him. "I know you think I'm unreliable or attention-seeking or having a breakdown. All those things might be true. But you must believe me about last night. I chopped logs, someone banged on the windows and rang the doorbell, someone left a crucifix on the porch, Mink ran off barking and I stood there calling her. All that really happened, I swear. I don't know why the camera didn't film it and I almost feel like I can't trust myself." He paused for a moment. "I wish Mink could talk. She'd vouch for me."

"What time did you chop the logs?"

He thought about it. "Before my shower. Around seven, I think."

Beatrice located 18.50 on the timeline and let the footage run. Nothing. She fast-forwarded, stopping occasionally to watch the rain spatter the empty porch. She peered hard at the ghostly monochrome image, trying to search every detail. She looked at the time counter and noticed the date. 11.12.15. The eleventh of December. She rewound to where the section began, at 18.00. The date was the same. She skipped to the next section, in which Adrian appeared on the porch. This time the date read 12.11.15. Twelfth of November? Unless...

She minimised the open windows and searched for the security system's user manual. The company's address was in Palm Beach Florida. She brought up the footage from between six and nine last night. 11.12.15, according to American date stamping was the twelfth of November. Everything else the cameras recorded was from yesterday evening, except one chunk, which was recorded one month ago. Beatrice scratched her forehead, thinking.

"What? Adrian demanded.

"Ssh," she replied. She found the files from November the twelfth and compared the six till nine recording with yesterday's in a split screen. Frame for frame it was exactly the same. It even had the movement marker in the same place when a piece of white flashed over the porch roof. The Recycling Bin showed no sign of the missing footage and recent activity had been erased. An expert would be able to find it, no doubt, but...

"Am I right in thinking the only person who accessed this computer since yesterday was Holger?"

"Yes. He went through it last night while I was downstairs waiting for Mink. Why?"

"One section of footage has been removed and replaced with film of the same three hours in November. Same sort of weather, dark, no change to the layout and the dates are so similar, most people wouldn't notice. Whatever the cameras recorded last night has gone missing."

Adrian stared at the computer. "I don't understand."

"Nor do I. But I think it might be best if you stay with Daan for the next few days."

The sound of a doorbell made them both tense.

"That'll be Stein. Go and let him in while I clear my traces. I need some time to figure this out. Adrian! Say nothing about this to Daan or Holger or anyone."

His face grew paler. "I won't."

"Go and answer the door. Tell Stein I'll be a few more minutes. Say I'm attending to my natural needs. That always shuts men up."

Chapter 24

The journey down the island, across to the mainland and back to the city of Hamburg should have provided Beatrice with plenty of time to think, but Herr Stein had other ideas. As soon as they'd established that Adrian and dog were well, he guided her attention towards their case.

The surveillance operation had borne fruit. Coded conversations and increased activity between the Hague and Bremen aroused enough suspicion to refer the transcripts to a specialist intelligence officer in Wiesbaden. She described the code the thieves had used as 'laughably simple' and analysed the messages in under an hour. She was able to give them specifics as to the planned theft. Äusserer Schweinehund, a George Grosz in a private home was the target for Saturday night. The family had gone to London for Christmas shopping and one of the security guards was in communication with the Dutch theft ring. He would disable the alarm, ensure the gang could access the property and allow them to leave with the painting before the police were alerted.

"And we will let that happen," said Stein.

"We will?" Beatrice asked.

"Yes. We don't just want the thieves, we want the whole organisation. The intelligence service in the Netherlands is working with us and Wiesbaden. We're planning a double attack. How do you say...?" He took one hand off the wheel and mimed plucking something with finger and thumb.

"The pincer effect. How will that work?"

"The gang intend to take the painting to Osnabrück. There they will hand it over to a middle man, who will travel back to the Hague and place it in storage until it's safe to transport it to the collector.

The thieves themselves will return to their hole until their services are next required. Except they won't get that far."

Beatrice folded her arms with a smug grin. "No. Because we're going to finger their collars."

"We're going to what?" Stein shot her a look of bewilderment.

"It's a British idiom – means arrest someone. Is that what we're going to do?"

"Yes. As soon as the middle man leaves with the painting, we either follow or surround the gang and take them back to Hamburg for interrogation."

Beatrice watched the scenery flicker by, although her mind was already in a blacked-out surveillance vehicle filled with screens, consoles and tension.

"Presumably the Dutch force will grab the middle man on the other side of the border? Or wait till he gets back to base?"

"We'll track him and see what happens. We hope he'll go directly to the industrial estate in The Hague, where he'll be arrested and the painting placed in the hands of professionals. We're just not sure if there might be one or two more switches of vehicles to misdirect the police."

"Yes, they can be extremely slippery, these types. What's our role, Herr Stein? I assume Tomas and Herr Meyer are running the show."

"I don't know yet. Briefing at eighteen-hundred hours. I estimate our arrival in Hamburg at twelve-thirty and then we must go to bed."

She bit her lip, amused. "If you insist."

"You need your sleep, DI Stubbs. It's going to be another long night." His stern tone was undercut by the crinkling of his eyes.

They were both quiet until Stein parked in the queue for the car train. He made a call in German, very clipped and professional sounding, while Beatrice peered through the windscreen. The weather was foul, sleet hitting the windscreen in irregular furious bursts. When he rang off, she leaned back in her seat to look at him.

"I still haven't said thank you. For driving me all this way, giving up a decent night's sleep, being so kind and reassuring all the time and not once losing patience with this wild goat's chase. I really am most grateful."

He twisted his torso to face her. His cleft chin and sculpted jaw impressed her all over again but the real danger was in those deep brown eyes. She blinked to break the hypnotic pull.

"I told you. I was pleased to help. Adrian seems like a nice man." He rubbed behind his ear, still gazing at her. "Do you think it was a... how do you say that in English? A trick to make someone pay attention?"

"A ruse? No, I wouldn't think so. Why would he want *my* attention anyway?"

"Not yours. Didn't you say Holger is his ex-boyfriend?"

"Yes. But the split was amicable. They're friends."

"People sometimes change their minds. Maybe Adrian wants him back."

Beatrice blinked, surprised to hear hypothetical gossip from someone who looked like he'd just stepped out of a razor commercial.

"In which case, why would he stay on the island?" she asked. "Holger all but begged him to come back to Hamburg. If he wanted Holger, why opt for a Danish bloke and his dog instead?"

"To make Holger jealous?"

Beatrice's laughter died in her throat.

Stein started the engine. "Here we go." He drove onto the car train with typical precise caution, while Beatrice thought about his words.

What if it was the other way around? What if Holger had engineered this whole charade to restart their relationship? Adrian might not love him, but he could certainly be forced into needing him. Her mind turned over the issue of the CCTV and she realised she had no idea why Holger had popped up four hours from his home when Adrian was at his most vulnerable. The situation preoccupied her all the way to Hamburg.

She woke at quarter to five after a succession of frustrating, alarming dreams with a head like tar. She showered, took her medication and tried to assess whether this distance from reality was due to exhaustion or withdrawal. Focus, she ordered herself. She checked her emails, trying to shake off the thick black fug between her ears. Admin from Scotland Yard, updates from the Hamburg operation, but nothing Stein hadn't told her. A gentle query from Matthew and two hellos from friends in London, including Dawn Whittaker, apparently loving her new role. Beatrice smiled. A note from Hamilton, thanking her for dinner but with a classic dig at the end. *Your company much appreciated, at least for two courses.* Nothing from Adrian, but she'd received two text messages on the journey enthusing about Daan's beachfront shack and assuring her of Mink's continuing recovery.

Time was getting on so she dressed in practical stakeout gear – dark layers – and spent several minutes choosing a snack from room service. With the possibility of being stuck in an enclosed space with members of Hamburg's police force for hours on end, she did not want her body to betray her. She opted for a cheese salad with a high energy drink. A combination which would have appalled Matthew, no doubt.

While she waited, she called him, just on the off chance. He picked up.

"Professor Bailey?"

"It's me."

"Hello stranger. Are you having fun?"

With a sudden rush of longing, Beatrice wanted to be there, to crawl under a duvet with him, tell him everything that had happened, share her concerns and quite simply offload. So much had altered since they last spoke that the sheer volume of things she had to tell him choked her.

"Fun? Other words leap sooner to mind. It's been rather more hectic than I'd like. Never mind that, because I can't go into detail anyway. Tell me what's happening in Brampford Speke."

"Very well. Mince pie failure, early carol singers, tree decorating with a three-year-old, mulled wine spice spilt on the carpet, wrapping paper coming out of my ears and I can't find the sellotape. Half my Christmas card list is either dead or divorced. Can one apply to be excused from the festive season, do you know?"

"Oh you Scrooge. I'm rather enjoying the Germanic take on Christmas. Their Glühwein and markets make Oxford Street look tacky."

"There is nothing on this earth that does *not* make Christmas on Oxford Street look tacky. When will you be back? The way things are going, I'm fearful of even preparing the pud without your guidance. Leave alone the roasted parsnips."

"Monday. I need to smooth Hamilton's feathers so I'll have to put in a full week. Office party on the eighteenth, so what say I come down on the Saturday? Stay for the whole holiday fortnight."

Matthew's smile could be heard in his voice. "If you bring authentic German goodies, I could probably put up with you for that long."

A knock came at the door. "That'll be room service. I must dash. Shall I call you when I'm back in London?"

"Yes, please do. Give my very best to Adrian. Take care, Old Thing."

She replaced the receiver, her mind on roasted parsnips and that wonderful man. Matthew could never advertise grooming products. Which was precisely why she loved him.

Considering this was a five-way operation involving the BKA, three German police forces and a Dutch one, Beatrice expected to be sidelined, perhaps attached to Tomas Schäffer. He would direct operations from the Hamburg base, using intercepted communications to guide his decisions. The most useful thing Beatrice could do, especially as she wouldn't be able to follow the language, would be making tea. Three sites were the focus of attention. The house in Bremen from which the Grosz would be stolen, the hypermarket car park where the gang would hand over the painting and the final destination, assumed to be The Hague, where the Dutch intelligence service would be poised to make the arrest.

So she was surprised and delighted to discover that she was to accompany Herr Stein and his team to Osnabrück, in order to assist in making the initial arrests. Right slap bang in the middle of action, just the way she liked it.

Stein's briefing was meticulous. Safety was paramount as the gang were likely to be armed and had proved themselves violent. Bulletproof vests, protective helmets and weapons for the arresting officers, roadblocks prepared in detail and GPS slap-and-track devices tested and ready. One of the blonds, Kurt, was tasked with attaching the devices to the vehicles. This meant using a launcher, hence a distraction was required. Two younger officers were briefed on their roles as boy racers using the car park to test their souped-up saloons. They wore baseball caps and saggy jeans and looked as if they'd yet to learn to shave. Margrit's shrill cackle at her colleagues' appearance drew a frosty look from Stein.

Finally, Beatrice received her own instructions. While Stein, Margrit and Rudi moved in to arrest the gang, she was to record the whole operation on camera. She fixed her attention on the map, listening to Stein's explanation of who, what and where, her sense of anticipation wobbling on the brink of nerves. Briefing over, Margrit accompanied Beatrice and Tomas back to the glass-walled room to demonstrate how to use the police video camera.

"There's also a zoom function on top. It makes more noise, but you're only capturing pictures tonight. We'll need detailed close-ups of everything. Not just faces and number plates, but shoes, watches, hair, everything."

Beatrice practised using both functions by filming Tomas, who looked as shifty as any criminal. "Right, got it. Thanks Margrit."

"You're welcome. Oh, I've got something for you." She pulled out a folded sheet of paper from her back pocket and handed it over. "That convent you asked me to check out. You said you didn't want anything overly religious, right? This is a translation of their homepage. I'll let you decide." She boggled her eyes in an expression of exaggerated alarm as she left the room. Beatrice read.

Here at Kloster St Ursula, we are at war.

Christianity is under siege. Today children learn that there are no values, there is no right, no wrong, no God.

We wage war on a number of different fronts. On protecting the church and Christian principle according to the teachings of the Bible. On making the womb a place of safety, by protecting life from the moment of conception. On resisting all earthly claims such as family bonds, as our ultimate allegiance is focused on the imminent return of Jesus. On defending the erosion of the only true marriage, between a man and a woman.

We use every means at our disposal and all the strength that God supplies to fight this war, including negotiations with the earthly whilst always staying mindful of the powers in the unseen realm.

Here at Kloster St Ursula we are committed to a Biblical worldview, where Creator and created are separate, and where the marriage supper of the Lamb is distinctly between the Redeemer and those redeemed through the blood of Jesus.

-Sister Immaculata

"Good God."

Tomas looked up from his screen. "What's the matter?"

"Nothing." Beatrice shook her head. "People can be very strange."

"I know exactly what you mean."

Stein opened the door. "Time to go."

Butterflies started their nonsense in her stomach again as she wished Tomas good luck and followed the police unit down to the car park. A sudden seriousness permeated the atmosphere. The team piled into a van, but Stein gave a murmured instruction she should ride with him in the unmarked Mercedes. The clock showed

19.00 on the dot as they belted themselves in for the two-hour journey to Osnabrück.

Stein flicked on the wipers to clear the screen of snowflakes. "The theft is due to occur at half past eleven. It will take the gang around ninety minutes to reach Osnabrück. Which means we have six hours to prepare the trap and conceal ourselves. Are you ready?"

Wide-awake and eager, Beatrice gave a decisive nod. "Let's go."

Kurt stood in police combat gear apart from his helmet, holding something like a cannon in his arms. His blond hair shone white in the moonlight while the matt-black weapon reflected nothing. He looked like Rutger Hauer in *Blade Runner*. The team had concealed themselves at the furthermost points of the car park: in a thicket of trees, behind the recycling bins, in the neighbouring lot. Everyone found their positions, waiting for the opportunity for a cautious rehearsal. The hypermarket was still open and Friday evening shoppers hauled trolleys across the tarmac, full of pre-packaged Christmas-in-a-box. Beatrice thought back to Matthew's query. *'Can one apply to be excused from the festive season, do you know?'*

In the shadow of the police van, Kurt took aim at tree trunks without pulling the trigger.

Stein spoke at Beatrice's shoulder. "It shoots fake bullets which embed themselves in the vehicle body. They contain GPS trackers so we can follow, but the problem is the sound when they hit. This is why we need the distraction. If the 'racers' can make enough noise, Kurt can attach trackers to the Dutch vehicle without raising alarm. The only risk is attracting their attention. Kurt's timing is crucial."

Beatrice whispered, despite the strains of the supermarket's piped *Der Tannenbaum* drifting across the night air. "What if he does attract their attention?"

"We have to make the arrests immediately. Right here. We cannot lose the middle man, with or without the painting. If he suspects we're in pursuit, he'll change tactics and hide. He won't lead us to HQ and then all we'll have is a stolen painting and a bunch of goons playing dumb." His tone was patient even as his keen eyes ranged over the area.

A tannoy released a series of warning bleeps, followed by an announcement. The shop was closing for the night. Stein made a brief gesture, as if turning a key to his lips. The team gave varying signs of assent and retreated to their positions.

She followed Stein into the surveillance van, clunked the door shut and settled into position. "Radio contact only in an emergency, I assume. What about the roadblock people?"

"Radio contact will be essential, but any movement or conversation outside the vehicles should be kept to a minimum. We expect our visitors in approximately three hours. I want total silence and stillness for at least two hours before that. Just in case our friends from the Low Countries arrive early. Any 'natural needs' should be managed now."

She shook her head. "My natural needs are under control. What about you?"

To her surprise, Stein laughed. Quietly and with more shaking shoulders than sound.

"Yes," he said, on an intake of breath. "Mine too."

Chapter 25

Everything had gone exactly to plan, right up until someone else had natural needs. Via radio, Tomas assured them the operation in Bremen met all their expectations. A security guard had admitted a Mercedes-Benz Viano with blacked out windows at 11.15. Three men entered the house, removed the Grosz painting, covered it in protective wrapping and took it to the van. While they were inside, a police officer had attached a tracking device to the vehicle, out of sight of the getaway driver in the cab.

Once the Mercedes had left, the guard let exactly thirty minutes pass before calling the police, claiming he had just managed to untie himself after an aggravated burglary. The van's movements were visible on the GPS screen, heading directly for Osnabrück. Contrary to expectations, the wait passed quickly. Only fifteen minutes to the van's estimated time of arrival remained when a Hummer cruised into view and parked behind the shopping trolley shelter.

The atmosphere in the van, already charged, changed into something deeper, the feel of gears engaging.

"Commence filming," said Stein. The camera's position was almost perfect, just a few degrees left. Beatrice adjusted the angle, twiddled with the focus and sat forward, observing the dark, silent, tank-like lump. More of a hippo than a Hummer. Activity buzzed behind her and she turned to watch. Margrit fed the number plate detail back to HQ and Stein was giving sharp instructions into the radio as he pulled on his combat gear.

Margrit gave her a quick smile. "He's talking to the racers. They must be visible to the gang but not too noisy or someone might report them to the police!" She pulled a quizzical face.

Beatrice returned her smile, her expression far more relaxed than her mental state. Her nerves grew more taut with each click of buckle and metal. She ran over the plan once again.

The thieves would arrive any minute now. They would hand over the painting to the man, or men, in the Hummer. Under the cover of backfiring exhausts, Kurt would shoot GPS trackers at the Hummer. Both vehicles would depart. If all went according to plan, the Mercedes would run into a roadblock. What then?

Existing evidence presumed the van contained four men, but could they be sure? Such a brutal, professional crew would do anything to resist arrest. Up to now, her main concern had been how to arrest the gang without giving them time to warn the Dutch middle man. Now, faced with the blank armour of the squat vehicle less than thirty metres away, her fears slipped into the cracks between certainties.

Headlights swept across her face and she froze before reminding herself she could not be seen. The Mercedes Viano circled the car park, in no hurry. It passed horribly close to their concealed spot behind the trees and she sent a silent thank you to the cloud cover. Finally, it parked alongside the Hummer and switched off its lights. For a few seconds, nothing happened and it seemed the entire empty expanse was holding its breath. Then an interior light came on as the door opened.

This was her moment. She zoomed in on the vehicles, watching silhouetted figures emerge. Faces, features, expressions, narrowed eyes, a lit cigarette; everything came sharply into focus.

"Four men out of the Merc. One looking around the car park, two gone round the back, one leaning down to talk to... aha, the Hummer window is down. Can't see a face. They've opened the side door of the Mercedes. A man just got out of the back seat of the Hummer. He's going inside the van."

Stein listened and muttered something into the radio. Seconds later, a jarring screech of tyres ripped across the car park and Beatrice saw all three men guarding the Mercedes reach inside their jackets and withdraw handguns. The driver of the Hummer got out and beckoned to his colleague inside the van.

"Three men are armed and have their weapons ready."

Two absurdly customised VW Golfs shot across the forecourt to the hypermarket, revving and changing gears with such a racket Beatrice worried they might be overdoing it. At some invisible signal, both drivers hit the accelerator, so that the cars emitted startling bangs and flashes from their exhausts. They screamed around the car park, engines whining and exhausts popping, setting Beatrice's teeth on edge.

The men in her viewfinder watched the spectacle, their heads following the trajectory until the two cars burst out of the car park and back onto the street. A moment of stillness passed, until every echo of the intrusion had faded. Then the Hummer's driver opened the back door and a large padded package was transferred carefully from the interior of the Mercedes.

Stein's radio scratched into life. He replied and Margrit gave Beatrice a thumbs-up. Kurt had hit his target. She looked back to her screen and saw the occupants of the Hummer close the door, get back inside and wind up the windows. When the vehicle's lights came on, Stein spoke into his radio, his voice calm but urgent. The Hummer peeled away, steady and slow, out of the car park and onto the street.

Margrit got behind the steering wheel and Beatrice braced herself for the moment they would pursue the Mercedes van. Yet nothing happened. One man was still smoking and the other three stood around, apparently shooting the breeze. Taking advantage of the close formation, Beatrice zoomed in, making sure she got each face on film. Then one man broke from the group and started walking straight towards her.

"Herr Stein!" she said, her eyes fixed on the approaching figure. In direct contradiction to her sudden alarm, the other three men burst into laughter and shouted something after their friend. He bent into a crouch and waddled a few steps, eliciting more laughter.

"*Scheisse!*" spat Margrit.

Stein leaned over Beatrice to watch as the figure grew steadily larger. "*Scheisse* is the right word. It seems our friend has some 'natural needs' that cannot be relieved in the car park. So he is coming into the trees to..."

Beatrice was horrified. "He's coming over here to take a shit?"

Stein's eyes darted around the interior. "We'll have to move now. If he sees us and raises the alarm... we can't risk it. No, we snatch him here and surprise the others immediately. It's too late to wait for back-up."

He spoke into his radio, his voice guttural and harsh, nodding to Margrit as he did so. She waited till he'd finished, then cocked her gun and slid open the panel door before melting into the darkness. Stein pointed at the camera and followed Margrit, closing the door behind him.

Beatrice's fingers shook as she put her hands back on the camera. The looming man had moved out of her sightline so she trained the focus on the trio by the van. Her peripheral vision picked up shadows scuttling across the car park. The three men, sheltered by the van on one side and the trolley station on the other, continued smoking and chatting, oblivious of the tightening noose.

Several things happened at once. A volley of yells ricocheted across the tarmac, headlights from concealed police vehicles threw the scene into harsh illumination and the boy racers squealed back through the entrance. The three men scrabbled for guns or phones, but at the clicks of readied weaponry, they lifted their arms in the air, hands visible. She watched as Rudi, Kurt and Stein arrested the men, removed their weapons and eased them into waiting Polizei vehicles. Margrit came into the picture from Beatrice's left, marching a handcuffed man ahead of her. Only when the patrol cars left with the suspects did she switch the camera off.

The side panel swung back and Stein stooped to enter. He was sweating, but had an air of triumph. He threw her a crooked grin before picking up his radio and relaying the successful result. Beatrice clambered out to stretch her trembling legs. Margrit and Kurt came over to shake her hand, as if she'd done something useful. She just managed to express her admiration of their slick professionalism when the atmosphere changed. Stein stood with his hands on his hips until everyone gathered into a semi-circle around him.

He addressed the team in German, but Margrit whispered a translation for Beatrice's benefit. "Suspects taken to Hamburg... BKA officers interrogating... our team stands down... good job, no shots fired... debrief tomorrow at fourteen hundred... congratulations...

get some sleep." She grinned at Beatrice. "He's pleased, I can tell. I'm going to have a couple of beers with the boys when we get back. Surplus energy, you know? You'd be welcome to join us."

"Thanks Margrit, that's very thoughtful. But wild horses couldn't keep me from my bed tonight. Enjoy your beers, you deserve it."

Margrit held out her hand. "Another time. Goodnight."

Beatrice shook it with a warm smile and made her way back to the van, in weary anticipation of another two hour drive.

"DI Stubbs!" Margrit hissed, running after her.

"What is it?" Beatrice's heart began the adrenalin pump all over again.

Margrit's smile lifted her cheeks into crab-apples. "The guy who started all this, the one who came into the trees? Guess what his name is?"

Beatrice stared at her, lost for words.

"He's called Anton Baer," said Margrit, barely suppressing her amusement.

"I don't..."

Margrit leaned forward to whisper. "You have an English expression I learned. Do Baers shit in the woods?" Laughter escaped and she covered her mouth.

Beatrice's eyes widened and a bubble of mirth rose from her stomach. "I don't suppose this bear...?" Her voice wavered as she tried to control her giggles.

Margrit shook her head, squeezing her eyes shut. "He didn't have time."

Beatrice bit her lips and sang in a stage whisper, "If you go down to the woods today, you're sure of a big surprise..."

Margrit clutched her arm and they doubled up in the shared laughter of relief and complicity, drawing puzzled stares from their colleagues.

Chapter 26

Six hours of dreamless sleep. She couldn't believe it. The alarm was set for midday but Beatrice awoke, bright-eyed and smiling, at half past eleven. Serene and rested, she ordered brunch, had a shower, caught up with emails and almost enjoyed her brisk stroll through the crisp salty air to the police station.

The atmosphere inside was equally upbeat. Margrit and Kurt, both on their phones, lifted hands in greeting as she made her way through the open-plan section. She waved back with a happy grin. Stein was in the glass office, peering over Tomas's shoulder with a coffee cup in his left hand. Even from this distance, Beatrice could tell they'd both been here for hours.

Stein spotted her and beckoned. Clean shaven he might be, but tell-tale grey skin shadowed his eyes. Part of her was relieved. Even Mr Perfect had off days. Tomas looked up briefly and offered an unusually broad smile. Stein opened the door for her.

"Good news, DI Stubbs! In addition to our four arrests, the Dutch police followed the middle men to The Hague and caught the gang in the act of receiving the stolen painting. Six men were arrested at four o'clock this morning and another ten individuals are being questioned."

"Ten? This thing is bigger than we thought!"

Stein exhaled a short laugh. "You have no idea. Come."

He led her back through the building to a small cubbyhole with several screens and a console. He gestured to the seat and fiddled with the controls while she settled herself.

"Obviously most interviews were in Dutch or German, which I'm having translated for you. One man they arrested is a New Zealander. This is significant for two reasons. Firstly, they interviewed him in English. Second, he agreed to cooperate if the threat of deportation was removed. He has a partner and children in Amsterdam. There's a lot more to the case than his testimony, but it will give you an idea of what we're dealing with. Press this button to play and this one to pause. The good bit is at around fifteen minutes in. I'll get you some coffee."

She pressed play as the door closed and focused on the picture in front of her. A police interview room with stark overhead lighting which made the faces on screen look more chilly and tired than they probably were. An interviewee sat opposite two police detectives, leaning his forearms on the table and yawning as the interview commenced. They spent some time establishing his identity and the events of the evening. Beatrice twigged he was the driver of the Hummer.

She listened to the initial questions and stonewall response. Then his attitude changed. The insolent folded arms and closed mouth changed as the Dutch detective laid down his offer. In exchange for cooperation, he would not be charged and would be permitted to remain in the Netherlands with his pregnant partner and child. She watched as the sullen posture altered and a decision was made. He asked for it in writing and agreed to tell them what he knew. Beatrice wrinkled her nose. Snitches were solid gold from the police perspective, but it didn't stop her despising them as self-interested cowards. After a few more minutes, she attuned to his curious habit of accenting his statements as questions. She could see he was telling the truth. She speeded up the film to fifteen minutes into the interview.

The detective asked another question and the man hunched his shoulders, tucking his hands into his armpits.

"Like an agency, we deal with buyers and sellers. Look mate, it works like this. People send a request for a particular painting, or a kind of painting. We find out where it is and by that I mean exactly? Not just the house, but the room, the alarm system, the exits and what condition it's in? We instruct our people to take it. Gently. Like with all the care of museum curators? We have perfect storage conditions for even the most delicate artwork. Our team are professionals. The important thing is that the artwork is not damaged. We keep it safe until the noise dies down and then we do what the client tells us. Offer it to the insurance company, ransom it to the owner, hand it over to another dealer or collector, whatever they want us to do, hey?"

One of the detectives flicked through a file and spoke. "The artworks themselves may not be damaged, but several people were seriously hurt during these aggravated robberies. A cleaning woman in London is still recovering from a head injury. A householder in Hamburg spent six months in hospital."

The New Zealander rubbed his nose with the palm of his hand, a casual gesture of weariness and lack of concern which Beatrice suspected indicated the opposite.

"Outsourcing. What can you do? Their methods aren't our concern. All we ask is to get the right piece at the right time and in pristine condition? You can chuck the book at us for receiving stolen goods, but we can't be implicated in bodily harm. It was up to him to clear the place. He knew when the boys were coming. That's not my problem, mate."

"Sorry. *Who* knew when the boys were coming?"

"Waring. He commissioned us. A private collector bought the Dix piece and Waring wanted the insurance on top? No worries, we're happy to help. We take it, hand it over to the collector, Waring claims the insurance and everybody's a winner."

"To be clear, the man who commissioned the Otto Dix *Salon II* theft was its owner, Mr Chet Waring?"

"Yep. We only ask one question – can you afford us? That's all we need to know. In fact, it's easier when you work with the owner? Precision intel, you know?"

The door opened and Stein returned with two coffees. He handed one to Beatrice and stood behind her, watching the screen for a couple of minutes. The interviewer asked if any of the other thefts under the scope of the Interpol investigation were committed with the knowledge of their legal owners.

The lanky Antipodean bent over the table to look at the images the officer had drawn from the file. "No. Nope. We've had a request for that Schad with the boar, but security is way too tight. Aha, now you're talking! That was one of ours."

"Can you please indicate which picture you're identifying for the tape?"

"Sure. Max Beckmann's *Exile*. We had orders from de Vries to move that one fast. Stolen, secured and off the continent before the theft was reported? These were all for the same collector but we only ever dealt with intermediaries. Yeah, I recognise several others. This one, *Nina in Camera*, we should have lifted last week until we heard you guys were watching."

"*Nina in Camera?* Did your instructions to steal that piece come from Herr Walter?"

For the first time, the Kiwi looked uncomfortable. "Nah, not him. His son. The collector got hold of some stuff on the kid, I don't know the details, but he blackmailed him into fixing things. He's only nineteen with more bollocks than brains."

"And the painting you took last night. The Grosz from Bremen? Was that theft also arranged by the owner?" asked the interrogator, voicing Beatrice's next question.

"Yeah, Frau Birmensdorfer was ready to sell fifteen years ago. That Grosz featured in our private catalogue. No one bid. Now, with the Schad under police surveillance, we managed to persuade her to drop the price? In under six hours, we got confirmation the money was in escrow, to be released when the painting was delivered to the collector."

The interviewer raised his head. "*The* collector. All these pieces were destined for the same person?"

"Yeah. Whether they were for him or he was a dealer selling them on, I don't know. But this guy knew exactly what he wanted."

Stein leaned forward to press pause. His thigh brushed Beatrice's and she found herself acutely aware of the confined space.

"As far as our case goes, four thefts were either commissioned or inside jobs. Waring, de Vries, Walter Junior and Frau Birmensdorfer."

Beatrice shook her head. "So Tomas was right all along. Despite Herr Meyer's insistence the anonymous collector is nothing more than a myth. Someone, somewhere is coveting Expressionist eyes. You know, that bloody slimy git Waring said as much when I interviewed him. 'Some wealthy oligarch is amassing German

Expressionist art from the 1920s and needed a Dix for his collection.' He was so cooperative and pleasant, after I'd been warned he was difficult. I should have realised. A classic criminal tactic."

"Classic, I agree. Tell a partial truth with a sin of omission – the fact that the wealthy oligarch had a willing seller. No surprise he was pleased to see you. A police report equals insurance claim. He never expected your investigation to get this far."

"Nor did I, to be honest. Did that bloke give us much more?" Beatrice jabbed a finger at the screen.

"Enough detail to implicate another ten people and a whole network of leads and connections. But we won't find him." Stein's shoulders slumped.

"Who?"

"The collector. Even if we had the time and resources to follow up every last lead, we'd get no closer. Whoever he is, he's made sure there are no direct connections to him."

Beatrice narrowed her eyes. "You can't know that. Sounds to me as if you're settling for a consolation prize."

"I'm not settling for anything. This is an Interpol operation. They call the shots. They've fulfilled their mission and arrested a gang of fine art thieves. Meyer's already writing a concluding report."

"What? This is nowhere near concluded! What about all the complicit owners? Surely they will be charged with aiding and abetting, and fraud, and acting as an accessory?"

Stein switched off the monitor and leaned back against the desk, facing Beatrice with a sad smile. "Yes, they'll be charged. Their legal teams are already rubbing their hands in the sure knowledge they will be acquitted, or in the unlikely event they are found guilty of some charges, it will be a minor matter of paying fines they can afford and restoring reputations. We plugged a leak, DI Stubbs. Just one hole in the dam. While we prepare the paperwork to dismantle this ring, another will quietly take its place. The collector will continue to collect and those paintings will never be recovered. At least not in our lifetimes."

His voice carried a cynicism and defeat she recognised from the howls of her own black dogs. She had learned to manage hers but to hear that same tone in one so young and decent seemed heart-breaking.

She met his eyes and he shrugged with his eyebrows. "We did our job," he said. "And if we finish the paperwork today, you can return home tomorrow. Or do you plan to go back to Sylt?"

Beatrice released a huge sigh. "I have absolutely no idea."

The rest of the team, as well they should be, were demob happy. As Beatrice was packing the last of her paperwork, Rudi tapped on the door of the glass office to invite her for a drink with them all. She opened her mouth to offer an excuse but caught sight of Tomas hovering a few paces behind with an expression of concern. Further back still, she saw Stein feigning jovial high spirits with Margrit, but he too was watching for her reaction.

"I think we deserve it," she smiled at Rudi, giving him an un-necessary and uncharacteristic double thumbs up. Out in the open plan area, three faces broke into a smile.

Margrit yelled across the room. "No one can resist Rudi!"

Beatrice laughed and allowed the large blond to take her suit-case. She would make sure she sat next to Tomas.

An hour later, the party was getting into full swing. Everyone had been toasted for their role in the operation, Tomas twice. His discomfited delight was apparent to all, but the banter was good-natured and inclusive. Several times she caught Stein's eye and exchanged an almost parentally proud smile.

After the second beer, Beatrice judged it an opportune moment to take her leave. She shook hands with everyone, thanked them repeatedly, wished them all a good festive season and then Stein stood. She assumed he would only escort her to the door, but he made a few rapid-fire wisecracks in German and gave a mock-salute to the team before picking up Beatrice's case and guiding her to the door.

"I hope you're not leaving on my account, Herr Stein? I'm per-fectly capable of getting back to my hotel alone, you know."

He shook his head and led her outside through a curtain of

snowflakes to his car. He opened her door and went to the boot to stash her case. Only when they pulled into the flow of Saturday evening traffic did he speak.

"Do you want to go to your hotel or can I take you somewhere else?"

A wash of weariness overtook her. A younger, livelier, better-rested Beatrice would have invited him for dinner, but she needed time to herself and space to think.

"That's very kind of you. Lack of sleep and two powerful beers have left me running on empty. So if you wouldn't mind, the hotel sounds the best option."

"Of course. It's been a heavy week."

They drove in silence, Beatrice gazing out the window at the Christmas scenes, humming a vague tune even she didn't recognise. In a few minutes, she realised they were passing the station and only moments from her hotel. She remembered her manners.

"Herr Stein, it's been a real pleasure to work with you. You've been extraordinarily kind, not to mention tolerant. I hope we meet again one of these days."

He smiled at her while they waited at the traffic lights. "Yes, I'd like that. It was an interesting experience meeting you. Maybe in future, we could use first names? Mine is Jan."

"Good idea. Please feel free to call me Beatrice..."

The lights turned green and Stein pulled away slowly only to hit the brake as a last pedestrian dashed across the road.

"Bloody fool!"

Beatrice glared at the idiot whose impatience could easily have got him killed as he continued running towards the station.

"Beatrice Bloody Fool? If you insist." Stein grinned.

The figure disappeared into the crowd and Beatrice squinted. That was when a familiar figure crossed her line of sight.

"Did you see that man in the puffy jacket just then?"

"Sorry, I was watching the road. What about him?"

"I could have sworn that was Holger."

"Possibly it was. He does live in Hamburg."

"But why would he be heading to the train station at ten to seven?"

"No idea. Did you speak to Adrian today?"

"That's my number one priority as soon as I get in."

Stein slid the car into the forecourt, stepped out and retrieved Beatrice's suitcase. He offered his hand.

"Goodbye Beatrice. Safe journey and it was a pleasure to meet you."

"You too, Jan. You're an impressive leader and a very decent person. We could do with more like you. All the best."

He squeezed her hand. "I meant what I said. I would like to see you again. Call me if you need anything."

"I will. Goodnight and Merry Christmas."

"Goodnight. Same to you."

Beatrice waited on the pavement to wave him off. As soon as his car turned the corner, she asked the doorman to take her bag inside, then hurried across the road and back towards the station.

Chapter 27

Only a dog could recover from such an ordeal without a backward glance. Just before the sun set, Daan fed Mink some cold rice with chicken pieces and peas. She devoured the lot in seconds, checked the bowl ten more times and scratched at the door.

Adrian laughed as he slipped his feet into his boots, harried by the dog. Mink was eager to get outside, bunting Daan's legs and Adrian's hands, her tail a constant happy pendulum. They strolled down to the beach, grinning at Mink's antics with lumps of driftwood, relaxing into the expanse of sand and sky in silence. Neither spoke, content to observe the rhythm of the waves and the darkening sky as the sun slipped below the horizon. Tangy scents of seaweed mixed with the ocean spray, encouraging hearty breaths.

Daan stopped and looked out to sea. "There she is," he said.

Adrian followed his sight line to a small fishing boat. "That's yours?"

"Yes. I spent two years getting her seaworthy. Inside isn't luxurious but comfortable enough. You should come back in the summer. We can do an island tour from the sea. Less traffic."

"I'm not much of a sailor, but I'd give it a go."

Daan bent to tug at the stick Mink had brought him but she wouldn't let go, throwing all her weight backwards with her jaw clamped firmly on the wood. With a twist, he succeeded in wresting it from her and threw it in a long boomeranging arc down towards the sea. She took off after it, her white scut like a leader's flag.

"As if last night never happened," said Adrian.

Daan nodded, his eyes watching the dog, the fondness in his face evident. "She's a tough one." His expression changed, a frown tensing his brow. "The thing I don't understand is why someone would do that. The farmer swears he didn't lock her in there and I believe him. She doesn't trust many people. She likes you. She likes Holger. But you're the exceptions. So why did she follow whoever it was?"

The mention of Holger gave Adrian an internal twinge he chose to ignore. "Maybe she didn't. If they left food in there, they could have waited till she went in then locked the door."

"But why? Who would be hanging around with a lump of meat on a deserted beach at midnight?" Daan kicked a pebble which tumbled ahead of them.

"I wish she could talk. I don't suppose we'll ever find out what really happened."

They walked further along the dunes, Adrian lifting his collar against the bitter blasts of sea air. The lights of a distant ship glittered on the far horizon. Daan was unusually silent as they both gazed it.

"Daan, you know it wasn't me who shut Mink in there, don't you?"

Daan stopped in amazement. "Of course I do! You were as worried as I was. Shit, I know it wasn't you and it wasn't Holger."

Adrian sighed, a mixture of relief and a surge of concern. He'd heard nothing from Holger, or from Beatrice, and kept his promise to say nothing about the CCTV anomaly.

"Thank you."

"Let's turn back now. It's freezing. Don't forget it's your turn to cook tonight. Mink, *komm jetzt*! *Fuss*!"

Mink bounded towards them, her face sandy from digging. During the walk, the night had assumed control, bringing a vicious, skin-flaying wind. Both men bent their heads and Adrian walked the last stretch with his gloved hands over his perished ears. The glowing windows of Daan's ramshackle house acted as a beacon. Unlike Holger's place, which had the reassuring twinkling lights of distant neighbours and the nearby town of List to remind you of civilisation, Daan's boatyard was the only sign of life along this stretch of coast.

Outside the house sat a red and white *Strandkorb*, the beach basket chairs everywhere on the island. Daan lifted a corner. "Spare key under here, in case you get locked out."

"Thanks Daan. It's really good of you to let me stay."

As they took off their boots, Daan looked at his expression. "Don't worry about Holger. He'll get over that scene this morning. He's just very proud. Typical Bavarian."

"You reckon? I just want to speak to him. Do you mind if I try him again now? And then call Beatrice about flying back together tomorrow?"

"OK, but be quick. You need to start dinner because I'm already getting hungry. What are you going to make for us?"

Adrian's mood lifted. "Typical British."

Daan's eyes lit up. "Cornish pasties?"

"No, not pasties. Fish and chips."

Hundreds of people swarmed around Hamburg Hauptbahnhof, all in a hurry to get somewhere. A disproportionate number appeared to be tall, blond men in padded black jackets. The chances of finding Holger in this melee were zero – a weevil in a haystack. Unless, of course, one knew where he was going. Beatrice scanned the departures board for trains to Westerland and found the 19.16 was due to depart from platform 11. She had four minutes.

She speed-walked the length of the concourse and slipped onto platform 11, already crowded with noisy groups of youngsters. For fear of being spotted, she hid behind taller folk, which wasn't difficult. Around a third of the way along, she saw the one she wanted. His stillness gave him away. Everyone else was shifting, reading, fidgeting in impatience, pressing buttons on phones, staring at screens or laughing with their friends. Holger stood in silence, his gaze remote. Beatrice assessed her options. The most sensible, not to mention appealing, course of action was to go back to the hotel, phone Adrian and casually mention Holger was on his way to Sylt. Just to warn him. Warn him of what? She had no reason to mistrust Holger, other than the CCTV issue. He could well be heading back to build bridges with his friends.

The huge bulk of the Deutsche Bahn engine cruised into the

station. A four-hour train journey was the last thing she needed. She'd be far better off going back to her room for some dinner, packing and sleep. Even if she got on this train, how could she ensure Holger wouldn't see her? It would be a busy journey, people wandering up and down looking for seats. The answer presented itself as the train eased to a halt. A door opened right in front of her and a few passengers disembarked. The sign on the window said First Class Dining Salon. An obvious invitation. She boarded the train.

She had her choice of seats in the first class carriage so selected a rear-facing seat in the Quiet Zone. It was plush and hushed and suited her mood perfectly. She switched her phone to silent and shoved it back in her bag, intending to call Adrian from the toilets once she had decided what to say. Then she left her coat on her seat and went in search of the conductor and the dining-car.

After a fruitless half hour trying to get a signal on his phone, Adrian used Daan's landline to leave a message for Beatrice, but couldn't reach Holger. He gave up, went into the kitchen and started peeling potatoes. There would be various possibilities for flight times to London. He'd book as soon as he spoke to Beatrice. It would be much nicer if they could travel together. A lovely warm airport taxi on police expenses was infinitely preferable to trains or Tube. Despite himself, he mentally planned his route from London City to Boot Street and experienced an unexpected pang of homesickness. He made up his mind to leave first thing in the morning whether he'd heard from Beatrice or not. Facing fears could be done anywhere. In fact, he should never have run in the first place. It was time to go home.

Outside in the shed, Daan whistled as he hacked blocks of wood into fireplace shapes. Mink had opted to stay indoors, in the warmth of Daan's rough and rustic kitchen and in pole position when it came to the chances of food.

The domestic comfort of the situation could not be further removed from the solitary terrors of the previous night. Adrian chopped up the potatoes into wedges and mixed the beer batter, his mind calming with the ritual gestures of food preparation. He was just skinning the fish when his phone beeped. He washed his hands and checked.

A message from number he didn't recognise. He opened it and recoiled as if he'd been slapped.

YOUR NO SINNER.
A SINNER CAN REPENT.
THE DEVIL MUST BE DESTROYED.

Then the phone vibrated in his hand, emitting its shrill song. It gave him such a shock that this time he dropped it onto the fishy work surface. He snatched it up immediately and saw Beatrice's name on Caller Display.

"Beatrice! Finally!"

"Yes, sorry I missed your calls. My phone was on silent for a while. Is everything all right?"

"It was till about ten seconds ago. I think I just got a death threat."

"What do you mean? Another note?"

"No, a text message. Unknown number." He read the words and the number to her, aware of Daan talking to Mink in the living room. "Should I call the police?"

"Hmm. Not sure. We could make a strong case for harassment or stalking, but it's a bit oblique for a death threat. I mean, it doesn't mention you specifically. If I were you, I'd report this to the police in the morning. Don't delete it but don't let it unnerve you."

"So do nothing tonight?"

"Where are you?" She raised her voice over the sound of a loud rattling in the background.

"At Daan's place. I'm making fish and chips for us. Where are you? It sounds very noisy."

"Fish and chips? I'm in a restaurant, just about to order and you've just helped me make up my mind. Is Daan there?"

"Yes. He's laying a fire."

"Do you think I could have a quick word?"

Adrian was offended. "To discuss my paranoia? That text message is right here in front of me. I can show him."

"Adrian, the only paranoia here is your suspicion of my motives. In point of fact, I'm following up one of my theories on who's trying to scare you as we speak."His offence dissolved into curiosity. "Are you? Which one?"

"Not over the phone. I'll tell you when I see you. Will you put Daan on now?"

"Hang on, what time are we flying back tomorrow?"

"Not sure yet. I'll talk to you later."

Adrian sighed, took the mobile to the living-room and handed it to Daan. He stood in the doorway while Daan listened intently and answered a series of questions. He gave her his full name, his address, a few mysterious yes and no replies then bid her good-night. He handed the phone back.

"Show me this message," he demanded.

Adrian showed him.

Daan screwed up his face in distaste. "What the hell is that supposed to mean? You know what I think? This is some religious freak. A closet case himself, deep down he's attracted to you and blames you for it."

The theory made a perverted kind of sense to Adrian. "I'll tell Beatrice. Why did she need all that info about you?"

"Paperwork, she said. Has to get the facts right for her report. How's dinner coming on?" Daan went into the kitchen to wash his hands.

"It's on its way. But even if this is a stalker, what kind of weirdo would follow me from London to Hamburg to Sylt to try and freak me out?"

"Food first, talk later. I'll heat the oil. And before you do anything else, wash your phone. It stinks of fish."

Train travel was so refined, so classic, Beatrice sensed she'd been born for it. Each table bore its own lamp, casting a pool of intimate light over the linen, glassware and silvery cutlery. Other diners were few and all better dressed than Beatrice.

She chose sea bass with a lemon sorrel sauce on olive oil mash, her tastes swayed by Adrian's menu. Dawdling over the wine list, she polished off all the mini seeded rolls with their chilled pat of butter before selecting a glass of Spatlese. When the dapper little waiter brought her wine, she sat back to absorb the genteel ambience. Matthew would love this. Perhaps next year, when her retirement released them from time pressures, they could finally fulfil their dream of the Orient Express.

But she'd not yet retired and had work to do. She dragged her notebook from her bag and prepared a variety of scenarios:

A: It's not real:

> 1. Adrian - under stress, over-sensitive and a little paranoid connected unrelated incidents in London and invented those in Germany to gain sympathy. From??? Me? Holger?

> 2. Holger - London events weren't connected but Adrian's vulnerability gave Holger an opportunity to act as protector. Isolated him in a place he knew well and tampered with the video footage.

> 3. Daan – amused by Adrian's fears, plays practical jokes to add to the alarm, returning to "find" his own dog. In which case, Adrian is not in the best place but at least not likely to suffer physical harm.

B: It is real:

> 4. An ex-boyfriend – perhaps unable to deal with rejection, own sexuality, collision of faith and love sets out to punish his former lover. Holger dressing as a nun?

> 5. An admirer – perspective or circumstances make him resent the temptation and act as avenger.

> 6. A nun – taking the hard line against homosexuality decides to pick a gay man at random to terrorise.

The Kloster, or convent of St Ursula, had plenty of hard lines, but she hadn't found any connection to Holger or Adrian.

Her food arrived. A delicate citrus aroma met her nostrils and the artful presentation displayed the dish at its most appetising, rather than hiding a miserly portion with pretentious flair. The dish, the wine and muted ambience of the carriage brought a smile to her lips. The kind of moment which tempted one into a selfie. *Look at me!* She dismissed the idea with a snort and tucked into the mash.

After her meal, she returned once again to the toilets to make a call, this time to a taxi service in Westerland. She spelled her name and gave them Daan's address. By the time she returned to her seat, there were just under two hours of the journey remaining. She switched her phone to silent, but put it in her jacket so vibrations would wake her, and settled down for a post-prandial nap. It was essential to be one of the first off the train.

The smell of frying still filled the house. Adrian opened the kitchen window while rinsing the plates in the sink but the blast of minus-five wind soon changed his mind. Daan made coffee and they sat in front of the fire in the same desultory gloom which had hung over the meal.

"That was a great dinner," said Daan, again.

"Yeah, you said. I couldn't really taste it."

Daan nodded. "It was good, trust me. Adrian, there is nothing more you can do. Beatrice is right. Someone is trying to scare you. Meanwhile you're safe here with me and Mink. Tomorrow you can join Beatrice in Hamburg to fly back to London. First job in the morning is to visit the police station to discuss that SMS."

"Also known as death threat."

"Also known as Stupid Message Shit. Come on. What do you want to do? Sit here shivering in fear and let this freak achieve his aim, or carry on with life and ignore him?"

A sharp report like a bursting balloon came from the direction of Mink's back end. She whipped her head around to the source of the sound. Both men laughed.

"Fish as well as bones?" asked Adrian.

"Bones, fish, peas, everything makes Mink fart. Talking of digestion, I want a drink to help me sleep. Have one with me."

"Akvavit? I don't think so."

Daan leapt to his feet and rummaged in a cupboard. "Not akvavit. This is different. Bliss in a glass. Stay there."

He clattered about in the kitchen as Adrian checked his phone. Nothing. He brought up the message again. YOUR NO SINNER. A SINNER CAN REPENT. THE DEVIL MUST BE DESTROYED. 'Your' no sinner. Not 'You're'. A rushed typo or an error? A non-native speaker of English? An anti-grammar troll? He recalled the graffiti on his shop – HERE SODOMY. Something unnatural about the syntax, something mere millimetres off...

"Daan's Dangerous Liaison!" Daan burst into the room with such energy, Mink jumped to her feet, her tail wagging. "*Nichts für dich*. You can't have any. Well, maybe some milk."

"Milk? We're having hot chocolate?" Adrian asked.

"No. My version of a Dangerous Liaison is Cointreau and chocolate milk with a dash of cinnamon. You will love it."

"Sounds revolting. Surely it will curdle?"

"Wait and see." He poured a healthy measure of Cointreau into two scratched glass tumblers, shook the bottle of chocolate milk and filled them to the brim. Then added a sprinkle of cinnamon.

"Taste it."

Adrian bent to take a sip. "That *is* nice. Dangerously innocent."

"Exactly. A Dangerous Liaison to send you to bed happy. *Prost!*"

"*Prost!*" The warmth of the orange liqueur permeated the silky sweetness of the milk and comforting spice. Adrian wondered why he'd never discovered this before.

Daan settled back with a smile. "Jochi introduced me to the idea of a Dangerous Liaison. It should have Kahlua and other ingredients but we adapted it to use what we had. We were camping in Zealand and this was the only luxurious thing we experienced in two weeks."

"You were in New Zealand?" Adrian asked.

"Old Zealand. We travelled all over Denmark and Germany trying to get laid. Then our first weekend in Sweden, we both lost our cherries. That country will always have a special place in my heart."

Adrian laughed at Daan's wistful expression. "Who's Jochi?"

"Joachim, Holger's brother! I showed you the photo. He must have told you about Joachim. Those two... I love them both like family. We were all born in the same year and they're the closest thing to brothers I ever had."

Mink sat up and stared into Daan's face. She dropped her nose but kept her eyes on him, as if she were looking over a pair of spectacles.

"*Was willst du*?" he said. He hauled himself out of the chair and poured a glug of milk into the dog's bowl. She waited till he had finished and began to drink.

"She's got you well trained," Adrian observed with a yawn.

Daan nodded. "It's the eyes. She hexes me and I have no choice but to obey." He topped up Adrian's glass. "One more Dangerous Liaison before bed. It will help us sleep. Yes, summers on Sylt were always Holger, Joachim and Daan the Dane. Every year we had a project, got in trouble, broke bones, made discoveries and grew up a little. My parents only saw me at bedtime. Right after breakfast, I cycled across to the Waldmann house." His face in the firelight radiated happy summer memories.

The Cointreau was working its magic. Laughter bubbled up from Adrian's stomach. A sleepy relaxation lulled him into an almost horizontal position on the sofa as he pictured the two blond boys and their dark Danish friend growing, experimenting and bonding. For the first time, he regretted being an only child.

"What does Joachim do for a living?"

"He's a master carpenter. Teaches apprentices how to make furniture. He and Holger have a way of encouraging people to learn. Holger with his instruments, Joachim with his furniture. It's funny if you think about it. All three of us grew up to work with wood."

"And their sister?"

"God knows." He laughed, throwing his head back. "Actually, God is the only one who does know. She's a bride of Christ."

"A what?"

"She took holy orders. That's why she won't accept Holger's

sexuality. It's against the scriptures so he must confess his sins, repent and be pardoned or cast out forever. I tell you, the language she uses, it's mediaeval."

Adrian sat up, all warmth and comfort draining from him. "Holy orders? You mean to tell me she's a..."

"Nun? Oh yes." His laughter died in his throat as he caught Adrian's expression. "Oh shit."

A gentle hand shook Beatrice's shoulder and she opened her eyes. An elderly woman pointed to the window. "Westerland. *Endstation*."

Beatrice jerked upright. The carriage was empty, her back was stiff and her eyes gummy. She'd slept through their arrival. Passengers had departed and had it not been for this kindly lady, she'd still be snoring.

"*Danke*," she said, gathered her things and scrambled to her feet. Holger would be long gone. All she could hope for was the cab driver would still be waiting. She stumbled onto the platform, still not fully awake and followed the sign for the taxi rank. As she turned the corner, yawning and cold, she collided with someone coming in the other direction. The impact knocked her sideways and she fell onto her side, dropping her handbag. Pain pulsed through her hip and elbow as a hand reached down to help her up.

"Beatrice?"

"Holger!"

He pulled her upright and retrieved her handbag, his expression both solicitous and surprised. The temperature drop after just waking up was cruel, so Beatrice brushed herself off and dragged her coat on, trying to gather her thoughts.

"What are you doing here?" he asked, handing over her bag.

"Protecting Adrian. And you?" Her tone was aggressive, partly because she'd been caught out, partly because she'd just woken up.

"The same." He shook his head. "No, not only that. I want to stop a person I love doing something stupid, but it's the same thing. We must get to Daan's place as soon as we can. The next bus isn't due for twenty minutes. That's why I came running back this way to see if there were any taxis."

"I booked one earlier but he might have given up on me."

Thankfully, the cab was still waiting and after Holger confirmed their destination, the driver took them off in the direction of the west coast.

Holger glanced at his watch. "We'll be there in half an hour."

"So will you please tell me what the hell is going on?"

His eyes rested on hers for a second then stared beyond her head, out into the freezing night.

"Holger? Talk to me. If you know anything about what's been happening to Adrian, you'd better tell me now."

"It is not me, Beatrice. I am not the person trying to scare him. I'm another victim. Earlier this year, I had a very similar experience. My way of dealing with it was to ignore it and hope it would go away. Not cowardice but a specific strategy. If these people get no reaction, they move on to the next target. This person is imbalanced and delusional, but not dangerous."

"You know who it is?"

"Yes. It's my sister."

Chapter 28

By the time Adrian had told Daan the whole story, from his first sighting of the nun opposite his shop to the crucifix wedged in the door, the fire had died to nothing and the chocolate milk was empty. Daan was horrified at the level of fear Adrian had undergone while he'd taken such a casual attitude.

"Shit, I'm sorry. I showed more concern for the dog. Holger said to keep an eye on you, that's all. No one told me what was going on."

Adrian shook his head, his gaze absorbed by the embers in the grate. "No one knew what was going on. I'm still not sure myself. If it's really Holger's sister and she's trying to frighten me off, how does she know so much? My shop, my flat, my mobile number. How did she know I was here? Who's helping her?"

The room fell silent as both men considered the implications.

Daan spoke. "At least we know she's not dangerous. Patti is sly and sneaky and very good at mind games. But the worst she can do is make you afraid. Tomorrow we'll report her to the police and make her stop this bullshit."

Adrian closed his eyes and took a huge breath, exhaling with immense weariness. "The funny thing is, for an inveterate drama queen, this is not my style. Ask Beatrice. I hate being tense and freaked out and nervy. All I want is to go home to my own little rat run, drink good wine, cook lovely food and sleep with gorgeous men. I don't judge other people's choices. Well, apart from clothes, soft furnishings and tastes in music. Whoever she is and whatever her beliefs, she has no right to judge me. Seriously, I am sick and tired of being scared."

Daan heaved himself across the sofa, looped an arm around

Adrian's shoulders and pulled him into a sideways hug. His beard bristled against Adrian's temple.

"I'm giving you the night off. Tonight, you will not be scared. I was going to make up a bed for you on the couch, but I changed my mind. You will sleep in with me and Mink. With me and her either side, you'll be safe as houses. Apart from the farts and the snoring, it'll be the best night's sleep you ever had."

Adrian relaxed into laughter and Mink wedged her nose between them, eager for her share of affection.

After they cleared up the kitchen, Daan locked the doors while Adrian got ready for bed. The wind rattling at the bathroom windows didn't bother him as he cleaned his teeth, so mellow did he feel. His face in the mirror looked a bit more than mellow, if he was being honest. Certainly soft around the edges, thanks to the Cointreau. In the living-room, Daan clattered around raking the ashes of the fire, locking the doors and speaking unintelligible words to Mink. The bedroom was cold in comparison to the fireside sofa, so Adrian dived under the layers: a duvet, a pleated quilt and a sheepskin. He curled up to fend off the chills, wishing he'd kept his socks on as well as his T-shirt and boxers. The bottom edge of the bed bounced and Mink landed beside his feet. She circled the same spot a few times, scratching the sheepskin into shape before settling with a heavy sigh on Adrian's feet. He smiled at her but the blue eyes had closed.

Daan yawned and scratched himself as he emerged from the bathroom. "Be warned. She sleeps down there for about half an hour, then she gets cold and comes up here to get as close as she can and shares my pillow. If you wake up and find you can't move, you've been Minked." He got into bed and switched off the lamp.

"She's the best hot water bottle ever. Goodnight Daan. And thanks for everything."

"Sleep well. We've got a busy day tomorrow. Goodnight."

The taxi rolled along the coast road, its headlights swooping across the dunes, reminding Beatrice of Ingmar Bergman landscapes.

"I don't understand. Why on earth is your sister terrorising Adrian? And how long have you known about it?"

"I suspected that evening after the zoo. When he told us the details of what was happening, too many elements pointed to her. She joined a convent years ago and has very strong views on sin. In her weird way of looking at the world, Adrian is to blame for my sexuality. When I told my family, she did the same kind of thing to me. Sending me leaflets about the church's view on homosexuality, offering to pray for me, asking me to repent, generally freaking me out. Then I found out she was in Hamburg. You see, I have a wall in my studio where I pin pictures, photos and so on."

Beatrice said nothing, glad of the darkness to hide her blush.

"After a while, I noticed certain things were going missing. Usually postcards from Adrian. Or pictures of the two of us together. I kept replacing them, they kept disappearing. She can be very determined."

"Why didn't you tell him?"

"I had to speak to her first. To be sure. That's why I suggested Adrian get out of the line of fire while I dealt with her. Unfortunately, when I went to the convent, they told me she'd been asked to leave over two months ago. Her behaviour, they said, was not suited to a place of prayer and contemplation. I had no idea where she was, so I contacted her via her blog."

"She has a blog?"

"Her withdrawal from the secular world did not include the virtual. She used to run the convent's website until she became too extreme. Now she posts weekly updates or rants against every aspect of modern life. I sent her an email asking her to leave Adrian alone and explaining he did not 'turn me gay'. I told her she could spend the rest of her life chasing away any man that came near me, but it wouldn't change who I am." He slipped a hand into his padded jacket and pulled out a folded sheet of paper. "Today, I got a reply."

"And?"

"It's in German so I'll paraphrase. She accuses me of unnatural sins and offers me redemption. If I renounce evil and embrace Christ, I can be forgiven. But for the devil that turned me from the path of righteousness, there can be nothing but destruction. He must burn in hell forever."

"Good Lord. What kind of woman is she?"

Holger gave a helpless shrug. "I don't really know her any more. Even before I came out, we didn't get along. My brother and I were closer to Daan than to her. Then when she got obsessed with the church, it got worse. I don't have a problem with religion, unless she tries to pressure me to 'find Jesus' and 'save myself from earthly torment.' I cannot have that kind of conversation."

"Rhetoric of drama. Extremists love it," Beatrice huffed.

Holger looked at his watch again. "She's certainly an extremist. I feel many things for my sister: pity, incomprehension, sadness and even occasionally, loss. But before now, I never felt fear."

"You think it was her at the house on Thursday night?"

Holger gave her a level look. "It was someone with a key, who removed family photos and replaced them with a crucifix. I checked all the security camera footage. No sign of her, or anyone else. But she knows that system better than all of us, because she was the one who had it installed. We used to call her Paranoid Patti."

"When was the last time she was at the house?" asked Beatrice.

"In November, I think. I didn't know she used it any more. My grandparents say she has never asked their permission, but a neighbour saw her last month. She must have stayed up there when she got kicked out of the convent. She has a key. We all do."

"Holger, if you think she's dangerous, perhaps we should call the local police. Do you really think she is capable of doing more than scaring people? Would she hurt you?" She reached for her phone.

"I don't think so. But she's still here, on Sylt, watching." He lifted the paper in his hand. "She rages at me for allowing 'that pervert' into our grandparents' house and talks about purging the place of his sin. What worries me is that she must have seen Adrian with Daan."

Beatrice snapped her head round to stare at him. "She hates Daan too?"

"No, that's the problem." Holger exhaled and shook his head. "He was her first love. But he couldn't stand her. We were all young and stupid, thoughtless teenagers. Patti took rejection badly and became very bitter. That's why I came back to talk to them. I don't want to alarm anyone, but they need to be aware that she's here. She's irrational and angry and I just don't know how her mind works. I have no idea what she's planning to do." His eyes were as bleak as the coastline.

"Holger, I'm sorry, but I would feel better if you called the police."

Beatrice saw defeat in the angle of his head. "All right. We can't handle this on our own."

She squeezed his shoulder and handed him her phone.

The bed was bouncing. Not like an earthquake kind of judder, more an irregular bumping as if someone was trying to heave it over. Adrian opened his eyes and tried to shake off sleep. Something feathery brushed his face in the darkness. He flinched. A muffled grunt to his right reacted to the next bounce. All he could make out was a weight on the bed and a strange snuffling. His breath quickened.

"Daan?"

The sounds stopped, the mattress beside him sank and something cold and moist touched his face. He squealed and brought up a hand to defend himself. A familiar shove pushed into his palm. Mink's muzzle. She prodded again, less playfully, and Adrian protested. Then she barked, right in his ear.

He inhaled sharply in fright. That was when he smelt it.

Gas.

He wrestled his way out of the covers and shook Daan. It was like rousing a black bear. Mink leapt to the floor, her claws clattering on the wood.

"Daan! Daan! Come on!" The smell was stronger now he was upright.

"DAAN! Wake up now!"

"*Was ist?*"

Adrian sensed him turn and roll towards the lamp. "NO! I can smell gas. Do not turn on the light! We have to get out. Please move!"

The bed seemed to heave upwards as Daan sat up.

"*Scheisse!* Out the back door. Mink, *wo bist du*? Grab a blanket, let's go."

They fumbled out of the bedroom and into the passage, where enough faint moonlight shone to indicate the door. The smell was thick and noxious. Mink whined and scratched until Daan found the key. Adrian's panic rose as the fumes filled his nose. He couldn't remember if you should get lower or higher with gas. His shoulder brushed against a rail of jackets and he scooped up an armful, his head beginning to throb.

Mink whipped her way through the door before it was fully ajar. Adrian and Daan ran after her, leaving the door wide open, and raced over coarse grass and shingle until they stumbled down the beach side of a dune. Panting and shaking, they collapsed into the sand. The heat of exertion and adrenalin in an outside temperature of minus seven degrees evaporated faster than it took for their breathing to return to normal. Without speaking, they shared out the coats, wearing some, sitting on others. Daan searched the pockets of each garment while Adrian lured Mink closer by patting a spot next to him. She gave in, but sat bolt upright, still tense.

"Are you OK?" Daan asked.

"Yeah. Shaken. You?"

Daan sat back. "One hell of a headache."

"What do we do now?"

"Get away from the house, keep warm, call for help. We have no phones or shoes. That's bad. But we have winter coats and I found a torch, gloves, a couple of lighters, a bunch of tissues and some chocolate."

"Should we go up to the road and flag down a passing car?"

"There's no traffic at this time of night and the nearest neighbours are around two kilometres away. The quickest way to get help is the radio on the boat."

"How are we going to get out there? You don't seriously want us to get in the sea?"

"Not us, just me. I don't want to either, but I have no choice as the dinghy is back at the house. It's too dangerous for you and Mink. I can't look after you two as well as wade out there in bare feet. You stay on the beach and light a fire. Not here, we're still too close. Let's move."

Adrian's feet were stiff with cold. He scrambled upright and gathered the coats, with a glance back at the top of the dune.

"Adrian, come on! The house could blow at any second with the amount of gas in there. The only reason it hasn't gone up yet is because we left the back door open. As soon as the generator kicks in or any other thing sparks, it's toast. I have no idea how far a gas explosion will throw debris. We must get farther away. Mink! *Fuss!*"

He snapped his fingers and Mink trotted to his heel, her tail tucked between her legs. The three trudged down the beach, each cowed against the fear of what was behind them.

The taxi driver was unhappy about the pot-holed track so dropped them at the top of the lane. Cold pierced Beatrice's coat the minute she exited the warm interior of the cab. Her mother's voice returned. *If you don't take it off indoors, you won't feel the benefit.* She surveyed their semi-visible surroundings. The moon played searchlight tricks, offering teasing glimpses of the landscape before clouds concealed everything like a magician's cloak.

Daan's boatyard bore no advertising, not even a sign, just a rough track leading to a hollow. You couldn't even see the house from the road. The red tail-lights of the taxi faded into the distance and Beatrice switched on her Maglite. She crunched across the stony, pot-holed ground beside Holger, illuminating the path ahead in steady sweeps. Despite his confident step down the track, Holger maintained a tense silence.

In a break between the clouds, the house hove into view along with a scrubby yard rather than a garden. A large shape to the right seemed to be a breeze-block garage, although Daan's Jeep was parked right in front of the house. The wind lashed Beatrice's face, whipping strands of hair into her eyes and strafing her skin. With a grudging sense of relief, she saw that up ahead wooden steps facilitated access on foot. Rough, mismatched planks, but infinitely preferable to the pitted track.

She glanced upwards to see the cloudbank moving north, taking the wind with it to leave a starlit sky and the promise of frost. The moon added an eerie wash to the spotlight of her torch.

Down in the hollow, not a single window was lit in Daan's squat shack. If they weren't home, where were they? It was barely midnight. As they started down the steps, Holger placed a hand on her arm. He pointed. Away to the right, far down the beach near the sea, a small fire was burning.

"There they are!" Holger's smile was audible. "I bet they're drinking beer on the beach. In December! Poor Adrian. This is a typical Daan rite of passage." He cupped his hands to his mouth and yelled. "HAAALLLOOOO!"

Bitter cold, exhaustion, stupidly dangerous male rituals and the downright foolhardy nature of the entire enterprise blew a fuse in Beatrice's patience.

"Holger, don't be ridiculous! They won't hear you from this distance. I'll call Adrian's mobile. Can we get in the house?"

Holger seemed oblivious to her sharp tone. "Sure. I know where he keeps a spare key. But I'm not sure your mobile will work down there. Daan always has problems with the signal at his place."

"Fine, I'll try from up here or flash the torch to attract their attention."

"Yes and I'll go inside and use the house phone." His boots sounded solid on the wood as he followed the steps towards the house.

She yelled after him. "Put the kettle on!"

He gave her the thumbs up.

The cold bit at her fingers as soon as she took off her gloves. She wedged the torch under her arm to reach for her phone and pushed her damp hair from her face. The Maglite beam shone against the back of Daan's garage. In the pool of light was a disembodied female face, staring back at her with saucer eyes. Beatrice jolted in fright and the torch fell to the ground. She scrabbled to pick it up and directed it back at the same spot, her breath short. A black-clad figure raced out from the shadow of the garage away from her and towards the house. An unearthly scream ripped through the air, sending a primal shiver through her scalp and spine. She froze and heard a thud, a scuffle and a peculiar hiss. She swept her light across the hollow below but the vehicle obscured her view. She hurried down the steps, her skin prickling with fear, crept along the wall of the garage and listened.

"Holger?"

The next second, an almighty bang followed by a white blast punched her backwards, lifting her off her feet and slamming her onto the ground. Her torch somersaulted off into the sky. All the air left her chest and around her there was nothing but silence. Seconds passed before she managed to haul in a breath. She curled instinctively into a ball, her lungs heaving, her nostrils full of singeing heat and the stench of burning hair. Liquid ran into her eyes and beyond the echoing ring in her ears, she heard the crackle and spit of flames.

Chapter 29

The fire was starting to take. Adrian pushed another piece of driftwood into the pile and leaned forward to feel the warmth. Mink's attention remained on the sea, at the precise spot where Daan had gone into the waves. She had sat and stayed, as per his instructions, but didn't take her eyes off the huge black bear of a man as he waded out, swearing at the freezing water. For the hundredth time, Adrian switched his gaze between three points. The boat; still no lights. The house; dark and silent. The fire; damp wood burning and giving off more a sense of comfort than actual heat. He stood, straining his eyes for any hint of Daan, but the shifting midnight ocean camouflaged him perfectly.

He glanced back at the house and did an immediate double take. A shaft of light was coming down the track. He checked out to sea, where the boat bobbed on the tide, its cabin still unlit. Had Daan managed to radio for help already? The moon came out, turning the beach grey and shedding enough light for Adrian to pick out two figures making their way down to Daan's house. They stopped and Adrian caught a noise, as if someone had yelled. For the first time, Mink's ears twitched and she looked back up over the dunes, a low growl in her throat.

"Stay, Mink. Sit."

Whoever it was, they shouldn't go any closer to the house. Adrian waved his arms, feeling futile and helpless. He put two fingers in his mouth and whistled. Pathetic. The torch wobbled about and one figure moved out of sight. They must have heard him! One of them was coming down to the beach. Adrian looked out at the boat and with a wash of relief saw the cabin lights on. He couldn't see Daan at this distance but knew he must have made it.

"He's safe, Mink! Help is on the way." He selected a few more sticks and was just dropping them on the fire when a horrible screech reached his ears. His whole body seemed to drop several degrees in temperature. He reassured himself. It was an owl. A seagull. Some kind of predator killing a rodent. Then he saw Mink's ears flat against her head, her hackles in spiky ridges along her back, staring up at the house and his mouth went dry.

At that moment, the night exploded. A shocking boom echoed across the beach and a ball of flame erupted above the dunes. A wave of heat washed over him and strange splatting sounds began hitting the sand. He grabbed Mink's collar and they ran, away from the shower of objects and into the sea. The icy water was brutal but Adrian pulled Mink further until he was thigh-deep in the sea and she was swimming. He stopped, clutching the dog to his chest as her feet kept paddling. While missiles hissed into the shallower water, his focus was on the fire blazing above the dunes. He waited till he could hear no more falling debris and carried Mink back onto the beach, his teeth chattering and legs numb. She shook herself, spattering him with wet drops he could barely feel. Adrian peered out at the boat. Still no sign of Daan but the boat's headlights came on, adding to the illumination of the beach. He could stand it no longer.

"Mink, come with me. *Fuss!*" He turned to the dunes and broke into a run.

Adrenalin and nerves charged his veins as he approached the scene and the cold no longer seemed to matter. He pushed up the sandy bank in the direction of the garage, Mink hard on his heels. Close up, the damage was shocking. Over half the house had gone. The back section, where he'd been asleep less than an hour ago, was still standing, but judging by the ferocity of the fire, it wouldn't be for long. He recalled Daan's voice. '*You sleep with me and Mink... you'll be safe as houses.*'

Thick black clouds of smoke rolled inland and the Jeep lay on its side, its windows blown out. He kept away from the heat, creeping around the back of the garage, his hand on Mink's collar. A series of small explosions stopped him in his tracks and he heard the sound of broken glass shattering. Mink balked, so he gave her a reassuring stroke. But she stiffened and sniffed, the tension in her body tangible. Adrian's own hairs rose. There was something there, lying on the ground.

It moved and Mink leapt backwards like a spooked cat. Whatever it was let out an odd moan, like an elderly person does when getting to their feet. Not agony, but discomfort. Adrian despaired, faced with the idea of administering first aid, in German, in pitch darkness while trying to control an unnerved dog.

"Umm, hello? *Guten Tag*? Are you OK?"

"Adrian?"

He started in disbelief and reached out a tentative hand. "Beatrice? What in the name of... ?" He touched something warm and heard her suck in air through her teeth.

"Sorry, sorry. Are you hurt?"

"Adrian, listen to me. Holger's down there. Much nearer to the house. Call emergency services. Don't you go any closer."

"I don't have my phone, but Daan's radioing for help. Are you hurt?"

She shifted and drew a ragged breath.

"Beatrice! What is it?"

"Phone... my jacket. Help him! Help Holger!"

Her voice cracked in desperation. Adrian ran his hands along her coat and located a lump in her pocket. He'd just withdrawn the device when he sensed Mink bound away, back down the beach. Out of the shadow of the garage, moonlight shone on the figure of Daan, powering up the dune, wearing a wetsuit. Sirens grew louder, overcoming the noise of the burning house and Adrian watched five vehicles approach.

"They're already here, Beatrice."

She didn't respond.

"Beatrice, talk to me." His cold hands fumbled for hers, trying to find her pulse. A fire engine came down the track, its headlights penetrating the shadows. Adrian gasped when he saw Beatrice's face. Her eyes were closed and a tributary pattern spread from her forehead, like Leigh Bowery face paint. Except this was not makeup.

Chapter 30

The Westerland Klinik, quiet during the winter, was having an unexpectedly busy night. Adrian received a full check-up and a cup of coffee. The nurse answered all his questions with great patience. Beatrice was still in surgery. No, she couldn't say how long it would take. Daan was fine and waiting for him in reception. She had no information on Holger, because he was not being treated at this hospital.

When Adrian was given the all-clear, he returned to reception to find Daan. But the only person in the waiting area was Herr Rieder, the same police officer who had come to the Waldmann house. He stood up.

"Hello again, Mr Harvey. Is everything in order?"

"I'm fine, apart from being worried sick about the others. Where's Daan?"

"He's at the police station, helping Herr Weiss understand what happened. He's the detective in charge and he would like to talk to you too."

"First I need to make sure Beatrice is OK. I want to wait till she's out of theatre. Do you know where they've taken Holger? He's not being treated here, they said."

Herr Rieder dropped his eyes. "Herr Weiss can give you more information. I can tell you the dog is also at the police station."

Adrian gripped his arm. "Please tell me. Is Holger...?" The word stuck in his throat. He swallowed.

"Two people were airlifted to Hamburg with severe injuries. I have no further updates, but if you come to the station, they can tell you more."

A headache loomed with the remorseless progress of a

steamroller. Tension, exhaustion and the knowledge that things were far from over made him want to cry. He closed his eyes, imagined lying down on a cream-coloured sofa, covering his head with a pillow and just drifting off on a cloud of cinnamon.

"Mr Harvey?" A doctor approached, with overnight beard growth and a white coat over jeans and trainers. "You're waiting for news of Ms Stubbs?"

Adrian jerked to his feet. "Yes! Is she OK?"

"It seems so. She suffered a fractured bone in her forearm, which required setting. There are several skull contusions resulting in concussion. In addition, various abrasions and some bruising. We'll monitor her over the next few hours and do further tests. But my opinion is that with care and rest, she will make a good recovery." He looked at his watch. "Come back this afternoon and you will have the possibility to see her."

Adrian thanked him and drew on the last reserves of his energy to accompany Herr Rieder to the police station. At least this time he was not under suspicion.

Morning broke, sunlight forcing its way into the interview room. An officer brought a new pot of coffee, more bottles of water and this time, warm breakfast rolls. Daan immediately tore into one and asked for some butter. A sour caffeine bitterness in Adrian's stomach made him refuse until the smell of fresh bread proved irresistible.

Once the separate interview sessions had been completed, the atmosphere was collegial and workmanlike. Somehow, the normality of morning took the edge off the weary piecing together of events. Although the two detectives and Rieder joined in with the impromptu breakfast, the questions kept coming. The same questions already answered, alone in other rooms. What time was it when they left the house? How long did it take Daan to get to the boat? How many people could Adrian see coming down the track? Who had a key to Daan's house? Where is the gas tank? How is it possible the emergency call was made before the house blew up?

Adrian and Daan answered all the questions again, only foundering when it came to the whys.

Why would Beatrice Stubbs and Holger Waldmann travel to Daan's house at midnight without warning them of their arrival? Why was Patricia Waldmann at the scene? Why would anyone want to poison them with carbon monoxide? Why had she attacked her own brother? Why had the house exploded?

They didn't know.

After the long lonely silence of the night, the station had woken up. Three times, an officer knocked at the door with a message for one or the other detectives. Each time, Adrian held his breath, willing it to be news of Holger. Eventually, it was.

Herr Rieder showed the message to the two detectives, both of whom scanned the words with impassive expressions. Then he cleared his throat.

"I'm sorry to say it is bad news."

Daan gripped Adrian's hand but kept his focus on the police officer.

"Patricia Waldmann was pronounced dead at six-twenty this morning. Internal injuries caused a fatal haemorrhage."

"What about Holger?" Adrian asked, his voice constricted and high-pitched.

Rieder glanced back at the printout. "Holger Waldmann – third degree burns on 10% of his body. Condition stable. Next of kin notified."

Daan shoved back his chair and got to his feet. "We must go. We've done all we can here. Please bring me my dog. We're leaving."

Adrian couldn't leave Beatrice, Daan couldn't leave Mink. So they compromised. Daan left for Hamburg while Adrian stayed the night in the hospital's accommodation for relatives, sharing a narrow single bed with the flatulent husky. Other than walking the dog, he spent his time at Beatrice's bedside, arguing.

In spite of the stitches down her forehead, half her head obscured by a bandage and her arm in a cast, her stubborn defiance did not waver. She refused to let him talk to Matthew.

"If I was him, I'd want to know," Adrian insisted.

"No. He can't do anything from Devon and God knows I don't want him travelling all the way up here. I'm fine. I'll be out tomorrow or the next day. This looks worse than it is."

"Well, it looks terrible."

"Thank you. Adrian, please let me deal with this my way. I promise I'll talk to Matthew. But I'm going to play this down and you may not contradict me, do you hear? Go and visit Holger then get back to London. Once they've done the scan, I'll follow you. I want to see Holger myself and apologise in person."

"Me too."

Daan returned on Monday afternoon with positive news about Holger's condition and they switched places. Adrian prepared to depart for Hamburg, leaving Daan in charge of his obstreperous neighbour who insisted on getting out of bed and trundling around the hospital at every opportunity.

It was a strange farewell. In such a short time, this huge hairy man and his beautiful dog had become his close friends. On the station platform, he dug his fingers into the thick ruff of hair around Mink's neck and scratched. She leaned into him, her back leg kicking. With one last stroke of her muzzle and a look into her trusting china blue eyes, he said goodbye.

Daan had obviously spotted the welling tears and saved them both embarrassment by opening his arms for a hug.

"Come back in the summer. We're going to rebuild the house. Me, Holger and Joachim. Another pair of hands would be very welcome. Plus I never did give you the island tour."

"I will. I don't need asking twice. In fact, I'm already looking forward to it."

Daan released him and looked down at Mink. "She's going to miss you. So am I. Look after yourself, OK?"

"You too. Take care of Beatrice for me."

"Don't worry, you can trust me. See you in the summer! And Adrian?"

"What?"

"When you come back, can you bring me a Cornish pasty?"

As the train pulled away, Adrian strained to catch the very last glimpse of the hairy pair on the platform. Daan was still waving.

Chapter 31

How to look hot when seeing the most handsome man in the world? Head partially shaved with cumbersome bandage, stitches down forehead, left arm in sling and burnt-off eyelashes. In the grand cinematic tradition, set in the monochrome romance of a German railway station, Beatrice imagined Clark Gable meeting the Bride of Frankenstein.

Unlike all the other passengers on the train, Jan Stein didn't flinch when he saw her. He was waiting at the end of the platform, looking chiselled and elegant in a long grey coat. When he spotted her, he smiled and came to take her suitcase. He didn't even attempt a greeting over the constant noise of the Hauptbahnhof and simply guided her outside to his car. Once the door closed, he turned to look at her, his stare unreadable.

"Last time we spoke, you asked me to call you Beatrice Bloody Fool. Then you left for Sylt, alone and without back-up, to walk straight into a life-threatening situation which left one person dead and another seriously injured. Every single judgement call you made earns you the name Beatrice Bloody Fool ten times over."

Beatrice lay back against the headrest, too tired even for sarcasm. "You're right and I'm sorry. You can call me all the names you want and I'll accept every one. Thank you for meeting me."

"You're welcome. How's your head?"

She touched her bandage. "Bit of a mess."

"Inside or out?"

"Both. Can I go and see Holger now?"

He drove through the city with no questions, no probing glances, no more comments on her behaviour. The silence acted as an unguent, soothing and healing.

She was the first to speak. "I don't suppose there's any news of the art collector?"

Stein gave her a sideways smile.

"There is?"

"Yes, there is. Tomas never gives up. Dutch police analysed all the communications logged by the art theft 'agency'. The collector was using various re-routing IP addresses to hide his tracks. One was in St Petersburg, and another in Amsterdam."

Beatrice snapped her head up and wished she hadn't. "De Vries!"

"You're spoiling my story. Tomas remembered what you said in your report about de Vries and his business interests in Russia. He passed the information on to Meyer. This time, Meyer took him seriously. The BKA followed up that line of enquiry and Dutch intelligence forces made an arrest early this morning. Geert de Vries is an art dealer in more ways than one. He has a private gallery filled with stolen artwork on his country estate in Amersfoort. Some but not all of the paintings have been recovered."

"What an absolute swine! Getting his own paintings stolen, claiming insurance and then selfishly depriving anyone else of the pleasure. His greed beggars belief. Will the Köbels get their picture back?"

"I don't know yet. I have no information on which paintings they seized. But I hope so."

"So do I." Beatrice wondered if that sweet woman's blank face might react to seeing her favourite picture again.

Stein continued. "Not only that, but Waring has agreed to a plea bargain and given a full statement, implicating seven other high-profile businessmen in arranging to have their own artworks stolen. It seems we lifted the lid on an international operation. Red faces from here to Washington."

"But bloody Waring weasels his way out of a jail sentence by squealing on everyone else?"

"He'll serve a few months, I expect. Somewhere comfortable."

Beatrice snorted and looked out at the city streets, the sparkling shop windows, Christmas lights and shoppers. For the first time since her arrival, she missed the familiarity of London, of Matthew, even of Hamilton.

She spoke. "Human nature still surprises me."

"Me too. Which is why we need people like Tomas, Margrit and Rudi. They still have a lust for justice."

Beatrice studied his fixed expression and accepted the confidence without question. She thought of DS Pearce and his intellect, Dawn and her sympathy, Ranga and his open mind, all battling the endless effluent of London's underground.

As if reading her mind, Stein spoke. "I booked you on the 16.40 flight to London City. I can take you to the airport when you've finished at the hospital."

"That's kind of you. But a detective has better things to do with his time than ferry me around. I'll call a cab when I'm ready."

He didn't speak for several minutes. "Do you want to tell me what happened at Daan's house, or would you rather not talk about it?"

"We don't have the whole story yet," she sighed. "Current theory is Patricia Waldmann got into the house via Daan's not-so-secret key and switched on the gas rings in the kitchen while Adrian and Daan were asleep. Whether she intended to cause carbon monoxide poisoning or create an explosion, we don't know. The dog woke them and they got out the back door. They ran down to the beach and Daan called the emergency services from his boat. A taxi dropped Holger and me at the end of the lane and we saw a fire on the beach. We assumed it was them and I stopped at the top of the steps to call Adrian. I sent..." she clenched her teeth and swallowed. "I sent Holger down to the house. Patricia was hiding behind the garage. I actually saw her face. Frightened the life out of me. Then she attacked Holger. The gas ignited and the house exploded, burning Holger, injuring me and killing Patricia."

Stein shook his head. "Why did she want to kill Daan and Adrian?"

Beatrice sighed more deeply. "God only knows."

The Mercedes finally peeled out of the traffic and into the hospital drive. Stein reversed into a parking bay and switched off the engine. "I'm happy to wait. I'd like to make sure..."

"... I leave the country? I promise I'll go this time. Thank you, really, but a taxi will be fine."

He came round to open her door and helped her heave herself gracelessly out. She extended her right hand.

"Thank you. For everything."

He took her hand and reached for her shoulder, his fingers squeezing gently yet with a particular pressure. "Please take good care of yourself, Beatrice. We need to keep you." Leaning closer, he brushed his lips against both her cheeks. "Goodbye. Or better, *Auf Wiedersehen*. Till we see each other again?"

He held her gaze and the magnetic pull of those eyes might have drawn her closer, had she not caught sight of her reflection in the glass doors of the hospital behind him.

"Yes, *Auf Wiedersehen* sounds about right." She dragged herself and her suitcase away.

She'd expected worse. A tent lay over Holger's legs and gauze bandages covered the lower parts of his arms. Tubes snaked under the sheets and he appeared to be hooked up to an extraordinary number of monitors. One ear and the left side of his face looked raw and painful but his eyes and smile were as genuine as ever.

She couldn't speak at first, pressing her fingers to her mouth, holding back tears which were both inconvenient and painful.

"I want to hug you," she said. "But I can't see a safe place to touch."

His voice was hoarse and breathless. "There isn't one. Virtual hug?" Holger raised his arms and shoulders a few millimetres but she could see it cost him considerable effort.

She embraced the air in front of her. "I can't tell you how relieved I am to see you. We were all so worried."

He indicated his throat and pointed to a thin tablet computer on a side table. She passed it to him and watched him use one finger to type. When he'd finished, he turned the screen to her.

The specialist says I will be fine. It is going to take some time and I don't want to think about what I would do without morphine. My worst fear was that I had permanently damaged my hands, which is not the case. There will be some scar tissue but I will be able to use them and that is the important thing. What about you?

Beatrice sat on the visitor's chair and pointed to her bandage. "Fifteen stitches and a fractured ulna, plus a few other bangs and scrapes. Good news is it gets me off work for a week. I should have been back in the office this morning."

He typed some more, his eyes reddening.

Beatrice, I am so sorry. I want to apologise to you, Adrian and Daan for this whole stupid, ugly mess.

"This mess is not your fault. You can't blame yourself. Your sister is not your responsibility. For her own twisted reasons she wanted to destroy you all, so she alone bears the guilt."

He shook his head and spoke. "She tried to save me."

"Holger, she attacked you!"

He shook his head again and typed. In a way she was glad of the enforced wait for a reply. It gave her time to control her temper.

No. She stopped me from going into the house. When she screamed, I turned around. She was dressed in black so all I saw was a white face coming at me. I stepped backwards and fell over. She helped me up and pushed me behind the Jeep. All the time she was hissing at me to get away. When the blast came, her body took most of the impact. That's why I'm still here and she is not.

Beatrice chose not to argue. Painkillers could do funny things to the brain and even if the woman was an attempted murderer, she was still his sister. Her own speech, apologising for mistrusting him, now seemed surplus to requirements.

"You've seen Daan and Adrian, I gather? How was that?"

Half his face smiled.

Emotional! My family visited too. They said Daan and Mink should live in our place on Sylt over the winter. After I get out of hospital, I am going there to recover. My brother and I are going to help Daan build a new house, in spring, when the weather improves. Adrian plans to take a holiday and join us. I think the four of us could make a good team.

He'd added a smiley at the end. Beatrice touched a finger to his unburnt cheek, the only gesture of affection which would not cause him pain.

"Four men and a dog. Sounds wonderful. Will you invite me to the house-warming? Sorry, poor choice of phrase. How about a Phoenix Party?"

He lifted a hand in a gesture of triumph and rasped, "You can be Guest of Honour."

Chapter 32

The taxi driver who took her the final leg of the journey, from London City Airport home to Boot Street, was a wellspring of advice. The best thing for bruising was to drink pineapple juice. He should know. Twice he'd been beaten up while working nights and the last time, he tried pineapple juice. Bruises faded almost overnight. Like a charm. Beatrice should try it. She promised she would.

As she paid him and waited for her receipt, she noticed with surprise and disappointment Adrian's windows were unlit. He'd sent her a text last night to assure her of his safe arrival, so there was no call for alarm, but she'd been looking forward to a debrief and a hot dinner. He was probably still catching up at the shop. It was not yet seven o'clock. She asked the driver to leave her case in the hallway, exhausted at the thought of trying to heave it upstairs one-handed. She tipped him and trudged up to her flat.

Bless Adrian. He'd collected all her post, put the heating on and watered the plants. She opened the fridge. And to crown it all, he'd bought milk. She made a cup of tea and sat back on the sofa, savouring the sense of peace and sanctuary. Her head and neck throbbed so she lifted the weight of the sling from her shoulders and rested her cast in her lap. Just for this evening, she would ignore the pile of letters, overlook the blinking light on the answer phone and forget her promise to Dawn to phone as soon as she got home. All of it could wait till tomorrow.

Everything except Matthew. She reached for the landline, grateful it was not her right arm in plaster, about to press speed dial 1.

From the dining-table, her mobile rang. *Great minds think alike.* She got to her feet in anticipation, but the caller display showed Rangarajan Jalan. She answered.

"Hello, Ranga."

"Beatrice, I heard about your accident. How are you?"

"Could be worse. Bashed about a bit and totally shattered but glad to be home in my own flat."

"You're home already? I wasn't sure if you were fit to travel. Did your neighbour come home with you?"

"Adrian flew back yesterday."

"I mean is he with you now? Is someone there to take care of you?"

"No, but I'm fine, Ranga, really. I'm relieved to be alone and enjoying my own company."

There was a pause. "The reason for my concern is that I have some bad news and despite the awkward timing, I wanted to let you know personally."

"What do you mean, bad news?" Beatrice's mind seemed to seize up entirely, incapable of even fearing the worst.

"Superintendent Hamilton passed away this weekend."

She sat down with a thump, jolting her arm. "Hamilton is dead?"

"A terrible shock for us all, I know."

"He told me he was seriously ill, but I had no idea it would be so soon."

"None of us did, except for him. Beatrice, he chose the timing. Hamilton ended his life at a clinic in Switzerland on Friday."

Beatrice's skin cooled. "Friday? So he came to say goodbye," she whispered.

"Sorry?"

Tears stung her eyes and her face grew hot and swollen. "He came to Hamburg on Thursday. We had dinner. He told me about his illness and mentioned taking some time out. I assumed it was a holiday."

"Beatrice, are you sure you're OK?"

She swallowed. "I should have realised. It's classic Hamilton, controlling to the last. Literally." Her voice lacked any bass tones.

"Everyone said the same thing. Myself included. I only wish he'd given us the opportunity to say goodbye. At least to say thank you. But you're right, this is classic Hamilton. As always, he did things his own way."

She sniffed and dug in her pocket for a tissue. "What happens now?"

"Chief Super asked me to act up over Christmas and the board will make some decisions in January. Beatrice?"

"What?"

"Both our names are on the table as replacements. Can we talk about it, just between us, before the end of the year?"

She held the receiver away while she blew her nose.

"Of course. I think that's best. Thing is, I'll be in Devon over the Christmas holidays but let's ring-fence a breakfast meeting on the first Monday back to work."

"Perfect. Thank you. Listen, I don't know when you plan to leave for Devon, but there's a memorial service for Hamilton on Friday. Eleven o'clock. Sharp."

She released a snort of tearful laughter at Ranga's use of Hamilton-speak. "I'll be there. Thanks for letting me know, Ranga. Goodnight."

The desire for solitude instantly transformed itself into the opposite. Beatrice became a communicator. She made a series of calls.

Reassuring Matthew she was well.

"*Ready whenever you are and already steeling myself. Worse or better than the incident in Vitoria?*"

"Worse, I'm afraid. Fractured ulna. You'll have to peel all the parsnips."

"*So long as you are here with me and supervising the Christmas pud, I'm sure we'll muddle along. I miss you, Old Thing.*"

Exchanging shocked exclamations with Dawn.

"*Nope, not a bloody clue. Board must have known as he'd helped them choose a successor. Cooper's talking about organising a wreath from the whole team – want to contribute?*"

"Of course I do. I'm officially on sick leave, but can we have lunch on Wednesday?"

"*Deffo. I want to see your bruises. Can you drink wine?*"

Checking on Adrian's whereabouts.

"*Happy Hour somewhere on Dean Street. You will not believe who's at the bar right now ordering me a cocktail!*"

"You're on a date?"

"*Hell yeah! Detective Sergeant Quinn! The one who interviewed me after the allegations. He popped into the shop this morning to ask me out! Looks like my luck is changing! God, I so love the police.*"

She launched into her emails, tackling everything urgent and ditching the rest.

After more tea and a painkiller, she ran a bath. In an uncomfortable position, shower cap protecting her head wound, the cast resting on the soap shelf in the steam, grazes stinging in the warm water, she recalled every conversation she'd ever had with Hamilton, including the last one. She closed her eyes and bid him goodbye. Salty moisture – sweat or tears, she wasn't sure – slipped past her bruises into the bathwater and dissolved.

At ten to ten, she got into her pyjamas, made herself a hot chocolate and switched on the TV, ready to watch the news. While waiting for Huw Edwards, she flicked through the post, sifting it into three piles: Christmas cards, bills and junk. Some items didn't fit. A postcard from an old friend in Spain. An appointment reminder from James. A letter with a Swiss stamp on hotel stationery in familiar handwriting. With an unsteady hand, she opened the envelope and sat down to read.

Dear Beatrice

Please excuse familiarity of address.

Our conversation last night was curtailed sooner than I might have wished or there would be no need for this letter.

As you will know by now, I have taken my leave. The outcome would have been the same had I let the disease take its course, incurring pain and indignity for myself as well as inconvenience and expense for others.

This is not a decision taken heedlessly. I spent some considerable time putting my affairs in order and setting the record straight. One element of the latter required my coming to Hamburg to talk to you. However, as often happens when Beatrice Stubbs is involved, things did not go to plan. (By the way, I hope your friend is safe and well.)

I came to Hamburg firstly to apologise. For fifteen years, I have patronised, goaded and bullied you, rarely giving you the credit you deserve and worse still, never admitting the reason why. Allow me to state now that you are one of the finest detectives I have ever known and for every cowardly, selfish time I vented my frustrations on you, I suffered twice.

There is a second reason I had to speak. Fifteen years ago, one Monday morning, you joined my team. My fate was sealed. You were happily not-married to another man. I was your boss. Most of our colleagues believed I was either celibate or homosexual. Our personalities clashed and we fought like cat and dog. Nevertheless, I fell in love. For me, no other woman could ever come close to Beatrice Stubbs. When you tried to end your life, I wanted to follow. Yet as luck would have it, I go first.

You have been, for better and worse, the most powerful force in my life. From the moment we met, I loved you. If there is such a thing as a soul, I always will.

I wish you well.
Paul Hamilton

Bad Apples

Extract from *Rogue* by Anonymous

Bears, clowns, cats, butterflies, demons and angels cavort along the banks of the canal, dancing, laughing and twirling their capes in ceaseless balletic arcs. Music drifts through the night air from the square up ahead, growing louder and more frenetic as I approach. My feet stamp along with the beat.

A black and white chequered mask looms out of the crowd. Man or woman? I have no way of telling. It points directly at me and beckons. A strange force compels me forward. As if under a spell, I have no choice but to follow. The light-footed creature tiptoes onto a tiny bridge, stands in the middle, claps silently in time to the music then runs backwards, drawing its arms together, suggesting an embrace.

Aroused and afraid of losing sight of this hypnotic stranger, I cleave from the crowd and speed up, breaking into a run over the ancient stone edifice after the disappearing figure. A flash of white down an alleyway catches my eye and I give chase, my breath ephemeral clouds in the February chill. Moonlight barely penetrates these tiny backstreets, and when it does, merely illuminates skeins of gauzy mist rising from the Venetian waters, creating a theatrical dry ice effect. A whistle from above makes me look up.

The china-faced harlequin, high above me on a crumbling balcony, lit by an arcane street lamp, genuflects in an elaborate bow. I tilt my head back as far as it will go and stare up at the apparition. How did it get up there so fast? Impossible, unless whoever it is has wings. And how am I supposed to follow? I pace backwards across the deserted street until my back grazes the stone wall and fix my attention on the balcony – a stage no bigger than a dining-table – as the performance begins.

The harlequin spreads its arms wide, revealing the dramatic scarlet lining of its black and white cape. Each arm makes a sweeping gesture, once left, once right, acknowledging a vast imaginary audience. The head rolls in figures of eight, apparently seeking someone in the crowd. Then with catlike precision, the mask looks directly at me. One hand floats to its mouth and it blows me a kiss. I press my fingers to my mouth, offer them upwards and blow one in return.

The harlequin clutches at its heart with one hand; the other reaches out to snatch the kiss from the ether. The clenched fist remains in the air while the head is bowed in gratitude. Long hair, black as midnight, spills around the frozen features. This is a woman, I am now sure. With a slow, ritualistic gesture, the figure brings her fist to her mouth and raises her chin in ecstasy.

Once more the arms widen, as if receiving rapturous applause, and then the figure bows to the left, right and centre. She brings both hands to her painted mouth and blows an expansive kiss to her public. Her arms mime a giant heart shape as she embraces her watchers and holds them close. She repeats the gesture, her beautifully chiselled mask somehow evoking modesty, pride, love and passion without a single movement. The third time her hands return to her heart, they are no longer empty.

In the left, a single red rose, striking against the white diamond on the front of her cape. In the right, a handgun, aimed upwards beneath her chin. She kisses the rose and lets it fall from the balcony to the street below. I watch it tumble to the ground, its petals scattering on the cobbles. The shocking report of a gunshot whips my head upwards.

Against a blood-spattered backdrop, her body crumples over the stone balustrade. Long black hair dangles from the remnants of her blasted skull and the white diamonds of her cape turn dark. Something breaks at my feet. Her mask, cracked into shards. I lift one to the light. Her mouth, painted in a silent, frozen smile.

He jerked upwards with a gasp, his torso covered in sweat. The sheet fell to his waist and his breathing rasped in the silence of the bedroom. He stared at the mirror on the opposite wall, replaying the flamboyant brutality of his dream. The monochrome cape, the crimson rose, the decaying balcony and those scarlet china lips. In the mirror, his own face reflected back at him through the roseate light of dawn.

Beside him, the girl shifted, curled up like a dormouse. He laid a hand on her shoulder to ease her back to sleep. When her breathing had deepened, he slid out of bed and used the torch on his phone to locate his clothes. He backtracked, recalling the feral passion of the night before. His jeans lay in the bedroom doorway, his shirt was on the living-room couch and he found his jacket in the entrance hall. His wallet was still in the inside pocket, its contents intact.

Two problems presented themselves. His boxer shorts and shoes were missing. Underwear he could manage without but no way was he going to tramp the streets of Venice barefoot. He closed the bedroom door silently and risked switching on a lamp.

He found one sock dangling from the lampshade. The other could have been anywhere. His brogues, dusty from the previous night's dancing, lay half under the sofa. In the absence of his boxers, he was forced to go commando. Time to leave. On the glass coffee table, he spotted her handbag, all quilted leather, gold chain and to his amusement, his own initials. He opened it, took out a lipstick and wrote on the table. *Grazie. CC xx.* The front door creaked as he crept away into the early morning light.

As he wended his way back to his hotel through the detritus of last night's *Carnevale*, mist wreathing over midnight-blue canals brought back his dream. His subconscious had ways of making itself heard, so he did not simply dismiss his nocturnal visions as after-effects of a night on the town. Turning his collar up against the frosty air, he concentrated on revisiting each lurid element to articulate what he'd seen.

A caped reveller in black and white with the classic mask, at once beautiful and unnerving. The performance, just for him. The rose, the gun, blood dripping from the long black hair onto the petals.

He crossed a little bridge over Rio de San Andrea and came to a sudden halt as he saw the sign. *Albergo Arlecchino*. Harlequin Hotel. The morning chill was forgotten as he stared at the multi-coloured joker.

Harlequin. In the dream, he had thought of her as a harlequin. But now, awake and lucid, he knew Harlequins were male, colourful characters, figures of fun. Not a black and white image of bloody suicide.

That was when it clicked. He broke into a run, sprinting through grey littered streets, past empty café tables and overflowing bins. It took him fourteen minutes to reach his apartment, during which time he'd worked the whole thing out.

Out of breath after leaping up two flights of stairs, he opened the safe and fired up his laptop. He logged into PIN and entered his high-level access code. Ten seconds later, he received a second code via his mobile and punched that into the security portal. After speaking his name into the microphone and allowing the camera to compare his right eye to his left, the Police Intelligence Network granted him permission to enter. Sweaty and uncomfortable after racing across the city wearing one sock and no underwear, he adjusted himself and began his search.

It took him three minutes to review the entire Code Red report on potential terror attacks during a major European national festival. Intelligence services had earmarked suspected agitators with allegiances to three right-wing groups and intercepted a certain amount of traffic which pointed to Venice as a potential target. As a high-level undercover agent fluent in Italian, he'd been the natural choice for the task of locating this gang and preventing a terrorist action. Venice at party time. Perhaps he'd thrown himself into the celebrations with too much gusto.

But he'd done his homework and now it began to pay off. One of the names under surveillance was Zanni2, whose avatar on the chat site was a coat hanger bearing a black shirt. This faceless commentator had made occasional references to *My Darling Columbine*, leading the police to suspect a planned mass shooting.

He printed out all the comments from Zanni2 and sat in the kitchen with an espresso, underlining what he could see as an emerging pattern. It was not yet seven in the morning, but he was so close that the excitement buzzing through his whole body rendered the caffeine surplus.

Harlequin. A character from the theatrical *Commedia dell'arte* tradition involving two characters named Zanni. The first Zanni always took the lead, driving the plot, backed up by his comic sidekick. The second Zanni was a trickster clown in a colourful diamond-patterned costume, half masked, known as *Arlecchino*, or Harlequin. His love was for Colombina, although he slaked his lust wherever he could.

Decoding the simple disguises became child's play. He identified Zanni2's collaborators from their use of similar terminology or characteristics and put them through a simple program to search for lexical overlap. What words were these guys using and what did they mean?

The first, *Littorio*, an Italian emblem from the days of Mussolini. Intelligence had correctly labelled the term as the terrorists' utopian ideal of a return to Fascism. The second, *Colombina*, was the name of Harlequin's true love. This was harder to pin down as all four collaborators used it differently. He decided to identify it as Venice itself. Thirdly, *la spiacevole sorpresa*. The unpleasant surprise.

He recoiled in horror, his cup clattering into its saucer. It wasn't a shooting Zanni2 was planning. It was a bomb.

He reached for his phone but hesitated. Yes, he now knew what and where and why. But a crucial element was missing. When. He scrutinised the exchanges again and picked out key words: Glory. Right. Joy. Fight. People. Flight. Angel. Dove.

He stopped and reread. *Il Volo dell'Angelo*. The Flight of the Angel. He checked the date on his watch, smacked his palm on the table and snatched up the phone. He hit number 7 on his speed-dial list, typing his notes into PIN as he waited for a reply.

"Good morning sir, how can I help?"

"Wake him up. I've got bad news."

Twenty minutes later, this time wearing cotton briefs beneath his black jeans, he ran back downstairs. While intelligence agencies were comparing notes and alerting *carabinieri* across the city, he had a job to do. Few taxis patrolled the streets this early, so he swung a leg over his rented Vespa and sped towards Piazza San Marco.

Street cleaners, security officers, city officials and pigeons still had the freedom to roam the enormous square. In a matter of hours, every inch of space would be packed with costumed revellers, hawkers, food stands and media, awaiting the annual Flight of the Angel. From the bell-tower of San Marco, a wire ran to the Doge's Palace, where the angel would 'fly' across the crowds, a tradition stretching back centuries.

Originally known as the Flight of the Turk, a real acrobat used to cross the square on a high-wire, to the thrill and delight of the crowds below. In 1759 they renamed the event *Il Volo della Colombina* – The Flight of the Dove. That was the year the acrobat performing the stunt fell to his death.

Human beings were replaced by a large wooden dove for some time after that tragedy until the performer's safety could be guaranteed. Nowadays, he or she would be winched across the square in a harness, scattering glitter and confetti onto the celebrating crowds below.

He put himself in the mind of a terrorist. How could one cause maximum damage during such an event? If the high-wire artist scattered something else, such as hydrofluoric acid, he could inflict horrific carnage on those upturned faces. A homemade bomb made less sense. Detonated at that height, the device would wreak limited damage, even if it was filled with nails or ball bearings. Most would fly harmlessly into the air. No, he was sure the attack was a ground-based explosive. He was equally sure this was not a suicide bomber. These individuals had bigger plans. The perpetrators had no intention of dying or getting caught. This was merely their opening scene.

Angel. Dove. *Dove?* He snorted in not-quite amusement. Good question. *Where are you, you bastards?* His stomach clenched as he considered the possibility that these people had long since planted their little box of tricks and were now watching from a comfortable distance.

He had just parked the Vespa up a side street when his earpiece buzzed. He listened in silence. Latest intelligence on the suspects' communication included repeated mentions of The Triumph of Venice. Could he shed any light? For the first time that day, he allowed himself a smile.

Yes, he could. Although the café was no longer called *Alla Venezia Trionfante*, it had a long history of hosting revolutionary ideas and described itself as the oldest café in Europe. With its famous artworks and live concerts, it had attracted the powerful and beautiful for nearly four centuries. Most crucial of all, it nestled under the arches of the Procuratie Nuove in Piazza San Marco. Which, in a few hours from now, would be crammed with people.

He set off with a purposeful stride while giving his intelligence agents all they needed to know. They'd found him.

Get ready, Zanni Two, I'm on my way.

The café was almost empty this early in the day. The waiters had little interest in a solitary coffee drinker, and after serving his espresso they retreated to the counter to argue about the distribution of tips. Most patrons, sitting in his spot, would be looking outwards, absorbing the architecture of the most famous piazza in the world.

Not him.

He took in the café's interior, its distinctive decor and proud heritage, trying to comprehend the layout of such an historic building. With a yawn, he got up and went in search of the bathrooms. The waiters ignored him as he passed and descended a stairwell bearing the universal male/female toilet signs. At the bottom, he stopped and checked the other doors.

The clanging of utensils and scent of baking bread came from the kitchen, a smell of detergent and air freshener seeped from the toilets and the only other room released no clues other than the sign on the door. PRIVATO.

He pressed himself back into the doorway of the Gents and listened. Clattering cutlery, voices raised in banter, the thin sound of a radio from the kitchen. Not a sound from either toilet and the private room stayed silent. An unoccupied cellar office, probably. It looked like he was in the wrong place. But his job was to chase each lead till it ran out. He had to be sure Zanni2 was not on the premises, and flush the terrorising little bastard out if he was.

Like every field agent, he had an ASK – an Access Skeleton Key – which could open pretty much anything. In this situation, it was unnecessary. The lock was old enough to be defeated by sliding in his credit card. He withdrew his gun and pressed himself up against the PRIVATO door for one final check before he attempted to prise it open. At that moment, he heard a whispered curse.

"*Merda! Mi manca la quarta sorpresa.*"

'Shit. I'm missing the fourth surprise'.

Two things sent a chill through his veins.

One: He had found Zanni2, preparing to detonate no fewer than four bombs in the heart of Venice during the most popular event of the year.

Two: Zanni2 was a woman.

He messaged PIN, calling a ground team for back-up, and slid his platinum AMEX into the gap. Silent as he was, he still couldn't prevent the door mechanism from clicking. In the dim basement light, she turned from the laptop, her long black hair swept over one shoulder, eyes dark hollows in her pale face. An oil-fuelled heater sat in the centre of the room, its paint peeling and one wheel missing.

"Put your hands up. It's all over. We have everyone now," he lied. "You were the last, Zanni Two. Hands in the air, please, and back away from the computer."

Seconds ticked away. He took a step forward and repeated his instructions in Italian.

Her hands floated upwards and she swivelled slowly in her chair, obscuring her left arm for a second. With a twist she lifted a handgun and aimed it at him.

On instinct, he dived right and shot at her wrist as a bullet smashed into the door jamb behind him. He rolled backwards out of the doorway, scrambled to his feet and listened. He could hear liquid dripping onto tiles.

He crept back into the room, his weapon readied, but it proved unnecessary. His shot had done double duty, passing through her wrist and into her face. Zanni2 flopped across the radiator, a broken puppet. Her long black hair hung down like a stage curtain. Blood pooled from her shattered skull and dripped from the remains of her left hand. A small square of sunlight streaming through the stained glass rhomboids of the basement window threw colourful diamond patterns across her white shirt.

With one eye on the doorway, he picked up her undamaged right wrist to feel for a pulse. Tattooed on her forearm was a crimson rose. He let her hand fall and stepped past her dead body.

He had a bomb to defuse.

Chapter 1

"Ah-kah."

The muffled cough was barely audible in the quiet of the third floor bedroom, but Doctor Elisabete Silva heard it. She held her breath and tilted her head so both ears were free of the pillow. Another cough and an accompanying snuffle. She reached to throw the duvet off her legs, but a hand pressed on her chest, fingers splayed.

"Stay there," he said.

"No."

"Yes."

"Samuel, you have to get up in an hour. I'll go. You need your rest."

"I'll see to her," he replied. "My last chance before I leave." He rose from the bed like a wraith and pulled on a T-shirt, graceful and grey in the chiaroscuro of the shadowed room.

Elisabete relaxed and smiled up at her husband even though she couldn't quite make out his face in the dark of their bedroom. "Thank you, *o meu amor*. Call me if you need any help."

She closed her eyes and her head sank back into the pillows, listening to the rasp of the door, the slap of bare feet on tiles and the soft murmurs and groans as Samuel lifted their daughter out of the cot. Sleep dragged at her consciousness and the creak of the rocking chair next door lulled her body into a doze.

But her mind refused to go back to sleep. Part of her brain was awake and ready for duty, running through a checklist. His suitcase, his documents, itinerary and police issue weapon all floated across her vision. His presentations and handouts all prepared, almost as familiar as the first photographs of Marcia. Once more she calculated his journey time from leaving home on Rua dos

Anjos. Crossing Lisbon by car to Santa Apolónia station, taking the train to Porto, another to Viana do Castelo and a taxi to the venue. Samuel would be travelling almost the length of the country.

She stretched and faced the fact the night was over. Instead of getting into the shower, she wrapped a robe around her nakedness and padded into the adjoining room, her need for them both a palpable thing. The nightlight on the landing shed a soft pink glow, illuminating her husband rocking gently back and forth, his hand supporting the child's dark head against his shoulder. She watched him, returning the contented, weary ghost of a smile when he looked up.

"I'll miss her," he breathed.

"She'll miss you," Elisabete said, resting her head against the door. "Maybe I will too, just a bit."

"I already regret doing this conference. It's too soon and not worth..."

"Sssh. It is worth it. This is your career. It's only a week and it's a high-profile, well-paid appearance. Anyway, you can't cancel now..."

He pressed his lips to their daughter's forehead, his long lashes brushing the thick hair on top of her head.

"But the timing..."

"Samuel, she's still only two. She's absorbing everything and finding her place. Yes, the absence of Papa will confuse her to begin with, but as long as I'm here to take care of her and shower her with love, she'll continue to adapt. Then when you come back she'll be delighted to see you all over again. Seven days, that's all."

He eased out of the rocking chair and with great tenderness, placed their daughter back in her bed, where she clutched her pillow with her small fist.

"I think I meant the timing for me." He reached out and Elisabete slid into his arms. They gazed at the sleeping figure, as if unconvinced she was real.

"After everything we did to bring her here," he whispered, "it feels as if every minute without her is a waste of time. I wonder if natural parents think the same."

"Some, maybe. Those who tried and tried and then conceived a child after they'd given up all hope. But many others regard children as a nuisance. So when Marcia grows up and we tell her the story, she'll know she was no accident or afterthought. We wanted her so badly we went through two years of bullshit to rescue her. Now we are her parents and her daddy loves her so much he doesn't even want to go to work."

Samuel laughed softly through his nose. "I do want to go to work. I just don't want to think about a week without you two."

"When she's older, we'll come with you. I want her to see the whole of Portugal and then travel all over the world. I just don't want to drag her away when she's only just getting used to this place as her home. This time, we stay here. You go to the conference. Speak, socialise, network and tell everyone about your plans for publication. Build a fan base and make sure the name on every police bigwig's lips is Samuel Silva. Then come home to your family."

Morning light spilling through the window began to add shades of clarity to the pink glow. She studied his complexion as he faced her. His usual frown of concentration was absent but the lines on his skin remained. The grey in his hair stood out against the black and even his stubble was now stippled with white. He kissed her and pulled away to direct his intense stare into her eyes.

She knew that look. "We don't have time! You should get into the shower while I finish your packing. Nelson will be here at seven to take you to the station and it's already half past five. Samuel, listen to me!"

His arms slipped around her waist and he nuzzled her ear. Her body responded as inevitably as an egg on a hot pan.

Samuel murmured in her ear. "I'll be ready by the time Nelson arrives. Of all people, he would never let me miss the train. But as my daughter is now asleep and I won't see my wife for seven days, not to mention nights, I think I should say *até logo*, in my own way."

He took her hand and led her back to their bedroom. She paused for a second, then ran ahead of him and flung off her gown as she leapt onto the bed.

"The doctor will see you now."

Chapter 2

Acting Detective Chief Inspector Beatrice Stubbs. 'Acting' was about right. She was making it up as she went along and the sense of being an utter fraud was omnipresent. Even her new desk made her uneasy. This was the headmaster's office; the place one was summoned to be carpeted or given bad news. The usual chatter, banter, laughter and inexplicable smells of the open-plan area were all shut out of here. She craved the hum of a busy office, grease stains from a half-eaten pizza, stale whiffs of lunchtime booze and damp of tobacco from those who forced outside to smoke in the rain. This was Hamilton's place, not hers. This room smelled of polish and whisky and punishment. It smelled like politics.

Her discomfort was exacerbated by the knowledge that every time she'd stood here fuming with dislike of the man behind the desk, his feelings had been quite the opposite. Six months had passed since she received Hamilton's final missive before he chose to end his life. Time had not healed and she still found the realisation too much to bear. It was odd to discover your nemesis had actually loved you.

And as the gods love to play with our fates, so they had in this instance. The powers-that-be at Scotland Yard met and came to a decision. The Superintendent's position was to be awarded to Rangarajan Jalan, a choice universally approved, especially by Beatrice. The man was a diplomat, an admirable detective and made of the sort of moral fibre immune to erosion.

Which left the position of his junior – Detective Chief Inspector. Despite her insistence that she intended to take early retirement, that she hated managerial responsibilities, that she would be far better employed as a detective than a boss, Beatrice Stubbs was appointed to 'caretake' the role of DCI until a suitable replacement could be found.

Beatrice scowled at the brilliant London summer sunshine streaming in past the plants Melanie had added to the windowsill.

"Hamilton wouldn't even of had a cactus in here, even though I told him about Feng Shui. Bit of green, few flowers, instant karma, innit?"

She decided to avail herself of one of the few privileges the position afforded and picked up the phone. The administrator answered immediately.

"Hello, Beatrice! What can I do you for?" That particular joke had never worn thin. At least for Melanie.

"Hi, Melanie. Could you bring me a coffee, please? Latte macchiato, no sugar."

"You want that much caffeine before the meeting with the Super? If you're thirsty, Beatrice, I'll bring you some water or a camomile tea. Thing is, you don't wanna go over there wired even if it is only Ranga. You know what you're like. Gotta keep a clear head, know what I mean?"

"Never mind, I'll get it myself."

So much for privileges. She considered visiting the coffee machine and ignoring Melanie's advice, except the interfering little cow was right.

She sent a text message to DI Dawn Whittaker.

Feel like I'm in solitary confinement. What did I do wrong and when can I get visitors?

Dawn pinged back in seconds.

It's what you did right that counts. Word is, time off for good behaviour. Large glass at The Speaker tonight?

Beatrice smiled and sent a thumbs-up icon, entering into the whole txt-spk shorthand for civilised communication with barely a regret. She checked her hair, picked up her brand-new briefcase and walked the length of the building for her meeting with Superintendent Jalan.

"Beatrice, punctual to the minute. Come in, sit down and let's have some coffee. This machine can make the concoction of your choice and I ordered a pastry selection from Paul's. This whole position of power deal has its perks, don't you think?"

The elegant glass table sat in a corner window with a view across St James's Park, where swans glided across the water and the perfectly maintained lawns were as yet free of tourists.

"If you can get the staff," replied Beatrice, dumping her bag on a leather chair and reaching for a plate.

Ranga laughed and sat down opposite, the skin around his warm brown eyes crinkling. Apparently he was pleased to see her. "Melanie has our best interests at heart. By the way, are you going to her wedding?"

Beatrice bit into a plump doughnut filled with sweet yellow custard. "God, I love these things. Of course I'm going. She's been bending my ear with the planning phase for over two years, so I bloody well deserve a sit-down meal, some fizz and a spoonful of trifle. Are you?"

Ranga opened his palms. "I wouldn't dream of missing it. She's the nerve centre of this place and I think we're all very fond of her. Latte macchiato?"

"That would be just the ticket. Thank you." She raised her voice above the buzzing of the machine. "You didn't get me in here to discuss wedding outfits. What's this about? We had the weekly stand-up yesterday so this is either a problem or an issue and I'm not wild about either."

Ranga sat down, set their coffees on the table and selected a sticky croissant, still wearing a relaxed smile.

"No problems or issues. But something interesting has come to my attention and I wanted to share it with you before you leave for Portugal."

"Something interesting?" Beatrice brushed sugar crystals from her mouth, leaving most of them on her knuckles.

Ranga bit into his croissant and chewed. Impossibly, the man made no mess apart from a few crumbs on his napkin.

"Gossip. Nothing more. Word is there's a book. Creative nonfiction, thinly disguised facts, whatever. But it could expose, embarrass and possibly even indict senior officers across the continent. It's due for release this year."

"How bad? Who's behind it? Can it be stopped?" Beatrice put down her pastry.

"That's the difficulty. You see, we don't know. All we have is rumours and conjecture. No one can get close enough to find out who, when or exactly what. However, you'll be mingling with all the likeliest suspects for almost a week. My advice would be to say nothing but keep your ears and eyes open. Ask the right questions. Sniff the wind and follow your nose."

"That's not much to go on."

"I know, but it's all I have," Ranga opened his palms. "Someone or someones in the senior ranks of international law enforcement has hired the services of an expensive legal firm for personal reasons. We wouldn't normally take any notice. It's not an unusual occurrence, but it seems the same lawyer is in correspondence with a fairly well-known publishing house. Preliminary enquiries, through mixture of deceit and flattery, seem to show these legal checks are related to the imminent publication of a ghost-written book. But everyone involved is close-mouthed and cautious. Which gives even greater cause for concern."

Beatrice looked into Ranga's eyes. "How would you play it?"

"How I'd play it is probably not relevant. Whoever is writing an exposé must have quite an ego. In your shoes, I'd be unimpressed and under awed."

"Give them room to show off and let them come to me?" She returned her attention to her doughnut.

"Precisely. And I will be doing the same. We don't know whether this individual or partnership is internal. I am going to be observing your potential replacements very carefully, as it could just as easily be one of them. We have at least five internal candidates who want to be sitting in your chair when you finally retire – three of whom you know personally. So while I send you on useful collaborative missions to benefit the force as a whole, this conference being an example, your shoes will be tried on for size. The job continues as usual and you hand over the baton for a few days every couple of months. Then we evaluate their performance and make a decision as to your worthiest successor."

Logical. Inarguably astute management practice. And now that she had a secondary mission to fulfil she was less disgruntled about spending a residential week with a bunch of Euro-stiffs attending workshops with titles like 'Data-transparency: ingress, egress and mining'. She'd been dreading it. The worst bit would be the fact it was 90% men all itching to wield ego-sabres over canapés.

"Really Sven? We vastly prefer sequential presentation over simultaneous in witness ID. Have you read the study by... blah, blah, bloody blah."

But if she was covertly gathering information on them at the same time, the tedium would at least be alleviated a little. Ranga wouldn't exaggerate just to pique her interest, she knew him better than that.

She ate. Ranga drank. Pigeons purr-cooed on the guttering above the huge glass vitrine.

"So I spy on my peers while you spy on our colleagues?"

Ranga's face creased into one of his good-natured smiles. "Spy might be too strong a word. What we need to remember is that information is power. You are a perspicacious judge of character and that is an extraordinary skill. I want to know everything you find out, but in particular I want your opinions…but there is one small catch."

Beatrice sighed. "You want me to sleep with them all and tape their pillow-talk."

Ranga smiled again. "Not quite, but you might be better placed to judge if you spend at least one evening in their company as well as the daytime activities. Now before you erupt, I know you're mixing business with pleasure on this one. But if you flew out earlier, on Friday, you could go directly to the venue, attend the opening night dinner and stay overnight. Then join Matthew, Adrian et al on Saturday. You would get two days in lieu as compensation. Am I being unreasonable?"

Beatrice thought it over and shook her head. "Suppose not. You're just as devious as Hamilton was, aren't you? "

"Perhaps. But he was by far the better actor. So you'll go for Friday evening? I want the best pair of ears I've got on the ground from the outset."

Beatrice lifted her shoulders as high as they would go and

dropped them with a sigh. "You can dispense with the flattery. I'll go. But I should make you tell Matthew."

Ranga grinned. "There is one piece of good news. One of the delegates is an ex-colleague of yours. Do you remember Xavier Racine?"

Chapter 3

Catinca burst through the doorway of Harvey's Wine Emporium just before five o'clock, still sporting the Frida Kahlo look. That made it almost a whole week now, but the look definitely suited her. She wore a white peasant blouse with an embroidered collar, a voluminous yellow skirt and black leather clogs, her hair was plaited and rolled on her head, with three silk roses in her crown. Over her arm hung a scarlet shawl and a tote bag printed with wildly coloured parrots.

Adrian greeted her with an affectionate smile. "You can't just come into a room like a normal person, can you? It always has to be an entrance. But you're looking good. As always."

"Feeling good an' all. Done my application to remain today."

"You're definitely not going back to Romania?"

She gave an emphatic nod. "Staying here, if they let me. Got meself nice flat, decent man and the job's not too bad."

Adrian reached up for a high five. "From an employer's point of view, I am relieved. I really want to keep you."

She smacked his palm. "Cheers! You all ready for Portugal?"

"I've been ready for approximately three weeks," he admitted. "The final item, my mobile boarding pass, arrived an hour before you did. The big question is are *you* ready?"

Catinca cackled and bustled off into the office to deposit her things. Her voice carried back into the shop.

"I gonna do a top job while you is gone. So good you want go away every other week, mate. Plans coming out my ears!"

The bell rang as a young couple entered the shop. They held the door open for three women following them in.

Adrian readied himself for rush hour, reminding himself to

check exactly what 'plans' Catinca had for his beloved business. She emerged from the back room and made for the group of women just as he offered assistance to the browsing couple.

"Good evening. Were you looking for anything in particular?" he asked.

"Wotcha ladies! What you after? Bookclub or hen night? Come on then, Catinca gonna sort you out."

An hour and a half later the rush hour had died down and the heat of the day subsided as a golden sunset bathed the street outside. Adrian was laminating his DO NOT FORGET document for Catinca when the sound of a car horn tooted twice outside the shop. Catinca dropped the calligraphy chalk she was using on the blackboard and rushed to the window.

"Is Will! With new Audi! God, I love your boyfriend!"

Adrian stayed behind the counter, serving customers and shaking his head at the sound of Catinca's oohs and aahs from the street. The car pulled away with the top down and Catinca in the passenger seat waving back at him, her mouth set in a wide grin. Will would probably drive her round the block at least. Adrian gave an indulgent laugh. His assistant's enthusiasm would please Will, because try as he might, Adrian couldn't really see what the fuss was about. If it started when it was supposed to, didn't break down, was an inoffensive colour and emitted no attention-seeking roars on city streets, it was a perfectly acceptable means of transport. Not a source of breathless joy.

But Will wanted appreciation of the upholstery, the fuel consumption, the range of instruments at the driver's disposal and even the non-slip drinks holder. And that was before he'd even started the thing.

Within ten minutes, Catinca was back, face glowing. "That is one sexy beast! And not just talking about the driver!"

Adrian laughed, a little demob happy, and handed Catinca his list. "Here. Be good. Be creative. Be careful. Any problems, call me. And thank you so much for giving me a whole week with my wonderful man."

"Awww!" Catinca grabbed him in a hug and squeezed. "Have a great time, maties, I mind the shop so don't worry. I offer to mind his car, but he's not very trusting. Probably 'cos he's a copper. Go, have fun, bring me a present! Go now! He's on double yellows."

Adrian went, and jumped into the car beside Will with one last look back at the shop. He waved goodbye to Catinca, who was miming heart pumps in the window.

"She loves it. And you." Adrian leaned over for a kiss.

"Course she does. The girl's got taste." Will drove along the street and waited to join the main artery, still clogged with traffic at the tail end of rush hour.

"You can't really appreciate it when all we do is stop-start. The real test will come when we're cruising down a motorway. That's when you'll notice the smooth handling. Travelling will be a pure pleasure," said Will, raising his hand to thank a driver who let them out.

"Does it have a radio?" asked Adrian, his mind on whether he'd mentioned fire alarms to his assistant.

"It has every means available of playing any sound. Can you imagine? Roof down, music playing, wind in our hair and sun on our faces."

"Something to look forward to when we get back. I always feel deflated after holidays," Adrian said.

"Do you? I love coming home. But I'm looking forward to this holiday more than I did Mauritius, you know."

Adrian looked across at his partner, unable to resist his enthusiasm. "Me too. Though I doubt the weather will be quite the same."

"Don't care. Good company, fine food..."

"And when we get back, a new toy to play with. Are we going out for dinner tonight? I think we've pretty much emptied the fridge."

Will reversed into a parking space opposite the flat and turned off the ignition, grinning at Adrian.

"As we'll be eating Portuguese salads and fish for a week, we could be forgiven a pie and a pint tonight."

"I'm sure we could," Adrian reached for his seatbelt and spotted a familiar figure crossing the road. "There's Beatrice! Shall we ask her to come too?"

"Of course. If you'll forgive us a bit of police gossip."

"As if I have a choice. Hang on a minute, she's got a face like a wet weekend. Let's go and see what's wrong."

Any hopes Will might have had of the Audi garnering a little more admiration from Beatrice were soon dashed.

"It's very nice," she said, patting the bonnet. Adrian gave up on the car and ushered Beatrice into the building, through the front door of his own flat and straight to a stool in the kitchen. By the time Will joined them, Adrian was adding a slice of cucumber to three gin and tonics.

"I have to travel to Portugal earlier on Friday to be there for a welcome dinner." Beatrice blurted out. "So I can't fly with you and the others. Not only that but because I've been given extra duties, I'll have to attend workshops on the Saturday. So our first weekend is going to be severely hampered. To be honest, it's a bloody pain."

"That's a shame. But if you can't get out of it, we'll just have to make the most of the time you do have. Cheers!" Adrian raised his glass and his eyebrows at Will, a silent signal to join in with the positive spin.

Will picked up his cue. "Cheers! I don't suppose you can tell us what the extra duties might be?"

"Not really. We have some intelligence which I am supposed to explore, basically." Beatrice screwed up her nose. "It's pretty vague."

"Well, look on the bright side. You get to spend an extra two days with some seriously big fish. I'm a bit envious, actually. Am I allowed to pick your brains every evening?"

Beatrice chinked her glass against theirs. "Cheers and thank you for being so upbeat about this. Matthew and the girls won't take it so well, I'm sure. Yes, it would be a golden opportunity to network and make contacts for someone keen to pursue a career with the police. But for me, it's a curate's head. I'd send you instead if I could, Will. For someone intent on retirement like myself, it will be an exercise in gathering information and making space for Ranga to trial run a replacement."

Will opened a packet of pistachio nuts and poured them into a bowl. "Do you know who the Super has lined up for the job? Sorry, you don't have to answer if it's confidential."

Beatrice peeled apart a nut. "All Ranga said was three of the five are known to me. I assume he means our existing DIs – Cooper, Bryant and Whittaker. By which I mean Dawn, not her husband. That would be politically awkward, having one's ex as line manager. I suspect they may be looking at a sideways transfer from LTP or another force."

"The Thames Valley DCI is keen, I hear. But with so little inner-city experience, I can't see it happening."

Adrian yawned with great ostentation. That was the only downside of his partner and neighbour being in the same line of work – talking shop.

"DCI Stubbs, DS Quinn, let me read you your rights. Next week, you are allowed half an hour over aperitifs to discuss police politics and that is your daily ration. Do I make myself clear?"

"Sorry," Beatrice held up her hands. "It is a bad habit. Blame Will for encouraging me. I promise I'll try and behave next week."

Will laughed. "Me too. Beatrice, have you got plans for dinner? Adrian and I were thinking of heading over to The Morgan Arms for something to eat."

She grimaced. "I can't, much as I'd love to. I have to phone Matthew and break the news. Then I need to pack and do my homework for the course. The Morgan Arms...is that the one that does those pies?"

"'Fraid so," Adrian pulled down the corners of his mouth in a moue of regret and Beatrice sighed before draining her drink.

"Life is *so* unfair. Thank you for the gin. I feel slightly fortified but still awfully hard done by. Enjoy your dinner and I'll see you in Portugal." She kissed each of them on the cheek, heaved up her briefcase and trudged towards the front door.

Once the door had closed, Will indicated the bottle of Sipsmith's.

"If we have another, I can't drive. Shall we walk to the pub instead? Or would you prefer to stay in and get a takeaway?"

Adrian used his fingertips to push his glass towards Will. "Of the many reasons why I love you, the fact that Action Man occasionally indulges my inertia is one of my favourites."

Chapter 4

All things considered, Matthew took it very well. Beatrice's biggest concern – that police work always taking precedence over her private life – was not even mentioned. Weekends with Matthew and his daughters were a regular occurrence. To Beatrice, Marianne and Tanya were more like good friends than anything resembling step-daughters, and Tanya's son Luke, now five, was a sociable, well-behaved child, comfortable with adult company.

But this would be the first holiday they had ever spent together, and they'd been planning for months. Their first time abroad as a family. The first time with the additional company of Adrian and Will. Her neighbour and his partner were both urbane and social, yet the connecting factor was Beatrice, who would be absent for the first two days, leaving poor Matthew to hold the fort.

"I'm really sorry about having to do this. I feel rotten about arranging it all then leaving you to provide the social glue," she told him.

"Not to worry. Marianne's had to reschedule their flights too. She and her new chap will arrive for Saturday. Something to do with his work. So we'll be an advance party setting up base camp. Tanya and Luke won't mind and I assume you've already told Adrian and Will. We can take care of ourselves for the first day and you'll be with us on the Saturday evening. We can manage, Old Thing. Then when we all fly home, you and I can have a few extra days to ourselves. We'll have to think about how best to use our time together."

"Practising?"

He was silent for a moment. "Yes. Practising sounds like a very good idea. Stay home, garden, potter and get used to having each other about." He snorted a laugh.

"What's so funny?"

"That it's taken us twenty-five years to try cohabiting. Marianne and Liam moved in together just two months after they met."

"I thought his name was Leon, not Liam."

"Is it? Perhaps you're right. I'd better check that before we get to Portugal."

"Matthew, do you mean to say you haven't you actually met him yet?"

"Yes, I have, if more by accident than design. I was in the iron-monger's in Crediton on Tuesday, getting some grouting for the downstairs bathroom. Walked out the door and bumped right into them both. He – Leon, Liam, whatever – was charming. Respectful, polite and jolly well turned-out, in my opinion."

Considering the way Matthew dressed, Beatrice had a broad interpretation of 'well turned-out'.

"Look forward to meeting him myself. She seems quite smitten."

"Yes. She is."

Beatrice picked up on the reserved tone. "You just said you liked him."

"I do, judging on the little I've seen. It's just... I wish her absorp-tion with him left a little more room for the rest of us. She's not seen Luke or Tanya for over a fortnight now and I've hardly spoken to her. She came over here once but only to drop off her cat. I'm actu-ally surprised she agreed to come on holiday with us, to be honest. She seems to have no time for anyone else."

"That's just the heady rush of young love," Beatrice said. "The honeymoon phase. It'll wear off. And to be fair, Marianne was overdue some romance in her life."

"You're right, I'm being selfish. I'll be on my best behaviour next week and I'll cook for us all on Saturday evening. You'll definitely be able to join us by then?"

"Yes. I'll get a taxi from the conference and be there as close as I can to dinnertime. Matthew, I really am sorry about this. Genu-inely sorry and not just pretending because I'm a bit excited about the alternative. I wish I didn't have to do this and could spend the time with all of you instead."

"This is where I could say something about having the rest

of our lives together but that might put you into a flat spin so I'll simply say, I know."

Chapter 5

On the flight to Porto, Beatrice studied the conference programme in order to manage her expectations. A key event in the law enforcement calendar taking place from Friday to Friday, this would be the fifth and last time she'd have to attend the European Police Intercommunication Conference, or EPIC.

EPIC, for pity's sake. She loathed these cutesy acronyms. This one was bound to provoke police websites across the continent into endless bad puns and tired headlines.

Think positive, she muttered to herself. She spent a while checking the various workshops on offer, entering her options and wondering whether she'd made the wrong choices. Then she read the list of participants, checking ranks and positions and looking for names she might recognise.

At least there would be one friendly face – Xavier Racine. She smiled. Four years earlier, after an extended break, she'd got back into the saddle with an assignment in Switzerland. It wasn't the easiest case, but she'd respected and enjoyed working with her international team in Zürich. Xavier Racine was intelligent yet endearingly shy, and worked as part of a specialist task force. She remembered a few details about the young man. He was eager, clumsy, prone to blushing and one of the top ten marksmen in the country. She'd grown very fond of him and had even put in a word with his superior.

She had no idea whether that had made any difference or not. But here, near the end of the list, was a photograph of Herr Xavier Racine of Swiss Fedpol – a little older with a receding hairline, but the same freckles and awkward grin. He was a speaker, no less, leading a workshop she'd never have thought of attending – Markers of

Terrorist Activity in Online Communications. Perhaps it was not too late to change her mind.

The second factor to lift her gloom was the location itself. Gerês College of Hospitality promised five-star cuisine, an expansive wine cellar and silver service to train its students before they graduated to take roles at key hotels, discreet homes, yachts and private jets across the world. Its grounds and 120 rooms looked luxurious and Beatrice even considered for a moment the wisdom of travelling to and from their holiday villa each day. She was extraordinarily partial to a nice hotel room and the sense of freedom that came with it. At least she'd have one night to experience its comforts.

Maybe the week would be rather more enjoyable than she'd first thought. Certain names on the list of speakers and attendees she recognised, including Commander Gilchrist, a high-profile UK senior officer charged with the task of promoting European police cooperation. A regular on various news sites with his white smile and reassuring wrinkles, Gilchrist was the popular face of international law enforcement. Beatrice found his approach informed and wise, if a little media-flashy. Still, she could not deny looking forward to meeting the man in person.

A car collected her from Aeroporto Francisco Sà Carneiro and drove her north. She gazed out at the terracotta roofs, window shutters, dusty summer foliage and roadside hoardings with a familiar sense of excitement. She was back on mainland Europe, where things were just a little different and always unpredictable.

The taxi crossed various bodies of water, each reflecting the afternoon sunshine and deep blue sky as they entered the natural park and drew nearer to their destination. Buildings became scarce and the terrain grew more mountainous and verdant. If a moose or a wolf had strolled out of the forest, Beatrice wouldn't have been in the least surprised.

Low sun hit the fields surrounding Gerês College of Hospitality as the car rumbled up the drive to the grand-looking castle. The facade was slightly marred by damage to the uppermost stonework, where part of the crenellations had crumbled, leaving a gap resembling a missing tooth. Red and white plastic tape secured the area but detracted from the charm of the building.

She tipped the driver and pulled her suitcase behind her into an equally impressive portico lined by blue and white tiles depicting scenes of country life, reminding her of her mother's willow pattern crockery.

She checked in, received her welcome pack and made her way to a first floor room without seeing anyone she knew. Large, modern and practical, the room had all the necessaries, including a mini-bar. The most luxurious element of all was the view. She stepped out onto her balcony and soaked it all in.

Below, a terrace stretched the breadth of the building, and in its centre a few steps led down to a tidy lawn which sloped away towards a lake. A path meandered through the shrubs between cerise bougainvillea and blousy pink camellias. To her left, another path led under a walkway of climbing roses to a sort of temple, complete with white marble columns. The perfect place for a wedding.

Beatrice sighed, opened a bottle of water and dithered. Once she left her room, she would be exposed and forced to find a conversational partner or fake a certain business-like air by muttering into her mobile. She wandered back to the balcony, watching small groups and pairs stroll the grounds in the summer sunshine. She would much prefer to stay indoors alone. But how could one gain intelligence without actually talking to people?

The pressure of enforced sociability hemmed her in. She paced the room and rehearsed casual introductions while inwardly wishing she was back in her intimidating office in Scotland Yard. The ring of the room telephone startled her.

"Hello? DCI Stubbs speaking."

"DCI Stubbs, hello! This is Xavier Racine from Zürich. Do you remember me?"

"Xavier! Of course I remember. I was so pleased to see your name on the list of participants. How are you?"

"Thank you, I'm very well. I'm calling to see if you would like to join me for a drink before dinner?"

Relief flooded through her. "I would love to. Shall we say in ten minutes, on the terrace?"

"Perfect. See you then."

Beatrice replaced the phone and began digging through her case to find her hairbrush.

He'd barely changed at all. A few fine lines formed a delta at the corners of his gentle hazel eyes, his hair had receded but it was still the same copper colour, and his eager smile radiated from a clean-shaven face. She held out her hand and he took it in both of his.

"Beatrice! So good to see you again! Oh, can I still call you Beatrice now you are DCI?"

"Of course you can. It's lovely to see you too. You don't look a day older since the last time I saw you."

"Thank you. You actually look a lot better than last time I saw you. Shall we sit here?" He indicated a table beneath the green and white striped awing." I ordered us a bottle of white wine and spar-kling water. If I'm not wrong, your preferred drink is a spritzer?"

"You are not wrong. So how's life in Zürich? Do you still work with Herr Kälin?"

"No, he retired last year. Before that we worked closely together. He was a great support to me and recommended me for promotion to Fedpol. That's why I'm here. And you are now Detective Chief Inspector! Congratulations!"

"Acting DCI. I plan to retire at the end of this year."

"So soon? That's a shame. For the Metropolitan Police, I mean. Ah, the wine."

Beatrice watched him as he tasted the Chardonnay and thanked the waiter in Portuguese. She revised her opinion. He *had* changed. There was an assurance to him now which had been absent four years ago. All that gauche awkwardness had disappeared, leaving a confident, measured man comfortable in his own skin. She noticed the gold wedding band.

"And you got married!"

He smiled, a touch of the old bashfulness surfacing.

"Yes, last year. I still can't get used to saying 'my wife' but it's the best decision I ever made. What about you?"

"Still happily unmarried, but I'll be moving in with my

long-suffering partner at the end of the year. It's about time, really. We've been together over a quarter of a century."

"That merits a toast. To success, professional and personal!"

"Success!" Beatrice beamed as they touched glasses and drank.

"I see you're a specialist in spotting terrorist activity now," she said.

"Specialist? Well, I hope to share some techniques. I've been training in Germany and want to pass on what I discovered. Will you be at that workshop?"

"Of course I will. Even if I wasn't interested, which I am, I'd come along anyway to support you. Which other sessions are you attending?"

"My priority is to attend everything by Samuel Silva."

"Who's that?" asked Beatrice.

"A Portuguese psychologist who works for the Lisbon Intelligence Unit. He's developed an exciting new profiling tool to assess levels of sociopathy in social media behaviours. It could be helpful in monitoring potential domestic incidents."

"Home-grown terrorists?"

"Yes, but more of the individual variety than organised cells."

"I see," said Beatrice. "More Brevik than Brussels."

"Exactly," Xavier nodded, his expression serious.

They chatted about the week ahead and strayed into police 'news' – which a casual observer might have construed as gossip – as they emptied the bottle. Shadows lengthened across the table and the cooling dusk attracted mosquitoes enough to eventually drive them inside.

In the dining-room, eight tables of six were laid out with sparkling glassware and floral centrepieces. It looked more like a wedding than a conference of senior police officers. On the stage sat the bigwigs, with Commander Gilchrist at the centre, and suddenly Beatrice was reminded less of weddings and more of school assemblies. There seemed to be no seating plan so Xavier led Beatrice to join a group of three on the second table. She was relieved to see another woman amongst them. Xavier made introductions and the reason for his choice became clear.

"Good evening, may we join you? My name is Xavier Racine

from Swiss Fedpol and this is DCI Beatrice Stubbs of the London Met."

A tallish chap in a tweedy jacket stood up. "Please do. My name is Samuel Silva of the LIU. This is my colleague André Monteiro and we have just introduced ourselves to Agent Cher Davenport of the FBI."

The Monteiro boy stood up for the handshakes. Beatrice tried not to gawp at him, as he really did appear to be no more than fourteen years old. The American lady remained seated and Beatrice realised she was in a wheelchair. Her sleek fox-red hair framed an open, bright face with a broad smile. Like Xavier, she had freckles. Unlike Xavier, she had pretty green eyes.

Silva had a friendly demeanour, a wise expression and a touch of grey at his temples. Xavier took the seat next to him and the two immediately fell into animated conversation. Beatrice sat the other side of Xavier, opposite the FBI agent, with a space between herself and the Portuguese lad.

"Can I get you some water, DCI Stubbs?" asked Monteiro.

Beatrice smiled. A teenager he might be but he had excellent manners and the hint of an American accent. "Yes please. And seeing as we're going to be colleagues this week, shall we use first names? You can call me Beatrice."

Cher Davenport's face broke into another wide smile. "That is exactly what we were just saying. So: Cher, Beatrice, André, Samuel and Xavier."

"And Roman."

A deep voice came from behind Beatrice. She turned to see a surfer-type with tanned skin, blond hair in a ponytail and a neatly trimmed beard. He looked around the table with a half-smile, his steady eyes the colour of dawn.

"Hello everyone. Roman Björnsson from the Icelandic *Víkingasveitin*, or Viking Squad. Can I sit down?"

Dinner, despite Beatrice's reservations, turned out to be thoroughly enjoyable, in terms of both food and company. She and Cher bonded instantly, in firm agreement that the gender imbalance in senior international law enforcement and intelligence was an embarrassment for all concerned.

Fishcake on a lake of beurre blanc accompanied by a Pinot Gris was their first course, during which she grilled the Viking on Icelandic culture. An easy-going, relaxed young man with a ready laugh, he answered all her queries with good humour and batted several more in her direction. Their conversation attracted André's attention. He added his opinion on how a country's cultural outlook affected its policing, offering his training experience in Brazil as an example. That explained the American accent. His voice and opinions were mature and Beatrice wondered if his boyish looks had deceived her.

Roman asked André about the effect of differing climates, citing long, dark Reykjavik winters and corresponding crime statistics. By the time the pea, asparagus and nettle risotto arrived, the whole table was in lively discussion. The staff made sure the diners' glasses stayed filled and the noise of cutlery, crockery and chatter rose to a boisterous rumble.

The conversation turned to national legends, and Beatrice had just finished regaling her party with the story of the Beast of Bodmin Moor when Commander Gilchrist stood up on the raised podium and switched on the microphone. There was a brief squeal of feedback and the hubbub hushed to an expectant silence.

"Good evening ladies and gentlemen, and welcome to Gerês College of Hospitality. I hope you all enjoyed this evening's meal. I think you'll all agree with me, these young people have a great career ahead of them. If I were the judge, I'd give this restaurant five stars!"

Enthusiastic applause rang out and heads nodded in assent. Gilchrist joined in the clapping, directing his approving smile in the direction of the kitchens.

"This week is going to be EPIC!" he said, and Beatrice sighed at the early onset of the puns. "I'd like to start by thanking all of you for giving up seven full days to attend this exciting event. In unprecedented circumstances across Europe, closer cooperation matters like never before. Many of you have left crucial posts and travelled significant distances to better your police management skills and align practices. This marks each of you as a true leader in the field."

He patted his hands together and rotated in a semi-circle, as if to applaud them individually.

"Gathered in this room are some of the finest senior police officers on this continent, not to mention lecturers representing another three: America, Asia and Africa. This week will see a packed programme of cutting-edge technology, superlative exemplars of best forensic practice, game-changing advances in psychological research and theories on detection as prevention, alongside some of the grassroots work done in community and social cooperative projects. We'll learn from each other, network and connect, build relationships and get back to basics.

"We're a relatively small group, but I want us to share our learning widely. In addition to feeding back to your own teams at home, it's essential to involve our colleagues across the globe. This year, the tech boffins have made that possible, via a brilliant new app called BluLite! In your welcome pack, you have instructions on how to download BluLite, which will enable you to add content to our exclusive international video-platform! Please download the app, use it according to the professional guidelines and spread your EPIC experiences on our unique intranet. You could start right now!

"Taking a week out from those whom we strive to serve, we must remember why we became police officers. I am quite sure we're all going to come out of this week tested, challenged but above all improved. I wish you all an unforgettable and EPIC week!"

Beatrice and her colleagues clapped and smiled, as did every other table, but she caught the Viking's eye roll and André's complicit grin. Xavier excused himself and made for the bathroom. To Beatrice's surprise, Samuel Silva slid into his seat.

"I understand the hierarchy at the Met is undergoing some changes," he said with a diffident air. His expression of genuine interest and his attentive listening manner led her to go into rather more detail than usual, encouraged by his gentle questions. Their superficial small talk soon became a serious and frank conversation about fears for the future.

Xavier returned and held out a palm to indicate the seating arrangement was fine with him. He took the empty seat next to Cher. Their conversation sounded interesting but Beatrice was drawn back to Samuel Silva's unassuming yet perceptive eyes.

Sotto voce, he enquired how she felt about retiring.

"Truthfully, I feel dread and anticipation in equal measures. I worry about getting bored in retirement and maybe even missing the pressures of this job. I worry about my partner finding me far less interesting when I'm attainable. I worry about what I'm going to do with all that free time." She gave an embarrassed shrug. "My worries are most people's dreams."

"None of us can truly envy or pity each other because we are not wearing each other's shoes." Samuel sighed. "I was just talking to Xavier, who admits nerves about his upcoming presentation and wishes he had my speaking ability. Whereas I can address 200 international police professionals with confidence but confess pure terror at something the rest of the world takes for granted – becoming a parent."

He looked a little old for a first time father, but Beatrice was poor at judging ages. She sought a diplomatic reply. "Is that a recent development?"

"Yes. I left everything too late," he confided. "I was forty-five when I met my wife and we knew we were unlikely to conceive a child. But now, after two years of red tape, we just succeeded in adopting a little Romanian girl. She's two years old."

"Congratulations! That is a huge step."

"Thank you. It is. A first-time father at the age of fifty-two, I don't have the blind braggadocio of a young man. My job makes it worse. An entire career studying sociopathic behaviours and their consequences tends to test one's faith in humanity. On top of that, I have the added pressure of leaving them alone to come to places like this. I'm sorry, I shouldn't have said that. It was rude of me."

"Not at all. It makes perfect sense," said Beatrice. "You found something you thought you never would. Then to experience the emotional wringer of the adoption process, to bring her home after so long and have that precious little life in your care, no sane person would wish to be anywhere else but by her side. What's your daughter's name?"

His face creased into an expression of such heartfelt gratitude that his eyes almost closed. He slipped out his phone and showed her pictures. Marcia in the hospital, Marcia with her new parents, Marcia on the balcony with views of Lisbon's castle beyond, Marcia sleeping, her tiny fists beside her head.

Beatrice could see his point. "I'm not a baby person as a rule, but I have to say she is completely adorable. I'm not surprised you're in love. How did you..."

"And here I see some familiar faces!" Commander Gilchrist placed his hands on the back of Cher and André's chairs, as if he was Jesus at the last supper. "Silva, you old rogue! It's been years."

He reached across and shook Samuel's hand before flashing his teeth at the whole party. "Silva and I used to go to the football together. Then I think he got sick of England winning! Now, Acting DCI Stubbs I recognise. Holding the fort for Jalan, I believe."

Beatrice smiled as they shook, aware there was no need to reply.

"Monteiro Junior! How's your father doing?" He loomed awkwardly over André to offer his hand, forcing Cher to lean sideways in case she got an elbow in the face. "So, who's doing the introductions?"

Xavier stood up. "Good evening, Commander. My name is Xavier Racine from Fedpol, Switzerland, and this lady is Agent Davenport of the FBI. Here is Roman Björnsson of Iceland's Viking Squad. Pleased to meet you."

Beatrice watched Gilchrist turn his spotlight on each, throwing out a charming compliment or brief mention of common interest, to make everyone feel included. The man was a professional, she recognised.

He stood back and drew out his phone. He filmed the table, introducing each delegate and signed off his mini-reportage with his signature speech. "Good to meet you all, and I hope you'll learn a great deal from this EPIC experience. You're going to work hard, but this week will reignite your passion. That much I guarantee. Enjoy your dessert and coffee and see you all bright and early in the morning!"

He saluted and moved on to the next table. Beatrice and the Viking locked eyes. His smile was brief yet sardonic, and made him all the more interesting. The week ahead was beginning to develop quite some potential.

Dessert was a sorbet of melon and port. It was delicious, but no one at the table felt the need to film or photograph it and share the results online with their colleagues. After coffee, Roman suggested an after-dinner drink in the bar. André, Cher and Xavier agreed with enthusiasm, but Samuel demurred.

"That's kind of you, but I want to prepare for my lecture in the morning and call my wife. So I'll thank you all for such an enjoyable evening and go back to my room now."

Beatrice folded up her napkin. "Me too. I need to find out if my friends made it to the villa and get my beauty sleep. As Samuel says, you've been very good company. The rest of the week has a lot to live up to."

"Not if you always sit with us," said Roman, to general laughter.

Xavier and André stood as Beatrice rose from her seat and said her goodnights.

In the foyer, Beatrice and Samuel stopped for a moment.

"It was really interesting to talk to you, Beatrice. I hope we can manage another conversation together over the next week."

"So do I," said Beatrice, with genuine sincerity. "I'll be at your seminar tomorrow and will probably want to pick your brains. Thank you for the pleasant company over dinner."

"How about having breakfast together? Not tomorrow – I promised the Commander my undivided attention. He wanted to have lunch today but I always eat my midday meal in my room. It's the only chance I have to call my wife and talk to Marcia. Any other morning I'm free?"

"I'd be delighted. Let me check which night I'll be staying again and we can fix a date."

As they stood there, Roman and Xavier headed towards the bar, the tall blond inclining to listen to the shorter redhead. Behind them, André walked beside Cher's wheelchair, laughing at something she said.

Beatrice grabbed the chance to ask her burning question. "Your colleague is a charming young man. Such maturity for one so young. How old is he, exactly, if it's not impolite to ask?"

Samuel chuckled. "Exactly? He will be twenty-six on September the fifth. Between you and me, Beatrice, André is not just a colleague, he's also my godson. His father is my oldest friend."

They watched as the foursome settled at a table by the window, André solicitous over Cher's comfort.

"Well, you should be very proud of him. He's a credit to you."

"Thank you. I am proud. I'm a very lucky man. Goodnight Beatrice."

"Goodnight Samuel. Sleep well."

Chapter 6

Considering his usual allergic reaction to children, Adrian would go as far as to say he didn't actually mind Luke. A quiet, introspective child, he listened to conversations and asked thoughtful questions of his mother and Matthew. Luke had met Adrian before but this was the first time he'd been introduced to Will. He tucked his cuddly dolphin into his armpit and shook hands, but regarded the newcomer with watchful eyes until his attention was claimed by the complexity of the security procedures at the Queen's Terminal at Heathrow.

Luke followed his mother's instructions and cleared the checks with ease. The only hold-up was Matthew, who had forgotten to remove his belt, keys and phone. Tanya shrugged and shook her head at Adrian and Will as Matthew submitted to a hand-held body scanner.

Once in the departure lounge, Matthew, Will and Luke went in search of a vantage point to view the planes taking off and landing, while Adrian and Tanya made a bee-line for the Duty Free. On the escalator they had to stand and wait as a family of five had clearly never heard the Stand on the Right, Walk on the Left maxim. The father carried a baby and travel bag, while two knee-high children held their mother's hand and blocked the entire space.

Adrian suppressed his impatience and bounced his right leg as the steel staircase bore them upwards. In front of them, one of the children was trying to pull free of its mother while the other trotted a plastic toy along the handrail. Adrian took a deep breath but chose not to make a comment. After all, the children were not that much smaller than Luke.

A sudden shriek jolted his senses. One child had lost its grip and its toy tumbled downwards. Immediately, the kid tried to clamber onto the handrail. The mother panicked and let go of the struggling one to grab the potential jumper with both hands. The released child bolted past his father, racing for the top of the escalator, but tripped and fell forwards onto his hands and knees.

Adrian saw the tiny fingers approaching metal teeth, heard the screams of the parents and acted without a rational thought. He ran past them and scooped up the child, but its weight overbalanced him. With the force of fear and shock, he got to his feet before the stairway ran out and stumbled onto the steel platform, the child held firm in his protective grip.

Adrenalin pulsed through him long after he'd returned the child, shaken the hands of the parents and various onlookers, and even posed for a photograph, ruffling the boy's hair as if he were Jimmy Stewart.

When they finally got away, Tanya took his arm with a squeeze. "You, Adrian Harvey, are a class act."

"With torn Paul Smith trousers and a massive bruise to wreck my tan."

"It's not a bruise, it's a mark of bravery," said Tanya. "Come on, we should be able to get all the ingredients for the perfect martini and a great big bottle of champagne to toast our hero."

"Hero, schmero. But I never say no to some classy spàrkles. How about I get the gin and you choose the vodka? Let's make it quick because Will is obsessed about getting to the gate early. As for the rest, I'm sure Portugal has shops."

"Yep. Or we can get Marianne to bring anything we've forgotten when she flies later."

With practised efficiency, Tanya selected a litre bottle of Grey Goose and a bottle of Mumm, while Adrian dithered over a bottle of The Botanist or Hendricks.

"Why didn't she come with us this morning?"

Tanya shrugged once more. "Because Leon had to work, and she can't do anything without Leon."

Adrian opted for the Hendricks, added a chocolate selection for Luke and they moved to the till. "Well, it's always nicer to fly together."

Tanya snorted. "If you've got the cash to chuck away on rescheduling two flights, I'm sure it's much nicer."

"Look at it this way. At least we get the pick of the bedrooms before they arrive."

Tanya flashed him a wicked grin and showed the cashier her boarding pass.

Eight people, two cars. They could have hired a people carrier, but two separate vehicles were actually cheaper and allowed for more independence. So Tanya took the wheel of the Peugeot estate while Will assumed control of the Fiat Panda.

"Bit of a comedown from the Audi," observed Adrian.

Will buckled his seatbelt and adjusted the mirror. "Yes, but imagine how happy I'll be to get back to it next week."

They ignored the motorway and took the coast road north, passing through quiet villages with beachside bars, black-clad old ladies and the occasional chicken scratching in the dust. After one ice-cream stop and two bathroom breaks, they turned inland and soon found themselves in the national park area of Gêres. Adrian could see why it was protected. For almost an hour, he said nothing more than "Wow!" and "Look at that!".

Lilac mountains soared into a cloudless sky around midnight-blue lakes. The landscape alternated between rocky cascades and dense forests or sudden bursts of flowering shrubs which erupted like fireworks alongside the winding road. Best of all, other vehicles were scarce and they encountered remarkably few people apart from occasional clusters of old men sitting outside tiny cafés, smoking and squinting at them as they passed.

The GPS told them they were approaching their destination.

"I am officially excited!" said Adrian, almost bouncing in his seat. The square sand-coloured house had its own driveway off the main road and sat on a terrace above a shimmering green lake. Will parked up in front of the main house. Between it and a small outbuilding to the left, Adrian spotted a trapezoid of brilliant blue.

"Swimming-pool!" Pointing with a chocolatey finger, Luke jumped from the Peugeot before Tanya had switched off the engine.

Will threw the keys over the bonnet to Adrian and called to Luke. "Race you!"

Luke took off immediately and the two disappeared around the corner. By the time Matthew, Tanya and Adrian caught up, the pair were exclaiming over the range of pool toys available in the little cabana.

Tanya and Adrian followed the terrace that surrounded the villa. It was a heavenly spot. The house jutted out towards the lake, meaning two sides enjoyed a lake view. The mountainside tumbled away below them, strewn with orange and purple flowers, boulders and occasional thickets of trees. On the opposite bank, less of a village and more a scattering of houses clustered around a little harbour. Cicadas chattered away in the foliage and a breeze brought the faint scent of lemons.

"This is gorgeous!" Tanya breathed.

"Perfection," Adrian agreed. "I plan to lie on that sun lounger with a chilled martini always in reach, working on my tan until I get too hot, then a cool swim, a lazy lunch and back to it."

"If Action Man will let you."

"Good point. He'll sit still for a maximum of half an hour before suggesting a hike, or a quick water-ski round the lake, or an exploration of the nearest village."

Matthew eased off his jacket and came to stand beside them. "I say. This looks jolly nice. Let's take the bags in, explore the house and open a bottle of something local. I have a feeling this will be a most relaxing week."

Chapter 7

Towards the end of Samuel Silva's seminar on Common Psychological Factors linking Mass Shootings, Beatrice's stomach began rumbling, growing increasingly louder until she drew amused glances from those around her. When Silva had finished answering a question on gun licensing, he checked his watch, apologised for over-running and announced lunch. Beatrice shoved her notes into her bag and got to her feet. Cher Davenport, sitting beside her, made a suggestion.

"Beatrice, you wanna steer me out? People always make way for a wheelchair and that way we get to the front of the lunch line."

"Brilliant idea. I'm starved."

"Yup, I kinda guessed."

They took full advantage of the salad buffet and chose to eat on the terrace in the sunshine, Cher carrying both their meals on a tray in her lap. Sharing their thoughts on Samuel's excellent talk led naturally to a conversation on US gun control, a subject on which Cher was well informed. Xavier arrived with a plate piled high and immediately joined in the discussion with some facts on Swiss gun ownership.

"And as Samuel mentioned," he said, "the American culture surrounding weapons couldn't be more different."

Cher nodded, waving a celery stick to emphasise her words. "Damn right. He totally nailed it by looking at the issue from the prevailing cultural values perspective. The right to bear arms for self-protection is individualism in a nutshell. Where is Samuel, by the way? I have a whole bunch of questions I didn't get chance to ask. We shoulda invited him to join us."

Xavier swallowed a mouthful of bread. "I did. He said he was going to have lunch in his room so he could call his wife, but he'd catch up with us later. And it won't be long before we can all read his book."

"He's writing a book?" asked Beatrice, flapping open a napkin to disguise her curiosity.

"Sure," said Cher. "He told me about it last night. But if you've heard the same stories I have, we're not talking about *that* book. Samuel's publishing his research, that's all."

"Ah," said Xavier. "So this mysterious soon-to-be-published novel is already common knowledge?"

Beatrice shook her head. "Is it? Unless you two know more than me, the problem is exactly that. The knowledge we have is far from common."

Xavier and Cher shook their heads.

"Nope," Cher replied. "All I got was the order to watch and listen. So let's cut to the chase. Either of you two writing a fictional exposé on senior police officers?" Cher pointed her fork at them in turn.

"To be honest, I have no idea where I'd find the time," said Beatrice.

"It's not me. Telling stories is not my strong point," said Xavier.

"Well, that makes life easier. Which workshops are you two attending this afternoon?"

Beatrice consulted her participant pack. "Multiracial and Interfaith Cooperative Projects, as one of ours will be on the panel, talking about our own Operation Horseshoe. Then I want to catch the International Team Management session. Cher?"

"Presenting this afternoon. Oh wow, the nerves just kicked in. Bathroom break. I'll be right back. Don't let anyone steal my salad!"

She wheeled herself rapidly across the terrace and into the hotel.

"What about you, Xavier? Your workshop isn't today, is it?"

He shook his head. "Tomorrow. I'm trying not to worry about it. I've given this talk to hundreds of trainees but now that I have to address peers and senior officers, I'm having nightmares. Still, this afternoon I'll be at Cher's seminar on Hostage Negotiation then I can't decide between..."

A burst of laughter from a nearby table made them both turn.

Gilchrist joined in the amusement and inclined his head to accept the approval. Behind him, Beatrice spotted the Viking emerge from the French windows.

So did Xavier. He waved an arm. "Roman! Come and join us!"

The Viking's face broke into a crooked smile as he loped towards them.

"You're late for lunch," Beatrice observed. "Did your session run over as well?"

"No. I slept in this morning, so I had to go to my room before lunch and take a shower or stink all afternoon. That's the danger of having 'just one more' with certain people." He took a bite out of a chicken drumstick.

Xavier laughed and pulled an innocent face.

"Have you seen André today?" asked Beatrice.

Roman nodded and swallowed. "Just now. I passed him in the corridor. He already had a lunch appointment. Is anyone eating that bread roll?"

"Hands off, Blondie." Cher took her place and reclaimed her tray, a faint blush suffusing her cheeks. Beatrice was not surprised. He was a rather striking Viking.

"I was just telling Beatrice how you, Xavier and André led me astray last night," Roman said, gnawing on his chicken.

Cher affected outrage. "I don't recall Xavier or myself proposing a round of schnapps! Still, it was an educational evening."

"Ah yes," said Beatrice. "The bar is often underestimated as a seat of great learning. If I was twenty years younger, I might have joined you."

Cher threw her a sardonic look. "C'mon Beatrice, you're not milky drinks and slippers just yet. Why not join us for a glass or two tonight?"

"I would love to, but part of the quid pro quo for my attendance this week is the chance for a semi-holiday. A group of family and friends are staying nearby, so I'll divide my time between business and pleasure. Nevertheless, one night this week, I'll certainly stay for a snifter. And undoubtedly drink the lot of you under the table."

"Now that I would like to see!" Gilchrist materialised as if from nowhere and joined the conversation with his normal self-assurance. He clapped a hand on Roman's shoulder. "I'd say you young fellas would give her a run for her money, eh?"

Roman turned to address the Commander, subtly removing his shoulder from the other man's grip. "Perhaps when I've fully recovered from last night, sir. Did you have a successful morning?"

"Superlative. I popped in on the human trafficking workshop and then caught most of the forensics lecture from Oyekunle over there, before having to deal with the usual admin headaches before lunch. Extremely pleased with the live streaming via BluLite. This is the wonderful thing about social media. Immediacy and inclusivity. How is everyone's day going?"

There was a general murmur of positive noises, which appeared to please Gilchrist. "Excellent. We're off to an EPIC start. Agent Davenport, I will make every effort to be at your talk today. You of all people know what it means to take one for the team."

Cher seemed at loss to respond, but Gilchrist didn't wait. "DCI Stubbs, your room is booked for the entire week, so whichever night you plan your 'snifter', you have somewhere to stay. We're neighbours, in fact. I'm in Room 1101. I wanted Room 101 but that was the closest I could get!"

Everyone laughed, even those who clearly didn't get the reference.

"Enjoy the afternoon, one and all." With that, he sallied forth to join another party, soon eliciting a round of polite laughter. The man really was a pro.

"He reminds me of someone," said Cher, following her eye line. "An actor, perhaps. Or a newsreader."

"I know what you mean. He has that way about him. Very slick, very practised. Like a politician," said Roman.

"I wish I could do what he does," said Xavier, a touch of wistfulness in his tone.

"Really?" asked Beatrice. "I wouldn't want his job for all the peas in China."

"Not his job, at least not for another ten years. I mean his ability to talk to everyone, to be so comfortable with crowds and at ease when he's the centre of attention."

"I suspect that's exactly where he wants to be," said Beatrice. "Anyway, Xavier, you have something much more valuable."

"What is that?" Xavier asked, with a puzzled look.

Roman got there before her. "Sincerity."

All three of them nodded and Beatrice was delighted to see two spots of pink on the Swiss redhead's cheeks.

While it was a familiar feeling to learn something useful at events like these, it was rare to feel an emotional surge of pride during a workshop on community projects. However, hearing to what various forces had achieved by listening to religious leaders and encouraging dialogue delivered exactly that. Beatrice grew oddly fond of the human race, a sensation she seldom associated with her job. All the initiatives were encouraging and inspirational. None more so than when her own colleague, Dawn Whittaker, appeared on the screen from London to explain the aims and achievements of Operation Horseshoe, Scotland Yard's interfaith initiative.

When she'd finished, Beatrice slipped her phone from her handbag to try this BluLite thing. She couldn't make it work and found the whole thing rather intrusive, so she reverted to text message and sent an exclamation-filled pat on the back to Dawn. Two missed calls from Xavier with voicemail alerts made her frown. There was no way she could listen to messages in the middle of a lecture. The next speaker ascended the podium, a heavyset man who began describing the intercultural challenges of dealing with the refugee crisis off the coast of Greece.

She sent a quick text to Xavier.

Something wrong?

The phone vibrated almost instantly.

Silva AWOL. You saw him this morning?

Beatrice sensed heads turning her way in disapproval as she typed a hurried reply.

Yes. Session overran – maybe asleep?

Then she put the phone in her bag and returned her attention to the Greek chap, who was introducing a collaborative venture between NGOs, police and the Refugee Council.

Only when the applause had died down after the moderator's summation did she pick up her mobile again. There was one message.

Silva found in his room. Not asleep. Dead.

Chapter 8

A loud report, a splash and burbling laughter woke Adrian from a light doze. He lifted his head and shielded his eyes. Will had dived from the board, swum the length of the pool and surfaced underneath Luke's lilo, toppling him into the water. Adrian watched as Luke attempted to clamber back on, impeded by his water wings. He spluttered giggles as Will circled him, swimming one armed, with the other hand vertical above his head, presumably to indicate a shark's fin. His menacing noises were no more than bubbles under Luke's squeals.

By eleven, the heat had become too strong to lie on the loungers, so Adrian and Matthew moved to the shade of the cabana, sighing with contentment, reading their respective publications and sharing smiles at the energy of the two in the pool. True to his promise, Will had agreed to stay at the villa for their first day. Sitting still, however, was impossible. He swam, dived, played Swing ball with Luke, harassed Adrian into a game of volleyball and helped Matthew with the crossword.

Tanya had left after breakfast to collect her sister and Leon from the airport. If all went smoothly, they would be back in time for lunch. Thinking of Tanya reminded Adrian of her stern words on sun protection.

"Luke? Luke! What did you do with your hat? Your mother's going to kill me. Will, come out of there and let's get some sun cream on him. It's all right for you, with skin like a saddle, but Mr Blonde here will turn into Mr Pink if we're not careful."

Like a pair of obedient otters, they hauled themselves out of the water, leaving wet prints on the tiles as they came towards the cabana. Adrian held open a towel for Luke to run into, wrapped it around him and pressed his nose with a firm finger. The skin turned white for a second then back to pink.

"As I thought. Already glowing. Sun block this afternoon. You don't want to spend two days in bed with heatstroke, do you?"

Luke shook his head vigorously, sprinkling droplets onto Matthew's paper.

"Where's Mum? I'm hungry."

Matthew folded his copy of The Times. "I was just thinking the same thing. They should be here within the hour, so let's make a start on the food. No reason you can't have a banana to keep you going, Small Fry. You and Will have used up quite some energy this morning."

"I could hardly keep up with him. He's a natural in the water. Can't wait to get into the sea tomorrow," said Will. "Right, I'll put some clothes on and set the table."

The four of them were in the kitchen – Adrian assembling the salad, Matthew baking whole trout, Will slicing bread rolls and Luke eating them – when a horn sounded outside.

"Mum!" Luke dropped his bread and rushed to the front door.

Matthew wiped his hands and followed, but Adrian motioned to Will to hang back. He didn't want to overwhelm Marianne's new boyfriend as soon as he arrived. They continued preparing the food and Adrian took the opportunity to steal a kiss from his incredibly sexy man. A whiff of burning came from the oven and Adrian checked the trout. Skin already blackened, but just about salvageable.

After rescuing the fish, they went to greet the new arrivals. Adrian followed Will out for hugs and handshakes but stopped in the doorway and stared at Marianne. Last time he'd seen her, she was pasty and overweight, hair scraped back, with an aggressive attitude. Not anymore. Her smile was broad, highlighted hair glossy and her summer dress indicated a curvaceous, healthier figure.

"Adrian! Look at you!" She held out her arms for a hug.

Adrian obliged then stood back to admire Marianne's transformation. "Look at me? What about you? You look amazing, Marianne! What have you done?"

She gave a delighted laugh. "Ain't love grand? Meet Leon. The guy who changed my life."

Adrian had a lifetime's experience assessing men. In the time it took to smile, reach out a hand and say 'Pleased to meet you, Leon,' he had made several not entirely conscious judgements.

Average height, a looker in that backroom-of-a-dirty-club sort of way, a stylish dresser who tried to look careless, black hair falling over one eye and a day's growth of stubble on his angular jaw. Handshake firm, smile less so.

"I took a risk, Adrian. Knowing your profession, you'll be even more critical about wine than Matthew." He held out a bottle wrapped in green tissue paper. "So I thought I'd bring a Touriga red. Going local kind of thing."

"Touriga? That's very thoughtful. We'll enjoy it this week. How was the trip?"

Marianne interrupted. "Apart from getting up at stupid o'clock, fine. Can we dump the bags and then eat? I'm itching to get in the pool."

Tanya, Luke and Will took the arrivals upstairs while Adrian set out the salads. Matthew was deliberating on which white wine would go best with the trout when Will came back into the kitchen.

"Might have to rethink the rooms. Leon is less than chuffed at sharing a bathroom with Tanya and Luke. Shall we offer to swap? I really couldn't care less."

Matthew grunted. "First come, first served. They'll have to lump it. *Vinho verde*, with lunch, I thought. We have three bottles of this. What do you say, Adrian?"

"I say yes to wine and no to swaps. I've unpacked now anyway. I think we'll just serve the trout as they are and call them peasant-style. Bit of blackened skin never hurt anyone. For future reference, it seems that oven cooks on max regardless of setting. Will, look in that drawer for a fish slice, would you?"

Lunch was polite and chatty, with everyone trying to make Leon welcome. Skin removed, Matthew's fish was delicious and the wine slipped down easily as the party relaxed, aided by Luke's happy chatter. Tanya's expression relaxed, Will's cheeks bloomed and Marianne babbled away like a bride at the top table.

"Did you see that little village with the fabulous church?" asked Adrian.

"Yes! I made Tanya stop so I could get a photo. And that dinky little square!" Marianne exclaimed.

"Looks like we have a bit of everything." Will said, extracting a bone from his teeth. "Mountains, villages, countryside, interesting cities within driving distance and the seaside."

"Yay! Seaside tomorrow!"

Will joined in Luke's excitement. "Yay! Seaside tomorrow!"

Tanya reached over and kissed her son's cheek.

Just before dessert, Leon admitted with endearing shyness the reason they had not been able to fly on Friday.

"Yes, sorry for the delay. My boss asked me to come to a meeting. I was a bit concerned, to tell the truth, but in fact, they offered me a promotion."

Marianne glowed with pride.

"A promotion! That's worthy of a toast, I'd say!" Matthew topped up all their glasses and they offered congratulations.

"Great news!" said Will. "What line of work are you in, Leon?"

"Consulting. A business advisor, basically. I just got made partner in the firm, which means a better salary and more civilised hours. More time for life." He exchanged a loving glance with Marianne.

"Exactly. Just what we all want," said Matthew.

Tanya swigged from her glass. "Too right. Though Beatrice's promotion has had the opposite effect. I can't wait till she's retired and we can actually spend more than one meal at a time together."

"Beatrice is a police officer, I hear," said Leon, folding his napkin neatly into a triangle.

Will raised his eyebrows. "Bit more than a police officer. She's an Acting DCI with the London Metropolitan Police. A senior detective with years of experience whom I would love to have as my boss."

"You're out of luck there," said Matthew. "She'll be retiring at the end of the year to become my boss instead. Now who's for some cheese and quince jelly? Luke, do you want ice-cream instead?"

Tanya and Matthew gathered the plates and Leon addressed

Will. "When you say you'd like Beatrice as your boss, I'm assuming you're police too?"

"Yeah. I'm currently a DS, but aiming for promotion by the end of the year. I want to be an inspector. Just like Beatrice Stubbs, but with better hair."

Marianne and Adrian laughed loudly, both cuffing Will for his cheek. Leon looked bemused.

"You'll see when you meet her, Leon. She has the most unruly mane," Adrian explained. "She'll be here this evening – so whatever you do, don't stare."

Leon gave a brief smile. "I look forward to meeting her and promise to be discreet. One thing I meant to ask, the garden flat. Do we have access?"

Tanya returned with a platter of cheeses, grapes and a solid-looking jam in one hand and a basket of crackers in the other.

"Cheeseboard! Yes, we have access. The house can accommodate ten if we want. But we thought we'd all stay together in the main house."

"Can we have a look at it after lunch?" asked Leon. "Don't mean to be rude, but I do need a bit of space. As an introvert, I like to have a bolthole where I can decompress. "

Tanya blinked. "Sure. I'll find the key and it's all yours."

"That's very kind. Marianne and I would be most grateful."

"Knickerbocker Glory!" Luke marched into the room carrying a ludicrously ornate dessert of multi-coloured scoops, glitter and Smarties, topped off with a lit sparkler.

Tanya covered her eyes. "Dear God, Dad, you are a Health and Safety nightmare."

Will stood up to applaud. "All the best granddads are."

Adrian beamed at the party as the sun streamed across the table, lighting Luke's dessert with a honeyed glow. Birdsong trilled from Matthew's mobile. He took the call out on the patio.

While Marianne, Will and Tanya argued over regional British cheeses, Luke finished his dessert and ran upstairs to change into his swimming trunks. Adrian asked Leon his opinion on European holiday destinations and found him well travelled and informed. The chatter died when Matthew returned through the French windows, his face drawn and concerned.

"Bad news, folks, I'm afraid. Beatrice is going to be late, if she gets here at all tonight. Seems one of her colleagues has been shot."

Chapter 9

Beatrice quite literally couldn't believe it. Everything about the situation seemed unreal. When Gilchrist gathered all the participants into the dining-room to give a briefing, his demeanour was completely inappropriate.

"Good afternoon one and all. As you all know, we lost a dear colleague today. What you may not know it that the sudden death of Samuel Silva was not an accident. He was shot in the head at close range. Next of kin have been informed and the local police will be in charge of the murder investigation. I would like you all to assist in any way you can, but as civilian witnesses. Regardless of our profession, we cannot interfere in the Portuguese jurisdiction."

Beatrice saw the same concerned, shaken expression on the faces of her colleagues. No one spoke, waiting for Gilchrist to continue.

"Those of you planning to attend the Briefing the Press session will be able to learn on the job via a real-life example, or perhaps I should say real death? I will be making a press statement tomorrow morning and must ask you all to keep the event quiet until then. Please tell no one what happened until we have formulated an official response. I apologise for the disruption to your schedules this afternoon and hope you understand. However, I encourage you to put the incident behind you and concentrate on making the rest of the week an EPIC success. One final reminder regarding the BluLite platform. I would like to see far higher usage of the app to share your experiences, today's sad loss excepted. Now, afternoon tea will be served on the terrace before the final sessions of the day. Thanks to all of you for your patience."

Judging by the bewildered expressions of those around her, Beatrice wasn't alone in finding his tone a touch too convivial.

Conversations ebbed and flowed around her as she tried to make sense of it all. An idea took root. It was quite absurd but she found it hard to shake. She retreated behind a large flower display to give herself a moment to think.

She had seen no body. None of them had. Apparently it had been removed to the pathology lab and Scenes of Crime Officers now occupied the room. Without the evidence of her own eyes, she really couldn't conceive of that gentle, diffident man having gone, leaving his poor wife and their new baby daughter alone. Beatrice squeezed her eyes shut. It was too much to bear.

Several peculiar circumstances gave her cause for concern. A murder at a country house amidst a bunch of strangers who happened to be police detectives? It was ridiculous, exacerbated only by the fact that said country house hotel was a hospitality college, or to look at it another way, a school for butlers.

The final element of the sense of farce was Gilchrist's near glee at the drama of it all. As if the entire thing was an elaborate set-up to test their mettle as detectives setting out to solve the case of the murdered psychologist. At that moment, in the gap between her flowery screen and the wall, she spotted a black-clad figure at reception. She narrowed her eyes. *Enter a priest? Who wrote this script?*

"Would you like a cup of tea?"

A waitress holding a tray full of cups and saucers peered around the foliage. Behind her stood a man with a large china teapot.

Beatrice emerged from her hiding-place with as much dignity as she could manage. "Yes, please. Milk, no sugar."

"Certainly, madam. On the table by the staircase, you will find a selection of cakes and sandwiches for afternoon tea. Dinner will be about half an hour later than expected this evening."

"Oh, I'm not staying for..." She stopped, aware of her mood and her preoccupations. She would be terrible company for Matthew and the others, and what a way to meet Marianne's new boyfriend. She'd be better off staying until things calmed down. "Actually, yes, I am. Thank you very much. Can you tell me something? Is that man..." she gestured at the priest, "staying at the hotel?"

"No, madam. This week, the hotel is for the exclusive use of EPIC, the police convention. We are at capacity."

"I see." Beatrice watched the man pour the tea and a thought occurred. "Capacity? But there can't be more than sixty of us. It says in the brochure you have 120 rooms."

"That is correct, madam," said the girl, handing her a teacup. "But currently, the top two floors and roof terrace are undergoing refurbishment because of extensive storm damage this spring."

"Thank you. So if he's not staying here and the body's already gone, what do we need with a man of the cloth?"

"The priest is here to bless the room where... where it happened."

Beatrice thanked the girl again and made her way to the cakes. After a scone and a slice of sponge, she went to reception where a clerk confirmed her room was available all week. She was on her way upstairs when footsteps pounded up behind her. Roman, taking the stairs two at a time, pointed a finger at her.

"Where have you been hiding? We were looking for you."

"A secret place. Who's looking for me?"

"Me, Cher and Xavier. Which secret place?"

"I'm not telling you in case I need to use it again."

Roman's lip curled into a half smile. "I see. And where are you going now?"

"To my room. I'm staying here again tonight. Shall the five of us have dinner together?"

"That's why we were looking for you. We thought we might get away from here and eat in a local village. Xavier is trying to find a taxi service with wheelchair access."

"That's a good idea. I don't want to inflict myself on my friends after what's happened, but I do want to talk about it with people who understand. Are we allowed to go off campus, do you think?"

Roman snorted. "Who's going to stop us? Let's meet on the terrace at six-thirty and make our getaway. By the way, we are only four. André has gone back to Lisbon."

"Of course. Samuel was his godfather. That poor boy."

"Beatrice, are you OK?" Roman's expression invited confidence.

"Not sure yet. What about you?"

"I feel bad. About Silva and about this whole situation. Something feels wrong in here." He pressed a fist against his stomach.

Beatrice looked into his grey-blue eyes. "I know exactly what you mean."

A wheelchair-friendly taxi at such short notice was too much to expect. Roman dismissed the issue as insignificant and asked Cher if she would object to being carried. After some consideration, she decided she would not mind. So at six-thirty, four guilty-looking detectives convened on the terrace while most of the other participants were preparing for dinner. When the cab pulled up in the driveway, Roman scooped Cher into his arms, Beatrice opened the back door of the taxi and Xavier folded the wheelchair into the boot. Within two minutes, they were on the road, with as much relief as if they'd just pulled off a heist.

Xavier, in front, gave the driver the address in what sounded like flawless Portuguese and they drove along a road that paralleled the river towards the town of Ponte de Barca, its dusk lights twinkling in invitation. The atmosphere had a peculiar charge, as if each was silently acknowledging the fact that together they had formed a discrete, complicit bond of trust. Beatrice looked backwards on several occasions, but they had not been followed. She shook her head. Why on earth would anyone bother?

The arrival of four *estrangeiros* would inevitably have attracted attention in the small town, and they certainly looked like an odd collection of foreigners. But while Beatrice and Xavier drew only mild curiosity, the tall long-haired blond guiding a pretty redhead in a wheelchair invited open stares. The waiter showed them to the table, rearranging the seating to give Cher sufficient space.

As the waiter distributed the menus, Xavier gave him a brief instruction. He nodded and hurried off. No one spoke for a moment, a self-consciousness hanging over them, not helped by the unashamed observation of the other diners.

Beatrice and Cher spoke at the same time.

"Why is your Portuguese so good?"

"You guys deserve an explanation."

Beatrice held up her hands. "Sorry. You go first."

Cher smiled. "Thanks. And I agree, I want to know Xavier's secret too. No, what I was going to say is you're all being very cool in accommodating me, and I'd like to explain the wheels."

"You don't owe us any kind of explanation," said Roman.

She bumped his shoulder lightly with her fist. "I appreciate that. But after Gilchrist dangled it out there, I wanna give y'all the full picture. So here goes. Until 2007, I had a pretty good pair of legs. I used to play tennis in summer and ski in winter. In the fall of 2007, I was on patrol in Boston. My unit was called to assist in an armed robbery and siege situation at a print factory. We secured the area, released the hostages and moved in to make the arrests. It all went well until one guy panicked. He was hiding behind a curtain, can you believe? He shot me twice in the lower back. I was wearing body armour, so if it had been higher up, I'd have escaped with a nasty bruise. But his aim was off and one bullet shattered my pelvis while the other penetrated my spine."

Beatrice sensed rather than saw the collective wince.

"The result was Brown-Séquard syndrome, where only half the spinal cord is affected. So after a year and a half of rehab, I have as much of my muscle function back as I'm gonna get. On the bright side, I love the office job. I get to use a whole bunch of other muscles." She tapped the side of her head.

There was a moment of silence, as the group digested the information.

"I'm sorry you had to go through that, Cher," said Xavier. "You are a very strong woman, and thank you for sharing your story with us."

"Well said," Beatrice agreed. "I'm so pleased that horrible incident didn't put you off the police force. You're an asset we could ill afford to lose."

Cher smiled. "I had no choice. No way would my boss let me give up. She pushed me all the way up that hill. Amazing woman. You know what, Beatrice? When I first saw you at dinner last night, you reminded me of her."

"I'll take that as a compliment," Beatrice replied, smiling.

"Cher," said Roman. "Can I ask a question?"

"Sure."

"From what I know about spinal injury, especially if only partial damage is done, patients still have a certain amount of feeling in the affected area. So they can control bladder and bowel movement, enjoy a good sex life and live independently of carers. Tell me if I'm getting too personal."

Cher and Xavier blushed, and Beatrice's own ears got a little warm.

Cher took a deep breath. "Pretty close to the bone there, Roman, but hey, we're amongst friends. Truth is, it depends on the person. I can only speak from my own experience. I live alone and since my apartment's been adapted, I manage just fine. I can go to restaurants and fly and stay in hotels and use the bathroom same as anyone else. As for my sex drive, same as it ever was."

Roman locked eyes with her. "Thank you for being so honest."

"You're welcome."

Sex, violence and bowel movements all before the aperitifs? Beatrice was casting around for a light-hearted remark to break the tension when thankfully, the waiter arrived. Xavier examined the bottle he was shown and gave his approval. The waiter pulled the cork and started pouring sparkling wine into their glasses.

Xavier glanced around the table. "I hope you don't mind, but I ordered a bottle of Espumante. I thought we should raise a glass to say goodbye to Samuel Silva."

"Oh what a lovely idea," said Beatrice. "And let's spare a thought for his wife and their new little girl."

Cher's face paled. "They had a new baby?"

Beatrice bit her lip and nodded. "Just finished the adoption process. He showed me the pictures. A two-year-old called Marcia."

Cher pressed the bridge of her nose and closed her eyes.

Xavier went to stand, changed his mind and lifted his glass instead. "To Samuel Silva, an extraordinary man, police officer, husband and father. None of us who ever met you, no matter how briefly, will ever forget you. To Samuel, may you rest in peace."

Beatrice, Cher and Roman tilted their glasses to his and repeated, "To Samuel, may you rest in peace." They all sipped and stayed silent in thought for a moment, the waiter sensitively keeping his distance.

Somehow, Xavier had become the natural leader of the four-some. He suggested they choose the set menu and get down to business. Everyone fell in with his plan and the waiter was despatched for four orders of *Arroz de Marisco* and a bottle of Dão.

Beatrice offered around the bread rolls, helped herself and started buttering.

Xavier began. "I can't speak for anyone else, but Samuel Silva's death has affected me deeply. Not just the shock of such a sudden and brutal death, but the situation, the environment and the circumstances. To me, this whole situation feels very bizarre."

"That's pretty much what I thought," said Beatrice. She relayed the thoughts that had occurred to her whilst concealed behind the flower display. No body, the artifice of the crime, a country house full of butlers. Shaking her head, she laughed with more disbelief than humour. "If I didn't think this was ludicrous, I'd honestly suspect hidden cameras. I feel as if we're in a reality TV show and Gilchrist is our puppet-master."

Cher was nodding energetically. "Yup, there was something weird about his reaction. Where was the shock? Where was the grief? Goddamit, I only met Samuel yesterday and I'm hurting. You know what I think about Gilchrist's speech? It was rehearsed. I don't know if it comes across that way because he's so media-savvy, but his reactions were not natural. And as you say, Beatrice, no one saw a body."

"I did," said Roman.

Everyone stared at him, awaiting an explanation.

"He was on the first floor, same as me. When I tried to go back to my room this afternoon, the corridor was taped off. I was explaining to the uniform that I only wanted to drop off my computer when a gurney came past with the body bag."

Beatrice hesitated. "Seems a stupid question, I know, but could you be sure it was Silva?"

Roman shook his head. "No. Those Portuguese cops are way too efficient. They didn't leave a hand hanging out with a distinctive signet ring on a finger, and they didn't drop his ID card as they passed. All I can say is it was a body of similar height to Silva, coming from the direction of his room, where he was reported as shot." He shrugged, but offered a crooked smile to temper his sarcasm.

The waiter brought the wine and a bottle of sparkling water. As Xavier thanked him and received a gracious smile in return, an idea occurred to Beatrice.

"Xavier, you didn't answer my question. How come you speak such good Portuguese?"

He looked up from tipping oil and vinegar onto his side plate. "My wife Yasmin comes from Florianópolis in Brazil." He tore off a piece of bread and dipped it in the oil-vinegar mixture. "She taught me how to mix *caipirinhas* and make *feijoada* but I still can't dance the samba. Portuguese is not so different from Italian so I picked it up quickly."

"You speak Italian too?" asked Roman.

Xavier shrugged, apparently modest about his linguistic abilities. "I'm Swiss. We have three languages."

Cher narrowed her eyes at Beatrice. "Are you thinking what I'm thinking?"

"If you mean that the four of us should work this case as a private investigation without bothering the local police, using Xavier's language skills to find out as much as we can, then I'd say yes."

Cher looked at Roman. "What do you say?"

"I can't offer any relevant language skills, but I think four detectives at our level could combine a lot of intelligence, ability and a very healthy disregard for protocol. Yes, I want to be a part of this, if you'll have me."

"So that's settled then. Now we just need a game plan," said Beatrice.

Xavier pulled a notebook from his jacket. "I already wrote down a few ideas, just in case."

"You planned this all along, you dog!" exclaimed Cher, with a broad smile.

"As I always say," said Xavier, with mock dignity, "be prepared for the worst, but hope for the best."

"I'll drink to that," said Beatrice, triggering another hasty toast before they had to clear space on the table for a huge gleaming tureen borne by two waiters. The smell of saffron, spice and fish enveloped them and Beatrice saw the appetite for food and investigation dancing in everyone's eyes. With the help of this unconventional team, she would find out exactly who was behind the death of Samuel Silva and see justice served.

For Marcia's sake.

Chapter 10

When it came to cars, Adrian seemed to be missing the point once again. The debate over breakfast was all about who should travel in which vehicle.

Will phrased his claim as an offer. "How about I drive the Panda for our trip to Braga and take Leon and Marianne as passengers?"

"If it's OK with you, I'm happiest behind the wheel," said Leon. "Maybe I could drive Marianne and Matthew in the Peugeot while you take Tanya and Luke in the back seat."

"Wait a minute." Tanya frowned. "Why is it only blokes have access to car keys? I've driven the Peugeot so far and don't see why I should be relegated to passenger status just by the arrival of another man."

"I want to go with Will!" said Luke.

Matthew stirred his coffee. "Personally, travelling in the back seat is not a pleasant experience for me. I get queasy and there's never enough leg room. I don't mind who drives but I would put in a request for the front passenger seat."

Everyone had strong views on the subject apart from Adrian. So long as they went somewhere nice and considered cars as nothing more than a means of getting there, he was happy.

Bored of the discussion, he took his coffee onto the terrace. The sun was beating down already, heating the tiles and warming Adrian's skin. Far below, boats puttered across the lake and a riot of birdsong populated the shrubs. He drank his latte in peace and inhaled the herby scents of nature. He wished Beatrice was here.

Eventually they struck a compromise. Leon would drive the Peugeot to Braga, Will would drive it back. Tanya would chauffeur her father and son in the Fiat. In the spirit of cooperation, they cleared the breakfast detritus and got into their respective vehicles.

In the back seat of the Peugeot, Adrian rested his hand on Will's thigh and gave him a 'you OK?' look. Will smiled and leaned over for a brief reassuring kiss.

"No snogging in the back seat!" said Marianne, laughing at them through oversized sunglasses.

Leon opened the window. "Tanya, you follow me. Shouldn't be difficult to find, but we've got a satnav."

Tanya's mouth opened to respond, but Luke was cavorting around, pulling faces and distracting her attention.

Adrian spent the entire drive oohing and aahing at the views. Thankfully, for fear of losing Tanya, Leon had slowed to a pace more suited to holiday driving, so they could enjoy the constantly surprising landscapes of the national park. Will read out historical facts from the guidebook and details of the protected species in the park.

"I'd love to see one of those Minho horses. But if they're that rare, it's probably unlikely," said Adrian, while trying to capture the scenery on his phone.

"I expect they're much like Dartmoor ponies. You only ever see them at a distance," Leon answered.

The tourist board had helpful signs warning motorists of upcoming photo opportunities, and Adrian persuaded Leon to stop at every one. He and Marianne were the first out of the car, but for different subjects. Adrian wanted sweeping views, details on lichen on rock or a sunbathing lizard. Marianne wanted pictures of herself and Leon in all variety of affectionate poses. When Will was unavailable, she took selfies. Leon didn't seem to mind.

"Here, let me take one of you two," he offered, as Adrian snapped a shot of Will against an oak tree.

They posed for the camera and Marianne came to look at the result. "Aww, you two. You're so photogenic, it's sickening."

The sound of a chirpy horn tooting made them look round. The Panda whizzed past, hands waving from within. "Eat my dust, suckers!" yelled Tanya, as the car sped up into the bend.

"She's such a tomboy," said Marianne.

Leon returned Will's phone. "I hope she doesn't get lost. She's supposed to follow me."

"Don't worry about Tanya. She's a terrific driver," said Will. "Right, let's get on or we'll be the ones left behind."

"Oh my God! Is that a salamander?" Adrian gasped. "One sec, I have to get a shot of this."

Will rolled his eyes, but Leon merely grinned, leaning against the car. "Take your time, Adrian. We're on holiday."

Braga had the most divine architecture. Literally. Austere yet ornate, the whitewashed buildings and towering edifices were designed to invoke a higher presence. Stone crucifixes, arches, turrets and clocks threaded a motif of religious piety through the streets. They wandered past so many churches in sparsely populated squares that Adrian wondered where all the worshippers came from.

As always with a group of disparate people with differing interests, it was a stop-start progression around fountains, cafés and beautifully decorated buildings. The souvenir shops appealed to everyone, and even Matthew found something local for Beatrice. The heat intensified towards mid-afternoon and Adrian understood why so few locals were on the street. Everyone must be enjoying a siesta after lunch.

"I'm hungry," said Luke.

Matthew glanced at his watch. "Good heavens, it's half past two. Yes indeed, we should set about finding a place to eat."

"Is it that late already? We've probably left it a bit too long," said Will. "My guess is most places have finished serving lunch by now. We might find a chain or something still open."

Leon agreed. "If we'd got here by twelve, we might have had a chance. But we didn't bargain for so many photo opportunities!" He nudged Adrian with a wink and a smile. "Sorry to put a dampener on things, but we'll be lucky to find a local restaurant still open and prepared to seat such a large party."

"Don't they have a McDonald's?" Luke asked.

"I never eat junk food. Sorry. We can do better than that." Leon gestured to a nearby café with empty tables and drawn curtains. "Sit down in the shade for a moment and I'll have a scout around." He strode off up the nearest alley.

Assuming the restaurant was closed, Adrian was surprised to see a weary-looking waiter emerge from the front door once they had rearranged tables to suit their party of six and a half.

"Food finish. Drinks only. Coffee? Beer? Water?"

Marianne counted heads. "Six bottles of water and a Coca Cola, please."

"With gas?"

Marianne's forehead creased. "With what?"

"He's asking if you want still or sparkling water," said Will. He spoke to the waiter. "Four waters, two with gas, two no. *E duas cervejas, por favor. Obrigado.*"

"Where did you pick up the lingo?" asked Adrian.

"It's just a few phrases from the guidebook. How are you feeling, Matthew?"

"I'll perk up as soon as I get some food inside me. Luke and I are very similar in that way. Feed us regularly and we are docile as lambs." He brushed the hair from Luke's forehead, which flopped right back into his eyes.

When the drinks arrived, Adrian appreciated Will's choice of beer over water but regarded the bowl of small yellow pods which accompanied them with some suspicion. Will asked the waiter what they were but couldn't really understand the reply. The man demonstrated by picking one up, squeezing to release it from its skin and popping it in his mouth. He smacked his lips and winked at Luke, who naturally wanted to try one as soon as the waiter had returned inside. Tanya gave her permission.

"Are you sure that's a good idea?" asked Marianne. "You don't know where they've been."

"I'll volunteer as taster," said Will, copying the waiter's movements and chewing cautiously. "They're nice. Salty, like soybeans. Probably make you want to drink more."

Luke and Matthew followed his lead and soon everyone was snacking on the odd little pods, leaving the carapace of skins around the bowl. The restaurant door opened and a short, white-haired man in a light blue suit approached the table, bearing another two bowls. His face was lined and brown, and his blue eyes sparkled under wild eyebrows.

"Good afternoon, my friends. I see you like our *tremoços*. Here, I bring you another bowl and some potato chips. Are you hungry? Would you like some proper snacks?"

Will spoke. "You are open for food? We thought it was drinks only."

"We are open. Restaurant service finish at two but we can make toasted sandwiches, salads, fishcakes, French fries or our special, the *francesinha*."

Marianne began to refuse. "Thank you, but we have plans to..."

"What's a *francesinha*?" Tanya asked.

The old man made a face of exaggerated disbelief. "You never tried a *francesinha*? What are you, vegetarian?"

"No, I just don't get out much." Tanya cast a meaningful glance at Marianne, who made a show of looking up the street for Leon rather than meeting her sister's eyes.

Their host was in his element. "Imagine the king of sandwiches. A slice of bread. Piled on top you have pork, chorizo, bacon, steak and another slice of bread. Cover the whole thing with spiced cheese sauce and a fried egg. If this is your first, young lady, I will make it myself. It is an experience you will never forget."

"Oh God," moaned Adrian. "Carbohydrate City here I come. I want one so badly it hurts."

"Me too!" Matthew and Luke spoke simultaneously.

They ordered six full *francesinhas*, with three bowls of chips on the side and a salad for Marianne. She sent Leon a message to announce they had found sustenance. Adrian and Will pored over the guidebook and suggested a visit to Bom Jesus, a religious pilgrimage site after lunch. Matthew and Tanya agreed, despite neither having any religious proclivities.

After a few minutes, Leon arrived, hot and irritable. He muttered something about unhelpful locals and a lack of flexibility. "You'd think they'd realise how much the tourist trade is worth in a backwater like this."

Matthew tried to cheer him up. "It was awfully good of you to go in search of something for us. We didn't even think this joint was open. The owner is friendly, you know, and has offered us his house special. Seemed a bit off to refuse. Would you like one of these?" He offered the bowl of *tremoços*.

"Thanks, I won't. Just some still water, cold if possible. I think once we've eaten, I'd like to head back to the villa. Catch a nap and perhaps..."

"Your lunch, ladies and gentlemen!" The little man in the powder blue suit carried three plates and the waiter followed with more. "Hello, Mister!" he said to Leon. "One of these is for you. Enjoy, a Portuguese speciality!"

Leon stared at the yellow lump in front of him and Adrian burst out laughing.

"It's a sandwich, Leon, not an alien life form."

"Try a bite, you might like it," said Will.

Leon did cut off a corner of the impressive slab, but made a show of forcing it down and shook his head. "Not for me, I'm afraid. I prefer something light at lunch. Could I get a green salad?"

The owner shrugged his shoulders and turned down the corners of his mouth in a 'what can you do?' pout and returned to the kitchen while the rest of the party moaned and groaned in delight.

"We were planning a trip to the religious pilgrimage site this afternoon. It's supposed to be spectacular in itself with amazing views," Tanya said.

"According to the guidebook, pilgrims used to climb the stone steps on their knees as a show of penitence," added Will.

Marianne looked at Leon, who was taking a long draught from a glass of water. "That could be interesting, don't you think?"

Leon swallowed, wiped his mouth and said, "We'll see."

After the food had been attacked with intent but not quite finished off, the group drank coffees and chatted about nothing in particular. Tanya told Adrian all about her business idea for outdoor summer schools, to educate children about the value of nature. Matthew and Will played I-Spy with Luke while Leon and Marianne spoke in low voices on a topic Adrian couldn't catch.

The owner emerged with the bill, which Matthew insisted on paying. The man asked several times for their opinions on his *francesinhas* and then asked where they were staying. When Will told him the name, his face lit up with recognition.

"Beautiful place. And only a few kilometres from the best fish restaurant in Northern Portugal. The *Marisqueira do Miguel*. My cousin's father-in-law owns it and it has a fantastic reputation. You must go! Here, I write down the name." He scribbled on the back of one of the paper napkins. "Tell him Pedro Pereira sent you and you will get five-star service. Try the *Bacalhau a Zé do Pipo*. Paradise!"

They thanked him and he shook everyone's hands, even Luke's, as they said goodbye. The amenable atmosphere left Adrian with a very good feeling about Braga. Back at the cars, Marianne announced she and Leon would prefer to miss Bom Jesus and head back for a rest by the pool.

"Can we go back to the pool too, Mum?" asked Luke.

"Don't you want to come and see this church with us?" Tanya's question was addressed to Luke, but Adrian sensed there was a broader target.

Luke shook his head with great conviction.

"If you like, we'll take him back with us, Tan," offered Marianne. We can keep an eye on him while he's in the pool. And I won't forget sunscreen and hats and all that."

Luke cheered. "Do you want to come too, Will?"

"No thanks. You practise your shark-wrestling techniques and I'll test you when I get back. Why don't you guys take the Panda and we'll take the Peugeot? We'll see you back at the ranch later this afternoon. Tanya, do you want to drive?"

Adrian and Will sat in the back, Adrian reading out some of the titbits from the guidebook. "Eighteenth century sanctuary, commissioned by the Archbishop, Baroque stairway with Stations of the Cross, sculptures on each landing depicting Christ's Via Crucis, some alarmingly graphic, 300 feet up, journey of purification... it sounds fabulously gothic. I can't wait!"

A full afternoon of gothic religious architecture was certainly intimidating, and the climb to the church in the late afternoon heat wore Adrian out. In the car on the way back, he tried to keep awake to talk to Will while Matthew dozed off in the passenger seat. Shortly afterwards, Tanya's head dropped onto his shoulder and his own eyelids grew heavy. Next thing he knew, Will was parking outside the villa. He glanced at his watch. It was half past six.

A figure appeared in the doorway, holding a glass aloft.

"Beatrice!" exclaimed Will, waking his sleepy passengers. He was out of the Peugeot and across the drive before Adrian had even gathered his belongings. He roused Tanya and Matthew then hurried to join in the greeting hugs.

"Finally! So pleased to see you!" he exclaimed.

"I'm so pleased to see all of you! Sorry to take so long. What a glorious spot you chose, Professor Bailey! This is the perfect retreat from it all. Hello Tanya, you look tanned and relaxed already."

"Just woke up, that's why. Great to see you, Beatrice. When did you arrive? Have you seen the others?"

Beatrice kissed Matthew and clutched his arm. "Yes, I have. Well, Marianne and Leon for a few minutes, before they retired for a nap. Luke was already in bed when I got here. Bit too much sun this afternoon, I believe. How was Braga?"

A frown of concern flashed across Tanya's face. "I'll go check on him."

Matthew squeezed Beatrice to his side. "Braga was quite out of the ordinary. An experience I would not want you to miss. If you get time, Old Thing..."

"I'd love to see it, if I can get away from this whole sorry business. I'm not going to bore you with the details, but I hope you'll understand this week will be more work than play. A dustman's holiday, unfortunately. But at least we're all here together at last." She indicated her drink. "I thought you'd understand if I started without you all. It is cocktail hour, after all. Can I make anyone else a martini?"

Will stroked the back of Adrian's neck. "I'd love one. Can I have an olive in mine? I'll just grab a quick shower and start cooking. We'd planned stuffed squid tonight."

"Yes please to the martini and the olive," said Adrian. "We'll freshen up and then get into the kitchen. It really is great to see you, Beatrice. I hope the work situation... well... works out. Back in ten."

He followed Will upstairs, admiring the view and calculating how much could be achieved in ten minutes.

Sounds of splashing, gargling and brushing came from the bathroom as Adrian billowed the sheet, wafting a gust of air over his damp body. The cool cotton settled on his skin and he released a contented sigh. Five minutes lie-down and then get dressed to say hello properly to Beatrice. He wished she could be there tomorrow for their day at the beach. She always managed to act as a dynamic force of perspective. He would miss her terribly when she finally moved to Devon.

Will came out of the bathroom and leapt onto the bed, bouncing Adrian three inches off the mattress.

"The boy who never grew up," murmured Adrian.

"The old fart who grew up too soon," said Will, wrapping himself around Adrian's body.

They lay in silence, temperatures adjusting.

"Seaside tomorrow," Will whispered. "Can't wait."

"Don't know who's more excited, you or the five-year old child."

"Me, of course. No contest. As for the child, I'll mind him."

Adrian rolled over to face Will. "We'll all mind him. You might be the strongest swimmer, but everyone looks out for Luke."

Will didn't answer.

"What?"

Still no reply.

"William Quinn, if you have something to say, spit it out."

"I have nothing to say. Yet. But the thing is, you don't watch like I do. Beatrice got here at six o'clock and Luke was already in bed. Why? His mother told us yesterday his bedtime is seven o'clock, even on a school night. Did you notice the tension between Tanya and Marianne at lunchtime? Why were none of the pool towels even damp when we got home?"

Adrian laughed, his eyes closed. "Stop it. You are on holiday and are forbidden to see suspicious signs, clues or footprints till we get back to Boot Street. There is nothing to investigate here, DI Quinn. Although, on closer inspection..."

Adrian caught Will's hand and pulled it under the sheet.

Chapter 11

Beatrice enjoyed dinner enormously. It was a lively affair as she did her best to make up for her absence by catching up with everything at once. She avoided any mention of the sudden death of her colleague, but engaged and teased and entertained throughout. It wasn't easy to get a handle on the new addition to the family, as Leon and Marianne conversed quietly together, whispering sweet nothings as new lovers tend to do. The stuffed squid was perfection, and Adrian assured everyone he now understood the quirks of the cooker. The Gerês hotel might boast five stars but Adrian's culinary skills were of an equal standard. Beatrice sighed happily and tucked in.

Luke flatly refused to even try the squid, claiming it looked like an alien. He'd been crotchety and irritable since he woke up, so Tanya made him beans on toast and took him off to bed once he'd finished. He wouldn't say goodnight to anyone, burying his face in his cuddly dolphin.

When Tanya returned, Beatrice voiced her concern. "Is he all right, Tanya? He seems a bit upset about something."

"Don't think so. Just overtired and probably not that hungry after that mahoosive lunch. You should have seen it, Beatrice. A sandwich the size of a pillow containing an entire farmyard's worth of meat. I am going to put on at least a stone this week."

"No you won't," said Will. "Tomorrow we're at the beach, so we can swim it all off."

A pang of envy pierced Beatrice. She loved the seaside. "Stop it. I've got to attend dull seminars with stiff suits in air-conditioned rooms. I only manage to stay awake because the chairs are too hard." She waved her empty wine glass at Matthew, who duly filled it.

"Don't you have a pool at the hotel, Old Thing? I can lend you a shower cap if you're worried about your hair."

Beatrice pulled an expression of outrage as everyone burst into laughter.

Matthew had been on top form the whole evening, cracking jokes and including everyone in his merriment. Holidays obviously suited him. The room rang with laughter, so much so Beatrice wondered if they might wake Luke.

Just before dessert, Tanya brought in two champagne bottles in ice buckets, distributed glasses and popped both corks.

"We're toasting our local hero. Adrian won't tell you himself, but when we were at Heathrow Airport, his quick thinking saved a child from getting mashed into an escalator. The parents were in tears, other passengers wanted to shake his hand and I was so proud, I could burst. Raise your glasses, ladies and gents, to Adrian Harvey, aka Superman!"

Glasses chinked, Tanya told her version of the story with bells and whistles, Adrian delivered a downbeat, modest version and everyone applauded both. The intensity of Will's expression delighted Beatrice. She herself was puffed up with pride for her friend but recognised the look in Will's eyes as much more than that.

The clock struck eleven. Tanya drained her bubbles and announced it was her bedtime. Leon and Marianne went shortly afterwards, wandering across the garden path along a trail of solar-powered lights. Once the newcomer had departed, conversation naturally turned to opinions on his character.

"Polite, well mannered, if a bit fussy about food," pronounced Beatrice. "And looks-wise, I'd give him an eight if he tidied his hair up a bit."

There was a moment of silence until Will, Adrian and Matthew caught each other's eyes and burst into an explosion of laughter. Beatrice, feeling the pink in her cheeks, joined in with a knowing grin.

She was curious how the first two days had played out in her absence. It was one thing to talk about what had happened on the surface, but it was the subtext that interested her.

Matthew rubbed his face, still smiling. "He's all right. A bit prickly, which I can understand. He's in enemy territory and an obvious outsider being judged by a tight-knit pack. I have a feeling he'll settle down. Thing is, he needs to do it on his own. While Marianne insists on acting as his spokesperson, he can't realistically engage with us on his own terms." He paused. "Did that sound a bit esoteric?"

"Yes, it did," said Beatrice. "But enough of Pater's fence-sitting. Will, you're a pretty good judge of character. What do you think?"

' Will looked into his champagne flute. "Jury's out. He's tender and sweet with Marianne, which is what counts, I guess. But a good guide for me is how people behave with animals, kids and waiting staff. So far, I'm not impressed. All I can see is an almighty ego."

"Will!" Adrian sounded truly shocked. "Is this all over the who-gets-to-drive issue? Because you, Tanya and Leon were all waving your petrol-head credentials about this morning. It's unfair to pick on him for that."

Will lifted a shoulder in a half-shrug, which could have meant anything.

Beatrice fixed her eyes on Adrian. "We haven't heard from you yet."

"He's insecure, probably a bit defensive as he's in the lion's den. He has an ego but let's just look around this table. We all have reasons to be proud of ourselves and not one of us can claim to be self-effacing. Imagine what he's heard about each of us. Wouldn't you come out sabre-rattling in such company? And aside from all of our irrelevant opinions, Marianne loves him. For that reason alone, we should give him a chance."

His speech seemed to chasten the party and conversation turned to safer waters, such as how many visits to castles and waterfalls could be fitted into one day.

Chapter 12

The post-prandial sensation of well-being and familial contentment was punctured as soon as Beatrice checked her emails before bed. Gilchrist had called a breakfast briefing for all senior officers at eight in the morning and would she please confirm attendance on receipt.

Three things about this put Beatrice in a furious temper.

First, she had to get up at six in the morning in order to make the journey back to the hotel in time. It was already quarter to midnight.

Second, breakfast was a time for re-engaging with the world, adjusting to other people and most importantly, eating.

Third, Xavier, Roman and André were not deemed sufficiently senior to merit an invitation.

She sent a curt reply in the affirmative then picked up her phone, pressed a number and launched into a whirlwind of ranting as she applied moisturiser to her face. When her annoyance had blown itself out, Xavier's calm voice at the end of the phone soothed her.

"No, listen. This actually works in our favour. Roman and I have two paths to pursue and need some time to do so. I'll explain tomorrow. The briefing means we can disappear for a few hours in all innocence, come back with our findings and share all our news over lunch. Don't raise any objections on our behalf, B. We can use the time."

She softened at the use of her initial. "OK. I suppose that makes sense. See you at lunch for a general catch-up. Sorry for disturbing you."

"I planned to call you actually. We need to keep in touch, even if we have to be quiet about it. By the way, André is back. We had dinner together tonight. He's a very useful source of information. Sleep well and see you in the morning."

She wished him the same and got into bed beside Matthew, who was reading some tome about explorers.

"I've got to get up at six, I'm afraid. A bloody nuisance I know, but the boss wants all senior personnel in early for a briefing. I'm sorry."

He placed the book on the table. "So we should get some sleep. And yes, you are a bloody nuisance but I'm awfully glad you're here. By the way, I bought you a present."

He rustled in his bedside cabinet and handed over something heavy wrapped in tissue paper.

She tore away the wrapping to reveal a six-inch highly coloured metal cockerel with bright red comb and yellow feet. It looked both sharp-eyed and cheerful; a ferocious defender of happiness.

"It's lovely, thank you!"

"Very local and somehow, it reminded me of you."

"And I'm supposed to take that as a compliment, am I?" She smiled and kissed him goodnight, and placed her cockerel beside her phone before she turned out the light.

Six hours later, the sunrise was a bonus. Foul-tempered and dry-mouthed, she couldn't even doze in the taxi, as the driver's choice of radio station played endless howling laments. Instead, she observed the dawn scenery as the sun emerged over black silhouetted trees. As the not-yet-brilliant ball of fire ascended, a rush of wonder and awe filled her, erasing all her negativity. Even the music seemed to fit.

She made a promise to herself. She would pull every trick in the book to solve this case. If that meant spending less time with Matthew, Adrian and the gang, then so be it. Some things were more important. With a deep intake of breath she prepared herself for a heavy week ahead. In her pocket, she ran her fingers over the little cockerel, another harbinger of dawn.

Within the first minute of his speech, Gilchrist took the wind out of her sails. The murder of Samuel Silva was being treated as a botched robbery. The man's wallet had been emptied, the watch removed from his wrist, and the murder weapon, also missing, was his own revolver. The likely scenario was that someone had been in his room when he returned. Silva disturbed the burglar who panicked and used the psychologist's own gun against him. There were no fingerprints, but the window had been forced from the outside. Local police were following several leads and were optimistic the perpetrator would be found in the next twenty-four to forty-eight hours. The conference would go ahead with some minor changes, but Gilchrist exhorted everyone to focus on the task in hand. A memorial book would be available at reception for colleagues and friends to leave their thoughts. At the end of the week, it would be sent to his widow.

He finished with a warning. "The press already know there has been a homicide and are desperate to get more on the story. From their perspective, a murder at a convention of police detectives is great entertainment. In order for the local force to do their job and for us to maintain our collective reputations, I must ask you not to speak to anyone on the issue, either formally or informally, and refrain from discussing the incident in front of the hotel employees."

Beatrice looked around at the empty salvers in the serving area where a buffet breakfast would normally have been waiting for them, with staff on hand to refill the salvers, coffee dispensers and bread baskets. Her stomach rumbled.

"Please continue to share pictures and videos of our EPIC event but on no other social media platform than BluLite, which is the only one we can be sure is secure. I'm sorry this tragic event has happened and I am as shocked as the rest of you. However, we are professionals and must continue in our duty out of respect for our colleague, one of the most honourable men I have ever known. Ladies and gents, would you get to your feet for a minute's silence to remember a great detective, teacher, friend, colleague, husband and father. Samuel Silva."

They rose, bowed their heads and remained perfectly still for sixty seconds, united in the subject of their thoughts. Beatrice recalled the last funeral she had attended, that of Superintendent Hamilton. The silence as his friends, family and colleagues paid their respects contained such a range of emotions and feelings towards the suddenly departed. Not just his choice of exit – a clinic in Switzerland – but how much of his manner had aroused resentment and animosity. As if he had made enemies to save himself the trouble of being liked.

Somehow, here in this room, there more harmonious warmth towards the man they had lost. After the minute was up, Gilchrist thanked them and invited them to eat. The doors opened and the staff hurried in with stainless steel trays of eggs, bacon, sausages, hash browns, tomatoes, toast, beans, pancakes and warm plates. Junior officers, who had been waiting outside, swarmed in after them.

Beatrice was out of her seat immediately, barrelling directly towards the buffet with ruthless intent. She heaped her plate with all the elements of a full English, added two slices of brown toast and turned victoriously towards her seat when André hailed her from across the room.

"Beatrice! Join us!"

He and Cher occupied a table near the door. She changed direction and set her tray on the table next to Cher's.

"Whoa, Beatrice! You got some appetite!"

Beatrice looked at Cher's bowl of fruit and yoghurt with some disdain and gave André's American-style selection a nod of approval.

"I have been up since six this morning so I deserve every mouthful. If I ate nothing more than a bunch of berries, I'd faint by eleven o'clock. Hello André, good to see you again. I'm truly sorry about the loss of your...colleague."

She chose not to mention the personal information Samuel Silva had shared. André met her eyes and gave her a brief nod of understanding and a warm smile.

"Thank you, Beatrice. Everyone in our Lisbon office is shocked and saddened more than we can express. He was one helluva guy, not just to me, but the entire force." He reached over to the coffee pot and poured them both a cup before filling his own. "For such an incredible life to end this way is incomprehensible. I just don't get it. On any level."

Beatrice added milk. "A tragedy, for all concerned. I must add my own comments in the book of remembrance."

"There'll be a whole bunch more now," said Cher. "Yesterday's new arrivals."

Beatrice looked around. "Yes, I saw a few unfamiliar faces this morning. How was dinner last night?"

Cher cupped her hands around her coffee mug. "Nothing special. Only one topic of conversation at every table. To be expected, I guess, but so much speculation is just so much speculation, know what I mean? How was your evening?"

"Good fun. Some of my favourite people all in one lovely place. And a stuffed squid dish I will never forget. Did you see Xavier this morning?"

"I saw him." André cut into a pancake, added a slice of bacon and dipped it into some maple syrup. "He and Roman left in a taxi. Must have been around six-thirty? I was just warming up for my morning run. Xavier said they were going to watch the sunrise at a local tourist spot. Those guys. I think it's very romantic." He forked his creation into his mouth.

"Romantic?" Cher twisted her body towards the young man. "You don't think...?"

André swallowed and nodded. "Come on. Two good-looking men, obviously attracted to each other, spend every minute together and get up early to watch the sunrise?" He pulled down his lower eyelid in a gesture of 'you don't fool me'. He drained his coffee and looked back at them. "And why not? This is the twenty-first century. My philosophy? Your happiness is no one else's business. I wish them nothing but the best."

Cher hadn't touched her breakfast. "I thought Xavier was married."

"He might be," said André. "But this morning when I met those two, their eyes were alive, excited and full of joy. I might be kinda green and naïve in some ways, but I can recognise two people in love. This pot is empty, I need to order more coffee."

Beatrice said "Good idea."

While he attracted the attention of the nearest waitress, Beatrice nudged Cher's elbow and shook her head. She gave a pointed look at the neglected berries and Cher picked up her spoon.

"So André," Beatrice chirped, "what sessions are on your agenda today?"

Two hours of 'Culture and Connections', a short coffee break during which Beatrice wrote in the memorial book, followed by ninety minutes on human trafficking initiatives made for a long morning. The prospect of lunch loomed large – and not just for the opportunity for much-needed nourishment. She was eager to hear what Xavier and Roman had discovered and wanted the chance to talk as well as listen.

Her session finished on time so she waited for Cher in reception. The plan was to grab a couple of salads and eat on the terrace. But when she switched on her phone, a message was waiting.

INVITATION: Stubbs, Davenport, Racine. Lunch with Björnsson. 13.00, Room 1126. Room service ordered for 4 guests.

When Cher eventually rolled into the foyer, she flashed her phone to show Beatrice she'd got the message. Avoiding an overfamiliar ex-colleague and two seasoned researchers who wanted to discuss 'functioning dysfunctionals', Beatrice excused herself and followed Cher away from the restaurant to the lifts. She hoped Roman had checked the room for bugs.

Xavier opened the door. "Here you are! Finally!"

Beatrice raised her eyebrows.

Xavier understood. "The room is clear."

"We only just got your message," said Beatrice as she helped manoeuvre Cher's wheelchair over the threshold. "It's been a long morning."

"Come in, Roman's in the bathroom, but we have food, drink and news."

Cher took over the steering and parked herself at the dining table, where she began lifting lids. "Let's do it in that order. We only have an hour and I gotta eat."

"I wouldn't like to say I told you so, but that's what happens when you only have a handful of berries for breakfast." Beatrice flung her bag on the bed and sat at the table. "Xavier, do you already know what Gilchrist said in his speech or do you want the condensed version?"

"We heard. But what we learnt this morning doesn't quite fit."

The bathroom door opened and Roman emerged with a towel around his waist. His chest, muscular and lean, was decorated with a tattoo across his left shoulder. His long hair was wet and his feet left damp prints on the carpet as he padded across the room. "Aha! Our guests have arrived. So, who's ready for a debrief?"

Beatrice bit her lip and examined her fingernails, not daring to look at Cher.

Happily, at least in terms of Beatrice's concentration, Roman put on a hotel robe before joining them at the small table. Xavier took his plate to the armchair to give them some space and relayed their morning's discoveries. They'd made contact with the police and hotel management on an informal basis.

The robbery was the only line of enquiry and the police already had a list of suspects. Xavier had spoken to two different officers off the record, both of whom were willing to chat and share experiences with a fellow detective. Silva had been shot twice at close range in the back of the head whilst he was at his computer. So much for surprising a thief. The second detective had referred to it as 'execution-style'. The window had indeed been forced, but contrary to Gilchrist's assertion, several fingerprints had been found. The window pane had a recent set of prints which did not match those of Silva.

Apart from the hotel's closed floors, the conference had booked all available rooms, and more than a dozen casual workers had been taken on as gardeners, cleaners, drivers and kitchen staff. Work on the upper stories had been stopped for the duration of the conference so as not to disturb the participants, so at least they didn't have to check out dozens more workmen and suppliers. Of the casual staff, four had no alibi and two could not be located. It was simply a matter of time until they were found, fingerprinted and a suspect arrested. And time was crucial as the pressure was on, both externally and within.

"And you?" asked Roman, wiping his mouth on a napkin. "What's the news on the grapevine?"

"Not much more than you know," said Beatrice. "Gilchrist made his speech, we attended our seminars like good girls and kept our ears to the grindstone. Everyone's talking, but nobody's saying anything of note."

"Apart from André," said Cher, with a light flush.

"Oh yes. André saw you two leave this morning and assumes you've become lovers. We didn't argue."

Roman yanked the fruit bowl towards him and pulled a grape from the bunch. He popped it in his mouth and chewed, his gaze distant. Finally he swallowed and turned his glacial gaze to Xavier. "That could be a very useful cover."

Xavier's eyes widened and a slow smile began to spread. "I would never have thought of it, but you're right. A hint here, an absence there, don't ask, don't tell, but let the rumours do the work. And no need to hide the fact that we are always together at mealtimes, or in each other's rooms."

Roman clapped his hands together and laughed. "Perfect. We'll have to pretend to be hiding our affair, but everyone knows. I love it. We couldn't have designed it better ourselves. But how do we explain these two?" He jerked a chin at Beatrice and Cher.

"Fag hags?" suggested Beatrice.

Roman and Cher burst into laughter, but Xavier held up a hand.

"Leave it up to them. No explanations. People will create their own story. B, you and Cher can drop lots of hints about the side-benefits of inter-force co-operation, without stating facts, which should create enough of a distraction for us to follow up on the case."

Cher frowned. "Wait up. The case is over, right? In a couple days, they're going to make an arrest. You said so yourself. What more can we do?"

Xavier shook his head with some impatience. "Yes, they'll make an arrest. But all of us who call ourselves detectives can see this case is far from over."

"He's right." Roman reached behind his head and wound his long blond hair into a man bun. "Someone took Silva out. It wasn't a casual thief, it was a planned hit. I want to know where the internal pressure is coming from and why it's so vital for the local police to wrap this up. My guess is they will pin this on someone and file the paperwork while the real killer walks away."

Beatrice frowned. "So whoever owns those fingerprints is as much of a victim as Silva himself."

"Exactly." Xavier pointed his pen at her. "I'd like to take this to someone high up in Interpol, but we need more than second-hand circumstantial evidence. We have work to do. First, throw doubt on whoever has been set up as the suspect. Second, investigate who really engineered this killing, bearing in mind it could be one of our colleagues. What concerns me is how much we can achieve in the limited time available. We could use some help. André Monteiro seems the obvious choice, but can we trust any of our colleagues outside this room?"

A pensive silence descended. Beatrice understood. The question in everyone's mind was could they trust everyone *inside* the room? They knew so little about each other and a true sociopath would be very skilled at making others like them.

She looked into each face and made a decision. "If we suspect a police officer could be involved, perhaps we'd be wise not to confide in anyone else at the conference. I like André, but he was more than a police colleague to Samuel. He was also his godson. Without any more background information on the relationship, we can't eliminate him as a suspect. My view is we should use someone outside law enforcement. And I think I know just the person."

Chapter 13

Inside *Casa das Noivas*, Lisbon's premier bridal shop, no one was happy. The bride thought the neckline of her dress was too high, her mother thought it too low. Two of the bridesmaids were bickering over a pair of heels, the assistants' patience was running low and the maid of honour was bored out of her mind.

Ana Luisa Herrero rested her elbow on her knee and her chin on her hand, gazing past all the chiffon, gauze and satin, out at bright morning sunshine in the cobbled street. Workers hurried out of the Saldanha metro stop, tourists dawdled to window shop and ladies with designer handbags sat outside cafés enjoying a coffee, a *nata* and a gossip.

Ana wondered if she could sneak across the road for a *tosta mista*. She wasn't really hungry; she'd do anything just to get out of this air-conditioned dressing-up box. She looked over at the group in the changing area, but her aunt, famous for eyes-in-the-back-of-her-head, was one step ahead of her.

"Ana! Please show some enthusiasm. As *madrinha*, you are supposed to be the bride's constant support. Your cousin's not sure about the alterations on the dress. I think..."

Gisela interrupted. "I know what you think. But I'm the one getting married and I think it's all wrong. I look like a doll."

The other bridesmaids whose names Ana couldn't remember stopped their circular debate on kitten heels and rushed to the bride's side.

"No, not a doll! You look perfect!"

"Definitely not a doll. It's very glamorous but without being too obvious."

"The cleavage is too low, in my opinion."

"I WANT to show some skin."

"Skin maybe, but half your breasts?"

Ana hauled herself out of the chair. "Gisela, come here."

Her cousin shuffled over, pouting. Ana got it. Neither of them wanted to be in this position. Gisela wanted one of her best friends as *madrinha*. Ana would have been fine with that. Playing chief bridesmaid for her self-absorbed cousin ranked lower than an extended session with the dental hygienist. However, Aunt Candida believed family came first. So Ana must be Gisela's best woman, despite the fact that they barely tolerated each other.

"Show some skin but be subtle. Channel Brigitte Bardot. Pull the dress just off the shoulders like this. There. Beautiful neckline and it lifts the front to suggest at the cleavage. Sexy but sweet."

Gisela looked at her reflection and her eyes softened. Aunt Candida clasped her hands together and nodded. The bridesmaids applauded, the shop assistants sighed with relief and Ana's phone rang.

"I'll take this outside in case it's urgent." No one was even listening.

She shoved her way out the door and across the road to the café, while checking her screen. She widened her eyes at the name of the caller.

"Beatrice Stubbs? No way! Is this really you?"

"Ana, hello! It's great to hear your voice. How are you? Is this a good time?"

"It's a bloody brilliant time. I'm so happy to hear from you. Is everything OK at your end?"

Beatrice paused. "Personally, yes. Professionally, I might need some help. I'm in need of a Portuguese-speaking mine of information with an intelligence network, who's also trustworthy and discreet."

Ana leaned on the bar and beckoned a waiter, mouthed *uma bica* and indicated a sparkling water. She continued speaking into her phone with a huge grin.

"I know just the girl. I have to warn you she's half-Irish and curses like a trooper. "

"Sounds just what I'm looking for. Are you still in the Basque Country?"

"No. After that whole wine fraud story, I got offered a job back home in Lisbon. I've been here almost a year now. Is that a problem?" Ana took her drinks outside and sat at an empty corner table, turning her back to other patrons and donning her sunglasses.

"Not in the slightest. Your physical location is immaterial. I know you can dig out all kinds of information from anywhere with your phone, laptop and charm. And for this case, Lisbon is a very good place to be."

"Is it now? Come on then, what do you need?"

"Well, if I could give you an exclusive story only to be reported once this case is over, would you do a little subtle investigation for me? It's about a crime in Portugal. Obviously, off the..."

"...record. No need to ask. You're in Portugal? Where?"

"In the north. Gerês. Half-holiday, half-work. Are you terribly busy at the paper?" Beatrice's voice sounded tense.

"Not a paper, I'm on the telly now, don't you know. But it's too damn hot to work and shag-all happens in the summer. I'm officially on holiday for the rest of this month anyway because my cousin is getting married. I'm the *madrinha*, sort of chief bridesmaid. So come on then, tell me what you want me to do."

"Do you have time? I imagine you've got your hands full with bridesmaid duties." Ana could hear the smile in her voice.

"Yeah, you can just imagine how much fun I'm having. Flowers, dresses, decorations... Beatrice, I am bored out of my mind. Rescue me. Give me a job and a story and I'll name my first-born after you."

"Deal! But I'll let you off if it's a boy. I need you to find out all you can about a Portuguese psychologist called Samuel Ramiro Silva of the LIU. You'll have to be very hush-hush and I'll send you an email with the details. I'm particularly interested in any tensions between him and his colleagues in international law enforcement."

"Silva?" Ana sat up straight and dropped her voice to a fierce whisper. "Shit! He's all over the news! Of course! Sometimes I'm so slow I could kick myself. OK, so if we're talking about that situation, hush-hush won't be necessary – just a bit of discretion. Everyone is scrabbling for information. Send me everything you've got and I'll do whatever I can to help. Can you really get me an exclusive on this?"

"Yes, I can. Thank you, Ana. You're one of the few people I can trust. I don't suppose you could bring me your findings in person? Matthew and I are renting a villa near here with Tanya and Luke. And Adrian's here too. We have a spare room. Or am I being too demanding?"

Ana slugged her coffee in one. "You're all there? I'd love to see Adrian and the Prof again! And I've not seen Tanya since we were exchange students! All this and a shit-hot story? It must be my birthday or something. Count me in. Thanks, Beatrice, you've saved me. This week was rammed with duties, but now I have a get-out clause. I'll start digging today and if the schedule works, I'll get on a budget flight to Porto tomorrow. I can't wait!"

Ana paid the waiter, declined to give him her number and took a second to compose a suitably sad face before returning to Casa das Noivas to break the news. Tragically, she would be unable to fulfil her duties as *madrinha* due to an urgent work commitment. A great deal of feigned sadness and regret later, five women left the shop vastly happier than when they'd gone in. Ana was making calls before she even got on the tram. Work versus wedding? No contest.

Chapter 14

All things considered, Adrian was quite pleased with the way things had worked out. The only missing element was Beatrice. Breakfast was long and haphazard, as everyone rose at different hours. Adrian, always a light sleeper, had woken on hearing the sounds of Beatrice's departure. He slipped out of bed, sat on the terrace and read the news on his phone until Matthew came down. They discussed international politics over coffee until Luke arrived, at which point the conversation turned to Coco Pops.

When Will came down, Matthew began frying some bacon and Adrian brewed fresh coffee. The smells woke Tanya, who emerged barefoot in her shortie pyjamas and the early part of the morning passed in comfortable banter. Finally, Marianne and Leon joined them for coffee. Marianne announced their intention of travelling across the border to Vigo and Pontevedra in Spain. Would anyone mind if they took the smaller car?

There was a puzzled silence. Tanya was the first to speak.

"If you like. You don't fancy coming with us to the beach, then?"

Leon shook his head, his expression regretful. "I'm afraid I get bored sitting in the sun. Marianne and I are well matched that way. Neither of us is a beach person. We'd far rather go exploring."

Tanya's eyebrows lifted. "Yeah, right. I remember how much she hated Lanzarote. Sun, sea, sand... she said it was her idea of hell."

Marianne gave her sister a dry look. "Tastes change. OK, so if no one objects, we'll see you back here for dinner. Leon and I are cooking tonight. Chicken piri-piri with wild rice."

"Piri-piri? That's chilli, right? I'd better make something else for Luke," said Tanya.

"Yeah, it's pretty spicy. And we plan to eat about eight, so it would be too late for him anyway," Leon replied.

"I like chicken pirry!" said Luke.

Leon shook his head again. "I don't think so. Is Beatrice joining us? Just to know if I should buy enough chicken for seven."

"Buy enough for eight, if you don't mind," Tanya said, her voice tight. "Beatrice said she'd be here and Luke likes to eat with us. I'll do a lighter version for him and he can sleep late tomorrow."

"Sure. No problemo. Will, where can I find the car keys?"

Packing for the beach was almost as much fun as being there. They borrowed beach umbrellas and windbreaks from the villa's cabana and crammed them into the Peugeot's boot along with sun creams, insect repellent, football, bucket, spades and naturally, the picnic. Adrian and Tanya organised the latter, leaving everything else to three excited males of varying ages.

Tanya was soothing company. She worked with cool capability, achieving six dishes to Adrian's one, although his was a truly sublime tortilla. She hummed and sang random tunes and didn't seem to expect a constant flow of small talk. The hamper gradually filled with three different salads, sardines for grilling, a batch of mini fishcakes and a flask of chocolate ice-cream.

"So all we need now is water, wine and fresh bread, which we can buy in Viana do Castelo. Are we ready?"

Adrian wrapped his tortilla in foil. "Yes! I'll just add the ice-packs to the cool bag and we're good to go. Do you think we have enough?"

"There's only five of us, remember. Well, four and a half. Luke stuffed himself at breakfast so he won't eat much. You know what? I'm pleased it's just us today."

This was a tricky moment. *Tread softly*, he advised himself. He wasn't family, and a careless comment could still give offence years later.

"Me too. I like Leon, I really do, but I feel we're on best behaviour when we're all together. I feel much more relaxed when it's just you and Luke and Matthew."

Tanya wrinkled her nose. "That's as much her fault as his. She's watching us all, marking our reactions to Mister Wonderful on some kind of score sheet. Do you really like him?"

Adrian zipped up the hamper. "He's pleasant, polite and makes Marianne happy. He might be a bit defensive, but how do you think he feels, under such scrutiny? I think we should all give him a break and get on with our holiday. Come on, let's go to the beach, sunbathe, swim, build sandcastles, grill fish and indulge ourselves. I intend to pursue my latest hobby, which is finding you the perfect man."

Tanya sniffed. "I'm off men. Present company excepted."

"The perfect woman, in that case. Can you manage that cool bag if I carry the hamper? Come on then, tell me the top five characteristics you want in your ideal partner."

Viana do Castelo was not exactly the dream beach Adrian had envisaged, but it was certainly the perfect location for a family day out. On this Monday afternoon, the sand was sparsely populated, the sea calm and the sun brilliant. The heat drummed down relentlessly and Adrian decided to be judicious with his tanning. Burning would be an amateur error and red skin was dreadfully gauche.

Luke, impatient to get to the sea, harassed and chivvied each of them in turn as they unloaded the car and set up camp under two large sun umbrellas. He squirmed and wriggled under sufferance as Tanya smeared him with Factor 50, then raced Will into the surf, shrieking all the way. Matthew drew his fedora lower and donned aviator shades to watch his grandson splashing and laughing in the shallows.

Tanya peeled off her sundress and headed off to join them. Reminded of his mission, Adrian scanned the beach for any gazes following her shapely form across the sand. He counted at least four.

"I'm glad you and Will are here," said Matthew.

Adrian lifted his sunglasses to look at him. Matthew's attention was directed at the sea, where Tanya was running into the water, chased by Luke and Will.

"We're glad to be here. And at least we get our Beatrice fix once a day. I have to say, you're taking her absence very well."

"Par for the course. We never get enough time together. Always wringing out the moments until we part. Our relationship thus far has been built on missing each other; either savouring the last time or looking forward to the next. So this is no surprise. The real shock will come when we have all the time in the world."

Six teenagers ran past in baggy swim shorts, their skins the colour of toffee.

"You're as nervous as she is, aren't you?"

Matthew dragged his gaze from the shore to Adrian's face. "If you'd spent twenty years trying to persuade her to move in, wouldn't you be nervous? The funny thing is, you are part of it. You and Will represent her London life, something she feels she'll lose when she retires. That's another reason I'm glad you're here. You are more than a neighbour."

"I should damn well hope so! She's nearly got me killed twice so far. She'll be fine, Matthew. You'll both be fine. I wish you wouldn't worry." He lathered sun cream onto his skin, wincing as he touched the bruise on his shin. It had developed into an ugly inky smudge, toned down by his tan but still sensitive. If only heroism could be achieved without personal injury.

"Worrying is an integral part of having a relationship with Beatrice Stubbs. That and the 'nearly killed' thing. Anyway, I rather think I might chance a paddle. Would you keep an eye on our things?"

"Of course. I'm busy working on my tan anyway. Paddle away and bring me back any nice shells you find. I'm amassing a collection."

Adrian lay back and stared up at the impossible blue of the sky, recalling times when he'd sneered at a future with one person for the rest of his life. How things change. Now he found himself envying Matthew and Beatrice their future contentment, their pretty Devon cottage and their kitchen garden filled with sweet peas and courgettes. If Will got a transfer to the countryside, Adrian could sell up in London and open a wine emporium somewhere on the coast. Less violent crime, more romantic sunsets, endless relaxing weekends and maybe a dog to walk on the beach...

He sat up with a gasp of shock as cold wet droplets spattered his skin. Will stood over him, shaking his wet hair and laughing. "Come on. Matthew's got his knees wet and is coming back to start the grill. Time for a serious swim before lunch."

"You play hell with my tanning routine," Adrian said, accepting Will's hand and hauling himself to his feet. Hot sand forced him to run towards the sea, and exhilaration overcame his self-consciousness as he plunged into the waves, gasping as the cool water made contact with sun-warmed skin. He struck out towards the horizon in a powerful crawl, trusting Will would overtake him in seconds.

He was right. Adrian slowed and rolled onto his back, kicking lazily and scanning the beach for their friends. He spotted the two red polka-dot umbrellas and a wisp of smoke. So Matthew had managed to light the barbecue. He was about to raise his arms in a wave when a sudden tug on his shorts dragged him underwater. He swallowed a mouthful of sea and coughed, his vision blurred. He surfaced to see Will a safe distance away, grinning like a dolphin.

Adrian pulled his shorts back up, took in a deep breath and allowed himself to sink under the next wave. Then he took off beneath the surface with a deadly purpose. No one debags Adrian underwater.

By the time the two men finished fooling around and made their way back up the beach, the picnic was all prepared. Matthew was using his fedora to fan the coals under the sardines while Tanya had opened all the salads and distributed plates, cutlery and glasses around the mat-tablecloth. Luke, huddled under a towel, was gnawing on a slice of tortilla.

"This looks amazing! Thanks, Tanya and hats off to Matthew. Luke, how's the tortilla? You may answer using any of the following words: divine, fabulous, absolutely," Adrian said, sitting cross-legged in the sand.

Luke giggled. "I like it. It's got cheese and potato and egg. Cheese and potato and egg are my favourite foods. As well as sausage and tomato sandwiches."

Will pulled a beer from the cool box and offered it to Adrian.

"I'll stick with wine, thanks. Luke, you should go to Spain. They make a tortilla just like this but with tomatoes and a special Spanish sausage called chorizo. All your favourite foods in one dish."

Luke's eyes widened. "Marianne's in Spain now! We could call her and ask her to bring some back!"

Matthew ladled sardines onto everyone's plates, crisp, slightly blackened and with a hint of smoke. Adrian was salivating.

"That's not a bad idea," Matthew agreed. "They're going to a supermarket anyway so I could put in a request for chorizo. Tanya, would you give her a call or send her an app, however you people communicate these days."

"Yeah, OK. I'll text her after lunch. Adrian, do you want vinho verde or this white Rioja?" she asked.

Adrian glanced briefly at Matthew and shared a knowing look while tearing off hunks of bread.

"Vinho verde, I think. Let's go local. Did you two have a good swim?"

Luke nodded with enthusiasm, reaching for some bread. Tanya poured three glasses of white wine, her face relaxed and glowing.

"Yeah, it's brilliant. Can't believe the beach is so quiet and the water is gorgeous. I'm going back in when I've digested all this."

"And me!" said Luke.

They ate in silence for a few moments, savouring the pungent sardines and sampling Tanya's salads.

"What to have next, Small Fry?" asked Matthew. "I rather fancy something eggy and cheesy, and if it had potatoes or onions, that would be a bonus."

"Tor-*tee*-ya!" yelled Luke.

"Me too ya!" yelled Will, sending Luke into a fit of giggles, his towel dropping from his shoulders.

Matthew sliced a portion each for everyone, including a second piece for Luke, and conversation became nothing more than appreciative murmurs.

Will reached across to squeeze Adrian's knee. "It's delicious. You are a domestic god." Then his attention was caught by something else. "Luke, what happened to your arm?"

Adrian followed his gaze and saw four small bruises on the boy's upper left arm. Luke glanced down and shrugged.

"Oops, did we get a bit too rough in the water just now?" asked Matthew.

"Bruises don't develop that fast," said Tanya. "How did you get those, Luke?"

Luke shook his head. "Dunno."

"Probably all the rough and tumble in the pool on the first day," Adrian suggested. "You need to be more careful, Will."

"Will didn't do it," muttered Luke, scooping the towel back over his shoulders. Adrian understood the signal. *Stop staring!*

"Can you imagine what it must have been like?" asked Matthew, his eyes on the horizon. "Six hundred years ago, to step off the only land you've ever known and set sail with nothing more than optimism, courage and hope? Knowing nothing of what might be out there, yet risking your life in the name of discovery? Could you board a wooden ship and sally forth into the open sea, with only the vaguest idea of where you were going and no idea if or when you might return? The people of this country did. The Portuguese took off from these shores in fragile crafts and mapped the world. We owe these explorers more than we realise."

Despite Tanya's sigh as she spooned out the ice-cream, the entire party was enthralled, including the five-year old.

"Think about it. Here we stand, a family of fisherfolk in the fifteenth, sixteenth century, unsure of what's out there or what mythical monsters lurk beneath the roiling waves. We wave goodbye to our courageous sailors, our hearts full of fear and dread. What terrors will they endure, what strange lands will they encounter?

"Many will never return, but those who do shall be forever heroes. Henry the Navigator, da Gama, Magellan, Dias and Cabral were the astronauts of their time, going bravely where no man had gone before. We owe these extraordinary intrepid adventurers a profound debt. They connected the atlas and discovered the world we know today."

They applauded his monologue, turning heads from other parties on the beach. For the first time, Adrian understood why

Matthew was such a valued professor. He loved his subject and made it human.

Will tilted his head backwards to catch the sun on his face. "This is what holidays should be like. Sunshine, seaside, lovely food, beautiful views, good company and a great storyteller. But nothing puts the cherry on the cake as much as beach volleyball!"

Luke leapt up so fast his plate went flying. "Beach volleyball! Three against two! Come on Granddad!"

"Granddad doesn't want to play beach volleyball," said Will. "He wants to doze with the crossword. Listen, you and I will play against your mum and Adrian. Why don't we let them clear up while you and I go set up the pitch? We also need to warm up and talk tactics."

Matthew's expression was one of relief and Tanya gave Will a grateful smile, so Adrian overlooked the number of assumptions made in that comment and resolved to discuss it later. Matthew retired to his deckchair as Adrian and Tanya cleared up the picnic. They both gazed down the beach to watch the mismatched pair playing Head, Shoulders, Knees and Toes. Then with a handshake, Tanya and Adrian stepped out into the sunshine to meet their opponents.

By the time they got back to the villa, sandy and sun-pinked, the Panda was parked outside. Will lifted a sleeping Luke from the back seat up and took him upstairs to finish his nap, with Tanya yawning in his wake. After unpacking the remains of the picnic, Adrian wandered outside to the pool. Marianne and Leon lay in the shade, him face down, her reading a gossip magazine.

"Hi! How was Vigo?"

Marianne looked up. "Hi there. It was OK. Nothing to write home about. What about the beach?"

"Perfect. Loads of space, hot, sunny and Matthew grilled some sublime sardines. But after beach volleyball and swimming in the sea, I think we're all fit for a nap. Luke was asleep before we left Viana do Castelo."

Leon rolled over, shielding his eyes with his hand. "Sounds like a fun day. What time should we plan dinner?"

Adrian looked at his watch. "It's half past five now and Beatrice won't get here for another hour and a half. So shall we say aperitifs at seven, and dinner at eight?

"Ideal. The chicken is already marinating so we'll start the roasting at seven."

"Oh, one thing about the oven. The temperature dial is a bit dodgy so you need to watch whatever's cooking."

"Don't worry, Adrian, it's all under control. Can we leave you in charge of the cocktails?"

"Cocktails are my speciality. See you later."

Leon put on his sunglasses. "So I hear. See you at seven."

Marianne snickered.

The sun reflecting off the pool and the scent of rosemary made Adrian dozy. With a salute to the reclining couple, he returned indoors, wondering what Marianne found so funny.

They overslept. Will kissed his shoulder, told him it was quarter past seven and dragged on some clothes. Laughter from the poolside rippled through the window and Adrian recalled his promise to be barman. He threw on linen trousers and T-shirt, checked his hair and followed Will downstairs. Leon was adding the finishing touches to the dining-table, which looked spectacular, with orange napkins, sparkling glasses and a centrepiece of dramatic red flowers to match the sunset. Marianne was in the kitchen, rinsing rice. Everyone else was poolside, nibbling on nuts, olives and breadsticks while Will made martinis.

Adrian spotted Beatrice and opened his arms. "Are you coping?"

She leaned into his hug. "I am. Are you?"

"Actually, we're having fun. Have you got a cocktail?"

"I have an Old-Fashioned, made by that handsome barman over there. If I were you, I'd get his number."

As if he'd heard her, Will looked up from his preparations and grinned.

"Hmm, you might be right. He looks the sort to go for a golden tan, which you have not yet noticed." Adrian pulled up the arm of his T-shirt and Beatrice responded exactly as she ought.

"Adrian! You look so sun-kissed! Have you been on holiday at all?"

Luke wandered over with a closed hand. "Guess what? Do you know which way is north?"

Beatrice looked to the sky. "My guess is that way." She pointed east.

Adrian shook his head. "I'm afraid you're wrong about that, Beatrice. I think you'll find north is that way." He pointed south.

"Wrong!" Luke opened his hand to reveal a tiny compass, the sort one might get in a Christmas cracker. "North is up there," he whispered, his eyes wide with drama. "Beatrice, is your working place in the north?"

"No, a little bit south. But the weather is the same. My only problem is we have no beach. Can you believe it? One week in Portugal, a country full of beaches and what do I get? A big pond!"

Luke laughed and started to tell Beatrice about the picnic when the smell of burning and the sound of swearing drifted from the villa. Matthew broke off his conversation with Tanya and went indoors.

The group drew together near Will's makeshift bar and took turns to reply to Luke's knock-knock jokes. Adrian winked at the barman and got himself a second martini. He was just requesting an olive when Matthew emerged from the French windows and clapped his hands.

"Folks, change of plan. The oven malfunctioned and burnt the chicken. So I suggest we head down the hill to the fish restaurant tonight. Apparently we get five-star service if we mention our friend from Braga. Anybody sober enough to drive?"

Twenty minutes later, Will parked the Panda next to the Peugeot beside a very dark, closed restaurant. Adrian's spirits sank. If it were only Will and himself, they'd laugh and go exploring elsewhere. But tonight there were seven adults and a hungry child to accommodate.

"You didn't think to book a table?" asked Leon.

Matthew shook his head. "No, not at such short notice. I'm

sorry, I thought we could just walk in on a Monday. Do you suppose all restaurants close on Mondays? Like hairdressers?"

Beatrice walked to the door. "Ah. The notice is in five languages. 'Closed for two weeks for the annual family holiday.' What a shame, I love that little pier and the boathouse on the lake. Too pretty. Still, there's no food on offer here and time's getting on. Back to the ranch for omelettes or a local café for a toasted sandwich?"

Will rested his chin on Adrian's shoulder. "I'd chance the local, but happy to fall in with what everyone else wants to do. What do you say, Luke, omelette or toastie?"

Luke didn't answer. Adrian looked around the car park, but there was no sign of him.

"Luke!" Tanya called. "Luke, where are you?"

After calling his name a few times, Will gave the party instructions. "Split up. He's probably hiding from us. Leon and Marianne, look round the back of the restaurant, Tanya, you check the terrace. Beatrice and Matthew, search in and under both cars. Adrian and I will cover the pier and the boathouse."

They spread out, calling Luke's name with a false cheerfulness. Adrian tiptoed along the short pier, squinting into the black water, his mind playing out all kinds of nightmarish scenarios when a voice rang out.

"He's here!"

Will guided Luke out of the boathouse onto the wooden boards of the pier, his hand on the boy's shoulder.

Tanya rushed down the steps. "Luke, where have you been? Don't you ever do that again! Wandering off in the dark! You scared me half to death. You always stay with the family, understand?"

"I only wanted to have a look." It was clear from Luke's expression he had no idea what all the fuss was about.

"Well, don't! If you want to go somewhere, you only ever go with one of us," said Tanya. She turned back to the others. "Look, can we just get back to the villa and eat whatever we've got in the fridge? I'm kind of done with today."

Leon and Marianne shared a look and stalked back to the car. The drive back was cold and awkward, unlike the villa, which smelt of burnt food. Everyone congregated in the kitchen for omelettes and toasties, but despite Matthew's best efforts at inclusion, Marianne and Leon would not be mollified and retired to the garden flat.

Adrian was not sorry to see them go.

Chapter 15

One advantage of getting your face on TV most evenings is that people tend to know your name. This can open a whole lot of doors.

Yesterday Ana had sent out a dozen emails to colleagues, relatives and contacts of Silva's hoping for at least one bite. She got four. One of whom refused her enquiry in the bluntest possible language. Two offered some personal platitudes and information on Silva but neither added much to what she already knew from her research. The fourth, however, made all Ana's efforts worthwhile. Silva's sister, Olivia, was willing to talk. Even better, face to face.

Ana stood at the faded wooden door on Rua Mirabilis, took a deep breath and rang the bell. She tilted her head towards the fish-eye lens so her face could be seen and pulled out her press pass. A tinny voice came through the intercom.

"Ms Herrero?"

"That's me. Here's my ID." She held the card up to the camera.

"That's not necessary, I recognise you from *Telejornal*. Come in. Directly across the courtyard and I'm on the second floor."

A buzzer released the door and Ana pushed it open. The gloomy hallway gave way to a beautiful interior courtyard with trailing plants and tubs of flowers. Parakeets chattered and squawked from a cage on a balcony above and a cat lay in a patch of sun, watching her with indifference.

When she reached the second floor, an apartment door opened and Olivia Tavares appeared, a silhouette against the sunlight. Ana moved towards her, hand outstretched and was met by a study of grief. Not just the black clothes, wan complexion and puffy eyes, but a palpable feeling, like a musty smell. It was a salutary reminder that loss could be unexpectedly violent, attacking when you are least prepared. The two women shook hands and Olivia made a valiant effort to return Ana's smile.

"Come in."

Ana did as she was asked and stepped into a large room in which every surface held a plant. The profusion of greenery against blue walls gave the impression of an aquarium.

"You are alone?" asked Olivia.

Ana nodded, puzzled by the question.

"I'm glad. I'm not ready to face a camera crew today. Please, have a seat. You'll take a coffee?"

Ana recalled the fictitious commission she had invented. The Life of Samuel Silva, a profile of the man and his achievements. Not entirely a lie, she argued with her conscience. If she found enough material, she could try to get the green light for some in-depth reportage. In return, her conscience gave her an arch look.

"Just water, thank you. No, it will be some time before we start filming. I have a lot of research to do before then. That is why I'm so grateful for your help. To be able to start with the family is exactly what I wanted. Thank you for meeting me, especially at such a difficult time." She sat at the dining-table and took out her notebook.

Olivia poured a bottle of Salgados into two glasses. "Of course I will help. To be honest, I want to talk about him."

"I can understand that. My aim is to profile the man as a whole, not just the professional. Can you tell me a little about your family? I know there are three children and Samuel was the eldest."

"That's right." She sat opposite Ana, her face partly shadowed by an overgrown spider plant that hung from the ceiling, filtering the light. "Samuel, then me and Salvatore is the youngest. There are two years between each child. Our parents were good planners. We grew up in Sintra, on a beautiful *quinta*, with vineyards. My father inherited money and my mother had land. A wealthy, respectable family and three children destined for great things."

"Were you three kids close?"

Olivia's face crumpled and she pulled a tissue from her sleeve to press to her eyes. She held up a shaky hand as if to ask for patience. She took several uneven breaths and started to speak.

"We used to be. Samuel was the oldest and we both adored

him. He was clever and kind and very protective of his siblings. He defended us against my father. Papa was an authoritarian, very old-fashioned with a quick temper. Samuel was always smart. He went to university and studied psychology, even though our father wanted him to be a doctor. Our mother was so proud of him and displayed all his certificates on our living-room wall.

"The trouble started when Mama died. She was the calming influence, a force for balance. Without her, my father became more conservative, less tolerant." She heaved an enormous sigh.

"He was obsessed with class and education. He wanted Salvatore to study like Samuel, to become an engineer, but Salvatore trained as a mechanic and now works for the railway. As for me, his only ambition was to find me a good husband. I refused to cooperate and trained as a teacher. When I got married, it was for love, not for status. Our choices were a constant source of conflict between us, and family occasions became a source of stress, not comfort. But until our father's death, the three of us were a unit, a team who looked after each other.

"Papa died four years ago and left his estate to Samuel as the eldest male. It was profoundly shocking. Of course Samuel was ready to be generous and share his good fortune, but Salvatore disputed the will in court. That put a terrible strain on the family. After the verdict, which was to uphold the will, Samuel and Salvatore no longer spoke. I hoped that one day they would reconcile, but now..."

Her voice cracked and Ana handed her a clean tissue.

"Take your time. There's no rush," Ana lied. To catch the 11.25 flight to Porto, she would need to leave within the hour and that was looking unlikely.

Olivia gulped some water. "It's heartbreaking. My father and his money have made us angry and unforgiving. Even from beyond the grave he still divides us."

"You too? Because you had to side with either Samuel or Salvatore?"

A grimace crossed Olivia's face. "It was horrible. I tried to stay neutral but when I heard the terms of Papa's will, I had to support Salvatore. You see, the will states that in the event of Samuel's death, Salvatore inherits our father's estate, bypassing me and ignoring

Samuel's own family. My father intended to ignore Samuel's wife. It was an injustice I could not bear."

"You can't have been too happy yourself."

Olivia shook her head, a quick, impatient gesture. "I don't want it. That place holds nothing but bad memories and ghosts. What made me so angry was the unfairness of his final gesture. Papa wanted to keep stirring trouble long after his death and by writing such a bequest, he made sure he succeeded. When Samuel met Elisabete, a successful, independent doctor who had no need of financial support, my father called her a gold-digger. Grace be to God he died before they adopted Marcia. An orphan from Romania as his grandchild? He would rather have me inherit his estate. Me, a woman!"

The venom in her tone surprised Ana, but gave her cause for optimism. Anger has all the energy grief lacks. She drank some water and checked her watch. Forty minutes to mine this seam. It could be done.

"You said Samuel and Salvatore weren't on speaking terms. What about you?"

"I talked to both my brothers. I love them and that will never change. Family is everything to me. After the court case, I tried to build bridges. Samuel and Elisabete embraced me immediately. Salvatore did not judge me for being in the middle, but refused to listen to any attempts at reconciliation. He just switched off whenever I mentioned Samuel's name."

Ana calculated. So the younger brother certainly had a motive. One of the oldest in the book. But why wait four years and take revenge at a conference of police detectives?

"Is Salvatore married?" she asked.

"Yes. He has a wife and two lovely boys. When Samuel and Elisabete adopted Marcia, I thought the children might provide some common ground." She shook her head sadly. "Salvatore did seem to be softening, but when he heard about the court case, he shut down again."

"The court case? For adoption?"

"No, this was a claim against the adoption agency. Those terrible people! They delayed the process, inventing red tape and

_*Bad Apples*

administrative fees to extort more and more money from Samuel. Marcia's case was so badly handled that when Samuel finally got custody, he sued the agency for emotional distress and damages.

"The judge found in their favour, but the agency declared itself bankrupt. Samuel didn't mind about the money. He said he was happy no one else would suffer the way they had done. Then the whole situation got very ugly. The boss of this disgusting company, who made children's and prospective parents' lives a misery, threatened to take his revenge. He targeted Samuel in particular. It cast a dark cloud over the joy of bringing Marcia home."

Ana stopped writing and stared at Olivia. "He threatened to hurt Samuel? When was this?"

"Almost three months ago. He threatened to do more than hurt him. He said he would take Marcia away and he promised to kill my brother." She covered her face with her hands.

"Olivia, have you shared this with the police?"

She wiped away tears and met Ana's gaze. "Nobody asked me. Do you think I should?"

"Listen, I need the name of this guy, the adoption agency and anything you can tell me about the court case. If you can give me everything you know in the next twenty minutes, I'll make my flight. I'm heading north, to Gerês. I know someone who can help us both."

Half an hour later, Ana dashed through Portela Airport and arrived at the check-in to find her flight had been delayed by ninety minutes. She checked in, sent Beatrice a message and found a quiet seat facing a wall. She opened her laptop and inserted earphones which weren't connected to anything, but would ward off chatty fellow passengers. She had work to do and there was no such thing as wasted time.

Chapter 16

Beatrice knew from experience that in any investigation, the urge to get a result is like acid, eroding principles and burning its way through assumptions of moral superiority. When four upstanding officers of the law combine forces, no matter how informally, a code of conduct will be required. This is why investigative ethics are so important

But at Tuesday morning's coffee break, while Roman charmed hotel security, Xavier bought the local police coffee and Cher spent every spare minute with André Monteiro, Beatrice looked the other way. After all, she would be fraternising with a journalist in a couple of hours, so who was she to judge? Instead, she walked the grounds, called Matthew in anticipation of their dinner party that evening and spent the time on a logical assessment of the circumstances. It didn't help much.

She returned to the hotel for all the EPIC events of the day, her mind turning over each piece of evidence, even while attending a seminar on Big Data – Finding Needles in the Haystack. Her problem was the opposite. She and her impromptu team were searching for clues based on almost zero data. She cocked her head in a simulacrum of attentiveness and went over the facts again.

Clumsy window entry and fingerprints on the pane pointed to either an amateur burglary or a professional set-up. Every element of an interrupted burglary offered the local police an easy resolution.

Beatrice worked both theories. Two shots to the back of the head indicated a planned hit, not a disturbed burglar. This person gained access either via the window, a key or as a welcome guest. In the former two scenarios, someone had entered, waited and struck.

In the latter, turning one's back on a visitor seemed an unnatural thing to do.

So the Bond-style assassin theory gained the upper hand, but a huge gap of logic remained.

Motive.

Then there was the rumour. Ranga's comments echoed in her mind. *Word is, there's a book ... due to expose, embarrass and possibly even indict senior officers across the continent.* If Silva was connected, the international police convention could have been the opportunity to silence him, the book and its revelations.

If Silva *was* connected with the book at all. His work was professional research, not a vengeful memoir. He didn't seem the type, based on Beatrice's limited knowledge of the man, but she had only conversed with him for a few short hours.

A police detective would know every foolproof method of avoiding detection and how to throw enough circumstantial evidence to implicate someone else. Who would have known he would be in his room at that time? If Xavier had made his lunch invitation to the professor in public, any one of the seminar goers might have overheard. Then whoever it was could have preceded him before the doting family man made it back to his room to phone his wife.

When lunchtime rolled around, Beatrice ducked out of the seminar in full awareness she'd learned nothing about Big Data and it was all her own fault. Hurrying up the stairs to Xavier's room for their previously agreed meeting, she checked her messages and cursed. She had hoped Ana would arrive in time to join them, but according to the latest message – 'Sodding plane delayed. ETA circa 14.00.' – the girl had just touched down in Porto.

Xavier opened the door and welcomed her in. Cher was sitting at the table, waiting. A deliciously fishy scent emanated from the silver cloches at each place setting.

"That smells heavenly!" Beatrice tossed her bag on the bed and joined Cher at the table. "Ana's flight was delayed, so I'll skip the first session of the afternoon and hang around to meet her. Where's Roman?"

"Just gone back to his room for a shower," said Xavier, pouring water into her glass.

"The man is obsessed!" exclaimed Beatrice. "How many times a day does he perform his ablutions?"

Cher laughed. "I'm pretty sure it's only once. He overslept again this morning. He'd better hurry because I want to eat."

"Let's give him a minute before we start," said Xavier. He picked up a basket covered in a napkin. "These rolls are still warm. Anyone?"

Beatrice and Cher both took one and Beatrice started buttering.

"How did you get on with André Monteiro?" she asked Cher.

"Smart kid. Like us, he thinks something about all this stinks. I agreed but didn't say too much. He knew Samuel his whole life and talks about him with real affection. But he has a little chip on his shoulder. His father and ..."

The doorbell rang and Xavier admitted Roman. The Icelander squeezed both Beatrice's and Cher's shoulders before flinging his long body into a seat and lifting the silver cloche.

"Right, let's get down to business. We need to talk."

By the time the plates were empty, everyone had shared their information and thoughts. Xavier summarised them above the buzzing clatter of the coffee machine, where Roman was making each of them an espresso.

"Key information is this. Cher discovered a potential motive in jealousy. Samuel is André Monteiro's godfather and best friend to Nelson Monteiro. Nelson and Samuel are peers, but Samuel is the one who got promoted and received all the accolades for the work he and Nelson have done. André feels some injustice on his father's behalf.

"For my part, my police sergeant contact told me there is CCTV footage of the first floor corridor at the time Samuel Silva was killed. I did not see it, but he tells me no one enters Samuel's room but Samuel himself. Then André Monteiro knocks on the door, receives no reply and leaves.

"Roman's conversations with the staff show that only reception and housekeeping have access to master keys. The Do Not Disturb sign was on the door and the key log confirms the video footage. The only person to go in and out was Samuel Silva.

"Access from the window would be difficult. The room is on the first floor so you would need a ladder to climb onto his balcony. During lunchtime, when people are milling around the grounds, it would be unmissable."

The room fell silent and everyone sipped their coffees.

Beatrice looked at each face in turn. "Thank you Xavier, but this is all hearsay. We are not in control, we cannot see the footage for ourselves, we can't interview the staff as police officers, we can't take official statements. We're basing an entire investigation on gossip and we don't know any of it is true. Some of these suppositions sound plausible but could be inverted by testing the hypotheses. Come on, let's think like detectives, not nervous house guests."

Roman rolled his shoulders, arched back his neck and fixed his gaze on Beatrice. "You have a point. Based on reading people as opposed to forensic evidence, these are the facts as we know them. I have faith in professional detectives' opinions but you're right, we need to challenge our assumptions. What might we be reading wrong?"

Cher raised a finger. "Access to Samuel's room. If someone in uniform was up a ladder, I wouldn't think twice. I'd guess the guy was doing his job. There's all sorts of renovation work on the upper stories. I know it's been suspended for the week, but there are still ladders and equipment lying about."

"True," said Beatrice. "And there's a balcony outside. If it's anything like mine, you could hop over onto next door's as easily as getting out of the bath. Which means it could have been anyone who has a room on the first floor."

Xavier stirred his coffee. "All of this is true. We need more facts. But the one thing we must find..."

"... is a motive," Roman interrupted, placing a bowl of sugar on the table.

Xavier inclined his head. "My thoughts exactly."

"Oh you two," Beatrice laughed. "Finishing each other's sentences? You should get married."

Roman rested his chin on Xavier's head, his blond locks framing both their faces. Beatrice smiled while Cher took a picture. She turned the phone to show them.

"We would have made such a beautiful couple." Xavier exaggerated a sigh.

"Listen, we have ten minutes before the afternoon sessions start," said Beatrice. "This is how I suggest we proceed. Xavier, you need to get the details about the fingerprints in Silva's room. Were there any others? Where were those deemed to be the suspect's? Any other relevant information on the room? Roman, we need to know who's on the first floor, especially the rooms either side. Can you also try and get a look at that footage of Saturday lunchtime? As for you, Cher, try to get close to André Monteiro, earn his confidence, ask more about the relationship with his godfather, you know what to do. Listen very carefully to what he doesn't say. I'll meet Ana and hope to high heaven she's found something for us."

Xavier slapped his thighs and got to his feet. "OK, let's meet up at afternoon coffee break at the end of the terrace. Hopefully Beatrice's friend will be here by then. Let's keep digging."

Beatrice hid in her room, studying the list of delegates until two o'clock, and then descended to the gardens. She wandered aimlessly behind some shrubs with half an eye on the drive, trying to appear interested in horticulture. While she walked, she added up all she knew and reached a different conclusion every time.

"Oi!" A long-legged figure waved at her from the terrace, a rucksack dangling from one shoulder.

"Ana!" Beatrice waved back and hurried up the slope to greet her guest, already elated by the sight of the girl.

Ana dropped her rucksack and bent to embrace Beatrice in a crushing hug. Her long hair was the silvery-brown of melted chocolate, the same colour as her Fiat 500, carelessly parked on the forecourt. A delightful smile illuminated her lovely face.

"You look more beautiful than ever! I am *so* pleased to see you," Beatrice said, holding Ana's shoulders.

"You look shitloads better than the last time I saw you. Thanks so much for giving me this tip. This story is the dog's bollocks and getting to see you, Tanya, the Prof and Adrian is the custard on my plums. Come here to me, I've got some intel and a ton of questions for you."

"I thought you might. Let's drop your bag in my room and I'll order room service so we can get up to speed in private."

Ana scribbled notes in shorthand and interrupted frequently.

"Do we know which publishing company is handling the book?"

"I'll get the names of everyone who had rooms on that corridor."

"How do you spell Gilchrist?"

"Have you a minibar? I could murder... sorry. I mean I'd love a beer."

Beatrice's fetched Ana a bottle of Super Bock. "Your turn," she said.

Ana swigged at her beer then flipped open her tablet. "First thing I can tell you is there's plenty of motive. I spoke to his sister."

Beatrice stared at her. "His sister!"

"Don't worry. This wasn't a pushy journo intruding on grief. I dropped her a note saying I'd been commissioned to do a reportage on his life."

"Have you any such commission?"

"Not yet. But I will get one. Beatrice, you're going to have to trust me on methodology, OK?"

Beatrice nodded, aware she'd asked Ana to get information off the record. "OK. I just don't want to..."

"Neither do I. His sister is a lovely person. She adored her brother. Silva's wife is a doctor and they recently adopted a child from Romania."

"Marcia."

"You knew about her? So you heard all about the adoption agency hassles?"

"No, just the child's name and where she came from."

Ana rotated her laptop so Beatrice could see the screen and navigated to the website.

"Cloverfield – Creating Happy Families. Or more accurately, ripping off well-heeled couples and making kids miserable until they squeeze out every last cent. Silva sued them for emotional damage to the kid, himself and his wife. Their lawyer accused Cloverfield of 'naked profiteering from the vulnerable' which by all accounts was a pretty generous description. These guys were traffickers in all but name. Judge found for Silva, Cloverfield went bankrupt and the disgraced manager made a death threat. Motive One."

"Where is the manager based?" asked Beatrice.

"Bucharest. I've looked him up and it seems he was at a wedding on Saturday, but this guy has connections. He could easily have called in a favour."

"Go on."

Ana slugged her Super Bock. "There's another possible motive tucked away in family history. Samuel Silva fell out with his brother after their father died four years ago. Pops left his estate to Samuel as the eldest male. We're talking a valuable property. Unless you flog it, you can't exactly divide it by three. Little brother Salvatore disputed the will and the two fell out. The real kicker is that Pops was typical old-school. The will states that on Samuel's death, Salvatore inherits his estate, leaving second-born Olivia and Samuel's wife – and, as of then, hypothetical kids – out of the picture. So we've got money as Motive Two. Here's a picture of Salvatore. Geeky, right?"

Beatrice studied the bespectacled image, a screenshot from his employee page on CP Railways. He looked harmless and rather sad. Yet the same could be said of many of the world's worst serial killers.

"Then there's Motive Three – Jealousy. We both reached the same conclusions about Nelson Monteiro. He and Silva were colleagues and friends, working on the same subject. But only Silva was offered a contract to publish his findings in a book..."

Beatrice snapped her head up.

"Wait, I'm not sure it's *the* book. Silva was working with a ghostwriter to produce something called *Lone Wolf*. It's not fiction, more a sociological or psychological study on individual terrorists. Don't give me that look, I'm using the term terrorist correctly. Not random violence but driven by a mission to change the status quo. And before you start, no, I've not attended a seminar on politically correct phrasing, but I do my homework."

Beatrice nodded as she scooped the froth off her coffee. "Fair enough. I assume you know the name of the ghostwriter? Then we can find the publisher."

"Not yet. I called Olivia from the airport and she'd never heard of the book. I asked her to find out what she could from Silva's widow. I took the opportunity to mention Monteiro and she dismissed the jealousy motive out of hand. As you said, the two men were godfathers to each other's kids and Monteiro even testified as a witness for Silva in the court case. She insists Nelson Monteiro and Samuel Silva have always been like brothers."

"In which case, two of Samuel Silva's 'brothers' are under suspicion," Beatrice muttered.

"True. As I see it, we have three leads. Revenge, family money and professional rivalry. Which one do you want me to work first?"

"I'd like to put that question to the rest of the team. We're due to meet on the terrace in ten minutes. I suggest you use this room as a makeshift office while I attend the last sessions of the day. As soon as I'm done, which will be five or near as dammit, we leave for the villa."

"Sounds like a plan. Can I use the loo?"

Over many years of managing teams, Beatrice had learnt that regardless of how well you balance skills, cultural compatibility, gender and experience, there is one factor that can wreck the most harmonious and focused of groups.

Sex.

Introducing the undeniably attractive Ana to a new, loosely formed team was a risk. Especially if Beatrice's instincts were right, and the accidental team already contained a level of sexual tension. Not to mention the fact Gilchrist had issued an explicit order, asking them not to discuss the case with anyone external. All of this had flammable potential.

So as they strode across the terrace to meet the Swiss, American and Icelander, all Beatrice's senses were on high alert. She noted the curiosity in Xavier's eyes, the appreciative interest in Roman's expression as he stood to meet them and Cher's brief assessment of this naturally lovely creature as they shook hands. The one thing she'd not considered was Ana's forceful personality and direct expression.

"Good to meet you all. I want to say that I'm willing to chuck everything I've got into helping you solve this. For me, the story comes second. You can count on my discretion. Beatrice called me for a favour because she trusts me to keep my trap shut. You don't know me from Adam, but I hope you will all give me the benefit of the doubt. What I do best is find information. It's up to you what you do with it."

A silence lingered for several seconds then Cher's eyes bulged. "Beatrice, Gilchrist is heading our way. What is our story? Who is Ana and why is she here?"

"An old friend. Exchange student from years back. All true."

"And what innocuous job does she hold?" Cher hissed.

"Good evening!" called Gilchrist, as he took in the group of five. "New face on the block if I'm not mistaken." He flashed a dazzling smile at Ana.

Beatrice stepped up. "Commander Gilchrist, this is Ana Herrero, an old friend who lives in Portugal. As mentioned, I'm combining work and leisure, so invited Ana here to meet me today."

"Delighted to meet you, Ms Herrero. Do you live in the region?"

"Porto. It's just over an hour away. I'm a tour guide of the port wine caves. Like a bat, I spend a lot of the time in the dark."

Everyone at the table laughed just a touch too heartily.

Gilchrist grinned. "How fascinating! Are you staying the night? I'd love to hear more about your insights."

"No, much as it looks a grand place, I can't. As Beatrice said, I'm a friend of the family. Tonight, we're all having dinner together. A reunion I'm looking forward to more than I can say."

"Oh well, perhaps I'll be able to visit the caves before I return home. Do you have a card?" Gilchrist bestowed another charming smile.

"If I worked for a single company, I would. As a freelancer, I'm not tied to a particular house, so I don't know which one will hire me from week to week. Vila Nova da Gaia isn't that big, though, so you'll probably find me coming up for a few minutes of sunlight. How do you all like Gêres?"

Cher spoke first. "We only saw a little but it is incredibly beautiful. I want to come back here for a holiday. I think Beatrice organised this work-life balance perfectly. I envy you, Ana."

"Ah yes, you can count on Stubbs for European cooperation," said Gilchrist. "Well, nice to meet you and enjoy your reunion. Good evening, all."

Cher looked from the retreating Commander's back at Ana and spoke in a low voice. "You are one class act. Even I believed you. I think you're going to work out just fine." She raised a clenched hand and Ana returned the fist bump while Beatrice exhaled a guttural sigh of relief.

But she knew that from now on, Gilchrist would be watching.

Chapter 17

Porto's art installation, the steep cobbled backstreets, the blue-tiled station, the cathedral, the bridge, the port wine-caves and all the little squares, statues and parks were each uniquely absorbing. Adrian could have spent hours meandering around any one of them. Hours were not an option with Will, who urged him from one sight to the next, cramming as much as possible into their day.

The heat grew so oppressive that by midday even Action Man began to flag. They walked back across the Dom Luis bridge and sought a restaurant on the Ribeira to sit, rest, eat and people watch in the shade. Will ordered two beers and scrutinised the menu, while Adrian sat back and relaxed. Children chased each other along the quay, oriental-looking boats bobbed in the river and cats prowled the walls in an attempt to charm tourists in the same way their ancestors must have beguiled fishermen.

"That guy in Braga recommended something with *bacalhau*, or salted cod, didn't he? Do you remember the name of it? They've got several *bacalhau* dishes on the menu here and I'd like to try it at least once."

"No idea. I gave the note to Matthew. Let me have a look and see if anything jogs my memory."

Will handed over the menu. "Then after lunch, what about taking the tram up the river to the beach? Spend a while exploring Foz before we head back to the car."

"As long as it involves sitting down, I'm ready for anything. This one looks possible. All I can recall of what that bloke said is it sounded like peephole." Adrian pointed to a dish described as *Bacalhau a Zé do Pipo*.

The waiter placed two beers on the table and Will asked him

to describe the cod dish. Adrian tuned out, his curiosity piqued by three vociferous old women on the quay, all dressed in black, yelling and gesticulating at each other as if about to throw a punch. Then the most grizzled of the three burst into wheezy laughter and the only punches thrown were gentle bunts on the shoulder.

"It sounds delicious so I ordered it for both of us and a half bottle of white," said Will. "I have to drive later, so you can finish it. Are you listening?"

Adrian reached across to squeeze Will's thigh. "I wasn't, but I am now. So we're having Peephole Cod? Good. Which wine did you choose?"

"Vinho verde. I wish we had time for a cruise up the Douro. I'd love to see the vineyards at sunset."

"We can always come back. Anyway, we hate cruises. Far too many other people. Look at that kitten! It's actually squaring up to a Jack Russell!"

Will looked and laughed. "The dog's backing off. It may only be a ball of fluff, but it's fluff with attitude."

"Too cute. If only we could pop it in a pocket and take it home. A little kitty-kat around the flat until we have space for a... what's the matter?" He followed Will's sightline.

Leon and Marianne, arm in arm, strolled along the quay laughing at something on Marianne's phone. Adrian's spirits sank. That morning, when discussing plans, Will had announced their plan of visiting Porto. Leon and Marianne said they wanted to explore the national park of Gerês. Matthew, Tanya and Luke were happy to stay by the pool, so the party set off in different directions. Now, it appeared, all four were in the same place. He knew Will would chalk this up as another instance of Leon's bad character. Adrian didn't want any embarrassing drama or fuss.

"Well, well, well. A long way from the park, aren't they?" Will's tone was snide and Adrian sensed a tension, an urge to challenge.

"Leave them. They don't want to be with us and we don't want to be with them. So they told a little porkie? What of it?"

Will took a long draught of his beer and got to his feet. "I want evidence of this. I won't talk to them or make a scene; I just want proof that he's a liar. Stay there, I'll be back before the food arrives."

"Will!" Adrian protested, but DS William Quinn had already joined the slipstream of tourists thronging the promenade, camera at the ready. Adrian shook his head, irritated by his boyfriend's obsessive behaviour but still appreciative of how good he looked in a pair of shorts.

Lunch was tense and awkward. Will, fired up by what he'd seen, wanted to discuss the other couple's behaviour. Adrian did not want to hear anything about Leon or Marianne or listen to Will's theories. They ate in silence, both pretending it was companionable. The coolness persisted even as they boarded the rickety wooden tram to Foz. It trundled along the riverside, affording the occupants a variety of views; fishermen drying nets, boys playing football in bare feet, two older women smoking in a doorway. Anger subsided and Adrian pressed his shoulder against Will.

"You should get a shot of that," he said, pointing to a line of washing, quite literally all the colours of the rainbow, fluttering across an alleyway.

Will obliged and replaced his camera in his bag. "Sulk over?"

"I wasn't sulking. I was angry with you. But I've said my piece and we moved on. All I want is a peaceful, friendly holiday and I'm prepared to compromise. Your contribution is a promise not to stir the shit. Can we please just enjoy ourselves?"

Will gave a slow, guilty smile and draped an arm around Adrian's shoulder.

"I love you," he whispered.

"I love you too. Especially when you're off duty."

They rumbled along, the silence more harmonious. A woman in a flowery pinafore boarded the tram carrying a bag of salt cod. The smell pervaded the whole carriage and Adrian turned his face to the open window.

Above the noise of the tram, Will spoke into his ear. "The thing is, Adrian, I'm never off duty. Can you live with that? A detective who never stops using his eyes and ears? Or is that going to be a deal-breaker? I'd like to know sooner rather than later."

Adrian turned back and shook his head. "Don't be so Inspector

Morse. I already live with it, from you and from Beatrice. All I want is a nice peaceful holiday without inventing theories and spying on our companions. Look! There's the sea! Portugal is so beautiful. I really think I could live here."

The camera snapped and Adrian saw Will had photographed him rather than the sea. "Me too. In fact, I could live anywhere with you."

"You're changing the subject," he said, but moved closer till their legs touched on the creaking wooden bench.

Chapter 18

As the Fiat 500 pulled up outside the villa, slightly later than expected due to Beatrice's inexact navigation, Tanya careened across the drive, arms spread wide with a grin to match. Ana leapt out of the driver's seat and rushed into her embrace. The gasps and laughs echoed across the courtyard and Beatrice found herself beaming as she heaved the bags from the boot.

"Talk about a rabbit out of a hat!" Tanya said, her arm around Ana's shoulders. "What is it, twenty years? I'd never have thought of finding you. Yet again, DCI Stubbs, you're full of surprises."

"Frankly, both of you need a kick up the rear," said Beatrice. "When you find a friend, someone you connect with, regardless of what personal dramas you have in your lives, keep in touch. There. That's your lecture for today and I'm ready for an aperitif."

The welcoming committee had prepared canapés and chilled white port by the poolside. Beatrice stood back to allow the party to reunite. While Ana had first met Tanya as an exchange student under the charge of herself and Matthew, her familiarity with Adrian was relatively new. Yet for all the effusive hugs and squeals, it looked to Beatrice as if they'd known each other for ever.

"You look fabulous!"

"So do you! Look at the colour of you!"

"I take tanning seriously. I'm so happy you're here!"

"Me too! Where's this gorgeous man of yours?"

"Will, come meet Ana."

While introductions were made, Beatrice sat down with a thump on a sun bed. Matthew joined her and placing his hand on her back, asked in a low voice, "How was today?"

"Useful. I'd go so far as to say we have a lead or two. Yours?"

"Very relaxing. We explored the valley and found hundreds of lizards. Luke will show you photos of every last one. However, storm clouds have gathered over the sisters. Couple of tiffs and a bit of tension. Hopefully, the lovely Ana will defuse all that. It really is a pleasure to see her again."

"Nice for Tanya too, having a friend her own age. So, what's for dinner? I'm ravishing."

A small voice came from behind her. "So am I."

Beatrice half turned and saw Luke's steady blue eyes flick between her and Matthew. She got to her feet. "In that case, let us demand to be fed. After all, we've both had a hard day."

"Have you been swimming too?" Luke asked, slipping his hand into hers.

"Yes, but not in the water. Did you go back to the beach?" she asked, as they made their way indoors.

"No. Grandad, me and Mum stayed here all day. Will and Adrian went to Porto and brought me a hammer. I'll show you." He rushed back outside and returned with a large squeaky plastic hammer which he bounced lightly off Beatrice's head.

"The perfect present! Mind you don't mess up my hair. What about Marianne and Leon? What did they do today?"

The smile left Luke's face and he shrugged. "Dunno. Are you staying here now? With that lady?"

"For tonight, but we have to get back to work tomorrow. It's a shame because I really wanted to explore this park. Apparently there are a lot of lizards. I wish I could have seen some."

Luke's cheeks rose into apples. "Wait there! I've got something to show you!"

He pelted up the stairs and Beatrice wandered into the kitchen. Tea towels lay across a variety of dishes, actively encouraging curiosity. Salads, breads, cold meats and several colourful dishes rested beneath and a tray of potato wedges glistened in the oven. Beatrice stole a slice of bread and a glance at the door.

Will leaned on the door jamb, a reproachful look on his face.

"It's a fair cop, guv," said Beatrice, with her mouth full.

"Hard day?"

"Yes, but Ana made it easier. How was yours?"

Will frowned. "I'm a bit concerned and wouldn't mind picking your brains. If we could find five minutes for a chat sometime this..."

The sound of small feet thundering down the stairs made them both turn.

Beatrice swallowed her bread. "Course we can. But first I need to look at some lizards."

The meal went perfectly until dessert. Ana had a wealth of stories to tell and made an instant connection with Will. Adrian's food and wine choices were sublime, as expected, and almost everyone ate heartily. Having her own friend seemed to release Tanya's sparkle, so the table rang with laughter and memories. Beatrice was surprised how much the girls could remember from the exchange trip nineteen years previously. In her own mind, it was all a bit soft-focus and vague. So much energy and congeniality filled the room; it was almost possible to ignore the near-silent couple at the end of the table.

Matthew made several attempts to offer them more ham or peppers or wine, which were consistently refused. Marianne ate a small portion of potatoes and a few fried whitebait, but Leon merely shoved a few pieces of meat around his plate and left a single bread roll untouched. He drank only water and made no eye contact with anyone. Passive-aggressive attention-seeking infuriated Beatrice into active aggression, so she chose to completely ignore him.

Just after nine, Luke said his goodnights and Tanya took him off to bed, while Beatrice helped Adrian clear the table. The second time she came out of the kitchen, she sensed something had changed.

Will was speaking. "We thought Porto was beautiful. So atmospheric, and the architecture is a constant surprise. Even the train station deserved a photograph. As for the riverside, it's a people watcher's dream. Did you and Marianne like it?"

"Sorry?" asked Leon, his expression so contemptuous it was close to a sneer.

"I asked if you liked Porto. We saw you there this afternoon. Obviously we were a bit surprised. When we announced we were going to Porto today, I could have sworn you told us you were going to tour the national park. Had we known, we could have taken the one car and left Matthew with the Panda."

Adrian brought out a large plate with oranges and meringues and set it on the table. Only then did he notice the atmosphere. "What?"

Marianne rested her hand on Leon's arm. "Easy to make a mistake in a bunch of tourists. I imagine there are a lot of couples who look like us."

"I'm a detective, Marianne. I don't make assumptions. To be honest, I don't need to when you walk right past our table. I even took a picture, want to see?"

An unpleasant silence hung over the table and Beatrice saw Adrian throw a thunderous glare at Will.

Marianne began. "Look, the thing is..."

Leon pulled his arm away from Marianne and stood up. "I can speak for myself, thank you. Yes, we were in Porto. We chose to tell a white lie and go alone because the truth is I don't want to spend every single second in the family pocket. I respect the fact that you want to organise your lives around the whims of a child but I don't. This is my holiday too and I want to do what I enjoy and spend some time with my partner. And I am not going to apologise for that. Thanks for dinner. Goodnight."

He threw down his napkin, reached for Marianne's hand and they left the room, to the sound of Marianne's sniffs.

"Will!" Adrian put his hands on his hips and faced his partner. "Why do you insist on winding him up? I thought we agreed not to mention seeing them!"

Tanya came back into the room with a big grin and a bottle. "He's crashed out. Now who's for a vinho do Porto? What's the matter?"

Matthew patted the chair next to him. "Sit down, my dear one. It seems Will and Adrian saw Marianne and Leon in Porto today, despite their apparent intention of going to tour the park. Will just challenged them in the deception and Leon took offence."

"Which was completely unnecessary and ruined the evening," said Adrian. "If they want to sneak off, it's up to them. What is your problem with him?"

Will revolved the stem of his glass between his fingers. "My problem with him is his attitude to Luke. Didn't you just hear what he said? *I respect the fact that you want to organise your lives around the whims of a child but I don't.* Look, I've been watching his behaviour and I'm sorry, but really, really don't like the way he treats Luke."

"He said what?" gasped Tanya.

"That's enough." Matthew didn't shout, but the gravitas in his tone stilled the room. "Ana, I apologise for such a scene in front of a most welcome guest. I think the best thing would be to retire for the evening and consider our respective behaviours. Beatrice and I will adjourn to our room. I appreciate you have things to say, Will, but we can discuss any issues in the cold light of morning. Tanya, I expect you and Ana might enjoy a glass of port on the terrace. Just be aware that sound carries. Thank you all for dinner and I'll be up for breakfast at seven. Beatrice, do you want to bring your dessert upstairs?"

Beatrice hesitated. "Yes, good idea. But before all this blew up, I had planned to talk shop with Will. If you don't mind, Adrian, I'd just like to borrow him for a few minutes."

Adrian shook his head, his face set and stony. "I don't mind."

Ana put her hand on Adrian's shoulder. "Come and have a glass of port with us. I want to try a bit of your Orange Eton Mess or whatever it is."

"It's called a Good Luck Charm cake. Perhaps we could have done with it a bit earlier before *someone* decided to wreck the atmosphere. Yes, let's leave these two to their police gossip and enjoy our pud outside."

Beatrice left them to their desserts and followed Will out the back door towards the pool. They walked to the garden chairs at the far end, the furthest they could get from the house. The evening air, still warm and fragrant, had a soothing effect as they sat and gazed at the underwater lights.

"I assume it's Leon you wanted to discuss?" Beatrice said.

Will nodded twice. "Adrian thinks it's an ego thing between us, but I'm afraid it's worse than that. He forgets that I trained in behavioural psychology. Beatrice, I really believe Leon has a worrying number of signs to indicate Narcissistic Personality Disorder. Did you know Marianne gave her cat away because of him?"

"Gave it away? Why?"

"He told her he's allergic and said he wouldn't move in with her if the cat remained. So she gave it to Matthew. Now, when we saw them today, we were having a beer and they walked right past our table. I left Adrian people-watching and followed them. I was determined to get a photograph. They stopped at a restaurant on the Ribeira, not far from us, and ordered food. I got several shots of their faces with the river and the bridge in the background. Then I noticed movement on the wall behind them. Cats. Lots of them. Sunbathing, scratching or washing themselves, right behind the man with an allergy. And Leon was smiling, chatting and completely fine."

"That's odd, but hardly enough to classify as NPD."

Will hunched forward and dropped his voice. "Narcissists have to be the centre of attention. They dislike anything that takes attention away from them. Luke has bruises on his upper arm in the shape of a handprint. Someone has treated him pretty harshly. Remember how fractious Luke was the evening after Marianne and Leon brought him back to the villa? Often, especially with new partners, narcissists push away the partner's family, friends, children or pets and insist on a hundred percent devotion."

"If you think he hurt Luke, we need confirmation of that. Otherwise I'd class his behaviour as just a bit too possessive," Beatrice replied. "It's quite common, especially with a couple who've found each other later in life. They've both been single a long time."

"Well, that's what he told her. He said he couldn't find anyone who matched up to his ideals. Another narcissistic indicator, incidentally. But I did a little bit of research on social media and found some direct contradictions to what we know. His Facebook profile is squeaky clean, but by befriending a few of his contacts under a false profile, I found a lot of photographs and conversations which at the very least catch him out in blatant deception."

"Everyone exaggerates on Facebook," said Beatrice.

"There's exaggeration and outright lies. Six months ago he had an engagement party with his Polish girlfriend, Iwona, after a 'whirlwind romance'. Shortly before that, a girl called Nicky blogged about Love Rat Leon, who broke her heart. The photos are clearly of him, the most recent dated a year ago.

"It's not just Facebook. He describes himself as a business consultant. The reality is that he works as a salesman for an amusements company, flogging gambling machines to pubs and arcades."

Beatrice placed her hand on Will's forearm. "Why are you doing this?"

He didn't answer right away. He rubbed at his stubble and stared into the pool, his eyes reflecting the turquoise ripples.

"He's a fraud, Beatrice. I have an instinct for people like him. He's going to damage your family and I can't stand back and watch that happen."

They sat in silence for a few seconds, listening to a faint burst of laughter and some subsequent shushing from the other side of the house.

Beatrice sighed. "Marianne is an adult. We have to let her make her own choices, or mistakes."

Will shook his head emphatically. "I don't think she is, emotionally. Even so, Luke is a child. Having such a toxic person around makes him vulnerable."

A light went on above their heads and Matthew's silhouette filled the window frame. He looked down for a moment and Beatrice waved. He turned away.

"Leave it with me. Don't provoke any more confrontations with Leon or Marianne. Don't inflame Tanya with your concerns, but make sure Luke is never left alone with him. I'll arrange some background checks and see if we have legitimate cause to alert the others. Where Adrian and Matthew are concerned, my feeling is to play it down. How do you see it, DS Quinn?"

"Fair enough, Ma'am."

Beatrice stood up and bent to kiss Will's cheek. He reached up an arm to embrace her and she squeezed his shoulder.

"I'm very glad you care, Will. Tell Adrian I said that. Night night."

"G'night and thanks for listening."

Matthew was in bed, reading. Or at least pretending to. Beatrice brushed her teeth, moisturised and sent two rapid emails. One to Dawn Whittaker, with a request for background information on Leon Charles. One to her own counsellor, James, asking for advice on Narcissistic Personality Disorder.

She put the laptop back in her bag, donned her pyjamas and got under the duvet. Matthew accepted her kiss goodnight but said nothing. She lay back on the pillow, unable to resist replaying Will's observations.

Matthew turned out the light. "Stop it."

"Stop what?"

"Thinking. Go to sleep and save it for tomorrow. Otherwise you'll fidget-arse all night and keep us both awake."

"Fair enough. I'll try."

He turned his back to her, pummelled his pillow and let out a deep sigh. "Matthew?"

"What?"

"I never had my dessert."

He didn't reply, but his silent laughter shook the mattress.

Chapter 19

By the time Adrian showered, dressed and descended at half-past eight, the only person up and about was Matthew. In his cargo shorts and blue shirt, he looked like a dishevelled David Attenborough, making coffee after a long night of observing gorillas.

"Good morning! I suppose Beatrice and Ana are long gone?"

Matthew looked up with a vague smile. "Good morning, Adrian. Yes, they left over an hour ago and even then they were running late. How did you sleep?"

Adrian sat at the table and reached for some juice. "When we finally got to sleep, which must have been after two, I slept well. Obviously we had a few things to hash out. Will's in the shower now and before anything else, he's going over to apologise to Leon for last night."

Matthew switched the kettle on and spooned coffee grounds into the cafetière. He selected three cups and poured milk into a jug.

"I'm pleased to hear that. Beatrice and I had a serious discussion this morning. Will's heart is in the right place and we both appreciate his concerns. I feel we should be nice yet watchful."

"So do I. But I hate atmospheres. First thing, I'll go over and get Marianne to come out on some pretext or other, leaving the coast clear for Will and Leon to talk man to man. Then we can all have breakfast like civilised human beings."

An expression of relief smoothed Matthew's features. "That sounds very grown up to me. As to breakfast, I'm toying with the idea of scrambled eggs with bacon. Could I tempt you?"

Adrian slugged more grapefruit juice, relishing the acidity on his palate. "Oh yes, you most definitely could. Have we got any salmon? Because Will..."

"Oh God!" Tanya wandered into the room in shortie pyjamas and fluffy socks, with bed hair and traces of last night's make-up. "I need caffeine and I need it now. Whose idea was port wine and cigars? My mouth feels like a pub carpet."

"Port and cigars?" Matthew poured boiling water into the cafetière and replaced the lid. "Were you founding your own gentleman's club?"

Tanya slumped into the chair beside Adrian and made feeble clutching motions at the table. "Juice! Juice! I blame that wicked Portuguese-Irish female. She always has led me astray. Oh thank you so much."

She wrapped both hands round the glass Adrian gave her and drank deeply, making noises like a suckling calf. Matthew rummaged around in the fridge, pulling out eggs, bacon, milk, salmon, butter and cream, humming something by Vivaldi.

"Is Luke still in the Land of Nod?"

Tanya put down her empty glass. "Yep, flat out when I just looked in. Don't wait for him. Sometimes he'll sleep through till ten if he's had a late night. Feed me and feed me now. Adrian, your cake last night was to die for. Confession time. After you went to bed, I had seconds. Where's the coffee, Dad?"

"Good morning everyone, how are we all today?" Will entered, freshly showered and shaved, smelling divine. Adrian watched him with a mixture of admiration, love and lust.

He met Adrian's eyes as if he could read his thoughts and jerked his head in the direction of the garden flat. "I'm ready when you are."

Adrian checked his watch. "They rarely emerge before nine. Shall we have a coffee first?"

Tanya glanced between them. "Don't tell me you're going to apologise. Will had every right to say what he did and I for one..."

"Tanya?" Matthew interrupted. "Do you want bacon or salmon with your scrambled eggs?"

"Both. But first I need some coffee. Anyway, Will, I really don't think...."

"It wasn't Will's decision, Tanya, it was mine," said Adrian. "I want us to have a nice holiday with no tensions. If Will says sorry, we can get back to enjoying ourselves and perhaps give each other a bit more space. For all our sakes, I think it's best."

Matthew had his back to them, slicing bread, but his silence acted as tacit approval.

Tanya groaned. "Oh God, everyone is dancing attendance on him as if he's a VIP. Well, I'll tell you one thing, when we get back, he can forget the kid gloves and stop being so precious. Because I don't need another attention-seeking child in my life. Luke is five. He's allowed to try it on. Leon is an adult and needs to bloody well grow up. Right, if no one else is making the coffee, I'll do it myself."

Will looked away, towards the open doorway. "They're up. Marianne's sitting on their terrace in a robe. Let's get it over with."

"OK." Adrian drained his glass and got to his feet.

An agonised scream shattered the peace of the kitchen. Glass, metal and liquid hit the tiled floor. Adrian whirled round to see Tanya's shocked face, the smashed cafetière and coffee grounds all over her left arm and down both her bare legs.

"Oh my God!" Matthew exclaimed. "What have you done?"

Will pushed past Adrian and put his hand on Tanya's back. "Cold running water on it, as soon as possible. Quick, let's use the pool shower. Watch your feet."

White-faced and trembling, she allowed him to guide her outside.

Adrian waved a hand at Matthew. "You go and see if she's OK. I'll clear up in here."

He'd just finished mopping the floor and wrapping the broken glass in newspaper when Matthew returned.

"Adrian, the burns look rather nasty. Will's going to drive her to the nearest hospital to get a professional assessment. He says we should cover the scalded areas with cling film. Do we have any? And where are the car keys?"

"Keys on the windowsill and the cling film is in this drawer. Here. Are you going with them? I can hold the fort here, make Luke's breakfast and so on."

Matthew hesitated. "If you're sure you don't mind? She's still my little girl, even if she does drink port and smoke cigars."

"Come on. Let's get her wrapped up and into the car."

When they got outside, Tanya's trembles under the cold water had become teeth-chattering shivers. Will's forehead creased with concern.

"Adrian, could you fetch a bottle of water and a blanket? And in my sponge bag, there are some painkillers."

"It doesn't hurt," said Tanya, her voice wobbling.

"Not as long as it has cold water on it. But we have a bit of a drive ahead, so you should take some now."

By the time Adrian had gathered pills, tissues, blanket, water and a handful of energy bars, the party were already in the car, Tanya half-wrapped in plastic.

Matthew sat in the back seat beside her and draped the blanket around her shoulders. "Adrian, look after Luke, would you?"

"Of course. Don't worry about us and call me as soon as you know anything," he said and kissed Will goodbye. The Peugeot crawled across the bumpy track to the road then picked up speed once on tarmac. Adrian watched till it turned the corner and disappeared.

Back in the kitchen, he dug around in the cupboards until he found an old aluminium Moka coffeepot and started the essential process of getting his morning fix of caffeine. It would help him think straight. He was just smiling to himself at the pun when the door opened. Marianne walked in without looking at him, went straight over to the windowsill and picked up the second set of keys.

"Seeing as someone's already taken the Peugeot without even discussing it, I hope you won't mind if Leon and I use the Panda?" she said, heading for the door.

Adrian's mouth fell open in disbelief. "Will took the Peugeot to drive Tanya to hospital. You weren't consulted because serious burns take priority over petty squabbling about cars."

Marianne's sour expression turned to one of confusion. "What are you talking about?"

"Tanya spilt the contents of the cafetière over herself. Will thought the burns were serious enough to need medical attention, so he and Matthew have gone to the local A&E to get her checked out."

"Oh shit. Is she all right?"

"No. She's badly scalded. And for your information, before that happened, Will was coming over to see you this morning to apologise. We don't want any tensions to spoil this holiday, so it would be really helpful if you could drop the attitude so that we can all behave like adults."

"Yes. Sorry. We were both upset, that all." She sat down, her voice quiet. "We thought some space would be best."

"I disagree. I think clearing the air with an apology and accepting your wishes to do whatever you want would be best. Especially for Matthew and Luke."

Marianne's eyes flicked to his face. "Where is Luke?"

"Still in bed. I offered to stay and look after him. Tanya said he..."

"Problem?" Leon stood in the open doorway, addressing Marianne.

Marianne's expression was a mixture of guilt and concern. "No...well, yes. Tanya scalded herself with coffee this morning, so Will and Dad took her to hospital."

"Sorry to hear that."

The coffeepot began to gurgle.

Adrian took a deep breath. "Good morning, Leon. As I just told Marianne, Will and I were about to come over and apologise this morning when Tanya had her accident. We don't want an atmosphere between us. Would you like some coffee?"

Leon kept his eyes on Marianne. "No thanks, I think we should go."

Adrian continued as if he hadn't spoken. "And Marianne agreed it's better if we all behave like grown-ups and enjoy the holiday." He poured coffee into three cups. "As far as Tanya will be able to enjoy herself after this morning. Boiling water burns are very painful. I just hope she won't end up with any scars." He placed the cups on the table. "Help yourself to milk and sugar. I'll just pop upstairs and check on Luke."

He bounded up the tiled staircase, releasing some of the pent-up anger triggered by Leon's petulant expression. He sulked more than a five-year-old, which was a frankly unattractive trait in a grown man. Adrian pushed open the door and looked in on the sleeping figure of Luke in his Spiderman pyjamas. His duvet had been kicked to one side, but even so his fringe seemed damp with sweat. Adrian tentatively pressed the back of his hand against Luke's cheek to gauge his temperature. Warm, but not feverish. Good job. He had no idea what to do with children when they were healthy, let alone when they were sick.

He crossed the hall to his own room, for no other reason than to give the couple downstairs time to review their stropping policy. While he was there, he went into the bathroom to check his hair and wash his face. Voices floated up from the terrace, through the open window. Despite himself, Adrian crept closer to listen. He knew eavesdroppers rarely hear good of themselves, but they often hear worse of others.

Marianne and Leon were leaning on the terrace railing.

"Because I don't want to!" hissed Leon.

Adrian noted he was carrying a coffee cup. One point to Adrian.

Marianne's voice was harder to hear, her tone low and her face directed out over the valley. A few words floated up. "...can't just leave him here... surely?"

"I'm not staying here. I want some space. I thought you understood that."

Marianne stayed silent. *Go on. Tell him to piss off*, Adrian willed her.

She turned to Leon with an imploring look and Adrian could hear her more clearly. "How about we take him with us?"

Leon's head retracted, affecting mock disbelief, as if he were an affronted turtle. "Take him with us? How does that give me space? I can't believe how my needs are always at the bottom of the list. Everyone treats that bloody child like some kind of princeling, as if his welfare trumps all. So his dad left. Happens to half the population. He's nothing special. If you want to stay here, you're welcome. I'll go on my own."

Marianne's pitch rose. "No, darling, I don't want that. But you know why I can't leave Luke here, alone with Adrian. You must understand that."

Leon placed his empty cup on the terrace table. "Let me ask you this. Who is more important to you? Your sister's kid or the man you say you love? Think carefully, Marianne. I'm leaving in five minutes, with or without you."

Adrian stepped away from the window and rested his head on the shower stall, trying to block the echo of her words. *I can't leave Luke here, alone with Adrian. Alone with Adrian. With Adrian.*

When he heard the car drive away, Adrian washed his face again and went downstairs. As expected, the kitchen was empty. Their coffee cups, still wet, rested on the draining board. He made a fresh pot of coffee and sat down to read the online news till Luke awoke. He checked his mobile every few minutes but it showed no messages. At quarter to nine, he heard a toilet flush upstairs. He closed his laptop and waited.

"Where's Mum?" Luke was dressed in an Ice Age t-shirt, shorts and trainers. He carried a mini iPad.

"Popped out for a bit. She'll be back soon. What do you want for breakfast, or should I say brunch? I can do scrambled eggs with bacon or salmon."

"Bacon, please. Salmon pongs. What's brunch?"

"What do you call the first meal of the day?"

Luke sat on a chair and put down his iPad. "Breakfast."

"Correct! Do you want juice?"

Luke nodded.

Adrian poured half a glass and asked, "And what do you call the meal in the middle of the day?"

"Lunch."

"Correct once again. You may have extra bacon. Now, what happens if you combine breakfast and lunch?"

"Brunch! Oh."

"What?"

"Does that mean I can't have any lunch if I have both together?"

"It depends. Some people don't want lunch as well as brunch. Brown or white?"

"White, please."

"Others, who run about a lot, swim, dive and expend a lot of energy, get hungry at lunchtime. Those people definitely deserve lunch. Shall we see how you feel when your mum gets back?"

"Yes. Because I think I probably am going to be hungry at lunchtime. And Will is definitely going to want lunch. He runs about a lot and swims and things."

"I think you might be right. We'd better make an extra huge lunch for them when they get back. Luke, does your mum let you have ketchup?"

"Yes, but only on burgers. With fish fingers we have tarty sauce."

"Right. Scrambled eggs aren't really either so I'll just leave it on the table and you can have some if you want. Here you go. We can make more toast if that's not enough."

Luke tucked in and Adrian searched for a topic of conversation before realising it was unnecessary. He ate his eggs, read his news and kept half an eye on his young charge in case he overdid the ketchup.

"Where's Grandpa?"

"He went with them."

"Why?"

"Luke, your mum had a little accident this morning. She spilt some hot water on herself. Don't worry, she'll be fine. When she gets home, she might have a few bandages and we'll have to take good care of her."

Luke's long-lashed blue eyes fixed on him. "OK. I had a bandage one time when I fell off my bike. All up here was covered in blood." He indicated his shoulder.

"Really? I would have fainted. Did you faint?"

"No. I cried though."

"Of course you cried. It must have hurt. I always cry when things hurt. Somehow that makes things better. But blood makes me faint."

Luke patted a pile of egg onto his toast and dabbed it in some ketchup. "My friend Ben says only girls cry." He stuffed the toast into his mouth.

Adrian curled his lip. "Then your friend Ben needs to grow up and develop a little emotional intelligence. More toast?"

"Yes please. Are you and Will going to have kids?"

Adrian popped two slices in the toaster which gave him time to frame his response.

"It's not something we've discussed. Even if we wanted children, it would be complicated. Biologically, men can't have babies, as I'm sure you know. We could adopt or use a surrogate, I suppose, if we really wanted a family."

Luke squirted a blob of ketchup onto his plate. "You totally should. You'd be great dads. I wish Mum would marry both of you. That'd be so cool!"

"Enough of the ketchup now. Here's your toast." Adrian started the washing-up so Luke couldn't see his face.

"Good morning, Flukey Lukey! That looks yummy!"

Adrian turned to see Marianne enter the kitchen, a bright smile on her face despite her puffy, reddened eyes. He watched her stroke Luke's hair, keeping her face averted from Adrian's gaze.

"It is! There was bacon too but I ate that already."

"Would you like some, Marianne? There's salmon if you prefer," Adrian offered, with an olive branch smile.

She shook her head. "Thanks, but Leon and I already had breakfast. Any news from the hospital?"

Luke looked up at her. "Who's in hospital?"

Adrian shot Marianne a glance and her complexion flushed salmon-pink.

"Oh, no one you know, darling. Just a friend of mine," she smiled down at him.

"Is it Mum? Adrian said she had an accident."

Marianne glared over Luke's head. "Mummy will be fine. In fact, I expect she'll be back any minute. Why don't you go outside and see if there's any sign of the car?"

"OK." Luke picked up the last bit of toast, hopped off the chair and ran out through the kitchen door.

With her scowl and folded arms, Marianne epitomised judgement. "You had no business telling him that. You'll only worry him."

Adrian struggled to keep his voice calm and his temper in check. "He came downstairs to find his mother and grandfather weren't here. What was I supposed to tell him? I told him the truth but played it down. Tanya doesn't wrap him in cotton wool. As she left him in my care, I followed her example."

"Yes, well, thanks for making him breakfast but I'll take over from here. He'll feel more comfortable around family."

Adrian stared at her. She lifted her chin and gave him a defiant look in return, then turned on her heel and left the kitchen.

"Any sign of that car yet, Lukey?"

Adrian finished the washing-up, tidied the kitchen and went upstairs to change into his trunks. Thirty lengths of front crawl should take the edge of his rage.

When he finished his swim, he showered and rested in the shade until his pulse returned to normal. Neither Marianne nor Luke had made an appearance. He returned indoors to find his phone and saw a message from Will.

Tanya OK, but dr wants her to stay overnight. M & I leaving soon – back around midday. PS: Hungry!

Adrian checked his watch. Ten past eleven. He ran upstairs to change into a shirt and shorts before starting on lunch. He had his head in the fridge when a splash from outside caught his attention. Luke's head bobbed up in the middle of the pool, his water wings bright red against the turquoise water. He shouted something and Adrian followed his line of focus. Marianne reclined on a sun lounger, wearing oversized sunglasses and a floppy hat. She waved at Luke and went back to her laptop. An intense heat spread up Adrian's neck. She had waited till he left the pool before letting Luke go for a swim, as if Adrian represented some kind of danger.

His hands shook as he chopped onions for the fish chowder and he told himself that was the reason his eyes were watering. He followed the recipe and won a magnificent argument in his head.

Melt butter and fry garlic, leeks and onion.

Marianne, can I just pick up on something you said? 'He'll feel more comfortable around family'. You're aware that the vast majority of paedophiles are members of the victim's own family?

Stir in potatoes and season. Cook for three minutes.

And you should know that gay men are interested in other

consensual gay men, rather than anything with a pulse and a penis.

Add the stock, wine, herbs and fish. Simmer for five minutes.

Child abuse is less about sex or sexuality and more about power, so why would you think a happy, healthy gay man in a loving relationship cannot be trusted with a child?

Strain liquid and reduce by boiling.

And one last thing, regarding Luke's welfare, I'd like to tell you what he said this morning. Out of nowhere, he told me he wished Tanya could marry Will and I because we'd be great dads.

Blow nose, wipe eyes, put bread in oven to warm.

He was adding cream and parsley to the chowder when he heard the car pull up outside. He threw the tea-towel over his shoulder and went to meet them.

Matthew's tired, grey face lifted into a smile as he saw Adrian in the doorway. "All well. She needs to stay in overnight, but due to instant expert treatment from Will, she's likely to escape without a scar. Please hang onto this man, Adrian. He is a true asset."

Arms full of stuff from the back seat, Will gave Matthew a friendly shove with his shoulder. "Of course he'll hang onto me. Good looks, fast car and first aid, what's not to love? His side of the bargain is good food and wine. So what's for lunch?"

"Fish chowder. Is she in much pain?"

Matthew shook his head. "Morphine. No more sunbathing for her, I know that much. Where's Luke?"

"In the pool. I'll give them a call and we can eat."

He gave the chowder a quick stir and made his way to the back garden. The pool area was empty. There were splashes and wet footprints all over the tiles, but no sign of life. He hadn't heard them go upstairs so Marianne must have taken Luke back to the garden flat. She really wasn't taking any chances.

In the kitchen, Will lifted the lid and inhaled. "I could eat all of this on my own. Are those scallops?"

"Yes. Don't touch. Matthew, do you want to choose a wine? Something light, I recommend."

Matthew opened the fridge. "I concur. Perhaps something suited to a spritzer. If I drink a glass of something strong on an empty stomach, I will collapse."

Will replaced the lid and took his seat. "Five places? You, me, Matthew, Luke and...?"

The kitchen door opened and Marianne burst in, wild-eyed and tearful. "I need the keys. Please, I need the keys to the car. Leon's gone!"

Adrian was the first to recover. "He went hours ago. What's the emergency?"

"I mean gone permanently! He sent a text." She waved her phone at them. "Said this holiday wasn't working and he had to leave. I need to get to the airport. I have to talk to him and he won't answer his phone. Keys, Will!"

Matthew closed the fridge door. "Marianne, sit down."

"Dad, I don't have time! I have to catch him before he gets on a plane."

"I said, sit down. You are in no fit state to drive. I want an explanation first. But before anything else, where is Luke?"

Marianne looked out of the window. "Still in the pool, I expect. When I got the message, I went back to the flat to see if Leon had taken his stuff. I left Luke here with Adrian."

Matthew looked at Adrian, blinking just once.

"He's not in the pool. I thought he was with Marianne. He must be upstairs. Will, can you..."

Will was out of the room before Adrian could finish. Matthew picked up the car keys and put them in his pocket, without looking at anyone. He opened the back door and called, "Luke! It's lunchtime! Luke? Are you hungry? We've got a surprise for you!"

Cicadas chittered and a magpie rattled from a nearby tree. Other than that, silence. Will's footsteps thudded downstairs.

"He's not there. Floor dry, no swimming trunks, nothing. Marianne, go back and check your flat. Adrian, search the house. Everywhere a kid might hide. Matthew and I will comb the gardens."

Marianne let out a short sob. "The thing is, I..."

Will rounded on her. "Sorry, this is no longer about you."

Chapter 20

When Ana and Beatrice had arrived at Gerês College of Hospitality earlier that morning, Roman, Cher and Xavier were waiting on the terrace to tell them a suspect had been arrested in the Silva murder case.

"His name is Marco Cordeiro and he's a casual labourer. He works for the hotel every summer as a gardener," said Xavier. "His prints match those on the window and they found Samuel's watch in his bike pannier."

Cher chimed in. "We don't have much information. My gut says we need to get to that police station and find out more, but today it's going to be pretty much impossible. Some of us are giving seminars and the rest of us need to show our faces."

"Ana doesn't." Roman looked at her. "What were your plans today?"

"To hide out in Beatrice's room and make some calls. But if you like, I'll see what I can find at the station first. I'm guessing he was taken to PSP in Viana do Castelo?"

"I guess. They didn't give out that information," said Cher.

Beatrice spotted Gilchrist talking to another man just inside the foyer. "OK, let's make a big show of saying goodbye and I'll call you during our lunch break."

Ana got to her feet and shook hands with each member of the party, ending with a hug for Beatrice. She walked off to her car, waving and waggling her fingers as if to remind Beatrice to email.

"Beautiful girl," said Cher.

"Stunning," agreed Roman.

"Very useful ally too," said Xavier.

"Yes, yes. Have I missed breakfast?" asked Beatrice.

The bitter truth was that she had. Nothing more than coffee carried her through the dull-as-ditchwater Compliance and Governance workshop, but the Unconscious Bias session was a revelation. Especially as she looked around the room and saw the lack of diversity amongst her colleagues.

When lunchtime finally arrived, she scurried out of the seminar and shot across to the canteen. She added black pepper and Parmesan to a large plate of Spaghetti Puttanesca and went to find a seat outside. She chose a table away from the general hubbub, hoping for some privacy to check her emails and call Ana. But after one mouthful, a voice said, "May I join you?" and she looked up. Commander Gilchrist beamed at her, the sun behind his head creating a Christ-like corona, giving the impression of a divine visitation.

Beatrice swallowed. "I would be honoured, sir."

She removed her handbag for him to place his tray beside hers. Beatrice noted the abundance of 'superfoods' on his plate, the majority of which she couldn't even pronounce. He wore a pale grey suit with a pink shirt and lilac tie. Up close, he was undeniably handsome, in a slightly over-groomed sort of way.

"How was your morning?" he asked, placing his napkin on his knees.

"Extremely beneficial. Dr Ruishalme's presentation on implicit bias was a real eye-opener. I plan to repeat the exact same session for my colleagues."

"Ah yes. Ruishalme knows her stuff. Scientific minds fascinate me. I'm more of a people person, bumbling along on instinct."

"Likewise. But you've done rather well without the science, sir."

"Allow me to return the compliment. In fact, I have heard certain stripes say you could go still further." He smiled his TV-friendly smile and bit into a broccoli floret.

"As I'm sure you know, sir, my plans are to retire at the end of the year. I've had a good run and intend to quit before fulfilling the Peter Principle."

"Ah yes. Promotion due to competence till you reach a level at which you are incompetent? Does that ever happen in international law enforcement, do you think?" He widened his eyes in mock surprise, his smile still broad.

There was something in his manner that bordered on camp, as if he were playing to the gallery.

"It most certainly would if I were promoted any further. I'm already feeling a total fraud. A feeling which is exacerbated by having such a consummate professional and all-round nice guy as my boss."

Over Gilchrist's shoulder, she saw Cher, Roman and Xavier sitting at a nearby table, throwing concerned glances in her direction. She twisted strands of pasta around her fork.

"Of course," he said. "Rangarajan Jalan, known as The Incorruptible. A rare breed indeed," said the Commander.

Beatrice didn't like his tone. "Do you think so? In my experience, admittedly vastly inferior to your own, I have found my British and European colleagues to have the highest integrity, often in extraordinarily challenging circumstances. There might be the odd one whose motives are penal, but on the whole, I'd say I'm proud to be amongst our number."

Gilchrist had finished his measly portion of salad and dabbed at his lips with his napkin. "A noble sentiment I wish I could echo. My experience in the higher echelons is a different story, one of politics, intrigue and backstabbing. You know, the tales I could tell are downright Shakespearean. I suspect if one were to dig deeply, even the saintly Jalan has a skeleton in his closet."

At her feet, Beatrice's mobile vibrated silently through her handbag.

"I'm sure many senior executives in the business world would say the same, sir. Sharks, piranhas and jellyfish swim in every corporate sea. Still, I can honestly say I have never heard a bad word against our Super, at any level."

"You're very loyal, Stubbs, and I admire that. As for the worlds of business and politics, do you know why our television screens are dominated with crime series, police dramas and detective stories? I'll tell you. Because we are the front line. We are the ultimate good guys. Politicians and businessmen face the same kind of power struggles, but those worlds can never deliver the thrills of police work. The reality is that we have the sexiest job in the world!" He laughed loudly and heads turned at other tables. Beatrice laughed too, hoping she didn't have basil stuck in her teeth.

"On which note, I will leave you now as I must catch up with Fisher," he said. "We're doing a repeat session on media briefing in the morning, streamed live on BluLite. You should try to catch it. Do you know Fisher? Our man from Interpol?"

Beatrice resisted the urge to curl her lip. "The name rings a bell. I'm sure our paths must have crossed somewhere," she lied. "Well, thank you for your company today."

"My pleasure. Oh, one more thing. Your friend I met yesterday? The young woman who works in the port wine industry. I'm rather a hobbyist wine buff, so thought I might pick her brains while I'm in Porto this weekend. How might I contact her?"

"If it's alright with you, sir, I'll give her your number. I follow police policy and never give out anyone's number or email without their permission. Even to those I trust."

Just the tiniest tightening of the jaw before the smile came again.

"Very wise. Yes, here's my card. Feel free to pass it on. Thank you. Must dash and see you later."

She checked her mobile. A voicemail from Ana.

"Call me when you get this. Someone here you should meet."

The taxi dropped her and Xavier outside the Café Camões at half past one. Ana was sitting in the window with another woman. She raised a hand in greeting as she saw them arrive.

"Beatrice, Xavier, this is Sandra Cordeiro, the mother of the suspect. *Sandra, posso apresentar a minha amiga Beatrice e o seu colego Xavier. O Xavier fala muito bem portugûes.*"

Sandra stood, shook their hands with a firm grip and said "*Muito prazer.*"

Xavier repeated the words so Beatrice attempted the same.

"I just explained that I'll need to translate for you, Beatrice. When I got to the police station, Sandra was there, pleading with them to let her see her son. They told her she should come back later, so I caught up with her as she was leaving. She is adamant her son did not kill Silva. I know, I know, what mother would say otherwise? But Sandra has some important details the local police dismissed as irrelevant, and I think someone ought to hear this."

Ana gestured for the woman to speak.

Sandra's demeanour impressed Beatrice. She seemed calm and dignified, with steady brown eyes in a careworn face. She spoke slowly and with emphasis, addressing Beatrice and Xavier in turn. Without understanding a word, Beatrice was already convinced by her sincerity.

Ana waited for her to take a pause then rattled off a translation.

"Marco is a migrant worker. He goes wherever he can to make money. He gets repeat employment because he's reliable and he's strong. In winter, he works in Andorra at a ski resort. In spring and autumn he usually gets employment on a farm, but can spend the summer at home with his family because of the hotel. He started there as a teenager and is well liked by the management. They find something for him every summer, gardening, driving, painting, anything that doesn't involve dealing with the public. He's not good with people.

"He works five days a week and Saturday mornings. On the day Silva died, Marco went to work as usual and came home for his lunch. Sandra says she shouted at him for leaving bits of grass all over the floor and the green stains on his trainers. He said he'd been mowing the hotel lawns. After lunch, he played football with the village team and came home for dinner because it was his sister's birthday."

Xavier made a note and Ana opened a palm to Sandra. She spoke in a rush, a mellifluous waterfall of whispery sounds, intense and emotional, almost like a song. Finally, Beatrice saw the tears build and her eyes redden, but she did not cry. She stopped, inhaled deep breaths and waited for Ana to catch up.

"Her son is well-mannered, respectful and very kind. He is always bringing home stray dogs, cats, injured birds and won't even let her use mousetraps. He might be big and he's certainly strong, but his soul is gentle. He lives by the motto 'Do No Harm.' There is nothing that will convince Sandra her son could shoot a man. As for something as material as a watch and some money? Never. That is not her son."

Beatrice nodded and tried to look reassuring but Sandra was speaking rapidly and with some agitation, this time directly to Ana.

"He's not a good communicator. Being under interrogation will make him stressed and he will panic. She wants to get him out, but if that's not possible, she needs to be with him. She can't bear to leave him on his own."

The tears escaped, but with great dignity, Sandra Cordeiro pulled a tissue from her sleeve and patted them away.

Beatrice took a deep breath and turned to Xavier. "None of us has any authority here. All we can do is talk to the local police and ask for a sympathetic hearing."

"Could we get any of the senior officers at EPIC to use their influence?" he asked.

"Gilchrist is the obvious choice," said Beatrice. "He handed them this case and asked all of us to keep out. The thing is, if we go to him for support, how do we explain how we found Sandra and why we were digging in the first place?"

"Me," said Ana. "Tell him the partial truth. I'm a journo and I've sniffed out a story. When I find me old mate Beatrice is involved, I probe her for intel. A total pro, she gives nothing away, so I go snooping alone. When I meet Sandra, I take the info back to Beatrice, my professional police connection, and ask her advice. She does the responsible thing and passes it upwards."

Sandra's focus switched from one face to another as they cogitated.

"Gilchrist won't swallow that. He's already fishing for info on you," said Beatrice.

"So confess. I don't work in port wine caves, I'm a hack. You deflected all my enquiries but when I came back with a story, you felt it incumbent upon yourself to fill him in. You regret telling half-truths but ethics are more important than face-saving."

"He won't believe me."

Ana folded her arms, a challenge in her eyes. "He will if you play it right."

Chapter 21

By the time Beatrice left Gilchrist's office, it was four o'clock. Her hands were shaking and her knees were weak, but her fists were clenched in triumph. She hurried back to her room and tapped on the door. It opened in seconds and Xavier ushered her in, his eyes bright with curiosity.

Inside, Ana sat at the table, one ankle resting on her knee, a pen in her mouth and a large piece of paper in front of her. On the floor, Roman sat cross-legged with Cher in his lap, her legs flopped out in front of her, a computer on her knees. The windows were open and the pungent scent of honeysuckle wafted in on the breeze. Beatrice had an overwhelming feeling of coming home.

She threw her bag on the bed, looked into each face and made a theatrical eye-sweep of the room. Roman, Cher and Xavier all understood the question and gave the thumbs-up. Beatrice relaxed. If these professionals had found no bugs, there were none.

"So you're all skipping class this afternoon? Disgraceful."

"No classes to skip," said Xavier. "Instead there's a Wednesday afternoon excursion around the national park. We sneaked off."

Beatrice turned her attention to the couple on the carpet. "Have you two got an announcement to make?"

Cher laughed. "My butt got a little numb after all morning in the chair. Roman offered an alternative and threw in a free massage. No complaints from the FBI."

Xavier took his seat opposite Ana. "We've been waiting for you, B. What happened with Gilchrist?"

"He'll recommend bail. He had a whole barrage of questions and was less than happy, but yes, he'll advise letting Marco Cordeiro out this afternoon. Ana, he wants to talk to you tomorrow."

"He can. I've got my story straight. I can give him the family background and there's even a development on one of my leads. Pretty much public on the wire, but backs up my story as a journo on the trail."

"Of interest to us?" Beatrice sat at the desk, quashing another twinge of guilt regarding Matthew, Will and the gang. Tonight would have been her turn to cook.

"Could be. More info on the Monteiro angle." Ana flipped over the pages of her notebook. "Nelson Monteiro has been overlooked for promotion in favour of Samuel Silva no fewer than five times. The guy is a friend and supporter in public, but it's no secret that if Silva were removed, Monteiro's career would take off. We're talking a fifty-year-old man who's not got that much longer to climb the ladder."

Xavier threw Ana a disapproving frown.

"Chill out, Xavier, I've not offended Beatrice. She's leaving at the end of the year anyway. This fella is a career cop and getting to the stage where he's gonna need to skip a few rungs. Saying that, they're old pals and he's godfather to the little girl, so I can't really see him in the frame."

Cher sat up. "I'd have to second that. I spent a lot of time with André and he's totally determined to bring Silva's work to light. He respected and liked the guy and I don't feel any kind of insincerity there at all."

"Right," Beatrice wanted to remind them all to stick to facts, but she was not their boss. The only way was to lead by example. "Ana, what did you find out about the death threat from the adoption agency?"

"Dead end. The man's a chancer with a big mouth. He's practically bankrupt and has more enemies than friends. His own alibi is solid and the fella has a record of making wild threats. One even landed him in court. I'd say he's just a bad loser."

"It was a long shot," agreed Beatrice. "Silva's brother?"

"That was more of a challenge. He was away on a boys' weekend and neither his wife or sister knew exactly where. I started to get excited till he called me and confessed to a gambling weekend in Cascais. A whole list of folk who'll corroborate his story and credit card details at the casino match what he says. Incidentally, when I explained I was eliminating suspects, he mentioned more than one woman scorned. Samuel had quite a reputation, according to Salvatore. I've had a dig around but as yet, no info on any vengeful ex-girlfriends."

Roman reached into his jacket pocket, easing Cher forwards for a moment. "I got a list of all occupants on the first floor. My room is 1126, so I tested your theory, Beatrice. By sliding over the dividing rail, I managed to enter my neighbour's room, Silva's and Gilchrist's office. It wasn't difficult. The windows are simple to open from the outside."

"You went into other guests' rooms?" asked Xavier.

Roman reached up to pass Beatrice the papers. "Yeah. The BluLite app is very useful if you want to know where someone is at any precise moment. I waited till Gilchrist began filming himself as a panel guest and slipped into his office from the balcony. Nothing much to see, but I noticed a couple of strange things. It's a suite, but he's using another room for his private quarters, so you'd expect very few personal items in the suite. But in the wardrobe there's a full SOCO outfit. Shoe covers, gloves, the standard white non-contamination suit but none of the usual equipment. In the bathroom, there's a bottle of isopropanol, nail varnish remover and hand sanitiser. There's a hallway between his office and the corridor which is empty apart from a small table with a Bose speaker."

Xavier shook his head with a frown, his eyes flickering back and forth across the carpet as if seeking an explanation. "Maybe the SOCO suit is a demonstration sample. The liquids you mention sound like someone obsessive about hygiene. He shakes a lot of hands."

Roman gave a brief nod, but seemed unconvinced. "Maybe. What about you and the fingerprints?"

Xavier placed a scanned document on the table. "The fingerprints were poor quality, as if they were made earlier than Saturday. There's only one set, outside the French windows. The police found none of the same prints in the room."

Cher, reclining in Roman's arms, took a deep breath. "Guys, this is a wild card, but what if we're talking about a different sort of jealousy? We all know Silva was writing a book, to be published on the internet. It's a collection of all his teachings, kinda non-fiction research on sociopathic tendencies. Then there's this other book, a novel on similar themes, which might cause a few red faces. It's supposed to be hush-hush, but pretty much everyone at this conference heard the same jungle drums."

Roman's forehead wrinkled. "A literary rival? No way. That really is something out of a TV series. It could only be more clichéd if he'd been poisoned. You don't really think someone would shoot him over a book?"

Cher hunched her shoulders. "Just throwing it out there."

Beatrice sat on the end of the bed. "But the book in question is apparently an exposé of some of the most senior figures in international policing, disguised as fiction. I can't see why Silva publishing his work would clash."

Cher shook her head. "Nope, me neither. But I keep circling back to the idea that there's something more to this. Call it a hunch."

"A hunch?" Roman laughed. "Have you been reading crime fiction?"

"Never dismiss a hunch," said Beatrice. "Ana, this is a lead we need to work. Can you locate that ghostwriter, sniff around publishers, legal firms and recent deals? The rest of us should test the waters internally and find out which kind of ego would risk his or her career for a story."

Roman exhaled in derision, blowing Cher's hair over her face. "Ninety percent of the people in this hotel, for a start. I think we need to prepare a strategy, split up and start asking the right questions. Ana, it might be better if you stay out of sight. You're a little too memorable."

Ana shrugged. "Not a problem. I need to get to work on all this, so I'll stay here and see you all later."

Xavier looked at Beatrice with an expression of concern. "Do you have to leave or can you join us this evening?"

"I'll stay. I won't be popular but it's absurd to rush off now." Beatrice pressed the bridge of her nose. "Especially with Ana here to help."

"Right. Beatrice, Xavier, Cher and I can work the room between us." Roman looked down at Cher. "Now we should get back to our lines of enquiry. Ready?"

"Aww, I was just getting comfy."

Xavier cleared the table of papers and laptop. "Good idea. Enjoy your evening, Ana. See you in the morning. Breakfast at eight?"

Roman scooped Cher up, placed her gently back into her chair and the three of them left with the minimum of fuss and noise. As Beatrice closed the door, she had a thought.

"If I'm staying here tonight, I'd better organise a room for you. I'm far too long in the hoof to share a bed. I'll nip down to reception and sort it out now."

Ana looked up from her screen. "Oh thanks, but no need. Xavier already gave me his room key. He's sleeping in Roman's room."

Beatrice stared but Ana's attention was back on her laptop. "Well, I must say they're taking this gay couple cover very seriously. All credit to them."

"What? Oh right. Yeah, that's part of it, but the real reason is that Roman spends all his time in Cher's room. Those two are getting it on. You didn't miss that, surely to God?" She snorted. "Call yourself a detective?"

While Ana tapped away at her keyboard, Beatrice fetched a bottle of water from the mini-bar and wondered exactly when the world had started moving so fast, and why sometimes it seemed to be leaving her behind.

Room 1106 hummed with activity. Ana spent her time alternating between calls to various contacts and rattling off emails. It didn't disturb Beatrice. Firstly, all Ana's conversations were in Portuguese and secondly, it reminded her of the office back in Scotland Yard. Noise, work, action, progress, it was all rather comforting.

Beatrice was scanning the profiles of every conference attendee to find personal or professional connections to Silva when Ana's mobile trilled.

Ana answered, stating her name. Whoever was on the other end had a remarkable effect on Ana's hunched, screen-facing posture. She sat up and stared at Beatrice with wide eyes as she replied.

"*Si, estou aqui, Senhora Doutora. Obrigada para a chamada.*"

She reached across to a hotel notepad and scrawled the words *Silva's wife!* before returning her attention to the call.

Beatrice watched her body language and listened to the conversation as far as she could, but could only detect an empathetic intonation and one word in fifty. She couldn't even read Ana's notes, typed directly onto her screen in some kind of shorthand. After Ana opened several other tabs and ran searches, Beatrice realised she was wasting time trying to second guess her. Patience and persistence would be the best way to proceed.

She continued her cross-checking of the delegate database and created a grid. Of the fifty people on the course, eight had previously worked with Samuel Silva—all of them men, including Xavier Racine. That came as no surprise; Beatrice knew her Swiss friend was a fan of the professor's work.

Of the eight, two had enjoyed a closer friendship, one of whom was Gilchrist. Close friends for some time, attending football matches together, they seemed to have drifted apart of late. The other was Portuguese detective sergeant André Monteiro, godson and colleague. She trawled BluLite for any interaction between them to reinforce her findings but found precious little. She was making notes on her file when Ana ended her call.

"How on earth did you manage to get his wife to call you?" asked Beatrice.

Ana shook her head in disbelief. "The way I always try. Contact them or close relatives, explain I want to share their story, emphasise that I want to help bring justice to the victims. Two people advised her to talk to me. Samuel's sister, Olivia, and remember I mentioned Nelson Monteiro?"

"Good Lord, I was just digging for info on André Monteiro online. Why would his father advise a grieving widow to talk to a journalist?"

"André thinks there's something wrong and his dad agrees. Bear in mind what I said, though. Nelson has good professional reasons to wish Silva out of the way. And his son is right here with easy access. Wait now, I'm getting sidetracked." Ana glugged a third of a bottle of water and checked her phone.

She took a deep breath. "His widow is wrecked. New kid, start of the rest of their lives, coasting on their successes and now he's dead." Ana ran a hand over her face. "The poor creature."

"I'm amazed she could even talk to you," said Beatrice.

"Me too. But she wants us to find who did this and she's not buying the casual worker chancing his arm either. She thinks it's either politics or jealousy. We'd be wise to keep an open mind on that one. Mind, according to her Nelson Monteiro could never be in the frame. She swears André's dad has wings growing out of his shoulder blades but we'll be the judge of that."

"Of course we will. So who's jealous, if not Monteiro?" asked Beatrice.

"The ghostwriter. We know Silva was writing a book. He has no time to do it himself so he hired a ghostwriter. He sends her a set of notes for every chapter and she turns it into something readable. They'd been working on this for eighteen months, then it suddenly stopped. Silva never told his wife why, just said it wasn't working out. After his death, she heard some rumours. Seems there'd been a brief affair or possibly one sexual encounter. Hard to tell. But apparently this ghostwriter woman was obsessed, convinced they were destined to be together and threatened to tell his wife, wreck the adoption and basically ruin him."

Beatrice considered the idea. "Motive for him to kill her rather than the other way around."

"That's what I thought. The interesting thing is there is no record of any dialogue with a ghostwriter on Silva's computer. Either he deleted it all, or used an email address she doesn't know anything about. Now, Nelson Monteiro calls bullshit. He says Silva dropped the ghostwriter due to a conflict of interests. Apparently, a colleague in international policing was using the same ghostwriter for his own book. Monteiro Senior says either Silva didn't know or wouldn't say who it was.

"One thing I don't get is why there's a conflict of interests. Like you said, Silva was more or less publishing his teachings as a manual. We only have rumours about the other book. But to all intents and purposes, it's a very different beast. Fact disguised as fiction, designed to embarrass a shitload of head honchos. Bottom line, Beatrice, I need to talk to this ghostwriter."

"I know! But we don't know who or where she is."

"Sure we do. Elisabete Silva told me why her husband chose this particular woman. She used to work in the Communications Department at Europol. The only other details she knew were the woman's first name and two other books she's written. She's in the acknowledgements of both, so it took me five minutes to find her details. She's based in Paris and her name is Georgina Bow."

Beatrice gave her a gleeful grin. "Ha! I knew you were the right one to find this level of detail. Is there a phone number?"

"Yeah, but I think I've a better chance of getting her to talk if I go there in person. I could probably get a flight out tonight."

"Right, let's do it. Check she's home, and if she is book the first available flight. I'll reimburse you. This woman is the answer to several questions and we need to act fast."

Ana snapped her laptop shut and grabbed her bag. "On it! I'll go back to Xavier's room and collect my stuff. Good luck with pack hunting tonight and I'll keep you informed every step of the way."

Once she'd gone, Beatrice decided to bite the bullet and call Matthew to offer an explanation for another night's absence. As she composed her speech, she brushed her hair. She was interrupted by her mobile ringing and winced when she saw Matthew's name on Caller ID.

"Matthew, hello. Bad news I'm afraid."

"You too? What's wrong?"

"Nothing serious. Just need to spend another night here. Is there a problem at your end?"

"Not too sure yet. We had a mishap this morning when Tanya spilt hot coffee all over herself, but she's all patched up and staying overnight in hospital."

"Good heavens! Is she badly hurt?"

"She has some burns on her arm and leg, complicated by the fact her skin was already overexposed to the sun. The doctor says she'll be fine and back home tomorrow. What's bothering me now is we can't find Luke."

"What do you mean? He's missing?"

"We're still looking. Adrian and Marianne were supposed to be watching him while we were at the hospital, but each thought the other was responsible. It's all rather complicated, but the point is, no one has seen Luke since around two o'clock this afternoon. Will, Adrian and Marianne are still out searching but before it gets dark, I wondered if I should call the police. Hence seeking your advice, Old Thing."

Without even wondering why, Beatrice asked "Where's Leon?"

"Ah yes. Another complication. He left this morning, by all accounts, in a bit of a huff. It's a very awkward situation but my concern is that my five-year-old grandson is somewhere out there and I am closer to panic than I can ever remember."

Beatrice squeezed her eyes shut. "Right. You stay home and check the entire house, cupboards, attics, under beds, every possible hiding-place. Get the others to check all the outbuildings and the nearby area. I'll alert the police and explain the situation. I'll call in an hour and if there's no news, we'll decide how to proceed."

"Thank you. I'm sorry to ask, but truth be told, I'm at my wits' end."

"I understand. He's most likely somewhere close by, hiding or asleep. But let's take all reasonable precautions. Now I'm going to hang up and phone Will directly. Easier to discuss procedures with a fellow copper. Try not to worry. If you've not found him in the next hour, I'll come back. Everything else can wait."

If the afternoon had been buzzing, the next hour was frantic. Beatrice spoke to Will and got the number plate of the Fiat Panda, then called the Viana do Castelo police force and alerted them to a missing child. Meanwhile, the sun began to sink towards the horizon. Beatrice scoured her hard drive for images of Luke to share with the search team and spoke to border control regarding the possibility of an abduction.

She phoned Matthew exactly one hour after his previous call. He confirmed there was no sign of the boy, but the police had arrived and begun a search using dogs.

"In that case, I'll order a taxi and join you as soon as possible. I doubt I can be of use, but at least I can be there for moral support."

"I'd be most grateful if you would."

Beatrice repacked her suitcase, her mind on Luke and any reasons he might have to run off. Just as she was ready to leave the room, a knock came at the door.

Gilchrist stood in the corridor, his expression grave.

"Good evening, Commander. What can I do for you?"

"I'm the bearer of bad tidings, I'm afraid. I relayed your information regarding Marco Cordeiro to the local Inspector as soon as you left my office. As a result, the detectives released him on bail. A few minutes ago, I received word of a street brawl involving the Cordeiro boy. It seems he suffered a serious stab wound. He's currently in ICU."

"A street brawl? He didn't seem the type."

"One can never tell, especially when the only account of his character came from his mother. Anyway, you know these Latinos. Hot-headed and ready to defend their honour. His family is with him as we speak but the detective I spoke to was less than optimistic. Sorry to put a dampener on your evening. However, I thought perhaps you and your friend could join me for dinner?"

"I can't tonight, Commander, much as I appreciate the gesture. I'm heading north to be with the family. Thanks for letting me know and see you in the morning."

"Ah." Gilchrist shook his head. "I'm afraid I must ask you to stay put for the time being. Your connection to the injured party means you need to help the local police with their enquiries first thing tomorrow. Same goes for your colleague. It would be preferable if you would both remain in the hotel. Just until we clear this up. I would like to be civilised about it. So, dinner at my table?"

Beatrice opened her mouth to explain about Luke but stared past the plastic smile into his cold eyes instead. Appealing to his human side wasn't going to work. She could make a fuss and leave anyway, but something told her to feign obedience.

"I see. Dinner is fine. If you'll allow me to shower and change, I'll join you downstairs in an hour."

"And your journalist friend?"

"Ana's already gone back to Porto, I'm afraid. She'll be back sometime tomorrow." It was not a lie, just an omission of certain truths.

"The police would like to speak to her first thing in the morning. She needs to be here at eight o'clock for an informal interview."

"I'll let her know. See you shortly."

She gave him a tight smile, closed the door and looked through the peephole. Gilchrist stood there for a few seconds, apparently checking his phone. The second he'd gone, Beatrice hurried into the bathroom and switched on the shower. Then she dialled Ana's mobile, hoping she had already left the hotel, if not the country.

The girl answered on the first ring. "Beatrice? What's the story?"

"Where are you?"

"About half an hour from Porto. I've booked the ten to seven flight and made an appointment with Georgina Bow for nine o'clock tonight. She thinks I'm a potential client."

"Ana, listen. Gilchrist has grounded us both as witnesses. I'm not allowed to leave the hotel and he wants you back here for eight in the morning."

"Why? Witnesses to what?"

"It's our connection to Marco Cordeiro. He's just been stabbed in a street fight."

Ana exhaled. "Dead?"

"No, but he's in Intensive Care and Gilchrist says it's not looking good."

"Shitting shit on a shitty stick. If he dies..."

"There is no way he can be proven innocent. Which is convenient for whoever really killed Silva."

"Bastards! Do you think I should come back?"

"No. I think you should stick to Plan A and we'll improvise tomorrow. I really can't see why the police need to talk to both of us. We're certainly not suspects."

"What about you? What do the others say?"

Beatrice bit her lip. "I'm telling Xavier, Cher and Roman nothing yet."

There was a pause at the other end of the line. "Feels a bit weird not to share developments with the team. Is there something I need to know?" Ana's voice, clear, sharp and intelligent, cut right to the heart of the matter.

"Who else knew the Cordeiro boy was about to be released? The five of us and Gilchrist. You and I were together all afternoon, but what about the other three? I suspect we have a mole. If one of our 'team' is party to this, we have a problem. That I can deal with on my own. Go talk to this woman, keep communications open and please be very, very careful."

Ana's voice, when it came, sounded uncertain. "Ooh-kay. Is everything else all right? You sound nervous."

Telling Ana about Luke's disappearance was impossible without admitting her worst fears. She just had to keep working. "Just unsettled, that's all. Talk to you tomorrow. Good luck."

Outside her window, the onset of evening created a spectacular lightshow as the sun sank behind the trees, radiating fiery spotlights like angels' wings. It would be dark in a couple of hours. Tears of frustration, isolation and fear welled up to blur the beauty of the scene. Beatrice shook her head and shucked off her clothes. Shower, dress, call Matthew, dinner, focus. *Concentrate*, she told herself, *you cannot afford to lose it now*.

Chapter 22

Once the police took over the search, there was nothing else for Adrian, Will or Matthew to do but gather in the villa's kitchen, waiting for news or darkness. No one spoke, their faces drawn. Adrian made a pot of tea which went untouched. The news that Beatrice was unable to join them had come as a real blow, adding to the sense of abandonment. As the light leached from the sky, police officers returned sniffer dogs to their vehicles while the detective in charge came up to the house. Marianne materialised from the living room, phone clutched to her chest. Adrian did not acknowledge her, convinced the news she craved was of Leon, not Luke.

Detective Machado seemed unsure as to whether to address Matthew or Will. He chose both.

"As expected, my officers found nothing. The search was only a formality, as the dogs traced the child's scent to the end of the drive, where it disappeared."

Marianne clutched a hand over her mouth to stifle a sob.

"Thank you, Detective. I understand why you are no longer searching the grounds," Matthew's voice was weary and defeated.

Adrian glanced at Will, expecting him to ask more questions, but his gaze was distant, lost in thought.

"When you say his scent 'disappeared', what do you think happened?" asked Adrian.

The detective, who smelt of aftershave and tobacco, blinked while formulating his reply. "The scent is traceable to the end of the drive. Then there is nothing. We think the boy walked to the main road where he got into a car."

Matthew massaged his forehead. "Luke is only five, so one can never be sure, but he has been drilled never to accept sweets, lifts, presents or anything from strangers. I don't know why he would wander down the drive on his own and I cannot imagine he would get in a car with someone he doesn't know. The boy is shy with people."

"Unless it wasn't a stranger," Will said, his arms folded as he leaned against the worktop. "As I said before, you need to locate that rental Panda."

Marianne shot Will a look of pure venom and stalked out of the room. In a way, her absence was a relief. She added nothing but tears and an endless loop of alternating self-blame or exoneration.

"We will follow every lead, I assure you. As soon as I have any information, I will telephone you. We are doing everything we can. I will return in the morning. Goodnight, everyone."

Matthew, Will and Adrian returned the farewell.

The three men listened to the cars drive away, leaving them in a hollow silence. Moments ticked by. No movement, no sound apart from the cicadas, nothing to say. Finally Will took a deep breath.

"We need to keep our strength up. Matthew, you've eaten nothing since breakfast. Let's eat the fish stew or we'll be useless. Adrian, warm it up and I'll ask Marianne if she wants to eat." He strode out the door towards the garden flat.

Adrian got to his feet and switched on the hob. If he was hungry, how must Luke feel? He stirred the chowder and glanced at Matthew.

"Will's right, we have to eat. I'll slice some bread."

Matthew twisted in his seat to face Adrian. His eyes, shadowed and hollow, bore no warmth. "The last thing I said to you was 'Look after Luke'. I distinctly remember. *Look after Luke.*"

Adrian's mouth opened to protest but found his throat had closed. Matthew dropped his forehead into his hands and turned his back. The only sound in the kitchen was the bubbling chowder until Will returned.

"Can't find her. Come on, let's get this down and leave some in case she's hungry later. Any bread to go with it, Adrian?"

The three men ate steadily but without enthusiasm in a gloomy silence. Matthew emptied his bowl and pushed back his chair. "I'm going to have a lie down. Please call me if there's any news at all."

Will and Adrian cleared up and left a plate for Marianne. For want of something better to do, Adrian made another pot of tea.

Will checked his mobile, shoved it in his pocket and caught Adrian's arm.

"You've got something to say and I want to hear it. What exactly happened this morning? Keep your voice down but tell me the whole story."

In urgent whispers, Adrian told him everything. He explained with as little emotion and as much fact as he could manage, but his voice broke as he relayed Matthew's accusation. Will sat still, intent on his words until Adrian ran out of steam.

"I just don't know what happened. I wasn't there. I know I should have been. I should have ignored her and watched out for Luke, regardless of her opinion. This is my ego getting in the way. I got offended and stomped off, leaving Luke in the care of..."

"His aunt." Will hissed. "His aunt, for God's sake. You've no chance against someone pulling the family card. Adrian, this is Marianne's fault and I won't allow you to take any blame for it. Leon has taken Luke to make a point and hurt Marianne."

"Well, I don't work for Scotland Yard, but I'd worked that much out for myself." Adrian pressed his own cold palms to his face. "The question is, what's Leon going to do with him now?"

Will rested his chin on his fists and gazed out at the night.

"Will? What do you think Leon is planning?"

"I don't know. I honestly don't know."

Chapter 23

Entering the bar for pre-dinner drinks, Beatrice scanned the scene and noted several points of interest. Cher having a flirtatious chat with one of the hotel staff. Roman with a group of men in the humidor, laughing at someone's joke. Xavier in earnest discussion with André Monteiro, walking in the direction of the dining-room. Two plain-clothes officers feigning nonchalance by the door, fooling no one. Gilchrist was doing his usual butterfly act, gliding from table to table until he spotted her and excused himself.

"Good evening. Lovely dress. Can I get you a drink?"

Conscious of her mission, Beatrice opted for a lime and soda. While he ordered, she checked her phone.

Message from Adrian: *No news. Everyone tense as hell just waiting.*

Gilchrist guided her in the direction of the dining-room. She passed Cher, who looked up with a friendly acknowledgement. Beatrice returned the smile but pushed on, fearful of what signs even the blandest small-talk might reveal.

The menu offered some cheer. Chicken and cherry tomato skewers with chilli oil, followed by pork with clams and a dessert of chocolate salami. Gilchrist's table was similar to that of a head teacher – elevated above the crowd and occupied on one side only, leaving its occupants exposed. Gilchrist sat on her left, and her neighbour on the right was a pleasant surprise. Dr Ruishalme, whose workshop on implicit prejudice she had enjoyed, greeted Beatrice with a strong handshake.

The two women dispensed with small talk and fell into intense conversation, ignoring the men either side of them. Beatrice could have happily chatted to her all night. But as the starters were cleared away, Gilchrist slanted his head towards her and tapped her arm.

"Can I suggest a glass of wine to accompany the main course? I know you fancy yourself a connoisseur. Try this one."

Beatrice registered the patronising tone but accepted the glass. As she sniffed, she surveyed the room. Xavier sat beside the Monteiro boy, while Roman seemed to be in the thick of it with the Russians. Cher was nowhere to be seen.

Gilchrist claimed her attention once more. "This is one of my favourite Portuguese reds. Light yet full of flavour. I believe it would complement the pork perfectly."

"Just the one. If I'm to be interrogated tomorrow, I'd like to keep a clear head."

Gilchrist smiled, an attempt at reassurance. "It's not an interrogation. Just a clarification of your connection to the victim."

"Commander, I had no connection to Silva whatsoever. I met him for the first time here, on Friday night."

"I was talking about the boy. Marco Cordeiro. You certainly had a connection to him. It was you who brought him to my notice."

Beatrice swivelled in her chair to address Gilchrist face on. His smile had vanished and his expression gave her every reason to feel that he was the predator and she was his prey. A vision of Sandra Cordeiro floated into her mind, a mother fighting back tears as she defended her son.

"Indeed. Due to the diligent work of my friend, we met his mother and found out a few basics about the young man. Any element of which should have been obvious to the police. We did the correct thing and brought the information to you. I fail to see why myself or Ana should be under any kind of suspicion."

"Oh come now, no need for melodrama. The police want you to share what you know, that's all. As do I, to be honest. You may remember I did make a point of asking delegates not to investigate by themselves or involve any external parties, especially journalists."

"I remember and I followed your edict. I had no idea Ana was already on the trail. She reads the newspapers and when she found out I was representing Scotland Yard at the conference, seized her chance. You can hardly blame her. What else would a good journalist do?" Beatrice tasted her wine.

"Her doing her job is one thing. Your compromising the police investigation is another. Nevertheless, I appreciate your confidence and shall say no more about it. I'm assuming no one else apart from the three of us knew the boy was due for release?" Gilchrist looked pointedly across the room to where Xavier sat, fork in his right hand, gesticulating with his left.

The waiter placed two steaming plates in front of them. Beatrice inhaled, giving herself a second to think.

"Thank you. That smells delicious!" she told the waiter.

Returning her attention to Gilchrist, she added, "Not unless my room is bugged. Sorry, I didn't mean to be flip. This is not a Bond movie. *Bon appétit.*"

"*Bon appétit.* No, it's not a Bond movie. Real life is far more dramatic. If the general public knew half of what goes on in our world, they wouldn't believe it."

"If the general public knew half of what goes on in our world, they'd die of boredom. Let's face it, Commander, ninety percent of what we do is dull and dreary paperwork. About as gripping as watching stains dry."

Gilchrist cut his pork into small strips. "Oh I don't know. You've had a few adventures yourself, so I hear. Ever thought of putting your escapades on paper?"

On paper? Beatrice chewed, shaking her head with emphasis, trying to control her amusement. He must have heard the rumour and was doing exactly as she had been instructed to do by Ranga. Sniffing, trying to find out who was writing that book. However, he was rather less than subtle.

The waiter topped up their glasses.

Ranga's words echoed in her mind. *In your shoes, I'd be unimpressed and under awed.* She swallowed and responded to her host's question, consciously casting a lure. *Patience, Beatrice, is the angler's friend.*

"Oh God, no. Sharing some of the situations I've encountered would result in calls for my resignation as a result of gross incompetence. No, I think the old adage holds true. Everyone may well have a book in them, but most of them should stay there. Unless of course it's question of sharing practical knowledge and expertise, like Samuel Silva. His work I would have loved to read. It's a real shame."

"How do you know what he was writing?"

Beatrice dabbed her mouth to hide a smile. *The fish approaches the hook.*

"He told us at dinner on Friday night. That's one of the reasons I switched sessions on Saturday. He was so fascinating on the subject, I had to hear more. It pains me to think he won't be able to finish it. Oh, this is a super combination, don't you think? I'd never have paired pork with seafood, but it works a treat. And you were right about the wine. Perfection!"

Gilchrist nodded with a hum of assent but said nothing. Moments passed as they continued eating and Beatrice was considering throwing out another worm when Gilchrist put down his knife and fork.

"Yes indeed, Portuguese cuisine is underrated. This place was an inspired choice, if I say so myself. As for Silva, I always found him rather dry. Great on science but not much of a one for entertaining stories. My view is whether you're expounding a theory or spinning a yarn, you have to draw the reader in."

Either the man was feigning literary ambition or trying to trip her up. *Reel him in sideways. No sudden movements.*

She took another sip of wine. "I'm sure you're right, Commander. I know nothing about his writing, but he was one of the best speakers I ever heard. I wonder how far the two skills cross over."

"Depends what you're writing, I suppose. Presenting slides and statistics must be pretty similar to writing a textbook. Creating a full-length narrative based on fact is a wholly different proposition. Have you read Rimington's stuff?"

"The fiction, yes. Very enjoyable. But I'm afraid I abandoned the memoir. Even if the thing hadn't been so heavily censored so far as to make it moth-eaten, it seems impossible to me to write your own life story with any kind of objectivity. It would be a constant clash between facts and ego, surely. Not my sort of thing."

Across the room, she watched as Xavier walked over to whisper something in Roman's ear. She didn't miss Roman's meaningful squeeze of Xavier's hand and the exchange of looks. Neither did Roman's companions, judging by the good-natured nudges and winks around the table.

The waiters cleared the plates and presented something resembling a Yule log. Beatrice accepted a portion but excused herself briefly for two reasons. She wanted Gilchrist to stew and come to the boil. She also needed to check her phone.

Ten emails in her inbox and three messages awaited.

Matthew: *Still no news of Luke. Wish you were here. Mx*

Dawn: *Mr Leon Charles is very interesting. Emailed with detail*

Ana: *Arrived Paris CDG. RU OK?*

She replied to each and took her time getting back to the table, composing herself and packing all these issues into the 'Nothing you can do, worry later' compartment of her brain.

Her chocolate salami was still there, but Gilchrist had gone. She had just picked up her fork and resumed her conversation with Dr Ruishalme when a waiter hovered at her elbow.

"Excuse me? Commander Gilchrist would like to see you in his office. Please will you follow me?"

Beatrice abandoned her dessert and companion with some reluctance to follow the young man through the dining-room. An uncomfortable sense of threat dogged her and she opted for an insurance policy. As she passed Xavier and young André Monteiro, she stopped.

"Gentlemen, I know I promised to join you for a digestif after dinner. I intend to fulfil my promise but first I have to meet the Commander in his office. I shan't be long. See you in half an hour?"

Xavier's expression showed full understanding. "We'll look forward to it."

Beatrice knew he had decoded her message and would act accordingly. He knew where she was going and if she had not returned in thirty minutes, he would come looking for her. She continued to the first floor and stopped at Room 1101, but the waiter kept walking.

"I think this is it," she called after him.

The waiter stopped, surprised. "No madam, that is the Commander's personal room. He uses a different room as his office, at the other end of the corridor. Suite 1120. This way."

"Really? I assumed he'd have them next to each other," she said with some disingenuity.

"He did two rooms. Unfortunately he found Room 1122 too loud to sleep, so changed his personal accommodation to 1101."

"Oh, I see. How many nights did he spend in Room 1122?"

"Just the one, madam. Here we are."

Gilchrist's temporary office was crowded with police officers. Phones rang, screens glowed and a smell of stale coffee clouded the air. A small balding individual ushered her towards the central desk, where Gilchrist was ending a telephone conversation. His eyes flickered over her and he indicated a seat. Two young men in suits tapping at laptops on a sofa shifted sideways to make room without lifting their eyes from their screens. She spotted the hotel manager standing by the door, his expression concerned.

Gilchrist ended his cryptic conversation and addressed a heavy-set plain clothes detective to his right. How these men could ever call themselves 'plain clothes' was a joke. They were the most obvious plants you could imagine. Their conversation was incomprehensible to her but the effect was immediate. The detective made a hissing noise between his teeth and the uniforms dispersed. The laptop lads clicked their machines shut and followed, leaving Beatrice, the hotel manager and Gilchrist in relative silence.

"Marco Cordeiro died just over an hour ago. Internal bleeding," Gilchrist announced.

"*O meu Deus!*" The hotel manager crossed himself and muttered a prayer. He seemed genuinely distressed at the loss of his casual worker.

"Yes, very sad. My condolences to you and your staff." The manager shook his head in regret, wished them goodnight and left the room. Gilchrist continued, addressing Beatrice. "And in a further development, the murder weapon used to kill Samuel Silva has been found. It was in the compost bin behind the kitchens. A dishwasher-cum-dogsbody emptied the green waste this evening. The local detectives confirmed it matches their records and the case is now closed." He looked rather pleased with the intelligence.

"And the people who killed Cordeiro? I presume the police are on the hunt?" asked Beatrice.

"I am sure they will be. But enthusiasm for finding a knife-happy thug who took out the murderer of a police professional may not be high on their list of priorities. Plus we now have Silva's gun, dumped in a staff area, Cordeiro's prints on the window pane and the watch in the boy's bag. I'd say that's our final loose end tied up. Sorry to abandon you in the middle of dinner. How was dessert?"

"It looked delicious. Why did you need me here, Commander? Seems you have it all under control."

"Courtesy, DCI Stubbs. Given your interest in the case, just thought you'd like to know it is now closed, bar the paperwork. In the morning, I can offer your friend an exclusive quote, if you like."

"In the morning? We're still being interviewed despite the case being closed?"

Gilchrist looked back at his screen. "Not my call, really, but the local lads want to dot the Is and cross the Ts. Formalities, that's all. Nothing to worry about."

"Well, that's good to hear. Thank you for your excellent company at dinner. See you bright and early for the police interview. Goodnight Commander."

She returned to her room and called Matthew. His voice was thick and slow, and he admitted to taking a sleeping tablet. She told him she approved of his getting some rest and called Will instead.

"No news, and there won't be any till tomorrow. Adrian and I are staying awake though, just in case. I know Leon took him, I just don't know why."

Beatrice clenched her fists then remembered her emails. "I agree. I have some intelligence on Leon, for what good it might do. I haven't had a chance to read it all yet, but I'll do so immediately and forward it to you. This is confidential police data, obviously."

"Obviously. Thank you. I have to do something. Sitting here drinking tea is driving me mad."

"As soon as we've done our interviews tomorrow, Ana and I will travel up there and do whatever we can to help."

"Good. We need you. All of us."

Beatrice brushed her teeth and took a mood stabiliser. Her

emotions in flux, she sensed an emotional downswing looming. Before she switched off the light, she set her alarm and pictured Luke's serious blue eyes.

Keep him safe, please.

Chapter 24

Parisian traffic. What a pile of crap. The cab crawled along Rue du Renard and Ana looked at her watch. Again. Ten-minute train journey from airport to city, twenty minutes from Châtelet-Les Halles station to Voie Georges Pompidou. She was going to be late. She shouldn't mind; she was the 'client', so it made no difference. But Ana detested lateness in everyone, especially herself. A wave of brake lights ahead coloured the taxi interior with a sordid rouge. Ana checked her watch.

"*Deux minutes, mademoiselle!*" The taxi driver was watching her in his mirror. His expression was probably intended as kindly reassurance but the red uplighting twisted it into a demonic grimace.

"*Merci, monsieur,*" she replied, with little enthusiasm.

Ghostwriter Georgina Bow had chosen Chez Julien just off Pont Louis Philippe for their meeting. 'Just around the corner from me and the waiters are divine!'

The cab eventually deposited her outside the restaurant at ten minutes past nine. She hurried in to find that Georgina had not yet arrived. The waiter, who was admittedly damn close to divine, suggested she enjoy the house cocktail until her guest arrived. Ana agreed and made a decision. This was work and therefore a legitimate expense. Cocktails, haute cuisine and fine wine would suit her role perfectly. She repeated her cover as an internal monologue.

Ana Herrero is a Portuguese journalist who needs help with an exposé on wine crime. She heard of Bow via a security officer. Discretion and ethics are essential. Tonight's meeting is simply testing the waters.

The waiter brought her a French 75 and did something subtle with his eyebrows. Ana thanked him and returned the charming smile. *OK, so Parisian traffic may be a bag of shite, but the city has some fine-looking men.*

She sipped her drink and considered her surroundings. St Gervais and Le Marais equals expensive. Ghostwriting as a profession is unreliable. Unless Ana was very much mistaken, the girl she was about to meet would probably be some kind of trustafarian. The minute the door opened, Ana knew she was right.

Georgina Bow wore denim shorts, cowboy boots and a voluminous, ruffled white shirt over a dishcloth-coloured crochet vest. Her blonde-streaked hair was woven into a messy plait and topped with a battered top hat. Around her neck and both wrists were various bits of silver, leather and feathers, all presumably deeply meaningful and highly symbolic.

Ana stood up. "Hi Georgina, I'm Ana Herrero."

Georgina's face broke into a broad smile, a testimonial to her dentist. She took Ana's hand and leaned in for the cheek kisses.

"So pleased to *meet* you!" she breathed, her entire vocal range exercised in a mere five words. She smelt of citrus fruits and rosemary.

"Likewise," said Ana, sitting down again. "One of your divine waiters talked me into a French 75. Would you like one?"

"Oh wow, they are a*maz*ing! Yes, please. Have you been waiting for me long?" She glanced at her watch.

Ana noted the Breguet steampunk timepiece and smiled. *Yes, living the dream on the Bank of Dad.*

"No, not really. Fifteen minutes or so." She hailed a passing waitress who took her order with nothing more than a nod and glance of disapproval at her guest's Glastonbury-style attire.

Georgina rolled her eyes. "The waiters here are to die for, but that waitress? She has *such* an attitude problem. What can you do? Haters gonna hate. French fashion, at least at the bourgeois level, is just *so* conventional. I mean, really? This is *Paris*, for Chrissakes!"

And a spouter of clichés. Please don't say City of Light or I may have to slap you.

"You've lived here a while?" she asked, just to cut her off.

"Oh yeah, it's been over a year now. I *adore* it. London was special, but here in the City of Light, I'm at home. What about you?"

"I live in Lisbon," muttered Ana through gritted teeth. Then she remembered her cover story. "But the book I want to write is set in Spain."

"Right, your book! Sounds intriguing! Let me take some notes." Georgina dug around in something that looked like a black leather designer bin bag as the waitress placed their drinks on the table.

"Oh thank you. And could I get a bottle of sparkling water?"

"*Oui, madame.*"

Ana rubbed her nose to disguise a grin. *'In the City of Light, I'm at home'. Yeah right. So at home you can't even order a bottle of water in French. You may well be able to write, but you are a typical rich kid, living in a bubble, insulated from the real world. Time to wake up and grow up.*

In that instant, Ana made the decision to drop all pretence and go on the attack.

"Georgina, forget the book. It's time I put my cards on the table. I'm not here as a client. I'm here to help you. Very soon, you're going to need professional support and advice. I am a journalist, that much is true, and I'm working on a story at the request of the police. Unfortunately, you are implicated in a murder enquiry. Everything I tell you must be kept confidential, for obvious reasons. But if you can fill in some blanks, we can keep this out of the press and preserve your reputation."

The waitress brought the water but Georgina didn't move, her grey eyes staring at Ana in alarm and mistrust.

"Last week, a Portuguese police psychologist named Samuel Silva was shot twice in the back of the head. There are various lines of enquiry, one of which centres on his book. The one you were ghostwriting."

Georgina pressed her hands to her cheeks. "Oh my *God!*"

"Listen, you can talk to me, off the record. Or I can report back that you were unwilling to help and let the police do their thing. All I want to do is strike this line of enquiry. I have no reason to cause you any trouble; I just want to know what happened with you and Silva. The rumours are..."

"I know what the rumours are!" hissed Georgina. Her face

segued from horror to angry frown to mask of misery. She covered her eyes with her hands.

Ana noted the silvery sparkle of her nail varnish. She sipped her cocktail and waited for Georgina to compose herself. The young woman who finally looked back at her seemed suddenly different, the artificial poise and the brash confidence replaced by a serious expression and maybe just a glint of intelligence.

"I didn't ghost his book. I started, but... it didn't work out. I really can't say more than that. I've had no contact with him for months – and as for the rumours, they are as untrue as they are unpleasant. He and his wife were trying to adopt a child. Can you imagine how she must feel, hearing false and hurtful stories about him having an affair with me?" Georgina pointed a painted fingernail at herself. "I met Samuel twice and the only contact we had was a formal handshake. When I read about his death, I cried. He was a lovely, sweet person with the highest code of honour. I'm sorry, I can't help you."

She yanked her ugly bag onto her shoulder and got to her feet.

"Maybe not. But I can help you," said Ana. She leaned back and folded her arms. "I can tell you exactly what the police think and why they believe you are involved. Sit down, Georgina, you've not touched your drink. Talk to me. I'm serious. I really do want to help. Anyway, you can't leave without paying. That waitress would detest you even more than she does now."

Georgina hesitated. "I'm sorry, that's just not possible."

"Sure it is. Now she simply disapproves of you, but I can tell she's capable of hate. Sit down. Let's talk. All I need is for you to fill in the gaps. You might not even need to do the whole statement-to-the-police thing."

Patrons of Chez Julien were openly staring at this mini-drama, so Georgina sat, hugging her lumpen bag to her chest like a comfort blanket.

"What gaps?" she whispered.

Ana leaned forward and clasped her hands under her chin. "The obvious. Why did you stop working on his book?"

"A conflict of interest."

Ana waited for more. Georgina fidgeted with her jewellery and played with her hair. Ana sat stock still and focused.

"Look, discretion is incredibly important in this line of work. I cannot name names but another senior civil servant employed me to write his book. I soon realised some of the fiction in his work was based on Samuel's facts. I told both men I had found a conflict and could not work on both books. I asked if one of them would find another ghost. Samuel agreed immediately and asked me to delete all his notes. Which I did. The other party..."

Ana interrupted. "Man. The other man. You already mentioned his gender. And I know he's also police."

A flush bloomed in Georgina's cheeks. "Yes, I did say a man. But you're making assumptions by saying he's a police officer."

"Why else would there be a conflict of interests?"

If Georgina had possessed a sharper mind, she could have come back with several feasible reasons. But her face gave far too much away.

Ana was winging it, but still flying, so saw no reason to stop. "I'm not making assumptions. I know Silva's case studies provide the essence of the other narrative. I know one is fact and the other is fiction. The other thing I know is that the relationship between these books is the motive for Samuel Silva's murder. This is why the police will be knocking at your door in the next twenty-four hours."

Georgina shook her head. "Dragging me into this is completely unfair! I did the right thing and told them I couldn't do both books."

"Who? I need the other name. You might think I'm going to take your word for it, but how far will you get feeding the police that bollocks? Unless you can give me the name of the other officer, I'll have to report back that my findings were inconclusive and hand this line of enquiry over to Interpol."

Georgina bit at the side of her thumb, her brow arched in concern. "As I said, discretion is incredibly important. I signed a confidentiality contract and I could get into a lot of trouble."

"More trouble than being a witness in a murder trial?"

Seconds ticked by in silence while Georgina played with her crescent-moon necklace and looked down at the table.

"Let me ask you a question," said Ana, changing tack. "You met Samuel Silva twice, right? What did you think of him?"

"Samuel was *so* sweet. Very clever and well-read, but totally a people person, you know? We connected immediately. Actually, I was sorry it was his book I had to stop writing. It was much more cerebral. Samuel was a lovely, warm, intelligent man."

"So I hear. Which is maybe why everyone who met him is pulling out all the stops to try and find his killer. Of all the people who had any contact with him, you're the first one I've met who refuses to help."

"I'm not refusing, honestly I'm not! I just can't divulge names. I mustn't break client confidentiality. As a journalist, wouldn't you protect your sources?"

"Nice try, Georgina. This is not a source. This is not someone sticking their neck out to give me information. This is a client of yours who is implicated in a murder investigation. And to answer your question, I do try to protect my sources unless I can see I'm impeding police work. The basic question? Which is the lesser evil? Protecting your credentials or pursuing justice?"

Her voice had risen and the waitress was watching with a certain curiosity. Ana drained her glass. Sick of playing games with Four Non-Blondes, she decided to call the girl's bluff.

"OK, I can see I'm wasting my time. If you won't help, I'll let the police question you. No doubt they'll get a search warrant and find the information that way." Ana stood up and threw twenty Euros on the table. "That's for the drinks. And here's my card in case you change your mind."

"Wait." Georgina was actually chewing a strand of her hair and looking at Ana from under lowered lashes. The brash character was rising to the surface again. Her style, affectations and entire personality were lifted from a magazine, and not a particularly good one. "I'll tell you as much as I can. Just not here."

Ana picked up her bag but left the money and her card on the table. The waiter hadn't actually asked for her number, but it wouldn't hurt to let him have it, just in case. You never know.

"Come on, let's walk."

Without discussion, they headed towards the Seine, through patches of shadow and lamplight, past bright shop windows and classical architecture, dodging packs of tourists and eager purveyors of tat, ignoring it all. Away from the café, Georgina's assumed persona faded and a more genuine face showed through.

"What you said before, regarding Samuel Silva. There's something you should know. I worked in Communications for Europol, and that's where I met both the clients in question. When I started to make my main income as a ghostwriter, I went part-time. The regular cash is useful because now I'm ghosting more for politicians. They can be a bit unreliable when it comes to payment, so I still keep my hand in with the police. Samuel Silva approached me about two years ago to work on his opus, *Lone Wolf*. It was to be a mixture: part theory and part real life cases to demonstrate theory in practice. Terrifically interesting stuff."

"But then you had to stop," prompted Ana.

"Yes," Georgina sighed. "We'd done about a year together when I was contacted by a rather bigger fish. His project was different, more of a fictionalised memoir. Some might call it creative non-fiction. As soon as I started the outline, I realised there was a conflict of interests. Either Samuel Silva had got his facts wrong or the other party intended to appropriate his colleagues' achievements as his own."

"The name, Georgina," Ana demanded.

"Commander Anthony Gilchrist. You've probably seen him on telly."

"Right. Go on. The facts informed the fiction?"

"One incident leapt out at me immediately. A planned act of terrorism was anticipated and defused by exactly the sort of intelligence-gathering Samuel Silva described. The similarities were too close for coincidence, and the key difference lay in style. Silva's facts showed international collaboration, no heroism and the safe apprehension of this particular lone wolf."

Ana gave a dry laugh. "Let me guess. In Anthony Gilchrist's 'novel' the lone wolf is a maverick cop who finds all the data himself and prevents a demented powermonger from releasing nerve gas into the New York subway. And his name is Anthony Bond."

Georgina giggled. "Close! The book is called *Rogue* and the main character's name is Christian Crow."

Ana rolled her eyes.

"Anyway, the real event Silva and his team prevented was due to happen in Porto. There's a big festival in June where tourists, locals, children and old folk gather to celebrate, eat sardines and watch the fireworks. The man had planned to detonate several devices right along the riverside, killing partygoers and probably many more in the ensuing stampede."

"*São João*," Ana muttered, her mind tumbling with images of sardines, music, lanterns, plastic squeaky hammers and revellers. Laughter, dancing and hundreds – if not thousands – of joyous bodies packed into the Ribeira. She squeezed her eyes tight shut, refusing to imagine the carnage. "Sorry, carry on."

"In Anthony's book, the fictional terrorist attack was set in Venice during the Carnevale. Masks and disguises as opposed to sardines and fireworks. But the details were exactly the same. I told Samuel his case was being used in a work of fiction. I mentioned no names and he didn't ask. He immediately cancelled our contract, gave me an excellent recommendation and advised me to get legal advice regarding my own implication. The book might even be libellous, he said, in which case I shouldn't let my name anywhere near it."

They crossed the bridge onto the Ile de France and passed Notre Dame, slowing their pace to a stroll. The warm evening wind brushed Ana's cheek like a caress and she gazed at sparkling lights reflected in the Seine. She took a deep breath. *Paris is like one of those ex-boyfriends you thought you were over. But it turns out you're never immune to classic charm.*

Outside the cathedral, Ana halted to look Georgina in the eye. "Do you think Samuel Silva knew who the other writer was? Is that why he didn't ask?"

"No idea. But I can tell you, Anthony Gilchrist didn't need to ask. He knew it must have been Silva and wanted to know everything about my work with Samuel. He made subtle threats as to my position in the Communications sector unless I was willing to communicate the content of Silva's work."

"Did you comply?" Ana tried to keep judgement out of her voice.

Georgina lifted her chin with a certain pride. "No. I refused and told him I was no longer working with Silva."

Ana was unimpressed. *Ethics are a fine thing if you can afford them.*

"Next thing I know, rumours of an affair are whizzing round the grapevine. After that, I heard nothing from Gilchrist for months. Then less than a fortnight ago, he suggested he was ready to publish and wanted me to agree to an extra confidentiality clause. He was in a terrific hurry so I signed. That's why I was so worried about talking to you."

They walked in silence along the Ile de la Cité. Ana stopped in the middle of Pont au Change, her nerves jangling. "Georgina, have you an agent? A legal representative? Someone else who knows who you're working with and what you're working on? Has anyone checked these contracts you're signing?"

"Umm… sort of. My brother is in law school and he thinks it's all fair and square. I'm a freelancer so I'm pretty much independent. "

"When and where were you due to meet Anthony Gilchrist next?"

"Sunday afternoon at my apartment. We usually meet in *Les Deux Magots*, but this time he said he'd come to me."

Ana plunged her hands into her hair and stared down at the water beneath her.

"Oh shit."

"What's the matter?"

Ana took a deep breath. "You wouldn't happen to have your passport with you at all?"

Chapter 25

Shortly after eleven o'clock that evening, Xavier, Cher, Roman and Beatrice convened in the hotel gym. They checked the pool for late-night swimmers and decided to retreat into the sauna, which had long since cooled from the afternoon's activities. As Xavier said, the chance of a functioning bug in there was remote, but they performed the usual checks anyway.

Everyone had news. Beatrice waited till last, glad of the opportunity to observe her colleagues. Her radar was alert for any hint of a potential mole. Each face exuded sincerity and enthusiasm, but spies are nothing if not excellent actors. If the motive for Silva's murder sprang from internal politics, it was entirely feasible that someone had been bribed or blackmailed into a hit. Regardless of how much she liked them, any of the people in front of her could be the killer.

Xavier, the self-confessed fan who knew all about Silva and his work. Beatrice knew from their previous dealings that he was well-known as a brilliant shot. She tried to envisage a situation in which this upstanding young man could be turned traitor. But Xavier had joined herself and Cher on the terrace almost immediately after the Saturday morning seminars had ended. He couldn't possibly have had time to follow Samuel Silva, enter his room, kill him and arrive at their table with a plate full of salad. Unless he'd done it *after* lunch.

On the other hand, there was the Viking. He told them he'd been back to his room for a shower and volunteered the information that his room was just around the corner from that of Silva. His 'romance' with Xavier was perfectly acted to fool most of the delegates. It wouldn't be much of a stretch to employ the same level of deception to the inner circle of investigators. A double double-cross.

As for Cher, she could be the classic innocent. A disabled woman would engender more sympathy than suspicion. She'd been with Beatrice for most of the lunch hour, only leaving briefly to visit the bathroom. How long had she been absent? And this sudden closeness between her and Roman could signify a different kind of collaboration.

She listened to each person's discoveries with a dual filter. One eye on the case, one eye on the messenger.

Xavier began by exonerating André Monteiro. After an unsuccessful experience with a ghostwriter, Samuel Silva had decided against publishing his teachings as a book. Instead he wanted to give his ideas away for free. He had been working together with Monteiro Junior on a website where people could access his case studies and a blog where theories would be up for discussion. Monteiro's web design skills, Silva's material. On the day of the murder, Monteiro received a note from Silva, asking if he would come to his room to discuss the project. He arrived and saw the Do Not Disturb sign. Due to the fact he had an invitation, he rang the bell twice. No reply came but he could hear Gilchrist next door, giving someone a hard time on the phone.

Roman had talked to the Russian intelligence team. None of them believed the violent burglary theory, but they put it down to politics. "Their confusion is around the victim. Silva was an international star in high-level detection methods and universally well-liked. The Russian theories centred on personal vengeance and a professional hit. No weapon, no prints, a simple local lad framed, job done."

Beatrice spoke. "Except the gun was found this evening in a staff only area of the hotel. Confirmed as the murder weapon, property of Samuel Silva. So the professional hit angle gets my vote. Cher, where did you disappear to?"

"I managed to persuade Sergio, the charming hotel concierge, to show me the security system. I told him I was advising an hotelier friend on state-of-the-art systems. While chatting, I asked him about cameras. He told me about the footage of the relevant first floor corridor on Saturday. I said I wish I'd seen it myself. After a little eyelash-batting, he showed me the digital recording. For what it's worth.

"As mentioned, Silva had the Do Not Disturb sign on the door. Just before lunch, Gilchrist goes back to his room. Roman can be seen heading back for his shower. Silva enters and no one else follows. Monteiro comes to the door and rings. No reply and he tries again before leaving. A little while later, maybe ten minutes, Roman walks past, followed by Gilchrist about five minutes after that. Over an hour passes until the concierge knocks on Silva's door. He unlocks it and finds the body."

Xavier nodded his approval. "Cher, that is most impressive! You've now confirmed what we heard from the police."

"You said Gilchrist went to his room?" A chill settled over Beatrice. "Which one?" She already knew the answer. Room 1101 was on the other wing of the building. If the footage Cher had seen was of Silva's corridor, it had to be Gilchrist's office.

"Room 1120," Cher said.

She closed her eyes as a sudden clarity of understanding and a flurry of interlocking images flooded her mind.

When she opened her eyes, all three of her fellow detectives were staring at her. She spoke in a whisper. "You know when the unthinkable becomes thinkable?"

Cher frowned. "Beatrice?"

"Xavier, will you go and fetch André Monteiro? We're going to need all the help we can get."

Fifteen minutes later, Xavier and André entered the tiny sauna and sat on the bench. The wood creaked with a sound like old bones resting.

Beatrice aimed for a friendly smile, aware how shadowy their faces must look, lit by pale blue pool lights.

"André, thank you for joining us. I know a midnight invitation to the sauna must be alarming. But we figured this would be a safe place to talk. We believe, and I think you are of the same mind, that Marco Cordeiro did not kill Samuel Silva. He was framed and murdered so the truth could be buried. We've been investigating and think the perpetrator..." she broke off as her phone trilled.

Her first thought was news of Luke until she saw Ana's name on the display.

"Sorry, I need to take this, it's Ana." She swiped the screen. "Hello?"

"Beatrice, I think we're in trouble."

"I tend to agree. Listen, Ana, I need to put you on speaker. We're all here, including André. We have some more information to share with you but first can you tell us what the ghostwriter said?"

The team listened to Ana, each of them intent and silent. She finished her summary by urging extra caution.

"I've already told Georgina to scram, hide with her folks in the Home Counties until this is over. I think anyone who knows what Gilchrist has written in his book is potentially in danger. Beatrice, that includes you and me."

"Wait, we need to think this through," Roman pressed his palms together. "Who knows we're working as a team?"

Xavier was the first to respond. "Anyone who's watched us over the past few days. Which is pretty much everyone. We're detectives, for God's sake, it's our job. Beatrice hangs out with Cher, you and I are apparently lovers, and Ana and André are implicated by association."

"Which means we gotta act," said Cher. "We need to take this case to the senior officers in charge and get the guy arrested. And I mean right now!"

Ana's voice came from the phone. "I agree with Cher. Don't wait any longer. We have evidence, witnesses and motive. Take this to the police."

Beatrice considered. "Whistle blowing on one of our own is complex, even in the same country. This situation is a bloody nightmare. We need to get the senior detective here to take us seriously and he or she may take a little convincing. We might want to follow a parallel line by reporting Gilchrist to his own superiors, Europol and Interpol. Then we need to get him home. There's department there that deals with police crime, but I don't expect they can drop everything and fly out here to arrest him at a moment's notice. This is not going to be easy."

She clasped her hands over her face, thinking about how to block every loophole. The room stilled, awaiting her advice.

"Here's what I suggest. First thing in the morning André and Xavier as our Portuguese speakers make a statement at the local police station in Viana do Castelo. At the same time, Cher should contact Buckinghamshire's Assistant Commissioner while Roman seeks out the Interpol rep here, a man by the name of Fisher. Good luck, he's as slimy as frogspawn. We need Gilchrist taken in for questioning at the very minimum, but I would push hard for an arrest."

Roman spoke. "Yes, we should cover all bases. What about you and Ana?"

"This is where the timing comes in. The police are coming here to interview Ana and myself at eight in the morning and Gilchrist wants to be present. I'll make some sort of excuse for Ana, but I can waffle enough to ensure that Gilchrist will be with me until nine. If you can all report to your respective forces at seven, you can get authorisation for an arrest within two hours."

From Beatrice's phone, Ana spoke. "I'm calling in some favours so I might get into Porto on an early flight. If so, I'll head straight to Viana. I'm giving the hotel a wide berth. I'm away to get sorted now but if you need me to do anything, just shout. Goodnight all. And in the immortal words of Beatrice Stubbs, please be bloody careful."

They each responded in kind and sat in silence for several seconds.

André ran a hand over his face. "There are still a couple of things I don't get. When I knocked on Samuel's door, I could hear Gilchrist in the next room, shouting into the phone. How could he be doing that and shooting Samuel at the same time?"

To Beatrice's surprise, Cher asked a question. "Xavier, when you came to my room yesterday afternoon and knocked on the door, did you hear anything from inside the room?"

Xavier thought about the question. "No. It was silent. Why?"

"Because Roman and I were making a helluva lot of noise. You interrupted us in the middle of something. Hey, no need to blush, it's fine. We're the ones who should be embarrassed. But if you really couldn't hear us, how come a loud phone call is audible when the door muffles the sound of uninhibited lovemaking?"

"Good point," agreed Beatrice. "Plus Gilchrist's office room is a suite. There's a hallway between the front door and the room with his telephone."

"So you'd need to amplify your voice, or a recording of it, to play right behind the door at the exact time you expected someone to be passing," said Roman. "For example, via a speaker."

"And the note," said André. "Samuel sends me texts or emails but this was the first note I ever got."

"Lemme guess, it was typed," Cher added.

André gave her a wry smile.

Xavier got to his feet. "We need to prepare our case. It's nearly one in the morning, so I suggest we get a few hours' sleep. I'll order room service breakfast for us at six a.m. in my room, including very strong coffee. Today we'll need to be at our best."

Chapter 26

From: dawnwhit70@btinternet.uk
To: beatrice@beatrice-stubbs.com
Subject: Leon Charles

Hi Beatrice

Thanks for your feedback on the seminar. I thought it went pretty well so I'm glad you agree. Your praise matters more than most.

I would say something trite like 'hope you're having fun', but with a murder on site and background checks required on one of your house guests, I'll just say I hope you're OK.

Leon Charles. I found out plenty from his own profiles then filled the gaps with a few calls. There's a pattern here and you're not going to like it. Our generation would label this sort of man as an egomaniac. Modern psychologists have a variety of terms, mostly involving the word 'narcissism'. You and I would probably just call him a tosser.

Facts: He has been married and divorced twice, and had a string of engagements. Mostly to women from Eastern European countries. I spoke to a Polish woman and a girl from Lithuania, but there are several others. None of these relationships ended amicably.

He meets these women via his job. He's a salesman to pubs, arcades and shopping malls. His company rents and services fruit machines and all their variants – pinball, quizmaster, and one-armed bandit type of thing.

On his police record are two cases of assault (both trying to prevent women from leaving his flat) and one restraining order. The case notes on the latter are worrying. He'd been seeing a nurse for about six months. In her statement, she says she ended the relationship because he was too possessive. After the split, she made him return her house key. But he'd made a copy. She came home to find him waiting for her in bed. She changed the locks. When she left the hospital one night, she found flowers on the windscreen of her car. Then her cat went missing. After she'd spent three days frantically searching for the animal, he turned up, pretending he'd found it. That's when she got the restraining order.

Not Quite Facts: His online profiles are 80% fake. Several pictures of parties in Ibiza, Monaco and Hawaii are stock images. His work history is 90% invention, as are his qualifications. He has a profile on three separate dating sites, each with a slightly different identity and/ or age. The one consistent factor is he wants a life partner without children.

Personality: He's possessive to the point of psychosis. He has a compulsive need for attention. Both those women I spoke to told me he often lost his temper if she looked away while he was talking! He is also a fantasist who fabricates tales of heroism. A busy boy, according to his stories – ex-SAS (yawn, who isn't), undercover agent for the drugs squad (!) and Red Cross volunteer/White Helmet.

Bottom line: A man with serious reality issues. Steer well clear.

HTH, love Dawn

Chapter 27

From: james.parker@IGTT.com

To: beatrice@beatrice-stubbs.com

Dear Beatrice

Thanks for your note. I am glad to hear you're well and look forward to our next appointment in September.

I'm happy to share my ideas with you on an informal basis. You didn't say if the person you describe is a friend, colleague or suspect. So here's the usual disclaimer: please remember none of this could be regarded as official psychiatric opinion for the CPS or other legal processes.

To summarise your concerns, your colleague's observations lead you to believe a particular person demonstrates behaviours associated with NPD, such as passive aggression, attention-seeking, self-aggrandisement and possessiveness towards his partner, including rejection of close family.

It's impossible to label a person based on so few examples so all I can do is direct you to further studies on the subject – see attached. You will see there are a whole range of disorders under the Narcissism-related umbrella and often from directly opposite causes; e.g. insufficient nurturing/excessive praise in the developmental phase.

I would add a word of caution – there might also be a range of other reasons for this person's behaviour. NPD is a hot topic in popular *culture, with all kinds of blame being laid at the feet of these three letters, and subsequent assumptions made.*

However, your question was quite specific. Do you think he might have NPD?

My answer, subject to my caveats above, would be yes, he might. That is precisely the first condition I would suspect, and I'd work towards greater clarification of his attitudes to himself and others before eliminating it as a possibility.

I hope the material attached expands on the above and I look forward to our next meeting. Incidentally, I would like to discuss your ongoing treatment once you leave London at the end of this year. My thinking was monthly check-ins, in person or online. Let's discuss in September.

Best wishes

James

Chapter 28

Hours passed after Will had received Beatrice's emails. He sat in front of his laptop, reading, making notes, checking various websites and emitting the occasional grunt.

Adrian paced the house and garden every twenty minutes, just to keep himself awake and to reassure himself he was still doing something. He made more tea, most of which went undrunk.

Just after midnight, Will got to his feet, opened the fridge and took out the tinfoil-wrapped plate of chowder left for Marianne.

"What are you doing?" Adrian asked.

Will tore off a hunk of bread and laid it on top of the plate. "I'm going to talk to Marianne. Gloves off. I want some answers."

He slipped on his jacket and went out the kitchen door.

Night noises kept Adrian awake. Clicks and creaks from the cooling house, chitters and squawks from outside roused him whenever he fell into a doze. Each time he awoke, he prowled the grounds with a torch, always with a glance at the garden flat. Two silhouettes faintly discernible, no movement. Still talking.

He saw his reflection in the windowpane. White, drawn and with a heavy woollen throw around his shoulders, he looked like a Porto fishwife. He rubbed his face and checked his phone. 05.04. No messages.

It would be light in an hour and they could resume the search. In two hours, the police station would be open and they could call. Soon they could do something. This endless dark night of horrors, most created by his imagination, would be over. Tomorrow, they'd find him. They would find Luke and he would be fine. Of course he would.

The kitchen door opened. Adrian turned, as he had done for the last six hours, hoping to see a short blond-haired figure. Instead, he saw Will's tall blond-haired figure, his eyes bloodshot.

"No sign of... anyone?" Will asked.

Adrian shook his head. "I've just done another check and Matthew's still upstairs. I doubt he can sleep either, but he'd rather keep his distance from me."

Will threw himself onto a chair and dropped his head on his forearms.

"Should I make tea?" asked Adrian.

His voice, when it came, was muffled. "I'm shit-sick of tea. Can we not have a livener? I need a whisky and Coke. Have one yourself, bar-keep."

Adrian made the drinks, happy to have something to do. When he placed them on the table, Will's head jerked up.

"Good man. I damn well deserve this." He took two enormous swigs and blinked.

Adrian watched him and waited. "I'm feeling a bit underinformed here. You had those emails from Beatrice and a long conversation with Marianne to add to your own observations. So what do you think is going on?"

There was no reply. Will stared into his drink, his face blank.

"Can you at least summarise what Marianne told you? You've been over there for hours."

Will rolled his head from side to side, the muscles in his neck clicking audibly. "Sorry, I was just thinking. What she said, in a nutshell, is that he's special. An introvert who's desperately insecure and needs constant proof of her love for him. Also known as a self-obsessed wanker. I apologise, I shouldn't rant at you. It's just that after listening to hours of that bullshit, trying to be diplomatic for half the night, I need to vent a bit."

Adrian squeezed his arm. "For the record, I think he's a wanker too. But what the hell is he doing taking Luke?"

"He's trying to hurt her. He feels undervalued," Will clenched a fist and mimed a backhander. "So he lashes out by taking something precious to Marianne. She doesn't think he'll try to leave the country, although I wouldn't set a lot of store by her opinion of what he may or may not do."

Will swirled his drink around his glass and Adrian waited for him to continue.

"There are medical names for Leon's issues, but in layman's terms, he's basically a dickhead. Interests include he, himself and him. Ego out of control. Only interested in what people can do for him and desperate for attention. An emotional parasite. The damn shame is Marianne is the perfect host. Needy, clingy and willing to make excuses. Luke took up more attention than Leon. So the bigger brat had a tantrum. And he's done it before."

"Leon has taken kids before?" The fishwife shawl fell from Adrian's shoulders as he clasped his hands to his mouth.

"No, I meant he's had a tantrum over Luke before. Marianne used to babysit Luke every Thursday night for Tanya's night out with the girls. She'd cook his tea, put him to bed and watch TV with a glass of wine. When Tanya got home, they'd have another glass and a chat and Marianne would stay over.

"But Leon kept getting tickets for the cinema or booking restaurants for Thursday evenings and when Marianne couldn't make it, he'd throw a hissy-fit. Those weren't her words. She said he got very upset and emotional. In other words, a hissy-fit, a wobbler, a tantrum, call it what you will. When he moved in, he insisted he couldn't spend a night without her by his side, so she had to stop babysitting. Things with her and Tanya have been difficult ever since."

Will took another swig. "You know what else? I think Leon was affected by the fuss we made of you."

"Me? What have I got to do with it?" Adrian gaped.

"The saving-a-kid-at-the-airport story. You were the centre of attention and it pissed him off. Did you notice how quiet he was when Beatrice arrived because she stole the limelight? He has to be the star or he sulks. I reckon he's taken Luke somewhere and will bring him back in a big 'rescue' event tomorrow or the day after. He'll be expecting a hero's welcome. Instead he's going to get a kick in the fucking bollocks." He drained his drink.

Adrian got up to make another, wincing as Will cracked his

knuckles. He gazed out at the night, his mind less panicky now his man was back. Then he laughed inwardly, realising that everyone has a touch of Leon in there somewhere. He started thinking about the sequence of events. "Do you think Luke liked him? I mean, would he get in the car with Leon willingly?"

"No." Will was emphatic. "He avoided Leon whenever he could and I'm convinced those bruises on his arm came from that nasty git pushing him around. But if Leon told him they were going to see Tanya or something..." Will tapped a nail against the table. "But where could he take a small child? After a while, Luke would get restless, tearful, and hungry. You couldn't check into a hotel or a B&B with a five-year-old screaming for his mother. He'd have to go somewhere quiet, private."

A chill crept up the back of Adrian's neck and he hunched his shoulders against the panic rising in his chest. "Private? Why? You don't think he'd hurt him?"

Will clenched one hand around his own fist. "It's impossible to guess. If he has Narcissistic Personality Disorder, which I think he does, he will do anything to cover himself with glory. This kind of person, often described as a Lone Wolf, has a distorted world view. In their minds, they have an inflated sense of their own worth and get frustrated when events don't reflect that. A surprising amount of mass shooters have been diagnosed with the condition. Ask Beatrice.

"I don't know Leon very well, but I can see his ego has taken a bashing this week. Marianne's attention is often claimed by her family, and by Luke in particular. We treated Leon as one of us, and didn't put him on some kind of pedestal, which he may feel is his right. No coincidence they made a late entrance, apparently due to Leon's 'promotion'. He resents anything or anyone who draws attention away from himself. He wants the spotlight on him and him alone. Whether he plans to do that by abducting Luke then bringing him back as a generous act, all I can say is that I hope so."

A voice came from the hallway. "I'm afraid you didn't answer the question, Will." Matthew emerged from the shadows, still fully dressed. "Do you think he'd hurt Luke?"

Will pressed his fingers to his eyes. "I can't say either way with any degree of certainty, but I think we should operate on the basis that it's possible."

Moments of silence ticked past. Adrian held his breath.

"Is there anything we can do?" asked Matthew.

Will didn't look up from the table, his head bent over his clasped hands.

The inertia was unacceptable. Adrian smacked his hands together, making everyone jump. "Of course there's something we can do. Marianne and Leon went to particular places each day, so we can trace their routes from here. Realistically, Leon won't have gone too far and will most likely take Luke to a place he knows or has seen before. The last thing he wants to do is get himself lost with Luke. The Panda's not been found so he probably went to ground about an hour, two at the most, after he snatched Luke. Come on, get that laptop open and let's add everything we know to a map of their movements. Where has he been since they got here?"

Will straightened and an optimistic light shone in his weary eyes. Matthew pulled up a chair and the three began to superimpose a record of Leon's movements onto a map of the region, according to their memory. Within twenty minutes, they had drawn a radius around the limits they calculated.

Adrian was reassured by the concrete nature of the activity, but unsettled by the fact it was all based on assumption. Perhaps all detectives start this way. He got up to make coffee. The first pale ribbon of dawn floated on the horizon, offering all the clichés it always did. Hope, optimism, light, a new start and all the brightness of reality to chase away nightmares. As he waited for the pot to bubble, half listening to the conversation behind him, he gazed out over the valley as it came to life. The lake emerged from a velvety blackness to reflect the lightening sky, in which ripples of pink heralded the sun.

He poured the coffees and handed one to Will. Matthew had gone onto the terrace so Adrian took two more cups outside.

"Coffee?"

Matthew looked over his shoulder. "Yes, please. I think I may need more than one. Is there any warm milk at all?"

"Already in. I know how you take it. Quite a sight, a Portuguese sunrise, don't you think?"

They watched the mist lifting from the valley like lace curtains. The sky announced morning by flame-throwing its entire palette of fiery colours onto the underbelly of a shoal of cumulus clouds. On the lake, a fishing-boat puttered away from a pier, its motor chugging as a bass note to the dawn orchestra of a million birds.

"Quite a sight, as you say. I imagine how one experiences such a natural wonder depends on the state of mind." Matthew sipped at his milky coffee. "I might well be impressed by the delights of dawn, but my mind is wrestling with the stark horror of what I say to Tanya in a few hours' time. What would you advise? I'm not being sarcastic, I'd like some help. How do I tell my daughter her five-year-old son has disappeared from my care and we have no idea where to look for him?"

Adrian's eyes followed the small craft across the water as he tried to frame his apology, but he couldn't find a way of explaining without attaching blame to Matthew's other daughter. He simply didn't have the words. Far below, internal lights illuminated the little fishing-boat and Adrian involuntarily imagined the cramped, smelly interior. He'd experienced a particularly horrible journey across the Irish Sea in a similar vessel. Since then, he'd never quite felt the same about boats.

With a dizzying rush, random elements connected in Adrian's brain, like the tumblers of a lock mechanism falling into place. He grabbed Matthew's forearm, spilling his coffee.

"The boathouse! At the fish restaurant the other night. Remember? Luke disappeared and we all panicked. Will found him in the boathouse. He said he only wanted to have a look. The restaurant is closed for two weeks so the place is empty and private. It's a fifteen-minute drive from here and Leon knew no one would be there."

Matthew stared at him. "Good God. You might well be onto something."

Will's reaction after Adrian breathlessly announced his brainwave was disappointing. Surely a detective should have leapt out of his seat and grabbed the car keys, shouting 'Let's go!'. But he didn't.

"Hmm. Could be a possibility." He returned to his screen, checking a map of the area.

Matthew had obviously held the same expectation. "I wonder if we ought not just get in the car? Creep up on the place while they're still asleep? Or do you think we should call the police first?"

Without lifting his gaze from the screen, Will said, "I am the police, Matthew. Which is why I want to do this properly. I'm going to inform Detective Machado of our suspicions and ask him to stand by with back-up. Adrian, on the off chance we do find Luke, can you get milk, biscuits and a towel or something comforting? I suggest we don't tell Marianne where we're going. If she's with us, her concern for Leon could override Luke's safety. Plus, someone should stay put in case we're wrong and Leon or Luke returns to the villa. Matthew, would you leave her a note saying we've gone out searching? Just don't mention where."

Matthew went off in search of pen and paper.

"Will, do we tell Beatrice what's going on?"

"Yes. But I don't want to wake her at this hour and leave her worrying about all of us. I'll drop her an email and hopefully we'll have Luke home before she gets up and sees it. I'll do that the minute I've called Machado."

While Will was on the phone, Adrian went upstairs to collect Luke's cuddly dolphin and a bath towel. He shoved them both into a carrier bag along with a bag of chocolate chip cookies and a carton of milk. As an afterthought, he added the First Aid kit from under the kitchen sink. Matthew returned and waited till Will had finished typing before offering his note for approval.

"Perfect. Right, I've spoken to the police and emailed Beatrice. Now I want you both to sit down and listen to me. We are potentially looking at a hostage situation and this is how we're going to play it. Follow these instructions to the letter, even if things go pear-shaped. Adrian, where's that shawl you were wearing?"

They sat, they listened, then they prepared themselves and trooped out to the car. Will drove, his mouth a hard line.

Chapter 29

Fifteen minutes later, the Peugeot passed through the village and into the forest. Two hundred yards from the turning to *Marisqueira do Miguel*, they stopped and parked between the trees. Through the copse, they could make out the restaurant and a little farther, the boathouse. The tension in the vehicle was heavy and the air not much lighter. As if reading Adrian's mind, Will turned the ignition and pressed the window button. Cool morning air flowed inwards, easing the pressure a notch.

Will twisted to look at them both and the smallest flicker of a smile crossed his face as he appraised Adrian.

"Right, one more time. What are we going to do?"

Adrian checked his costume in the rear-view mirror. Black T-shirt, black double sheet wound round his waist and fastened with a belt. Black shawl around his head like a caul, safety-pinned under his chin. Black trainers and the sleeves of one of Matthew's jumpers cut off and acting as woolly socks.

"I'm a fisherwoman heading down to my boat. I get out of the car, walk down to the turning as if I came from the village, go down the driveway and past the boathouse to the fishing boats at the end of the pier. I move slowly, like an old woman. I keep my head down, so my face is obscured by the shawl. I watch where I'm going and try not to trip over. When I get to the boats, I sit with my back to the boathouse and pretend to do something with nets. If I see the Fiat, I send you both a message. The aim is to keep Leon's attention on me. I do not even look at the boathouse until I get your order to approach."

Will nodded once and looked at Matthew.

"I stay behind the tree line and watch. I must not fidget or attract attention. I stand still, watch and wait for your shout or message. If you say 'Retreat!', I go back to the car and call the police. If you say 'Approach', I come to your assistance. If I hear nothing within fifteen minutes of your entering the boathouse, I call the police regardless."

Seconds ticked past and the only sounds were those of the village waking; in the distance, the church bells struck seven, a cockerel crowed and a cacophony of barks responded to a moped's waspish rasp. Sunlight grew stronger, changing the colours of the foliage from dewy grey-green to a thousand brilliant hues.

Will pulled a black beanie down to his eyebrows to cover his blond hair and instantly transformed himself into someone terrifying.

"I'm moving left through the trees to approach the boathouse from behind the restaurant. If he's there and he's watching, his focus will be on the driveway and the old fishwife. I'll creep under the pier and enter the boathouse from beneath. If Leon's there, my priority is to disable him. Then I'll call for you two to get Luke out of there. He'll need to see a familiar face as soon as possible. Keep a cool head. If you panic, so will he. Mobiles on but switched to silent. We're now operating on stealth mode. Let's go and don't slam the doors."

Adrian had an urge to salute, not out of sarcasm but obedience. Instead, he crossed his fingers. They emerged from the vehicle and pressed the doors closed. Will seemed to melt into the foliage, while Matthew pressed himself against a tree trunk and peered through the branches. Adrian crossed the road and began the downhill slope to the lake while managing the uphill curve of learning to walk in a skirt.

After a minute's walk, he left the shade of the trees and found himself exposed, in full view of the boathouse. He kept his head down and concentrated on his character. *I do this every day. Down to my boat where I go fishing to feed my family. This is just a normal morning for me. Nothing to see here. This is just my normal gait, a bit of a limp and eyes on the track. No need for alarm. Just a fisherwoman off to work. Poor thing, widowed young and wearing mourning clothes. I have a family of five to support.*

He descended the dusty drive, passed the restaurant and the boathouse, then headed for the pier and its cluster of boats at the end. Apart from the riotous noises of nature, he heard not a sound. No voice calling his name or ordering him to approach. No one rushed out of the door and rumbled him. So far, so good.

Until he looked up. Four fishermen trudged along the lakeside from the opposite direction, heading for the same destination. Real fishermen, who very probably owned the boats. Dressing the part and faking the walk was one thing, but blending in with the locals? Adrian slowed, noting the curiosity on the approaching faces. He wished to God he'd shaved.

Chapter 30

The fishermen stopped in their tracks and gawped at Adrian with a mixture of surprise, suspicion and bewilderment.

With no other grasp on Portuguese than how to say hello and thank you, Adrian opted for mime. Performance, after all, was his forte. He pressed a finger to his lips and pointed back over his shoulder. He made sure his back was to the boathouse and his face to the fishermen. His impromptu audience watched intently, saying nothing, every brow a frown.

Adrian mimed rocking a baby and stroking its face. He indicated behind him again and then snatched the imaginary child from his own arm. He considered tracing his tears but judged that a touch too Marcel Marceau. Instead he pulled a face of pure panic. Two of the fishermen widened their eyes in an echo of his pantomime fear.

They were with him so far. He tapped his temple to signify thinking, followed by a Eureka! expression, backed up by a roll of the eyes to direct their attention to the boathouse. The men nodded and talked amongst themselves, articulating the narrative so far.

The youngest of the four made a beckoning gesture which Adrian translated as 'Do go on'.

So he did. He tapped his chest, waved a hand around his head, pulled his shawl tighter and spread a hand across his face. He could see from their faces they understood the reason for disguise. He jerked a thumb behind him and changed character. He pressed three fingers to his shoulder, having no idea how many stripes a Portuguese detective might wear, hardened his expression and pulled an imaginary gun. Then his fingers crept up his forearm, slowing towards the elbow until one 'foot' hovered in the air. The tension was unbearable. Eyes flicked from Adrian to the boathouse and the men discussed the situation in urgent whispers.

Adrian placed his finger to his lips once more. He pointed to his chest, pointed at the ground and glanced at his watch. He added a nibble of his nails and showed them his mobile phone. He received nods of understanding and sympathy.

The youngest asked a question. Faced with Adrian's incomprehension, he too mimed a babe in arms, then placed his hand palm-down by his knee, his thigh, his waist, with an enquiring look.

It clicked. Adrian splayed his hand. Five fingers. Luke was five years old.

One of the older men placed a hand at thigh-height and pointed first to Adrian's skirt and then at his own trousers.

Uncomprehending, Adrian looked from one to another for elucidation.

A second whiskery old bloke tutted and shook his head. He cupped his hands under imaginary breasts, then mimed waving his penis.

For the first time, Adrian spoke. "Oh I see! He's a little boy." He repeated the penis-waving mime, a gesture incongruous on its own, let alone dressed as a Portuguese fisherwoman.

The penis-waver's impressive eyebrows rose. "English?"

"Yes!" He dropped his voice. "Yes. You speak English?"

"A little bit. My name is Pedro Quintela. I come from Portugal. How do you do?" He held out his hand.

Adrian shook it. "My name is Adrian Harvey and I come from..."

At that moment his mobile vibrated and sent shockwaves through his system. He grabbed it and answered.

"Will? Are you OK? Will?"

The voice in his ear was a whisper. "They're here. I can see Leon watching you at the window and Luke is asleep in the corner. I'm going to tackle Leon but I need you to get Luke out of here. Retrace your steps as if you're going back to the village then as you pass the boathouse, rush through the door and look to your right. Luke is on a pile of tarpaulins. Grab him and get him out. I've alerted Matthew."

"OK," Adrian whispered. "The thing is, Will, there are some..."

A series of beeps indicated Will had ended the call.

Adrian looked at his new friends and made a decision. With a wave of his arm and a jerk of his head, he invited all four men to join him. Together, they walked back towards the boathouse. A movement to his left caught his eye and he spotted the Peugeot crunching down the drive. Matthew!

Right beside the entrance to the boathouse and out of view of its windows, Adrian tore off his 'skirt' and pointed at the door. He mimed again, this time for reasons of silence. He pointed at his chest, made a grabbing motion and rocked a baby. Then he counted with his fingers.

One, two, three.

He burst through the door and saw Will crouched on his haunches restraining a struggling, swearing Leon. The fishermen rushed past to help hold him down.

To his right, a small figure wrapped in a blanket sat up.

Adrian's heart thumped as he saw Luke's exhausted little face appear from beneath the folds. He reached out his arms.

"Luke! It's OK, we've got you."

Tears flooded the little boy's eyes and he scrambled up into Adrian's embrace, dragging his blanket with him. Adrian thought it best that Luke did not witness to the ugly scene behind him, and took him to the doorway.

"Come on, let's go. Grandpa's outside."

The Peugeot had just come to a halt. Matthew emerged, looking pale and gaunt, but determined. As Adrian walked out into the sunshine with Luke in his arms, Matthew's eyes creased with relief.

"Hello, Small Fry."

"Grandpa?" Luke got down and ran across the dusty car park, trailing his blanket. "Where have you been?"

His intonation, unconsciously mimicking his mother's, forced tears to Adrian's own eyes. He brushed them away and watched the pair embrace, Luke's small hand patting Matthew's back, as if he were the comforter. Which in a way, he was.

He went back inside to see what more he could do, but it was clear that Will had all the help he needed. Leon sat on an upturned rowing-boat, trussed like a pheasant between the two whiskery fishermen, who were watching him with belligerent expressions. Will shook hands with all of their unexpected helpers, with an *Obrigado* for each of them. He came towards Adrian, his face dirty but with the ghost of a grin.

"Don't know where or how you found these geezers but they're pretty handy with knots. He's not going anywhere until the police get here."

Under the circumstances, Adrian chose not to fling his arms around his hero.

"Considering I'm the first bearded fishwife they've encountered, they took it pretty well. Luke's outside with Matthew. What should we do now?"

"First priority is getting Luke home. He needs to get away from here and rest. I'll stay here to meet Machado, who should be here in around twenty minutes. You go with Luke and Matthew. Give Luke something to eat and drink then put him to bed. Don't give him a bath or a shower. We may still need to take physical samples." He gripped Adrian's shoulders and fixed him with an intense stare. "Listen to me. We don't know what he's been through. Take no risks. Resist the urge to cuddle or hug him unless he wants. Let him dictate terms, don't ask questions but listen to everything he has to say."

Adrian, too horrified to even consider the worst, gave Will a nod.

Will addressed the fishermen. "If you guys will stay with me for half an hour, we can keep the site secure."

"No problem," Pedro replied.

Adrian clasped his hands together to say a heartfelt thank you to all four men who had simply taken him at his not-quite-words. They all gave the universal thumbs-up and genuine smiles.

Outside, grandfather and grandson were still clutched in an embrace. On Adrian's approach, Matthew lowered the boy to the ground.

"Where's Mum?" asked Luke.

Matthew's eyes were still damp so Adrian jumped in.

"She's coming back today. We're going to fetch her later on. But we really should have breakfast before we go, don't you think?

Talking of food, there's milk and biscuits in the car if you're hungry."

Luke rubbed his grubby face. Matthew took his hand and they started walking towards the Peugeot when Luke stumbled, dragging Matthew sideways.

Adrian stepped forward. "Did someone call for the Piggyback Taxi?" He hunkered down, allowing Luke to clamber onto his back and felt two little arms wrap round his neck. Matthew got into the driver's seat to chauffeur them home.

"Not awfully certain of the route, so all navigational advice is welcome," said Matthew, crunching the gears.

"Blind leading the blind," said Adrian, looking down at the small blond head beside him. He managed to swap the cuddly dolphin for the filthy blanket, which he dropped on the ground outside.

After two chocolate-chip cookies and several slurps of milk, Luke sat back and leaned against Adrian. Mindful of Will's advice, Adrian put his arm around the boy with great caution. Luke nestled closer and shut his eyes. Next time Adrian looked, he was fast asleep. Which was just as well, because Matthew's driving would have given anyone nightmares.

The jerky, hair-raising journey lasted twenty-five minutes after a couple of wrong turns, but finally they spotted the villa.

Adrian let out a huge sigh. "Has anyone called Beatrice?" he asked

"Not yet," said Matthew, his focus on the road. "I'll do so as soon as we get in. It is early, but I am sure she'd like to know he's safe. My other concern is ..."

"What to say to Marianne."

Matthew glanced across at the garden flat. "Precisely. Do you have any ideas? Other than 'your psychopathic boyfriend abducted your nephew and terrified your entire family', of course."

Adrian looked down at the small face resting against the seat. "Unless I get an hour's sleep, I'll never have another idea in my life. Why don't you go over and tell her we found him, at least. She must be worried. Leave the rest till Will gets back. I have faith in his judgement."

Matthew nodded. "So do I."

Luke barely stirred when Adrian lifted him out of the car, still clutching his dolphin. Matthew trudged across the lawn to inform Marianne of her nephew's return. Following Will's instructions, Adrian carried Luke upstairs, took off his little trainers and laid him in bed, still in his grubby shorts and Ice-Age t-shirt. He covered him with the duvet and watched for a few moments as the child slept soundly.

His own exhaustion dragged at him but he was reluctant to let Luke out of his sight. Footsteps on the staircase jolted him alert and he looked around to see Matthew coming through the door. He glanced at Luke with a sigh then turned to Adrian.

"She's gone," he whispered.

"Marianne? Why?"

Matthew shrugged. "No idea why or how. We had the only vehicle. But all her and Leon's things have disappeared."

"She must have called a cab. Where do you think she would go?"

"Home," said Matthew, rubbing his eyes. "Where else?"

Chapter 31

At seven o'clock, Beatrice bade Cher good luck, took one more chocolate croissant from the trolley and returned to her room. First priority now was checking on Luke. André and Xavier would be at the police station in Viana do Castelo already, Roman had left to seek out Fisher and Cher was waiting for the Buckinghamshire Assistant Commissioner to return their call.

Beatrice wished she could have spoken to the AC herself. She knew him in a nodding acquaintance sort of way. But as the man was unlikely to be in his office before eight, she had no choice but to put her trust in Cher.

While dialling Matthew, she looked out at the grounds, the pale morning sunshine casting a rosy light onto the white pagoda on the hill. The delicate beauty of the edifice and perfect natural illumination made Beatrice catch her breath. A summer wedding at sunrise would be a photographer's dream.

Matthew sounded far more relaxed than he had during his previous phone call an hour earlier. He assured her several times that Luke showed no obvious signs of physical or emotional damage and that he was still fast asleep. His voice was weary but cheerful, despite his concerns for his daughters. He was vague about what was happening with Leon.

"Really couldn't say. That's Will's area of expertise. Talking of whom, he called twenty minutes ago to say they're filing the paperwork, whatever that means. Then he's going to the hospital to collect Tanya."

"I imagine he'll need her to make the decision about pressing charges against Leon. Poor Tanya, as if she doesn't have enough to cope with."

"Quite. I'm rather glad Will's handling this. He always knows what to do. As for Marianne, she's done a bunk. Cleared out the garden flat and gone. No note, nothing."

"Good grief! Are you all right? This must be immensely stressful for you," Beatrice asked.

"I'm fine now I've got my grandson back. I'll wait up till Will and Tanya come home, then I am going to bed for the rest of this holiday. You can join me if you like."

"I'll accept that offer. Will truly is a Superman. If Adrian does his usual trick of getting bored of his boyfriend after a few months, I will give him such a fourpenny one. William Quinn is perfect for him."

Matthew released a deep sigh. "I know. I can't even attempt to tell Will how grateful I am. I'm likely to break down and weep. Anyway, the most important thing is Luke is safe and asleep in his own bed. Likewise Adrian. What's the latest with you?"

Beatrice dissembled. "Everything is coming to a head. Should all be over very soon."

"Cryptic. Which is fine with me. I would rather avoid any drama for the next ten years. Plays havoc with my digestion."

"Oh you poor old devil, this must have been a wretched holiday for you. Well, we start anew tomorrow. Give the boys my love and ask Will to call me when he can. I have an interview this morning but plan to leave here at lunchtime, or just as soon as Ana can drive me. The more I think about it, the more retirement appeals. See you later and look after yourself."

"Will do and same to you, Old Thing."

Beatrice put down the phone and began making her third coffee of the morning. Her phone buzzed. A message from Cher.

Phone conf confirmed for 08.00 with AC of B.

Beatrice sent a thumbs-up icon in reply and returned to her deliberations over a ristretto or an espresso. After a sleepless night and with a dramatic day in prospect, she decided on both.

At seven forty-five on the dot, someone rapped on her door. Beatrice expected Roman with Fisher in tow, or possibly the local police detectives. Yet there stood Commander Gilchrist, dressed to impress, complete with smile.

"Good morning! The interview is taking place in my office. As I was on my way back from breakfast, I thought I'd escort you both. Are you ready?"

"Good morning to you, Commander. Unfortunately, Ana is still en route and unlikely to be here before ten. However, I'm ready to talk to the police and share everything I know."

Gilchrist's smile faltered. "Ah. That could be awkward."

"She sent her apologies and is prepared to drive to the station at their convenience."

"Let's deal with that later. Now we should get going, we don't want to keep them waiting. I take it you've eaten?"

"Indeed. Room service is a wonderful thing. Isn't it a glorious day?" She reached for her jacket.

"Glorious. Forecast is for 28 degrees, so I doubt you'll need a coat. Shall we?"

Beatrice picked up her bag and put on her jacket. She wasn't sure why, apart from her innate loathing of being told what to do. She followed Gilchrist out into the corridor, slipping her hand into her pocket to reassure herself the heavy little cockerel was still there. Somehow, he felt like good luck.

"Incidentally," he said as they walked along the hotel corridor towards his office, "I hear there was a touch of drama at your holiday home. The little lad is back safe and sound now?"

Beatrice narrowed her eyes. "Good gracious, news travels fast. Yes, thankfully Luke is home and none the worse for his ordeal."

"I'm in constant touch with local police, so naturally they mentioned the situation. Very pleased to hear it all turned out well."

Her phone pinged. A message from Cher asking her to confirm where the interview would take place.

Beatrice replied in two words. *His office.* She looked up. Gilchrist had opened his door and was waiting for her. She stuffed her phone in her handbag and stepped inside.

Chapter 32

A private jet left Paris Orly at 04.20 with four passengers, two pilots and one not-quite-flight attendant.

If the four businessmen had been less focused on planning their negotiation strategy, they might have observed a certain clumsiness to the in-flight service, a worrying amateurism to the security announcement and an ill-fitting uniform on the young stewardess.

Yet the weather conditions were perfect, no coffee was spilt, the flight landed on time and a car was waiting to take the negotiating team to Matosinhos. Everyone was happy. Especially Ana Herrero.

She changed in the tiny toilet, yanked her bag from the rear cupboard and came down the aisle to hug the pilot.

"Antoine de Puits, you are the best. I know this was a mighty favour. Call me next time you're in Lisbon, OK?"

Antoine shook his head. "You are one crazy female. And I'm even crazier to take such risks for you. I will call you, don't think I'll forget. At the very least, you owe me a decent dinner."

"Deal! I have to run!" Ana clattered down the steps and raced across to the terminal. If she got out of Porto before rush hour, she could make Viana do Castelo by eight.

Sometimes, Fate is on your side. The car starts, the lights are green, the traffic is going in the other direction and music is your positive affirmation. Today, the stars are aligned. Christina tells me I'm beautiful, Annie says sisters are doing it for ourselves, George insists I gotta have faith and everything Bryan does, he does it for me.

Ana slugged her second shot of caffeinated fizz and switched off the radio. Awake, nervous and in no danger of napping, she needed to focus. The next few hours could be life-changing.

When she parked at the police station, it was a quarter to eight. She allowed herself a fist pump before announcing herself at the desk. Within minutes, she was shown to a waiting room containing Xavier, André and most importantly, a coffee machine.

"Ana!" Xavier leapt to his feet and kissed her on both cheeks. "Here so early?"

"I hitched a ride with an ex-boyfriend." She held out a hand. "Hi, you must be André."

André shook her hand. "Yes and I already know who you are. I watch you every evening on the news. It's a pleasure to meet you."

"Likewise." She yawned involuntarily. "Sorry, that wasn't meant for you. I need a shot of the black stuff to perk me up. What's the latest?"

André pulled some coins from his pocket for the machine while Xavier summarised the morning's events.

"Team meeting in the hotel at six, where we aligned our plan of attack. André and I arrived here at seven. It seems buying coffees, beers and sharing confidential chats with the local force paid off. They know me already. Although André is a new face, he commands respect through his own status, his father's reputation and of course, his Portuguese, which is so much better than mine. Detective de Sousa came in half an hour ago and listened to what we had to say."

André handed her a cup. "*Um cafezinho.* Then we had to repeat it all over again for his senior officer, Inspector Gaia. They have gone to make some calls but once protocol is satisfied, they'll order Gilchrist's arrest or apprehension."

"*Obrigada.*" Ana slugged the little coffee back in two gulps. "And what are the others doing now?

Xavier checked his phone. "Last thing I heard, Roman had filed a report with Interpol and was heading south to Porto to complete the formalities. Cher is going to speak to Gilchrist's superiors at eight. She'll have to do that alone as that's exactly the same time as the police will be questioning Beatrice, in the presence of Gilchrist himself."

"Where…" Ana was interrupted by the door opening. A

crumpled-looking man in an open-necked shirt started to speak, spotted her and frowned.

André explained Ana's role in the investigation and introduced her to Detective de Sousa. He nodded, unsmiling, but shook her hand and asked them all to come to the interview room. Inspector Gaia awaited.

To Ana's surprise, Inspector Gaia was a tall, silver-haired woman with a firm handshake and impressive dark eyebrows. She welcomed Ana with good grace and invited them to sit. She spoke Portuguese in a slow, formal style, which may have been for the benefit of Xavier or all part of her dignified persona.

"We have contacted Interpol, Europol, the PGR or attorney general for Portugal, and informed the British Home Office. An arrest warrant is seen as unnecessary at this stage but all agencies agree the commander should be invited to answer some questions and that the investigation be reopened. In the light of this new information, the case will be handled by a senior detective from Lisbon, assisted by Detective de Sousa."

André cocked his head, rather like a puppy who heard the word 'walkies'.

Inspector Gaia gave a faint smile. "Your father would have been the ideal choice, Senhor Monteiro, but as I am sure you appreciate, personal involvement disqualifies him in these circumstances. Detective de Sousa will take two officers to Gêres and request the commander's assistance with our enquiries."

The crumpled-looking man gave a brief, weary nod and glanced at his watch.

Ana looked at the clock. Two minutes past eight. She caught Xavier's puzzled expression and she spoke without thinking. "Why not use the officers on site? It will take Detective de Sousa at least an hour to get there, but your officers are all in the same room as Gilchrist and DCI Stubbs as we speak."

Inspector Gaia frowned. "I'm sorry? De Sousa, you already have officers at the hotel?"

De Sousa shook his head, his frown more pronounced. "No. The case is closed. Why would I send men..."

"Officers," Gaia corrected.

"... officers when we filed the paperwork yesterday? All my officers have been reassigned new caseloads." He glared at Ana. "Who told you there were police at the scene?"

Ana stared at Xavier.

His face paled as his eyes grew large. "Commander Gilchrist asked DCI Beatrice Stubbs to be present for an interview with the local police at eight o'clock this morning. If there are no police at GCH, Gilchrist is acting alone."

Ana swallowed. "And he has Beatrice." She got to her feet.

"Hold on, you guys!" André called. "She's not alone. First off, the conference is full of police detectives. Second, Cher is on site. Someone can intercept him and get Beatrice out of there. Where is the interview taking place?"

All four faces focused on Ana.

"She didn't say. I'm not even sure she knew."

Inspector Gaia slapped a hand onto her desk. "De Sousa, call the hotel and see if the commander reserved a meeting venue for eight this morning. Authorise Housekeeping to open it, his office suite and even his own room if requested by nominated officers. They must also be given access to any security camera footage of relevant areas. Mr Racine, please alert your colleague and give her name to Detective de Sousa. I will arrange transport to GCH for all of you."

"I have a car!" Ana yelled. "Sorry." She dropped her voice. "I have a car right outside."

Inspector Gaia picked up the phone. "In that case, go ahead. Senhor Racine and Senhor Monteiro, go with her and take a police radio with you. De Sousa and his team will follow and I must insist you take no action without their permission. I will do all I can to ensure the safety of DCI Stubbs."

Ana jumped up so quickly that she bashed her knee on Gaia's table. She bit back a violent imprecation, rubbed her kneecap and limped to the door. She turned to say goodbye but de Sousa and his boss were already on their phones.

Rush hour, such as it was, drove Ana to the point of apoplexy. She swore and cursed and gesticulated at every single obstacle in their way, using the horn with abandon and wishing she had a flashing blue light. In contrast, Xavier and André spoke on their mobiles with a sense of calm urgency. Police training, Ana assumed, releasing a stream of expletives at a driver who halted traffic while he took three attempts to park.

André looked up, his hand over the mouthpiece. "Roman and Mr Fisher managed to get a meeting arranged with local government officials and senior police officers this morning in Porto. He asks if they should come back."

Ana watched Xavier in the rear view mirror.

"Can you hold one second, Cher?" He muted his call and replied to André. "How long will it take them to get back if they turn around now?"

André relayed the question and listened. "He's guessing an hour. They're on the outskirts of the city."

"In that case, they should continue and deliver the report in person. This must be done through official channels. We can get to the hotel sooner, so there's no point in them turning around."

Ana exhaled. "Xavier, we're a good thirty minutes from the hotel. Looks like we need Cher to step up." She scrunched her eyes in apology as she realised what she'd said, but opened them again to accuse the driver in front of bestiality.

Xavier returned to his conversation with Cher. His voice carried a quiet authority. "Use the hotel security cameras. Ask for assistance from the staff but do not put them in danger. Find out where she is and..." He broke off and listened in silence. "Whose office?"

Ana flicked her eyes to the mirror and saw Xavier's brow crease. She overtook a bus, with her eyes on the road but her ears straining to hear one half of this crucial conversation.

"You're sure that's where they are?"

" "
...

"In that case, get your friend to show you the CCTV, just to be sure. And Cher, please wait for back-up. We'll get local police to..."

" "
...

"Half an hour, I think. Maybe less. We'll try to mobilise local forces to support you but you cannot go up there alone."

André's thumbs began twitching over his phone.

"..."
...

"I understand that, but no officer should approach a hostage situation without back-up. You know that."

"..."
...

"Cher, I agree, but as a colleague I am asking you, please, not to try this alone. You will put yourself and Beatrice at risk. Wait for us. We'll be there in...?"

Ana slammed on the brakes as a tractor pulled out of a field. "Twenty-five minutes if we're lucky, and it's not looking good."

"Listen to me, Cher, this is no time for individual heroism. You must wait! We'll be there in half an hour."

"..."
...

Ana watched Xavier in the mirror. He took the phone from his ear and shook his head. She waited till André had ended his call.

"Xavier?"

"She says half an hour is thirty minutes too long for Beatrice."

André twisted in his seat. "She won't try to tackle Gilchrist alone?"

The tractor indicated left and drove off down an overgrown track. Ana floored the accelerator and raced along the road, dangerously over the speed limit. She knew without a doubt Cher would tackle Gilchrist alone. Because that's exactly what she would have done.

Chapter 33

"Come in and take a seat, DCI Stubbs."

She perched on the end of the sofa where she'd sat the night before, her handbag on her lap.

Gilchrist leaned against his desk, watching her with an intrusive intensity. "We have a few minutes before we talk to the police, so how about a little chat? I believe you and I can come to an agreement which will benefit us both."

Beatrice stared straight into his dead-fish eyes and shook her head. "I think that highly unlikely, Commander."

The silence solidified. Beatrice dropped her gaze, looking down at her own clasped hands. Dry, wrinkled, bearing small scars and large veins, these scruffy old tools had served her well. Every action, whether peeling a grapefruit or handcuffing a suspect had been decided and directed by her brain. A rather unpredictable organ. But in these circumstances, it was all she had.

Gilchrist's voice continued, smooth and assured. "I am in a position to be very supportive of your career, Acting DCI Stubbs. A word in the right ear and we could easily drop the 'Acting'. Or perhaps you'd prefer an advisory role, comfortable and well-remunerated."

"Commander..."

"As for your friend the journalist, there's every chance of aiding her career too. She seems like a smart young woman. I'm sure she'd recognise the value of a series of exclusives."

"Your offer is conditional, I presume. You would like us to lose interest in the murder of Samuel Silva."

Gilchrist flashed those showy teeth. "That case is closed. The perpetrator has been identified, but sadly not brought to justice.

Local police are satisfied and it would be arrogant and patronising to assume our opinions are in any way superior. I think the best thing to do is respect the conclusions of the Portuguese force and move on. Both you and your friend should go back to your respective employments, at which you're both doing so well, and concentrate on the task in hand. Raking over the coals would be disadvantageous."

Anger surged through Beatrice's veins like molten lava. She clenched her fists as if holding the reins on her temper. Her imagination helpfully provided a slideshow of the photographs Samuel Silva had shown her. Marcia in the hospital, Marcia with her new parents, Marcia on the balcony with views of Lisbon's castle beyond, Marcia sleeping, her tiny fists beside her head.

"All my life, Commander, I've been raking over the coals. It's what I, what we, were trained to do. I turn stones, despite dreading what I might find under there. Some of the things I've found have had a permanent effect on my mental health. As I am quite sure you know, I have struggled with depression for many years. The first time I met my counsellor, he advised me to resign. In his words, I would have far less need of his services or medication if I took up a different profession. But that was not possible. I'm a detective and I do my job to the best of my ability. I've brought bad people to justice and set good ones free, if not as many of either as I would have liked. As for my career, it's over. I'm retiring at the end of this year. Further rungs on the ladder don't interest me as I'm not right for them. There are far better people for the job."

Gilchrist studied her. "I'm aware of your condition, yes. After your most serious episode, many of my management colleagues thought it might be time for your retirement. Hamilton stood in the way of that. So here you are. Personally, I'd like to see you leave us as a success story."

Donkey refuses carrot. Here comes stick.

"So would I, sir. But perhaps in a different way to Samuel Silva." She held his gaze.

"Let's make this simple. I expect no further muddying of waters in a case already closed by the investigating officers. This conference has already suffered from the consequences of an unexpected death. I would like you either to refocus or retreat to enjoy the rest of your holiday. The latter would be understandable under the circumstances."

Beatrice pretended to be in deep thought and considered her options. She could lie and accept his deal, then retract her promise when at a safe distance. She could refuse and deal with whatever consequences he planned. The one thing she could not do was forget it and move on. Gilchrist was no fool. He'd want some guarantee if she agreed. She played for time. The longer she kept talking, the greater chance there was that help would arrive.

"Commander Gilchrist, forgive me. I just don't understand. Samuel Silva was a friend of yours."

This time, Gilchrist laughed aloud. "And with searing ingenuity, the lady detective elicits a full and frank confession from the criminal mastermind, whilst fashioning a pair of home-made handcuffs out of crochet hooks. Don't be ridiculous, woman. I had nothing to do with Silva's death. If I can be accused of anything, it's putting the conference first and allowing the local jurisdiction to take control. Now can we step away from the conspiracy theories and work together to make this event the success it deserves? It's time to move on."

Beatrice checked her watch. "Yes, it is. The police are running late, aren't they? It's ten past eight already. "

When she looked up, she expected hostility. Which was exactly what she got.

Gilchrist levelled an Abadie revolver at her, while holding out his hand for her bag. His manner was as matter-of-fact as an airport security guard.

She gave it to him, clenching her fists to disguise the tremble in her hands.

"Walk ahead of me to the lift at the end of the corridor. Please do not attempt any theatrics or give me any reason to cause you unnecessary injury."

Adrenalin pumping through her, she could think of nothing

else to do but obey. He stepped backwards, his eyes never leaving hers, and deposited her bag in a drawer.

Beatrice's mind scrambled to comprehend what he might have in mind. He couldn't be planning another execution. The man was a megalomaniac, undoubtedly, but even he must realise that the murder of another delegate would result in his eventual arrest. As an intelligent officer of the law, no matter how deluded he might be by his own potency, he had to know he was cornered. If he killed Beatrice, what of Ana? What of Xavier, Roman, André and Cher? No. He couldn't kill them all.

Gilchrist, still calm, still smiling, slipped the gun into his pocket and gestured for her to precede him through the door.

"Commander, I think it's time to..."

He shook his head. "Move, please. Walk to the lift at the end of the corridor. I should inform you that I have disabled the security camera on this wing."

Without a word, she did as she was told, frantically wondering how she could get a message to Cher. But even if she were able to make contact, she had no clue where this man intended to take her.

The lift doors opened and he pressed the button for the fifth floor. The top three buttons had a sign taped beside them.

DUE TO RENOVATION WORK, FLOORS 3, 4 AND THE ROOF TERRACE ON FLOOR 5 ARE CURRENTLY CLOSED TO THE PUBLIC. WE APOLOGISE FOR ANY INCONVENIENCE.

The roof. Somehow a sense of relief washed over Beatrice. Outside, in the open air, with birds singing and sun shining, the feeling that nothing bad could happen was irrepressible. She reprimanded herself for such stupidity.

The lift doors opened onto another corridor, one distinctly less manicured than the one they had just left. Underfoot plastic sheeting protected the carpet from dusty footprints and cables snaked their way towards a door at the end that led to the roof terrace.

The commander withdrew his gun and used it to point in that direction.

Beatrice picked her way among the builders' detritus; past rooms labelled Suite Douro, Suite Tagus, and Suite Dão and opened the heavy fire door into the fresh air. She rounded the corner to see the roof terrace stretching the length of the building, the size of an Olympic swimming pool. On the fifth floor, she realised, the two wings of the building were occupied by luxury suites leaving the long rectangular central section open for patrons to eat, drink and admire the view.

Tables and chairs were stacked against the back wall, next to metal shutters that probably concealed a cocktail bar. A stone balustrade ran along the front of the building, broken by a taped off section where the wall was missing. Beatrice eyed it, assessing how many tons of stone had fallen onto the ground floor terrace below. It must have been quite a storm.

"Take a seat, please." He motioned to the circular pond with a sculpture at its centre which formed the focal point of the empty expanse. Huge scallop shells decreased in size in three tiers, each bearing occupants. Dolphins arched out of the lowest, a female nude reclined in the second, her long hair covering her modesty and in the smallest and highest, seagulls perched around the edge, wings extended as if about to take to the air. At night, when the water flowed and the lights illuminated the arcs and curves, it would surely be a delightful sight.

At intervals around the water feature were benches made of the same polished granite as the fountain itself. Beatrice sat on one, her back to the bar, facing out to the view. Gilchrist sat on the next bench and swivelled to face her, his gun no longer visible.

"Sorry to play rough, but I think it only fair to remind you there is a less pleasant way to do this." His voice had taken on an ugly harshness.

Far below, a blackbird sent its distinctive alarm call. The terrace remained cool despite the morning sunshine and Beatrice pulled her jacket tighter, the comforting weight of Matthew's souvenir against her leg.

"What do you say, Stubbs? Shall we let sleeping black dogs lie?" He laughed through his nose without a trace of amusement.

Her scalp prickled. Black dogs. What a low blow to use her

depression as a weapon against her. The man was amoral. Even if she agreed to back down in return for some fictional promotion, she would never be anything more than a loose end. Sooner or later to be tied up. She had come too far and it was time to confront this inveterate liar, whatever the consequences.

If only she had a little more time. She looked straight at his face.

"I'm sorry, sir, I don't think we should lie any more. Least of all you."

His nostrils flared but he said nothing.

Beatrice continued, her voice calm. "The truth is that when Samuel Silva's book was published, it would have exposed you as the charlatan you are. His work would reveal yours to be plagiarised and self-aggrandising. Not a problem for an anonymous author, but I believe you planned to be 'outed'. A self-regarding personality such as yours could never remain in the shadows for long. You expected your 'creative non-fiction' to shake the world of law enforcement and eclipse previous insider works from such sources as MI5. You would never have been able to resist the glory.

"So you decided to publish first and call Silva out as the plagiarist. However, he chose to release his findings as a blog, inviting discussion, offering proof, citing sources. Completely undermining your claims and exposing you as the cheat.

"I think you invited Silva to this conference with every intention of killing him. You switched rooms, staying one night in 1121 before requesting relocation. Of course your own fingerprints were all over the room, because it had been yours. And while it was, you got one of the gardeners to help you fix a stuck window. The gardener's name, which you took as you tipped him, was Marco Cordeiro.

"You put Silva in that room, next door to your office, from where you had access via the balcony. You knew he always returned to his room to call his wife at lunch because he told you so when refusing your Friday lunch invitation. You asked André Monteiro to come to that very room on Saturday lunchtime by faking a note. You recorded your own voice shouting into the phone and played it while Monteiro passed your door to provide you with an alibi. You shot Silva twice in the back of the head, framed Cordeiro and had him killed by local thugs.

"Samuel Silva was a husband, a new father, a great mind and altruistic educator. You killed him for purely selfish reasons, inflicting enormous suffering on his family and then covered your tracks by doing the same to Cordeiro. All this at a conference for police detectives. To think you could pull this off, you must have extraordinary levels of confidence. One might even say epic.

"Incidentally, my journalist friend Ana was included in our investigations at a later stage. Much of the legwork had been done and she merely filled in some gaps. As we speak, six high-profile international detectives are reporting our findings to your superiors, Interpol and the local force. We're not as stupid as you think, Commander. Neither are you as smart as you believe. I've come across some immense egos in my time, but you? You are off the scale."

The quiet following Beatrice's words seemed to echo back at her. She'd lit the touch paper and now she waited for the explosion. In the next few seconds, he might very well decide to silence her permanently. He had the means. A shot to the head and he could attempt a getaway. Or he might try to push her from the roof and frame it as suicide. If he took her words at face value and realised he couldn't get away with Silva's murder, he had nothing to lose by killing her.

"Well, that is very disappointing."

Beatrice looked up and her heart began to race. His face was a mask of cold determination, his pupils shone dark and the only movement was the professional way he was putting on a pair of sterile gloves.

With a plummeting drop in her gut, she knew she had reached the end. Plenty of times she'd stared death in the face, but she'd never really believed it would happen. This time was different. She had finally run out of chances. No one was coming to help and she would face this alone. After all these years serving the force, she was going out at the hands of one of her own. Fear and self-pity pricked at her eyes and she hoped his choice of method would be a bullet. Falling from the roof or strangulation would be so much worse than a quick and sudden exit.

She tried to remember her last words to Matthew and experienced a profound sadness that they never would enjoy their long-anticipated retirement together.

Gilchrist stood up. "The tragedy due to unfold was for the mentally unstable detective to throw her journalist friend off of the roof and then shoot herself. I can still make that work. Come, Stubbs, on your feet."

Beatrice rose, her eyes fixed on his cold face. A movement behind him caught her attention as a wheelchair rounded the corner and a voice rang out.

"Here you are!"

Cher sat at the end of the terrace, phone held aloft. "Hello everyone, we're live on BluLite!"

Chapter 34

"Day Six of EPIC and we're onsite in Gerês! Today's BluLite reportage coming from Agent Cher Davenport of the FBI. Right now, we're on the terrace on the roof of the hotel. Beautiful spot, don't ya think?"

Cher rotated her phone around the scene and brought it back to focus on the couple in front of the fountain. "And did we just get lucky! Here's Commander Gilchrist, kingpin of the entire project. With him is Acting DCI Stubbs, of the London Met. Quite a coup to get these two guys in one place, if I say so myself. Let's share a few words with two of the most influential figures in British policing."

She steered her chair one-handed towards them, using the other to continue filming, but stopped at a distance of around fifteen feet. Well out of reach. Her smile was bright enough for daytime television.

"Good morning to you both!"

Beatrice returned the smile with a nod, watching Gilchrist in her peripheral vision. "Good morning, Agent Davenport, it's a pleasure to see you again."

Gilchrist switched on his beam. "It certainly is a surprise. You caught Acting DCI Stubbs and I having a quiet chat." He laughed heartily. "We assumed everyone was at breakfast so we sneaked off for a policy discussion. We should have known nowhere is private at a conference for detectives!"

Cher beamed right back. "Too right! Say, lemme ask you how you think the conference is going."

Gilchrist glanced at his watch. "In a word, fast! We hardly have time to cover all the topics and conversations we want to discuss with our European colleagues. Every moment counts. My next session begins at nine, in fact. I should be heading back."

"Just one last question, to both of you. How has the death of Samuel Silva affected morale? Of course the press are making the most of it but how did this event impact the conference itself? Is it business as usual?"

Beatrice turned her face to Gilchrist, in an ostensible gesture of politeness; in full knowledge the Commander saw it as a challenge.

"The death of a colleague is always a tragedy. Not one single delegate is unaffected, but we are professionals. We are here to do a job. The best way to honour our comrade is to carry on. The case is closed and my only regret is the perpetrator was not brought to justice. Thanks for the chat, but unfortunately, I need to get to my next appointment." Cher ignored him and kept the camera on them both.

Cher turned her attention to Beatrice. "DCI Stubbs?"

Beatrice took a deep breath. Their colleagues now knew where they were, so all she had to do was sit tight and wait for the cavalry to arrive. She had to filibuster.

"Commander Gilchrist has done an EPIC job at this year's European Police Intercommunications Conference. His achievement has been to bring international detectives together, encouraging collaboration in all kinds of unexpected ways. I am sure, in time, all his actions will be deservedly recognised.

"If I may, I'd like to pay a personal tribute to Samuel Silva. The loss of such a pioneer of intelligence is a blow to the entire law enforcement community. His research benefitted us all, in Europe and beyond. He knew this, yet he sought to take no profit. Instead he planned to share his work as a public resource. I still hope his colleagues can make that happen. He was also a husband and father, mentor and godfather. He was a wise, decent man who will be greatly missed."

Gilchrist applauded. "Well said! Marvellous speech. Thank you. However, Acting DCI Stubbs, Agent Davenport, I have to get to..."

"So I would like to ask you all," intoned Beatrice, addressing the camera, "wherever you are in the world, to bow your heads for one minute and give thanks for a truly exceptional fellow officer. Ladies and gentlemen, Samuel Silva."

Sixty seconds. Gilchrist stood beside Beatrice, his head bowed and hands clasped behind his back. He couldn't go anywhere for the next minute without appearing a crass oaf. Then what? Beatrice bowed her head and squinted at her watch. 08.46. Come on! Roman? Xavier? Someone? Out of the corner of her eye, she saw Gilchrist slip a hand into his pocket.

The sound of a gunshot behind them both gave Beatrice such a shock that she stumbled sideways, the heavy ornament in her jacket pocket thumping against her hip. Gilchrist's head snapped up and he stared past Cher, at a wide open space.

"What are you doing? Get away from her!" Gilchrist launched himself forwards, as if at some invisible assailant. Cher attempted to spin round but couldn't turn quickly enough before Gilchrist ran behind her, snatched her phone and threw it over the edge of the balustrade.

The oldest trick in the book. *Look behind you!*

Before Beatrice could move, he trained his gun on Cher. "So Plan A it is, with a minor adjustment. Sorry ladies, no time for niceties. Let's make this quick."

He shoved Cher's chair in the direction of the red and white tape flapping in the breeze, his gun pointing at the back of her head. Time seemed to slow down as the chair rolled noiselessly towards the gap in the low wall. Cher released a howl of protest and yanked on the brakes. Gilchrist swore, shoved his gun in its holster then tipped the chair back and physically dragged it to the edge.

Beatrice's hand slipped into her pocket and took hold of the metal cockerel. Her fingers fitted around the sharp curves of its tail and comb as if it had been designed for her palm. Gilchrist lugged the chair closer to the crumbling stone, his face red and ugly.

Two could play at old tricks.

"Commander, *look out!*" she shrieked and hurled the cockerel with all the strength she had, aiming directly at his head. His face snapped up a second before the spiky souvenir hit him full in the mouth. He released the chair and recoiled, his hands covering his face. Cher reacted instantly, using both arms to wheel herself away and snatch the chance to escape.

So only Beatrice watched Gilchrist stagger backwards through the plastic tape and lose his footing. Only she saw his arms flail outwards and his mouth open to scream through broken, bloodied teeth as he fell. Only she covered her ears and counted the seconds until he hit the ground.

Chapter 35

Pancakes for ten, fruit salad, yoghurt, bread, poached eggs, bacon, cheese and ham for the continentals, all accompanied by plenty of coffee. Adrian whisked and chopped and arranged and brewed for over an hour until Matthew wandered into the kitchen, dressed in wrinkled linen.

"Something smells rather wonderful."

"Apart from me? Might be the strawberries. Can I pour you some freshly squeezed orange juice?"

"Yes please. Beatrice is in the shower, so you may as well pour her one too. Can I do anything to help? We've a few more mouths to feed."

Adrian smiled. "All in hand. Will drove me to the shop first thing and now he's tending Tanya. She wants to come downstairs today."

"Only because she hates being left out. Missing all these new faces, it must be more painful than her burns." Matthew cleared his throat, as if about to make a formal speech. "Adrian, while it's just the two of us, I have something to say."

"I see." Adrian poured two glasses of juice and sat down. Time to clear the air.

Matthew gave him a frank and direct look. "I blamed you for losing Luke. That was wrong and unfair. I realise now you could not possibly have overruled Marianne and I respect you even more for not assigning negligence where it was due. I am sorry, and I want you to know that I trust you and Will as family members with my grandson. Probably a lot more than some family members. Please accept my apologies."

Adrian reached over to shake his hand. "No need to apologise. I felt wretched about what happened, but only about a thousandth of what you must have been feeling. Thank you, anyway. I hoped you would feel that way, but it does my heart good to hear it."

Matthew's forehead smoothed. "I heard from her this morning."

"Marianne? Where is she?"

"Back in the UK. She's trying to get legal representation for Leon." He shook his head in a gesture of disbelief.

Adrian debated whether to speak his mind and decided against. "Shall we make a start on the pancakes?"

Several minutes later, Will helped Tanya into the room and eased her with great care on the chaise longue he'd dragged in from the living room. He laid a cotton sheet over her and poured her some juice.

"Adrian, are you very attached to Will?" she asked. "Because if not, I would be happy to take him off your hands."

Will laughed and kissed Adrian's cheek. "Sorry, Tanya. I'm a one-man kind of guy. I'm guessing you don't want any coffee?"

"Oh well, it was worth a punt. Actually, yes I do want coffee. Just add lots of milk and serve it in a sippy-cup."

Ana wandered in, phone glued to her ear, laptop under her arm. She gave everyone a thumbs-up, took some coffee onto the balcony and continued chatting and tapping away. Her story had the whole of RTP in a state of huge excitement.

Voices came from the hallway and a peal of laughter announced Luke and Beatrice.

Matthew's eyebrows rose. "Up before ten, Luke? I never thought I'd see the day!"

"Grandad, Beatrice taught me a rude song!"

"I don't doubt it. Go and enquire after your mother's health."

Luke planted a cursory kiss on Tanya's cheek. "Morning, Mum. Are you better yet?"

"Hello Trouble," she replied and stroked his hair. "It's getting better. But no swimming or sunbathing for me today. I'll have to stay inside and watch Poldark videos."

Adrian grinned. "What an awful ordeal. I might have to join you."

Luke returned to the table to help himself to pancakes. "Beatrice?" he asked, in a whisper.

"No, not in front of your mother," Beatrice replied, her hair a strange explosion of peaks and tufts. "Pass that maple stuff."

He giggled and handed her the syrup. "I wasn't going to ask you to sing it again!" He glanced at the garden flat and whispered. "Is that man really a Viking?"

Beatrice had a mouthful of pancake.

Adrian spoke for her. "Maybe we should go and ask him. Xavier went over there an hour ago to start work, so they must be hungry by now. Luke, wanna come with me to get Xavier, Roman and Shoop-Shoop..."

"Cher," offered Matthew.

"I know. I was just giving it the right build-up," said Adrian. At least Tanya and Will found it funny.

Luke dropped his fork and scrambled down from the table. He ran ahead across the lawn but hesitated as he got to the door. The three were clearly visible through the French windows, all bent over laptops on the dining-room table. No one had noticed their approach. Luke reached up for Adrian's hand.

Their polite knock turned all three heads.

"Just wondered if you're hungry? There's bread and coffee and other things I've forgotten. What did we make, Luke?"

"Pancakes! Bacon! Eggs! Juice! Maple syrup!"

Cher stretched. "That sounds exactly what the doctor ordered. C'mon, you guys, I need to break my fast. Luke, lead the way."

Breakfast was a success. Cher parked her chair beside Tanya and helped her by passing pancakes or juice as required. Will, Xavier, Beatrice and Roman ate with gusto, while Matthew and Adrian brewed coffee, poured juice and poached eggs to order. Luke spread honey on a piece of toast and cast covert glances at Roman as the adults discussed developments.

"Politically it's complex," said Xavier. "The case will be a collaboration between Inspector Gaia's team, Interpol, LIU and the British Home Office. Assuming Gilchrist survives his injuries, it will be at least a year before he can stand trial."

"He'll survive," Cher snickered. "So what if he got lucky with an awning instead of concrete? He's still due a sucker punch from the long arm of the law."

Will applauded. "Calamity Jane is alive and well and hiding in Gerês!"

When the laughter died down, Roman spoke. "Gilchrist will get what he deserves. Once the paperwork is filed here, he's the UK's problem. Interpol will actually enjoy dumping this on the Brits, according to Fisher."

Beatrice wrinkled her nose and Xavier spotted her reaction. "What is it, B? Not a fan of Interpol?"

She shook her head. "I have a great deal of respect for Interpol. But bloody Fisher rubs me up the wrong way. He's so... smooth. Like an oil slick."

Roman laughed, throwing his blond head back. Luke gazed up at him in awe.

"Well put. Not my kind of person either. Although I must say he was pretty effective when I tackled him yesterday morning. Listened, checked, acted and knew the right people to call. No hesitation in suspending the conference either. I respect him for that."

Will addressed the new arrivals. "It leaves a bad taste regarding EPIC as a concept, doesn't it? Rumours are getting more and more dramatic. Even if you have managed to keep it out of the press so far." He threw a curious look at Ana.

Dark rings shadowed her eyes but her expression remained animated and alert. "The way things look from the press side, I get an exclusive. Plus budget not only for reportage, but a full documentary. So I can spin this however I like. My gut is to tell the truth and praise EPIC for the good it achieved. Shame it was derailed by one power-crazed egomaniac who tried to get away with murder and shot himself in the foot."

"He didn't shoot himself in the foot," said Roman. "Beatrice knocked him off the roof with a cockerel."

His black humour hit the mark and no one could resist laughing.

Luke gawped at Beatrice. "You knocked somebody off a roof?"

"Only because I had to. It was a last resort."

Matthew coughed politely. "Luke, what about you and I going

on lizard patrol? They'll be out sunning themselves on the rocks now."

"In a bit, Grandad."

Beatrice dabbed her mouth with a napkin. "I think now would be a good time, Luke. We need to have a police conversation and we'll need to borrow Ana and Will. Perhaps we should retire to the garden flat, out of the way? Adrian, thanks for a lovely breakfast. If you don't mind clearing up, I'll promise to take charge of dinner."

Luke released a disappointed sigh, but slipped off his stool and took Matthew's hand. "I'll take photos for you."

"You better had," replied Beatrice and led the team out through the garden door.

Chapter 36

Dear All

Hope you're all managing to chill after the stress of this past week. Sorry I couldn't join you today but I'm more useful here.

Just a few lines to let you know what's happening in Lisbon. Communication is constant between ourselves and Inspector Gaia's team. The case against Gilchrist is clear and it is simply a question of the jurisdiction in which to charge him. Due to his senior position and the international nature of EPIC, it is likely to be the UK. (TBH, we fought to keep it here, in honour of Samuel, but this is a political hot potato our domestic affairs department could do without.)

My father and I are arranging a widow's pension for Elisabete and we both intend to be very present and responsible in her and Marcia's lives. We debated trying to monetise Samuel's blog, but Elisabete agreed with his ethics and insists on making it free. I will test the blog in Beta version next month, with Xavier and Cher's help. If anyone else is interested, let me know and I'll put you on the list. Ana, that goes for you too. This is not exclusive to police.

I guess we'll all meet up at the trial, wherever and whenever it is, so right now I'm just going to wish you a relaxing weekend. On a personal note, I'm really glad I got to know you and earned your trust. You people made this happen and on behalf of Samuel's friends and family, I thank you.

Kind regards & beijinhos
André

Chapter 37

The sun-baked tiles around the pool radiated warmth, the sky was melting towards another spectacular sunset and the scent of grilling meat wafted across the pool. Cher, Roman and Will supervised the barbecue, while in the kitchen, Xavier instructed Matthew and Adrian on how to cook the bean stew. Ana and Tanya mixed *caipirinhas* behind the bar and did a fair amount of sampling, judging by the bursts of raucous laughter. Luke and Beatrice set the table, placing *citronella* mosquito candles at strategic points.

The vestiges of a mild headache induced by dealing with emails, a lengthy discussion with Ranga and endless repetition of yesterday's events ebbed away as Beatrice looked forward to the evening. Despite her promise to Adrian, she'd actually contributed very little to dinner.

Xavier's suggestion of a traditional Brazilian *feijoada* earlier that afternoon had met with general enthusiasm. Will and Adrian took him shopping for ingredients. Cher, Ana and Tanya prepared the salads and by the poolside, Roman taught Luke some kind of martial arts.

This gave Beatrice and Matthew an hour or so for a nap. They lay on the bed with their eyes closed but neither slept.

"Are you really OK?" she asked him, for the fourth time that day.

"Yes, I am. I do have a whole bagful of concerns regarding my daughters, in the light of recent events. If Marianne does side with her nephew's kidnapper, I really can see no future relationship between herself and Tanya. I struggle to comprehend her myself."

"If it comes to that, which I doubt. Leon's relationships rarely last long. Marianne will wake up to him sooner or later. Keep the doors open."

"The doors will always be open. She's family. By the way, I apologised to Adrian," said Matthew. "I should have known it wasn't his fault."

"Good. It's obvious Adrian and Will both adore Luke."

"Yes, and they're both good role models in the absence of a father figure." He sighed and reached for her hand. "For some reason, perhaps because I almost lost two people closest to my heart, loved ones seem awfully precious today. Your rooftop drama will give me nightmares for months. Isn't the DCI post supposed to keep you safely in a carpeted office?"

They lay side by side, hand in hand.

Beatrice decided to put it into words and thereby make it real. "The DCI post will keep me in a carpeted office for one more month exactly. I called Ranga for a debrief and asked to resign from the post of Acting DCI. My time is up and I know it. He promised to replace me within a month and then I can officially retire."

He released her hand to put his arm around her and she curled into his shoulder, watching a tear leak from his closed lids. The time, she sensed, was finally right.

She closed her eyes, drawing peace and restoration from his presence. For five minutes. Then she sat up.

"Don't know about yourself, but I'm hungry."

"Ah-ha. Normal status restored."

Beatrice took another paper napkin from Luke and rolled it into a hanky shape to poke in a wine glass. Pure elegance.

"Beatrice?" asked Luke.

"No! Never. Pinch me, tweak my ears or take away my bean stew, if you must. But I shall never sing in public."

Luke creased up with laughter. "I know! That song is just for us. Guess what I learned from Roman today?"

"Karate chops and kick-boxing?"

"No. He says feet and fists are your weakest weapons."

Beatrice stopped and raised her eyebrows. "Give me another napkin."

He handed her one, his face eager.

Beatrice rolled and stuffed. "So what is my strongest weapon? No, don't tell me, I want to guess. Is it my bottom?"

"No!" he giggled and handed her another napkin. "Guess again!"

"For your information, my bottom can be pretty lethal, depending on what I've eaten." This time Luke laughed out loud. "All depends on the individual, I suppose. It must be something superior to your opponent. Hmm." She placed a knife, fork and spoon around a place setting. "Whoever I'm up against might have bigger fists, bigger muscles, bigger guns or in extremely rare cases, a bigger bottom. How can you deal with all of those?"

Luke placed the pack of napkins on the table and pressed an index finger to each of his temples, his eyes wide. "Your mind."

"Oh really? So where does the karate come in? You two were pulling some judo moves this afternoon, I saw you."

"Not judo or karate, it was Tai Chi. Roman says it's a very different kind of discipline."

Beatrice moved on to position cutlery, but her eyes had filled with tears. Luke was an open book, influenced by everyone he met, easily convinced and enthused. She made a decision to offer as much support as she could to Tanya and to her sort-of-grandson. She had to fill his life with good people and the Viking was an ideal example.

"Maybe in the morning, you can teach me how to do it?" she said, beckoning for the napkins.

"OK. It's very slow and easy so I reckon you could handle it. Why are there only nine places? We're ten, including me."

Beatrice laughed at his accurate assessment of her level of fitness. "Mum can't sit at the table so she's on the sun bed. You will have to act as waiter for her."

"Oh yeah. Course. Beatrice?"

"What?"

"I don't want to go home tomorrow. I like this place."

"Good. So do I. Anyway, we're not going home tomorrow but on Sunday. That's the day after tomorrow. So you have one and a half more days to swim and play and watch the lizards and learn Tai Chi. Feeling sad on Friday about leaving on Sunday is a waste of time, so we'll have no more of it. Right, the table's done. Go put a napkin in your mum's wine glass and let's get this show on the road."

By sundown, the table stood testament to a feast enjoyed by all. Empty plates, a few wilted lettuce leaves, bones, bits of bread and an almost-empty pot of black bean stew sat among wine bottles and shot glasses of *aguardiente* muddied with bean juice. The night air rang with laughter and a giddy sense of release. Beatrice started to clear the table, assisted by Xavier and Adrian, both pink of cheek and magnanimous. The *cachaça* had worked its magic.

Will joined them as they took the citrus sorbets from the freezer. He produced three bottles of champagne. Beatrice beamed at him.

"That's a thoughtful gesture. Such a nice way to celebrate the rescue of Luke and Gilchrist's downfall."

Adrian and Will stared at her in disbelief.

"I can't believe you just said that!" said Will. "Sometimes I think you do it on purpose."

"Of course she does it on purpose." Adrian placed a tray of sorbets on the hostess trolley and pushed it at Will. "Put the bubbles on the bottom shelf. I'll load the dishwasher and be with you in a sec."

Beatrice stood in the doorway for a moment, inhaling the night, listening to the cicadas, anticipating the sorbet and champagne, watching the pool lights ripple and flicker across the party.

Adrian appeared behind her, his hands on her shoulders. "Come on, you of all people must be present for this."

"For what?"

"Ssh. Listen."

Will was on his feet, tapping a spoon against a glass, while Xavier and Roman distributed glasses of champagne. With a gentle shake, Matthew woke a dozing Luke who blinked at Beatrice as she sat down.

"It's been quite a week!" Will announced. His voice rang down the table as far as Tanya's sun bed, where she sat with Ana.

"This has been a holiday to remember. There's been fun, sadness, drama and more than the usual amount of stress. Some were lost, some were wounded, and we also gained new friends. Welcome to Xavier, Cher, Roman and Ana, again."

Laughter and smiles bounced around the table. Luke applauded.

"All these are things we should celebrate. But there's one more cherry on the cake I want to share with you all. Yesterday, I asked Adrian Harvey to marry me. I still quite can't believe it myself, but he said yes!"

Beatrice leapt to her feet with everyone else, except Tanya and Cher, who applauded with hoots, cheers and whistles. Will and Adrian accepted all the hugs and congratulations with tears and delight. Matthew proposed the toast and they raised their glasses to 'Will and Adrian!' at least three times.

"When is the wedding?" asked Tanya. "Can you at least give me a couple of months to get better? Assuming I'm invited, of course."

Will took Adrian's hand. "Everyone's invited! We want a massive party, but we've not discussed a date yet. Probably next year. Plenty of time for you to heal."

Conversation turned to possible locations and the optimum season for nuptials, with opinions ranging from springtime in Venice to Brampford Speke in early autumn.

Xavier fetched more champagne from the fridge and set off another round of toasts. The clock struck twelve and Luke began rubbing his eyes. Beatrice beckoned Roman.

"Luke is ready for bed. Tanya isn't but if you could help her upstairs and Ana takes a bottle of fizz, the girls can party on while the little chap gets his rest. None of us wants to leave him unattended."

"Sure. I'd be happy to. You ready?" Roman raised his eyebrows at Tanya, who pretended to fan herself.

Cher wheeled herself up to Beatrice. They watched Tanya lean on Roman and limp indoors. Ana scooped up two glasses, a bottle of champagne and held out her other hand for Luke.

"Coming, little fella?"

He nodded and took her hand. "Tomorrow is Saturday, you know. Not Sunday."

"Thanks be to God! Otherwise I'd have to go to Mass."

"So we have another holiday day here. All of us together."

"Isn't that grand?"

"Yes, it *is* grand," he agreed.

The small group went inside and closed the curtains. Beatrice sat down on the stone bench and faced Cher.

"Love is in the air..." she sang, quietly.

Cher laughed, a throaty contagious sound. "Love is all around us..."

Beatrice snorted. "Feels like it, I must say. What about you and the Viking? Is there a future?"

"Who knows? We've had such a great time together. He's like no one else I ever met. But long-distance relationships are not really my thing."

"Bugger. We could have had a double wedding."

"Nah. If you're going for the full house of political correctness, you need gay, disabled *and* black. That tall handsome blond ruins the whole damn thing." Cher threw back her head and gave a gurgling infectious laugh.

Adrian joined them, his eyes shining. "Is this the rowdy ladies' corner? If so, may I have guest privileges?"

"Sure you can! Hey, congratulations again. He is one helluva catch," Cher said.

"I think so." Adrian chinked glasses with them both. "Mind you, yours is rather easy on the eye. Love his hair."

Roman sauntered across the terrace, making for the group at the bar, with all the grace of an inhabitant of Asgard.

"Is there a place you can go where they teach you to move like that?" Beatrice asked. "Catwalk school, or something?"

Cher sighed. "With some people it's genetic. Look at Ana. She comes into a room and jaws drop. Roman's got damn good genes. And while I still got the chance, I'm going to get into them thar jeans." She gurgled again, setting Adrian and Beatrice off into laughter, and wheeled herself away towards the Viking.

Beatrice nudged Adrian. "You're getting married."

"I know. Beat you to it by a country mile."

"Seeing as I've been running in the other direction for twenty-five years, that's no surprise. But honestly, I could not be happier for you two. Will is a lovely, kind, smart man and he adores you. No surprise there either." Her throat constricted. "I feel like an emotional auntie with her favourite nephew. I'm going to miss you so much."

He pulled her into a sideways hug. "I'm getting married, not joining a monastery. We'll still be neighbours, at least till the end of the year."

With a sniff, Beatrice patted his leg. "End of next month, actually. I asked Ranga to release me early. I can retire at the end of September and move to Devon."

Adrian twisted his body to face her. "Oh my God, you're actually going to do it, aren't you?"

"Yes, I am. You can visit us, we can visit you, we'll go on trips, and on top of that, I have to come back every month to see my counsellor. I could use a friendly place to stay. If you like, I'll even help plan the wedding. Adrian, we want you and Will to be a part of our lives. And Luke's life. We're family now."

Adrian dropped his head onto her shoulder. "Yes, we are."

A gale of laughter drifted from the bar and a head poked out of an upstairs window.

"Oi!" yelled Ana.

"Sorry," called Xavier. "We'll keep it down."

"No, don't worry, Luke's next door and he's out for the count. The thing is, has anyone got a cigar?"

Will reached behind the bar and threw a small flat tin up to Ana, who caught it one handed in the dark. She blew them all a kiss and retreated within.

Adrian's voice was low and discreet. "Beatrice?"

"You sound like Luke. Are you going to ask me to sing smutty songs?"

"No." Adrian faced her, his expression serious. "I'm just a bit worried. You've always been so preoccupied by your job. How will you deal with retirement? What are you going to do with yourself?"

Beatrice drained her glass and gazed up at the night sky. Stars twinkled back at her, reassuring in their permanence. She met Adrian's eyes with a mischievous smile.

"As a matter of fact, I'm thinking of writing a book."

Dedications

Cold Pressed
For Julie Lewis and Tracy Austin,
whose glasses are always half full

Human Rites
For Aine Kiely and Jo Rowling
Confidantes, conspirators and tosta mista sisters

Bad Apples
To Cooty, with all my love

Message from JJ Marsh

I hope you enjoyed *The Beatrice Stubbs Boxset Two*.

Also in The Beatrice Stubbs Series:
SNOW ANGEL
For more information, visit jjmarshauthor.com

For occasional updates, news, deals and a FREE exclusive prequel: *Black Dogs, Yellow Butterflies*, visit jjmarshauthor.com and subscribe to my newsletter.

If you would recommend *The Beatrice Stubbs Series* to a friend, please do so by writing a review. Your tip helps other readers discover their next favourite book.

Thank you.

Also by Triskele Books

The Charter, Closure, Complicit, Crimson Shore,
False Lights and *Sacred Lake*
by Gillian Hamer

Tristan and Iseult, The Rise of Zenobia, The Fate of an Emperor,
The Better of Two Men, The Rebel Queen and *The Love of Julius*
by JD Smith

Spirit of Lost Angels, Wolfsangel, Blood Rose Angel,
The Silent Kookaburra and *The Swooping Magpie*
by Liza Perrat

Gift of the Raven and *Ghost Town*
by Catriona Troth

http://www.triskelebooks.co.uk